TO SEE YOUR FACE AGAIN

EUGENIA PRICE

TO SEE YOUR FACE AGAIN

A Novel, the Sequel to Savannah

DOUBLEDAY & COMPANY, INC.
GARDEN CITY, NEW YORK
1985

Library of Congress Cataloging in Publication Data

Price, Eugenia.
To see your face again.

Sequel to: Savannah.
I. Title.
PS3566.R47T6   1985   813'.54
ISBN 0-385-15275-2
Library of Congress Catalog Card Number: 85-4434

FOR MARION HEMPERLEY

Part I

ONE

JUST AT SUNRISE on June 13, 1838, forty-six-year-old Mark Browning stood at the open east window of his mercantile office on Savannah's Commerce Row and stared out over the brightening expanse of water toward the wide bend that turns the river toward the sea.

From the moment of his first glimpse of this view when he was twenty and had cast his lot with this small city, the bend in the river had lifted Mark's spirit and confirmed his choice that Savannah was, indeed, his place-to-be for all the days of his life.

Year after intervening year, from this very window, even when the room where he now stood had been the office of his late, revered friend, Robert Mackay, Mark had taken delight in scanning the river traffic—an odd assortment of local boats and mighty sailing ships— as it moved slowly around that bend, each vessel nourishing the life of his city. Now, and for the past few years, steam packets plied the gray waters, speeding the town's growth, expanding his own pride in Savannah.

But on this early morning, so many troubled and contradictory thoughts tangled in his mind that he seemed almost unaware of what he saw. Trying to think his way through the vexing problem learned moments ago from his warehouse inspector, he crossed the spacious office furnished with a few fine pieces brought down from his old home in Philadelphia, and looked out the west window. Three slips away from his wharf, beyond the furled sails of two of his own schooners, he could see unusual bustle and activity where the new steam packet *Pulaski* now lay at anchor—white bow dazzling in the early sun, flags snapping in a rising breeze off the water. He could hear the commotion, far noisier than usual, because at 8 A.M., less than two hours from now, the *Pulaski*, carrying a large and prominent group of passengers on her fourth voyage, would steam away from the city and head for Charleston and then Baltimore.

Half an hour ago, when Mark left his home on Reynolds Square, the entire household had been in confusion. His wife, Caroline, their two children, Natalie, sixteen, and twelve-year-old Jonathan, and all the servants had been in a state of turmoil as everyone seemed to be checking at once to make sure that for her much-anticipated pleasure excursion, Natalie had everything she might need. Mark and Caroline had feigned cheerfulness at breakfast while inside both were anxious because their spirited, red-haired, willful firstborn was about to make a sea voyage without them. As far as Natalie was concerned, she was going for pleasure, although she had agreed to help Virginia Mackay, a family friend, care for her two small children during the journey and at Virginia's aunt's home in Baltimore. Some responsibility would be good for Natalie, but most worrisome of all was the girl's obvious delight to be going in the care of Mark's strange, troubling uncle, Osmund Kott. Both parents had exchanged concerned glances when Natalie announced as they sat down to breakfast that "the very best part of all this is that dear Kottie will be watching over me. No one, but no one understands me the way Kottie does!"

Their daughter's stubborn devotion to Mark's uncle had deepened the strain Kott's very existence had caused between him and Caroline for all the years of their married life—and before.

Still looking out at the *Pulaski*, in which he had invested heavily, Mark struggled with his helplessness, his inadequacy to deal with what he had learned about his uncle only this morning. For years, he and Caroline had endured the awkward relationship, never truly coming to terms with it. Against Caroline's wishes, Mark had made his uncle overseer at Knightsford, the large Savannah River plantation left to Caroline by her beloved grandfather, the late Jonathan Cameron. That Cameron had turned out to be Mark's grandfather, too, still had little or no reality to him.

The young, eager, ambitious Mark Browning, orphaned at eighteen, had then determined to spend his life, not in his home city of

Philadelphia, but in Savannah, the picturesque town where his wealthy father had found his beautiful young wife, Mark's mother. She died when Mark was only three. Every memory of Melissa Cotting Browning was shrouded—not only in mystery and beauty and fragrance—but also in shadow. Mark's misty portrait of her was more real than the actual memory of the young woman who, so long ago, had been his mother. Full of dreams and hopes and a romanticized notion of the city gleaned from his father, Mark had come to Savannah with no knowledge of his own connection either to Osmund Kott or to Jonathan Cameron. As though it were only yesterday, Mark shuddered at the sharp memory of the day at Knightsford, before his marriage to Caroline, when embittered Ethel Cameron—married in name only to Jonathan—had told him the truth about Kott and about Kott's sister, Mark's own mother, Melissa Cotting. First Osmund and then Melissa had been born out of wedlock to the respected planter Jonathan Cameron and an indentured servant named Mary Cotting, whose job it was to cut and sew Ethel Cameron's fine gowns.

Mark buried his head in his hands, hoping to shut out the odd immediacy of that shattering discovery, now more than twenty years ago. He could not shut it out. What his illegitimate uncle had done this time seemed to send the clock whirring back to that day alone in the Knightsford parlor with rigid, perfectly groomed Ethel Cameron and her shocking story. Her shocking *true* story.

Now, looking down on the bustle and confusion of the wharf where the *Pulaski* was docked, Mark felt less able to comprehend the facts than he had all those years ago. Then, he had not yet realized how lovely, young Caroline Cameron had been scarred by her grandparents. Orphaned too as a child, she had known no other home but Knightsford, no parents but her grandparents who, day after day, year after year as she was growing up, spoke to each other only through her. Caroline almost worshiped her grandfather, had been able to forgive her long-despised grandmother only on her deathbed.

Eighteen years of being married to Caroline, nearly perfect years marred by nothing except the always uneasy presence of Kott, had seemed to weaken Mark's ability to live above the family tragedy of which Kott was the symbol. Both Camerons had died, but because of Mark's sense of duty, Kott had so fastened himself on to his and

Caroline's life that, time after time, Mark had been able to come close to his wife again only by making love to her. The wonder they had shared from their first night together had never failed them. They dared not discuss Osmund Kott because Caroline's fear of the man kept her normally honest and balanced nature askew. Year after year, Kott had blackmailed her beloved grandfather—blackmailed him to the day he died in the mysterious fire that had consumed the cottage at Knightsford where Mary Cotting had given birth to Osmund and Melissa. Caroline tried to forgive Kott, Mark knew, but even after his years of superior work at Knightsford as overseer, could never trust him. She would not allow him to visit the Browning home in Savannah; though she managed, for Mark's sake—and for Natalie's—to be civil with him when they visited Knightsford. Osmund Kott, to Caroline, meant only treachery.

Mark sighed heavily. Today, alone in the empty office, he knew that she had been right. Dead right. In spite of Kott's showy profession of religious conversion, his faithful attendance at Christ Church, his profitable management of Knightsford, Caroline had been right. Through the years Mark had defended his now aging uncle, feeling that, as Kott's nephew, he owed it to him to try, at least, to understand Kott's bitterness toward the widely respected Cameron. Bitterness over Jonathan Cameron's secret arrangement to have Mark's mother, little Melissa, reared in a modest, but good Savannah home, while depositing young Osmund in Bethesda Orphanage without telling anyone that the boy was his son, his illegitimate son by the one love that had consumed Cameron for most of his adult life. Of course, Kott's revengeful blackmail had been wrong, but Mark, at least, had convinced himself that he understood its root. So far as most Savannahians knew, the Camerons of Knightsford—Jonathan and his wife Ethel—had had only one son, Caroline's father, who had died with his young wife in a long-ago epidemic.

There had been times when Mark had barely controlled his temper with Caroline over Kott, although he loved her with all his heart. Shouldn't their good life, their two children, Natalie and Jonathan, Mark's steady devotion to her, be enough to enable Caroline to put the past—including her loathing of Osmund Kott—behind her? To put the dark, cold, fear-filled years of her childhood lived in the oppression of her grandmother's hatred for her grandfather, Jonathan, behind her? In every other way, his wife was, except for their best friend, Eliza Mackay, the most fair-minded person Mark had ever known. Still, she could not forgive Osmund Kott for blackmailing her adored grandfather and, as she still believed—for killing him. Mark had watched her struggle and fail in her every attempt to accept Kott.

Today, he knew that Caroline had been right, at least in part.

He still doubted the murder, but learning of his uncle's continuing treachery in the face of what had appeared to be sincere reform —only minutes ago—had destroyed Mark's tolerance of him. He had never been so close to despising himself as in this moment, staring out at the glistening new steam packet that would take his beloved Natalie away—out of his sight for the first time in her sixteen years. Today—this very morning, when it was too late to stop Kott from accompanying Natalie on the *Pulaski*'s voyage north —he'd learned that, in spite of Mark's years of trust—Kott had been stealing from him. Humiliation consumed him.

He could remember no other time when having Caroline proved right had bothered him. He loved her so wholly that when she'd bested him in any situation, he honestly had felt only pride.

Though a few years younger, Caroline had indeed known first that she loved Mark—had known it long before he knew that she was the only woman he could ever love. When they met, he had merely been passionately drawn to the perfection of her body and face. By the time they were married, he loved her with his whole being, and yet—again the heavy humiliation—he had allowed Kott's continuing presence to torment her. Had stubbornly gone on believing Kott had changed, allowing the treacherous man to scar their lives. For Mark, at least, their years together had been happy in every way. The shame mounted when it struck him for the first time today that perhaps Caroline had struggled far more than even he knew. Both he and Caroline had been more than fulfilled with their two children. Both loved, admired, even leaned on their young son, Jonathan. Natalie, certainly a handful in all ways, was also a heartful. They all but worshiped the headstrong, infinitely beautiful daughter, who had, at the age of three, seemed almost shockingly drawn to her great-grandmother, Ethel Cameron—the forbidding, isolated woman loved by no one. Caroline still fretted when a stubborn, haughty streak showed up in Natalie that made her think of the grandmother whom she had merely endured throughout her own childhood. At the same young age, the child Natalie, had also seemed to worsen the old family trouble by her sudden adoration of Osmund Kott. "It's almost as though she's clinging to them both just to plague us, Mark," Caroline had once said. A three-year-old child wouldn't—couldn't—do such a thing. They both knew this but, especially after Ethel Cameron died, Natalie's preference for Kott and his for her grew with the passing of each year. Caroline and Mark were unable to explain Natalie's behavior and ultimately did not dare to discuss it. Spontaneously, they had named their son for Jonathan Cameron, although to Mark it was more as though they'd named the boy for a revered friend—not his grandfather. They were grateful to see that young Jonathan, unlike Natalie, was a born peacemaker. We need a peacemaker, he thought, now more than ever.

Slowly, wearily, even though the day had just begun, Mark moved toward his big desk and slumped in its leather chair, only to get to his feet again, a sense of anxiety and frustration overwhelming him.

He poured water from a pitcher into a matching bowl and splashed his face, then dried it briskly with a linen towel. Somehow he must enter into the joyous departure of the *Pulaski* in a little over an hour. He must also, somehow, keep Kott's latest chicanery from Caroline. He felt at this moment as though he could do neither. Little escaped Caroline's keen perception for long. She would know sooner or later, no matter how hard he tried to protect her from the latest blow. She would know because she knew Mark better than anyone on earth, except, he supposed, Eliza Mackay.

For the first time since he'd learned of Kott's deception from his warehouse inspector, Joe Blake, right after dawn, Mark forced himself to look again at the ugly ballast rock resting on the corner of his desk. Why today? Why had Joe Blake discovered Kott's thievery today? Wasn't it enough that Natalie was leaving them, to be gone until fall? Natalie, whose presence for Mark was as necessary as breathing, was going to be, not only away from her family all summer, but also under the guardianship of the man who now, more than ever, symbolized the only trouble he and Caroline had ever experienced together. At this moment, only one thing seemed clear: Until their beautiful, bright-haired, bright-spirited daughter was safely home again, Caroline must not—*must* not find out what Os-

mund Kott had done. With Natalie gone, Mark could not bear any
shadow between him and Caroline. He had found it hard enough to
convince her that Kott would take the best care of Natalie on the
voyage, not because Kott was so honorable, but because he had,
through the years, proved his devotion to the girl.

"I try to remember, Mark, that the hateful man *is* your uncle,"
Caroline had said again and again. "Remembering almost chokes
me, but I do try."

Mark had never felt exactly ashamed of the family connection, but
he was sure that no one in Philadelphia society, in which his father,
Mark, Sr., and Melissa moved, had even a hint of her Savannah
ancestry. For all Mark knew, his own father might not have been
aware of the whole story. He had simply fallen hopelessly in love
with Melissa on a trip to Savannah, and taken her back to become
the mistress of the Browning mansion on Locust Street. When
Mark, their only child, was still too young to remember her, she had
died. From that day, he had known no real family but his wise, loyal
Aunt Nassie, his father's spinster sister for whom they had named
Natalie. Swamped by a grief from which he had never recovered,
Mark, Sr., had simply left the day after Melissa's funeral and, except
for thirteen visits in eighteen years, had traveled the world until he
drowned in a storm off the Bahamas. A few months later, Aunt
Natalie had died too. One year after that, Mark, at twenty, was on
the schooner *Eliza*, owned by merchant Robert Mackay, en route to
spend the remainder of his life in Savannah, the city his father and
mother had loved.

That no one in a town as close-knit and gossipy as Savannah had
seemed to know that his mother had been born to prominent Jonathan Cameron and his servant, Mary Cotting, still amazed him. At
least no one had admitted knowing, or Osmund Kott's blackmailing
through the years would not have continued. The name Cotting did
not sound sinister or evil—Kott did. Had his uncle so resented
having to take his unmarried mother's name that he'd changed it to
Kott?

Slumped again at his desk, Mark shuddered, tried to stop his
thoughts. Was he disillusioned in his uncle? Was he really hurt? Had
he been so fooled by Kott's years of seemingly exemplary conduct
that he'd actually forgotten the rowdy, bold extortionist Kott was
before his seeming change of heart? Had Mark actually been taken

in by Kott's recent acceptance among respected southern planters? No mere overseer had ever before been invited to write for the widely read agricultural quarterlies of the day. His uncle had written three such articles on the cultivation of Sea Island cotton.

Mark banged his desk with his fist so hard it hurt. *Hurt.* He was hurt by what his inspector had told him this morning. After only one thrust of a four-edged sword cane into a bale of fine Sea Island cotton from Knightsford, Joe Blake had found the ugly fifteen-pound ballast rock that now rested on Mark's desk. His uncle had cheated him outright; may have been cheating him for years! He had never insisted upon close inspection of the Knightsford family cotton. Mark meant to confess to no one, certainly not to Caroline, but he admitted to himself now that indeed he *had* come to trust the man she never could. He felt his face grow hot with shame. Caroline had been right all along and he had been a fool. Still, only one bale had been checked when Blake gave him the shocking news. From habit, he caught himself, hoping that, by some means, the others had not been weighted.

At the window again, he could see people gathering on the *Pulaski* wharf—passengers scheduled to depart on the grand, swift steam packet, and with them friends and relatives to wave and cheer them on their way.

Mark's heart squeezed with fresh anxiety for Natalie. Why? As a major owner of the company that had built the *Pulaski*, he knew for a fact that there wasn't a safer, sturdier boat anywhere. Foolish anxiety, W. H. Stiles, his brilliant young lawyer, had called it, but as the time grew nearer for Natalie to leave, Mark felt smothered by anxiety. He had never seen Caroline so nervous as this morning. They loved Natalie no more than they loved their gentle, good-humored son, Jonathan, but Natalie was Natalie, and everyone who knew her lived almost shamelessly under her spell. Caroline concealed her adoration better than Mark, but neither parent would really rest easily until the girl was safely home again.

Somehow when he met his family at the *Pulaski* dock a few minutes from now, he would manage to behave as though he still believed Osmund Kott to be trustworthy. Mark took out his gold watch. Nearly a quarter to seven. He must arrive there no later than seven, his "piece of work at the countinghouse" done. There had been no work to do. He had lied to Caroline. Why? Why had he bothered to get to the office so early? A feeling of near nausea swept him. He had come so early, he knew, on the thin hope that his uncle might make the boat trip from Knightsford in time to visit him for a friendly talk about Natalie's welfare on the voyage. In spite of what he'd learned about Kott's thievery this morning, he could not help wondering—would it have done Caroline irreparable harm to have invited Osmund Kott to their Reynolds Square house just this once for breakfast? Wasn't he going along on the *Pulaski* specifically to protect Natalie and William Mackay's little family? Sensible, steady William Mackay, almost like a brother because the Mackay family had welcomed Mark as a part of their own brood during his early years in Savannah, surely would not entrust his beloved young wife and two babies to an irresponsible man! William had agreed at once for Kott to go. Weighted cotton bales did not necessarily mean Kott would not look after his charges. Besides, he did adore Natalie.

Helplessly torn again between Kott and Caroline, Mark felt only relief at the sharp knock on his office door.

"Hate to have to tell you this, Mr. Browning," Joe Blake said, his rugged face crinkled with sympathy, "but there's a ballast rock in every Knightsford cotton bale! I'd rather hang than tell you, sir. I know how proud you've been of Mr. Kott's work."

For a long moment, Mark stared at him. "You're sure?"

Joe nodded. "We opened every one of the two hundred bales. The boys are repacking them now. Hung every one on your big new scale. All told, there was over two thousand pounds of ballast rock in that Knightsford shipment. Haven't had time to figure how much, but that's a sum of money out of your pocket." When Mark said nothing, Joe added gently, "You look mighty pale, sir."

"I'm—all right. Have the cotton repacked into 150-pound bales. And, Joe—not one word to anybody about any of this, do you hear me?"

"Well, three of us checked the shipment."

"Swear the other men to secrecy. I—I have to see my daughter off on the *Pulaski* now—and Mr. Kott. I promised my wife I'd spend the day at home with her and our boy. Just repack the bales and I'll give you further instructions tomorrow."

" 'Scuse me, sir, but—you plan to mention this to the old man, Kott, when you see him off on the *Pulaski?*"

"Uh—no. No, I don't. I'm going to do my best to make that a

happy—parting. Kott's in charge of my daughter, William Mackay's wife and babies. I don't want him upset about it now. I'll handle it all when he gets back. I need legal advice first anyway."

"You're the best-hearted gentleman I ever knew, Mr. Browning."

Mark's laugh was brittle, helpless. "You're dead wrong, Joe. I'm sixteen kinds of—fool."

TWO

HURRYING DOWN the steep steps that led from the upper level of Commerce Row to River Street below, Mark prayed for the nerve to seem, when he met his family at the *Pulaski* wharf, as though nothing had happened. If that was acting a lie, so be it.

Caroline, Natalie and Jonathan would be there any minute. Mark's driver, Jupiter Taylor, would see to it. There was no doubt but that W. H. and Eliza Anne Mackay Stiles would be there, too, probably bringing with them her mother, Eliza Mackay, and the two unmarried sisters, Kate and Sallie, who now wanted to be called Sarah. Mark's longtime friend William Mackay would be on hand, of course, to say good-bye to his pretty wife Virginia and their infant children, Delia and William, Jr. This would be both a happy and a sad day for William, whose world revolved around his little family. Mark remembered when quiet William fell in love with Virginia Sarah Bryan when she was a young girl, too young to marry, and how patiently he'd waited for the day when he could make her his wife forever. Even though the *Pulaski* was the finest of all possible boats north, William would be on needles and pins until Virginia was back with him.

Mark had walked only a short distance along River Street when he caught up with his old friend and counselor, Sheftall Sheftall, in his usual out-of-style colonial knee breeches, cocked hat and silver-buckled slippers, heading also toward the festive wharf.

In spite of his inner turmoil, Mark felt pride in the very look of the prosperous Savannah crowd gathering now on the wharf, which had been swept and cleared of boxes and barrels for the big occasion. He felt pride, too, in the handsome, flag-bedecked *Pulaski*, broad, white and riding low at anchor, her gangplank already down and tall stacks smoking.

Slowing his own pace to match the old man's shuffling gait, Mark slipped an arm through Sheftall's. "Good morning, sir," he said. "Our fine breeze makes the day more like spring than a Savannah summer."

Ignoring the inane remark about the weather, Sheftall stopped walking and peered up at Mark through little round wire spectacles. He said nothing.

"They say not one more passenger could go aboard," Mark went on. "At least she'll be filled to capacity when the remaining passengers board in Charleston this evening. Just think—all the way to Charleston yet this evening!"

Still looking intently up at Mark, Sheftall said, "Browning, you're prattling. Not like you. Do you think anyone reads the daily papers more carefully than I? I know about the passenger list and all your claims for the boat. 'One night at sea—one night at sea!' I've read those *Pulaski* advertisements you stockholders have been running until I'm sick of them. Something's bothering you. Want to talk about it?"

Mark let his shoulders sag. "You're right. Something is—very wrong. I hoped it didn't show."

"Well, it does." Moving toward the *Pulaski*'s wharf now, Sheftall added, "I'm not prying. Just don't try to fool Miss Caroline. She not only loves you totally, she knows you like a book. She and I still have our little talks now and then. Just as when she was a child at Knightsford and I was her beloved grandfather's lawyer."

"I—I'd like very much to tell you what's wrong, sir."

"Then what's stopping you? You know by now it will go no farther."

Careful to match the older man's slower gait, Mark blurted out the whole sickening Kott matter, sensing more deeply as he talked that what worried him most was not the loss of money on the weighted cotton bales or damage to his reputation on the London market, but the loss of trust in his uncle. Trust that had been years in forming. "He's going to be in charge of my only daughter on the voyage, Mr. Sheftall! And of William Mackay's entire family."

They had almost reached the wall of barrels and cotton bales and crates that fenced off the cleared portion of the wharf where clusters of fashionably dressed people milled about bidding loved ones *bon voyage.* The laughter and shouts and general cheer only deepened Mark's misery. Caroline and Natalie were somewhere among those excited folk—and undoubtedly so was Osmund Kott. He would simply have to leave Sheftall behind and hurry on. One thing Mark had avoided through the years was allowing Caroline to face Kott without him beside her to help smooth the meeting.

When he attempted to excuse himself, Sheftall grabbed the sleeve of Mark's jacket. "Go to your loved ones. I can't hurry. But don't worry about the weighted cotton bales today. Later for that. And don't worry about Miss Natalie. Kott may cheat you, but you can trust him with your daughter! That girl is the reason he, too, gets up in the morning."

"I want to believe that, but—"

"Then believe it. We all decide what we do and do not believe. You can trust Natalie to your uncle and I'd stake my life on it. Better still, I'd stake my *reputation* on it, and that's far more important than my ebbing life. Now go—and *believe.* Don't merely try to act cheerful. You're a dreadful actor, Browning."

Sure that his family and the Mackays were already aboard, Mark made his way through the noisy, high-spirited throng on shore, each group intent upon its own friends and family members, so that he had constantly to excuse himself in order to keep moving toward the gangplank. Along the way, he was greeted by departing Savannah friends, prominent citizens most of them: Dr. John Cumming, Mr. Samuel Parkman and one or two family members, Mr. G. B. Lamar and what appeared to be his entire family plus a niece—Rebecca, from Augusta, if Mark understood correctly when Lamar insisted upon delaying him for introductions. He was sure he also saw Mr. James Hamilton Couper from Hopeton Plantation near Brunswick. There were strangers as well in the crowd. The passenger list was not made up entirely of Savannahians.

Nowhere did he see Caroline, Natalie, Jonathan—or any of the Mackay or Stiles families. But suddenly, there stood Osmund Kott, waiting alertly at the foot of the gangplank, dressed as would be any leading citizen, his elegant top hat at a rakish angle.

"I was watching for you," Kott called, his hand out, a smile wreathing his lined, but still striking face, the breeze ruffling his long, only slightly gray hair. "Natalie's already aboard. She commissioned me to stand here until I found you. You're to go aboard at once. Natalie's orders. Not much time left. About half an hour, in fact."

"I—I'm a bit later than I meant to be," Mark said, returning the handshake. "My wife's aboard too?"

"Nothing could have stopped her. She was bound to inspect everything about Natalie's accommodations. I'll take you straight to your family."

"Never mind." Mark's tone was curt. "I prefer to see them alone. Thank you anyway."

"Fine. I can give you exact directions. When you're aboard, turn toward the bow, follow the passageway to the Captain's quarters— plainly marked. Natalie and Miss Virginia Mackay have the stateroom directly across from the Captain. Third cabin." Kott all but bowed and laughed pleasantly. "I doubt you can miss hearing your daughter. I've never seen the child so happy!"

Aboard, Mark hurried along the passageway, unable to think of anything but that his uncle had acted as though the thought of a ballast rock in a bale of cotton had never once crossed his mind.

Approaching the Captain's quarters, Mark stopped to look around, relieved to see that on either side, in case of emergency, was a stair leading to the deck, which roofed the entire boat except the bow. He had been aboard before, the day the stockholders were given a special tour of the resplendent new packet, but the interior seemed more luxurious than he remembered—the polished wood and brass gleaming—even below, away from the sunlight.

"Oh, Mother, don't be a fuddy-duddy!" He heard Natalie's laughter ripple, underlining her words. "Not today, Mother. Today is— mine! Mine and Virginia Mackay's day. We're going to be snug as two happy bugs in a rug in this gorgeous stateroom. Only two others are as elegant as this one."

"Where is Virginia?" Mark heard Caroline ask, ignoring Natalie's sassy protest. "I want to remind her of a few things just in case you get too excited and forget."

"With William, of course." Natalie over-sighed. "Weeping and laughing in his arms, I have no doubt—just because they're going to be parted for one little short summer! Mother, do you suppose I'll ever love a man as Virginia loves William Mackay? Do you? Do you?"

Mark pushed open the stateroom door, his arms out to Natalie. "Here's the man you love, beautiful lady—and at sixteen, that's as it should be."

Natalie shrieked with joy and gave him a big hug. "Where've you been, Papa? I've had a dreadful time controlling Mother. She's nosing into everything, as though I weren't sixteen and about to take a sea voyage on the very grandest packet in America! Can you control her?"

"I think my sister's the one who needs to be controlled," Jonathan said, grinning.

Mark mussed his son's thick dark hair, the color of his own, then embraced Caroline. When she clung to him, he could feel the anxiety. Her body, still slim and youthful at forty-three, was trembling. "Help me, Mark," she whispered. "Help me not to worry so about her!"

"You see, Papa? A performance like this can spoil an otherwise perfect departure." Natalie turned her mother around to face her, literally jerking her away from Mark. "Mama, this is as good a time as any for us to get one thing straight. You haven't fooled me one bit for all these years. I know you despise my dear old Kottie, no matter how polite you try to be when he's around. I also know you won't allow him to visit us in town. It's not Papa's fault, it's yours. Do you deny I'm right?"

Mark gripped Caroline's arm to steady her, but said nothing.

"I've never once told you Osmund Kott could not visit us, Natalie."

"Then why doesn't he, Mama?"

"You two see a lot of each other at Knightsford," Mark said lamely. "He visits us in our Knightsford house."

Natalie gave him her most superior, demeaning smile. "Sometimes the two of you remind me of—children," she said, her voice suddenly almost casual. "Enough of all that. Kottie and I are going to have a gorgeous time on our sea voyage, and he'll be more than welcome at Virginia's aunt's house in Baltimore. Virginia told me so." Then she added sternly, "You two are to remember that I'll be as safe with my blessed old Kottie as I was as an infant in my mother's arms."

"You were a very wiggly infant and didn't particularly like being— in anyone's arms," Caroline said.

"Mother, this is a happy day, and if neither of you can manage a smile or wish me a beautiful time, I intend to have one anyway."

Mark did his best to smile. "We want you to have the time of your young life, don't we, Mother?"

"Of course," Caroline said, also trying to sound reassuring. "You'll be the belle of every Baltimore party, too, with all your pretty new gowns. Just promise you'll be a ladylike belle."

"She will be, Mama. Don't worry," Jonathan offered with his warm, encompassing smile. "Sister just tries to upset you sometimes. She doesn't mean anything by it."

Natalie stuck out her tongue impishly at her parents and at Jonathan. "Only I know what I mean, little brother, and I fully intend to be a *Natalie* belle." Then, abruptly, she kissed Jonathan and embraced her parents. "I do like being a Natalie-anything," she said, meaning it, "and I also like being your daughter. I like being my doting father's daughter and I like being my fussy mother's daughter." She stepped back, surveying them both. "You know, you're a very, very handsome couple. Perhaps when I get back from the North, I can teach you both how to have fun again."

Her seemingly casual comment stunned Mark. He was relieved when, as always, Jonathan tried to ease things. "We're going to have fun today," the boy said. "Papa's taking a holiday at home—with just Mama and me."

At that moment, William and Virginia Mackay, each carrying a child, appeared at the stateroom door and Natalie launched into an elaborate explanation, directed mainly at Virginia, of just how the well-constructed, somewhat ingenious extra bed worked. Each stateroom was large and roomy, containing every convenience, she pointed out as though she had designed them. There were two large berths in this room and another bottom berth was on casters—now pushed under out of sight, allowing more space. "So," she explained, "after we shut the door for the night, Virginia, the third berth can simply be drawn out with a tiny tug. Everyone come in inside and I'll show you."

"Won't it be a bit crowded?" Kott asked from the still open doorway.

"Oh, there you are, Kottie!" Natalie beamed at the older man.

"I should think it would be crowded," Mark agreed. "In fact, I'd say the bed can't be pulled out with all of us in the room, Natalie."

"Oh, all right. But isn't it a delicious stateroom?"

"Delicious, Natalie?" William Mackay asked, teasing her. "But what I want to know is, who will be the last one to bed?"

"I'll bet Natalie sleeps in the bed you pull out," Jonathan said. "She'll like that."

"You're right, little brother. After all, Virginia needs to be alongside the berth the babies will sleep in."

"That's unselfish of you," Virginia said. "Sure you won't mind hauling your bed out each night?"

" 'Only one night at sea,' Virginia, according to the advertisements. And anyway, I *am* unselfish as long as I get my way."

Everyone laughed. Natalie had always gotten her way, Mark thought, often by the altogether unchildlike method she was using now—the trick of seeming to laugh at herself. They all began to chatter pleasantly, and then Caroline reached for infant William Mackay, and told Mark to take two year-old Delia.

"You two grown-up Mackays need a minute alone for a proper good-bye," Caroline said as she herded the others out of the stateroom to look for Miss Eliza and her party.

"I wonder if anything's wrong with Miss Eliza," Mark said, as they all walked along the central passage. "It isn't at all like her to be late for an occasion like this."

"She's bound to be here somewhere," Natalie insisted.

"Of course she's here," Caroline agreed. "Kate and Sarah—the Stileses too. They wouldn't think of letting Virginia and the babies leave without a good-bye kiss from everyone in the family."

Once up the steep stair and out onto the deck, Mark called, "There they come! Look at Miss Eliza cut along. You'd never think she'd had her sixtieth birthday, would you?"

In the happy confusion of greetings and well-wishing, Mark couldn't help noticing his uncle. Osmund Kott, far from hanging back in deference to this intimate family moment, strode ahead and began bowing over the ladies' hands, shaking hands with William Henry Stiles, greeting the two spinster Mackay daughters as though he were one of the family. Mark thought he had conducted himself with Kott rather well so far, but his uncle's brazen manner right now filled him with fury.

He handed little Delia to Eliza Mackay and turned away from the laughing, hugging group to lean on the ship's railing, his back to them all. Instantly his young attorney, W. H. Stiles, was standing beside him.

"Finding it harder than you expected to say good-bye to that bewitching daughter of yours, Mark?"

"Yes, W.H., I guess I am." He looked straight at Stiles. "Natalie will be all right in the care of—my uncle, won't she? You do feel Caroline and I made the correct decision, don't you?"

Stiles's quick, puzzled frown would have been answer enough, but looking out over the river, Stiles asked softly, so as not to be overheard by the others, "Why on earth do you have such a question at this late hour? Your uncle is an elderly man, but in years only. He's straight as a pine, his mind's as sharp as yours or mine—he so idolizes Natalie it's almost pathetic. He'd die before he'd allow any harm to come to the girl." When Mark said nothing, William Henry asked, "Has something happened I don't know about?"

To avoid attracting attention, Mark pretended to inspect one of the lifeboats hanging from its hooks over the deck. "Yes," he said. "Yes, something has happened, W.H. I'd like you to be in my office this afternoon about four o'clock if you can be."

"Of course. But I thought you'd promised Caroline and Jonathan not to work at all today."

"I did. That's why I said four o'clock. I'll have most of the day with them. I have to talk to you. It's too late to stop Kott from going on the *Pulaski*—at least, without upsetting Natalie *and* Caroline. It may not be too late, though, to stop him from ruining me. That is, if you can find a legal way to help."

Back in the stateroom, embracing, kissing, embracing again, William and Virginia Mackay clung to each other.

"You do understand, don't you, dear William, why I have to go? Oh, I know you do. You always understand me. But tell me again," Virginia whispered, her cheek pressed to his, "that you do long for me to show our two darlings to my mother's only living sister. I can't

21

bear leaving you, but Auntie will die happy once she's seen them both."

Still holding her close, William tried to laugh at her melodramatic statement. "Virginia, your aunt isn't even sick! She's isn't about to die. But yes, yes, I understand."

"People sicken so quickly. My mother died and she was a lot younger than Auntie."

"I know, but"—he held her away from him just enough to look at her—"if you want to leave me with enough courage even to try to get along without you until fall, you've got to do one thing for me now. Smile. Please?"

Her pretty, trusting face contorted with the effort. All that came was a fresh torrent of tears.

"I'll write to you every day," he promised. "I'm not much of a letter writer, but I'll put my heart on a piece of paper for you every day. And you must write to me often—even today on board ship. Promise?"

She nodded, tried again to smile, failed and buried her face in the rough linen of his jacket. "Your shoulder smells so good, William. Your shoulder always smells so clean and good. I don't want to be away from your shoulder. . . ."

"The time will fly faster for you than for me, you'll see. I'll just be at our blessed place at Causton's Bluff. Thanks to dear Cousin Margaret's generosity, you'll have our own place to come back to. I'll just—be there, in the old familiar rooms, in our bed at night—missing you, trying to fix the place up nice for when you come home. The time will go faster for you, seeing new things and all."

Once more, he looked at her, his eyes begging for a smile. Once more she tried and failed. The *Pulaski*'s whistle blew. William held her close again, kissed her again, touched her cheek, then led her along the passageway toward the stair and the family up on deck. When they were almost there, Virginia said, "I'll try as hard as I can to smile before I'm—out of sight."

Looking down at her, William laughed softly. "Don't worry if you can't. I'll remember your smile anyway. Whether you manage or not, honey, I'll remember your smile."

Cheers swelled to a roar. From ashore and from the railing of the grand white packet, arms waved until shoulders ached, as the *Pu-*

laski, side-wheels churning, stacks belching smoke, whistle blasting, inched majestically out into the Savannah River and headed toward the sea.

Eliza Mackay, standing beside her son William, held tightly to his hand, giving him her strength, he knew. The strength that had held their family together through the first empty years after his father's sudden death on a trip to New York with William and his brother Jack and Mark Browning. William hadn't been with his mother in the months after Papa was gone. He and Jack were in the North, just starting school. But Mark had often told him of the strength in Mama during the weeks and months when they were all trying to learn to live in the rambling house on Broughton Street without the high spirits and cheerful sound of Papa's voice, and his laughter.

What a peculiar thing to come to mind right now, William thought, when with every nerve in his body he was straining for still another look at Virginia. Tender, loving little Virginia, holding their tiny son William in one arm. Natalie, with little Delia, stood waving a bright green handkerchief that exactly matched her traveling dress.

And, as big as you please, smack between the two young ladies stood old Osmund Kott, their protector. William had had to think a long time about letting Kott go as the sole escort for his wife and children. But once he'd talked it over with Mark, he'd agreed. Mark Browning, he guessed, could convince him of just about anything. And after all, Kott had behaved himself like a responsible gentleman for a long, long time.

William's married sister, Eliza Anne Stiles, moved now to stand on the other side of him and took his free hand. Most of the time, Eliza Anne, even when she was kind of smarty-pants and young, had been a good, loyal sister, who'd taken his side against their gun-loving brother Jack when William got sick the day he'd shot his first rabbit. He was glad to have her beside him now.

"Look, William," she shouted over the other voices of the crowd milling about them on the wharf. "Virginia's pointing to her mouth! She's trying to tell you something. I wonder what."

William grinned. "I know what she's telling me, Sister. I begged her to give me one smile before I kissed her the last time. She hated so to leave me, she couldn't do it. They're too far out for me to see, but I know she's smiling now and wants me to know it." He waved as hard as he could. "Virginia always wants me to *know* how she feels. She never is a bit tricky."

The *Pulaski* was moving faster, still gleaming white against the blue sky, gulls dipping in her wake. William watched her disappear around the curve in the river, and slowly, the crowd on the wharf turned away. William saw a few weep openly, but most were smiling, their admiration of the handsome new boat uppermost. Friends and loved ones could no longer be seen, so attention had turned to dockside talk and some began to walk slowly toward the steps that led up to Bay Street.

"Have you noticed Mark's face, William?" Eliza Anne asked.

"He hates to see Natalie go."

"I think it's more than that. I've never seen him so worried."

"I guess I've been so taken with watching Virginia out of sight, I haven't noticed much about Mark. He does look troubled, though."

"Mark Browning could never hide anything, no matter how hard he tried. I'm going to speak to W.H. about it. I know something beside Natalie's leaving is bothering him. You don't suppose Osmund Kott's caused more trouble between him and Caroline, do you?"

"That's silly, Sister. They both agreed to his going along."

"All I know is that nothing ever comes between them but Osmund, and I'm going to speak to W.H. about it. He *is* Mark's lawyer."

"What on earth could W.H. do to ease Mark's heart when he's just said good-bye to Natalie?"

"Mama! I didn't know you were eavesdropping."

"I wasn't. We're simply all standing here together," William's mother said. "And I saw Mark's face too. I agree. He needs help, but I'd say he needs a friend this time, not a lawyer."

"My husband is the kind of man who can be both at the same time." Eliza Anne flared a little.

"Nobody's trying to stop you, Sister, from telling W.H. anything," William said, only half teasing her.

"Well, he hates it when I pry."

"So do I," their mother said firmly. "But I think you're right about Mark needing your husband. I've been standing here longing to go put my arms around him."

THREE

BY THE TIME the dockside crowd dispersed, the Exchange clock had struck nine. Mark instructed Jupiter to drive slowly back to Reynolds Square. The day was not yet hot and he, at least, dreaded their empty house without Natalie. Suddenly, because she was gone, there would now be less playfulness in the big house, too much heavy silence without her startling opinions and declarations. Of course, Mark kept the dread to himself, knowing full well that Caroline shared it anyway. And since young Jonathan was trying so hard to make them laugh, to lift their spirits, mentioning how he would miss the unpredictable moods of his daughter would have been cruel.

At home, the three changed into comfortable cooler clothes—Mark, a favorite fine-spun white cotton shirt, open at the neck; Caroline, a soft blue voile; Jonathan, a play shirt and trousers, his feet bare.

"You look like a man ready for a day of no school," Mark said, as Jonathan hugged them both the instant they joined him in the small drawing room downstairs.

"You're a—joy, Jonathan," Caroline said, a bit absently, Mark thought.

"I'm ready for whatever we're going to do today," Jonathan announced, escorting his mother with exaggerated gallantry to her wing chair near the window. "What are we going to do, Mama?"

Mark felt, more than saw, Caroline's struggle as she tried to act naturally with her son. "Do?" she asked. "I'll be helping Maureen

with our dinner after a while—I have some letters I could write."
She managed to smile up at him now. "No school for the day and
your father a gentleman of leisure. Isn't it up to the two of you?"

"What would you like to do, Papa? I'm ready for anything."

With all his heart, Mark longed to think of something that might
please Jonathan. Nothing came. Nothing but the gnawing anxiety
over Natalie in the care of Osmund Kott. "I'll—uh—I'll have to give
our day some thought, son. And—I will, I will," he added lamely.

There was a long silence in the room, and then Jonathan said,
"Kottie's a good old fellow. I really like him fine. He'll take good
care of Sister. I wouldn't worry, Papa—Mama."

Mark looked at Caroline. Her face was turned away. "We're—
trying not to worry, son," she said. "I'm sure you're right that—
Natalie will be just fine."

"I wish you sounded surer, Mama. But I guess you are trying.
What would you like for us to do on this special day with Papa at
home? What would you *really* like to do?"

"I hadn't thought either, I'm afraid. Don't you have any bright
ideas? Your new books are here from London. Would you like to
read this morning?"

Mark jumped in quickly. "Good idea! I brought home a thick
batch of market reports last night. We could go in the garden out
back and have a good reading session. Would you like that?"

"What would Mama do?"

"I can always find plenty to keep me busy."

Mark watched his son turn and walk slowly to the tall front window facing Reynolds Square. Jonathan, he knew, was not pouting.
In every line of his shoulders, there was simple disappointment.
He'd expected something entirely different of this one day when his
father actually stayed home from his countinghouse. "We've both
made our quite inane suggestions," Mark said, trying to joke. "They
fell flat as pancakes, so far as I can tell. How about an idea from you,
son? What do you want the very most to do today?"

In one joyous leap, the boy was back beside them, beaming.
"Take a picnic to Knightsford! We could have a good long time out
there and still be home before dark."

Without one thought as to what his son might want to do, Mark
had made that four o'clock appointment at his office with William
Henry Stiles. Why had seeing his attorney today seemed so impor-

tant? Osmund Kott would be away until fall. He'd made the appointment in order to try to ease his own worry and anxiety, of course.
Involuntarily, he sighed, so loudly, Jonathan asked if he'd said anything wrong.

"No, no, son. Of course not. I'm—disgusted with myself. Not
you."

"Why, Mark?"

Without daring to look at Caroline, he answered, "I did a stupid
thing this morning and now I wish I hadn't." That much was true,
but he didn't need to look at his wife to know that she was fully
aware that he was not telling them everything. The room was filled
with such uneasiness that Mark got up abruptly and began to pace.

"If you have something to tell me—alone, dear, Jonathan
wouldn't mind running outside for a few minutes."

Mark forced a not very convincing laugh. "I know he wouldn't.
Unlike his curious sister, Jonathan respects privacy. Don't you, son?
But no. I haven't any secrets from either of you." That was a lie. It
sounded like it. "I simply made an appointment with W.H. at four
today. And now I'm sorry."

"Jupiter would gladly go by W.H.'s law offices to change it,"
Caroline offered.

"That's a good idea. I'll send him right over."

"No, Papa. It's fine with me if we don't go to Knightsford for any
old picnic."

Mark looked at his son. There were tears in his eyes.

"That old picnic doesn't matter. I'll just sit in the garden with you
—and read. Nothing matters except that you and Mama don't go on
—being like this together!"

Mark caught Caroline's quick, troubled glance. "Being—like
what, darling?" she asked the boy.

"You know. You both know. If you don't, I don't know how to tell
you."

"But you must try to tell us!" Caroline was suddenly almost
pleading.

Jonathan looked from one to the other. "I guess I wish you'd—
both go back to being close and happy, like I'm used to having you."

On impulse, Mark went to Caroline, pulled her almost roughly to
her feet and held her so close for so long, the old familiar rush of
desire surged up in him, blinding him to everything beyond this

unexpected moment. For the first time in weeks, he realized how long it had been since he'd touched her this way. "Caroline," he breathed, "oh, Caroline, everything has always come right when—I hold you!"

She was clinging to him too, almost desperately. "Mark," she whispered. "Mark, we must be careful!"

"Why? Why—must—we—be careful?" He spoke haltingly, forming his words between kisses. "Our highly—intelligent—son has—already left for the kitchen. I'm—sure Maureen—needs him to—to help her peel apples—or grind coffee. . . . Caroline! The boy's right. Don't ever be—away from me again."

"I never—want to be. But, Mark, you'll have to—help me."

By early afternoon the day had become magical . . . the kind of magic Jonathan had hoped for. The three together again—and alone. The Knightsford picnic forgotten, all three seemed even more excited to be setting a small Queen Anne table—carried from the parlor to the backyard—with the best crystal, the new Staffordshire china. When Jonathan appeared with Maureen, each holding a handle of the huge silver platter bearing a succulent, aromatic pork roast, Mark and Caroline hurried to take their places on either side, so that their son could sit at the head of the table.

"Dinner is served," Jonathan announced grandly, "and later, a big old chocolate pie!"

When Jonathan had seated his mother and taken his place at the head—his smile brightening the already sunlit day—Maureen cleared her throat. "Haven't you forgotten something, Master Jonathan?"

"Oh—oh yes. Mama—Papa? Maureen thinks that since I ground the beans and since this is such a special, happy day, I might just have my first cup of coffee with my hunk of pie!"

Mark and Caroline agreed that indeed the day had come for that first cup of coffee—with lots of milk, of course.

When Maureen went back inside the house to bring the vegetables, Mark thanked God for their food and for the enchanted day. Then, while he began to carve the roast, Jonathan said quite casually —putting his father completely at ease, as always, "There'll be plenty of time, Papa, for everything, you'll see. For our good dinner in the garden, for my first cup of coffee—and you won't even have to walk fast to make it to your office by four o'clock."

There was plenty of time for everything. Jonathan was fast asleep under the big live oak at the rear of the garden when Mark kissed Caroline and headed toward his countinghouse to keep his appointment with Stiles. True, he could have walked slowly. It was still not quite three-thirty, but making love to Caroline so unexpectedly in the middle of a workday had made him feel like striding. He'd also overeaten, but so much time had gone by since he'd known or recklessly satisfied any kind of hunger, he didn't care. Savannah's always embracing sky was cloudless and blue, the high sun pouring more heat over the city now that the breeze had changed with the tide. The problem of what to do about Kott remained, but Mark felt better—even found himself wishing he'd sent Jupiter to postpone the meeting with W.H. until tomorrow.

Still, something had to be done to rid both him and Caroline forever of the shadow his uncle had always cast between them. Upstairs, earlier, in his arms, his kisses still on her mouth, she had vowed that she did trust Mark wholly—in all things. Above all else, he had always wanted her trust. He had seldom lied to her outright about Kott, but her ongoing fear of the man had many times caused Mark to leave too much unsaid.

Slowing his stride a bit as he neared the entrance to his office at Number One Commerce Row, he felt the first small hope that by some means he and W.H. would find a way to control Kott. Being with Caroline today had set him on a new course. He was sick of misrepresenting his own conduct with Kott. His uncle had cheated him. There was now no more excuse for the feeling of responsibility toward someone who just happened to be his mother's brother.

Unlocking the front door of his countinghouse, Mark felt a fresh surge of determination to find a way to handle Kott. Certainly, there would be no problem in convincing Eliza Anne's brilliant young husband that his uncle needed handling. W.H. had fought Mark at every turn through the years of Kott's so-called religious awakening because he believed it all a sham. Still reserving judgment on his uncle's faith or lack of it, Mark was at last ready to take some kind of legal action to keep the threatening old man in check—he prayed without hurting Natalie.

• • •

In the afternoon of that first day at sea, Natalie spotted a wooden settee and a high-backed white rocker on the shady side of the *Pulaski*'s deck and motioned to Virginia Mackay and her shipboard acquaintance, Rebecca Lamar of Augusta, to join her. Rebecca, niece of successful Savannah businessman Gazaway Bugg Lamar, seemed pleased to have found Natalie and Virginia aboard. The two young ladies joined Natalie, who was seating herself dramatically in the white rocker, the long, full skirt of her green traveling dress spread just so.

"Sit here by me on the settee, Virginia," Rebecca Lamar said. "I love your pink dress. Or is it rose? And, Natalie, you're a picture in that white chair in your most *inconspicuous* bright green!"

"I thought I might be," Natalie said lightly. "I hope you're joking about my being inconspicuous, though, because, Rebecca—have you seen *him?*"

"Him?"

"Don't pretend innocence. You're single. It's all right for you to be looking around. Have you seen that gorgeous tall Adonis with an athlete's shoulders and golden curls?" She fanned herself and pretended to swoon.

"No!" Rebecca sat up, peering around the now almost empty deck. "All the oldies and children have undoubtedly gone to their quarters to take naps—out of the sun. How have I missed a gorgeous *young* man?"

"Where did you see him, Natalie?" Virginia wanted to know.

"On the wharf in Savannah, silly! I don't understand how anyone could have missed him. But at least, I have Virginia as my witness that you, Rebecca, did not see him first. He's mine."

Rebecca, about Virginia's age, winked over the head of the sixteen-year-old. "Virginia, did you notice anyone who resembles an Adonis?"

"Of course she didn't notice him," Natalie scoffed. "Poor Virginia is hopelessly hooked to good old William Mackay. She literally has eyes for no other man on earth."

Virginia laughed. "Happily, that's the whole truth, but I think I did see my William shake hands with the handsome young Adonis when our families were leaving the boat."

Natalie sat bolt upright in her rocker. "William shook hands with Adonis? Are you sure? Do you think he knows him?"

"I can't be certain, but I'd say no. He seemed only to be giving him a friendly handshake before he boarded. You know how kind my William is. This young man was evidently all alone."

"Hm-m. All alone . . ." Natalie was on her feet now, peering both ways along the deck. "Well, I certainly don't intend to wait until we get back to Savannah so old William can introduce me. Anyway, I don't think Adonis lives in Savannah. He may be on his way to—New York, or Philadelphia. I'm not going to wait. Not any longer than dinner tonight, in fact."

"And how do you propose maneuvering an introduction?" Virginia wanted to know.

Natalie, seated again, her bright, long skirt respread for the best effect, snorted prettily. "Virginia, you're an old married lady with two children, but you're not at all worldly-wise."

Unperturbed, Virginia laughed softly. "And why should I be worldly-wise? William's been in love with me since I was twelve years old!"

"Was your adoring husband worried about your taking this sea voyage with two such small children, Virginia?" Rebecca asked.

"Yes. He'll worry, bless him, until we're all home safely at Causton's Bluff again this fall. But my husband is the most understanding man in the whole wide world. It—it was really terrible for both of us —saying good-bye." Her eyes filled with tears. She tried to laugh. "I feel foolish, but it was far harder than I dreamed it would be."

"Truthfully, I almost didn't come at all," Rebecca Lamar declared. "My uncle really had to talk hard and fast to convince me that the *Pulaski* is absolutely safe. As safe as she is swift. He's a big stockholder in the company, you know. As I understand it, this splendid packet is owned mostly by Savannah men. Maybe some from Charleston."

"My father's a stockholder too," Natalie said, not much interested in the turn of conversation. "I would have come, though, even if he hadn't owned any of the ship. I was absolutely—dying to come!"

"I've known you only these few hours since we left Savannah, Natalie, but I'll wager you're ready to try most anything."

"Oh, Rebecca, you're right," Virginia agreed.

Natalie merely glanced their way and allowed them a somewhat bemused smile, as though to say, they're both so much older than I —and so much *younger*, really.

"I'm serious. I was downright frightened of the whole idea," Rebecca went on. "I'm terrified of water. Absolutely terrified of it." She pointed behind them. "Has either of you noticed those two skimpy little lifeboats? Don't they look puny when you consider that there are about ninety passengers already—before we take on any of the Charleston people—and thirty-seven crew members? Do you suppose they're the only boats aboard?"

Virginia shuddered. "I've never liked the water either, but I think I'd trust myself to the sea before I'd trust those boats. I do believe there are at least two more, though."

"Sh! *Look!*" Natalie whispered sharply. "Don't say anything silly, either of you. He's coming this way. *Alone.* Go on talking, but nothing stupid. And don't giggle! Don't sound *young.*"

Virginia laughed. "Here we are in our twenties, Rebecca, being tutored by a sixteen-year-old."

"I meant every word," Natalie said. "Go on, say something intelligent."

Virginia cleared her throat and gave it a try: "Of course, this *is* the time of year when everyone of means goes north to escape the heat and fever. Well, almost everyone. And our passenger list reaches beyond Savannah, too. I hear Judge Rochester of New York is aboard after a visit to Florida, with a party of some eleven persons."

"Well, 'one night at sea,' as the advertisements said, is a mighty drawing card," Rebecca picked up the "intelligent" talk. "I understand, too, that there were never such safe boilers as the *Pulaski*'s. Of the best copper and of enormous strength. I'm sure you know all this, though, Natalie, since your father is a stockholder. The boat's engine is also one of the best ever made. Just think, on her voyage before this one, she made the run from Charleston to Baltimore in only forty-eight hours!"

"I really can't believe we'll be in Charleston this very evening," Virginia said.

"Is your party going ashore for the night, Natalie?"

The tall, broad-shouldered young man stood within a few feet of them now, leaning on the ship's railing, looking out to sea. He had not yet passed where they sat, but had evidently been struck suddenly—just before reaching them—by the glory of sun and water.

Natalie waited a moment before answering Rebecca's question as to where she and Virginia and Kott would spend the night. Then, deftly rearranging her skirt, she said far more distinctly than necessary for her companions to hear, "No, we're not going ashore in Charleston. We much prefer to remain on board. It should be a gorgeous night. In fact, I'm longing to be right here on deck—under the stars—until a very, very late hour. You may go on to bed, Virginia, you and the children. After all, I have the caster berth. No problem at all if I come in late."

The young man turned to face them now, hat in hand. He smiled politely, bowed and strolled on down the spacious deck.

When he was safely out of hearing, Virginia said, "Natalie Browning, you're awfully forward to be so young! I'm sure he heard you say you'd be out here—late tonight. If you are, you know Mr. Kott will be with you, but you didn't inform him of that. I'm sure he heard you."

"Good!" Too excited to be quite as worldly-wise and mature as she intended, Natalie was now sitting bolt upright in her rocker, rather more like a fourteen-year-old. "Good," she repeated. "I think he *is* traveling alone, Rebecca, don't you?"

"Maybe. And I agree he's terribly handsome. A bit rugged, but definitely handsome. In his twenties, like us, would you say, Virginia?"

Ignoring that, Natalie blurted, "I don't see anything so marvelous about only one night at sea! I wish there were ten nights at sea." Abruptly, she asked—demanded, rather: "Tell me you two would like some iced syrups! I'll gladly go for some—or find a steward."

"Why yes—that might be nice," Virginia said. "But no stops along the way. Perhaps later some mutual friend can introduce you to your young man. Natalie, do please remember you're in my care."

Tossing her head as she hurried off, Natalie called back, "I'm really in Kottie's care. We both are. And I think it's time you relieved the poor man from playing nursemaid to your children."

When Natalie had gone, Rebecca Lamar asked, "Who is this gentleman named Kott?"

"Actually, he's the overseer at Knightsford, the plantation Natalie's mother inherited."

"Isn't it a bit odd sending an overseer to protect you?"

Virginia smiled. "It's a little hard to explain, actually. Mr. Kott is —very dear to Natalie. He adores her. It's almost as though he were related to her. In a way, Osmund Kott is more than an overseer. My husband thinks highly of him as an agriculturist. William says Kott is an expert at planting and managing a plantation. And William knows. He's also very smart about planting. Thanks to his wonderful cousin, Margaret McQueen, my husband now owns our plantation. She gave him Causton's Bluff east of the city. We've lived there almost since our marriage three years ago." She leaned her head back against the high wooden settee. "And oh, sometimes I have to pinch myself to believe such happiness as ours."

"I think I envy you that."

"You'll find it one day, Rebecca, I'm sure." She sat up. "Say, perhaps I should relieve Mr. Kott. I know he wants to walk in this lovely sunshine. He's been kind staying all this time with my babies."

"But shouldn't we wait for Natalie to come back with our ices?"

"I suppose so, but I'm going to find her if she isn't back soon."

"You know, Virginia, she is without a doubt the most beautiful girl I've ever seen."

"Every other young lady her age in the entire city of Savannah is in Natalie's shade where beauty goes. But she does need some watching. Oh, she's gracious and charming, not at all devious—just very, very headstrong and teeming with ideas about everything. Spoiled, too. Her parents all but worship the child."

"Speak of the beautiful scamp and here she comes, looking like a storm cloud."

"Also quite empty-handed. What's the matter, Natalie? Couldn't you find a steward?"

In a most unladylike manner, Natalie flopped in her rocker in sheer disgust. "No. I couldn't find *anybody!*"

After Virginia excused herself to see to the children, Natalie turned earnestly to Rebecca Lamar. "You—really didn't know that golden young Adonis who bowed to us, did you? You're not just pretending, are you?"

"If I'd known him, don't you think he would have spoken to me when he bowed to us as he strolled by?"

"I suppose so. Yes, yes, of course he would have." She sighed heavily.

"Listen. My uncle, Gazaway Lamar, knows just about everyone—from Savannah all the way up to Philadelphia. I'll speak to him. It just could be that after most of the others leave the boat for the night in Charleston, my uncle could—"

"Yes! Oh yes, let's cross our fingers that Mr. Adonis will stay aboard, too, tonight. Better still, I might even *pray* that he will. I'll also ask Kottie to help. Between God and Kottie, I'm sure there will be some suitable way for me to meet him!"

FOUR

MARK WAITED nearly half an hour for William Henry Stiles to arrive at the Browning Company offices, but the wait seemed almost pleasant because things had gone so well at home today, all thanks to his young son Jonathan. Still sick at heart over what his uncle had done, Mark somehow had gained new strength. He would have to live with the gnawing worry for Natalie's safety at sea until they learned of her arrival in Baltimore. The long summer without her stretched endlessly ahead, but the voyage obviously made his adored daughter so happy, he would manage somehow. The short wait for Stiles was almost welcome. At least, he could think more clearly than during the chaotic time spent alone in his office early this morning. This morning . . . what a long time ago it seemed. So much was still wrong, but so much had been set right with Caroline.

All thanks to my son, he thought, standing once more at the east window, still only half-seeing the river traffic. No two people in love can merely talk out a problem as shapeless as ours has been. Actually he and Caroline had been so in love, so close, that nearly a decade of their married life had passed before either could admit that a problem existed. Neither could have pointed to a time when their always eager passion had begun to cool. To cool? The hour together that began the magic of today proved there had been no cooling, just neglect. Not once had Caroline ever complained outright that Mark was too soft on Osmund Kott. She had merely implied it by keeping her distance from the strange, deceptive man.

That word "deceptive" was the key, Mark thought now, but Caroline had not been deceived. Her husband had been.

Back at his desk, his mind went again to Jonathan. Caroline and I both needed the boy's blunt, gentle honesty to draw us back into each other's arms again. What a difference between our two children! Natalie so adored Osmund Kott that she came close at times to resenting her mother for not liking him. What mattered to Natalie nearly always had directly to do with what or whom Natalie liked or did not like. What mattered to Jonathan was that they all stay close.

He leaned back in his chair and propped his boots carefully on the polished surface of his huge mahogany partner's desk. He smiled a little. Being careful of finely made furniture was a habit of years, thanks to Aunt Nassie, who had reared him. Her quiet, firm, careful lectures about the value and beauty of unscarred, polished wood were still a part of him today in late middle age. He wondered how much or how little he'd been like his own son for dear Aunt Nassie. Jonathan was certainly all boy, but gentle, bright, sensitive—a peacemaker. Maybe a born philosopher, who often secretly shamed his father.

How, he wondered, would Aunt Nassie have handled her namesake, Natalie? Fairly well, of course, being Aunt Nassie. Only fairly well, though, Natalie being Natalie. The Exchange clock struck the half hour. Aloud, he said, "In less than two hours, if all has gone well, my bewitching daughter will be in Charleston! *If all has gone well* . . ."

He welcomed William Henry Stiles's knock at his door.

"Cheer up! I'm certain all is fine aboard our magnificent new steam packet," Stiles said, after his apology for being late. "In fact, I wish I'd freed up still more cash to invest in the *Pulaski*. I'm that sure of her continuing success."

"I pray you're right, W.H.," Mark said, offering the armchair on the other side of the desk to his elegantly dressed young friend, whose almost perpetual enthusiasm seemed somehow not to match his aesthetic features.

"Of course I'm right, Mark. Why, by the time the Charleston passengers board her tomorrow morning, she'll be carrying more than a hundred and twenty paying fares. And in safety. One of our most assuring features on that boat is our duplicate crew. Passengers always in the care of a fresh crew. Lib and I are terribly eager to travel on her, but I'm determined to take my wife first to my beloved Etowah River country."

Still only amused by W.H.'s new passion for the Georgia upcountry, Mark asked, "You don't get that wild frontier off your mind often, do you?"

"I think of almost nothing else—except, of course, politics. My friend, if I established residence up there in Cass County among those mainly uneducated small farmers and mill owners, I'd win a congressional seat hands down. No wonder the Cherokees hung on to that land for so long. I swear to you, the richness of its soil, the sheer beauty of the terrain in the Etowah River valley is—" He stopped. "Look here, old man, you made this appointment because you had some urgent need for it. Not to hear me prattle on about my own affairs. Some other time, though, I mean to ask your advice on how to persuade my charming Lib to leave Savannah and flee with me to the wilderness."

Mark grinned. "You're asking *me* to persuade Eliza Anne Mackay Stiles—*against her will?*"

"Why not? You watched her grow up. Lived right in the same house with Lib and her family for nearly ten years. She still thinks you're the greatest Savannahian of us all." He leaned toward Mark. "Now, what's the trouble? Why the urgency to see me?"

Mark went straight to the heart of the matter—told him all he'd discovered that morning of his uncle's cheating. Stiles had been told, when he became Mark's attorney at the death of T. U. P. Charlton some three years ago, the whole story of Mark's strange blood relationship to Kott. Today, he filled Stiles in on another aspect of the problem about which Mark normally did not speak: Caroline's continuing mistrust—outright fear of his uncle, her near panic when Mark and Natalie had insisted that Osmund Kott should be allowed to accompany Natalie on the voyage north.

William Henry's seemingly irrelevant question, when Mark had finished, stunned him: "Why do you suppose Natalie has always shown such fondness—even dependence—on Kott? Lib tells me the child doesn't have any idea that Kott is your uncle, but that she has literally adored him all her life. Does that ever bother you?"

"Of course it bothers me! It's bothered me from the moment of their first meeting, when Natalie was just a little girl. He adores her, too. I've never seen one sign in him of anything but genuine concern for her. He's a—scoundrel, a liar, even a cheat—in spite of his Christian profession you've doubted all along. But I have to believe he's wholly genuine with Natalie. She's—the only one, in fact.''

"How old is Kott now?"

"At least seventy-one." Mark sighed. "And so far as I can tell, every year he lives, he seems to live more and more—for Natalie.''

"Adoring your daughter while cheating you for extra cash, eh? Well, men have lived for far less than a beautiful child and cash. What do you want to do about the shipment of weighted cotton bales, Mark? You'll have to pay out of your own pocket for what he's done. I'm inclined to doubt that he's done this before. You'd have heard from your British buyers. I shudder at the thought of Browning Company being accused of short-weighting.'' W.H. shook his head. "What an innocent you've been! Suspecting and checking nearly every other supplier to your firm—except Kott at Knightsford.''

Mark flushed. "I deserve every grain of salt you're rubbing into my self-inflicted wounds. Are you quite through?"

"Except to repeat my question. What do you want to do about him?"

"I know what I don't intend to do. My uncle won't be getting the gift of that new acreage I just bought adjoining Knightsford.''

Stiles stared at him in disbelief. "After all you've done for him, you were actually planning to—*give* him that valuable land? I grant you he's done fine work for you at Knightsford, but, man, that would be an outrageously preposterous reward—even if he hadn't duped you!''

"My uncle's always made a fool of me. Or maybe he's just managed to bring out the fool in me." Mark sighed. "This time, he's also managed to make me—almost despise myself.''

"That kind of talk will do us no good whatever."

"I want you to draw up some form of document for him to sign when he gets back, so that if he ever dares try such a thing again, I can take instant legal action."

W.H.'s eyes widened with shock. "Could you possibly mean that you intend merely to threaten him with a useless document? To say, in effect, 'Dear uncle mine, if you ever swindle me again, I'll rap your fingers?' Mark, that's no action at all! It's almost the same as old

Jonathan Cameron allowing Kott to blackmail him all his life for being his natural father."

"I don't see it that way."

"How *do* you see it? As a continuing act of charity on your part?"

"What do you want me to do, W.H.—throw him in jail for the remainder of his days?"

"I know perfectly well that life has not been fair to Osmund Kott. He is the bastard son of your grandfather—your wife's grandfather, too, as it turned out. He was certainly rejected—cast off by Cameron. Few know, but my father told me how the respected gentleman from Knightsford saw to a good home in town for your mother, but hauled Osmund off to Bethesda Orphanage and abandoned him there. I understand Kott's bitterness. I simply happen to believe that mistreatment does not give a man the right to blackmail or steal—to break the law as Kott broke it for most of his twisted life."

"I insist that you remember his age, W.H."

"You asked me here for my advice. There are two alternatives. You may get him to sign a worthless document *against* my advice, or you may confront him when he returns—in my presence—with the evidence of his thievery, give him a certain length of time to get out of town, and find a new overseer. That is my recommendation. I can threaten him with jail if he ever sets foot in Savannah again."

Without a word, Mark got up and went to the window, his back to his young lawyer.

"Of course," William Henry went on, "Kott may never return from his voyage on the *Pulaski.*"

"He'll see Natalie back safely! I'm sure he'll do that!"

"He's cheated you and you've paid him well. He could well be planning to live in the North. You have to face it, Mark. He may have no plans to come back at all. That may be why he was so eager to go in the first place."

Mark whirled around, his face white. "W.H., that would break Natalie's heart, if he didn't come back with her! Just as it would break her heart if I forced him to leave Savannah."

Stiles shrugged. "For a time, perhaps. She's young, though. Her heart will mend."

Standing very straight now, Mark looked piercingly at his friend. "William Henry, I don't like your advice."

"I can tell. It puzzles me that you don't. Unlike Jonathan Cameron, you have nothing to hide from society. Unlike him, you are *not* a weak man. You're too generous, but you're not weak."

"I do believe in giving any man another chance."

"How many chances does the old bounder deserve? You have no security at all if he signs a dozen documents vowing never to cheat you again. If you took that course, you'd only be giving him *carte blanche* to go on taking advantage of you and your family. Is that really protecting Natalie? As canny as she is, do you think for a minute that in this city of wagging tongues she won't find out about Kott someday? Find out what a sucker her father is? Young people seldom appreciate grand gestures."

Again, Mark turned his back, stared down at the river, but said nothing. Instead of helping him out of his dilemma, W.H. seemed to be exposing him to himself. Had he done Natalie an injustice by not discouraging her attachment to Kott—even at the risk of alienating Caroline? He had no doubt that Caroline had always wanted to shape and guide the child out of her spoiled temperament. He wanted that, too, but had he, at least in a passive sense, opposed his wife in favor of Natalie? Had he made "grand gestures" that would, in the long run, weaken his daughter when she was older? In his blind devotion to her, had he ill-prepared her for life's inevitable disappointments?

Mark turned around to his chair, sat down slowly, his shoulders stooped, his eyes downcast. "You make it sound so cut and dried."

"It is. You asked my advice—both as your lawyer and your friend, I assume. Confront Kott when he returns. Get him out of town on the threat of jail." After a moment, when Mark still said nothing, W.H. added firmly, "I'm too fond of you, I hold you in too high esteem to suggest any other course."

Mark looked up. "Thank you, W.H. I'll think about what you've said and we can talk again. After all, there isn't much that can be done about my uncle until fall—when they all come back."

FIVE

IN THE LATE AFTERNOON on that first day of the voyage, after the passengers spending the night in Charleston had gone ashore and while Natalie reluctantly helped Virginia Mackay bathe her babies, Osmund Kott stood alone at the ship's rail. A half-smile played at the deeply lined corner of his mouth. For this moment out of his long, often tortured life, a summer of joy stretched ahead of him. In it would not be one day to dread or worry about or scheme his way through. The summer of this year—his seventy-second—held the shining prospect of more time spent with Natalie Browning than any summer he had ever known—and the bright-haired, spirited girl filled his world. Contentment had come so seldom in his life that waiting alone for her now was near pleasure. Nothing to compare with the pleasure he would feel once she hurried back to him from the stateroom she shared with Mrs. Mackay and the children, but pleasure nonetheless. The anticipation of her return was sweet, like warm honey.

He felt a tinge of sadness that he'd failed to meet her latest dear demand of him, but he wouldn't fail tomorrow. She had simply given him his instructions a bit too late. "Find him, Kottie," the eager girl had ordered. "Find that dazzling Mr. Adonis we saw earlier today and invite him to dine with us at the Captain's table tonight! And don't take no for an answer. I'm counting on you to introduce us properly, so make friends with him—fast." Kott felt he had made a rather favorable impression on the good-looking, brawny young man, but the Parkmans from Savannah had invited him first to have dinner and spend the night ashore with Charleston friends. Kott approved the young man's integrity. He had refused to break his word—even to strangers. "I simply didn't reach him in time," he would tell Natalie, "but the boy was sincerely sorry to miss our dinner party." He had even confided that he'd had his eye on Natalie ever since they'd boarded the *Pulaski* in Savannah that morning. I can tell her that and it will ease some of her disappointment, Kott chuckled to himself. When his adored Natalie wanted a thing, she wanted it now—or maybe yesterday!

He glanced behind him toward the stair where Natalie would appear any moment now, then out over the Cooper River at the old city of Charleston, its handsome buildings reflecting the ball of red sun moving down the clear high sky to the west. Carefully, he weighed his own opinion of the young man, whose name he now knew to be Burke Latimer. That he was the handsomest young fellow aboard no one could deny. He was, Kott felt, also quite affable, though outspoken to the point of being blunt. Again he smiled to himself. Not exactly the kind of young buck his refined, Philadelphia-born nephew, Mark Browning, would consider a cultured gentleman, and Osmund Kott found that amusing. He felt sure it would not only be difficult for Burke Latimer to fake his way through a Browning or a Habersham or a Barnsley ball as though he really enjoyed it, Kott was sure the young man wouldn't even bother to try. Unless, of course, he were to fall under Natalie's spell, as did almost everyone who knew her.

Latimer was just up from the Florida frontier between St. Augustine and Tallahassee, he had told Kott. A red-blooded young American who knew what he wanted, no doubt about that. He must have trusted me, Kott thought, to have told me, on first meeting, that, as an orphan, he had worked hard in his native city of Baltimore to save enough money to be able to search out his own frontier at age twenty-four. He meant to be a successful builder, he'd said, "the best around, but I'll leave Florida to other men who enjoy sweltering and being chewed by mosquitoes." The young man had an infectious grin that showed strong, startling white teeth and the kind of self-knowledge Kott admired. He also liked Burke Latimer's ambition and decisiveness. "I plan to go far in my trade, Mr. Kott," he'd said just before they parted. "I'm on my way back to Baltimore now to get my tools and belongings. I've made up my mind where to settle. It's a spot in the old Cherokee Nation in north Georgia for me."

Osmund Kott looked at his watch. Nearly six. Surely Natalie would join him soon. They were to dine with Captain Dubois at a little after six. Deeply he breathed in the clean, damp evening air, feeling more alive, more needed than in all his life before Natalie had come to give it purpose. True, he dreaded her disappointment when he told her he'd failed to snare Latimer ahead of the Parkmans, but he felt he had quite a bit of good news anyway. Undoubtedly one of the Parkman young ladies had her eye on Latimer, too. No matter. He'd yet to see any girl who could hold a candle to Natalie. Tomorrow he, her protector, would not fail. The *Pulaski,* loaded with its Charleston passengers, was due to cross the bar and head for the open sea sometime between seven and eight tomorrow morning. Latimer would be aboard again and Kott would think of another way to help Natalie further what appeared to be her first romantic interest. Puppy love, perhaps, but whatever Natalie wanted, at whatever moment, was his command.

And then he saw her coming toward him. Her heart-stopping, lovely face flushed, she was running in a most unladylike manner.

"Kottie," she called. "Kottie, did you talk to him? I thought I'd never get finished with being a nursemaid! Honestly, Virginia Mackay acts as though no one else ever had children but her and William. Is Adonis dining with us? Where is he now? Tell me his name, Kottie!"

Gently, his arm around her shoulders, he told her everything he knew about her young man's courtesy and ambition, that he was a builder and that he, Kott, had found his smile most engaging—it almost made one forget what he was saying. He managed to keep her attention long enough to emphasize his own admiration of her Adonis for refusing to break a promise to the Parkmans.

Suddenly, she whirled and faced him. "Kottie, you haven't even told me his name!"

"Latimer. Burke Latimer. He's from Baltimore. Doesn't like the Florida land, but is set on moving to north Georgia, where—"

"You're repeating yourself now. I don't care where he's from or where he's going! I can handle all that." Abruptly she turned away from Kott and leaned on the railing. "Burke . . . Burke Latimer,"

she mused. "It suits him, Kottie. Burke Latimer is just right for him
. . . strong, hard of muscle, fearless. *Undaunted.*"

Kott laughed. "Oh, I'd say he's definitely undaunted."

"Go on and laugh. I don't mind one bit because I love you, dear
Kottie." She patted his cheek. "And I want you to be the first to
know that I do intend to become Mrs. Burke Latimer."

"I'm sure he'll be interested to learn that, too. I'm truthful when I
say his eyes lit right up when I told him I was traveling with you. I'm
positive he had already been admiring you and asked if I could
arrange an introduction. He wants to meet you."

Quite solemnly, she answered, "Oh, I'm not surprised. I was sure
of that. But just think of the time he and I are losing while he's being
bored half to death by Authexia Parkman! I know it was *Authexia* who
maneuvered him off the boat with them."

"She's pretty, but not to be compared with you."

"Kottie, I want you up early tomorrow watching for him to come
aboard again, do you hear me? No later than five; I want you right
here by this railing where you can see everyone who comes aboard."

"We don't cross the bar for two hours or more after that. How
about 6 A.M.?"

"Oh, all right." She gave him her bewitching smile—to him, always as though she handed him a gift. "I just might be taking an
early morning stroll around deck, too, along about six-fifteen or
so."

"You stay in that stateroom, young lady. No obvious behavior.
Now, do you hear *me?*"

Her larky laughter delighted him. "I hear you, but you never
sound gruff or unpleasant enough to force me to obey. I obey you,
though, most of the time, and I'll stay inside just because you're
better to me than anyone else in the whole universe!"

"I knew of my high standing with you," he teased, "but I swear, I
didn't know I spanned the universe."

"Well, you do." The solemn look returned. "Even Mama and
Papa—especially Mama—irk me sometimes. You never do. We simply have the best friendship in the universe. There's no other way to
look at it." The smile flashed. "I'll be good. I promise to stay in the
stuffy old stateroom with sweet Virginia and her pretty babies until
you knock on our door."

"Splendid."

"But you'd better not fail this time. I mean to be having dinner tomorrow with Mr. Burke Latimer as our guest. You know my patience won't last forever!"

Kott bowed over her hand. "At your service, ma'am."

"I do love you, Kottie."

A little after six the next morning, Osmund Kott, looking every inch the gentleman, stood waiting when Burke Latimer strode alone up the gangplank. The young man, cleanly shaven, though wearing the same rumpled, inexpensive clothes, was smiling, and on his open, rather snub-nosed face was the look of a man in a hurry. Kott thought even his voice sounded urgent as he blurted, "There you are, sir. Where is she?"

"Good morning," Kott said, his hand out. "I expected you to come aboard with the Parkmans. Did you have a pleasant time ashore?"

Latimer merely shrugged. "I excused myself early. Told them I had important business aboard. Where is she, Mr. Kott?"

"In her stateroom waiting for my knock. I do want to impress upon you, though, that Miss Browning is in my care—and is only sixteen." He grinned. "Only sixteen and—shall I say—impetuous?"

"Say it if you like, sir. What I care about is meeting her. Sixteen can be old enough. Or is she one of those silly young girls interested only in fashion and flirtation?"

"Natalie is just what I said, impetuous. And, of course, quite sheltered, although I imagine she'll try to convince you otherwise. Well bred, well educated, but impetuous."

"Are you related to her?"

"I—manage her father's vast land holdings. I've simply known and loved the child since the moment I first saw her when she was about three. She and I have enjoyed the rarest kind of attachment for most of her life. The highest honor I can ever attain is her affection for me. And there isn't anything in the world I wouldn't do for her."

Burke Latimer thought a moment, then said, "She's spoiled, I have no doubt. But I suppose such beauty breeds spoiling." He laughed a little. "Well, I plan to revel in the beauty, but I also plan to look quite carefully for what might be beneath it. I'll wait right here, Mr. Kott. Not patiently."

To Natalie, Kottie's flowery introduction was merely a formality to be endured. That over, she pecked him on the cheek, dismissed him and turned her full attention to the tall young man, as though between them they had already planned this time together. As they stood side by side at the ship's railing, Burke Latimer, she noticed, said very little as she kept up a running commentary on many of the passengers boarding from Charleston.

"You seem to know almost everyone," he said, as they watched the raising of the gangplank.

"Oh, if I don't know them myself, my family does."

Finally the *Pulaski*, her deck thronged with pleasant, sociable people, moved out to cross the bar on schedule. The weather was clear and apparently quite settled. A fresh wind blew from the southeast, so that the happy, pleasure-bound passengers and sea and sky seemed to Natalie in perfect harmony.

She could not say as much for her and the oddly silent but agreeable Adonis at her side. She had tried to make conversation with him and he showed all signs of attention, but plainly he was not a master of small talk. Oh, he did seem interested when she brought up one of her father's stories about how difficult a sea voyage used to be before steam, and agreed when she declared this voyage to be more like a long, festive party.

"We've had advertisements for months in the Savannah papers about the *Pulaski*," she said, when they headed into the open sea. "Of course, my father owns part of the boat, so I've known about it forever. He's very proud of it."

All Burke Latimer said to that was "I see."

"How did you happen to be in Savannah, Mr. Latimer, just in time to book passage? Were you teeming to travel on such a safe, fast ship? Had you seen the advertisements?"

He laughed. "Good heavens, no. Coincidence. The old tub I took from Florida just happened to make it to Savannah right then. I'm not particular about accommodations. This packet costs too much for me, but I do need to get to Baltimore as soon as possible, so I'm glad enough to be aboard."

"Is that the only reason you're glad to be aboard?" she asked.

He looked down at her with what appeared to be amusement for such a long time, she finally pressed another question. "Is it your business that takes you back north in such a hurry?"

His good, low laughter came again. "I don't have a business, Miss Browning. Not yet, anyway." He held out his wide, strong hands. "These are my business. I can build anything—everything. I'm an expert cabinetmaker and carpenter. My tools are in Baltimore, my few personal belongings. I've just been out scouting the country, looking for a place to establish myself. I found it, so I'm ready to pack up and go."

"Oh, you just think you've found it! I have other plans for you."

Again he laughed. *At* her? Or *with* her?

"Laugh if you want to," she snapped, "but Savannah, my father says, is going to grow by leaps and bounds. Papa keeps up with all that. The city council is even adding new squares—new streets. People are building new houses and stores—churches, banks, all sorts of things. They just built a new Jewish synagogue where the old one burned down, and something like thirty or maybe it's seventy miles of the Central of Georgia Railroad is already open." Natalie was watching the white wake of the *Pulaski* as she chattered, but she felt he was now even more amused. She raced ahead. "And I almost forgot, our church is Christ Church, and they've already laid the cornerstone for a new building. They did that last winter. You'd better think twice before you settle on any old frontier, Mr. Latimer. You could become wealthy if you settled in Savannah!"

When he said nothing at all, she looked up at him. He was smiling so broadly, a little shiver of anger ran through her. He had no right to take her lightly.

"I don't see anything funny," Natalie said, gazing off over the swelling water, so bright now with the new day's sun that she squinted. "What's wrong with considering Savannah? It's a highly cultivated city. If you're so ambitious to be successful at your trade, I'd think you'd jump at the chance. The pursuit of money is the rule of thumb there, I've heard my father say. He came to Savannah as a younger man than you are, and now look at him!"

"I don't know anything about your father, Miss Browning, and I want to succeed only because I love what I do. The pursuit of money is not my rule of thumb. Mostly, I want to—love the land where I settle. I want to belong to it. The fact that a piece of it might belong to me is secondary."

"Aha! Then you must meet my father! His merchant friends still tease him for loving Savannah the way he does. They say for twenty-six years he's had a love affair with the city. It's true, too. My mother accuses him sometimes of loving Savannah more than he loves her."

His expression became concentrated and serious. "I can understand a man loving a place that way. Especially if he picked it out for himself."

Natalie thought about that for a moment. Even that much understanding from him made her feel almost good inside. Suddenly it was terribly important for Burke to have a bond with her father. "My father did pick out Savannah as the one place he wanted to spend the remainder of his life. He was only twenty. And, you know? I think I understand that, too. I'll be sure to tell Papa I do—and that you do—when I get home. Up to now, I really hadn't paid much attention to his romantic talk about Savannah. It was just the town where I happened to be born. I'll think about—all this sometime. Would you like to take a walk around the deck?"

"All right. If you don't know so many people on board we won't have any privacy."

"Oh, I know lots of people, but you watch—I have a way of shutting them out when they slow me down too much."

"I'm sure you have."

Longing to slip her arm through his, but not daring to in broad daylight, she began to walk along beside him, their talk turning back to the *Pulaski*'s fine features. In all the detail she could remember, she told him about the steam packet called the *Home*, which had been wrecked last year and had killed a lot of people because the boilers blew up. He let her finish her story all the way to the end and then informed her that he knew all about the *Home*. She had to restrain herself to keep from hitting him. Since childhood, she had, when at all frustrated or embarrassed, hit someone. Instead, she told him that the wreck of the *Home* was the main reason her father and the other stockholders had the *Pulaski* built so they could be sure of its safety. Immediately, she remembered she'd already said that, and went right on. "Even so," she laughed, "poor Mama just did not want me to make this voyage. Not so much the danger, though. She simply does not like poor Kottie."

"He seems a pleasant enough old fellow."

"He's a perfect love! He's always treated me better than anyone else on earth."

"Do your parents mistreat you?"

"Of course not! But Kottie understands me better than they do. You know how parents are."

"No, I'm afraid not. I lost mine when I was only a boy."

"Then where did you live when you were growing up?"

"At an orphanage."

"Oh, so did Kottie! Right in Savannah. He grew up at Bethesda Orphanage." Before she realized it, her arm was hooked through his. "Growing up in orphanages must be good for people. Is it?"

"I never thought of it that way."

"But look at you and Kottie. You're both strong, yet truly lovable gentlemen."

"Both of us?"

"Yes. Kottie's past seventy and he's still strong and so smart he makes all sorts of money for my parents on our plantation."

"Your parents own a plantation plus a house in town?"

"Certainly. We have to live in town because my father's office is in Savannah. He's a factor and owns the Browning Company. Oh, not the big, worldwide Browning Shipping Company—his own factorage on Commerce Row. He just draws a lot of money from the big firm. His grandfather Browning started that one." She glanced at him. "Being such a good carpenter, you must make a lot of money."

Now his laughter rolled out. "If I told you how little, at least in comparison with your father, you'd walk away."

"I would not!"

"Oh yes, you would."

"You can't be clever enough to know what I might do!"

He looked straight at her. "But I am."

"You can be very irritating, can't you?"

"I expect so. You too, Miss Natalie."

The urge to hit him came again, but she tried once more to find an agreeable subject. "The truth is, I don't care a fig for money either. I don't even think about money. It's—just always there from somewhere and what matters to me is—is—"

He stopped strolling and held her arm tightly against his side. "What *does* matter to you?"

She gave him the smile that her father said could turn a man's blood to water. "Having a good time and being happy matter."

"I should have guessed that."

Up ahead, coming toward them along the spacious promenade deck, Natalie saw nice Rebecca Lamar and with her—hateful thought—Authexia Parkman. Deftly, she steered Burke Latimer in the other direction. "I think it would be fun to watch a big paddle wheel churn up the water, don't you?"

"If I were you, Miss Browning, I wouldn't give Miss Authexia Parkman a thought. I only went ashore with her family last night because I'd committed myself to go before I met Mr. Kott. I keep commitments."

She hit him on the arm. It was hard as a rock. "I don't know what you're talking about, sir!"

"Oh yes, you do." He was abruptly stern. "And one of these days maybe you'll even grow up."

This scared her. She'd only meant to give him a playful tap on his arm. She'd annoyed him without meaning to. Things weren't going at all right. She wanted him to be as good to her as Kottie, but young and heart-stopping and dashing. He was young and heart-stopping and dashing—but not very good to her. When she was even a little pert with him or said something that sounded to her just normal, he seemed almost to punish her.

Embarrassed that she had actually hit him, she tried a new tack. "You've had me talking about my family and myself too much. That isn't ladylike of me. I want you to tell me about you. I want to know all the details of your—big dreams for your life's work. What kind of place *are* you looking for?"

"I told you I've already found it. In north Georgia. The land just being vacated this summer by the poor Cherokees. However unwillingly, they'll all be gone soon. I'm not proud of my country for driving them out, but they're leaving. They have no choice. That glorious land they loved will be there—empty in the main. I want to own a piece of it. I want to belong to a piece of it. At least, I'll take care of what's mine. My few acres, at least, will be loved and revered as the Cherokees loved and revered it."

"You sound sympathetic to Indians. The Cherokees caused so much trouble!"

His laugh was short and flat. "Your father must be one of those

Georgians whose Christian compassion won't stretch to another human being who doesn't have a white skin."

"That's not true!"

"I know the kind of man he is. Not a bad man. Just a deluded man. Without thinking about it, he simply feels superior to all people with red or yellow or black skin."

She stopped walking, stamped her foot—hard, and cried, "You're the most impossible person I've ever met! My darling father won't even own a slave—not even one!"

The look he gave her was skeptical, yet curious. "He owns a plantation and no slaves? How does he manage that?"

"My mother inherited our plantation!"

"*And* its slaves?"

Desperately she wondered how anyone could be so attractive and so cruel at the same time. "My brother and I, what's more, have a German nurse and we have an Irish cook. Jupiter, our footman, is a free person of color and the maid who cleans our house is too. What's more, Papa pays them all salaries!"

"So only your mother is a slave owner. Does that make you proud of your father?"

"I don't know! It's just the way it is at our house."

"Where did you get the idea that the Cherokees caused all the trouble just because they were on their own land first? Did it ever occur to you that Georgians made trouble for them?"

"I don't have time to think about such things."

"Oh? And what keeps you so occupied, Miss Browning? Fancy dress balls? Lawn parties? Fittings for new gowns that cost so much a whole family could eat for weeks on the price of one?"

They had started walking again, but she stopped, and for a long, helpless moment stood facing him, fuming inside and filled with longing to touch his lean, sun-browned cheek. "I don't have to stand here and take such abuse from you, sir!"

"That's right, you don't. It's a free country for everyone but slaves and Indians. I wish you'd stay, though. I apologize. You're—so pretty. The prettiest girl I've ever seen. I guess I just hoped you wouldn't really be—your age. But that's my fault. I knew you were just sixteen. Mr. Kott told me. Some people are—older than their years. I was dumb enough to hope you might be." He held out his hand—somewhat a peace gesture. "You're really all right, though.

Especially for being the only daughter of such a rich gentleman—and so lovely you can make a man weak just looking at you." When she made no move to shake hands with him, he dropped his. "May I escort you back to your stateroom? Or help you find your devoted Kottie?"

He was saying good-bye. Almost tongue-tied for once, and in total desperation, she cried, "My father *agrees* with you—about the Cherokees! His lawyer, William Henry Stiles, wants to settle up there where you do. At dinner sometimes at our house, I've heard Papa kind of argue with Uncle W.H. about the way the Cherokees were treated. He isn't really my uncle. I just call him that because my father lived with his wife's family when she was growing up. Her name is Eliza Anne Mackay Stiles. Uncle W.H. and I are the only people who call her Lib. Of course, I call her Miss Lib. But even though Uncle W.H. isn't angry at the Cherokees, he and my father do argue about them and—"

Quite gently, but firmly, he laid his hand on her arm. "Don't try so hard to explain, little girl. Please don't try so hard. Our lives—are just too far apart. My point of view is as foreign to you as the Indians are. I find it—sad, but it's true. Won't you let me take you back to your stateroom now?"

Natalie felt her eyes burn with tears. There was no doubt that her heart had just broken for the first time. He didn't like her! He'd found her—too young. Well, maybe I even hate him, she thought wildly as she turned and ran as hard as she could run to find Virginia Mackay.

SIX

INSIDE THE STATEROOM, Natalie fell weeping into Virginia's arms, pouring out her shock and pain in such a torrent of complaint, Virginia made no effort to understand what she was saying—beyond the name of Burke Latimer—until a little of the sobbing subsided. As did everyone else they knew, Virginia Mackay adored this capricious, irresistible girl and felt more responsibility for her at this moment than she had ever felt for anyone not related to her. Something dreadful had happened with the handsome stranger whom Natalie vowed she already loved with all her untried little heart, and whatever it was, Virginia meant to find out.

"Oh, dear, Natalie—try to tell me what he did. Was—was he indecent?"

She felt Natalie stiffen in her arms, jerk away, her light, light blue eyes darkened with fury in spite of the tears. *"Indecent?* If I—know what you mean," she sobbed, *"no.* Far from it. He—he thinks I'm—a child! I'm not. I'm a *woman.* But, Virginia, he—made fun of me! He even made fun of Papa. He's so in love with himself, he can't—"

Little Delia began to shout, "Nattie! Nattie—Nattie!" When Natalie ignored her and went right on half-sobbing and half-fussing, Delia began to cry, too.

Rushing to the children's berth, where the infant, William, was still asleep, Virginia lifted Delia to quiet her, but in no time the baby was awake and crying, too. While holding Delia, Virginia tried to comfort him by patting his stomach with her free hand.

"Is that all you care about my broken heart, Virginia Mackay?"

Natalie demanded. "Here I ran to you for comfort and all you do is coddle your own children right before my eyes!"

In one swift, firm movement, Virginia went to Natalie and thrust Delia into her arms. "I need you to help me, too," she said in a rare scolding voice. "My daughter loves you, Natalie, and you promised to help me look after her. If you're really so grown up, prove it!"

At that moment, Virginia felt like shaking the willful young woman who had no notion of how to act in behalf of anyone but her own petulant self. Still, just being in Natalie's arms delighted Delia so that the tear-streaked, rosy face was already breaking into a hopeful smile. Natalie was paying no real attention to her, but Delia was in the arms of her adored friend with the bright, red-gold hair, and for Delia that was bliss.

"Go on," Virginia heard herself say again, still cross, "prove that you're a woman and not a spoiled child, Natalie. Not just because she's my baby, but because she is a very little girl who loves you, you owe Delia something. Not much—just a small show of affection." For an instant, Natalie held Delia's head against her shoulder, seeming almost stunned by the scolding. The child laughed and patted her. The instant was short-lived. She still held Delia, but Virginia saw the pale eyes fire with fury again as the two, each holding a baby, stood glaring at each other.

"Why should I prove anything?" Natalie demanded.

"Because it would—help me to see you act grown up about something—anything!"

"Why does someone always have to be helping *you*? I don't understand sweet, helpless women like you. You get your way by acting helpless with poor William so that he does everything you want." Tears began to roll down her cheeks. "I've just had my heart broken —broken right in two, and do you care? No, you don't care a whit. You just want me to help you with Delia!"

At the sound of her name spoken with such hostility, Delia's face began to contort again, the dimpled little chin to quiver. Quickly, as though she might be able to help, the child began to pat Natalie's cheek, to look straight into her eyes. Any show of anger had always frightened Delia because she had almost never sensed anger in anyone close to her—except Natalie. Virginia and William had discussed this tender trait in their firstborn only last week, when Delia had wept because she thought her papa was angry with Lon, the mule, just because he tried to yell Lon out of a balky streak. Just like her sensitive father, Delia had grieved when, one day, accidentally, she'd stepped on a sick baby chicken and it died. That was the day William confessed to Virginia that he had avoided fishing until he was a young man. "I just hated the thought of hurting their mouths like that," he said. Delia would grow up to be gentle and guileless like William, Virginia was certain. William, Jr., was still too young for her to be sure what kind of man he might be, but Delia would be very much like William, and for Virginia, that was an answer to prayer.

Natalie ended the long, strained silence, broken only by the infant's whimpering. "Don't you care, Virginia? Don't you care a fig—that I need to be comforted because of the way that—brute, Burke Latimer, treated me?"

With the baby, Virginia sat down on her own berth, motioned for Natalie to sit beside her. She did, still holding Delia. "Yes, I care, Natalie. I care much more than you can possibly guess. But comfort isn't all soft words. Real comfort means that something has been done to help ease the pain. Perhaps even to lessen the chance that the pain you've been showing during these last few minutes ever needs to be quite so sharp again."

"You're not making any sense!"

"Oh, but I am. I have no doubt that your young man hurt you. The hurt was worse, though, because you let it make you angry. You let it—hurt Delia, too. And me."

"I did no such thing!"

"We're all acquainted with your temper. If you *are* a grown woman, you'd better begin to act as though you are."

"I didn't come running to you for a sermon, you know."

"But you did come running to me, instead of Mr. Kott."

"That's where I made my mistake."

"No, that's where you showed a small sign of growing up."

For a time, Natalie said nothing. Virginia kept her eyes on the baby, but she could feel that she'd piqued the girl's curiosity.

Finally, Natalie said, "I have no idea what you're talking about, Mrs. Mackay." Her tone was flippant, but no longer angry.

"I think you know exactly what I'm talking about. Osmund Kott would have taken your side, sympathized endlessly. He might even have hunted down your young man and bawled him out good."

"He needs it."

"We can't discuss him because I've barely seen him. We can only discuss your reaction to the incident with him."

Still holding Delia, Natalie got up and began to flounce around the stateroom. "If you'd heard what he said to me, you'd never use a silly word like—incident. It was a *tragedy*."

"Natalie, I'm so glad for this chance to talk to you."

"That's quite obvious. You're reveling in it."

"In a way, I am. But not for the reason you think. I'm glad we're talking because I want to make a prediction." Virginia watched Natalie's face now. Watched it closely. The girl had stopped pacing about. She stood frowning.

"What kind of prediction could you possibly make? It's over. My romance didn't even get started!"

"That's my prediction—backwards. Romance is far from over for you."

"Virginia Mackay, don't you dare try to tell me that I'll find someone else to love! That I'm—still young."

"Oh, I wouldn't dare do that. Another thing—it's quite all right for you to accuse me of wrapping William around my finger by being sweet and helpless."

"Doesn't that make you angry?"

"No."

"Well—does anything make you angry?"

"Yes. But not your lack of insight. I love William with all my heart and soul and spirit and body. I've loved him since I was far younger than you. I know how things really are between William and me, so if they look another way to you, it doesn't make me angry. Natalie . . . I'm glad you came to me because even Mr. Kott might have tried to convince you that what you feel for your Mr. Latimer is— puppy love. That you're too young to know. You aren't too young to know. I knew and I was only twelve!"

Natalie stared at her for a long moment, then, quite gently, put Delia down, hugged the child and took her hand. "I'm not leaving you, Delia," she whispered. "It's just that you're such a big girl, my arms are tired. We'll hold hands for a while instead." Delia took Natalie's hand in both her chubby ones and laughed her pleasure at the whole idea. Then Natalie turned to Virginia. "Can you hate someone—and love him at the same time?"

"I doubt it. I suppose you can hate someone and still be—drawn to him. But I don't think you hate your young man. I'm sure he doesn't hate you."

"How can you be sure of that?"

"You're too—lovely to hate. He might have wanted to shake you —I do sometimes—but from the brief glimpse I had of him, he didn't appear to be dense. He might even suspect that your outer beauty goes as deep as I know it to go. I don't know him, though. We're talking about you. I do know you. One meeting, pleasant or unpleasant, does not a lifetime make. If you're sure you love him, don't even try to stop. Don't try to dislike him just because he—got the best of you once."

"How do you know he got the best of me?"

"Didn't he? Isn't that what this is all about?"

"I couldn't stand there and let him insult me, could I?"

"Did you try to reason with him?"

"Of course not! What does romance have to do with reason?"

"Everything, if it's going to last."

"I hate it when Mama says, 'Natalie, be reasonable!' "

"I don't always like it when William says that to me, either. But reason is the only way out of the corner you've got yourself into now."

"Well, it isn't my way! Old Reverend George White always said, 'Be reasonable, Natalie,' when I went to his school. I hate being reasonable because it just means that someone is trying to boss me."

When Virginia made no comment, Natalie asked with surprising earnestness, "How could I have reasoned with Burke Latimer when all he was doing was being nasty? And—what do we do about the invitation Kottie extended to him to dine with us at the Captain's table this afternoon?"

"Do you want him to dine with us?"

So fleetingly that Virginia almost missed it, Natalie smiled. "I wish I didn't."

"Then why don't you and I decide what you'll wear—just in case he does still intend to join us."

She hugged Virginia. "You know I say a lot of things I don't really mean, don't you? I think I see you suddenly in a way—I've never seen you before."

Virginia laughed. "Oh?"

"Yes! At heart, in spite of being in your twenties, you're a romantic! You're really—in love—with old William, aren't you?"

"For ever and ever. And you're not at all too young to know it if you're really in love with Burke Latimer."

"Well . . . I doubt that I am now and it's very, very sad."

"You doubt already that you're in love with him?"

"How could I be when he's—so crude?"

"Oh, I didn't know he was crude."

"Stop pinning me down! Maybe not crude—just blunt and—not a bit kind to me." She sighed heavily. "It's a pity, too. Because no matter how long I live, Virginia, I'll never find another man like him. I wish he were here this minute. I'd hit him again."

"You hit him?"

"On his forearm. It was hard as a—ballast rock. Even hitting him was—divine. But I do truly believe I hate him now, with every fiber of my being." She leaned down to kiss Delia's light hair. "Virginia, what do you think I should wear to dinner?"

SEVEN

SHEFTALL SHEFTALL'S belief that, in spite of his cheating, Kott could be trusted to protect Natalie, had reassured Mark enough for him to sleep some on that first night after the *Pulaski* steamed away toward Charleston. By nine o'clock the next day, though, he was in the large, high-ceilinged, familiar parlor of the Mackay house on Broughton Street, seated beside his best friend, Eliza Mackay.

"I'm sorry, Miss Eliza, if you had other plans for this morning," he said, taking a cup of coffee. "The years have spoiled me. You've spoiled me. You'll always be the one person I turn to when I can't manage things."

Her brown hair was silvery at the temples now, but still curly. Eliza Mackay, at sixty, was to Mark even lovelier than on the night so long ago, when, as a confused young man, he'd asked her to marry him. For years, they had been able to laugh about that awkward night—not *at* his boyish dream, but about it. Because Eliza was Eliza, their friendship had only deepened with the years. He needed her today, and as always, she was there.

"Whatever I might have done this morning can wait," she was saying. "You and Caroline are like my own. I could tell something was very wrong when we were all on the *Pulaski* yesterday. I know how I felt way back more than twenty years ago when my boys left—without me." Her musical laughter had not changed. It was simply softer now, perhaps a bit sad. "Even with their father and you to watch over them, I almost stopped breathing that day when I could no longer see the sails of that schooner taking William and Jack away."

That long-ago departure was still sharp in Mark's memory, too. Robert Mackay, his mentor, and he were escorting the two Mackay sons north to enroll them in a private school. Only Mark came back to Eliza. Her beloved Robert had died on that trip. Mark's own sense of loss was still painful at times. So painful, he had never stopped marveling that Eliza Mackay had been strong enough to carry not only her own crushing grief, but his and the children's grief too. "I manage, I suppose," she'd told Mark, "because I'm still Robert's wife. Whatever I do, I do for him." But neither grief nor the continuing love for the laughing man who was her husband had once shut Mark or Caroline out of her gracious heart.

"Do you want to tell me what's troubling you, aside from missing Natalie?"

He frowned. "Do you really think Kott will—look after her, Miss Eliza?"

"Oh, Mark, you know how uncomfortable he's always made me. Praying for poor Osmund is still hard for me, but he will take care of Natalie. And considering his early years here—the times spent in jail for causing every kind of trouble in town—hasn't he turned out remarkably well?"

Mark set down the barely touched cup, but said nothing.

"Mark?"

Slowly, he began to tell her the painful story of the weighted cotton bales, of his own shame in having trusted his uncle as he'd done, of W.H.'s advice to threaten Kott with jail if he refused to leave Savannah for good. When he had finished, Eliza Mackay sat silently for what seemed a very long time.

Finally she said, "I suppose you've thought of what it might do to Natalie if you forced her precious Kottie to leave town. Or if you actually put him in prison."

Mark got up and strode to the window. "I've thought of little else. Miss Eliza, Osmund Kott and—Ethel Cameron! The two most pathetic troublesome people you and I have ever known—and my daughter hopelessly drawn to them both from the start." He turned to face her. "Is that as—bizarre to you as it is to me?"

"You know it's always been. But I wonder if that doesn't have something to do with the difficulty of—being parents? Of truly

understanding our children. Heaven knows, my blessed William was
never headstrong or spoiled—"

"—like Natalie."

She smiled. "Yes, like Natalie. But I never felt I really understood
him, even when he was a little boy. You remember how silent and—
almost otherworldly he was? Oh, sweet and kind to us all, but
different—hating so to hook a fish's mouth or shoot a squirrel. Lost
in his own private thoughts, almost never confiding in anyone.
Children require superhuman understanding sometimes."

He returned to sit beside her. "But look at my son, Jonathan. I
can't imagine that he will ever *cause* trouble for anyone, can you?"

"No. William caused no trouble either. But I lay awake last night
picturing his melancholy aloneness out there at Causton's Bluff—
with Virginia and those two babies out of his sight. Out of his arms. I
worry about William, but he causes no trouble." She laughed a little.
"I knew Natalie was going to be a handful that day when I brought
her out into your upstairs hall for you to see her for the first time.
She put her mother to a lot of trouble, just by arriving! Oh, she
didn't intend to cause trouble for her mother. To this day, I don't
believe Natalie intends to make trouble—for anyone."

"No, she just—makes it. And in the process has her poor father
loving her more every day." Then he asked, "William wouldn't
agree to stay here even for last night, eh?"

"No. The only explanation he could give me for refusing to sleep
here after his family left was 'I have to be close to my land, at least.'
But, Mark, you came here to talk about Osmund Kott."

"Do you think I owe it to Natalie to—tell her that he's actually—
my uncle? Should I tell her the whole story about his and my mother's illegitimate births? About Osmund's troubled life? Please be
frank."

Eliza Mackay laid her hand over Mark's. "Dear boy, I don't know.
We've always said, 'Wait until she's older.' How old is 'older'?" She
patted his hand reassuringly. "You can't tell her today, anyway."

He sighed. "No. No, I can't."

She thought a minute. "It just might be better never to tell Natalie
that he's a blood relative. After all, he is past seventy."

"Should I have it out with Kott when he gets back and let him go
on his own sweet way with no punishment for what he's done? W.H.
thinks not. Definitely not."

"Have you told Sheftall Sheftall any of this? He knows more about Osmund and his past life than anyone, and he's a wise, wise old man."

"I told him the whole rotten story yesterday before the *Pulaski* sailed."

"And what did he say?"

"Sheftall thinks I shouldn't try to reach a decision about the—cheating right now."

"What about Caroline in all this? Have you told her?"

"No! And I don't plan to—not anytime soon anyway. You—you know what even the mention of Kott's name does to her. Whatever I decide to do, I mean to protect her from any more anguish over that man. That is, if I'm—able to protect her. I know my own anxiety about Natalie's being in his care on the voyage is greater for having found out what he did to me."

"Did Mr. Sheftall think you should tell Caroline the truth?"

"He didn't say so outright. He did warn me that my own worry—showed. And reminded me that Caroline knows me like a book. He just urges me not to act in haste—until we know Natalie's safely in Baltimore."

"Then you'd better take his advice." She paused, thinking. "Sheftall Sheftall is a Jew, but he does know our Scriptures. 'When I would do good, evil is present with me.' That verse, if I'm not mistaken, is right at the end of the seventh chapter of Romans. It sounds exactly like a description of Osmund." She took a deep breath. "In fact, Mark, it sounds like—all of us."

Thank heavens, the girl is still sound asleep, Osmund Kott thought, as he quickly picked up the infant Mackay boy before his outbreak of squawling awakened Delia. Seated again in one of the three small rockers in the stateroom shared by Natalie and Virginia Mackay, he felt the baby's bottom. Miracle—it was dry. Thank heaven again. Perhaps even such young babies have bad dreams that make them cry, he decided, and began to rock slowly, cradling the infant in his arms. In a blessedly few minutes, little William was again asleep. Osmund was free to go back to his own thoughts of Natalie and her young man. Another prayer couldn't hurt anything, he supposed, so, once more, he asked God to settle whatever differences the two had between them.

"She's the apple of my eye, Lord," he prayed. "I have no one else on this earth but Natalie. My dear, shining, willful Natalie. Lord, anyone as lovely as that child should want for nothing—ever. Give her her heart's desire. It's all right, Lord, that she doesn't know I'm her great-uncle. I've never longed to be an uncle! I've just longed for someone to love—someone to love me. Natalie loves me. Natalie does love me. Father in heaven, give her the desire of her heart. At least, Latimer kept his word. They're dining together right now. Cause that equally willful young buck to fall head over heels in love with my little minx, because, Lord, that's what Natalie wants."

He laid the sleeping boy back beside his sister, then returned to the rocker. After a time, he looked at the fine watch Natalie had given him last Christmas. Natalie and Virginia and Burke Latimer had been at the Captain's table now for nearly two hours. Instead of returning the watch to his pocket, he caressed it, smiling. He could just imagine how much fuss she'd kicked up at the Browning mansion on Reynolds Square when she demanded money to buy such an expensive watch for her old Kottie. They gave her the money, though. She got what she went after, that girl. Even her mother, Caroline, who still despised him, now and then gave in to Natalie. Of course, her father gratified her every wish and always would.

"My nephew's a charming gentleman, well loved, well respected. In many ways, though, for which I thank God, he's a weak fool," Kott said aloud. Alone, as he had almost always been, he enjoyed talking aloud to himself. It ensured interesting company. "Weak?" He chuckled. "Well, I doubt that I can honestly call my dead sister's son 'weak.' Lenient, overly trusting perhaps. Although he has managed to keep me at arm's length, with only a strictly business relationship between us. Still, he's had confidence in me. And I'm downright sorry those knuckle-headed niggers at Knightsford loaded the Savannah flatboat by mistake with what I intended as Charleston cotton. I had no inclination to let my nephew catch me cheating him." He smiled slyly. "Not directly, at least. Only I keep the Knightsford accounts. Only I know how many bales of sometimes weighted Knightsford cotton go to Hickman up in Charleston —how many go full measure to Browning Company to sell abroad. Old Hickman has too much on his own conscience to try to trap me or anyone else. Where he sells what I send to him every year is none of my affair. Those niggers have already paid dearly for mixing up the shipments this once, but evidently there's no harm done. Oh well. I thought Mark seemed friendly enough when we left Savannah yesterday morning. If he'd suspected me of any wrongdoing, would he have let Natalie come along under my care?" Kott felt no guilt. Without his expert guidance, the Knightsford land wouldn't have produced as it had for all these years. He had a perfect right to sell off, for his own profit, a discreet portion of the crops. He'd be more careful, watch the niggers more closely from now on.

His seventy-one years aggravated him only when he sat too long in one position. His legs were feeling stiff. Smoothing the finely enameled lid of his watch, he got to his feet, then put the watch back in the pocket of his waistcoat. A walk around the deck in the salt breeze would feel good, but little Mrs. Mackay freely entrusted her babies to his care. He would wait.

Kott was in the middle of a luxuriant yawn and stretch when the stateroom door opened and Virginia Mackay, her pretty face perplexed, said, "I think you'd better go to Natalie, Mr. Kott! She's waiting for you on the promenade deck—demanding to see you alone. Things didn't seem to go a bit well for her at dinner with her young man. He all but ignored her."

Giving her his undivided attention as they sat side by side on a deck settee, Kott noted the rising wind—shifting to the east now, and roughening the sea so that the promenade deck was all but empty of passengers. Natalie, not bothered by the motion of the boat, gave him a long string of what amounted to orders. Orders to be obeyed. Burke Latimer had indeed ignored her throughout the meal. He had conversed at length with Captain Dubois about what to Natalie was his foolish obsession with some remote Cherokee land on Georgia's northern frontier. He had, she declared, gone on about the same dumb thing with Mr. Lamar, who gallantly disagreed by telling Burke that he was much too quick to ignore the tremendous future of a thriving port city like Savannah.

"Lamar spoke right up to him, eh?" Kott asked, amused.

"He did, but, Kottie, listen to me. Burke Latimer is different from the gentlemen in Savannah. He paid no attention at all to successful Mr. Lamar. Burke's not like anyone I've ever met! He actually loves being uncomfortable, I feel sure. He thrives on uncivilized surroundings and work—felling trees to build his own house, planting wild land that's never been cultivated—peculiar things like that. So, I have an idea. You are to find him before the afternoon is any older —before time for tea—and offer him part of Knightsford Plantation!"

Kott stared at her. His beloved girl had managed to startle even him. "Offer him—part of Knightsford, Natalie?"

"Better still, I'm sure I heard Papa tell Uncle W. H. Stiles when he and Miss Lib came to dinner the other night that he had just bought a whole slice of Savannah River land—adjoining Knightsford. Offer Burke all of that!"

"News to me," Kott said. "I didn't know your father bought that land."

"I'm sure he did, but even if I wasn't listening very carefully, Papa's rich. He'll have an impressive acreage full of wild animals and trees and tangles somewhere he can give Burke. The point is, it's after three now, and you and I have only this evening to make our scheme work. I want him living near Savannah and we'll be docking in Baltimore tomorrow and he'll *vanish* in the crowds. Kottie, I couldn't bear that! I—I can't abide Burke Latimer, but I couldn't bear it if he—vanished."

Kott whistled, took a deep breath, then said, "Well, milady, you know there's nothing I won't try if you ask. Don't get your hopes too high, though. Your father will have a little something to say about such an offer."

"Pooh. I can handle him. Of course, he may resist some. He might even refuse at first. But Papa will end up doing exactly as I say."

"I don't doubt that for a minute, but—what if after you get to know Latimer better, you don't feel the way you do now? What if you change your mind about him?"

"I just won't, that's all. Now, go find him. I'm having tea with Rebecca Lamar and a few of her Savannah relatives not yet seasick. After that, I'll be in that stuffy stateroom, I suppose, helping Virginia with her babies. That's an awful bore, isn't it? I can tell you one thing right now: I'm not going to have any babies. They just don't fit into an adult's life."

Feeling a bit queasy from the rough sea, but chuckling to himself, Kott went to find Burke Latimer. Natalie had just hatched an outrageous scheme, but no matter. He liked schemes. What else was there to do aboard ship anyway? He would try to do anything she asked of him, and nothing else on earth was so important.

Braced now against the roll of the ship, he was glad Natalie had headed for her stateroom. The wind was so strong, he found walking difficult. Come to think of it, he saw no women on deck at all. Seasick, most likely. Or lying down to prevent it. He hoped Natalie would lie down, too.

At sunset, heavy clouds mustering toward the northeast, Kott still had not found Burke Latimer. The one or two men with whom he did speak feared a gale was brewing. Waves rocked the *Pulaski* so that few passengers appeared for tea or supper. Weary with struggling against the wind, his legs trembling from the sheer effort of keeping himself upright as he searched for Latimer, Kott felt queasy again. He longed to lie down, too, just for a time, but he had promised Natalie to hunt until he found her young man. He made himself keep circling the deck. Even after an hour or so, during which he was sick over the ship's railing, the old man went on searching. There was no sign of Latimer. He had met only Gazaway Bugg Lamar, the big booster of the *Pulaski*. The two men had exchanged a few words, G.B. still buoyant and hopeful that the sky would clear, thus giving the all-important passengers a pleasant night. Evidently, Gazaway Bugg Lamar had every confidence as well as a lot of stock in the new steam packet.

The sea did seem to be calming a bit, and overhead Kott could see bright stars flickering through breaks in the low clouds. By now, though weak from vomiting, he felt a little steadier. Resting on a wooden settee, he chuckled to himself, wondering what G.B. Lamar might have said if Kott had given in to something he'd wanted to do for years. "Gazaway Bugg Lamar" had always struck Kott as the most comical name he'd ever heard. What would the prosperous, agreeable gentleman have done if Kott had said, "Good evening, Gazaway Bugg Lamar. How are you, Gazaway Bugg Lamar?" He would remember to share that with Natalie. The same things always struck them both as funny.

The gale winds and rough seas had evidently kept everyone inside, perhaps brewing tea in their cabins and staterooms, including

Burke Latimer. Kott also felt the need for a cup of tea, but wouldn't disturb Natalie and Virginia for anything. He had no news to report to Natalie anyway. Her rugged hero of the wild could well be flat on his back—sick as a dog.

•

EIGHT

JUST AS DARKNESS SETTLED, Kott stood looking out over the black water and sky, both calmer now, the clouds almost gone. Certainly, standing was easier. The sea heaved in longer, less choppy, waves—invisible in the blackness except as the wind broke their crests into stark white foam. Striking the vessel under the weather bow, though, the force of the water was enough to slow the *Pulaski*'s progress. He was sure she was being given a full pressure of steam to enable her to overcome the resistance of these long, heavy swells. And indeed, she was overcoming steadily, gallantly.

Still wandering around the deck at ten o'clock, Kott longed to tell Natalie that he had tried with all his might to find her young man, but fearing to disturb her in case she was seasick, he decided to retire. Sleep should come rather easily, he thought. The *Pulaski* was driving through the dark water smoothly now, at the rate of at least eleven miles an hour. Only a few stragglers remained on deck, bidding one another good night and pleasant dreams. And then he felt her arm through his.

"Did you find him, Kottie?"

"I failed," he said, "but I haven't stopped searching more than a few minutes at a time, my dear. Your Adonis must be seasick. Lots of folks are, Mr. Lamar told me."

"He's hiding! He isn't likely to get seasick. You might know Virginia was. I wasn't a bit. She just wouldn't let me come back out on deck. Why should a big strong man like Burke Latimer be seasick? Kottie, what will we do?"

"Nothing tonight, dear girl. But I promise to be out here at the first sign of dawn. I'll find him. You have my word for it." He tightened his arm on hers. "I'm glad to be able to tell you good night. I was just thinking, before you appeared like a lovely apparition, how much I'd like to bid you a *good* night."

"Oh, Kottie, I love you. You always want everything to be good for me, don't you?"

"And I will be wanting that, pretty child, right up to the last breath I take."

"How romantic! You're part poet, I think. Do you suppose stubborn Burke Latimer ever has a romantic thought?"

He turned her around and they began to walk in the direction of the stair that led to the ladies' quarters. "We'll find out first thing in the morning, I promise. What matters right now is that you get your beauty sleep. I must get mine, too, so I'll be up bright and early to corner him for you. I won't fail tomorrow. I promise."

In the cabin shared with two other men, both snoring, Kott undressed and crawled into his berth. As always, he prayed first for Natalie, then Virginia Mackay and her children, thanked God that a storm had not materialized, that all was well, and that Mark Browning had quite evidently not discovered the mistake with the delivery to Savannah of the weighted cotton bales meant for Hickman in Charleston. He added a heartfelt request that he not fail Natalie, and fell immediately into a deep sleep.

Within what must have been no more than half an hour, he was jolted awake by an explosion so loud, so near at hand, he could think only that the ship had been struck by lightning or a battery of cannon.

Kott leaped from his berth and stood banging one ear and then the other. For a moment the crash had deafened him. The very air in the cabin seemed to go on bursting. Under him, the ship quivered. Wildly, he searched about in the darkness for some sign that his cabin mates were still there. He could tell nothing. Objects were falling, bells clanged. Glass seemed to be shattering endlessly. He shouted: "Anyone—here? *Say something!*" He shouted again. There was no answer. With the next step, pain shot through his right foot. He had stepped on the cabin lantern, smashed to bits.

After what could have been one or even two minutes, he was

thrown to his knees by a second loud crash, which felt as if the sides and deck of the boat had been, by an irresistible, wrathful force, crushed together.

With all his might, he screamed Natalie's name.

By some means, he must find the stairway that led to her stateroom. As he was feeling about in order to locate the cabin door, splintered boards and sharply wrenched rods of steel told him that the floor had been ripped apart, the door blown loose from its hinges. By chance, in the darkness, he felt a rail and, following it along, eventually saw a light at the head of the stairway.

Struggling to stand upright, he knew he was in the passageway between Natalie's stateroom and the Captain's quarters and began to call her name again—over and over and over. Shouting seemed to require no effort. Natalie's name tore out of him with every breath. And then, from behind the tightly closed stateroom door, he heard her voice, muffled, frightened: "Kottie! Kottie! *Help me!*"

Around him, there were no frantic screams, no panic—just shouts and calls and confusion and repeated questions: "What happened? What's wrong?" as the passageway filled with terrified women and children in nightclothes. Over and over Kott crashed his own body against the door of the stateroom where Natalie and Virginia and the children were trapped. Once, twice he cried out from the stabbing pain of blows that must have broken his shoulder.

"Stop it, old man," someone shouted.

Kott turned to see Gazaway Bugg Lamar beside him, ordering him to try to find out what jammed the door before he killed himself attempting to crash through it.

"It's the berth," Virginia Mackay called from inside. "We're trying to roll the berth back—under. We can't." Then: "Mr. Kott! Oh, Mr. Kott, Natalie's climbing through the transom! Catch her—please, catch her!"

Peering up at the narrow transom, Kott heard people begin to scream, "Fire!" and felt himself falling to one side as the deck slid steeply beneath him and the whole ship gave a gigantic lurch. On his back, he looked up to see Natalie's head and shoulders through the transom above the door, which had swung open when the sudden lurch released the berth's caster and sent it flying out into the passageway where he was struggling to get to his feet.

Kott no longer felt the agony of his broken body, did not know that both his bare feet were slashed and bleeding. Only one thing came clear: He would help Natalie down out of that transom and, by some means, he would save her life.

How he managed to get her down, he couldn't have told, but the next thing he knew for sure was that she was standing beside him and that he had hold of her shoulders, literally keeping her upright. As in a dream, he saw Virginia Mackay, her face white with terror, but quiet—not screaming, not questioning anyone—just leaning against a partly shattered bulkhead between the copper boilers, the right boiler across the passageway, torn open. In her arms, Virginia held both children, the little girl's tear-streaked face a mask, the infant boy staring. Both Mackay children were stunned into blessed silence.

"No need to worry about fire spreading," Kott heard himself say with authority. "The leaks will douse the fire."

Still holding Natalie, he saw a man dragging himself along the sloping deck, howling, "Oh, God—God, both my legs are blown off! My legs are blown—off!"

"Kottie, that's the barber who cut your hair. What can we do? Is the boat sinking?"

"The boat is sinking," Virginia Mackay said, her words measured. "The—boat—is—sinking."

"But we're going to make it all right, Virginia." Natalie's certainty somehow calmed Kott's own fear. "We're going to be—just fine. You'll see," she went on. "Look, those gentlemen over there by the wall—are calming their women down. Those *men* know we're— going to be all right! We have to—be. You and the babies are—going to be home soon, Virginia—with William! You'll see."

Virginia Mackay said nothing. She was peering as though into some far-distant place, still holding both babies, causing Kott to marvel that she was able to stand.

"Come up here, you people!" A voice shouted from above, not ordering—begging. "Please find a way to get up here and help us balance the boat. She's listing something awful!"

"We'll go," Virginia said, her voice strong, controlled. "We'll have to go, Natalie. We all have to help."

"I'm willing, Kottie—are you?"

"Yes! Yes, dearest Natalie. . . ."

"We'll all go together," Virginia ordered. "All together now, move! Just don't lose sight of the children, *please.*"

"Oh, Virginia—give me Delia," Natalie cried. "I'm sorry. Virginia, forgive me! I—I've let you carry them—both!"

Cautiously, they and others began to make their way up the broken stair to the main deck above. By chance, Kott noticed that Gazaway Bugg Lamar, his niece, Miss Rebecca, his wife and children were following them. Most adults carried or led a child.

About halfway up, the steps were gone and Kott, with a surge of strength, grabbed Delia from Natalie's arms and ordered his dear girl to grab a nearby rail and pull herself to safety. Natalie obeyed, reached the safer portion of the deck above, then extended both hands so that Kott could lift Delia up to her. He could hear Delia crying for her mother now, but Kott wrested tiny William from Virginia and handed him up to Natalie, too. As he did so, his broken shoulder and arm went limp, so that the baby dangled from his one usable hand. Somehow Natalie managed to grasp little William's thin nightdress and pull him to safety.

"Go on, Lamar," Kott yelled. "If a sixteen-year-old girl can pull herself up, so can you! Climb on up there—help me save the children!"

For the first time, Virginia Mackay's voice broke: "Mr. Lamar—Mr. Kott, save my children! *Please,* save—my children!"

"We'll try, Mrs. Mackay," Lamar called down from his new perch on the shattered deck a few feet above. "We'll try!"

"Mr. Lamar—are they all right up there? Please save them! Mr. Mackay will—bless you!" Virginia was sobbing now. "Mr. Mackay—will—bless you! He'll—need our—babies!"

"There's a lifeboat up here," Lamar shouted down, "but it won't hold us all."

"Mr. Mackay—will—*bless you!*"

"I'll do all I can to help, Mrs. Mackay—but I don't have hope—for any of us!"

"Kottie! Kottie—please give me your hands," Natalie screamed. "Let me help *you* up, Kottie—please!"

"Not yet, Natalie," Kott gasped. "Miss Virginia—first. Reach higher, Miss Virginia . . . higher!"

Kott saw Natalie's hand grasp one of Virginia's, but both were slippery wet and Virginia was losing her grip. "Lamar," Kott yelled,

"For God's sake, help Miss Natalie! She can't lift—a grown woman alone!"

"Where are my babies?" Virginia, he could see, was giving up for herself, and wasting precious strength weeping for the safety of her children.

"Mr. Lamar," she cried, as Lamar grasped her wrists in both his hands. "Tell me—please tell me who's taking care of—my babies!"

"They're safe," Lamar called down. "Natalie Browning—is holding them. Don't give up, Rebecca—Mrs. Mackay! Try to help me—lift you! Push them up, Kott! Then we'll get to you."

When at last Kott lay exhausted on the upper portion of the deck, he saw Virginia Mackay grab both her babies and stumble toward the one lifeboat hanging from its two davits about twenty feet down the now sharply pitched deck. With superhuman effort, Kott pulled himself half upright and crawled toward the lifeboat. How small it seemed! When he reached it he struggled to his feet and, with the one good arm, jerked at the canvas that covered the boat, shouting at Natalie to hurry and find herself a seat before the boat filled up.

"You're in my care," he shouted. "You're in—my care, Natalie! Climb in the boat—be the first one in!"

"Climb in, Rebecca," Lamar ordered his niece.

"I'm not getting in that rickety lifeboat," Rebecca Lamar cried. "I'd rather stay right here!"

"Climb in, I said! No promise of safety for any of us, Rebecca—but this is your only hope!"

Kott saw Miss Rebecca reluctantly climb in, but not Natalie. She was pushing and shoving Virginia Mackay, who still clung to both babies, trying desperately to get all three up and into the precarious little boat.

The useless arm hanging at his side, Kott managed to help the Mackays and Natalie into the boat. "Now you get in, Lamar! You and your nephew—can row. You don't expect—women to be able to—row a boat, do you?"

"No," Natalie screamed. "Kottie, no! I want *you* here!" She was standing up in the boat, as though about to jump back onto the wave-drenched section of deck where Kott stood.

Osmund groaned in anguish as, with one hand now, he began to release the ropes that held the lifeboat to the davits. He felt faint from the pain, but he lowered the bow onto the deck, slowly, carefully, so as not to dump its precious cargo. Someone was lowering the lifeboat's stern at the same time, so that when the *Pulaski* sank, as it surely would, the lifeboat could float free—those in it perhaps be rescued.

Kott tried to smile as he waved his good arm at Natalie, who was struggling against a strange man's arms, screaming that she did not want to be saved without Kottie.

And then, without warning, heavy planks and steel beams began to break and tear as the steamer reared and ripped apart, the severed ends lifting into the air. Within seconds, men, women and children were sliding, in shocked, frozen silence, down the steeply slanting deck and into the black water.

The last sound Osmund Kott heard as his own body slammed against the sea was Natalie calling his name.

NINE

FROM SUNRISE until after sunset on the second day at Causton's Bluff without Virginia and the children, William Mackay had worked even more steadily than usual alongside his field hands, hoping that hard labor would help him sleep. But here he sat on the new front steps alone, with darkness falling, dreading the thought of the big empty bed upstairs.

Work was usual for William. He thrived on it, but today, hour after hour under the hot June sun, even his strong, lean body had felt weak, almost useless. Still, he had worked on, stubbornly. He was aware even in his youth when his family—especially his mother—had been careful with him. He knew why they were careful. Knew that he wasn't acting like other Mackays, doing things his own way. Oh, his mother had never once accused him of being stubborn, but his outspoken soldier brother, Jack, made no bones about it, and neither did his sisters, Eliza Anne, Sarah and especially Kate.

With all his heart, he loved his family—each one. Summer was always hard to get through, even now, married to Virginia, because his father had died then. That was almost twenty-two years ago, but he still felt the loss and that always caused him to realize how much he loved all his family.

He looked up for a long time at the appearing stars, bright and close tonight. "Are you seeing them too, Virginia?" It helped to speak aloud to her even though she was so far away and maybe already asleep on the fine new *Pulaski*—spending this one night at sea before reaching Baltimore tomorrow. He remembered how bright the starlight had been on a particular night when he and Jack and Papa and Mark had all stood on the deck of Papa's old schooner *Eliza.* Papa and Mark had been taking him and Jack away to school in the North. That night, William, only a boy, had felt proud that Mark and Papa wanted him along for a man's last stroll on deck. Jack always seemed to take it for granted that everyone wanted him at all times.

"Virginia," he whispered. "Virginia? Look up, darling—at those stars. They're real close at sea, aren't they? Not as pretty as your eyes, though. Not as beautiful as you. Nothing is."

He and Virginia had been married three years last February. Dear, generous Cousin Margaret McQueen had given her own Causton's Bluff plantation outright to them "for love and affection." Otherwise, they might not be married yet. He had always loved every acre of his uncle John McQueen's land at Causton's Bluff. When Uncle John died, it had been natural to try to help his widow, Cousin Margaret, look after the land. Nor had William forgotten the daily walks he and Cousin Margaret took to Uncle John's grave in the old cemetery those first months when she stayed in town with the Mackays. She was away permanently, he now feared, although she'd only called it an extended visit to relatives in Jamaica. He certainly understood, maybe better than anyone except Mama, why Cousin Margaret had found it too hard to live at Causton's Bluff without Uncle John.

How he wished Cousin Margaret could see his two children. He smiled, trying to picture the quiet, happy face of his little daughter Delia, who was getting old enough now so that William thought he could tell that she was going to be a lot like her mother—poised, but full of life, pretty as a white violet surprising you in a spring woods. Just the opposite of Mark's daughter Natalie, when she was Delia's age. If he were honest, he'd have to admit that Delia wasn't as pretty as Natalie had been as a little girl. Delia's hair was soft and fine, sort of light brown—and straight. That rascal Natalie had been a carrot-top, a curly carrot-top from the start. William sighed. Virginia and I won't ever have the problems with Delia, though, that Mark and Caroline are apt to have with Natalie, and Delia is plenty pretty enough for her father.

"I'd give most anything to be hugging you right now, Delia," he said aloud. Then he laughed. I guess I've always been teased a lot, he thought, for talking to myself. Even Virginia catches me doing it now and then, but it helps me think. And the way she teases never hurts. "Hey, Willie, son—are you dreaming away right now in that fine berth beside your sister? I'll bet you are." He thought a lot about his sturdy son, who would carry on the name of William Mackay. At seven months, it was kind of hard to tell about young William, but his father had believed from the first moment he'd held the infant in his arms that he was going to grow up to be the spittin' image of his grandfather Robert Mackay, who didn't live to see him.

William stood up, stretched, yawned—his eyes itchy from lack of sleep. He couldn't have slept more than an hour or so last night. Not surprising, because he had never, since their wedding, been away from Virginia at night.

Reluctantly, he crossed the wide front porch, took his time pinching out the flames of the hall candles inside because Virginia fussed a little when he just blew them out. "It spatters wax all over, dear." Then he began to climb the stairs, carrying a lighted candle to show the way. The way to probably just another night of aching arms, of half-dreams in which he actually felt Virginia's warm, fragrant body against his. Another night of reaching, half-awake, finding only emptiness.

But she's so happy to be taking our babies for her aunt to see, he reminded himself, pulling off his socks. I wanted her to go. No, I did not want her to go, but I wouldn't have told her that for anything. Oh, I might have if she'd been taking any other ship but the *Pulaski.* If anybody knows how well built the boat is, it's Mark. And when he was willing to let Natalie go, too, that settled it for me.

Three months is an awful long time, he thought, trying to settle his body in the bed. It was too hot for cover. In his nightshirt he lay on his back, arms extended. Virginia . . .

In a moment, as though struck by a wave, he was almost swamped by a kind of chilling loneliness that seemed far, far more agonizing than the night before. In all his life, he had never felt so alone, so vulnerable.

The word "vulnerable" kept coming to his mind. It wasn't even the kind of word William used. But lying helpless on the wide, empty bed, it came again and again. Years ago, he had overheard Mama say to Papa, "Our eldest son is far more vulnerable than most." William hadn't quite understood. Until now . . . lying there . . . without Virginia.

The understanding brought another heavy wave of what he could now recognize as fear. "When you're afraid, William," his mother used to say, "remember that 'perfect love casts out fear.' " Virginia loved him perfectly. His own love for her was as near that as he knew how to make it.

After a while, the fear faded as mysteriously as it had come. The handsome corner clock Virginia's mother left her began to chime downstairs. Before he counted nine chimes, he was asleep.

A menacing crash, which seemed to shake the old Causton's Bluff house to its foundations, brought William up, out of the bed, down the dark stair and into the front yard before he came fully awake.

For a dazed moment, he stood—barefoot, in his nightshirt—trying to unstop his ears with his fingers. The thunderclap had been so loud it must have deafened him, he thought, frowning—surprised to find himself where he was, dressed as he was. There was no rain falling; at least, he couldn't hear any. "Just hasn't begun to rain yet, I guess," he said aloud in the night that seemed only to lie softly around him. No wind. There was not one flash of lightning. And no more thunder.

He looked up at the sky. Stars—single, bright, and in powdery, sweeping clusters, still lit the clear blue-black night. And then, slowly, as though they all were swarming back from a long way off, jar-flies and other night insects began to hum and buzz, some evenly, some in bunched, scratching phrases with silences between. His hearing had returned, he guessed.

"What's the matter with me? I couldn't have heard a thunderbolt! *The stars are still out.*"

He looked around, dazed and embarrassed to be outside in only a nightshirt. His field hands and the two house servants were asleep, he hoped, down at the quarters. Frowning, he hurried back into the house.

Upstairs on his bed again, he asked God to take away the dread that the nameless fear, which had earlier seemed about to drown him, was going to return. It did return. In no time at all, he was once more unexplainably, unbearably *afraid.* So afraid, so anxious that he dressed and went back downstairs to sit on the front porch and wait for dawn.

Moments before the *Pulaski* split in two, Burke Latimer had leaped from the seat he had grabbed for himself in the lifeboat that hung from the starboard portion of the broken ship and clung now, in the cold, undulating water, to a section of scantling nine or ten feet long. For the moment, hoping to catch his second wind, he folded his arms over the scantling as it lay across his chest and floated on his back. Deliberately, he tried not to hear the cries for help in the black water around him. He rested, seeing only the sky and the quiet bright stars.

He had just found the scantling in the water when the ship split— separating the fore from the aft—and began to sink. There was no doubt in his mind that one or both of the supposedly indestructible boilers had blown up. Burke had known—suddenly, helplessly— that he could not stay in that lifeboat. His was *not* the only life he had to save!

Floating felt so good, he postponed any action for a few more seconds, then, in desperate need of strength, tried to concentrate only on the eternal sky and the stars. He failed. The face of the exasperating, beautiful red-haired girl from Savannah had never left him after the explosion. He had tried, for the sake of his own future, to think of saving only himself. He had tried, before the explosion and after, to blot her out of his thoughts—and failed.

With a burst of effort, he turned in the water and, still holding on to the wooden scantling, began to make his way toward what appeared in the near blackness to be a floating portion of the wreck. *If Natalie Browning was still alive somewhere, he meant to find her.* Horror such as this would surely have knocked some sense into her.

Riding astride the scantling, he paddled desperately and tried not to listen to the screams and moans and prayers, the drowning gasps and pleas for help in the plunging water around him. Literally and figuratively, he closed his eyes to the sight of grasping hands, the occasional white face that in the black night could have been a grown man or woman turned child again by terror—or a real child— dying alone. He glanced only long enough at each face to be sure it was not *her* face.

After paddling what must have been two hundred yards, his hand struck something hard, rough, firm. In the blurry starlight, he recognized the stern from which he had been catapulted into the water when the ship separated. Grabbing an iron stanchion, he pulled himself up and onto the piece of wreckage. Still holding on to the stanchion, his feet braced against another, higher up, he hung for a moment head-down, the sea lapping against the flooded wreck. When a big wave struck, he drew on every ounce of strength to hoist himself up the steeply sloping plane of what remained of the stern deck until he reached the steamer's wheel. Thankfully, he grabbed a brass spoke. But he could feel, could actually see the deck rising more and more to the perpendicular. The stern was sinking, the water rising higher around him. The wheel could break off. Every muscle straining, he began to creep up, up to the far end of the stern still protruding in the air. Other victims—women, older children, young men, old men—were struggling to go higher, too, most wordless, all gasping and choking and grunting.

Burke had already seen so many deaths, heard so many last cries for help and mercy, he marveled that his stomach still sickened each time one of the terrified, climbing people lost hold or slipped on the wave-washed, dizzily slanting deck and vanished overboard forever.

Fighting as he was for his own life, Burke kept trying to look behind him, around him, hoping for a glimpse of Natalie. Once he put his life at even more risk by sliding sideways in order to reach the hand of a young woman about Natalie's age. Just as she stretched to touch his hand, a giant wave slapped her into the roiling water with only time for him to see her white, horror-stricken face. It was not Natalie Browning.

He rested for a few seconds and had just begun again the steep climb that was defeating one after another of his fellow sufferers, when, quicker than thought, he and the remaining few people were swept into the ocean. The stern deck had broken entirely away.

Drawn about by strong currents, he was one moment under a wave, another moment atop one that pushed him as though he were a piece of driftwood, toward still another that sucked him down, down until he felt his lungs might burst. His strong body was helpless against the force, but he couldn't remember when his mind had raced so fast. Old friends, distant relatives not seen since childhood, his pale, ill mother on her pillows just before she died, his always controlled, scholarly father sobbing in the woodshed out back of

their Baltimore cottage, then the gunshot that freed him of the grief
. . . and he thought of Natalie. Over all the faces there shone that
of the sublime, impish, petulant minx whose ginger and beauty
would not fade. Natalie, whom he'd never even touched, had been
the reason he had given up his seat in the lifeboat because he
couldn't face the thought of living if she died. *Why?* Mere beauty that
stops a man's heart would never be enough for Burke Latimer! So
far as he knew, she would make a dreadful wife—but as he was
tossed about, useless even to himself in the black chaos of this
moment, he was driven to find her. Suddenly he felt something firm
—a firm surface!

He stood up. The object under him was floating free of the wreck,
following the waves' motion, but floating—sturdy, blessedly intact.
In a moment, his eyes now adjusted to the starlit darkness, he
realized that he was standing on a portion of the torn-away starboard deck from which he had been thrown. It was easy to define—
covered with canvas, painted white.

A fresh surge of energy coursed through Burke's body. His hopes
soared. He pulled himself aboard the deck fragment. There was
another, much older man, already there, not ten feet away. The man
made no effort to hail Burke, so intent was he on inserting a key into
the lock of a carpetbag that somehow he'd managed to bring with
him into the sea and now onto the portion of deck.

As Burke stood catching his breath, looking about, another young
man, with a little girl in his arms, began to try to pull himself aboard
at the far end. Burke reached him in time to help them both to
safety.

"Whose child is this? Do you know?" the young man gasped.

"No," Burke said, comforting the little girl. She had not cried out,
but stared through strands of soaked hair from the young man to
Burke—bewildered.

"She's—mine! Connie, Connie . . ." The older man with the
carpetbag stumbled toward the child, who cried, "Big Papa!" and
fell into his reaching arms. "She's my—precious granddaughter,"
the older man breathed. "My—precious little granddaughter." Beginning to sob, the man went on: "My daughter, her lovely—
mother—" He stopped abruptly. Burke and the other young man
understood why. "Connie, sweet Connie, you'll be—my own little
girl—from now on."

In the confusion that followed the arrival of three other soaked, bedraggled people, Burke forgot his own exhaustion and helped them aboard. Once everyone in sight seemed safe, he sank down onto a coil of heavy rope still fastened to the deck. The newcomers, G. B. Lamar from Savannah, one of his children, a twelve-year-old boy named Thomas, and a niece, who looked familiar, all proved to be helpful arrivals on the makeshift raft. The boy, Thomas, cried briefly from weariness, but soon stopped and covered Lamar's niece with a camlet cloak that floated in on a pile of splintered boards as though from heaven, so that the cloak was barely damp.

The niece's name was Rebecca Lamar, Burke learned. "Here, forgive me," he said. "I—I didn't even offer you my—seat. Please. That coil of rope is—better than standing."

"Thank you," she said, allowing him to help her. Seated, she tried to smile—the smile including them all. "It would be nice to—be able to lie down awhile, wouldn't it?"

Their feet and legs were in at least six inches of water, often more, as waves lapped over the torn deck. The water was deeper at the end where the planks and canvas had been torn away.

Now standing, Burke looked around him. The men stood or squatted. Rebecca Lamar, holding three-year-old Connie on her lap under the cloak, stared into the darkness, saying nothing to anyone. The child slept. The old man sobbed off and on, plainly growing weaker. Gripped by helplessness, everyone fighting exhaustion, there seemed, for the moment, nothing anyone could do.

Bracing himself against the sickening roll of the torn deck fragment, Burke kept trying to scan the sea around them. He could not, would not accept that Natalie might be gone. The *Pulaski* had obviously broken near its midsection. Surely, there were other passengers still clinging to life on other parts of the ship, other fragments. Somewhere out there in the starlight and blackness, she had to be clinging to her life, too.

A lump rose in his throat when the child Connie, sensing her grandfather's grief and weakness, woke up long enough to say brightly, "Big Papa, look at the pretty stars up there!" Human courage, he thought, soars in odd places. On first meeting, no one would be apt to think of saucy, self-absorbed Natalie Browning as being endowed with much human courage. Somehow, by now, he'd bet against that. As the time dragged by, she was plainly taking over in his mind, persisting. Oh, he hadn't been wrong to try to forget her. Not according to the nonsense she'd talked at their first meeting. Still, for no reason that he could explain, at some moment before he left the lifeboat, his mind had been made up. If Natalie lived, he meant to find her.

After a while, Burke began to prowl about through the lapping water on the section of deck, hoping to come upon something on which he might float. He would not find her by staying where he was. A plan had begun to form, an impossible, wild plan, but out here any plan meant hope. At the far end, where the water stood a foot deeper, what appeared earlier to have been merely a piece of wreckage, now set his heart pounding. A sturdy, wooden settee stood there unbroken, as though securely fastened down, its joints firm and strong. It was a miracle that it had not been swept overboard. The settee was built entirely of good thick cedar, long enough to seat three people. No doubt in his mind that with a box or barrel to buoy it, the piece of furniture would float—might even float for a long, long time.

He glanced back almost furtively at the others. How much more comfortable Miss Rebecca Lamar would be, he thought, if she could sit on the fine settee while holding the child. Quickly, he dismissed the thought. He needed it himself, for Natalie's sake.

"Find anything, Latimer?" G. B. Lamar called from the other end of the deck.

"I'm—I'm looking, sir," Burke called back, only half lying. He was still looking for something he could use as a buoy. If he could find a buoy to fasten under it, he could push the wooden settee off into the ocean, swim to it, climb on it, and begin to move around the water among the strewn wreckage to search for Natalie. If she still had Mrs. Mackay and her two infants with her, he'd have to worry later about the manly thing to do. Right now, finding a way to move about in the water was a compulsion. He felt along the edge of the broken-away deck for a plank that might loosen if he pulled hard enough. The thought of a good oar in his hands filled him with anger. Oars were things men simply took for granted. He'd give five years of his life for an oar now! An oar and something buoyant enough to float. With rope from the spool on which Miss Lamar sat, he could lash it to the settee. Lurching about in the darkness, he stumbled and fell, his shoulder striking something hard and round that rolled away from him. On his hands and knees, he scrambled to it. An empty keg. *An empty ten-gallon keg.* His buoy!

From the far end of the wreckage, Rebecca Lamar's shout pierced the night: "Here! Someone take—the—little girl! We're going to be —struck! Dear God, she'll be killed if that thing hits us! Where's her —grandfather?"

"Sick," young Thomas yelled. "I think—he's dying!"

A massive, heavy object struck their section of deck with a splintering, scraping crash and Burke hurried back to where the others crouched, G. B. Lamar steadying the old man. Burke did his best to examine what had just washed onto the wreckage. It killed no one when it hit—but one glance told Burke that indeed the old man was dead. G. B. Lamar gently released the body and joined Burke, who declared that onto their life-preserving raft had slammed the heavy wooden cover of the *Pulaski*'s hold.

"A—gift right from heaven, Latimer," Lamar gasped.

Ten feet square, at least, nearly two feet high, the hold cover had settled near what appeared to be a deep chest or counter for stowing cables—seen by none of them until now.

"How did we miss—this?" Burke asked, running his hand over the sturdily built chest, which was twice as high as the hold cover— nearly four feet—too high for Miss Rebecca to climb up on, but not for the men. Together, they could help her, though, and then they could all sit on it and keep their feet out of the water. Young Thomas was already climbing onto the chest.

"Wait," Burke ordered. "I want to look inside."

Thomas jumped down and Burke lifted the chest's water-soaked lid. Inside lay five coils of good rope of varying sizes. The lid slipped from his hands and banged shut and as it did, one plank—one fine plank four inches wide and perhaps five feet long, simply fell away in his hand. For what seemed a long time he stood looking at the faces around him and at the sturdy piece of wood in his hand. There had been only time to pull on his trousers when the boiler exploded. His nightshirt having been torn off in the water, he was naked from the waist up. He reached in a trouser pocket. His good knife was still there! In an hour, he could whittle out a fair handle. He would have his oar.

TEN

ON THE MORNING of Natalie's third day away, with Mark at work and Jonathan in school at the Reverend White's Academy, Caroline walked swiftly across Reynolds Square toward the old Mackay house on East Broughton. Lowering her parasol, carried against the hot mid-June sun, she hurried up Eliza Mackay's front steps.

Seated in the cool, shaded parlor, she refused Eliza's offer of tea and went to the point of her surprise visit. "Has Mark been here to talk to you, too—since Natalie left?"

"Why, yes," Eliza answered a bit warily. "He dropped by yesterday. I hope I quieted some of his worry over that girl."

"Is that all he talked to you about, Miss Eliza? Was Mark worried only about Natalie?"

"The way he loves that child, he'd have trouble worrying about too much else, I'd think."

Caroline jumped to her feet. "Don't do that! Don't protect him— or me, please. Mark and I are closer than we've been in months, but—" She broke off abruptly, stood looking as helpless, she knew, as she really felt, then sat down again beside Eliza on the old love seat and took her hand. "Can you go back in your mind to those long-ago days when you let me live here right after my grandfather died? When I couldn't face staying on at Knightsford with my grandmother still in the house? Remember how deeply in love I was with Mark then?"

"Oh yes, Caroline, I do remember."

"Even when he thought he was in love with you, Miss Eliza, I didn't try to hide from you that—just his touch melted me all the way inside. In those days I lived for one kind word from him. I still love him that way." She thought a minute, then said, "We—Mark and I—made love the very day Natalie left. He stayed home with Jonathan and me and—unexpectedly, wonderfully, we made love. Something—I didn't know what—loomed so high and dark between us, I—gladly loved him because I couldn't think of any other way to be rid of whatever has been pulling us so far apart that even Jonathan noticed."

"And—that rid you of it?"

"Yes. It always has. I suppose it always will. I'd—tried to find my way back to him again—by reason, by talking. He—he went right on being dear, but so careful with me—as though I were Natalie's age! I can't bear that. Mark insults me when he's—careful with me. I've given him no reason to treat me with—kid gloves. Not ever."

"Not even about Osmund Kott?" Caroline looked quickly away. "Not even about Osmund, Caroline? My dear, I know you've tried, but have you ever managed to give Mark the freedom really to talk to you about his problems with Osmund?"

On a deep sigh, Caroline said, "No. No, I've never managed that. Miss Eliza, I can't forget the years Osmund—blackmailed my dear grandfather—his own father! I've tried. I—have tried."

"For Mark's sake—for Natalie's sake, shouldn't you keep trying harder to let go your own resentful feelings about that old man, Kott? Until God sees fit to take him?"

"I doubt that even God wants him around heaven! And don't tell me that's no way to talk, because it's the way I feel. And don't tell me how marvelously he's handled our interests at Knightsford, either, because I already know that and it doesn't help one bit."

After a pause, Eliza asked, "Does it matter that Natalie loves Osmund so, so much?"

"Of course it matters. It torments and infuriates me. It makes me shudder to think that my own flesh and blood could take so to—such an evil man."

"Natalie is part of—Osmund's flesh and blood, too, in a way."

"In a way I hate!"

Caroline knew exactly what Eliza Mackay was doing when she waited so long to speak again. She was giving Caroline time to simmer down, to think more clearly. "You're being careful with me too, just like Mark." She tried to smile. "And of course I don't blame either of you. I—I'm not at all Christian when it comes to that devilish old man. God actually helped me forgive my grandmother before she died for the way she mistreated Grandfather all those years. I—can't forgive Osmund Kott. Has God lost—some of His power?"

"You know the answer to that too."

"I have to ask you this. I'm sure you will protect Mark, but—did he come here to talk to you about—Osmund yesterday? To tell you something—I don't know about?"

"It does trouble Mark deeply, Caroline, that someone like—Kott could come between you. It troubles me, too."

Caroline sighed. "That's about what I knew you'd say. And I do know how hard I make it for Mark. I've even tried to—fake polite behavior toward Osmund."

"And don't you think that confuses both Mark and Natalie still more?"

"Mark, yes. Natalie?" She gave a short laugh. "When Kott's name comes up, she just flounces out of the room, or orders her father's boat to Knightsford to visit him. To spite me, I imagine."

"I think I'll just ignore that."

"I would, if I were you. But—you know Natalie."

"Yes. Caroline, does Osmund really *do* anything to—keep you so dead set against him? Does he act a certain way, or—"

"Butter would melt in his mouth when he addresses me before either my husband or my daughter. It's—the way he looks at me—when they both happen to be inattentive for a moment. It's—what I know him to *be!*"

"My, that kind of nervous situation must make for very trying visits to Knightsford. Poor, beautiful Knightsford."

"Yes. Poor Knightsford. I have come that far. I love it again out there. I feel close again to Grandfather when we're there. I even have some quiet, caring thoughts about—my grandmother."

After a long silence, Caroline took her hand. "Thanks for letting me spout. I didn't expect you to tell me much, but what would either of us ever do without you? And don't tell me to count my blessings. I know what an ungrateful wretch I am. What other woman has only one dark cloud on her horizon?"

• • •

Burke, alternately paddling with his makeshift oar, then resting, had floated the night away on his precious settee, the empty keg lashed beneath it as a buoy. Even so, water lapped over both feet. His companions aboard the shattered section of deck had thanked him for rolling the old man's body into the water while they slept. That is, they thanked him once he'd assured them that he'd said a proper prayer first. Funny kind of religion, he thought, watching the sun rise out of the water, all the time scanning the debris-tossed water for Natalie Browning. I doubt they'd have been so grateful if I hadn't said the proper words, even though God knows I rolled him overboard to spare them.

Burke honestly doubted that God dealt only in words. The sun came up swiftly and with it his spirits. Everything was going to be better by daylight. He would be stronger. Hungrier, but stronger, because hope gave a man strength. He meant never to tell a living soul that in the darkest part of the night—searching in the blackness for Natalie—he had wept. Exhaustion, he told himself then. He knew now that his tears had come from more than exhaustion, but admitting to fear that Natalie might be drowned was far harder than jumping overboard after he had pushed the settee off into the water. Far harder than swimming for the settee, with no assurance that its wooden frame, lashed atop the empty wooden keg, would hold his weight.

It had held. It held now as the night scattered. He was floating and the ruffling water only covered his ankles.

Bidding farewell to the others before he jumped into the sea had been far from easy, but once aboard his makeshift raft, the thought that he floated above the lifeless bodies of two young people who had begged him for help at some point in the night had made him vomit. "Help us, sir, please help us—! We love each other—please help us!" He could still hear their anguished calls, and although he had rowed toward them with all his might, both had vanished before he could reach them.

While still on the wreckage, Burke and G. B. Lamar had hauled another young couple—on their honeymoon, the wife told them— onto the fragment of deck. Within minutes, the pale young husband had died. Burke shuddered to think of plucky Rebecca Lamar back there now, trying to comfort the young widow.

A champagne basket from the *Pulaski* containing one quart and one pint of wine and a vial each of peppermint and laudanum had floated close enough to the little group so that Lamar could reach it and haul it aboard. Miss Lamar had been put in charge of the basket's precious contents. Burke didn't envy her the task of portioning it out because everyone desperately needed to quench the growing thirst that gripped them all, and most were in some kind of pain. Burke had jumped into the sea and now clung to the settee with nothing but his makeshift oar, a coil of stout rope and his pocketknife.

As the sun climbed in the cloudless morning sky, he remembered that before he'd left them, they had all shouted at the top of their voices when what appeared to be the lights of a ship had brightened the black horizon. He laughed a little now, because while they were still crying out, a nearly full moon had quietly sailed up into sight. There was no ship.

Grimly he vowed that, by some means, he would not see the moon tonight from the threatening waters of the Atlantic Ocean. Nor would he see it alone. He meant to save himself and he meant to find the red-haired girl from Savannah. Together, they would find a way to safety. A ship would surely pick up survivors today, tomorrow at the latest. The *Pulaski* was due in Baltimore soon, if he read the sun correctly. They would be missed and rescue ships would be sent out along the packet's scheduled route.

He could see for miles now, could tell that he had gone almost nowhere in the long night. The shattered deck where his companions huddled together was still in plain view. They waved. He waved back.

Carefully he turned on his settee, to face away from the blinding sun. There were still people on smaller pieces of wreckage in the water. Once he counted seven arms waving and felt a surge of pride in them—pride he knew they shared in him. In that silent way, by waving, they were congratulating one another.

Then he heard a woman's cry and, not a hundred yards away, saw another arm waving. "Help! Please—somebody help me! I'm here. Over this way—help! Help!" Almost at once, he saw *her* face.

For a choking instant, Burke was unable to move a muscle. "Don't just sit there," she called—more a command than a cry for help. "Here! Over here! This box won't hold me—much longer. *Help!*"

Tears coursed down his cheeks as he fumbled with stiff, swollen

fingers to untie the piece of rope with which he'd secured his whit-
tled oar during the last rest period.

"Hurry! This—box is—about to sink!"

Peering more closely now, Burke could see that indeed she was
floating in a wooden crate of some kind and that she held a baby in
her arms.

"Burke! Burke—help me!"

Finally, he had untied the oar, but until Natalie called his name,
for the life of him he could not make his body spring into action.
Then, as though untrapped from a nightmare, he began to slap at
the water with the crude short oar. Within seconds, he knew she
could drown before he reached her. His oar strokes barely moved
the makeshift raft. Without waiting to decide, he was suddenly in the
water, swimming across the distance that separated them. Neither
spoke as he pulled her from the box. She was still clinging to the
obviously dead body of an infant. With her and the baby, he began
to swim back in the direction of his settee. After only a few thrashing
strokes, he knew he was going to fail. "The baby's dead," he
shouted. "Let it go!"

"No!"

"Let it go!"

"No!"

"That's what we'll have to do with it—anyway," he gasped, near
tears. "You'll have to swim too! Natalie, can you—swim?"

"Of course—I can—swim!" Her voice broke. She was crying.

He reached for strength he didn't have, but they were getting
nowhere against the tide. In a moment, he felt the load lighten a bit.
Burke watched the tiny body slide to one side in the gray water and
vanish from sight.

In numb silence, shaken by their own near escape from death,
they sat side by side on the settee. The heaving water, with Natalie's
added weight, now reached to Burke's waist. The settee barely
carried them both. If only there'd been two settees, he thought
absurdly. Two lashed together with a length of the rope he'd
brought would do fine.

Suddenly, he thought of her box and leaped back into the water,
unmindful of Natalie's pleas not to leave her. When he caught hold
of the wooden crate, a severe cramp in one leg made the return

swim a blur of agony. But he reached the settee again and she reached through the slats and held the box securely while, treading water, he tied it to the back of the settee. Then, without a word, she helped Burke onto the wooden seat and with both hands began to rub the knotted muscle in his left leg.

"I—can—rub my own leg," he gasped, the pain lessening only a little as he dug into the hard calf muscle. After a time, his breath still labored, Burke slumped against the settee's wooden back. "Better," he said. "Couldn't be the water that caused the cramp. This morning air's—a lot colder than the water."

"I know," she said tonelessly. "Even with the sunshine."

"Sunshine's good."

She nodded.

For a time he lay there staring at her back, because something prompted Natalie to try her best to sit straight, as a proper young lady might, her back to him. Strands of wet red hair lightened as they dried in the sun's warmth; shone like gold, curled on her neck. She'd worn her hair in some fancy way, as he remembered. Now, it looked as though she'd been dragged about all night in the dark waves—in and under them. She had. "Where'd you find that wooden crate?" he asked.

"A miracle."

He laughed. "Did you get swept out of the lifeboat when the ship broke in two?"

Again, she only nodded.

"With—the baby?"

"Yes. Somehow—I got the baby."

"Was it—one of Mrs. Mackay's children?"

Natalie shook her head yes. "Her—little son, William, Jr."

"Mrs. Mackay and the girl? Are they gone, too?"

She only bit her lips.

His head against the wooden settee back, he was still watching her. She was clad only in a thin, once white, nightgown.

"I bet you nearly froze last night," he said. "How about the old man—Mr. Kott? Did he drown when she split apart?"

At that, she buried her face in her hands and began to sob.

Burke sat up, leaned forward, took her in his arms and held her head against his bare wet chest. "I'm—sorry, Miss Natalie. I'm so—sorry." When the sobbing eased, he said, "It's funny how strangers

—begin to care about one another when—we're all in a mess together. I've thought about that old man. I liked him. Thought about Mrs. Mackay too. She seemed as nice as she was pretty. I talked to her at the Captain's table. A really gentle lady."

In a moment, Natalie pulled away from him and sat up, as though trying to sort it all out for her own sake. "Let me see if I can—remember exactly what—happened. I need to remember—exactly. I'll have to tell—poor William, her husband. When the deck broke away, the bow—straight up in the air—I was holding the baby. Virginia had little Delia." A sob caught, then she steadied her voice. "Kottie—was trying to get to—me. He waved then I—*saw* him—slide past me—into the sea. *I—saw him.* I—kept calling to him." She shuddered. "Then, I remember—when I hit—the water. It was—so hard!"

"Were—you—still holding on to the baby?"

She nodded. "I'm a good swimmer, but—not very good—with only one arm."

"Hardly anyone is."

"I also watched—Virginia and little Delia—slide off the deck—right ahead of me. I was trying to help her and—Virginia was—really trying to help, too, but—I never saw either one of them—again." She buried her face against him. Once more, he held her. Then, without lifting her head, she said, "I don't know if William Mackay's baby son—drowned or if his little neck broke when we hit the water. But I felt the—life go out of him." She was looking up at Burke now, her face white and stark. "Burke, I—felt his life—leave!"

"But you didn't let go of him," he murmured wonderingly. "Not all last—night!"

"I—couldn't. It was little William! The box floated right to me. Don't ask me—how I got into it—with the baby. It *was*—a miracle. For a long, long time—in the water, in the box—I kept trying to breathe my life into Virginia's son. My father is very close to William. From the time Papa came to Savannah—when he was only twenty—until he and Mama married, he lived at the Mackays' house. William Mackay is like Papa's younger brother." She shuddered again. "Losing all three of them might—kill William! But I'll have—to tell him—all about it. He'll want to know—everything."

"And you and I are going to make it out of this—somehow," Burke said, hoping to encourage her.

For an instant, a flash of the old fire lit her pale blue eyes. "Oh, I've never doubted that for a moment!"

"Why?"

"Because God knows we're both out here."

"Didn't He know about—the others, too?"

"There you go," she snapped. "Being just the way you were on the boat before all this happened. Being opinionated. Arguing."

"I just asked a question."

"Have you swallowed much salt water?"

Her deft change of subject brought a short laugh. "I don't feel as though I have. How about you?"

"Some, I suppose, when I first slid into the water—but I haven't been sick."

Burke had been, but he decided not to admit it. "I'll bet you were really scared, though."

"Of course I was scared! So were you. So was everybody."

She asked then where he'd found the settee and Burke told her about the others washed up onto the split-off boat deck. She seemed genuinely glad to know that Rebecca Lamar was still alive. He weighed the matter awhile, then decided to tell Natalie that he had given up a seat in the only lifeboat at hand because he—had to find *her*.

Instead of gushing her gratitude as most young women who had just been rescued from the sea might, she looked straight at him and asked, "Why me instead of Authexia Parkman?"

"I can't answer that."

"Why can't you answer it?"

"Because I don't know. I only know that I had to try to find you."

"What made you so sure I wasn't already drowned?"

"I don't know that either."

"I thought you knew everything!"

"I don't. Sorry to disappoint you."

She appeared, he thought, to be mulling that over. At least, she was very, very quiet. Then he saw her eyes close and naturally, as a child would, she laid her head against him and fell into an exhausted sleep. For a time, realizing that her fair, clear, sensitive skin would

surely burn horribly when the sun climbed higher, he sat motionless, his free hand—the one not holding her—shielding her face.
When Burke could fight his own exhaustion no longer, he, too,
slept.

ELEVEN

ON SATURDAY, the fourth day after the *Pulaski* sailed, Eliza Mackay and her two daughters, Kate and Sarah, sat on the big side porch reading aloud a letter from the girls' brother Jack, now a captain in the Department of Army Engineers.

" 'Here in this seemingly godforsaken Cherokee Nation,' " she read, " 'I hear nothing of Savannah news beyond what you send me. I assume our little family group departed in style aboard the lauded *Pulaski.* I will hereby attempt to amuse you as you wait for word of the voyagers, with some scintillating news of my life at this army post in good old north Georgia, where nature outdoes herself—and white men, at least, seem content to live like pigs. My distinguished brother-in-law, W. H. Stiles, is right about the rolling hills and picturesque little valleys. I chuckle to think of his wife, my sister, contenting herself in these wilds, but she will love the beauty. Is William Henry still itching to buy land here? I realize that if anyone could civilize the area, W.H. could. I admit I so long to see someone from the family that I advise the gentleman to drag his lovely wife, if need be, all the way here to the upcountry he so admires. I could, at least, ride to Cassville to feast my eyes upon Eliza Anne's charms and listen to her fuss because I don't look elegant enough in my frayed uniform to be a captain.' "

"Jack is Jack—even in his letter." Kate laughed. "And can't you see William Henry dragging Eliza Anne *anywhere* she doesn't want to go?"

Eliza Mackay smoothed the letter over her knee, smiling at the thought of her eldest daughter keeping house on Georgia's frontier, and went on reading: " 'The Cherokees seem to me to be a peaceful people, and many are preparing to plant crops as though they harbor no thoughts of being forced to leave their beloved Nation. Time will tell, but the U.S. *will claim* their land—or rather, the state of Georgia will force the Feds to do so. Like W.H., I have quite fallen in love with its natural beauty, but my heart remains in swampy Savannah. I will say that trouble could be afoot here if the Cherokee's man, Chief John Ross, does not soon return from Washington with some settlement. At least, so far as I know, he has not yet arranged an emigration agreement. The Indians go on farming and trusting him to protect them.' "

"It doesn't seem quite right to force the Cherokees to leave the land the federal government has already given them by treaty," Sarah mused. "I think it's really somewhat of a problem."

Kate laughed at her younger sister. "There you go, making something that is so dreadful sound routine. Read more of Jack's letter, Mama. Does he want us to send his summer clothes yet? I should certainly think so."

"I'm just coming to that, Kate. In fact, I think we must have missed getting one of his earlier letters. Listen: 'Usually, you ladies on Broughton Street are quite prompt in complying with my requests. Why haven't I received my summer clothes? I do hope you are sending nothing too worn. You know how I hate the sight of threadbare garments, so give away all you know I won't wear. I plan to buy an entire new outfit if the creeping Army Bill ever passes the House of Representatives. About this I am not very sanguine, since those old boys in Washington talk far more than they act. Please tell me, Katie and Sarah, if any of those plants I sent from Florida sprouted. If they have, water them plentifully, since I dug them from the edges of ponds in low ground. I should very much like to hear of their blooming.' "

"Well, they didn't," Sarah said.

"I didn't think you gave them enough water."

"Then why didn't you do it?"

"Hush, girls. Listen to this: 'I put little stock in dreams, and suppose my nightmare about William was provoked by knowing the old boy is out there at Causton's Bluff alone, with his beloved Virginia and children at the North. Still, I can't shake last night's

depressing experience. As so often happens, the details of the nightmare are now missing, but I came fully awake out of my bed in a cold
sweat—frightened to my soul for poor William! This should not
worry you too much, Mother, but is my brother all right? Is he
bearing up without the light of his life? I do eagerly await the news
that he is all right in his quiet way, and that my dream was foolish. I
will write to Cousin Margaret McQueen, as you urged me to do,
Mother, sometime soon, although I doubt that my tedious surveying
trips from frontier outpost to frontier outpost will much amuse her.
Why is she staying so long in Jamaica? I'm sure my brother William
would love having her with him at Causton's Bluff while his family is
away. Love to all, Jack.'"

Eliza Mackay finished the letter and let her troubled eyes wander
out over the big side yard.

"Mother, don't frown so! That was only a dream Jack had. And,
Sarah, don't you frown either. You're as big a worrywart as Mama
is."

"Nevertheless," their mother said, "I want you to tell Mark, when
you're doing your shopping on Bay Street this afternoon, that as
soon as it's convenient, we want him to take us to Causton's Bluff."

Katie snorted her disgust. "Mother!"

"Do as I say, dear. We'll simply make sure."

"But what will you tell William? He's worried enough as it is. Do
you want to scare him even more with Jack's dumb old dream?"

"We're not going to scare him. We are just going to pay him a little
visit. I'm sure Mark and Caroline and Jonathan will enjoy it, too.
Caroline told me when she stopped by this morning that their beautiful house is like an empty, dim cave without Natalie."

"I know Mark has to attend a meeting tonight," Sarah said.
"When I stopped by to see if William Thorne Williams got in that
book he ordered for me, he told me some of the men in town are
going to form a society—to collect old manuscripts and things like
that. Mark's right in the middle of it."

"If Mark can't go this afternoon, he'll take us tomorrow after
church," Eliza said firmly. "The point is—we're going. I'll get Emphie to fix a picnic. We'll surprise William."

Natalie smelled the sea when she first opened her eyes sometime
on what must be Saturday morning—early Saturday morning, if the

first rays of the sun were any sign. Then she felt a hot, searing pain on her almost bare shoulder and stifled a cry. Gritting her teeth, she swiped hard at the ugly, slimy sea nettle splatted like jelly on her skin and watched it slip just beneath the surface of the sea and hang there, mocking her. Her face and nose and forehead hurt, too, and the back of her neck where the sun had blistered yesterday, but not as much as the stinging of the sea nettle. Her whole body burned from the sun and the fish's sting, but she was shaking with cold.

Burke still slept and she tried valiantly to think only that—they were together. Her skin hurt so and she was so hungry, so thirsty, her tongue felt huge and thick, but they *were* together. It's all right, she told herself, wanting him to sleep as long as possible. It's all right that I'm so cold and hungry and thirsty and burned—because so is he. So, she supposed, were all the others who might be still alive anywhere on the surface of the roughening water. The makeshift raft rose and fell more than last evening, she was sure, but they hadn't drifted much in any direction during the night. Burke would know. She would ask him after a while, when he woke up. He's here to ask, she reassured herself. *Burke's here.*

Carefully, she tried to turn a bit on the settee, to look around the open sea for signs of Rebecca Lamar and the others on their piece of deck. Still in sight last night, though too far away to reach, they had waved to one another until it was too dark to see. The back of her neck was so burned, it was agony to turn, but she could still see the forlorn raft. On impulse, she waved. From the wreckage, only three waved back.

"Some of them—must have—died," she whispered, not meaning to form the words audibly.

His groan tore at her heart. Coming awake was a terror-filled experience. She laid her hand on his. Not quite conscious, he jerked his hand away, stretched and groaned again.

"That's a rude way to treat a lady who only meant to comfort you," she said.

"Huh?" He touched the back of his own neck and winced.

"I just laid my hand on yours to comfort you through the first realization that we're—here in this terrible predicament. You snatched your hand away. Not very polite. Shall I order breakfast?"

For an instant, he looked at her, tried to smile and then retched over the arm of the wooden settee. Nothing came. There was nothing there. Quickly, Natalie pulled from under her one of the pieces of her nightgown which they'd used to wet their faces yesterday and then cover their heads. She dipped the rag into the ocean and held it under Burke's chin until the nausea passed.

"Where was that piece of cloth?" he asked.

"I slept on it all night. You didn't want anything so priceless to float away, did you?"

"You're a lot smarter than I thought."

Natalie almost smiled. "It hurts my face to smile."

"Mine, too."

"Burke?"

"Hm?"

"Gentlemen don't say 'hm?' They say *ma'am.*"

"In the middle of the ocean?"

"How far do you think we are from land?"

Involuntarily, he tried to turn, said, "Ouch," and straightened up again. "The *Pulaski* was supposed to be keeping to a course somewhere in the vicinity of thirty-five miles out to sea."

"Do you think we're drifting toward shore?"

"Have you seen any sign of the others on the wreckage yet this morning? My neck and back are not only burned—I've pulled a neck muscle."

She laid her hand on his again. "Yes, the others are still back there. Not as close as yesterday evening."

"Hm."

"I'd think, since we haven't a thing to do but talk, you'd say more than 'hm.' Are you still sick at your stomach?"

"No. Not any more. I'm trying to think."

"About what?"

When he turned to look at her, his deep-set brown eyes were still so sleepy and bewildered, she giggled. "We're both as stiff and puckered as old plucked turkeys, aren't we?"

"I'm trying to think what I'd better do next."

"Burke, what can we do but wait? Surely, someone has already sent ships to find us." He didn't answer. "Burke! Answer me. I can't bear it when you don't answer me."

"Sometimes I like to think awhile first."

"But where does that leave me?"

His eyes laughed at her. "Right where you are, sitting on a settee in the middle of the Atlantic Ocean—beside me. With the waves almost up to your breasts."

"Not if I sit up. And I hope you don't begin to be vulgar. You've been a perfect gentleman."

"I'm not vulgar and I'm not a perfect gentleman."

"Then what are you?"

This time, she was sure that at least a whole minute must have passed while he sat, half turned toward her, looking and looking right into her eyes, but saying nothing.

Finally, he asked, "What did I say that made you think I might be —getting vulgar?"

"You said—you said something about the waves being up to my— breasts."

"Should I have said your 'beautiful breasts'?"

"No gentleman would!"

"I'm *not* one of your Savannah gentleman. I'm me. And your breasts aren't the only beautiful part of you." His voice remained calm, almost matter-of-fact. "You're beautiful all over, Miss Natalie Browning. The most beautiful creature I've ever seen. Even now, with your hair as wild as witches' hair, your face as red as any beet or redder—and wearing that dirty, wrinkled, half-soaked nightgown, you're beautiful. So beautiful, I could look at you for the rest of my life."

Embarrassed, Natalie smoothed at the bodice of her once pretty nightgown, the long, partially shredded skirt floating around them in the water. Then she tucked uselessly at her shining, tousled hair. "I know I'm beautiful. Tell me other things you think about me. People have always talked about how beautiful I am. I can't help that. I was just born this way."

"That's right. You were. But aren't you vain about it?"

"No, because I have a brain, too, along with my beauty. I know why I'm beautiful. My parents are both handsome people. My goody-goody little brother, Jonathan, is a perfect picture—as boys go. I am vain about other things, though."

"What other things?"

"You said yourself I'm smarter than you thought I'd be. I'm vain about being smart. And about being a good swimmer and a good horsewoman."

"About your dancing, too, I'll wager."

She shrugged. "I should be a good dancer. I've had dancing lessons for years. That's simply because Papa's rich. So is my mother, too, I think, in her own right. She did inherit all that land at Knightsford, our Savannah River plantation. But those are family things. Tell me why you like *me*."

"Aren't you vain about your elegant, distinguished family?"

"I'm proud of my parents, if that's what you mean. Even when they cross me, I'm still proud of the kind of people they are. You'll like them both, Burke, a lot. But, my family doesn't influence me in the big, important things."

"That's nonsense if I ever heard it."

"It is not! What I mean is, I think you'll like them once we're back in Savannah where you can get to know them. But that's not the main thing. The main thing is—*you like me*."

"I do?"

"You risked your life to save me. And do you realize that we've gotten along just fine trapped here together on this settee?"

"Better than I dreamed we might."

She thought awhile, then said, "You told me you didn't know why you risked your life for me. I didn't believe you then. I wouldn't believe you now, so don't bother to say again that you don't know."

"I won't."

She fidgeted through another of his long silences. Then, when she was just about to break into it, he said, "Both things you claim to be vain about surprised me."

"Swimming? The way I handle a horse?"

"They're both outdoor things. Natalie, I'm heading—if we ever get rescued—to the frontier. To live and die there."

"I know that's what you think now, dear Burke, but you haven't been to Savannah except to board the rotten old *Pulaski*. You wait!"

"I hate waiting." He grabbed her shoulders. It hurt, but she didn't cry out. "We can talk later about other matters," he went on. "Right now, I need to settle something. God knows how long we'll be cooped up on this makeshift raft. Only He knows if we'll ever get off alive. He also knows that I am now—in love with you. I know it. I'm eight years older than you. I know myself better than you could possibly know yourself, but—I think you love me, too. I need to settle that. Do you, Natalie Browning?"

Without meaning to at all, she began to cry. "Oh, Burke, finally," she sobbed and clung to him. "I thought you'd never get it said!"

"I want to hear you say it. Do you love me?"

"Yes, yes, yes, *yes!*"

Holding her hard against him, he said, "One of us could die, Natalie . . . we could both be dead by sundown. We need—another miracle. You almost fell off this thing in the night, did you know that? No, you were too exhausted to know. A wind rose. The raft was careening up and over and down those big swells and—" He shuddered. "I just managed to catch you as you were—slipping over the side."

"Don't tell me things like that!"

"Natalie, if we only have a little time left together, I want us to be —committed to each other. Right here—now. Let's vow, before God." Tears were running down his cheeks. "If—we're going to die, please, Natalie, let's die—belonging to each other!"

She pulled herself upright. "I'm not going to die, and neither are you! I won't let us die, Burke. I mean to *live* my whole life beside you. For always."

"Is that—just *young* talk?"

"I can't help that I'm only sixteen. Inside I'm not. Inside, I know what I want and I love you. I love you. *I love you.* And I mean—I love you for *always.*"

"Natalie, our 'always' could be—now."

"Stop it! I don't want to hear talk like that, Burke Latimer. I knew I loved you long before you had sense enough to know how you felt. So stop it."

"Aren't you—afraid?"

"Of course I'm afraid. But I don't intend to let that spoil one minute of loving you. If we live on your frontier, don't you think we'll ever be afraid again?"

"I'm not asking you to promise to live with me up there."

His words sent a chill through her. "What—*are* you asking? Don't you want to—marry me?"

"Right now, all I ask is that—you love me. Natalie, I don't have any family—I don't have anyone." He held her head against his shoulder. "A man—doesn't want to—die alone. I won't now, will I?"

"I'll say you won't!" She pulled back enough to look at him, to force him to look at her. "Have you given up? Tell me the truth—do you believe we're going to die? I've never even thought we might die!"

He let her go and buried his head in his hands. "Neither have I—until now."

For once, Natalie couldn't think of what to say, but she must help him believe they *were* going to be rescued.

Again, she dipped the two torn-off pieces of her skirt in the ocean, wrung them out slightly and laid one over Burke's blistering bare shoulders, the other across the back of her own neck. Searching for something to say that would convince him, she turned to check on the other survivors. The wreckage was in sight. Natalie waved once—twice. Two arms waved back weakly. Had Burke said there were five or six aboard when he jumped into the water with his settee? She shivered, grabbed his hard, brawny arm and clung to it.

There was nothing to say.

The remainder of Saturday wore into darkness; their thirst was now almost unbearable. Burke slept so little through the long, cold night that Sunday's first light hurt his eyes more than ever. All through each dark hour, he had held her, his leg muscles aching so from being cramped up in such a tiny space that only Natalie's desperate need for sleep kept him from waking her, asking her to move a little. He needed to massage his legs.

She loved him. He believed her. At least, she loved him all a sixteen-year-old girl could love a man. She would, if God gave them a chance, love him more. He would see to that. Now and then, sitting there last night in the eerie darkness, or today under the torturing sun—forcing back nausea from hunger and thirst—he held to sanity by trying to imagine the two of them together. The two of them together—later, after this tormented, vicious nightmare had somehow ended. Man and wife, day in and day out. Thinking of them that way wasn't easy. They were more like a couple of squared-off, head-butting goats, he knew. Natalie would always be Natalie. He would always be Burke. Oh, he would be the head of their house. Living, as he'd done for so many hours now, a few inches from death, helped a man face facts—stripped away mere custom and social standards. He would be the head of their house, but Natalie would be the head of his heart.

He might even go back to Savannah with her to meet her parents, if God spared their lives. But only for a while. Marrying Burke Latimer meant settling where Burke Latimer wanted to settle. That would never be in Savannah society. He longed to rouse her, to beg her to promise to live on the Georgia frontier with him. Or had she already promised to do that? He shook his head. His mind was growing more and more confused, cloudy. He was no longer in charge of his thoughts, thoughts that seethed and slackened, seethed and slackened mercilessly, lulling him into near helplessness. At first, on their clumsy settee, he had felt strong in spite of the hard swims, the falls, the battering from the sea. He hated weakness. "I'm weak now," he said aloud and felt guilty. Guilty for being so absentminded as to risk waking her; guilty for needing her so much when she needed to sleep.

"Don't say that," she murmured, her eyes still closed. "Kottie? Kottie, don't you dare tell me you're weak!" And then she moaned, almost whimpered. "I'll keep—needing you—to help me—with lots of things, Kottie. So, do you—hear me? You are not weak! Not one bit weak . . ."

Burke held her closer, telling her over and over that she was in *his* arms. That he was Burke, not Kottie. That he loved her. That he would take care of her.

Hunger, he'd always heard, could blur a man's mind. A girl's mind too. Natalie was talking crazy. If only he had a piece of bread. It wouldn't have to be fresh or warm or buttered . . . one piece of plain, dry bread would do. If I had a piece of bread—he moved over the words in his mind as though forming an important plan—I'd rouse her and put it into her mouth, one little piece at a time, so she wouldn't choke on it. "I feed you with my—love," he whispered, forgetting already that he meant not to wake her. "I feed you, Natalie, with my strength—my dreams. I—feed you with my north Georgia hills, those high waterfalls, lovely Natalie. Poor, ill, lovely little Natalie! I feed you—with my—frontier, the house I want to—build for you with my—own hands. . . ."

When he regained consciousness, the sun was gone. A heavy, dark-clouded sky rolled above them as the sea rolled beneath and around them. Wind gusted, lifting the settee up and then plunging it down into great troughs of water. Burke could feel danger rise inside him—the danger of death, their death. Ill, unable to find any strength within himself now, he turned to look in the direction of the other survivors on their piece of promenade deck. He waved. No one waved back. Loneliness and panic seemed to be squeezing the very blood from his veins. In some useless, but important way, he had drawn a kind of consolation from those equally helpless human beings on the other raft. Now they were all dead. Or too ill to notice his signal.

Natalie screamed and grabbed him. He could feel her slender body tremble. She screamed again and cried for Kottie until Burke thought his heart would burst with anguish.

The wind, which had been rising, had now turned, as seawinds can, into a squall. He shook Natalie, desperate to make her say something—to *him*—not to the old man, Kott, dead and bumping around somewhere in the sea. "We're going to die now for sure, Natalie! Talk to me! Say something to *me*. It's Burke! Natalie— please talk to *me*. . . ."

The delirious whimpering and cries for "Kottie" went on until, on one steep fall down the side of a monstrous wave, she fainted.

"Our Father . . . who art . . . in heaven," Burke mumbled, only able now to hold her with one arm while clutching the side of the settee with the other—wrestling the power determined to destroy them. He prayed and held on, telling himself that if he let go for an instant, they would both be washed overboard. When his eyes closed, he forced them open, meaning to look at her face until the last minute left to him.

A squall at sea can be short-lived, something reminded him. Wordlessly, he prayed for that. Then he cried out: "God, if she has to—die—don't let her come to! Let her—die easy, God. Not knowing—anything about—any of it. . . ."

His own eyes were drawing shut again and maybe a minute or an hour had passed when they flew open on a heavy jolt at the back of their settee, splintering the empty box he'd lashed there to make it float high enough in the water. So weak that he could barely turn his head, he saw that a chunk of wreckage partially covered with white canvas had crashed into them. Deck canvas, he thought, dizzy now from the blow. Deck canvas . . . it's covered with deck canvas. . . . His mind wandered around the irrelevant thought. What did the canvas matter? Natalie still lay slumped beside him, her burned face chalky and swollen. Heavy spray enveloped them—spray both cold and smothering. Her bright hair was plastered across the little face.

He looked behind them again. The canvas-covered fragment was holding solidly against the back of the settee as though fastened there. It was big, too. A big, roomy, canvas-covered platform had floated miraculously to them and was being held there by the suck of the furious wind and the sea. Each time Burke and Natalie and their settee thrust up and over a giant wave, the platform went too. It also followed them when they dove down the other side. Up . . . down . . . up . . . down.

After a time, he realized that he had let go of the side of the settee by which he'd been holding them and was hitting his head, making sure that he wasn't asleep and dreaming. He was awake and it was all right that he no longer held them, because as quickly as it had blown up, the squall was dying down. If he could find the strength, the sea was now calm enough for him to cut some rope and try to lash the miraculous white platform to their raft. But first, after a little rest, he must tie Natalie to the settee. . . .

"Our Father, who art in heaven," Burke muttered over and over as he worked at securing the platform, his fingers stiff, swollen, bruised—his whole body feeble, like the body of an old man. A torn place in the canvas had revealed an opening through which he finally managed to slip one end of the rope. "Our Father," he breathed. "Our Father . . ."

On his knees at the back of the settee, he tied and hauled and leveled and tried to think about how he'd move Natalie onto the miraculous platform the sea had brought them. Ten feet long, he judged, and a good five feet wide. "I'll kiss her when I'm through," he said aloud, his voice raspy, trembling. "I'll—kiss her when I'm through here. Then she'll wake up. She's not dead. She's only fainted. I'll—wet our cloth scraps again, and that'll help her too. . . ."

And then the rain began to fall. Rain. *Real rain.* Water with no salt in it!

"Natalie," he shouted with all his might, then fell, more than turned, back into the sitting position and reached for her. "Natalie, darling Natalie, it's raining! It's raining water we can *drink!*" Hands shaking with excitement, he tried to untie her while lifting his own face to the gray sky, mouth wide open—parched, thickened tongue reaching as a helpless baby bird reaches—for precious drops of water that fell and fell and fell.

The rain peppered down on Natalie's still face. "We can cup our hands together, Natalie, and drink! We can let the rain wash the salt water out of our scraps and then—fill them with rain, Natalie—and we can squeeze them into our mouths!"

Always guarding their precarious balance, he had not dared before to face forward on his knees, but even the danger was forgotten now that the rain was falling and in his frenzy—near madness—Burke rose to his knees above her. "Our Father, who art in heaven," he whispered, "hallowed be thy name." . . . And then he kissed her mouth, parted in unconsciousness. There was no response. "Fall, rain!" He was shouting now. "Fall, rain—more, more! *Help me wake her!*"

Over and over he kissed her eyes, her nose, her cheeks, her lips, her forehead—parched, blistered, caked with salt. He could feel the pain in his own rough, eager lips, but he couldn't stop. The one thought that kissing her in the heavenly rain would bring her back possessed and drove him.

He could barely hear her over the roar of the ocean and the falling rain, but he did hear . . . she spoke . . . she was conscious! She knew he was there. He heard her speak *his name!*

Weeping, he said, "Oh, Father . . . our Father . . . our Father!"

TWELVE

AS ALWAYS, when Miss Eliza asked a favor, Mark was happy. Because of the important planning meeting of the Historical Society, she had said Sunday after church would be fine for their trip in Mark's boat to visit William at Causton's Bluff. The surprise picnic over, the women—Caroline, Miss Eliza and her daughters—along with Jonathan, had gone for a walk. Sitting beside William on the front porch, Mark hoped they wouldn't be gone too long. The bright sunshine under which they'd set sail early that afternoon now hung with low, angry clouds, and the wind had risen enough so that only the silvery underside of the gum and bay leaves showed.

For an hour, Mark had talked to William about Osmund Kott and the weighted cotton bags. He told him that Sheftall Sheftall had advised doing nothing unless it happened again; that W.H. had urged a confrontation with Kott the minute he returned and that he then force him to leave town.

"I need your opinion," Mark said, at the end of the story during which William, as always, had listened in attentive silence. "What do you think I should do?"

"I don't know that I qualify to say. I don't know the law and I don't know Kott the way Sheftall does. What does Caroline think?"

"Oh, I don't dare tell her!"

"Seems to me she's always been most reasonable."

"About everything—but Osmund Kott. Things went along pretty well with him for several years. Not good, exactly, because the atmosphere was strained every minute we spent at Knightsford.

Caroline is still constantly suspicious of him, but Kott has done a remarkable job out there, and our daughter adores him. We go out often."

William grinned. "Natalie has a lot of power over her papa, doesn't she?"

"Too much, I'm sure, but I've seldom been able to resist her. Of course she thinks I resist her all the time. I don't. Neither does her mother, although she manages to hold to a course with her far better than I. If I take Stiles's advice and force Kott to leave Savannah, I can't think what Natalie might do or say. I know it would break her little heart."

William sat up. "Did you hear something down at the end of the porch, Mark?"

"No."

"Listen." They stopped talking, but the only sound was the rattle of a stand of palmetto, a melody line from a thrasher somewhere nearby—and the rising wind in the pines around the house.

"Well," William said, "I guess I was wrong. A squirrel maybe. I'm jumpier than usual these days. I even imagined I heard a loud bolt of thunder the other night. Woke me out of a sound sleep, but when I ran outside, the stars were out. Guess I only imagined I heard something just now."

"You did not imagine it, William," Caroline said from the yard at the end of the porch, her voice cold. "I'm here, and I've heard the whole ugly story about Osmund Kott, Mark. I hate eavesdropping, but I was—planning to slip up and surprise you."

Mark hurried to her. "Darling, I thought you went with the others."

"I did, but when Katie and Sarah and Jonathan began to beg to go farther, I decided to come back." Her face was pale and angry.

Mark hooked his arm through hers to escort her up the front steps. Her body was rigid. "Here, take this chair," he said. "William and I were—"

"I know what you and William were doing—and no, I don't want to sit down. That was cruel of you, to expect poor William to advise you in something so—hopeless!"

"Caroline, no," Mark pleaded. "You and I were so close again. Don't shut me out. I beg you to try to see this from my point of view. I've tried all these years to see it from yours, haven't I?"

She didn't answer.

"I think he has," William said. "I don't mean to butt in, but Mark's tried hard to ease a family situation no man can really solve, Caroline. At least, not as long as his wife isn't—with him in it."

"You *are* butting in, William," she said.

"Darling, don't say anything you'll be sorry for."

Helplessly, she looked from one to the other, then threw her arms around Mark and wept.

Seated beside Eliza Mackay in the bow of the Browning schooner on their way back up the river, Caroline said, "I don't know how even God can forgive me for blowing up at Mark the way I did."

"Nonsense."

"But we went to comfort William today. To make sure he's doing as well as possible without Virginia and the children. I do have Mark and Jonathan in the house with me. Even so, Natalie's never off my mind. How must William feel with his whole family gone? He does seem all right, though, don't you think?"

"Yes," Eliza said hesitantly. "But even his own mother doesn't always know about what's going on inside William. He's so quiet most of the time anyway. Caroline, Mark and the girls and Jonathan are talking back there, so move closer and let me tell you something." When she scooted over, she felt Eliza's arm encircle her. "I've watched you and Mark struggle through your bad times over Osmund for all these years. It's past time that struggle ended."

"Miss Eliza, how? How can it end as long as that man is tormenting us the way he tormented my darling grandfather right to the end of his life? How? Tell me how it's going to stop!"

"You won't like this, Caroline, but you are going to have to forgive Osmund. For blackmailing his own father, your beloved grandfather, all those years—for all the trouble he caused in town when he was younger, for all his time in jail—for *everything*. Now, wait. Forgiving him won't necessarily change him. What he's done to Mark this time is very, very serious. That he's done it after all the years of Mark's trust and kindness makes it even worse. But if you could forgive him, you and Mark would be safe."

Caroline stared at her. "How? I don't understand that."

"If you could bring yourself to the place where, granting he bears watching, you also appreciate the good work Osmund's done for you and leave the rest up to God, you'd place yourself firmly beside your husband so that the poor boy would never have to come to me again with his Kott problems. He could confide in you, his wife, as he has every right to do. He wouldn't have needed even to tell William, although that was natural, since they've always been so close. Of course, it's natural for him to consult W.H., too, but—"

"That's enough. I know what you're saying. And—you're dead right." She sighed. Her shoulders sagged. "The problem is—I've thought a hundred times through the years that I have—already forgiven him. Or, at least, managed to sort of—live around him."

"There's a big difference, isn't there?"

Caroline looked straight at Eliza. "I love you, as much as Mark loves you. But—right now, penning me in a corner like this—I don't think I *like* you very much."

"I don't imagine you do. But we have to face it, Caroline. Osmund is the strangest mixture I've ever known. There's good in him, mixed in with the treachery. He cheats Mark, but I do feel certain that he will do everything humanly possible to take care of Natalie—Virginia and the little ones, too." She paused. "Can't you accept the old man as he is? As he probably will be as long as he lives?"

"I guess I can't. But I hope you're right about his looking after Natalie and William's family."

"There's a blow coming down from the northeast, ladies," Mark called from his place at the helm of the schooner. "But don't worry, we'll make it home before it hits—and the *Pulaski*'s been in dock in Baltimore since Friday, safe and sound."

"Do you really think William's doing all right, Mark?" Eliza Mackay called.

"As well as William could do without Virginia and those babies. I'm proud of him."

"You can check on him again Tuesday, Mama," Sarah said in her reassuring way.

"I can?"

"Mark's sure some word of the *Pulaski* should reach us from Baltimore by then. Don't tell me William won't be coming into town to find out for himself. He'll be looking for a letter from Virginia."

First thing the next morning, in spite of their weakened condition, Burke managed to get Natalie untied, up and over the back of the wooden settee and onto the section of canvas-covered wreckage. Holding firmly to one of her cut, swollen feet to make sure she didn't get washed overboard, he then pulled himself onto their newly arrived raft. Once there, he collapsed on his back beside her to rest, one hand holding her, the other the rungs of the settee.

Sprawled there, staring up into the low, scudding clouds, he wondered irrelevantly if he would ever want to see that settee again once they'd been rescued. *Rescued.* No one's going to rescue a waterlogged settee! Rescue . . . rescue. Now that he'd overcome the struggle to fasten the roomier piece of wreckage to the settee, he marveled that such a frail object had kept them alive for so long.

What day is this? Saturday? No. He tried to count in his mind. He was sure it had rained on Sunday, yesterday. It must be Monday, and if so, he and Natalie had lived together on their cramped, wooden life preserver for three nights and now into the fourth day. . . .

For the first two days, he remembered, they never ceased searching the horizon for some sign of a rescue vessel. Once they were sure they'd seen sails in the distance and had torn away another piece of her nightgown to wave until it felt as though their arms would drop from their sockets. It turned out to be a ship, all right, but no one aboard had spotted them. In their desperation and weakness, they had both wept—without tears. Their bodies were too parched to salivate or to weep tears.

They spoke little today. The small amount of rainwater had surely helped, or he could not have moved them onto the new raft, but as the clouds cleared with the mounting sun, they lay there in silence, suffering their separate pain and dizziness. During Natalie's moments of consciousness, though, she never once failed to smile back at him when he smiled at her. So burned and salt-encrusted were their mouths and cheeks, smiling was not pleasurable, only spontaneous for them both.

Toward noon, she said abruptly, with more vitality than she'd shown all day, "My family—had—better *not* object—when we—get married! If they do, Kottie will—" She broke off, unable even to cry out at the shock of remembering that her beloved Kottie had died trying to save her. By now, moments of realization had begun to come and go. . . .

Burke turned and looked at her with tender understanding. "Kottie—seemed—to like me—all right," he murmured.

"He did! He—liked—everyone I—liked. My—parents had—*better like you!*"

For the first time, Burke considered what it must be like to be the parents of such an independent, willful, altogether enchanting daughter. "I'll—do my best," he said, "to—make them—like me. Maybe—"

"Maybe—what, Burke?"

"Maybe—if I tell—them—old Kottie—liked me, they—"

"That's—the worst thing—you could do!"

Sometime lately, Burke had noticed that her energy seemed to come and go, too. Natalie now seemed, at least, to be momentarily stronger. Needing to talk, needing him to answer.

"They—had no use for Kottie! I pretended not to notice. That way, they were kind of—trapped into letting me see him. I—know my mother—despised poor Kottie. . . ."

"Rest awhile," he said hoarsely, his voice sounding old. "We—both need—to rest."

She lay still for a time, then, pulling herself almost to a sitting position, grabbed his arm. "Burke—will they—find us? Don't just—not answer me. I want to know!"

She had not complained once during their ordeal. Not once. She had a right now to an honest answer. "I—don't know," he said. "I—have no more idea of when—or if we'll be rescued—than you have."

Closing her eyes, she lay helplessly back on the canvas. "Don't shut your eyes, Natalie," he demanded. "We—almost—can't—talk anymore. I've—got to see—your eyes."

Slowly, she turned her head toward him. In her pale, but luminous eyes, he saw pain, ebbing hope, despair.

"Don't give up," he said with as much force as he could muster and looked at her with all the love and gratitude his heart felt when he saw the change come . . . almost imperceptible at first, but from under the puffed, burned eyelids, those eyes, still able to stir him, were trying to smile. She said nothing, but reached toward him. He clasped her blistered little hand, still watching her eyes. *They were smiling.*

With all his might, Burke tried to return the smile. Tried to show her that he, too, had hope to give her. He could not. Her point-blank question as to when they would be rescued had thrust him for the first time all the way into—stark reality. He, who had always prided himself on being a realist, saw that he had not really faced death until that moment. He had done all he could to keep them alive. Now he was failing her when she needed him most. He could not lie to her, but he should have tried, at least, to promise her that their love might keep them alive until help came. She was only sixteen and a girl. It was his place to give her hope. He could not. There was nothing in him that would permit him even to try to fool Natalie.

Fool her? Hadn't he been fooling her all along? God in His heaven, if He still remembered the two of them, knew that Burke *wanted* to marry her. But especially where their future was concerned, he had been fooling her. What did it matter if her parents didn't like him? Even if they were rescued, Burke Latimer now didn't have the price of a single meal! Every dollar he'd worked to save over the past four years had gone to the bottom of the sea when the *Pulaski* blew up. Even if they survived, he would have to begin again.

The sun told him it must now be midafternoon of the fourth day. He grabbed his stomach as if he could stop the hard wave of nausea. *Hunger* . . . Natalie was starving, too.

"Burke?"

Her voice was so weak, he barely heard her call his name.

"Burke, don't—give up. I—haven't."

The last thought before he lost consciousness was the realization that if she hadn't been there in his care, he would gladly have rolled overboard so as to end the ordeal.

Opening his eyes after what he believed to be only a short nap, Burke tried to sit up, then to stand. He could not, so crawled to where Natalie lay, again unconscious, her nearly naked body several feet away from where he'd last seen her—wedged against the back of the settee!

Horrified at the knowledge that only the settee had saved her, on his hands and knees, he stared down at her, trembling so that he nearly collapsed. His mind, which had blacked out sometime in the afternoon, struggled to understand why he seemed now to be intensely aware of color . . . gold, soft pink, shading to pure, nearly blinding light. Not sunset color. Surely, he hadn't slept that long. Staring numbly at the sky, the truth began to filter in—dawn was breaking! He had been unconscious throughout the long, danger-filled night. With enormous difficulty, he lifted Natalie's limp shoulders and held her to him. Blessedly, the sea was calm. Perhaps, in a moment, he'd try to stand.

Holding her, he scanned the horizon, blinked—looked again and then lowered Natalie back onto the white canvas and struggled to lift himself upright. Shading his burned eyes, he peered into the distance, clearer today, with no shred of mist.

And no illusions this time. . . .

He was looking—looking, really *seeing* the white, white, filled sails of a schooner, her black bow splitting the surface, already close enough for him to see men scurrying about her deck!

Was it coming toward them? Coming toward *them?* . . .

Energized by the vision, Burke leaned down and ripped the largest piece yet from Natalie's nightgown and began to wave it high above his head, back and forth, back and forth, until he fell to the deck. Back on his knees, he waved again . . . waved and waved.

When Natalie groaned, he did his best to make her hear: "Look! Natalie—*look!* Open your eyes and look—over there."

She did open her eyes, but they were vacant. Then she turned her gaze in the direction of the ship and said quite matter-of-factly, as though viewing a painting in a gallery, "How extraordinary . . . I —love white sails—in sunlight!" Her eyes closed and she was gone again.

Peering at the schooner, Burke could see now that the men on deck were lifting and carrying people from a lifeboat. They must be rescuing Rebecca Lamar and the others. But had the schooner's crew really seen his signal? Still on his knees, waving frantically, Burke felt his mind might break when Natalie began to mutter, "Oh, my—what shall I do? My mother would—have—a fit to see me back in Savannah—looking like this!"

Alarmed by her delirium, Burke stopped waving and watched her hysteria grow each time she tried and failed to cover herself. "Somebody—help me! Help me," she shrieked. "We're almost in town— and they'll never, never let me in—looking like this! I'm—so ashamed!" The more she tried and failed to pull and fold an imaginary skirt over her bare burned legs, the more uncontrollably she sobbed.

Still clutching his signal flag, Burke knelt again beside her. "Natalie, it's almost—over, my darling," he said. "Please, please—come back—so I can—tell you that—*it's almost over!*"

She was calling Virginia Mackay now, telling her that she could not expect her to go ashore looking like this. Then, a long, high wail: "Virginia! Vir-gin-ia . . . don't be dead! William—will die too, if—you're dead. . . ."

Abruptly, the wailing stopped and Burke tried to help her as she began to struggle to one elbow—her eyes no longer vacant, her voice no longer piercing, but startlingly calm. "I just had a—dreadful dream," she said. "About—Virginia—Mackay."

"I know, my darling, but—listen to me. It's—almost over! Oh, Natalie, I'm so—glad you're awake—because it's almost over, dearest!"

"What?"

"We're going to be—*rescued!* That beautiful ship—I showed you? Remember?"

She shook her head. "No."

"Look! Darling girl, look—over there. I've been—waving—waving this—a piece of your nightgown!"

She glanced down at what was left of her gown. "Who cares—about an old nightgown? Burke, hold me. I don't—care how much it hurts my shoulders—hold me!"

Above the now haunting, ceaseless roar of the ocean, clinging to each other, they heard a strong male voice call out through a trumpet: "Be of good cheer there on that raft! *I will save you.* . . ."

The sound of the first voice in nearly five days, other than their own, rang on and on in their ears as, huddled together, they waited, not speaking, arms and hands locked together.

On board the schooner *Henry Cameron*, Burke and the other survivors had to be restrained to keep them from rushing the ship's water kegs. In spite of his weakened condition, Burke had to be held back and forced to watch helplessly as two sailors carried Natalie and Rebecca Lamar into a cabin and out of his sight. In such a stupor, he had no memory of the actual rescue beyond falling as he tried to climb into a lifeboat. Now he fought against the arms that pinned him, shouting, "No! Don't—take her away! I have to care for her. She—belongs here—with me!"

"I beg you to conserve your own strength, young man," Captain

Davis said in a commanding voice. "And stop worrying about the young lady. She's being cared for. She'll be bathed and put to bed to rest." Burke fell into a stubborn silence and sat gulping the mere half pint of molasses and water Captain Davis allowed each of them. "That's better," Captain Davis said. "I know what you've been through, but you must trust me to see that my crew will show the suffering ladies every care and courtesy."

Burke said nothing. He had no choice. Even if he could have found Natalie, he was too weak to stand. Could do nothing for her.

After a time he heard Captain Davis shout to all the survivors: "The Lord in heaven guided my ship to you, so can't you trust us? Other ships have passed close by, unwilling to veer from their course so as to search for you. The *Henry Cameron* persisted! You are safe now. And we are heading for Wilmington, North Carolina. Can't you trust the Lord God in whose care we all sail toward land?"

Almost at once, a heavy, but sympathetic hand fell on Burke's shoulder. "Rest, son. You can't see the young lady now," the Captain said. "She's resting—and yes, yes, she's being given molasses and water, too. A little at a time."

Natalie's first moments of consciousness came as she was riding along—on land—in a carriage with a lady who kept trying to quiet her. She didn't know how they got there or who the woman was. She remembered only a ship and being carried away from Burke into a room with people and noise and the smell of molasses. From then until now, nothing. And all she could think of now was that she had to find Burke! The woman was trying to convince her, as they jolted along in the carriage, that even if she tried, she simply couldn't walk a step. She didn't believe it, and although the voice was kind enough, Natalie sat up wild with worry.

"My dear, dear girl," the kind voice kept saying, "your feet have been so cut and bruised, they're purple and green—and twice the size they should be!"

"My feet are fine," she cried. "If they weren't, wouldn't I know it? I—have to see *Mr. Burke Latimer.* You're gracious to look after me—but I think I—might *die* if I don't get to see him—*now.*"

"Do lie back, my dear, and rest."

Natalie could see that the carriage had been fitted out with pillows and blankets against the chill night air and that she was wearing a scratchy woolen sailor suit. The woman told her she was in Wilmington, North Carolina, and that Wilmington people were doing all in their power to help the survivors. Natalie had no doubt of that, but no one was doing what mattered most. She had to see Burke and no one would listen.

"I've been brought up to be courteous—at all times," she tried to explain to her companion, whose name was Miss Wheeler, "but this is a matter of life and death! If I'm not allowed to see Mr. Burke Latimer now, I may—never see him again. Miss—Wheeler, where are you taking me?"

"To my home, our family plantation, outside Wilmington. I will show you every kindness. Your young man is being taken to another house. Our people have opened their homes to all the survivors. Please try to rest, my dear. Please try not to make your—condition worse."

"My condition will be fine—if I can—just know where he is!"

"I promise, I do promise to do all I can to find out."

"But—they might just—take me back—to my parents in Savannah. . . ."

"That's right. If you're able to travel, you'll be taken back in just a few days—to be with your dear parents."

Her head tossing restlessly on the stack of pillows, Natalie kept pleading. "But they don't even—know—Burke. My parents don't—know him. And he's my—life now! He has to be taken back to Savannah—with me. On the same boat. Can't you—promise that? You've been so—good to me—can't you promise?"

"I wish I could. I do wish I could, but there's no way for me to promise anything tonight but that at my home you'll be lovingly cared for."

For the first time, Natalie tried to focus her eyes on the quiet-mannered, gentle woman. The cuffs of her once fine cloak were frayed, and she was old. She must have been at least as old as Miss Eliza Mackay—and she was sixty. "Oh, now—I see," Natalie whispered.

"What do you see, my dear?"

"That—you're too old—to understand—about being in love." Fresh tears ran down her cheeks. "I'm—so afraid my parents won't —understand either. They're also pretty old."

"Your parents—and even I—were young once, too."

"Can you get me on a ship to Savannah tomorrow? I'll start Papa searching for Burke—the minute I get home."

"Miss Browning, you can't walk."

"Of course I can walk!"

When the carriage stopped at last under the porte cochere of a large dilapidated, dimly lit house, Natalie threw back the blanket, stood up and promptly crumpled in a heap to the carriage floor.

"Oh, you poor child," Miss Wheeler cried. "Did you hurt yourself? Don't move—just stay there until I send for the servants. They'll carry you inside and I'll tuck you into a nice warm bed and—"

"Miss—Miss—the kindest thing you can do for me is—let me borrow those servants. Let them—go with me—tomorrow to—hunt for Burke! My father—will pay you well for my use of your people. Please?"

"We'll see about all that tomorrow. Right now, I must get you—inside."

"What day is this?"

"It's Tuesday, dear girl. Tuesday, June nineteenth. You were on that cruel, terrifying ocean for five long days and nights." Miss Wheeler cleared her throat. "How you stood it, I'll never know."

THIRTEEN

ON TUESDAY MORNING, June 19, William Mackay was waiting by the entrance to Number One Commerce Row when Mark arrived for work at a little after eight o'clock.

The two men greeted each other warmly.

"I figured you'd be in town today, William, but not this early. Expecting a letter, I'll bet, from your lovely Virginia."

The smile William had tried so hard to keep on his thin, pale face vanished. "Yes. She promised she'd write to me and have a letter ready to post as soon as the *Pulaski* reached Baltimore. I could get it today."

Mark's arm about his shoulders felt reassuring as William walked with his boyhood idol through the double front doors and down the familiar corridor to Mark's private office.

"We can check on ships docking from up that way. If not today," Mark was saying as he unlocked his door, "then surely there'll be mail tomorrow. Sit down, William. It's like old times to have you along at the beginning of a workday. Remember when I still lived with your family and you used to beg to come to work with me?"

"Those were good times," William said, walking to the high window to look toward the now empty slip where the *Pulaski* had lain at anchor seven long days ago.

Mark laughed. "With a wife like Virginia, two fine youngsters and your own plantation, I'd think these are the good days for you, old man. I know they're good for me—in spite of my troubles with Kott, which I suppose will go on until doomsday. Say, is something the

matter?" he asked. "William, did you come early to—talk about something? I'm sorry if I'm slow to catch on. Frankly, I won't think too clearly until I'm sure Natalie's all right. I'm eager for Virginia's letter, too. I don't expect my little scamp to write many."

William turned from the window to face Mark, hands quietly at his sides, a deep frown wrinkling his forehead. "Mark, sometimes I wish I were more like—other people. A lot more like you."

"All right, William. Sit down. I can tell you need to talk. What's wrong?"

"I—I don't know, except it—has to do with Virginia and—the children."

And then he told Mark what he'd wanted to tell him last Sunday, when Mark brought William's mother and sisters out to visit. Mark had had so much to tell him, though, about old Kott's latest deceit—something that was real and proved by the facts—that he barely mentioned his own nightmare or whatever it was that had seemed to shift the very foundation of his life.

"You thought the loud noise that woke you was a thunderbolt, you say?" Mark asked.

William nodded. "Sounded just like one of our coastal whoppers. I ran outside—still half asleep. The stars were out. It wasn't even sprinkling rain that night."

William could have kicked himself for bothering him on top of all the Kott trouble. Mark was also uneasy about Natalie, and here he was adding his own concern, which sounded ridiculous now that he'd spoken of it in detail.

"You haven't had any peace of mind since?" Mark asked.

"No. Not a minute's worth. When I doze off at night, I'm awake in a few minutes, sitting on the side of the bed, wondering."

"When did this thing happen?"

"Last Thursday night, about eleven o'clock, I guess it was. On the *Pulaski*'s one night at sea. Mark, I know how crazy it sounds." William sat straight in his chair. "But that's why I'm here so early. They were due in Baltimore on Friday. I figured that if Virginia wrote to me on board, and posted it when they got there, it might have been put on another boat Saturday morning. I'm being pretty silly, I guess."

"Not a bit silly, William. Perhaps just a bit—previous. I'd think tomorrow might be the day your letter gets here. Most likely on a sailing ship. Sailing ships don't make such good time as the *Pulaski*."

William only nodded, his face a mask of anxiety, but he couldn't help it.

"I imagine Virginia wrote a little off and on through that first night in Charleston and the next day," Mark went on. "I'm sure she'd want to write to you about the famous 'one night at sea.' Their stateroom surely did look spacious and comfortable."

"She'd want to tell me about how the babies did—sleeping at sea, I guess."

"Yes. And they passed Cape Hatteras by day. I'm sure she'd describe that for you, too."

"It's—it's just that I've tried to picture her—or Natalie—sending old Kott off to post Virginia's letter the minute they docked in Baltimore."

Mark laughed a little. "Natalie was ordering Kott around, you can be sure."

"I planned to tell you more about my nightmare on Sunday, but Caroline caught us, didn't she."

"She certainly did," Mark said. "I hate keeping anything from her. She's so intelligent, so understanding about—everything else but Kott. And she loves me. Thank God, she loves me through everything."

"No trouble when you got home from my place Sunday?"

"Not really. Actually, Caroline seemed to be trying very hard not even to bring it up." Mark gave William a knowing look. "Of course, on our way back upriver, she had time to talk to your amazing mother."

"You mean Mama had time to—talk to Caroline."

"That's undoubtedly it. What would any of us do without Miss Eliza?"

William sighed. "I guess we're going to have to do without her someday. I almost can't believe Mama's sixty years old."

"That's because her spirit is still so young," Mark said.

William stood, his hand out. "Thanks for talking to me."

"Feel better?"

He sighed. "I'm—not sure. Yes. Yes, I do. There hasn't been one time since the first day Papa brought you to our house that talking to you—hasn't helped."

"Eat dinner with us, William?"

"Thanks, no. I'm going to Mama's house—if I can bring myself to sleep away from Causton's Bluff for a night or two. Seems as though I can't—promise anything right now. I don't know, I—feel like I'm —lost, Mark. Even at Causton's Bluff, where I've been the happiest man on earth for the three years since Virginia and I got married. Ever since she went away, though, I've been—lost."

Aware, from the habit of many years, that young Bulloch, editor of the *Georgian*, would be at his desk with today's Wednesday, June 20, edition, Sheftall Sheftall walked east on Bay, crossed Bull Street and headed for the *Georgian* offices. Not only would Sheftall be able to collect his Charleston papers for the week, he would pick up today's *Georgian* and discuss its contents with his friend. Bulloch, thought the seventy-six-year-old Revolutionary veteran, seemed to enjoy their discussions as much as Sheftall did. Well, William Bulloch was a learned, thoughtful young gentleman. Thoughtful persons enjoyed Sheftall. He knew it was the commercially minded, shallow thinkers who fidgeted from one foot to another when he stopped them to exchange views, particularly on his own Revolutionary background. Shallow thinkers. Unaware that even the latest news could not throw light on today's events that the perspective of history could give. Bulloch knew that; appreciated it. Sheftall Sheftall, cocked hat, knee breeches, silver shoe buckles shining in the early sun, hurried as best he could toward his daily rendezvous with the editor, who was almost always waiting in the *Georgian* doorway long before Sheftall could spot him with his nearsighted eyes.

Bulloch was not in the doorway today. Once inside, Sheftall learned why. Across the editor's desk were spread three or four editions of Charleston and Wilmington Extras—and young Bulloch, his head buried in his arms, was slouched over the clutter of papers.

"Bulloch?" Sheftall said. "Bulloch! For pity's sake, what's wrong? Aren't you feeling well? Should I fetch a doctor? Lift your head, man, and tell me!"

When he looked up, William Bulloch's ashen face was twisted in agony. He gestured helplessly at the papers on his desk, and in a broken voice said, "Mr. Sheftall, an editor has to write the news— good and bad—an editor *has* to write it. Shape it into words. But—in a tragedy such as this—an editor has to shed his own tears first! Sit down, sir, and read for yourself. I'm—I'm too stunned to—tell you much yet, but the steam packet—*Pulaski*—blew up at sea and dozens, *dozens* of our—best Savannah people are—lost."

Sheftall sank into a chair, stared at the numbing headlines: " 'TERRIBLE DISASTER AT SEA!' " Sheftall read on silently, the words too shocking to speak aloud:

> The splendid steam packet, *Pulaski*, Captain Dubois, exploded on the night of Thursday, 14 June, some 30 miles from the nearest land, about 45 miles south of Cape Lookout, North Carolina. On a voyage from Savannah and Charleston to Baltimore, it is believed that most of those passengers aboard were lost forever.

Sheftall stopped reading, his dimming eyes too filled with tears to continue. For a long moment he simply stared, unbelieving at his stricken, young friend, who was looking back at him as though expecting some small word of comfort.

"Exploded?" Sheftall spoke his question aloud finally. "The boilers of such great strength and such expert design—*exploded*? The boilers that were 'never to be fired to reach a point of pressure higher than nineteen inches, although could carry with the greatest safety thirty inches'? Those boilers *exploded*, Bulloch?"

The editor shook his head. "Too early to know much," he said hoarsely. "There is some indication that perhaps only one boiler blew up."

"Enough, I'd say, to—drown our city in sorrow." Sheftall wiped his eyes, polished his small round spectacles with a clean handkerchief, replaced them and went back to the Wilmington, North Carolina, paper. " 'It is too early to provide a complete passenger list or the numbers of persons dead from Savannah, Charleston, and other points, but plus a crew of 37, it is believed the passenger list ran from 150 to 160 persons.' Dear Lord above," Sheftall gasped. "I've got to go to Mark Browning's office! His only daughter, Miss Natalie, was aboard the *Pulaski!* And—Osmund Kott." He sat up in the chair with a start. "Bulloch! Poor young William Mackay's entire family sailed on the *Pulaski* . . . his bride of only three years and his two little children!"

Bulloch wiped his own eyes. "Mr. Sheftall, some ninety passengers boarded the *Pulaski* here. Not counting the crew. A few meant to disembark in Charleston, I believe—but our loss is—staggering, old friend. How will—the city ever—recover from it? Members of our most prominent families—our most respected families—in the case of the Lamars, I believe the entire family sailed." Again, he looked almost pleadingly at Sheftall. "How—can I—write about it?"

"You'll find a way, Bulloch. An editor must have courage as well as integrity. You have both. Were any saved? Have you received no letters from up that way?"

Almost absently, Bulloch shuffled through a stack of mail just arrived that morning. "I confess I haven't—opened any of this. I—was so shaken by—these pages—" Looking at his friend, he asked, "Mr. Sheftall, sir, would you be so kind as to—examine some of these letters? One or two could have some news. I—I'm too dazed to think!"

Sheftall flipped through four or five pieces of mail, then stopped. "Here! Colonel William Robertson. You have a letter from Robertson written from Stump Sound Coast, North Carolina. He sailed on the *Pulaski*. Here's another from Captain R. W. Pooler. Why, I bid bon voyage to both Pooler and his son!"

"Open those letters, please!"

Hands shaking, Sheftall broke the seals, then glanced hurriedly at each short note. "Obviously both Pooler and Robertson are safe. Pooler's son, too, I see. Thankfully." The old man frowned. "How true his report could be, I don't know, Bulloch, but Robertson claims that 'of about two hundred persons on board, only twenty-one escaped from the wreck, of whom five afterwards perished in the surf on this miserable coast.'" Sheftall groaned. "That indicates only sixteen souls remain with us in this earthly vale. Too terrible to contemplate. But I, for one, mean not to let my despair engulf me until we've had more word—from somewhere. From someone. Robertson wrote on June sixteen. That's four days ago. He was safe when he wrote. Other letters will come. Other newspapers from north of us. There may still be hope, Bulloch." The old man got slowly to his feet. "The Exchange clock is striking eight. I'll be on my way now to—Browning's office. Your sad duty of writing about this tragedy will be no more difficult than mine. I'd rather swallow arsenic than tell Mark Browning that his beautiful young daughter—the light of his very life—could be lost."

"You didn't read all of Colonel Robertson's letter," Bulloch said as Sheftall started for the door. "He says that Mr. J. Hamilton Couper of Hopeton Plantation, near Brunswick, was saved in a lifeboat, too, along with two ladies under his care, Mrs. Fraser and her small son, of St. Simons Island, and Mrs. Nightingale of Cumberland Island. Perhaps you'd better wait for further news before you—"

"No," Sheftall interrupted, already at the door. "Mark is a strong man. Sensitive, but strong. And I don't want him to learn of it from anyone—but me. He knows of my deep regard for him." Wiping his eyes again, he added, "I doubt that anyone can—help him now, but —at least, I mean to try."

With the flicker of hope his reason and faith allowed, Sheftall told Mark what he knew of the wreck of the *Pulaski*. Told him not one untruth, withheld nothing, yet urged him not to give up hope that Natalie might well be among those saved. When Sheftall had first sat down, Mark was comfortably seated behind his wide polished desk in the high-backed chair that so became his dark good looks. At first mention of the tragedy, he only gasped, "Dear God!" As Sheftall went on, there was no more response at all, except for the healthy color draining from his face. He did not weep. He asked no questions. He merely sat—looking so searchingly into Sheftall's eyes that the elderly man felt more helpless than ever in his life. His friend, Mark Browning, was begging for his help. He had no help to give.

When Sheftall reached the end of what few details there were, both men sat for a long time in silence, Mark's eyes still imploring him. Finally, Browning got up slowly, as though his arms and legs were wooden, and moved to the tall window where William had stood looking out, where William had looked every day at the empty slip where the splendid, gleaming, flag-bedecked *Pulaski* had lain at anchor when the throng of merry, excited passengers had boarded one week ago—one short week ago—today.

Still neither man spoke. Sheftall began to pray to his Lord, silently. More earnestly than he'd prayed for a long time, the old man implored Jehovah to comfort the heart of this friend, who so loved an only daughter. He prayed also for Mark's courage to rise now as surely as the sun had risen this morning. He prayed for Mark's wisdom. It would take courage and wisdom beyond human resources to tell his wife, Caroline. He would have to tell Miss Eliza

Mackay, their dearest friend. He would have to tell Natalie's twelve-year-old brother, Jonathan. Undoubtedly, it would be Mark Browning who would have to tell shy, thoughtful William Mackay.

"Mark!" Sheftall heard the authority in his own voice and it surprised him. He hadn't intended to break in on his friend's first silent moments of realization and grief. "Mark," he heard himself repeat firmly. "There is darkness, yes. But this is no time to forget that hope is also in that darkness. We do not know that Natalie has not been rescued. We do not know that Kott is dead. We do not know that Virginia Mackay and her children are dead. We just do not know any of that, Mark!"

Slowly, slowly, Mark turned from the window to face him. "I—I'm trying, sir. I'm—reaching as far as I—can reach for—even a breath of hope."

"And have you been praying to—your Christ?"

Mark nodded.

"Good. The thing to do—the only thing to do right now. I've been praying, too. First, for you. You will carry the—weight of this awesome burden. You. If it helps, I want you to know that I, at least, am aware of that."

"Thank you."

"The town will know by noon, I expect. But it's only eight-thirty now. I'll leave you alone. I'll also pray that you will be able to weep awhile. I've never wept easily. Wish I could. I believe tears do ease a man's heart." He stood to go. "You know where to find me—if you need me. I promise that one thing I will not say is—'Be strong'. At a time like this, only God Almighty has the right to say that and He wouldn't be so stupid. He knows, Mark, that in the face of this—you *have* no strength of your own. The Almighty has enough—for us all, though." At the door, he added, "He even has enough for you to do —what you have to do today. The account of the explosion, as much as Bulloch knows of it, will appear in the *Georgian* tomorrow. But remember that I know you have to—tell them all *today*."

FOURTEEN

UNTIL MARK REACHED Bull Street, he had no idea of the time. No idea how long he had sat alone at his desk after Sheftall Sheftall left. He had not grasped much of the terrible truth that Natalie might be dead, but enough so that he had somehow walked out of his office to go to Caroline—to tell her that, until more word came—they *must* fight despair.

The Exchange clock struck a quarter past nine. The shortest route would have been to walk east on Bay, down Abercorn to Reynolds Square, where Caroline was undoubtedly in the kitchen planning the dinner menu with Maureen. Instead, he had gone west on Bay. Without actually deciding, he was headed straight for the Reverend George White's Academy to find his young son.

"I can't tell her without you, Jonathan," he whispered, as he moved stiffly toward the school. "You're too young for your father to be leaning on you, but I am."

At that moment, Mark saw even more clearly that, indeed, he had been leaning on Jonathan in small ways for a long time. Small ways? Last Sunday at Causton's Bluff when Caroline had overheard him tell William that Osmund Kott had weighted the latest shipment of Knightsford cotton, had cheated them from their own plantation, Mark had insisted, when they reached home that night, that Jonathan stay up. To help ease his mother back to her usual confident resilient self? To prevent her, by the boy's very presence, from discussing Kott at all? Yawning, Jonathan had stayed downstairs with them, and as always, she had responded to the beguiling boy.

Undoubtedly, he, Mark, was doing the same thing now, seeing to it that their son be present when he told Caroline that Natalie had never reached Baltimore. It would surely hearten her, he rationalized, if she could receive the blow with Jonathan there to remind her that should the worst turn out to be true, she—they—still had a fine young son to comfort them.

"It will help *me*," he said aloud, climbing the academy steps. Steps that had never before seemed steep. "I will need my son . . . I need my son now." The words kept sounding in his mind as, after jangling the brass bell that hung above the front door, he waited.

Mark stood alone in the small academy parlor where parents met their children when there had been trouble at home or at school; where stern, brilliant George White spoke with parents of the scholars who had misbehaved. Mark had never waited there for that reason. Jonathan was lively, but he loved peace and laughter too much to cause trouble of a serious nature.

In a few minutes, the boy hurried down the long stair from the classrooms above and, smiling broadly, called, "Hello, Papa! I wasn't expecting you."

"I know," Mark said. "Could we—sit down? I have to talk to you."

Seated beside him, the boy's smile vanished. "Is—it something—pretty bad?"

"I'm afraid it—might be. There's been a—ghastly accident."

"Mama?"

"No, no. Not your mama. Natalie. Son, there's no easy way to tell you. The *Pulaski* blew up at sea. Most of the—people aboard—are thought lost."

"When?" was all the boy managed to ask.

"It had to have happened a week ago tomorrow night. They were to be only one night at sea."

"It—blew up at—*night?*"

"Yes. We don't know details yet. But yes, at night."

"Maybe it isn't true. Maybe it isn't true at all."

"It's true all right. Mr. Sheftall got it straight from the editor at the *Georgian*. The papers from Wilmington and Charleston had already run their stories on it. It's true, son. But, some were—saved. Your sister's a plucky girl. She'd do all in her power to—save herself. To help. Don't you think she would?"

"Yes, sir. Oh yes, sir." His chin began to quiver. "Still, she's—a slender little thing."

"I know, but—Natalie's tough, too. And I know Kott did everything in his power to—save her."

Abruptly, the boy threw both arms around Mark and hugged him so tightly it hurt. Then, sniffling only slightly, he pulled back and gave his father the best smile he could muster. "I know Kottie—did all he could. He'd rather be—dead a hundred times than to have anything happen to Sister."

"Oh, son, thank you for saying that!"

"You don't need to thank me, Papa. It's true."

"I know, but—please, please tell your mother you believe that. She'll need *you* to tell her you're sure he took the best possible care of your sister."

"Poor Mama! What—did she—do when you told her?"

Mark looked down at the worn oriental rug. "I—haven't told her yet."

The boy stood up. "Oh." He squared his shoulders. "You wanted me with you."

"That's right. I—had to have you with me. Reverend White has already excused you from school. We can talk more, think more about how we'll tell your mother while we walk home."

Jonathan held tightly to Mark's hand as they headed toward Reynolds Square.

"The thing we have to keep uppermost in our minds when we tell your mother is that there is—always hope. If we just keep telling her that—over and over—it might help a little."

He glanced down at Jonathan as they walked along. The boy was thinking. Finally, he said, "Papa, I'll keep telling Mama there's hope, but she won't believe it if you and I don't—*feel* hopeful, too."

Irrelevantly, Mark envied Jonathan's young legs as his own barely pulled him up the high front steps of their house.

Caroline cried out when he told her, and tears streamed down her cheeks, but she kept her composure. Her questions, Mark thought, were clear, pertinent: When did it happen? There were two lifeboats of people who made it to shore? There were survivors still able to write letters? She expressed her thankfulness that their friends, Mrs.

Nightingale, and Mrs. Fraser and her child were safe in the capable
hands of James Hamilton Couper.

"And, Mama," Jonathan said, "we've got to remember that—no
matter what you think of Kottie—he would give his life to save my
sister!"

For a long moment, her face telling Mark nothing, Caroline
looked at their son. "Yes," she said softly, in a tone she might have
used for any other Savannah gentleman sent to protect Natalie.
"Yes, I'm sure—he did all he could—for her."

"Thank you, Caroline. Oh, thank you for saying that!" Mark knew
he had spoken too urgently, but he felt real gratitude.

She reached for his hand. "Mark, beloved Mark, I wouldn't taunt
you with—anything like that—now." In his arms, she whispered, "I
love you, dearest. I—am—me, you know. I can't help my feelings
toward that old man, but not now, Mark. We'll just believe that—he
did all he could do."

"Kottie's strong, too, to be seventy-one," Jonathan reassured her.
"He's got a lot of strength and—Sister's not very heavy."

For just a moment, at the mention of even the slimness of Natalie's nearly perfect body, Mark thought his wife might faint. Only for
a moment, though. "What we must all do," she whispered, "is—
remember that we're not going to be alone—in this. So many people
from Savannah were on that boat. Oh, Mark—Mark, poor William!
How could—anyone save two such small children—in a shipwreck?"

The two clung together for a long time. Jonathan waited, saying
nothing.

"How did I ever manage to find such a wife," Mark said at last.

"You didn't," Jonathan said, in his most hopeful voice. "Mama's
told me lots of times. She got you!"

Both parents smiled appreciation of their son. He's trying so
hard, Mark thought, to help us.

"Well," Jonathan went on in the manner of a grown-up, "the truth
is—we all have a lot to hope for. We don't know but that Kottie and
Natalie and William's family are all—safe and sound." Mark saw the
tears in his son's eyes, but the boy kept his voice steady. "There's
just—plenty of reason—to hope."

Caroline took a deep breath. "When will we know, Mark?"

"I suppose we'll find out a little more each day. Except for more
survivors' letters that might come, we won't know anything more

tomorrow, I guess. Sheftall told me everything Bulloch will run in tomorrow's *Georgian.*"

"We'll have to tell—Miss Eliza and William right away," Caroline said. "Mark, we mustn't let William find out from anyone but—us."

"I know. I'm—going over to the Mackay house now. He's there."

"William doesn't have a friend he likes as well as you, Papa."

"I'm on my way, son, just as soon as your mother promises us she'll—lie down awhile."

"Lie down, my foot! I'm going with you."

Caroline did agree to have their carriage sent around, and as the three got out in front of the Mackay place on Broughton Street, William came slowly toward them. Down the front steps, then along the walk he came, directly toward them. When Mark put his arm around the slender shoulders, William said in a toneless voice, "Something bad's happened."

"Yes, William. Something's happened. Caroline and Jonathan will tell Miss Eliza. You and I can go up to your room and talk."

Mark would have wagered anything that William had already guessed. The lean, sensitive face was deathly pale, the kind mouth set in a grim, stoic line.

"All right," William said. "Come on upstairs. I'm in my same old room."

Inside the front door, Mark saw Miss Eliza at the rear of the shadowy entrance hall, silently watching them, her hands clenched together. He longed to do what Caroline was free to do, run to embrace her. Instead, he labored up the familiar stair behind William. The last he saw of Caroline, Jonathan and Miss Eliza, they were filing silently into the old parlor where, in his youth, Mark had spent so many happy hours with all the Mackays. Like a stab, the pain of Robert Mackay's absence overwhelmed him. What he wouldn't give to have the buoyant, sensible, loving man here this minute! How William needed his father now. How he would need him when he learned that his life could be torn apart forever. Hope. *Hope.* He must remember his son's words ". . . the truth is . . . we all have a lot to hope for." William, you too, must hope, he thought, as they reached William's room.

There *is* still reason to—hope.

• • •

Wordlessly, Jonathan followed his mother and Miss Eliza into the parlor, watched his mother perch nervously on the edge of the love seat, while Miss Eliza eased herself down into her own dainty rocker with its fiddleback. She kept her eyes on his mother's face—peering, as though something in Mama's eyes could speak to her better, maybe, than words.

"It's—bad," his mother said. "It—could be the worst—tragedy possible."

Standing beside his mother, the boy looked from one anxious face to the other. "But—there's quite a lot to be hopeful about, Miss Eliza," he said. "Mama will tell you—what happened, but do remember about—hope."

Miss Eliza gave him a tender glance. "Thank you, Jonathan," she said, then turned to his mother. "Caroline?"

"The—*Pulaski*," she said, her voice hesitant, strange. "It—it blew up at sea. No one knows why. Mark—was so sure about those—boilers."

Jonathan felt more and more proud of his mother as, her own heart breaking with sorrow and worry, she controlled herself pretty well while she told Miss Eliza what little they knew about the calamity. She broke down once, but she tried, oh, how she tried, to convince Miss Eliza that her precious grandchildren could have been saved—somehow. "We just don't have any—details," Mama was saying. "And the worst part is that Mark says we may have to wait—days to know all that took place. More news should reach us, though—as the days go by. Those who were—rescued up in North Carolina are being cared for . . . I'm sure—well cared for."

Finally, Miss Eliza spoke, but she said just one word: "Yes."

Again, Jonathan looked from one to the other. If only he could think of something that would help. "Papa's the very best person to be telling—William, Miss Eliza," he said at last. "They're awfully close friends."

Miss Eliza nodded her head and said "Yes" again.

"You know what I've always thought of Osmund Kott," Mama was saying, "but Mark and I feel sure that he did all in his power—for all of them." His mother's voice wavered as she struggled not to weep. "Jonathan's right, of course. We must go right on hoping that they're all safe and sound." She turned and looked at him, then, for the first time, broke into sobs—such hard sobs that Jonathan's whole body felt numb. He could think of nothing to do but hold his mama and pat her shoulder, and just keep on doing it.

"Let her cry," Miss Eliza said in a funny, hollow voice. "Just—let her cry it out for now, Jonathan."

"Yes, ma'am. I—hope Papa can't hear, though. He's pretty—devastated, too, about all this."

Miss Eliza gave him a little smile. "That's a big—word for a twelve-year-old boy to use."

"Devastated? I just learned it. I—wish I hadn't found such a—terrible reason to use it, though."

"I know. I know. And your father will understand if he hears your mama weeping. I'm—so glad they have each other. And, oh, son, I'm so glad they have you."

"We all have each other," he said. "The whole town can be—glad we all have each other, I guess." He took a clean handkerchief from his pocket and wiped his mother's face gently. It was as though they had switched places—he was the parent, she the child in need of him.

Finally, Mama said, "Miss Eliza, Osmund Kott—could be dead, you know."

"Yes."

Jonathan felt his mother shudder. "Dear God, how—would I—deal with *that?*"

In a very quiet voice, Miss Eliza asked, "Had you—decided to forgive him, Caroline? To make things right when he comes back?"

Again the shudder ran through his mother's whole body. "I—don't know. I—can't think about it now."

Just then, they all heard a bumping sound and unsteady, slow footsteps on the stair. They all turned to see William, coming down alone, his valise banging with each step against the wall. Coming down the stair without looking to see where his feet were going. He stumbled, righted himself. Miss Eliza called to him, but he didn't answer. Straight through the front hall and out the door he went—without a word.

"Miss Eliza!" Mama gasped. "Shouldn't we try to stop him?"

"No. I know my William. Right now, he has to get back to Causton's Bluff."

Jonathan's mother ran into the hall to call up the stair to Papa.

"He'll be down soon, Caroline," Miss Eliza said firmly. "Give him time. Mark knows William, too. I'm sure he tried to go with him, but Mark knows exactly how far William—can be pushed. He's letting him do what he has to do."

When Mark turned from the front window upstairs where he'd watched William plod, valise in hand, up Broughton Street and out of sight, he did something that he supposed was selfish, with Caroline and the others waiting for him downstairs. Like William, though, who had to get back to Causton's Bluff to be alone, Mark felt a desperate need to spend a few minutes by himself in his old room at the Mackay house. Slowly, he crossed the hall and opened the door—engulfed in memories.

It wasn't his room any longer. The stamp of Jack Mackay's best friend and classmate, dashing, good-looking young army officer Robert E. Lee, was now in the big airy corner room. Lee, as the Mackays called him, had arrived in Savannah some nine years ago—Brevet Lieutenant R. E. Lee, with orders to report for duty to Major Samuel Babcock on nearby Cockspur Island to work on the initial engineering stages for federal Fort Pulaski.

Mark recoiled at the thought of the name Pulaski, now no longer merely the new United States fortification to be named in honor of the Polish Revolutionary War hero.

Inside the room, shuttered today against the hot June sun outside, Mark stood looking around. One of Lee's dress uniforms still hung on a peg against the far wall. Two of his drawings graced another wall. Lee had brought along a favorite candlestand and some books. These stood on the night table beside the bed where Mark had slept as a young man. In that big, comfortable bed, he had lain awake night after night, longing both for Caroline Cameron—and for Eliza Mackay.

Today, he tried to smile at the memory. Today, he could not smile at anything. In his boyish heart, he had indeed loved Eliza Mackay—even before his friend Robert Mackay's death. He had also adored the overwhelming loveliness of Caroline Cameron's face and form. Then, at last, he had loved all of her. As he did now. At seventeen, when she had known first of her love for Mark, Caroline Cameron had been as fresh and perfect in beauty as was—Natalie.

Natalie. His heart hurt so, he put his hand on it and pressed hard. There was no touching the area where the pain had already become a living, pulsing thing. If only he knew that his adored Natalie—lived!

His mother's portrait—all he'd known of her after his third birthday—once hung over the room's fireplace. The space was empty now. Miss Eliza hadn't been able to afford to repaper, and a dim, large rectangle still showed where Melissa Cotting Browning's portrait once hung.

The portrait was today in his house, in the family drawing room above the fireplace. It was good to have it there, but somehow he looked at it less often now. Caroline and Natalie—his own two treasured ones—filled his eyes and his thoughts. If he was truthful, it had become almost unbearable to think of his mother's face since the day, some twenty years ago, when he had learned that she was Osmund Kott's own sister by Jonathan Cameron and his indentured servant, Mary Cotting. Cotting to Kott.

Kott. What if Osmund Kott had been killed on the *Pulaski?* He was only a little ashamed at the quick thought that, if so, the one barrier between him and Caroline would be gone; that there would then be no need to decide about prosecuting his unpredictable uncle.

He was stalling upstairs, feeling guilty about leaving Miss Eliza and Caroline and Jonathan for so long. Surely, they had seen William go. Surely, he was needed down in the Mackay parlor. But he was reluctant to leave the shelter of the familiar room, even though it now belonged to Lee, back in Virginia this year, he'd heard. As with Mark so long ago, Miss Eliza had freely given the room to Lee to come and go as his military orders allowed. Robert Lee had also come to be like another son. When Jack Mackay worked with the engineers in Alabama a few years back, Lee had spent all the time he could spare from Fort Pulaski at the Mackay house. Eliza Anne Stiles didn't have a closer friend anywhere than Lee, who had married a young woman named Mary Custis. It still bewildered many Savannahians that Robert E. Lee had not married Eliza Anne. To this day, some six years after his marriage to her, William Henry Stiles held his head a bit higher than usual when the name Robert E. Lee was mentioned, because *he* had won the prize. Eliza Anne and W.H. were, Mark was certain, completely happy together. W.H. boasted of his conquest, but Mark had seen no sign of jealousy.

Stalling. His flurry of thoughts offered a brief escape from the tragedy—palpable by now in the old house. He was being unfair to leave such a burden on his young son downstairs. Softly, he closed the door, then opened it for one more glimpse of the room that had been his refuge so long ago when he had felt helpless or anxious. Both emotions gripped him now—not only for poor William, for himself. "Natalie," he breathed . . . "Oh, Natalie—be safe, please, be safe. . . ."

Again he closed the door, and hurried downstairs.

FIFTEEN

THE NEXT DAY, Thursday, June 21, the dreaded first account of
the tragedy appeared in the *Georgian* under the stark headline: AW-
FUL CALAMITY.

Knowing demand for that edition would be great, Mark picked up
several copies on his way to Commerce Row. While he waited for
William to knock on his door, undoubtedly early today, he scanned
the efforts of editor William Bulloch:

> We hasten to lay before our readers all the information received
> in regard to a calamity which has befallen our city, one the
> parallel to which we have never before been called on to an-
> nounce. We have no words to express our feeling. Sympathy for
> the survivors of those who have perished would be poor conso-
> lation in this hour of their bereavement. Our city has sustained
> a loss which years cannot efface.

Mark read on through the heartfelt, rather graceless lines and
found himself pitying young Bulloch in the exceedingly difficult job
of informing the city in the face of his own obvious sorrow. Normally, Bulloch wrote well. This time, his labored efforts were almost
pathetic. But one line kept Mark rereading again and again: "Our
city has sustained a loss which years cannot efface."

The years could never compensate for William's loss if the man's
premonitions that his family was gone turned out to be right. Still,
Jonathan had so fastened on to the resource of hope, he had his
father, Mark, hoping too.

During the long hours through which he lay awake beside Caroline last night, Mark had preached hope to her. Natalie would come back. Somehow, Natalie was too alive, too vibrant, too precious—too headstrong to die.

Now, as he read on, he fought to hold that hope. Plainly, the news story stated that, at eleven o'clock at night, when most passengers were in bed, probably fast asleep, a boiler on the *Pulaski* had blown up. Mark tried to absorb the ugly fact that the *Pulaski*'s boilers, in which all stockholders had placed such confidence, could have failed. And—at eleven at night. His thoughts were running wild as he read. He could see Natalie in her little nightgown, barefoot. Dear God!

The hope he'd tried so hard to nourish was ebbing fast when William's knock came at the door.

Mark got up to embrace his young friend, asking the useless question: "Did you sleep at all?"

"No." Grabbing a copy of the *Georgian*, William sank into the chair on the other side of Mark's desk and, in the terrible silence, began to read. Now and then, to clear his eyes for the fine print, he wiped at tears that hadn't stopped flowing since he sat down.

"Some *have* been saved," Mark said. "You see? Mr. Couper, Mrs. Fraser, Mrs. Nightingale, and Mrs. Fraser's child."

Still intently studying the account, William spoke flatly. "Captain Pooler and his son—Colonel Robertson, too. But nothing about—Virginia or—our babies." He looked at Mark. "There's nothing here—about them—because they're—all gone." William got up. "I'll be back tomorrow morning. Maybe even this afternoon, if the tide suits."

"William, this is only the first story. We all have to keep on hoping that—"

"I have to get home now. I wait better there. I sit in her chair a lot on the porch. I—lay on her side of the bed some last night. Used her pillow."

"You could even get a letter from Virginia when the Charleston boat docks this afternoon. Some *have* been—rescued. Pooler and Robertson were well enough to write letters."

"Men are stronger."

"Wouldn't you like to stay in town for dinner with us—or your mother? That way, you'd be here when the Charleston boat docks."

"No, thanks. I—can't be with anybody but you. Not long with you. Tell Mama I'm sorry. I can't control my own feelings—and hers, too." At the door, William turned back. "Remember what I told you about that big crack of thunder chasing me outside in the night? It says right here the boiler exploded that same night—about eleven o'clock. I heard it. Just—let me go home, Mark. I know—what I know."

Sometime in the late morning on Thursday, restless as a cat, Natalie was limping about her bedroom in the spinster Wheeler's plantation house outside Wilmington, when someone knocked.

"Come in, come in!" she called, both expectant and annoyed. Annoyed, in case it was just Miss Effie Wheeler bothering her with another cup of too-sweet wintergreen tea—which she loathed.

"Good morning again, Miss Browning," Effie Wheeler said. "Oh, my dear girl, are you sure you should be up going about on those poor feet?"

"Yes, ma'am. I'm sure." Natalie limped impatiently toward Effie Wheeler. "Have you found him? Did you send your nephew into town to find out about Mr. Burke Latimer?"

Evidently glad, Natalie thought, to have even a blistered, peeling, limping, shipwrecked guest in the house, Miss Wheeler took her time arranging her skirt and sat down. "Yes, Miss Browning, my nephew Olin went into Wilmington early this morning, as I told you he would."

Wanting to shake her for being so slow to get to the point, Natalie said curtly, "Then tell me! What did he find out? Did he find where Burke Latimer is staying? Is today Thursday?" Miss Wheeler looked so abashed at her rapid-fire questions, Natalie forced a beguiling smile and said, "I'm sorry. I wasn't taught such rudeness, especially when you've been so kind to me. I'm—I'm just nervous, I guess."

Plain Miss Wheeler jumped up and threw her arms around Natalie. "You poor, poor child! Of course you're nervous. I—I wouldn't have upset you any more than you're already upset for anything on earth."

Jerking free, Natalie smiled again. "Please tell me what you learned about him, Miss Wheeler!"

"I—I just don't express myself with your quickness. My father always said, 'Effie, your mind works all right, but your tongue is slower than a clock in need of winding.' Papa was always doing everything yesterday."

Feeling she might fly into bits and pieces if Miss Wheeler said another word about her papa, Natalie interrupted: "Burke Latimer, Miss Wheeler! *Where is he?*"

"My nephew Olin will talk to you if you feel you can let him—"

"*Let him!* Where is he?" Natalie started for the door.

Miss Wheeler grabbed her arm. "Not wearing that old—dressing gown of mine, my dear!"

Natalie was out the door, limping down the wide curving stairway before Miss Wheeler managed to call that she should at least brush her hair. At the foot of the stair, looking up as though he'd expected her all the time, stood a young man of medium build, his straight black hair trained in a big wave above his forehead. He was in elegant, but worn riding clothes and still held a crop in his hands. For a moment, they stared at each other—Natalie only halfway down the stair.

"Miss Browning?"

"Yes! Who else would I be?" Making no effort to hide the painful limp, Natalie braced herself by clutching the heavy banister. "Did you see Burke Latimer?"

For the first time, Olin Wheeler smiled. It struck her as a good smile. White, small, even teeth, eyes that showed both his confidence and the confidence he wanted her to have in him. "I saw Latimer. In fact, we talked for ten minutes or so before he left."

Natalie felt she might faint, but gripped the newel post hard and righted herself. "Burke—left? Where did he go?"

"I'm not sure. In fact, I don't think he told me. But he gave me this letter for you. After a lot of questions about your well-being, he —asked me to tell you that he expected you to go on being brave." Then, from inside his jacket, Olin Wheeler handed her a letter.

Still grasping the newel post, Natalie stared at the letter. Burke's handwriting was like Burke—strong, bold, self-willed. Unexpectedly, tears streamed down her cheeks. They stung her tender, raw face where the skin had peeled away. She didn't care. She didn't care that this accommodating, young man saw either her blisters or her tears. "Thank you, Mr. Wheeler," she said. "I'm—ever so grateful. Perhaps later, I can express my—gratitude." She turned and began to pull herself up the stairs by the banister. Miss Wheeler's slippers were so much too large, even for her swollen feet, one came off.

"Let me help you!" Olin Wheeler bounded up beside her.

"No! I mean—no, thank you. I'll be—fine." Reaching down to pick up the slipper, she barely glimpsed his face. He was horrified at the sight of her cut, bruised, swollen foot. At the top of the stair, courtesy caused her to turn to him again with what she hoped was a passable smile. "I do thank you."

Inside her room, Miss Wheeler blessedly gone, she fell across the bed and broke the seal on Burke's letter:

> Wednesday evening
> 21 June 1838
> Wilmington, North Carolina

Dearest Natalie,

Only day before yesterday, if I am finally straight on the calendar, we were still together and with little expectation of making it to shore alive. We both did. I am not much to pray, especially when I'm in trouble, since to pray only then strikes me as being rude to the Almighty, but in my way, I did pray for us out there. And now, we are safe and by that safety, jerked apart. My whole being, battered and bruised as it is, longs for even the sight of you. I grew accustomed to that face and form—the loveliest face that ever blistered or smiled under the sun; the perfect form. Undoubtedly, you will be furious, but the hours of rest and some good food have brought me to my senses. I know what I must do. I did not tell you, dearest girl, but I am now a poor man. On board the vaunted *Pulaski* I had in my possession nearly ten thousand dollars, hard-earned and saved over a long period of time. While we spent days on our raft, I kept hoping against hope that my trunk might be found. I no longer hope. I do not have enough money to buy even a piece of bread. And so, since there is no way in which a young lady of your standing could live on my present assets, I have found the strength to say good-bye, but only by letter. I could not, were I to see your dear face again. When you read this, I will be gone, so don't try to find me. If you love me enough, you will still want to marry me later, after I have recouped my losses. I will never have a large fortune. You must settle for being the wife of a man of modest means at best. If you do not love me enough to wait for me, then it will be better that you find it out. When the time is right, I will come to Savannah. In the meantime, I neither ask, nor expect you to wait for me. A young girl of sixteen should be having a good time. When I look into my own heart, I know I can never love anyone else as I love you. But I leave you free for now, because of my poverty, to enjoy whatever time may be required for me to prove myself worthy of asking for the hand of the loveliest, liveliest, bravest, dearest girl God ever created. I will not be in touch in any way, Natalie, until I am free to marry you. I know you will kick and scream at this letter, but I am eight years older and must do only what I know to be best for you. *Do not try to find me.*

Yr devoted
BURKE LATIMER

Natalie finished the letter, but she did not kick or scream. Instead, she stood up, let Miss Wheeler's dressing gown slip to the floor, pulled on the muslin nightgown she'd been given to wear, crawled into the high-postered bed and wept herself to sleep.

Miss Wheeler's clock in the hall downstairs was striking four times when she awoke. Natalie lit the candle on the nightstand beside the bed to find a tray of supper—beaten biscuits, a cup of that ghastly wintergreen tea, a bowl of gruel, an apple and a piece of sponge cake—everything cold and unappetizing. Ignoring the tray, she reached for her letter.

"Burke," she whispered. "Oh, Burke—no!"

Of course, she meant to find him. Papa would find him for her. The thought of her handsome, protective father moved her to fresh tears. Her parents must be wild with worry! She'd been too weak, too ill, too lonely for Burke to think much about them until now. But since he had done this pigheaded thing of leaving her stranded in Wilmington alone, she fought back a rush of tears for her parents.

Her muscles were still taut and sore as she dragged herself out of bed and slipped her feet into Miss Wheeler's slippers and the over-sized, musty dressing gown. The room was as chilly as the wind had been out there on the water at night. But Burke had held her out there and Burke was gone. Half-sobbing, she lit all four wicks in a candelabrum from the bedside candle and began to look through Miss Wheeler's guest-room desk for paper. A quill and an inkwell stood on the small curved desk, and in a top drawer she found a single piece of writing paper and sealing wax.

Seated at the desk, she began to write:

Dear Mama and Papa,

I am all right and in the home of Miss Effie Wheeler, a kind, quaint spinster lady on a plantation near Wilmington, North Carolina. I'm sorry not to have written sooner, but I was so tired after the shipwreck. It is the middle of the night and I am freezing cold. This is no way to tell you the terrible news, but I am too weak to write much. My beloved Kottie died trying to save us. I saw Virginia and little Delia slip into the sea to die together. I was swept overboard right after them, holding baby William. He died in my arms. In an empty box in the water, for a long time, I hung on to the little body. When Mr. Burke Latimer swam to rescue me at the risk of his own life, I had to let baby William go. I am in love with Burke Latimer, who cared for me on a settee and a piece of the promenade deck for five days and nights. Now he is gone, without telling me where. *Papa, you must find him for me.* This quill is dull and that is all I have the strength to write—except that as soon as the doctor allows, I want to come home. Please come and get me in one of your ships soon, Papa. Together, we will find Burke.

Abruptly, she was struck with longing for Kottie, seemed able only now to grasp the fact that he was gone, too. Forever. Kottie would have taken her right home, or—better still, north, to find Burke. But Kottie was gone and gentle Virginia and both her babies. They were all being slammed around somewhere in those big, brutal waves.

On the verge of collapsing at the desk, she quickly signed herself: "Yr loving daughter, Natalie," blew out the candelabrum flames and hobbled back to the bed.

In the dim light from the one candle on the nightstand, she glanced at the cold supper tray—felt a wrench of nausea that brought back black, always moving waves and the roar of water. Then, faint from the memory and exhaustion, she slipped out of the consciousness of Miss Wheeler's guest room and settled back on the settee again beside Burke. That's better, she tried to assure herself. Much better being beside you, Burke, even if those poor people out there *are* still praying and crying out for help. . . .

Wakened from a sound sleep by Natalie's screams, Olin Wheeler, hauling on a dressing gown, knocked urgently on his aunt's door. When there was no response, he banged.

"Go to her! Help her, Olin," Effie Wheeler gasped, appearing in nightdress, hair twisted around strips of muslin sticking out from one side of her sleep cap. "Whatever are you doing at my door? Go to her, Olin!"

"That's scarcely proper, Aunt Effie."

Natalie's screams were frantic now. Olin caught his aunt by a sleeve and pulled her down the hall after him.

"Of course," the sleepy woman said, coming somewhat awake. "Of course, I must be with you. It wouldn't be proper. Oh, that poor child! That poor—poor child! She must be having a nightmare."

Olin gave his aunt an irritated look. "Yes," he said, as to a slow child. "I'd say she is."

The screaming stopped when he knocked on Natalie's door. "Miss Browning? Miss Browning—may we come in?" Then, without waiting, he pulled Effie Wheeler inside with him and knelt by the bed. Holding Natalie's hand in both of his, he spoke gently: "My dear Miss Browning, everything's all right now. You're quite safe. You're right here with Aunt Effie and me, dry and safe and sound. We're going to help you through all this."

Natalie, half-sobbing, lay staring at him. "I'm—terribly sorry," she whispered. "You must—have been asleep. I—think I—screamed. Excuse me. You're—both kind."

"It's far more than kindness," he said. "We're here to—reassure you."

Natalie closed her eyes. Olin could see her body begin to grow less tense. As a small child might, she snuggled down in the covers. Even in her exhaustion, her face burned and, he was sure, somewhat swollen, her beauty made him feel almost a reverence. She was without doubt the young woman for whom he'd searched for all his twenty-six years. Well bred, spirited, even after such an ordeal. A highly respected, well-to-do family, at home in the cultivated life he meant to live. "That's better, isn't it?" He still spoke softly, comfortingly. "You're going to be fine, and something tells me you're just about to have a long, restorative sleep. When you wake up tomorrow, I'll—we'll be right here to care for you."

"That's right," Effie Wheeler said with more emotion in her dry voice than Olin had ever heard. "Oh, is this a letter to your parents, my dear girl?"

Natalie nodded yes, her eyes still closed. "I—wrote it in the night —sometime."

Taking the letter from his aunt, Olin said in his soothing way, "I'm glad Aunt Effie noticed it. I promise you, Miss Browning, I'll go first thing in the morning to find the earliest possible ship to Savannah. And—what's more, I intend to go right along with you when it's time for you to leave for home. You will not be alone again."

For an instant, he saw her open her eyes, look straight at him, murmur "Thank you" and appear to go directly to sleep.

Back in his room, Olin Wheeler lay wide awake, smiling into the darkness. Odd, that out of such a tragedy as the wreck of the steam packet *Pulaski*, could—for him—come such joyful anticipation. The joy most certainly included not only the irresistible Natalie Browning, but a trip to Savannah, too. His fortunes were, at long last, changing. He settled himself luxuriously in the warmth of Effie Wheeler's summer quilts. At this point, a man could ask for nothing more.

SIXTEEN

ON FRIDAY, June 22, the latest *Georgian* again spread on his desk, Mark waited for William, his thoughts—chaotic at best—turned back to last evening. He and Caroline had entertained Miss Eliza, her daughters and the Stileses at dinner, and Eliza Anne had urged Mark always to get to his office ahead of William each day—while the nearly unbearable suspense went on unrelieved.

"I know how hard it is on you, Mark," Eliza Anne had said, "but oh, I long to know that you're with William when he finds out—if the news is bad."

"I want to be with him, Eliza Anne. William and I need to be with each other when we find out. But I feel so—weak myself, what in God's name can I say to him if—"

"You'll know, Mark," Miss Eliza had interrupted firmly. "You'll know."

"That's just what I mean," Eliza Anne had pressed her point. "When we were all children and you still lived with us, you always knew how to tell us—the bad news, Mark. Remember when Papa had his first heart attack out at The Grange? I'll never forget the way you were the evening you came in from out there to be sure no one else prepared us—but you. You have to be with William when the news finally comes. I—shudder to think what William might do, if—"

"Hush, Eliza Anne," Miss Eliza had scolded. "Just hush!"

Today, Mark had left the house at a little after eight, without breakfast, because just before dawn, Caroline had fallen into a sound sleep. The thought of food sickened him anyway. Now, at a quarter to ten, he found himself rereading William Bulloch's heart-rending editorial. Somehow knowing that Bulloch—the entire city —shared the agony helped a little, as seeing every ship on the waterfront with flags at half-staff this morning had helped . . . some. Would that sign of city-wide concern comfort William when he maneuvered his boat into Mark's slip a few minutes from now? Would Bulloch's pouring out the sorrow in his own heart in his editorial help William at all?

> The Pulaski, a gallant boat which but a few days since, danced like a thing of life upon the waters of our harbor, and, under the mighty impulse of steam, boomed away from our port on her northward voyage, freighted with a living host variously intent on business, health or pleasure, and numerously composed of delicate females and tender infants, within a few hours after she joyously weighed anchor and proceeded on her trip—in a moment, in the twinkling of an eye, amid the quiet of night, when calm was on the deep and the head was pillowed in repose—was literally torn in pieces by the explosive power of that mysterious agent which propelled her on her course, and she sank beneath the ocean with her precious burthen. . . .

Bulloch had no family aboard, but like almost every person in the city, he had lost dear friends. The young editor, unmindful of the long, awkward length of his sentence—Mark found himself noticing inconsequential things such as this—had indeed poured out his own sorrow and shock.

Another short news notice declared that, according to present knowledge, "only 17 lives are believed saved of a crew of 37 and a passenger list of some 150–160."

Natalie . . . Dear God, let Natalie be one of the seventeen!

William's knock brought him to his feet. Neither friend could be false enough to say good morning. William merely nodded as he picked up the *Georgian* and began to read, his face a mask of torment.

Finally, William said, "Even if I've—lost my family—the Parkmans' loss is greater. Did you see that?"

For some reason, Mark hadn't.

"They lost four family members." In a voice that seemed unable to understand its own utterance, William added, "The Lamar family lost—*ten.*" Mark watched William slowly, carefully refold the paper, place it under his arm and start for the door. "Have you seen Mama, Mark? Is she holding up?"

"Yes. They were all at our house last night. Miss Eliza turned it into a prayer meeting."

William nodded. "That's good. But I guess it's late for that." At the door he said, "See you tomorrow. There's nothing in the paper to say any of our—loved ones—are dead or alive."

Along with his agony over Natalie, when William came the next day, Saturday, Mark was struggling with guilt as a principal stockholder in the Charleston-Savannah Steamship Company, owners of the *Pulaski.* Aloud, he read this to William:

"We are sorry on such a mournful occasion to raise the voice of censure and reproach, but we have reason to fear that a deep and criminal responsibility rests somewhere, in respect of this awful sacrifice of human life. There is a need for legislation to prevent ships from going above a certain number of knots per hour or of raising steam above a given pressure."

"I can't think about that," William said flatly. "I can't deal with—even *thinking* about somebody being to blame for this. Just don't bring it up, please."

There would be no paper on Sunday, June 24, the tenth day after the wreck, but Mark was waiting in his office, in case William made the trip in from Causton's Bluff. Promptly at ten, he knocked on the door.

"Nothing new to report," Mark said, "except that Bulloch told me late yesterday when I checked by his office that Monday's paper would carry a story concerning how much harder Savannah had been hit by this than Charleston. He also told me that last Tuesday, the steamboat *Washington* burned and sank off the coast of Maryland."

William sat for a long time, shaking his head. "It looks as though businessmen are bent on—destroying us all," he said finally. "Folks are crazy for speed. They can't just be still for long, it seems. Those of us who don't care about it are caught in the middle." Abruptly, William got up to leave. "You're a mighty powerful businessman,

Mark, but I can't believe you're like the others. I don't—dare believe it."

"I can't bear my own thoughts on that, either," Mark said. "If it was other than human error—I'll never put another dollar in anything but land."

"Land's—just right," William said.

"You don't think it might help to go to church with us today?"

"Not today. Maybe never. Right now, I'm closer to God—on my land."

"Mama, I'm almost ashamed to come to you with an—unrelated problem when everyone in town is—so heartbroken. When poor Mark and William still don't know—anything. But I need to talk to you. I need you to talk to me."

Eliza Anne, relieved to find her mother alone, her sisters making their Sunday visit to the Minises down the block—had come so close to an argument with W.H. after church, that she had no choice but to tell him she simply had to discuss it with her mother.

After changing from church dresses to cooler dimities, the two sat together on the side porch.

"Life goes on—for the living, Eliza Anne, no matter what. Was W.H. irked that you came to talk to me about—whatever you have on your mind?"

"Maybe, a little, Mama. Mostly, he was irked with me for being what he calls—afraid to leave you. I'm not afraid. I'm just—not sure."

"Still after you to leave Savannah?"

"I can't honestly say he's 'after me.' He's just a highly ambitious man, is my gorgeous beloved."

Her mother smiled. "I know. And he honestly loves that Georgia upcountry."

"Has he talked to you about it?" Eliza Anne knew her surprise showed and hated it. "He didn't tell me he had."

"Just a day or so after we heard about the—tragedy, W.H. came to see me."

"Sometimes I could shake him! How can such a sensitive man be so—insensitive?"

"He wasn't insensitive. Tragedies don't really stop the calendar, and if you do agree to move up there with him, he needs to know

now. He has his heart set on that acreage on the Etowah River." Her mother sighed, but, Eliza Anne thought, not unhappily. "For a young man born and bred here in Savannah, that's out of the ordinary. His roots are here. His reputation as an attorney . . ." She smiled. "But we all know William Henry Stiles is no ordinary young man. After such a happy friendship with Robert Lee, I doubt you'd have married W.H. if he'd been run of the mill. I take it he's pressing you hard again to make up your mind."

"You always know everything, don't you?"

"No, but after all the arguments you've given me since you were a child, I'm relieved to hear that you think I do."

"He's been excited about the Cherokee country ever since he made that trip up there to take those legal depositions last year. And he's so persuasive. Who else could have persuaded a busy man like Godfrey Barnsley to drop everything and go all the way up there with him? W.H. vows that Mr. Barnsley is as enthusiastic about the Indians' land now as he is."

"Do you think Godfrey Barnsley is going to leave Savannah?"

"He won't have a stubborn wife to stop him. That dear, submissive little Julia would move to the South Seas, if her Godfrey hinted that he wanted to go there. Mama, that's frontier country in north Georgia! I hate it when W.H. is out of my sight, but—our roots are here in the low country. How can I know it's the right thing to move up there?"

"You can't until you see it. I suppose W.H. knows more about the Indian situation than almost anyone in town. He's done so much legal work connected with the monies our government means to pay them for their land, but does he know for a fact that the poor Cherokees are really leaving?"

"It was in yesterday's *Georgian*. They're beginning to leave right now, I think." Eliza Anne sighed. "I doubt that many saw the article. No one's reading or thinking of anything but—the *Pulaski*. Oh Mama, am I terribly selfish to be bringing all this up now?"

"Not selfish at all. Any other subject is—almost a relief. In some ways, I wonder if you and W.H. shouldn't just keep to your plans to make that visit to his Etowah River land soon? Your sisters and I will be here for William and Mark, if they—hear the worst."

"Don't even mention that. I will not leave Savannah until we know —everything." She sighed again.

"For you, you're sighing a lot today."

"There's a lot to sigh about. I thought being United States district attorney and having big, profitable clients like Mark would be enough for W.H.—until our children are a little older, anyway. I want them to grow up near my family."

"You don't think the gold they've found in the Cherokee Nation has anything to do with his interest, do you?"

"No. Gold's too easy. My beloved has to be challenged. He's even talking about raising silkworms! Mama—what kind of life would my little Mary Cowper have in that wild, uncivilized place? I suppose the boys, once they're old enough, would thrive on it, but—"

"They'd all be far healthier than living here, I'd think."

"Maybe. But you know W.H.'s big challenge is politics. He even relishes being a member of the city council. But from what I hear, no one can understand Georgia politics right now. He feels that's just his cup of tea. He longs to step to the forefront and clarify matters. He insists he has a better chance of being elected to Congress up there, where so few men are educated, and candidates are so few." She stopped long enough for another sigh. "I suppose he's right too. He's very smart about almost everything."

"William Henry isn't objecting to postponing your trip up there until after we know about—our loved ones, is he?"

"Oh no! Whatever trouble I have now and then bending my own will to fit his, he's the most considerate of men. Postponing the trip was his idea. I—still feel selfish bringing up such mundane problems now. Oh Mama, what will my poor brother William, do if—"

"I don't know. He'll make it somehow. One does."

"I think I might go utterly to pieces if I lost W.H. or one of the children."

"I thought that when I lost your little brother Robert, before you were born. When your father died, I—longed to follow him. I didn't, though. And I'm here today, still plodding along."

"You never plod! But what will Mark and Caroline do if—Natalie is not one of the survivors?"

"What will we all do? I catch a few winks at night only by—praying God to take my sorrow, my fear—for an hour or so."

"We—can't let our hope turn to either sorrow or fear. You said that yourself when we first learned about the wreck."

"Thank you for reminding me." Then, "Eliza Anne?"

"What, Mama?"

"Why did you really come today? You've agreed to make that long carriage trip to see W.H.'s beautiful Etowah River country. Did you come hoping I'd say, humor him, go, but stick in your heels and never move there?"

Eliza Anne smiled a little. "I don't think I know what I wanted you to say. At thirty, I'm still a dreadful homebody. But I know that I love William Henry Stiles enough to go with him to the ends of the earth, if that's the only way I can keep him in sight."

Mark crossed Bay Street toward his office before eight on Tuesday morning. The *Georgian* was still not off the press, but editor Bulloch assured him there was little if any news. As always, he scanned the ships in the harbor. He knew most schedules by heart, and there was a good chance the *Star* from Charleston could reach Savannah on the high tide before William came at ten.

And then he saw her. Hurrying past his own entrance, he ran down the steep stairs to River Street and out onto the wharf where the *Star* was already being unloaded.

His loyal clerk, Johnston, who had met every ship that might bring some word of Natalie, was shouting Mark's name, running toward him as fast as his thick legs would carry him.

"Mr. Browning! Oh, Mr. Browning, sir," he puffed. "It's here! You have a letter from your daughter!"

Mark could only stare at him.

"See? Her name's on it. It's sent from Wilmington, North Carolina! Oh, Mr. Browning, sir—I'm so happy for you. That must mean —Miss Natalie was—saved!"

Almost fearfully, Mark grabbed the letter, ripped the seal open— tore the paper a bit in the unfolding, his eyes searching first for her signature. There, in a somewhat shaky hand, but unmistakably hers, he read: "Yr loving daughter, Natalie."

In full view of those on the busy wharf, he wept.

"Mr. Browning, shouldn't you sit down a minute on this barrel? Will you be—all right, sir?"

"Yes," he said, wiping his eyes with a handkerchief. "Yes, Johnston. I'm—all right." Then, abruptly, he shook his clerk's hand, turned and ran up the steps across Bay and cut through every back alley and yard possible to reach Caroline.

Inside their house, he shouted his wife's name at the top of his lungs. When she hurried down from upstairs, he was waiting in the entrance hall—his face glowing and wet with tears, his hand trembling as he handed her the precious, still unread, letter. "She's—safe, Caroline," he breathed. "Natalie—has written us a letter herself!"

"Mark! Oh, Mark—be sure!"

"Look! There. 'Yr devoted daughter, Natalie.' "

He thought for a moment that Caroline might faint. Then, as he'd seen her do so many times, she lifted her chin and asked brokenly, since she'd begun to cry, too, "What—does—she say, Mark? Where is she?"

"Somewhere in North Carolina—Wilmington, I think." He held out his arms, and as they clung together, he said over and over, "I—don't know what she says, my darling. I—just looked at her signature to be sure—and ran to you. Our girl is safe! I don't know what's in the letter—but, Caroline, dearest, our little girl is alive!"

"Jonathan! We must tell Jonathan. . . ."

Mark grabbed his head with both hands. "Dear God, yes. I ran to the boy for support when I first heard about the wreck. I couldn't even face telling you without Jonathan." He tried to smile. "This time, I forgot him. Your husband isn't a very strong man, is he?"

"How could anyone think straight at a time like this? I must hurry and tell Maureen and Gerta—you tell Jupiter and get the carriage. Better still, let's walk. First, the school to tell our son. Then, Miss Eliza and—oh, Mark—poor William. William still hasn't heard a word!"

Jerking his watch from his waistcoat pocket, Mark exclaimed, "I forgot William, too! He'll be at my office in no time. It is after nine. I didn't hear the Exchange clock, did you?"

"No. Oh my goodness—we'd better read her letter! Mark, we're not very sane. Surely there's news for William, too."

Hurriedly, they read Natalie's letter, black sorrow washing over their joy. No one in the little party had survived but Natalie. Not Kott, not Virginia, not little Delia, not the baby, William, Jr.

"Mark," Caroline gasped. "William has—lost his whole family!" Then she took Mark in her arms and soothed him as though he were a child. "You poor, poor boy. How can you—tell William a thing like this? Oh, my darling! I know he suspects the worst, but—Mark, this will be the hardest thing you've ever had to do."

He pulled gently away from her. "I—love you more than ever—for knowing that. Go tell our son now—and Miss Eliza. And—ask her to pray for William and me—both."

"I'll pray for you, too—all the way to the school and all the way to the Mackay house." For a long moment, they clung to each other again. Suddenly, Caroline asked, "Would you, *please,* let me take your place with William? Give me the key to your office. Mark, let me —do it for you, please!"

His hands on her shoulders, he looked at her. "You would, wouldn't you?" Before she could answer, Osmund Kott flashed as vivid as lightning before him. "Caroline! Do you realize? Kott is—dead, too!"

Not trusting her voice, he supposed, she shook her head yes and fresh tears sprang to her eyes.

"I'll go now—to William," he said softly. "And I'll find the courage to tell him. Nothing—can ever come between you and me again. Caroline, that gives me—courage."

William sat motionless in the chair on the other side of Mark's big desk, his eyes dry, his slender hands folded in his lap.

In a voice that sounded as though it came from a long way off, Mark read aloud the portion of Natalie's letter about Virginia and Kott and the babies. Then, for what to Mark seemed an eternity, there was no sound in the room except the shouts and whistles and wagon rattles—familiar wharf clatter—through the open windows. Mark waited.

"I'm—ever so glad for you," William said at last, his words straightforward, but spoken in a faint, old man's voice.

Mark's response sounded helpless, nearly foolish. "I'd—give—everything I own if you'd—tell me—how I can help you."

William got up. "Even you—can't do a thing."

"I'm on my way to your mother's house, William. You've got to come with me."

At the door, William said, "You've always let me be, Mark. Don't spoil that now—of all times."

Mark was on his feet too. "But, man, I won't let you—go back to Causton's Bluff—all by yourself."

"You can't stop me."

"You—*knew*—didn't you?"

William nodded. "And now, I'm free to—act on what I knew."

"What do you mean by that?"

"I'm not sure—yet. That's what I have to find out." In a gesture so unlike William, the stooped, grieving young man shook his finger at Mark, and in an angry voice said, "*You stay away from my place.* And don't you dare let Mama—or anyone else—come out there!"

By the time Mark reached the Mackay house, Caroline and Jonathan had told Miss Eliza and her daughters that Natalie was safe—and that her daughter-in-law and both her grandchildren were lost. Without a word, she had turned and fled the familiar old parlor. Kate and Sarah followed.

"Miss Eliza's still upstairs in her room, I'm sure," Jonathan informed his father the minute Mark walked in. "Mama thinks we should give her all the time she needs to be alone."

Mark laid a hand on his son's head. "You have a wise mother. That must be why you're so—wise, Jonathan." And then he did his best to recount the strange, frightening moments with William.

"Mark, whatever could he mean by being free to—act on what he already knew? That really scares me!"

"I wonder if we should even tell Miss Eliza that. William is so—desperate, I—I honestly don't know how much we should tell his mother."

"I can put your mind at rest, Mark," Eliza Mackay said from the doorway, her eyes red from weeping, but her voice strong. "You are to tell me everything. If you're all thinking that my William might—be considering—suicide, you're wrong. Even if he considers it, he won't do it. He's—he's just different from the rest of us."

"But can you—really leave him alone out there now?" Caroline asked.

"With God's help, yes. My heart wants to rush out as fast as Mark can take me. I'm not going. William knows himself far better than his mother has ever known him. Except—his heart. I think I do know William's heart. He has always been far more deeply hurt by—everything than most people."

"You know I'll take you out, Miss Eliza."

"I said I'm not going, Mark." She sat on the edge of her favorite rocker. "Now, when are you going for Natalie? I read her little letter."

"Today, this afternoon, if one of my schooners can be readied in time for the tide."

"Jonathan and I are going with you," Caroline said.

"This time I have to say no," Mark answered quickly. "It's quite possible that Natalie will be brought here on another ship headed this way before I could even reach Wilmington. You and Jonathan must be here to meet her, just in case."

"But, Mark, if she doesn't come we'll have to wait so long without knowing."

"We do know, Caroline. We know she's safe and being well cared for."

"I'll calm Mama down while you're gone, Papa," Jonathan said in his most grown-up manner. "Miss Eliza and I can handle her, can't we, Miss Eliza?"

The boy's tenderness and sensitivity, his almost unnatural maturity seemed to crack Eliza Mackay's control. Not since he and Caroline had heard her cry in the night right after her husband's death, had Mark heard such weeping. Only Jonathan seemed to know what to do. His parents watched, as the boy stood quietly beside Miss Eliza, slowly patting her shoulder until the sobbing stopped.

Helpless to do more than give her his handkerchief, Mark thought Eliza Mackay had never been so beautiful as when she looked up at his son and said, "Jonathan, you're like one of my own grandchildren. Would you please go find William's sisters and—comfort them as you've comforted me? They're—"

"Devastated," Jonathan finished for her.

"That's the word. They're both devastated."

When Jonathan had gone, Eliza said, "Your son is going to help us all—for as long as we live."

"Oh, Miss Eliza," Caroline said, "do you think it would help—William, if we took Jonathan out to Causton's Bluff today?"

"Yes," Mark agreed. "William didn't say anything about not sending Jonathan." Then, "Yes, he did. I can hear his last words to me: 'Don't you dare let Mama—or anyone else—come out there.' "

"We'll honor William's wishes," Eliza said. "That's the least we can do for him. Now, I'm all right. You two go home. Mark, you'll need to see to readying that ship so you can go get Natalie—and bring her back to us."

SEVENTEEN

WHEN MARK HURRIED to the Browning wharf after walking Caroline and Jonathan home, he found still another letter addressed to him from Wilmington, North Carolina. This one, written and posted the next day after Natalie's, was from a Mr. Olin Wheeler. It read in part:

> After a good talk with your charming daughter this morning, I learned that in the letter I sent for her yesterday, she had requested that you come for her in one of your own ships. For that reason, I hasten to inform you that will not be necessary. Dr. Silver has said that Miss Natalie is well enough to travel, and since she has brought so much joy to my aunt and me during her recuperation here at the family plantation, it will be my pleasure—indeed, my delight—to escort her personally to Savannah by the schooner *Supreme*, Captain Coffey, which should dock in your city on Thursday, 28 June. Rest assured that Miss Natalie is recovering from her dreadful ordeal at sea and, except for somewhat injured feet and the misery of her burns, you will find her still spirited. It has been a long time since any mission has given me as much pleasure as the glad prospect of reuniting this amazing young lady with her loving parents.

Mark read the letter at the wharf where he received it, canceled plans for making the trip himself and, once more, ran all the way to Reynolds Square to tell Caroline the good news.

Day after tomorrow, their adored Natalie would be home!

At the wide, welcoming front door of his house, Mark's mind raced downriver to Causton's Bluff and William's agony. On the hurried trip home just now, he'd tried to find words to thank God that Natalie was safe. Turning the polished brass knob, his heart cried: But why? Why, God, didn't you protect William's family, too?

If attentive Olin Wheeler expected her to be an entertaining travel companion on the creaky old *Supreme,* he'd been dead wrong, Natalie thought, propped among pillows on a deck settee. "Supreme, my foot," she said aloud to herself, frowning down at her own swollen feet. The cuts and scratches were healing, but they still looked ugly, and her right foot, in particular, was a bilious green color. She had long ago adopted her mother's favorite expletive, "Oh, foot!" and although she would never again take a foot for granted, she still liked saying it.

She had to admit that Olin Wheeler was a perfect gentleman. She merely hinted that she'd prefer to rest alone and he fled somewhere on the ship, eager to please her. That much was fine. In fact, she'd sent him away often, just to test his acquiescence. Still, it didn't seem quite as much fun, being pampered, as it once did. Being obeyed was still good, but loving Burke had taught her a lot, although she still thought he made far too much of the differences between her life as Mark Browning's daughter in Savannah and what he reveled in calling his kind of "simple frontier life." The wide gap he pictured didn't really exist. Love was love. Fate was fate. Burke Latimer wasn't going to get away because of some dumb idea he had about her. Of course, she loved gorgeous gowns and balls and parties. Of course, she liked being adored by eligible young men. Of course, her parents did all they could to make her happy. Why not? There's obviously something about me that makes other people—all kinds of people—want to please me, she thought. What's wrong with that? It makes them happy. She could also see nothing impossible or even improbable about her ability to leap right into whatever rough, wild things Burke imagined his frontier life would hold for them.

What right did he have to criticize the way she lived in Savannah with Mama and Papa? She certainly had every right, now, to criticize him! Just because his stupid money was lost on the *Pulaski* was certainly no reason to desert her. Her father had plenty of money for everyone.

"He did desert me." She spoke aloud again. And totally unintentionally, she began to cry. "He—deserted me and—I love him! I love him—*so much.*"

From out of nowhere, Olin Wheeler came, knelt beside her. To comfort her, he took one of her hands in both of his. "Could I bring you some tea?" he asked.

Olin knew she loved Burke Latimer. She had made that plain. Olin had even talked to him before bringing her Burke's foolish letter in which he wrote: "If you do not love me enough to wait for me, then it will be better for you to find out." She knew every word in that letter by heart. Find out, my foot!

She tried to smile at Olin, but didn't really succeed. Neither did she answer his dumb question about tea. Instead, she let her eyes wander out over the same plunging, heaving water on which she'd lived with Burke. How little Burke knows me the way I am now, she thought. I almost died, too, on that raft. The swelling sea seemed suddenly to surround her again and a familiar wave of nausea swept through her. Her other hand—the one not being held by Olin—rested on a wooden arm of the rickety settee. She was safe now. Going back to Mama and Papa, where she'd never be hungry or thirsty again. This minute, though, if it meant having Burke beside her, she'd gladly be transported to that other blessed, water-logged settee.

"This time tomorrow," Olin was saying, "you'll be at home, Miss Natalie. Back in your father's house on Reynolds Square. The nightmare will be behind you. What an ugly nightmare it must have been!"

He seemed to expect her to respond to that. "Ugly—and beautiful," she said.

"Your love for Mr. Latimer came out of it, you mean."

"And I want you and everyone to understand that I will always love him."

"Oh, I do understand that. I do."

She sighed. "Good. Then we can be friends."

"I'm honored that you want to be friends with me," he said.

"You are? That's nice. You and your aunt have been more than kind to me."

"Aunt Effie, whatever she is not, is the soul of kindness."

"Don't you get bored living there in that big old house with—only one old lady?"

He smiled. His fine, pearly teeth were so attractive, Natalie never failed to enjoy his smile. Not strong and white like Burke's teeth, smaller, one a little lapped on another, but attractive.

In a moment, he said, "Yes, I get bored. More to the point, I get—lonely. Your time spent with us was heaven-sent. We'll never forget you."

"Will you be going right back to Wilmington?"

"I'm not sure. All my life, since I've been old enough to know what I like, I've longed to visit Savannah."

Natalie thought a minute before saying more. She was sure her parents would invite him—even urge him—to stay on in their home for as long as he cared to. After all, he had paid for her passage from his own funds and was personally escorting her in as much comfort and safety as this old tub allowed. It would have been a far more comfortable voyage had Papa come in one of his schooners, but she did want to get home at the earliest moment, and Olin was doing his level best for her in all ways. "I think you'll like Savannah," she said more cautiously than she'd intended. "Are you interested in planting?"

"No, I'm not," he said firmly. "I'd like to make a place for myself in the mercantile world."

"Oh, then my father's the best possible connection you could find. He'll be so grateful to you for bringing me home, I know he'll help you. In fact, I'll see to it."

"Is the social life in Savannah as fascinating as it's reputed to be?"

She laughed a little. "It seldom stops or even slows down, if that's what you mean." Her face grew serious. "That's the part of Savannah Mr. Latimer—despises."

Olin waited, then asked, "Do you find that strange—that he does?"

"Strange, yes. But not insurmountable."

"I see."

She wondered what he really did see. "I'm sure Savannah's—changed now, though." She shuddered. Her mind had leaped back to the piteous screams and cries for help from the black water on that first terror-filled night, then leaped ahead to the dread moment when she would have to tell poor William about how his little family died.

"You mean the terrible grief in the city," he said.

Natalie nodded. "It must be—all different now," she repeated, as though realizing for the first time that it would be. "Olin?"

He beamed. "Thank you for calling me Olin. You haven't done that before."

She brushed that aside. "Does it seem to you as though I'm only partly here? I mean, my thoughts get so jumbled up. Sometimes I think clearly and feel in control again—then, I don't seem to know myself at all."

"The ordeal has left you in a state of shock, I'm sure. May I call you Natalie?"

"If you like," she said in a vague way. Then a deep sigh, a groan, really, brought her back. "I will have to tell poor William Mackay about how his wife and two children—died. If Kottie were here, he'd do it for me. Olin, you've no idea how I dread telling William! I'd give almost anything if I never had to mention or hear about the wreck—ever again. I'll hate having to answer all his questions. I'll— hate telling poor William. I want to forget all of it except Burke Latimer and that he loves me. He put it in writing in that letter." Suddenly, she could feel tears, the now too-familiar tightening in her throat. She was about to cry again and she hated crying.

"Shall I leave you alone for a while?" Olin asked.

"No, stay. I—won't—act like—a baby—if I'm not alone."

Still holding her hand, he tightened his fingers ever so slightly, ever so understandingly and whispered, "You're weak yet, Natalie. You've been through so much. Don't be ashamed of being human."

After a time, she disengaged her hand to dry her eyes. Then, deliberately, she gave him her melting smile. "Thank you for not— pitying me. You just state things as they are. You haven't said 'Poor Natalie' once. If Mama dares to say 'Oh, my poor baby'—or Papa either—I'll fight them! That kind of sympathy—embarrasses me." She sat up straight. "Burke didn't—really sympathize with me once —not once all the five days and nights we were on that raft. Olin?"

"Tell me what I can do for you."

"You can forewarn my parents not to gush over me and say, 'Poor baby!' I'm no longer—their little girl. Everything in me is changed. I am not the same Natalie who boarded the *Pulaski*." Her eyes swam again with tears. "What you call—my ordeal—was hideous. I'm pretty sure that I grew up in those five days and nights when—Burke and I knew that any minute we might die."

"I'll forewarn them and—would it help if I went with you to tell Mr. Mackay about his family?"

"No. My father will go. He'll know how to be—with William. They've always been very close. William was only a small boy when Papa lived at the Mackay house his first years in Savannah. I don't know that anyone will really know what to say to poor William, but Papa will try."

"You think a lot of your father, don't you?"

"Oh yes! Now that Kottie's gone, Papa's my favorite person."

"Your mother?"

"She's beautiful and intelligent—and can be lots of fun. They're quite the handsomest couple in town. I'm sure she doesn't know it, but I never felt quite as comfortable with her as with Papa, though."

"And why was that?"

"She couldn't abide my dear old Kottie. That may change now, but I won't ever forget that she—despised him." After a moment, she added, "In every other way, Mama is dear. I may never know now why she didn't like Kottie. But that's Mama's problem, not mine."

The tearful, joy-filled reunion with Natalie took place at Mark's wharf late Thursday afternoon. If they'd spoiled their daughter before the ghastly wreck, they treated her like a princess now. The young man, Olin Wheeler, so kind to Natalie, rather interested Mark. Within minutes, Wheeler had called him aside to say, with understanding and sensitivity, that Natalie dreaded the thought of their pity. "Above all," he'd said with his easy smile, "she doesn't want her parents saying 'Poor baby.' " Mark was grateful and gave Caroline the message at the first opportunity.

For two days, Jonathan, Mark, Caroline and the house servants simply tried to let the thin, exhausted girl know how happy they were to have her home. Caroline ordered all her favorite dishes, Jonathan read to her and, taking Olin's suggestion, no one mentioned that Natalie would soon have to see William, whose morning trips to Mark's office had stopped. There had been no word from him. At Eliza Mackay's insistence, they had all respected William's wishes.

Every morning, before he left for work, Mark paid Natalie a visit in her room. Sunday morning found him there, too, before church. "I've come to look forward to our little talks," he said, sitting on the side of her bed while she ate breakfast from a tray Maureen had fixed with loving care. "Do you like your father bothering you on such a regular basis?"

Natalie took a bite of biscuit, then reached for his hand. "Yes, Papa, I—love you even more—with Kottie gone."

For an instant, he wondered what to say to that. He decided to meet it head-on. "I—want you to know that I—understand why you said that, honey."

"Do you really think you do?"

"At least, I—try."

She held up her face to be kissed. "You're a sweet father." Then her smile faded. A cloud crossed her lovely face, still red-splotched and raw from the ghastly burns. "I—I worry a lot about William. Haven't you heard anything from him?"

"Not a word since the day your letter came with the—terrible news."

"I guess he's just out there at Causton's Bluff alone—with no one to comfort him. Papa, that's five days today!"

"I know, darling," Mark said. "He wanted it that way. I know how you dread seeing him."

"You do?"

"Yes. I waited for you to mention William. We all had a pact about waiting."

When she leaned over again from her stack of pillows to kiss him, he held her for a long time. "Natalie, Natalie—I love you so much. . . ."

Clinging to him, her face hidden on his shoulder, she said, "I—would have—died, too, except for—Burke Latimer."

"I know, darling. You told us in your letter."

"You will find him for me, won't you?"

"And *try* in some way to show our gratitude."

"He'd never let you do anything but—say thank you, Papa. Burke Latimer isn't like anyone else on earth!"

Mark watched her closely, but said nothing.

"He—he's—just Burke. And I think it's important for you and Mama to know once and for all that I love him and mean to marry him. Just as soon as you find him for me."

"Well, that sounds serious to me."

"I don't like the tone of your voice. I'm no longer a child. I'm a woman. I intend to be treated that way—even by you, Papa. I'm going to marry Burke."

"What about Olin Wheeler? He's more than a little attentive. He appears to be a real gentleman."

"Oh, he is. And Burke isn't. At least, he insists that he isn't a Savannah gentleman."

"What exactly does that mean—a Savannah gentleman?"

"If you don't know by now," she said with her bewitching smile, "you'll never know. You are one." Then her face quickly grew solemn. "Papa, you will go with me when I have to—tell poor William, won't you?"

"You know I will, my dear girl."

"Woman."

"I beg your pardon."

"Telling William something so—horrible will be no child's work. Should I tell him everything? Like when I—*felt* his baby son die? I had him in my arms in the water, just the baby and me, and I—could feel the life go out of him."

Finding it difficult even to speak, Mark said finally, "I—I'm sure William's questions will tell you—what to say, honey. You're the only one left who saw them all three—die."

Her lips trembled. "Yes," she said softly. "I—saw poor Kottie go overboard, too. Papa? Are you—sad that Kottie's gone?"

"Why yes, of course I am."

"Even though Mama despised him?"

"I don't think she despised him, Natalie. She—was just mortally afraid of him."

"I will never, never, never understand that, and I hope she doesn't ask me to. Even though I wish I could make Mama know how grieved I am over losing Kottie, I don't want her to bring up his name."

Mark sat beside her quietly, watching the beautiful face change with a confusion of emotions.

After a while, she asked bluntly: "If God loves everyone the same, why didn't I die too? Why did God save me, Papa? At first, Burke thought I was a selfish, spoiled brat. Sweet Virginia Mackay *died*. Her little innocent babies—died. Why didn't I die, too?"

Again, Mark swept her into his arms and held her. "Natalie, don't ever say that again!"

"I don't think I'm as selfish as Burke said at all—but I'm certainly no better than Virginia Mackay or her babies." She wriggled out of his arms. "Isn't there an answer to my question? Isn't there any answer to why I'm here—alive and getting better every day, and Virginia and her children are—gone?"

"No, darling. I—I guess there is no answer that can be put into words. At least, your father knows of none."

Tossing her bright, sun-streaked curls, she gave him a long, somber look. "I expect it will come as a shock to you and Mama, but I—did grow up on that old wooden settee with Burke."

"Natalie, did Mr. Latimer—conduct himself properly when you were out there alone all that time?"

She laughed. "He's not a Savannah gentleman, but he's a *gentleman*, if that's what you mean. Oh, he kissed me a lot. Blistered mouths and all, we managed. I kissed him back, too. Maybe more than he kissed me."

Mark studied the small pink flowers in the finely woven carpet. "I see."

"I hope you do, because just as soon as you find him, I'm determined to marry him." She took both of his hands. "Papa, I'm tired of feeling so happy that I found Burke—and *so sad* about William at the same time. Could you take me to Causton's Bluff today to see him? I want to have it over. I get terrified every time I think about it."

EIGHTEEN

FOR THREE DAYS, a blustery nor'easter kept them from making the short boat trip downriver to Causton's Bluff, but on the fourth day bright sunshine lit the clean, rain-washed air as Jupiter Taylor took his employer and Miss Natalie to see William Mackay.

For much of the nearly three miles to the Causton's Bluff dock, they sailed in silence, Jupiter praying earnestly for Natalie and for Mr. William in a soft, mellow voice.

"Do you have to pray out loud, Jupiter?" she asked finally.

Feeling ever so sorry, Jupiter gave her his warmest smile. "Excuse me, Miss Natalie. I didn't notice I was speakin' my heart to God out loud."

"Jupiter only meant to be helping," her father said.

"I know, Papa."

Miss Natalie was so nervous, it seemed to Jupiter as though she could hardly sit still on the hard wooden seat of the smallest Browning skiff. He thought they should have brought the bigger boat. Jupiter's heart was so torn by what had happened, he'd have liked fixing a nice pallet for Miss Natalie to lie down on for the trip. Dark and burdensome, he thought, for anybody to be the bearer of such sad news. Must be even worse for a sorrowful, wore-out little girl to have to do it.

"Are you praying for me too, Papa?"

Jupiter, his back to them, overheard her pitiful question and whispered, "Lord Almighty, help her!"

"Yes, darling. I've been praying for you ever since we left our wharf awhile ago."

"I'm glad. I'm glad you're praying for me too, Jupiter. I'm sorry I scolded. Please keep on praying while Papa and I are in the house with William."

Jupiter glanced back to see her father put his arm around her and hug her close, and he wished with all his own torn heart that he could somehow take her place when she faced the torment of William Mackay.

"Papa—I don't know how William can keep on living, do you?"

"No. No, I don't."

"I couldn't," Miss Natalie said. "I couldn't live—I wouldn't want to—if Burke died. And I was only with him for—five days and nights. William's loved Virginia for years and years! What—*will he do* without her? Everybody in his family is gone."

Glancing back again, Jupiter saw her cling to her father as though the horror of what had taken place had overwhelmed her afresh. They were in sight of the Causton's Bluff dock now, and as he maneuvered the boat toward shore, Jupiter saw Natalie pull away from her father's arms, straighten her shoulders and arrange her fancy straw bonnet with its bright ribbons atop her windblown curls as though ready for what she had to do.

Jumping onto the wharf, Jupiter tied the boat to the newly repaired dock—all fixed up so proud just before the family left—and once more, forgetting himself, he prayed aloud: "Lord, You gotta help Mister William too!"

When the Mackay cook, Mary, told them that William was "somewhere out in his fields," her father settled Natalie on the front porch, sent Jupiter to search the south fields and set out himself along the west road. Seeing Papa walk away and out of sight left Natalie shaken. She felt a chill of terror through her entire body. What if William weren't in his fields?

What if William had—followed Virginia and the babies?

Colliding with this ghastly question came another: What if William were only out at the barn? What would she do if suddenly—grieving, distraught William Mackay walked onto the porch so that she was forced to face him—alone? Without Papa!

In a kind of panic far worse than any she'd experienced at the strict Reverend White's Academy before an examination for which she'd failed to study, Natalie began trying to recall those first violent moments after the explosion—when people were crying out and struggling and running and slipping and falling and praying. How long Virginia had managed to carry both children, Natalie now had no idea. She remembered Kottie clearly—could almost feel his strong hands lifting her, the unwilling cry of pain because of his broken shoulder at the moment when he had lifted her up over a shattered opening in the steep stair. Someone had been pleading from up there for them all to climb up—to help balance the rearing bow—but who?

Was that before or after the boat had split in two? Ripped apart, the ends rising steeply into the air, sending furniture and coils of rope and people sliding helplessly into the sea.

Kottie had been holding her. Kottie and everything he did seemed so much clearer than anything else. Kottie, using even his poor, hanging arm to try to hold her—Kottie trying to grab Virginia and the babies at the same time. Kottie handing the infant boy to Natalie—or did Natalie take little Willie from Virginia herself?

Virginia, holding Delia, at Natalie's last sight of her, seeming almost ladylike as she slipped into the black water with the tiny girl still in her arms . . . Delia and her mother . . . as they both vanished from sight.

Had Kottie been swept down and into the sea before Natalie's own body slammed against the water? She had *seen* Kottie go. Was she still on the wreck when she watched him disappear?

"What are you doing here, Natalie?"

A gunshot could not have brought her to her feet in such stark terror as the sudden voice from the yard below the porch.

When stooped, tortured William began to climb the few front steps as though he climbed a steep mountain, she could only stare at him. This broken, unshaven, man *was*—poor William. William, loved and respected by everyone who knew him simply because he was William. She should hurry to embrace him, to give him a kiss on his pale, bearded cheek—to comfort him. She could only stand staring in frozen silence.

On the porch, moving haltingly toward her, he held out his hand. Still she only stared, afraid somehow to touch the skin of a man so filled with anguish and torment. She had seen that torment in the face of the barber crawling toward her and Kottie right after the explosion had blown off both his legs. She had seen at least a dozen other dead, gaping faces before being herself tossed into the sea that night. She had felt the life go out of little William's soft body. Looking at his father now was worse than any of those memories. Looking at William now was worse than death. He looked—dead, but he took one or two more unsteady steps toward her and stood offering her his slender young hand. Odd, how young that hand appeared to be—extending from the arm of such an old and shattered man.

"William," she whispered. No voice came, even when she tried again. "William . . ."

Then she moved to take his hand but she *could not touch him.* Finally, he dropped the hand and said hoarsely, "I've been expecting you to come to see me, Natalie. When you—could."

"Yes." Still only a whisper.

"Wasn't sure how long it would take you to feel strong enough to get here." For what seemed an eternity, his eyes studied her—head to toe—almost as though he were having trouble convincing himself that she was really there—alive and breathing. "I—couldn't bring myself to come into town to—see you. Felt ashamed. I know—how happy your father is that you're back. I—I thought about him a lot. Thought about all of you."

Natalie sank back in her chair. "You—thought about *us,* William? You—felt ashamed—for not coming into town to see—us?" She was not whispering now. William had helped her back to—where she was, to who he was. "It's—it's still—you, William, isn't it?"

"I—don't know about that, Natalie. I—just don't know."

Abruptly, he fell to his knees and buried his head in her lap. His weeping came in slow, jerking sobs at first and then broke into such helplessness that Natalie could only keep smoothing the soft brown hair . . . smoothing and smoothing, thinking of Virginia's hand smoothing that head, soothing the kind heart of the kind man that was William.

Once on the rising wind off the river, Natalie heard her father's voice in the distance, calling William's name. Then, silence again until a towhee, hopping about somewhere under Virginia's hydrangea bushes in the yard, began to call for its mate.

William lifted his head and listened. "Virginia always said that bird was talking to me," he said.

"She did? Why?"

Pain and fresh tears mingled with his shy smile. "She claimed he was saying 'sweet, sweet.' " Then he looked up at Natalie like a small boy. "Kind of foolish, I guess."

"Not a bit. You are a sweet man, William." Into her memory for the first time since she'd heard Virginia's plea came Virginia's words: "Please save my babies! Mr. Mackay will bless you! *Mr. Mackay will bless you.* . . . "

Almost before she realized what she was doing, Natalie was telling William that Virginia had spoken his name and had promised his blessing only minutes before the fragment of splintered deck had risen so high—so straight up in the air—that they were all plunged into the sea.

Somewhere during her careful, torturous telling of all she remembered of the last moments of his loved ones, William got up from his knees. He now sat very straight on the porch railing, the long, slender fingers folded together in his lap.

She spoke of all Kottie tried to do for William's family and for her —said right out that he had given his own life trying to save them. She tried to explain how hard the water felt when she struck it, but that since she had seen Virginia and little Delia go into it—Virginia feet-first and with a kind of unearthly grace—she was certain mother and daughter had not much felt the impact. "You see, William," she went on, longing so now to help him even in the slightest way—"I hit the ocean flat out—on my backside. But not once did I lose hold of the baby." She stopped. Could William bear to hear that she actually felt the little life leave?

"When did—my son die?"

"I'm—not sure. I—I just know that I was still holding his little body, both of us floating in a big box, when I was found by the man who saved my life the next morning."

William frowned briefly, blinking, shaking his head, as though trying to sort it all out, then asked, "You held—my dead son's body —all night?"

"That's right."

"I guess you finally had to let him go." After a long moment, William got up, gave her a stiff, small bow and said, "Thank you,

Natalie. Later, I can—try to thank you better for—all you did. For coming like this to tell me."

He went so deliberately toward his front door that Natalie asked, "Where are you going? William, are you coming back out?"

At the door, he said, not looking at her: "No. Tell your father I'm sorry, but I have a lot to do. I've—just been waiting. You've—brought me to where I—believe it now."

And then he went inside, softly, but definitely closing the door behind him. She heard the key turn in the lock. The sound was so ominous, she hobbled to the closed door and pounded on it. "William," she called. "Don't leave me out here on the porch alone like this!" That sounded stupid. "William, what do you want us to tell your mother? Miss Eliza's terribly worried about you. What must I tell her?" When he didn't answer, she screamed: "Your sisters—everyone's so worried about you, William!"

An upstairs window flew up sharply and William called down in that old man's voice: "Tell Mama not to worry. Tell 'em all I'm—doing the best I can. . . ."

"Come back to town with us, please!"

"I would—if I could, Natalie. That's a fact. I—can't do it yet. I'll come to Mama's, though—when I can. I—promise."

Somewhat eased in her mind that William wasn't going to try to follow Virginia because he promised he'd come to see his mother, she sat down in the porch rocker again and waited for her father and Jupiter to return.

For Caroline, the anxious hours while Mark and Natalie were at Causton's Bluff were made bearable by the company of young Olin Wheeler. She would have felt perfectly free to excuse herself, had she preferred waiting alone. Instead, she welcomed conversation while Natalie was undoubtedly enduring a kind of torment with William that could break an adult.

"Of course," Olin Wheeler said with a gentle, not at all mocking smile, "your lovely daughter insists that she *is* an adult now."

"Oh, I know. And I'm sure that dreadful experience did mature the child. Probably far more than her father and I can quite understand. Tell me, Mr. Wheeler, did Natalie talk a lot to you while she was being so generously cared for by you and your aunt—while you two were en route here by boat?"

"Not much at the plantation in North Carolina. She was still somewhat hysterical then—and of course, very weak." The good smile again. "Not weak in her spirit, though, I must say. She's a plucky young lady. She did have one nightmare at our house. My aunt and I awakened her right away, tried to comfort her as best we could."

Caroline sighed, shook her head. "Mr. Browning and I will find a way to thank you both." Then: "Mr. Wheeler, did you actually meet and speak with the young man who saved Natalie's life?"

"The young man she's going to marry?"

"Uh—yes. I believe that's her version of it."

"Excuse me, Mrs. Browning, but I don't believe you should—in any way take your daughter lightly on that subject."

Caroline stared at him. "Marriage to an—unknown person?"

"Well, at least, don't take her feelings about him lightly."

"Tell me, what does this young man named Latimer look like?"

She was fascinated by Olin Wheeler's expressive eyebrows. At times, they said more than his words. "He's—a fellow of impressive size, enormously powerful shoulders and forearms. Yellow hair as curly as Natalie's, white, strong, even teeth. A boyish, slightly snubbed nose. A somewhat startlingly direct manner."

"Like Natalie?"

"Frankly, no. I'd say their—backgrounds preclude too much similarity there. Latimer expresses himself quite clearly. He's even rather well spoken, but—"

"What do you know about his background, if anything? Did he or Natalie tell you anything?"

"Wouldn't it be far better for you to ask Natalie that question, Mrs. Browning?"

"I suppose so."

"I really know almost nothing about the man. He's—well, let's say he's undoubtedly a hard worker. A workingman—I'm sure, an excellent workingman. And proud of it."

"A craftsman of some sort?"

"Perhaps."

Abruptly, Caroline changed the subject. She was beginning to sound exactly like her grandmother, Ethel Cameron. The thought had never crossed either her mind or Mark's that Natalie might fall in love with anyone other than—other than what? A fine man was a fine man, whether he worked with his hands or his mind. She'd always believed that—and so she began to ask questions about Olin Wheeler himself.

An orphan, he told her, since the age of nine, when both his parents died in an epidemic. Olin and she had that in common, certainly. She had lost her parents in an epidemic as a child, so young, she only remembered Grandfather Cameron and the rigid, embittered, class-conscious woman who was her grandmother, Ethel. When Olin Wheeler told her that he had been reared by Aunt Effie Wheeler, his father's spinster sister, there was another bond— this one with Mark, who had known no parent other than his father's spinster sister, Natalie Browning. Casually, Caroline remarked about the similarities.

Olin's ready smile came again. "Another Natalie Browning, eh?"

"We named our Natalie for my husband's Aunt Nassie. He adored her."

"Mr. Browning obviously adores his daughter."

"Oh, my! He's her slave. I do my best to curb them both, but I doubt that he would—could refuse his firstborn anything."

"So she told me."

"She told you that?"

"Only in passing. Only in assuring me that she was going to find Burke Latimer because her father would see to it."

"We do hope to hear from the young man. After all, Natalie could be—gone now, except for his unselfish courage."

"I tried my best to thank him the day we met—just before he handed me the letter for Natalie."

"This Burke person sent her a letter by you?"

"Your daughter wouldn't rest until my aunt promised to send me to discover which Wilmington family was caring for Latimer. You see, he and Natalie were separated during the rescue. I found him at Dr. Silver's house. He gave me the letter then and she smiled her first smile when I handed it to her."

"I see." Deciding to change the subject, Caroline went on: "It seems to me you deserve more gratitude than we've shown you, Mr. Wheeler. You and your kind aunt. Could I send her a gift? What does she especially like?"

Olin held up his smooth hand. "Oh no. We were both only too glad to have such a remarkable young lady in our usually lonely house." He paused. "It seems to me you should understand clearly, Mrs. Browning—you and your husband—that Latimer does *not* want you to try to find him. He made it quite plain that he does not want Natalie to know where he was heading when he left Wilmington."

"Don't you think that strange?"

"Frankly, yes. But in spite of his good looks and—relative charm —I found Latimer himself a bit strange."

Caroline frowned, but said nothing immediately. What did this polished, well-bred young man mean by—strange? What is it in my own daughter that causes her to gravitate toward—odd people? I spent my young life dodging contact with my grandmother and Natalie loved her on sight. And Osmund Kott . . . the old dread rushed back. Kott was dead now, but at times her fear of him flared as real as ever. Natalie had loved him from the beginning, too. "Mr. Wheeler," she said, still frowning. "Did Natalie say anything about the man who went along to escort her and the Mackay family? Mr. Kott?"

He shook his head pityingly. "Oh yes. She's grieving for him. My understanding is that the old man gave his own life in a futile effort to save Natalie—the others, too, I believe. She—she's heartbroken that he died."

"I'm sure she is." Again, Caroline fell silent. How, without sounding prying, could she find out exactly what Natalie had told Olin Wheeler about Kott? The young man was obviously too well bred to gossip. "How like Mr. Kott to manage to die a—hero." She heard herself and was both startled and relieved that she'd actually said it.

"I gather you didn't particularly admire the man."

"I didn't. I was afraid of him." Attempting a smile, she added quickly, "Now, you know I'm a—very human being. I tried, oh, how I tried to get over my fear of that old man."

"Your fear evidently showed itself to Natalie as simple dislike," he said in a quiet voice. A quiet, understanding voice that made Caroline suddenly long to tell him more. "At least, your daughter believed that you disliked him."

"I'm—so afraid even his memory will come between Natalie and me. Do you understand at all what I mean?"

"Oh yes. There are skeletons in the Wheeler closet too. My aunt in Wilmington is a dry, parched old lady now simply because her sister, whom she adored, came to despise her—died despising her. I fully understand. The sister resented poor, helpless Aunt Effie because my father chose to leave me in her care." He laughed easily. "I must have been an enchanting little boy."

"But surely Miss Effie Wheeler meant no harm by rearing you. Why did her sister resent her?"

"She feared Aunt Effie's hold, through me, on the family property —such as it is."

Realizing that Olin Wheeler was equating Osmund Kott's trouble-making with his own family trouble, she felt suddenly uneasy. There was no possible way that he could know that Osmund Kott had been Mark's own uncle. Natalie had never been told, and Wheeler had spoken to no one but Natalie about Kott. Unless Mark had—no. She shut off that thought. He would never discuss such a personal matter with a stranger. And certainly she had no business whatever to be doing it. They knew nothing about Wheeler except that he had brought Natalie safely back to them and had been kind to her when she needed care. So far as this young man knew, Osmund Kott had merely been their plantation overseer.

Abruptly, although she could not have explained her instinct, she began to wonder about Olin Wheeler's motives.

Jupiter kept a respectful distance, but stayed nearby on the Mackay dock, so that if Mr. Browning needed his help in settling Miss Natalie as comfortably as possible in the small skiff, he would be there. The poor little thing had faced Mr. William's grief and questions about his dead wife and babies all by herself. She was tuckered out now. We shoulda' brought the big boat, for certain, he thought.

"Can you curl up on the seat if I roll up my jacket and put it under your head?" her father was asking her. "Your old papa's so sorry he didn't listen to Jupiter and bring the large boat." Jupiter saw Mr. Browning take her in his arms and heard him say, "You're a brave, brave girl—far braver than your papa, darling Natalie."

"Burke told me I was brave," she answered in a small, weary voice.

Jupiter chuckled to himself. She's wore out, but even in that tired little voice, I hear a favor about to be asked of her papa. He untied the boat, pushed it away from the dock and jumped aboard. Then he waited for what he was sure was coming.

"Burke said I didn't complain once the whole time he and I were stranded on that wreckage, Papa."

Letting the sprit sail catch the breeze as he steered the boat out into the middle of the Savannah River, Jupiter noticed Mr. Browning kept smiling back at his daughter.

"I'm so proud of you," he was saying. "Now more than ever in your life, dear girl. Your Mr. Latimer was right. You are brave. He'd raise that estimate, too, if he knew what you did a while ago—all by yourself, with poor William."

"I know I was right, Papa," she went on, "not to let you go in the house to look for William. I saw his face. I—felt his pain. He has to work this out in his own way. I hope you can convince Miss Eliza to let him."

"Don't worry about her, honey. She's always a fair and reasonable lady."

Natalie laughed a little. "Unlike me, huh? You and Mother never think me reasonable. And on one issue, I don't plan to be. Papa, *when* will you start searching for Burke Latimer?"

Uh-oh, Jupiter thought, looking out over the river to hide his big grin. There she goes. Who, I wonder, is this Mr. Latimer?

"When, Papa? I don't want a vague answer. I want to know when we're going to start trying to find him. I've figured it all out," she went on firmly. "Burke's as taken with that wild country up in north Georgia as Uncle W.H. is. Mother told me yesterday that he and Miss Lib had merely postponed a trip up there until you heard something about—all of us on the *Pulaski*. You can simply give Uncle W.H. orders as your attorney to find the young man who saved your precious daughter's life."

Jupiter caught his employer's warm, easy laugh, then heard him say, "Being half sick and exhausted in no way stops that mind of yours, does it, Natalie Browning?"

"I think about Burke every minute I'm awake. I—wish I'd dream about him when I'm asleep. The Stileses are going up there—right up to the Cherokee Nation—Cass County. Can you give Uncle W.H. his instructions yet today?"

"I suppose so," her father answered. Putty in her hands, Jupiter thought. Then he heard Mr. Browning's mild condition in response to her demand. "But maybe I should wait a few days. There's so much sorrow and grief in town, Natalie. We're all so heartbroken for

William, I doubt the Stileses make their trip for a while. They'll want to know more about William's plans. What he means to do now—stay out at Causton's Bluff alone or—"

"Oh, I agree with you on all that, Papa. Don't forget for one minute that I'm the one who—saw William's face today. But it needn't stop you from giving Uncle W.H. his instructions for whenever they do go. Now even you can't call that unreasonable."

"No, darling, I don't suppose I can."

Mister Mark had such a good smile, it always made Jupiter happy when he saw it. Miss Caroline, she smile' so pretty too, but Miss Natalie—Lord, have mercy—Miss Natalie's smile, it come from both her mama and her papa! The very best of both.

When father and daughter fell into a compatible silence, Jupiter began to hum softly to himself as the little boat skimmed over the quiet water. Life, he thought, is full up with mournin' an' joy. Poor Mr. William Mackay'll have to live all the years of his life in company with his agony. And here's Miss Natalie stirrin' up something new for her papa to handle.

He turned to peek at her, curled up on the cramped boat seat, her shiny head on her papa's shoulder. Blessed child. She'd been through more than any of the home folks would ever know about, but it was plain to see that Miss Natalie had come back from all of it still Miss Natalie.

NINETEEN

AS PART OF her recuperative treatment, Natalie, in the care of Olin Wheeler, went daily for long rides in the family carriage, or, when Jupiter was otherwise occupied, in a surrey, with Olin handling the gentle mare.

"I'll be so glad when I can walk on my own two feet again," she complained to her mother on the morning of July 11 as she dressed for a surrey ride with Olin. "I hate my feet for being so slow to heal."

"Darling, your feet were horribly bruised and cut—and burned—what do you expect? Miss Eliza and I are going to ride with you in the memorial procession tomorrow, so you won't feel odd."

"I want to *walk* in that procession—with the real mourners."

"But we're all mourners, Natalie. Everyone in town has lost at least a friend or close acquaintance."

In a firm voice, not looking at her mother, Natalie said, "I'll be the only mourner for—Kottie. It would help me to be able to walk—all by myself, for him." When her mother didn't comment, she added, "Don't worry about my mourning for Kottie, Mama. I promise not to let my grief disturb you. I—just happened to love him, that's all."

"I know you loved him," her mother said. "He loved you, too."

"I appreciate that you said that."

"Oh, my darling child, I want to be right about that man. If you knew how long I've tried to be right about him!"

"I'm sorry for you. I wish you'd succeeded a year ago."

Natalie could feel her mother's struggle as she said, "I—I hoped you didn't realize—how I felt about him. I'm heartsick that you knew."

Natalie balanced herself with a hand on her mother's shoulder while slipping her still swollen feet into the large-sized house slippers her father had bought for this awkward interim.

"Do you think William will come to town for the procession tomorrow?"

"Oh, I have no idea, my dear."

"I think he'll be here. For William to march in that procession would honor Virginia and the babies."

Her mother hugged her. "You're growing up, Natalie."

"Yes, Mama. I am." She leaned lightly on her mother as they walked into the upstairs hall toward the stair. "I wish Papa could drive me today instead of Olin."

"I thought you enjoyed being with Olin Wheeler. You certainly act as though you do."

"He's all right. Attentive, kind—so attentive and so kind sometimes, he's underfoot. Are you beginning to tire of his being here, Mama?"

"Well, your father and I do think it's a bit unusual that he hasn't said anything about going back to North Carolina, but he's a perfect house guest. And obviously quite smitten with you."

"I know that. But I'm already taken." Just before they started down the stair, she looked straight at her mother and said, "Olin does nicely for now. But wait till you meet Burke Latimer, Mama. I've told Papa all about my plans to marry him."

Her mother's smile was forced. I suppose I've hurt her, Natalie thought, but maybe it won't be so awkward telling her things now that Kottie can't have anything to do with my plans.

At the foot of the stair, looking up at them, stood Olin Wheeler. Natalie gave him her most enchanting smile.

Olin loved driving on Bull Street, but today it was blocked off to traffic so that its generous width could be raked and swept of trash and horse droppings from Johnson Square south toward the Independent Presbyterian Church. Memorial services in honor of those who perished on the *Pulaski* were to be held there once the sad procession reached the graceful white-steepled church.

"I'll feel foolish riding in a carriage tomorrow," Natalie complained—this time to Olin. "I long to walk in that procession. You'll have to be in the strangers' section, I guess. It's all been very strictly laid out. There'll be a definite order to things. After all, the committee's invited people from all over Chatham County."

"I won't mind walking with the strangers," he said. "But you can be sure I'll keep an eye on your carriage. I've memorized the order of march—you'll be between the committee and the clergy, with the immediate relatives and friends of those lost. My group of strangers will be last. I don't feel like a stranger in town anymore, though." He smiled down at her. "You and your parents and Jonathan have made me feel right at home. Am I staying too long, Natalie?"

"Oh, I don't think so. Has Aunt Effie written for you to come home?"

"No. I just don't want to wear out my welcome."

"We have plenty of room." Then, her mind not on him, he knew, she changed the subject. "Olin, drive me to Miss Eliza Mackay's house on East Broughton, will you, please?"

"Happy to. I like that lady. I've enjoyed both my short visits there."

"Oh, I'm not inviting you in today. I just suddenly feel I need to talk to Miss Eliza. You'll have to find something else to do while I'm with her."

His eyebrows arched in agreement. "At your service, Miss Natalie," he said, snapping the reins lightly so that the mare began to trot.

"Maybe you could pass the time at the Exchange Coffee House. I'd like at least an hour with Miss Eliza. Mama and Papa haven't let me tell her yet—all about my time with William. They pamper me too much. Only my stubborn feet are still not healed. I'm sure Miss Eliza needs to know. I need to talk to her too."

Natalie hoped she didn't offend Kate and Sarah Mackay too much when she just plain asked them to leave her alone with Miss Eliza. Of course, they left at once. Everyone jumped to do Natalie's bidding more than ever now that she had been so near to death. She could make it up to the sisters later. Her need to be alone with wise, understanding Miss Eliza Mackay was what mattered. Besides, making a real call felt good again. Sitting on the old Mackay love seat

across from Miss Eliza made her feel more like herself than at any
time since she'd been home.

"Being waited on hand and foot is fine," she said, after the Mackay's Hannah had brought tea and muffins, "but even I tire of it
sometimes." Frowning a little, she added, "It's only fun being
waited on when you want to be. Here, let me pour our tea."

"I've been waiting for this visit," Miss Eliza said, nodding her
thanks for the cup Natalie handed her. "I haven't waited very well,
either. Your dear father explained that he didn't want you to have to
talk about the wreck yet, or—"

"Oh, I know, I know! My dear father can be quite silly at times. I
wanted to come to you the very next day after I—told William." She
sighed. "One has to humor parents at times. Today, I just didn't tell
either of them that I was visiting you. I confess, though, that I
dreaded—having to tell you about poor William."

"The hardest thing I've ever had to do has been—to leave him
alone out there for nearly two weeks. Not knowing anything beyond
what your father could tell me."

Her tea nearly untouched, Natalie told her everything—every
word she could remember, every expression on William's face—
every detail of what she had been able to recall for him of the
manner in which his little family had died. She made a point of
telling Miss Eliza that it had seemed somehow to help William a
little that she remembered hearing Virginia speak his name just
minutes before the end. "She was pleading for someone to save the
children," Natalie explained. " 'Please save my babies—Mr. Mackay
will bless you!' "

Tears streamed down Eliza's face as she listened, her hands
clenched together in her lap. "And then what, Natalie?"

She described William's little stiff bow when he thanked her for
coming to tell him and the way he went directly to his front door. "I
begged him not to go inside, Miss Eliza. I begged him to come back
to the city with us, but he said he had a lot to do, that what I'd told
him had brought him to the place of—believing they were really
gone. After he went in the house, I still kept shouting for him to
come back, to tell me what I was supposed to tell you and his
sisters."

"That's what I need to know, Natalie! Your father tried to tell me,
but I need to hear it from you."

"He said to tell you not to worry, that he is doing the best he can."

"Is that all?"

"No. I pleaded with him again to come back to town with us. He said he would when he could." Miss Eliza's face was buried in her hands now and she was weeping quietly, helplessly. "But he did make a promise. He promised he'd come here to—you, just as soon as he could."

Slowly, Eliza Mackay looked up at Natalie. "William really promised—that?"

"Yes, ma'am. He did."

"Then he'll be here. William always keeps his promises."

"Do you think he'll come for the—citywide day of mourning tomorrow?"

"I don't know. William makes no pretense of it, but he has always had a deep, hidden kind of—strength."

For a time, they sat together in silence, then Natalie said, "I'm ever so relieved to have told you—finally."

"I'm sure you are." She blew her nose, wiped her eyes and tried to smile. "Now tell me about you, Natalie. You've—done some growing up, haven't you?"

"I—fell in love, Miss Eliza. On the makeshift raft where Burke Latimer and I lived for five days and five nights. I'm—going to marry him, practically as soon as we find out where he is."

"Your father told me."

"What else did he say about Burke?"

"Well, my dear, there really wasn't much he could say, not ever having laid eyes on the young man."

"Miss Eliza, you can help me! You're closer to our family than most blood relatives. You can help me with a lot more than just convincing my parents." The older woman's surprised look sent Natalie plunging ahead. "Burke's a frontiersman. And proud of it. He had money saved to build a house in the Cherokee Nation, but it was all lost on the *Pulaski*. They didn't take him to the same house with me after we were rescued and he—vanished. He sent a letter to me, though, telling me that someday, when he'd earned that dumb money again, he'd come to Savannah. Oh, Miss Eliza, he's the most gorgeous man you ever looked at! Big and strong—and not just in his muscles—in his *heart*. He saved my life. He cared for me, not like I was a little girl, but—a woman. He loves me. He'll never love another woman the way he loves me. He wrote that in his letter. But he can be maddening! Just because he's eight years older than I, he thinks he has to be manly now and earn back that stupid money. Isn't that maddening? When Papa is so rich?"

"I don't think I'll comment on that right now," Miss Eliza said, "but what is it I can do for you?"

"You can add your influence to Papa's instructions to Uncle W.H. After all, you're his mother-in-law. You can tell both him and Miss Lib that my father's instructions are to be carried out to the letter when they make their trip to the Etowah River country up in the Cherokee Nation."

"I don't think it's the Cherokee Nation anymore. In Jack's latest letter from up there, he seemed fairly certain that by now most of those poor Indians are being herded west. Do you know they quietly went on planting and tending their gardens this spring as though nothing was awry in their lives?"

"No, but I suppose Indians are peculiar. What matters right now is that Papa is going to give William Henry Stiles instructions, as his attorney, to find Burke up there!"

"You know he's somewhere near the Etowah River?"

"Well, not exactly. . . ."

"Your Mr. Latimer didn't give you any idea of where he was heading when he left Wilmington?"

She shook her head. "He's pigheaded as well as wonderful."

"Jack says there just aren't very many respectable white men up there."

"Probably that's true right now. But not for long. Once the Cherokees are really gone, splendid white men like Uncle W.H. and Mr. Barnsley—and Burke—will settle the land."

"Jack writes pages about its beauty. He's even bought a few lots himself."

"On the raft, Burke talked for hours about the scenery." Natalie stood up uncertainly, but shook off Miss Eliza's hand when she tried to help her. "Burke is going to be very successful. He's a master carpenter, and I'm sure he'll be rich in no time. He's absolutely made up his mind to settle there. I just know that if he isn't there already, he will be soon."

"And what do you think of the idea of living in the wilderness, Natalie?"

"If I'm with Burke, I don't care where I live."

"Eliza Anne isn't quite that agreeable to the idea of leaving Savannah."

"Oh, but she's terribly in love with Uncle W.H. She'll change her mind. I have it all planned. Miss Lib and I can be neighbors! You will help me, won't you? Everyone listens to you."

"Heaven help them, if true. But yes. I'll do what I can, my dear. Actually, I spoke with my old friend, Julia Scarbrough Senior, just before her beloved husband, William, died not long ago. She surprised me by showing quite an interest in the upcountry herself, just from listening to her son-in-law, Godfrey Barnsley, talk about it. He seems as determined as W.H. to move there. I'm sure you know Julia's older daughter Charlotte isn't exactly making her or the Barnsleys feel welcome at the Scarbrough house on West Broad."

"Maybe you could get your old friend Miss Julia—or her other daughter Julia Barnsley to convince somebody to help find Burke!"

Miss Eliza laughed a little. "You're still—Natalie, aren't you?"

"I mean not to leave a single stone unturned."

"I'll do what I can. Poor Julia Senior is too heartbroken to think of anything these days, though, beyond the fact that her William is gone. She's at her girlhood home in North Carolina now, anyway. I do promise to keep my eyes and ears open, though."

Natalie limped along beside Miss Eliza toward the front door. "I suppose Olin Wheeler's waiting for me in the surrey."

"And what's your opinion of your devoted Mr. Wheeler?"

She shrugged. "If he's still here when my feet are well, I'm going dancing with him. But he isn't—Burke Latimer." At the open door, Natalie said, "I'm glad you're riding with Mama and me in our carriage tomorrow, Miss Eliza."

"So am I. My heart's so heavy. Walking with such a load of grief wouldn't be at all easy for me."

Natalie hugged her. "None of—tomorrow is going to be easy for any of us. But at least, the whole town will be—grieving with us. Poor Miss Julia Scarbrough and the Barnsleys and Miss Charlotte are grieving alone."

Miss Eliza hugged her again. "I—love you, dear Natalie, for thinking of them—in the midst of everything else."

· · ·

At seven the next morning, July 12, every bell in town began its sorrowful tolling, and before nine, people were starting to gather in and around Johnson Square, where the procession of mourners was scheduled at ten. Two days earlier, the *Georgian* had carried a full account of how they were all to line up. The Reverend George White and his committee would come first, and, immediately behind them, the relatives and close friends of those lost on the *Pulaski*, then the clergy. Many carried the instructions clipped from the newspaper: Behind the families and friends would walk Mayor John C. Nicholl and the city officials, judges of all the courts, members of the bar, justices of the peace, consuls and agents of foreign nations, the collector and officers of customs, the postmaster, United States army and navy officers, members of the benevolent societies, harbor masters, sailors and, last, strangers and other citizens.

All present had been requested to wear some symbol of mourning, so that black armbands and black veils, even black ribbons in the hair of children, were everywhere. Those who were able would walk, but along with Natalie, her mother and Miss Eliza, driven by Jupiter in the open family carriage, there were other vehicles that carried the elderly and infirm—about seven conveyances in all. The death toll was so heavy, most formed up in the section called "relatives and family friends."

Natalie, in a black voile dress and hat with a black veil, sat between her mother and Miss Eliza—also in black—each hand being held, squeezed, by the older women. "We're just so grateful that you're here—alive, Natalie," Miss Eliza kept saying. And then she would sit up and search the crowd again for William. "I'm watching for him on this side," Natalie's mother reminded Miss Eliza often.

Waiting for the procession to begin, lost in her own now sharpened memories of the wreck, Natalie, on this her first real public appearance since the tragedy, felt an odd sense of not belonging; of trying to identify with the agony of those who had waited and wondered and grieved—not knowing. She had been there when the ghastly explosion ripped apart the boat; she had been there when all those people tumbled helplessly into the sea. Theirs is a different kind of agony, she thought, and I must be more tolerant when people, who mean well, don't understand why I want to put it all behind me. A lot of these people still don't know about loved ones— even family. Her father had told her that this morning. The latest tragic toll—not complete—was ninety-seven people lost, only fifty-four rescued.

Burke and I are two of those fifty-four, she reminded herself. If he hadn't rescued me, there might have been only fifty-three. And I'd never really have known him. Her heart pounded and her hands grew cold in the grasps of her mother and Miss Eliza.

Fragments of conversation in the crowd reached her again and again over the steady tolling of the bells: "No," a man's voice said sharply. "It wasn't caused by somebody's wager on speed! That's been proved." Another spoke of whose fault it was that such a carefully built boiler could explode: "Not Chief Engineer Kitchen's fault. That's a false rumor. Kitchen was having his rest when it happened. It was the fault of a Mr. Cannon, the second engineer. He let that boiler go dry and then, like a dumb ox, put in cold water!"

Every day since she'd been home, her parents had discussed what might have gone wrong. She'd heard Papa and Uncle W.H. discuss it endlessly. The *Georgian* ran countless editorials on how Congress should pass new safety laws; should make the ships' owners or captains responsible. "They have very few such accidents in England," Olin said one night. "Their laws are quite stiff."

Invariably, when they had spoken of the tragedy in her presence, she had tried to change the subject. She could do nothing now, though, in the midst of this pressing crowd, on a humid, hot day when all mourned the dead, but sit there sandwiched between her mother and Miss Eliza and—endure. Yesterday the procession had seemed a rather admirable idea, a chance for Savannahians to express sympathy, to honor those people, some of whom Natalie had seen die. She had longed to be able to step along on her own two feet, entering in, honoring the poor dead Lamars, honoring Virginia and her babies, honoring Kottie. Now, in the heat, with her choking concern for William somehow even more wrenching, she could only endure to the end of what would undoubtedly be an over-long memorial service at the Presbyterian Church.

At last, the procession began to move slowly, horses reined, the few conveyances barely rolling, and hundreds of feet shuffling along the sandy street. She could feel Miss Eliza's anxiety as the poor woman tried not to be too obvious while looking and looking and looking for William.

From Johnson Square, they moved along Bull Street toward

South Broad. William was nowhere in sight. "Maybe," Natalie whispered to her, "we just can't see him in the crowd. We don't know that he didn't come."

And then she heard Miss Eliza gasp and call out over the subdued noise of the procession and the bells: "Son! William—oh, William, you're here!"

From the shade of a giant magnolia, just before the procession reached South Broad, William stepped out alone, dressed in a white suit, a wide black armband on one sleeve, head high, stooped shoulders as erect as his grief would permit.

Wanting, as usual, Natalie knew, not to be noticed, he had waited on the sidelines until their carriage reached him. Then he simply stepped into the street to walk along in silence beside his mother.

In front of the church, he helped Miss Eliza down the carriage steps, then Natalie, giving her a brief hug. After he assisted her mother, too, William took Miss Eliza's arm for the climb up the church steps. Papa joined them, along with Jonathan, and as they helped Natalie into the church, she heard William say to his mother, "I'm coming home to live, Mama. By the end of next week, I'll have Causton's Bluff cleared out."

"Oh, William," Miss Eliza said, "I'll be—*relieved* to have you home again."

The service was so sad, Natalie cried. It was worse than a single funeral, so heavy with sorrow and questioning hearts, so oppressive, she could almost not wait to get back outside in the sunshine, hot as the day was. Would the grieving ever end? Yes, she told herself firmly, drying her eyes. *It has to end.* A lot of people are still alive. I'm alive and Burke's alive—and some day, even poor William might want to live again.

Back outside on the church steps, when the service was finally over, she saw Miss Lib and Uncle W.H. speaking privately to William and Miss Eliza. Not now, Natalie thought, but one day soon, I'm going to remind Miss Eliza of her promise to urge Uncle W.H. to be on the watch for Burke when he takes Miss Lib up north to inspect the Cherokee land.

She sent Olin Wheeler for the Browning's surrey so he could drive her home alone. With Olin she could talk or not, as she liked.

"You're quiet, Natalie," he said as they rode slowly back toward

Reynolds Square. "Was all this—too much? I couldn't help noticing how people stared at you. You're like a miracle to everyone."

"I'm not a miracle."

"Yes, you are. You're here. You didn't die."

All but ignoring him, she stared straight ahead. No, I didn't die, she thought. And—neither did Burke. Someday—I'm going to see his face again.

TWENTY

ON HIS LAST EVENING at New Echota, which had once been the civilized, flourishing capital of the Cherokee Nation, Captain Jack Mackay excused himself from the compatible, but somewhat downcast company of Colonel Lindsay and his other officer friends. Even in late July, the clear, light mountain air outside the comfortable old Boudinot house where officers had been temporarily bivouacked lifted Jack's spirits. If a man could enjoy anything at such a tragic time in American history, Jack had enjoyed the comforts of Elias Boudinot's well-built two-storied house. He breathed deeply now of the invigorating air, a continuing marvel to a man who had lived much of his early life in humid Savannah. Physical comforts, though, could extend only so far in lifting the human spirit. Eliza Mackay's son Jack, because he was a good officer, had obeyed orders to drive out the Cherokees, but not without distaste and loathing.

He had left his fellow officers this evening, depressed by the burden of having lived through what, to him, was the ugliest period in the history of the country he had been brought up to love and revere. Along with Cherokee chieftain old Major Ridge, Chief Elias Boudinot, missionary-educated editor of the only bilingual Indian newspaper, had once been a close ally of the Cherokee eighth-blood, Chief John Ross, the one man still trusted by a majority of the Indians. Jack knew Ross and understood why his people trusted him. A cultivated man, John Ross was not only a leader, but an authentically Christian gentleman, who had argued the Cherokee's cause in Washington City until the last possible moment. That moment, in spite of the fact that President Andrew Jackson was Jack's commander-in-chief, still rankled. Rankled more in Jack's heart, he supposed, than in his mind, which was obedient to all orders of the United States Army.

In 1835, Ridge, Boudinot and others had seemed to turn against their own people by signing a treaty that would remove all Cherokees from their beloved mountain land and send them packing to the country west of the Arkansas Territory. These chieftains, lesser in the eyes of the average Cherokee than John Ross, were already gone, having made the long, arduous journey in relative ease at government expense. But, to the last ugly moment, Ross had persevered. The ugly moment had come when, face to face with John Ross, President Andrew Jackson had said bluntly: "Ross, it's just too damned late!"

Since 1835, Jack Mackay had lived and worked with the engineers in and around New Echota, surveying the land for the federal government. Following that ugly moment in Washington City when even John Ross had accepted defeat, Jack had been ordered to oversee the building of rough stockades, into which his men had been forced to drive the peaceful Cherokee farm families at bayonet point.

This stretch of duty had spanned three of his thirty-three years that he would never, never forget. Three years of more physical discomfort than he'd ever known—of exhaustion, dull food, loneliness, long rides and agonizing treks on foot through the wilds of the Georgia upcountry. Never having climbed a real mountain, or even a hill, until he was assigned to the Cherokee Nation, Jack had done more than his share of suffering up the steep slopes that lay around the river valleys of the primitive north Georgia settlements.

No man in Savannah, no man anywhere in the low country could possibly match my leg muscles now [he'd written his mother]. The frontier has made a man of me, and in spite of my downright grief over the plight of the Cherokees, I have come to revel in the natural beauty of it all. I love the rich little valleys, always with a clear stream running through them. Indian villages dot the valleys, and unlike the generally greedy white settlers, the Cherokees are keen for education, justice and order. They even appear genuine for the most part in their pursuit of Christianity. But I see plainly why most whites are called "poor devils." Their log houses have but one room with a door and one stick-and-clay chimney. Windows are unnecessary, since the seams, which they don't pretend to stop, admit abundant rain and breeze. You may look in vain for a book, and two or three occupants in each house are always sick. By contrast, the Cherokees were mainly healthy and, as you know, published their own newspaper, *The Cherokee Phoenix*, at New Echota.

Strolling through the blue twilight, Jack tried to imagine the suffering and losses of those who, less than two months ago, had been driven by the brutal Georgia Guard, to begin the long march west. He could not. He dared not. By obeying orders, he had been a part of their suffering. One poignant, heartrending scene still tortured his dreams. On a cold, rainy May morning, after Chief John Ross had led them in prayer, Jack had watched one group depart. When a U.S. Army bugle sounded and the wagons began to roll, the children waved and waved good-bye to their dear mountain homes till out of sight. The scene would never leave him, no matter where he served his country in the future, no matter how long he lived.

One section of the dusky sky was now turning to coral, edging horizontally to gray and gold. Jack sighed heavily, then remembered a letter from his mother in Savannah still in his pocket. He would be writing to her next from Washington, where he'd head tomorrow for a visit to his best friend, Robert Lee, and to receive orders for his next area of duty. The thought of his mother tonight in hot, sticky Savannah worried him. His sister, Eliza Anne, was not yet keen on moving with W.H. to the upcountry, but she would be. No one complained more of Savannah summers than Eliza Anne. He took out his mother's letter and began to reread it. She had told him of the death of William Scarbrough, Savannah's once wealthy, social-minded merchant prince.

Poor Julia, his wife, and poor Julia, his daughter [the letter went on]. Young Julia has trouble enough attempting to keep peace between her husband, Godfrey Barnsley, and her own sister, Charlotte. Charlotte is such a brilliant scholar and yet, as the eldest of the Scarbrough children, she has demanded full and complete authority in family matters and seems to be behaving quite disagreeably even with generous Mr. Barnsley, who did, after all, rescue the Scarbroughs from their financial plight. Perhaps [his mother wrote], if I had a brain like Charlotte's, I'd feel superior too. She even told me the other day that Godfrey Barnsley and his family are living at what Charlotte now calls "the castle" on West Broad only because of *her* kindness to them. Young Julia isn't at all well, and her grief over the family trouble, and now her father's death, do not help. It seems such a short time ago that Julia and William and the Scarbrough house were the toast of Savannah's social life.

The sky was darkening too much to finish the letter. Passing the now deserted, hewn-log *Phoenix* print shop, Jack smiled, remembering Savannah's social madness. Compared to life here, the thought of those balls and parties seemed a contradiction. Refolding the letter, he recalled what his mother had also written of her eagerness to see him soon in order to discuss the obsession of his brother-in-law, W. H. Stiles, with this very upcountry whose horizon was now darkening to a burnished copper, cloud-streaked and wide above the Cherokees' almost empty land. He felt a tug at the thought of leaving tomorrow. But if, indeed, Eliza Anne and her husband moved here, he would return someday.

Odd, he thought, sauntering slowly back toward the Boudinot house, that Mama had written so little about William. He found himself being thankful that his older brother had actually joined the mournful procession memorializing those who had died on the *Pulaski,* and that William was coming home to Broughton Street to live. Poor William. A small ray of relief came when Jack thought of their longtime friend Mark Browning. At least, William would have the solace of Mark's friendship. Never one to pray on a regular basis, Jack breathed a prayer that God would do whatever it is He does for a man like William whose life has just been shattered.

He sighed again. He would nevermore be able to persuade his mother to leave the dangers of a Savannah summer—not with William at home. And maybe William was the one who mattered most now. He'd need both Mama and Mark Browning.

Maybe I'll be granted a furlough soon, he thought, and felt ashamed that even the prospect of looking at William in his grief filled him with dread.

· · ·

By the first week in August, not quite two months after the tragedy at sea, William had moved back into the Broughton Street house—into his own room, seemingly to stay. Mark, at least, believed Miss Eliza expected him to live there permanently. She evidently knows very little more about the true state of William's mind and heart than the rest of us, he thought, during his daily visit to the old Mackay house. As he and Miss Eliza sat now on the side porch together—in the kind of blessed, understanding silence they'd shared for years—he vowed not to press her for more details about her grieving son. She had already told him that in the nine days William had been home, he had not left his room once. What hurt her most, though, also hurt Mark more deeply than he dared reveal to her. William refused point-blank to see him!

As she'd done so many times in the years they'd known each other, Eliza Mackay again seemed to read his thoughts. "I'm so concerned about you, Mark," she said quietly, as though they'd been conversing all along. "You don't deserve the kind of treatment you're getting these days from Natalie and William. Sometimes I'd like to shake them both. And you're so kind to come to me every day. I know how busy you are. I read the papers. Savannah's business is picking up at such a rate, you don't have time for a daily visit here. You know what seeing you means to me, but you don't need to come every day, dear boy."

She had called him "dear boy" for as long as Mark could remember. He was fond of the name, could smile now at the memory of the only time he'd hated it—the agonizing months before he and Caroline were married—when he'd been so sure he was in love with Eliza Mackay. In answer, he reached for her hand—the same small, square, capable hand—a bit brown-spotted now with age. "You know I'll be here every day, Miss Eliza. I come for you, but I also come for myself. Just being with you helps me live through the—punishment my daughter is meting out to me these days. I come also, I admit, hoping one day William will agree to see me again."

"I know Natalie's punishing you for your quite sensible decision *not* to run off searching for her young man, Burke Latimer. We both know, though, that she's still young and—spoiled. But William—Mark, why on earth does William refuse to see you? There's never been a chink in the boy's loyalty to you, of all people. None of this is like the William we all knew!"

"He isn't the William we all knew anymore," Mark said. "He may never be again. There's no possible way we can understand the hell he went through out there at Causton's Bluff alone during those first weeks after he lost his family."

"No one's ever the same after grief, but why did he come back here if he can't stand to be with any of us? Oh, he's polite to the girls and to me when we knock on his always closed door, but I can sense his relief when we leave."

Mark took a deep breath. "I guess we all deal with grief differently. I—don't know what I'd do if I lost Caroline and Jonathan—and Natalie."

"Has she really not addressed you as anything but 'sir' in three weeks?"

"That's right. She seems about the same as always with her mother and Jonathan. It's as though I'm not her—papa anymore. All she talks about is the day Eliza Anne and W.H. get back from their trip to the Cherokee country. We both know why, of course."

"And they will be on the alert for any word at all about her young man. I can understand her interest in their return, but not at the cruel exclusion of her papa. This coldness toward you breaks my heart, Mark."

He gave a feeble laugh. "Mine, too. Obviously she now has the notion that asking W.H. to look for Latimer just isn't enough, that I should be doing more."

"What about Caroline? She's told me she could also shake Natalie for treating you the way she does, but—are things still so awkward at your house with Caroline where Osmund's death is concerned? Does Caroline feel at all guilty because she couldn't forgive him before he died? Does anyone ever mention the old fellow's name?"

"Natalie does. I've caught her crying over him twice, and the second time I hoped for a moment that my sympathy was about to soften her toward me. It seemed to for an instant, but then she withdrew again." He sighed. "Caroline and I are close still, though, when we're alone—which isn't often enough with young Wheeler in the house and Natalie, most of the time, at odds with me. When Caroline and I are alone we don't mention Kott. We're practiced at that, you know. All these years since her grandfather's death in the fire at Knightsford, she's believed Kott set the fire that killed the old gentleman."

"Oh, I'd hoped she no longer thought that. There's no proof."

"Caroline thinks only Kott would have known that, to Grandfather Cameron, burning Mary Cotting's house was the same as burning a shrine. Evidently Jonathan Cameron truly loved Mary Cotting —my grandmother."

"And he wasn't just Caroline's grandfather, either, Mark. He was yours too."

He smiled a little sadly. "I guess he didn't live long enough for that to become real to me. But don't worry about Caroline, Miss Eliza. She and I are going to be all right. My heart mostly aches for William—and Natalie."

"Mark, what more can you do? What more can you sanely do for Natalie?"

"At times I think everyone can always do *more* in my daughter's eyes. You—do think I'm right not to rush off myself to try to bring Burke Latimer to Savannah, don't you?"

"You're simply respecting *his* wishes."

"I owe him everything. He saved my girl's life."

"You certainly owe him some time to work out his own life. Why, Natalie told me what he wrote to her up in North Carolina. If the young man meant to be here now, he would be. Natalie believes he loves her. If he does, she'll hear from him, in his own time. But, dear boy, I know, I know how she hurts you with that—everlasting cold courtesy toward you."

Mark took out his watch. "I should get back to work, but could I ask you one other thing? What do you think of Olin Wheeler?"

The frown that pulled her even eyebrows together told him a lot, but he waited for her to speak.

"He seems very well bred, a gentleman. I—like him, I guess. He's obviously got his heart set on Natalie. I just hope it's only Natalie. You're a rich man, Mark. A very rich man, and Olin's family money is evidently gone. He makes no bones about that. I admit I've wondered at his leaving his maiden aunt up there alone all this time."

Mark got up to leave and Miss Eliza pulled herself stiffly to her feet, smiling. "These chairs haven't always seemed so—low to me."

He bowed over her hand, then tucked it under his arm as they walked along the porch to the front steps. "We all have a lot to wonder about these days, don't we? And until I come back tomorrow, I'll be wondering about you—and William—every minute."

At the steps, they stood, holding hands. "Caroline does agree with you about not sending out a search party just to please your daughter, doesn't she?"

"Oh yes. We're quite agreed on that."

"And does she like Olin Wheeler?"

"At first, yes. Now, I'm not so sure." Mark went slowly down the wooden front steps, reluctant as always to take leave of Eliza Mackay. "I like Wheeler, though. I'm thinking of offering him a position with my firm. Will you mull that over a little?"

He caught the fleeting surprise on her face. "Why yes. Has he asked you for work?"

"No, but it may be my place to bring it up. I remember how I used to bite my tongue with Mr. Mackay—hoping he'd be the one to make me the first offer."

"I—I promise to think about Olin Wheeler—in your firm," she said, "but maybe we should all just try to be patient about everything awhile longer." Mark saw tears well in her eyes. "So much has happened, in such a short time. Less than—two months ago, we all had—such a shock. Maybe we should just wait and see what tomorrow brings."

The next day and the next and the next brought nothing new. Mark visited Eliza Mackay every late morning, returned to his office to work until dinnertime at midafternoon, took his place at the Browning dining table and searched for some kind of familiar recognition in Natalie's eyes. Nothing. A formal smile and nod when he asked for the sugar or the salt server, a little polite conversation, but nothing more. No patting his hand as she'd always done—"just for fun"—no exchanged giggles at something strict Mama said. Nothing. Nothing altered with William either. He had still not left his room. He still refused to see Mark.

"Why won't William see you?" Caroline asked one August evening when they'd gone early to bed after Natalie, her injured feet healed, had gone out dancing with Olin Wheeler. "William has always adored you, Mark. Does Miss Eliza have any theories as to why he won't let you visit him?"

"None."

"She tells him you come every day, doesn't she?"

"Oh yes. She's used every trick she can think of to get him to see me. Sometimes I wonder if William has made up his mind—never to see anyone again but his mother and his sisters."

"I know he sees Eliza Anne when she comes over. Does he let W.H. visit him?"

"No. Only his mother and his sisters. And Hannah. He won't let Emphie in his room even to clean. Only Hannah."

"Well, I can understand that poor nervous Emphie's chatter would upset him, but—"

"Caroline," he interrupted, "I'm going to offer Olin Wheeler a place in my firm."

"You are?"

Her words told him nothing, her voice everything. She didn't like the idea.

"You don't approve?"

"It's your firm, Mark."

"It's our firm."

"Oh, foot. Men make business decisions. If you did, I suppose he'd go right on blithely accepting his room and board here, though."

"I'm not sure of that. The boy has no money to rent a room now. Darling, listen, the Mackays—"

"I know. I know how good the Mackays were to you when you first came to Savannah, and no one is any more grateful than I, but Olin Wheeler and you are as far apart as the poles!"

"How do you know?"

"You not only had your own allowance then, you left no one behind in Philadelphia who needed you as his poor aunt must need him. Mark, have you already offered him a job?"

"No. Of course I haven't."

"You're so generous, it wouldn't surprise me if you had. Oh, I take that back. You are too gracious for your own good sometimes— but I know you wouldn't do it without talking to me. I'm—I'm just uneasy. And I don't know why. Natalie's home, safe and sound. Other hearts are still bleeding all over this town for lost loved ones. Why wouldn't I be giving thanks night and day and never, never say a cross word to anyone—least of all to you?" She moved closer to him in the bed and buried her face in his shoulder. "Darling Mark, give Olin a job if you like. I don't ever want anything to come between us again. And I do know why I'm cross and jumpy. Believe me, it *isn't* only because I'm out of sorts with Natalie for treating you so cruelly. Mark—help me, please—help me!''

Holding her, his mind raced back to Eliza Mackay's question: "Does Caroline feel at all guilty because she couldn't forgive Osmund before he died?" Should he just come right out and ask Caroline if she was hiding her struggle over Kott? Quickly, he put the thought aside. For too many years the name Osmund Kott had come between them. With Natalie treating him as though he were a stranger in the house, he couldn't face anything that might rob him of a second of his closeness with his wife. His own pain that Natalie seemed almost to dislike him would be unbearable if he and Caroline weren't close.

"Do you need to tell me something, dearest?" he asked finally.

Abruptly, she sat up. "No, I need to ask you something." Only one candle burned on the night table, shadowing her face, but he could see that she was not looking at him. "Mark, is it—possible to forgive someone—after he's dead?"

For an instant, he felt afraid. Then, carefully, he said, "I usually ask Miss Eliza questions like that."

Caroline struck the bed with her hand. "Eliza Mackay will die someday, and then where will you turn?"

"I guess I shouldn't have put it that way," he said, trying to pull her back down beside him. "I'm sorry."

"Well, don't be sorry. Just tell me what you think. Mark, I love Eliza Mackay as much as you do, but it isn't fair for us to go on forcing her to answer the—hard questions for us. You're forty-six and I'm forty-three. Isn't it time we learned how to cope with our own lives?"

"Have we done so poorly?"

"Stop it. You're being careful with me the way you've always had to be when Osmund was still alive—and I won't have it! Not once more, Mark, do you hear me?"

Willingly now, she let him pull her back down beside him and both her arms circled his head, holding his face against her breast. To keep him from looking at her? To avoid having to look at him? He couldn't tell, but they had always made it through the strained times over Kott—made it best—when Mark waited for Caroline to, as she said, do all her spouting. He waited now.

Still holding his head against her, she said clearly, slowly, "If you'll help me—I'll try right now to forgive him for all he did to my darling grandfather—*our* grandfather. Even to—killing him!"

"We have no proof of that, dearest—"

"I know, I know. But who but Osmund *could* have thought to set fire to the cottage where poor grandfather spent his—happy, stolen hours with—Mary Cotting? Who else could have known that the old fellow would race into the cottage the instant he saw it burning?" She tensed. "Mark, don't try to reason with me. I'm serious about—wanting to forgive Osmund! No matter what he did. Don't move and don't say a word. I am—forgiving him down deep—*in my heart*—this minute. You're my witness. Keep me reminded. He—did try to save Natalie. Even Virginia and her children, if Natalie's telling us the truth."

As she spoke, Mark could feel her body relax, could feel forgiveness in motion, even though she still clung to him. Then she freed him, and in the dim candlelight, he knew she was looking straight into his eyes.

"I don't want Natalie to be like me, Mark—holding a grudge. And the way she's treating you most of the time these days, I'm afraid she might be. Worse still, she might be like—my grandmother. She's got to let go of her anger toward you for not calling out the state militia to find Burke Latimer. She's mulish—like her mother. I don't want her to be like me. Or—that bitter old woman, Ethel Cameron. I don't want her to hold bitterness in her heart against anyone. Least of all her tender, kind father. I—don't want her to be like—me."

"If I thought our girl would grow up to be like you," he said simply, "I don't think I'd ever agree for her to marry anyone because there wouldn't be a man on earth fine enough for her."

"Foot."

"Is that all you can say?"

"On that subject, yes." She lay back on the pillow. "But I *do* feel as though I've just had a long—wonderful rest. Mark?"

"What, beloved?"

"It *is* possible to forgive someone who's already dead."

"I can tell."

"You can?"

In response, he drew her closer, and for a long, quiet moment they just lay there together.

"Oh my," she said finally. "I just had a horrible thought! Do you suppose Osmund is—in hell?"

"You may not like this, but I think I know what Miss Eliza would say."

"What?"

"She'd remind us of the thief on the cross beside Jesus—the day they killed Him. The thief who simply turned to the Lord in his agony." After a moment, he added, "Aunt Nassie once told me that man's idea of justice is so inferior to God's as to be downright contradictory. We can leave poor old perplexing Osmund in God's hands, can't we?"

He could feel her nod yes. Then she said, "You know? Maybe I can—really help Natalie now. I'm well aware that she's always kept me charmingly at arm's length, and I know she did that because she knew how I felt about her—beloved Kottie. Do you think I'll have to tell her—that I've forgiven him now? I hope you'll say no. I'm afraid you might say yes."

"I don't have a right to answer that—either way."

"But you do! You've suffered through my despising that man all these years. You have a right to say everything. Only don't say anything because I already know that I'm the one who has to decide what to tell her. The child needs her mother now. Natalie's in dreadful turmoil." She sighed. "I suppose it will take her a long time, though, to believe I've forgiven Osmund. He was so perfect in her eyes, he needed no forgiveness from anyone." Then: "Mark, she might even—turn to Olin Wheeler!"

"I doubt that. I believe her when she tells me that she's in love with Latimer. It may be young love, but you were Natalie's age when you knew you loved me. I grant you she needs to confide in someone about Burke. I don't expect it to be Olin Wheeler."

"They're seeing a lot of each other."

"He's the perfect escort. She still thrives on Savannah social life, but I do believe her when she vows she loves Burke Latimer. I—I see him as a kind of protector for her still."

"Protector?"

"She thinks of no one else seriously. Because I won't search for him, she *feels* cold—toward her own father. At night, alone in her bed, she can dream of her love for Burke. Maybe it wipes out some of the horror of all she saw and endured after the explosion. She all but told me that herself before she went into this icy withdrawal. I even think loving Burke helped her face telling William how his—family died."

"You really believe she means to find that young man and marry him, don't you?"

"You and I may not be able to permit it once we know him, but she means to do it."

"In other words, she's just making convenient use of Olin Wheeler in the interim."

"Something like that. Natalie will always need someone to adore her."

"Are you really going to offer Olin a position?"

"I think I am, if, after I question him, he seems capable. I need a bright, ambitious young man right now. The market's picking up so fast after the so-called Van Buren panic. I need someone soon to make business trips for me."

"Do you realize that you leave Savannah less than any prominent merchant in town? For the past three summers, Natalie and I have almost had to bribe you to get you to take us to Newport, away from this ghastly heat."

He laughed. "And this year, because of Natalie's voyage, I got out of leaving altogether. It's too late to go now, I'm relieved to say. Business is too good."

"I'm warning you, though, that if Eliza Anne and W.H. move to the Georgia upcountry, we're going to spend a lot of summers up there. W.H. has already invited us."

"He swears the air along his Etowah River is superior even to Newport. Do you think Eliza Anne will agree to move?"

"If she loves him the way I love you, she'll go whether she likes his Cass County or not. Do you suppose the Stileses might, by some odd quirk of fate—actually meet Burke Latimer up there? There can't be too many white gentlemen in that wilderness now."

"I know only what I've read in the papers, but you're right, there are only a few. Once they learn that all the Indians have been driven out, though, more will go. Godfrey Barnsley is as taken with the place as W.H. is."

"Mark, has Natalie let you read the letter she got from Burke Latimer while she was still in Wilmington?"

Her question so stunned him, he waited to answer. He had seen the letter. Caroline had not. The day he told Natalie as firmly as he knew how that he would not go himself in search of a man who might be in one of three or four states, she had whisked out the already worn letter and handed it to him.

"Mark—answer me. Did you read his letter?"

"Yes. Natalie only let me read it, though, when she was desperate for what she thought would be a trump card with me. She and I—haven't been the same since that day. The child was sure his letter would convince me that he loves her, too, and—"

"Did it?"

He thought a moment. "Yes. I think it did. And he showed some good qualities in what he wrote. Some wisdom. Actually, the letter had the opposite effect from what Natalie hoped for. I was more convinced than ever that seeing each other again should be—Burke Latimer's decision." When she said nothing, Mark added, "She showed me what he wrote, Caroline, because she was trying to get her way with me."

"I believe you. I also know that she's always felt freer with you because I couldn't hide my feelings about Osmund."

"Still—feel rested inside—about him?"

She took a deep breath. "Yes. I also know I have to be patient until Natalie believes I no longer—resent him. And I don't. I really don't! Mark, you're free of it, too, at long last. And you need to be, dearest. I can feel the pain in you when Natalie treats you—as though you were not even related to her." She kissed his forehead and smoothed his hair. "We're going to find our way through this, you watch. Natalie's always been hard for us to—understand, but her mother is going to be a real help to her father from now on."

After a long kiss, Mark whispered, "No more barriers."

"Never again."

TWENTY-ONE

ELIZA ANNE and William Henry Stiles had been gone nearly three weeks when Jonathan Browning ran, in spite of the muggy August heat, from his father's office on Commerce Row to the Mackay house on East Broughton. In his hand, he held the first letter for Miss Eliza from her daughter. After greeting her, he carried two porch rockers out into the yard under an oak, eagerly accepting her invitation to stay for lemonade and a firsthand report from the travelers.

"You're growing up so fast, Jonathan," she said, filling his glass. "I didn't dream you could manage those heavy old chairs so easily."

"I'll be glad to do anything else you need done before I go, too."

"Oh, I know you would. In so many ways, you make me think of your father when he first came to Savannah. He was several years older, but always so glad to be of help—never a complaint that I remember."

"Papa would never turn you down for anything—even as old as he is now, Miss Eliza." His open, earnest face grew abruptly solemn. "How is Mr. William doing today?" When Jonathan saw her frown, he added, "I guess I shouldn't have asked."

"You must always ask me anything you like, son. But there's no change in William. He still spends all his time upstairs in his room—even in this heat. Won't see anyone but his sisters and me."

"That hurts Papa pretty bad, you know."

"I know it does. And I don't understand it at all." Then she made herself smile as she picked up Eliza Anne's letter and broke the seal.

"Now then, you and I are going to be the very first to know about our two sojourners in the upcountry. I do so appreciate your running straight here with this."

"It was Papa's idea. He knew how much you wanted to hear from up there."

Unfolding the long letter, Miss Eliza put on her spectacles and began to read aloud:

> "Cass County, Cherokee,
> 7 September, 1838.

"Dearest Mother and Everyone,

"We are here! The journey was as hard and tiring as W.H. warned, but moving out of lowcountry into this rarefied, bracing air helped. I will tell you of all our adventures on the way— trunks falling off the carriage rack, a squirrel jumping into the water pail, et cetera, when I see you. For now, we are in reasonable comfort at the good log home of a Mr. and Mrs. Brown, who settled here from South Carolina two years ago. Up here, we ride horseback. There is no getting around by any other means. Roads are called roads simply because there is no other name for them. Our city carriage made the journey, but bogged down two miles from the Brown's house. We walked the remaining distance in a steady rain. I looked like a disheveled porcupine when we arrived. W.H. was also soaking wet, but he is so handsome, nothing ever mars his beauty. Even wet, plastered hair becomes him, and the dear man is ecstatic to be here, among these breathtaking hills and in this quite pretty valley through which flows his blessed Etowah River. I have not yet seen the site he likes, but if the sun shines tomorrow, we leave for there at dawn. I hope his city-bred wife is equal to the trip."

Miss Eliza took a sip of lemonade, rearranged a page out of order in the letter and took her time smoothing it over her knee.

"Except when Papa goes on a journey north, I guess I didn't know how much fun getting a letter could be," Jonathan said, a big grin on his face. "I hope she writes something about the Indians."

"Well, this next part seems to be about her concern for William. How like Eliza Anne. Such an exciting trip for her with all those bright prospects of making William Henry so happy, but she's worried about her brother."

"I wouldn't expect you to read the private family things in the letter," the boy offered.

"You're part of our family, Jonathan, but here—I believe she's writing about the Cherokees on this page. Let me see—yes. Listen to this:

"Of course, I'm disappointed that we didn't reach the upcountry before Jack was ordered to Washington City, but oh, Mama, I certainly do understand his heartache over the treatment given the poor Cherokees at the end. Mr. Brown, our host, told us that he had never known a finer, more intelligent, Christian leader of men than Chief John Ross, who is now gone west, of course, with his people for whom he fought in the courts and at Washington City to the last. I actually seem to feel the Indians all around me! How they loved their homeland here, and how I hope that all white folk who may now rush in to settle it (as my beloved W.H. so longs to do) will remember that they walk on land that for eons was truly revered. The site W.H. has his heart set on for our house on a high cliff overlooking the Etowah River was actually the site of a Cherokee settlement. Just think, we may be entrusted to protect the same beauty they loved. I know many hard-nosed Georgians will think me silly for caring this way, but as you know, I am not easily shaken in my ideas. So far, in this tiny white settlement, some six or eight miles from W.H.'s favorite spot, there is little to love, but I confess my heart is stirred just the same. I think so often of Jack's letter to us telling of the Cherokee children waving their little hands as they were driven from their homeland forever."

"Why did the Indians have to go, Miss Eliza?"

"I guess, Jonathan, if we're honest, we must say that both the United States Government and Georgia drove them out so the white folk could have their land to settle on. None of it makes me very proud of either government, but I don't understand much about it. Jack used to tell us in his letters that, in his opinion, the Cherokee chiefs and representatives had a lot more intelligence and dignity than the men in Washington City." She laughed a little. "But then Jack is always a bit hard on any U.S. President and any U.S. Congress. Army men usually are. I can still hear him and his friend, Robert Lee, go after Congress." She refolded the letter. "I think that's about all. Seems that W.H. wanted her to get to bed for their horseback ride to the Etowah River the next day. She'll write again as soon as she's been there, I'm sure."

"It's pretty exciting, isn't it? The idea of maybe building a new house way up there in the wilderness?" He paused. "Miss Eliza?"

"Hm?"

"If this isn't a good idea, just tell me, but—I was wondering if maybe Mr. William might let me go upstairs and visit with him."

She looked at him, her face anxious. "Oh, Jonathan, dear, I just—don't know."

"He won't see Papa, but—maybe he'd like to talk to a twelve-year-old boy—just about things in general. I found a bluebird's nest near our coach house out back this morning. I could tell him about that."

Eliza Mackay stood up, her hands clenched together. "I'd—hate for you to be hurt—if he refuses, son."

"I won't be, honest. I just thought we might try. I'll come back tomorrow if you'd like to think about it some first."

She hugged him. "That might be a good idea. I think you'd do William a world of good, but—"

"I understand. Uh—in the parts of Miss Eliza Anne's letter you didn't read to me, did she happen to say whether or not they'd found any trace of my sister's—of Mr. Burke Latimer?"

"Goodness, you know about that, too, eh?"

"Oh yes, ma'am. I do. Papa's awfully hurt at the way Sister's treating him these days, and I just thought it might help him—and Natalie—if the Stileses had said anything about Mr. Latimer."

"No. Not a word."

"Well, thank you for the lemonade. It was awfully good. I'll see you tomorrow afternoon. I know Papa comes every morning, and if Mr. William would happen to let me visit him, Papa won't mind if he isn't here. Of course, maybe by tomorrow Mr. William will want to see my father."

"I hope so, Jonathan. Oh, how I hope so!"

The next morning, Mark paid his daily visit to the Mackay house, and again was not able to see his old friend William.

"Jonathan and I are going to try something when he comes by this afternoon," Eliza told Mark.

"Is Jonathan coming again today?"

"Yes. How he loves you!"

"I know. And I don't know what I'd do if he didn't. What are you two going to try?"

"I feel I should tell you, for the boy's sake in case it doesn't work. He wants me to ask William if he'll see him—as Jonathan says, just to talk about things in general, such as birds' nests."

"Oh, I hope it works! I'd give almost anything if William would agree to let me in to see him, but for William's own good, I pray he'll see my boy."

Sometime around four o'clock, the minute Eliza Mackay saw Jonathan coming, a bird's nest cradled in both hands, she hurried up to William's room. As always, he answered her knock in a quiet voice and asked her to come in. This time, though, he was not sitting in the big wooden rocker, eyes closed. William was at the small cramped desk writing in the Bible given to Virginia as a girl by her mother, Delia Bryan.

"Son," Eliza said, still in the doorway. "I didn't know you were busy."

William looked up at her, his cheeks wet with tears. "I was—just writing a little," he said.

"Someone very dear wants to—see you just long enough to show you a bluebird's nest he found yesterday."

"Who is it?"

"Jonathan. I think he said he found the nest near their coach house."

"Is he downstairs now?"

"Yes. He's brought the nest, hoping to see you."

"I'd like to see the boy. I got no reason to blame Jonathan for anything."

"Blame? William, are you blaming—someone?"

"Tell him to come on up and bring the nest. I'll know right off if a bluebird built it."

That night, Eliza Mackay and her daughters had supper with the Brownings, an ordeal they had all come to dread, loving Mark as they did. Again, Natalie kept the atmosphere icy by ignoring her father. Seated next to Olin Wheeler at the table, the girl talked mainly of her trip with Olin to Knightsford that afternoon, saying right out that she had no apologies for her swollen eyes. "I've just about cried my heart out, haven't I, Olin? I knew going to Knights-ford without Kottie would be bad—but not as bad as it was. I imagined I saw him everywhere. Still, I've done it. It can't be as hard the next time, can it, Miss Eliza?"

Careful not to meet Mark's miserable eyes, or Caroline's, Eliza said, "I'm sure it won't ever be quite the same up there again, Natalie, but yes, it should get easier for you with every visit."

Talk then veered from one far safer subject to the other—mainly the new Georgia Historical Society in which Mark was so interested. Later, when he stopped Eliza in the back hallway of the Browning home, Mark whispered, "Did William let Jonathan visit him today?"

"Yes. Yes, he did. And he's actually looking forward to Jonathan's coming again tomorrow."

"What do you think they talked about?"

"I don't know, but I could sing, I'm so happy for William!"

William seemed glad to see him when Jonathan came again the next afternoon.

"Come on in," he said, once more at the tiny desk, Virginia's Bible open before him.

"I hope I'm not interrupting any kind of important business," Jonathan said, taking a straight chair nearby.

"Well, to me it's the most important thing in the world," William said, still seated, staring at the blank page on which he'd written only one line in two days. "Not business. Personal."

"I see."

"Maybe I'll have it finished by the time you get back tomorrow. It just seems so hard to do."

"It does?"

"I thought I ought to do it, though. I plan to—write it all out here in her Bible. I don't know exactly why, but it seems like the thing to do. I thought maybe if I wrote out what happened—like a family history, it would—make us still seem like a family."

"You're about as brave as they come, I guess," Jonathan said.

"That's the last thing I am. But let's visit awhile now about other things. Maybe tomorrow I can show you what I've written—or read it aloud. Or maybe you'd read it to me."

Jonathan gave him his bright smile. "Either way. I just promise to be here, that's all."

• • • •

Through the open windows in his office on Commerce Row, Mark could feel an occasional breeze off the river, but the heat deepened his despair over Natalie's continuing detached manner with him. Glancing at his watch, he felt a twinge of impatience with Olin Wheeler, who had a three o'clock appointment to discuss a possible position in the firm. It was twenty past three. Impatience shifted to near resentment. Obviously Olin and Natalie were together somewhere. Young Wheeler saw a lot more of her than her father did these days. Still, Mark needed a bright young man at his factorage. Olin Wheeler needed money. No harm in questioning him. There was no doubt about Wheeler's abilities. He had checked on the Wheeler family in North Carolina. Olin, Sr., had been a respectable citizen in the Wilmington community. The financial squeeze that had gripped the nation for nearly two years had evidently hit the Wheeler plantation harder than most. Of the immediate family, only Olin and his aunt remained. Money sent by Olin regularly from Savannah would undoubtedly help. Having been reared by a spinster aunt, Mark felt unusual interest in Aunt Effie. Olin's attitude, when her name was mentioned, appeared to be merely tolerant. He was the kindest of young men, but Mark could only assume that Aunt Effie was no match for his own Aunt Nassie. Whether Effie Wheeler would dread living alone with only her Negroes and overseer, Mark had not found out.

The polite knock at his door almost startled him. And when Natalie herself walked into his office, he could only sit staring at her.

"Good afternoon, Father," she said in the merely courteous manner she now used with him on every occasion. "I know you're expecting Olin. I hope I'm not too much of a disappointment."

Mark leaped to his feet and went to her, hands out. "You—a disappointment? I'm so pleased you came to see me, I—I almost forgot my manners. Here, my dear, take this chair."

"I'm not staying, sir." Her "sir" was like a knife. "I just felt it only right to tell you that I'm taking your small boat this afternoon. I— I'm going back to Knightsford for another visit. I'll never feel the same about the place without Kottie, but I do have to go. After all, it will be *my* plantation someday."

Her casual manner concerning the day when he and Caroline would be gone left Mark staring at her again—unbelieving. There she stood, his own beautiful daughter, in a new soft blue dimity outfit matching, from her bonnet ribbon to the specially dyed slippers and parasol, addressing him as though he were merely an acquaintance.

Before he could respond, she said quickly, almost pleadingly, a catch in her voice, "I—I didn't mean that to sound the way—I suppose it sounded. Sometimes I—hear myself say—things I don't mean to say at all."

A tiny flicker of hope flared again in Mark's heart. "I know, darling. And of course, you may have the boat. In fact, your mother and I would love to go along. Jonathan too, I'm sure. We haven't been out there either for—"

Her face was a mask again. "I'm going with Olin. Just as soon as he keeps his appointment with you. And—I'm the reason he's late. I had to stop to pick up my slippers."

"I see. Do you think you should wear your new slippers to Knightsford? You'll undoubtedly do some walking out there and—" When she said nothing, Mark asked, "Do you think you'll—ever call me—Papa again?"

From the doorway, she looked at him for a long time. Again he felt the small hope. But what she said was: "I—don't know what I'll—call you. I guess only you know that."

"I love you as much as ever," he said, the hurt embarrassingly obvious in his voice.

"Thank you for the use of your boat."

His session with Olin took no more than fifteen minutes. The list of questions he'd worked out to test the young man's potential skills as a merchant stayed in the top drawer of his desk. Mark was too stricken by Natalie's visit to think straight anyway. As he tried to listen to Olin Wheeler's responses to the few superficial queries put to him, he could think only of completing their business so that his caller would leave him alone with his heartache.

In that moment of sheer confusion and anguish he made Olin Wheeler his assistant at a much higher salary than he'd intended. They shook hands and he watched the confident, exceedingly charming young man leave to join Natalie. The girl had so totally shattered Mark's poise that he hadn't once thought how foolish he'd been to have let her go alone yesterday—and again today—with an almost unknown young man. At Knightsford, no one was in charge now but aging, illiterate Matthew, the driver. Matthew would watch over Natalie if he happened to be anywhere near the house, but old Prince, the butler, was too senile to be wary. In any case, Prince so adored Natalie that she could and would keep him safely wrapped around her finger.

Mark sank back in his chair. What do I expect to happen to her? he asked himself, annoyed. I've just made Olin Wheeler my assistant. Don't I trust him to conduct himself as a gentleman with my daughter?

His clerk, Johnston, entered quietly with the mail picked up at the wharf where a boat from Charleston had docked an hour ago. On top of the bundle was a letter from William Henry Stiles. Mark jerked open the seal and began to read:

Cass County
20 September, 1838

My dear Mark,

Well, the decision is made. Lib, my marvelously perceptive wife, has fallen in love with my Etowah River land as I hoped she would. I closed the deal for the first acreage yesterday. Time does not permit details now, but my cup runneth over. Of course, it will require time to settle my Savannah affairs and time to clear my new land up here, but Lib is smitten with the country—is happily haunted by her own colorful imaginings about the recently departed Cherokees, and all is well so far. I am not certain exactly when we will return to Savannah, hence this brief letter to inform you that I have found no trace whatever of Mr. Burke Latimer. In the past few days I have spoken with most of the white settlers in this part of Cass County. No one has heard of him. This, of course, does not mean that the young man will not ride in any day, if indeed he is headed this way. I have little doubt but that Godfrey Barnsley will also settle here, and such an idea cannot and, I'm sure, will not be limited to merely two gentlemen such as ourselves, who happen to be close friends. Others will come once the financial panic of last year shows itself at an end. The upcountry is rich in farmland, timber and vast amounts of minerals. The railroad will

surely pass this way in but a few years. Be assured that as long
as we are here, I shall be on the lookout for Latimer. Please tell
the enchanting Miss Natalie that I have not, by any means, given
up.

Yrs faithfully,
WILLIAM HENRY STILES

Throughout the remainder of September and into October, except for occasional moments of hope, so little changed in Mark's life that he felt at times as though he were already an old man. He had always thought of old age as being a time of dull heaviness, of intense effort in the daily round, of only small anticipations. So these days had been.

When other letters came from the Stileses, but with no word that they had found any trace of Burke Latimer, Mark's dark mood deepened. In the family drawing room when he gave Natalie the continuing bad news, she received it with quiet courtesy, often her eyes filling with tears—or turning cold.

"Natalie, W.H. really tried—Eliza Anne tried, too. Ask them when they get back next month. They'll both tell you they mentioned Burke's name everywhere they went."

"I'm sure they did. The truth is, though, it was only a casual, social search. How much social life can there be, Father, up there in Burke's wilds?"

"They probably questioned fifty or more people. They've stayed longer than W.H. intended. And they're going back in the spring. Burke might well be there by then, unless he's changed his plans."

"I can assure you he has not changed his plans!"

"Then, honey, can't we—hope for spring?"

For the first time, she looked straight at him. "You really don't understand at all about being young—and in love, do you? Will you just go on being like this—for the rest of your life? An unfeeling stranger?"

His arms aching to embrace her, to convince her that indeed he did remember being young and in love, Mark steadied himself and tried to control his voice. "What else do you expect me to do, darling? Because I do remember what it's like to be in love and young, I can't bring myself to go against Latimer's wishes. It would be—worse than foolish. If he loves you as you believe, he will come here someday. What else can I do now?"

"I want you to send Olin Wheeler up there for no other reason than to look for Burke *now*. Not someday—now."

"Olin?"

"He vows he'll go gladly. You see, I'm sure of *his* love for me."

"I—I've surmised as much, but would you actually send him? Since he does love you?"

"Why not? I'd send him in a minute because I'm only fond of him. I find him pleasant and convenient. I can't send him, though. He works for you. Or had you forgotten? The way you treat him sometimes, I wonder if you do remember that you hired him to fill what you said was an important position."

Mark sighed heavily. They had been standing—facing each other. He sank into a parlor chair. "I did hire Olin. I hired him because I needed him. I need him now, here, in my Savannah office. Natalie, could I ask you one question?"

"Certainly."

"Do you really think that Olin would go up there to search for the man who could—"

"—keep Olin from marrying me? Yes, if he thought it would make me happy, Olin would go. He's a good, sweet person. Olin is—the way I always thought you were."

Trying one more tack with her, Mark said, "Captain Jack Mackay will be back in Savannah soon. He left the Cherokee Agency up there just this past summer. As an officer, he moved around almost constantly. We'll be sure to question him for any and all clues as to where Burke might be." He tried a hopeful smile. "Jack just may have run into him."

"I've already thought of that. But *I'm* asking Jack the questions. Not anyone else."

TWENTY-TWO

LATE IN NOVEMBER, on his first night at home in Savannah, Jack Mackay was determined to do his best to keep the mood at the family table as he'd remembered it—natural and pleasant. This, he realized, would not be easy. For the first time since moving back into their mother's house, his brother William had come downstairs for dinner. Two hours was not a long enough time to have recovered from the shock of seeing William's face so lined, tortured, closed—his shoulders bent as though from great age, his long-legged, once lithe walk halting. Oh, Mama and his sisters had tried, in letters both to the Cherokee Nation before his duty ended there and in Washington City for the past three months, to warn him about William, but they had failed. Jack had seen him last nearly two years ago, as the contented, happy father of little Delia—eagerly hoping for another child. He had fully expected his brother to be full of grief. He had not expected the isolated, trembling older man who only now and then glanced almost unseeing across the table.

"Of course, I'm eager to see Eliza Anne, but she's a Stiles now," Jack said, giving them all his contagious smile. "I think I came at just the right time. I like being able to concentrate these first hours at home only on the Mackays. I've so much to tell each one of you—so many questions to ask." In a characteristic exaggerated gesture, Jack clutched his forehead. "Poor Eliza Anne! I can picture her and W.H. slogging south over those muddy roads after all the rain Georgia's had. When do you expect them?"

"We thought they might beat you," Kate said.

"They'll surely be here by early next week," Sarah offered, passing William the big china bowl of rice, which Jack noticed he refused in silence.

"I'd rather hoped all four Brownings might eat with us," their mother said carefully—too carefully, Jack thought. "After all, they're family too."

"You can bet your bottom dollar I'll be at Mark's office bright and early tomorrow," Jack said, buttering another biscuit and reaching for the preserve compote. "I'm sure little Jonathan's quite grown up by now, and Natalie must be a raving beauty! By the way, why didn't they join us, Mama?"

Around the table, Jack sensed his question was like a silent explosion. He caught his sisters exchanging anxious looks with their mother, who was watching William.

"I—guess it's best that we're all—Mackays, as you said," Katie murmured, trying, Jack thought, to help Mama past a moment that appeared awkward for a reason unknown to him.

"We'll have the Brownings soon," his mother said hesitantly. "A young man named Olin Wheeler's living with them now. I'm sure I told you in a letter, Jack. He brought Natalie back from North Carolina. Olin works for Mark."

"And pines for Natalie," Sarah said.

Abruptly, William stopped toying with his almost untouched food, folded his napkin and stood up. "I can tell you why the Brownings aren't here. Jonathan visits me every day, but I won't see Mark again. Not ever!"

"William," his mother said, as though he were a small boy, "I want you to finish your dinner. Please sit back down."

"No, ma'am. I've had enough. I'm no good at a dinner table anyway." At the door to the front hall, he turned briefly back to Jack. "Good to have you home, brother. Good night, everybody."

"Good to be here," Jack called. "I'll be up to see you after a while."

From the stair, William said, almost as though speaking to himself, "I expect you will be. . . ."

No one said a word until they heard William's bedroom door close upstairs. Then Jack said, "All right, tell me about my brother."

"He's a lot better than he was," their mother explained weakly.

"Just a lot better, Jack. The boy's crushed. I have times when I doubt that even God can heal his poor, ravaged heart."

"But what's this about not seeing Mark? He all but worshiped Mark Browning!"

His mother and sisters looked helplessly at one another, but said nothing.

"You told me this is the first time he's come down for a meal, that Hannah has served him in his room—but surely he hasn't turned against Mark!"

"Your brother hasn't spoken to Mark once since he came back here to live," his mother said. "And please don't ask us why, because we just don't know. We've had to learn to accept a lot of things about William which we can't understand."

"But, Mama, this must be terribly hard on Mark."

His mother took a deep breath. "Only heaven knows how hard. Mark hasn't missed a single day since the tragedy visiting the rest of us. He comes every morning, rain or shine. Every day, he hopes William will agree to see him. It does seem to help Mark some that William enjoys being with Jonathan. And he does. They apparently talk about all sorts of—safe things." She shook her head. "He won't see poor dear Mark, though. If we had even a hint of William's reason, maybe one of us could do something about it, but—"

"We don't have even a tiny hint," Kate interrupted. "We've all tried and tried to imagine why he's turned against Mark, of all people. William always has been stubborn—to me, he's just plain cantankerous, but—"

"—we can't imagine." Sarah finished. "We can't think of a single reason why he's acting this way toward Mark."

Jack stood up. "I'm going to find out—right now. Excuse me?" He smiled somewhat sadly. "And—say a prayer for me?"

He waited in the upstairs hall for William to answer his knock. When he didn't, Jack tried the door. It was unlocked. Tapping softly again as he opened it, he stood motionless at the sight of his tall, thin brother at the familiar cramped little desk the two boys had shared in childhood.

"You're one of the big reasons I made an effort to visit Savannah before I head for my next duty in Florida, William. I haven't seen nearly enough of you yet." When William went on staring at the open Bible on the small desk, without looking up, Jack came on into the room and closed the door carefully behind him. "Are you busy?"

After a further silence, William said, "No. No, I'm not busy. I—just wanted to be sure I had this right."

Moving quickly to his brother's side, Jack asked, "Writing in the family Bible, eh?"

William nodded. "It—was a family Bible. Virginia's mother gave it to her when she was a girl. About thirteen or fourteen, I guess. You see"—he pointed with a trembling finger to the title page—"it says 'The Holy Bible . . . New York, for the American Bible Society, 1823.' She was born in 1810." William looked up with an agony Jack would never forget. "I was already in love with Virginia when she was twelve."

"I know you were. You're the sure one of us, William. The decisive one. I've loved a dozen or more young ladies. You always—only loved her."

"That's the truth." He turned one page. "See? It says here: 'Virginia Sarah Bryan, The gift of her beloved Mother.' Virginia wrote that herself. That's her handwriting."

Struggling to keep his own voice firm and encouraging, Jack said, "Yes, sir, I see it is. A real treasure, isn't it?"

Again William glanced up at him, agony so deep in his eyes, Jack coughed in order to look away for a moment. "I wonder if you'd mind if I read you what I've been working on here. I had young Jonathan read it over to me for about the tenth time. He comes every day to see me. He thought it was all right. But would you mind to listen? Won't take a few minutes."

Pulling up a straight chair, Jack said, "Oh, brother, I'd be—so glad if you would. I'd be honored."

"No need to be honored. I just want to make sure it's all right and —I thought it might be too hard on Mama if I read it to her." William cleared his throat once, twice. And then he began to read in an almost toneless voice: " 'The Bible of My Beloved Wife. We were married at Dr. Screven's house in Savannah on Wednesday the 1st of February, 1835. I was born in Savannah on 27th. March, 1803, and my dear wife, Virginia Sarah Bryan, was born on Wilmington Island on 22nd. September, 1810.' " Clearing his throat again, William went on: " 'Our children: Delia Bryan Mackay was born at my mother's in Savannah on the 27th day of November 1835. William Mackay, Jr., was born also at my mother's on the 3rd day of November, 1837.' "

Jack waited while his brother took out a handkerchief and wiped both eyes.

"Hard to see sometimes," William said. "Now, this is the part I worked on so hard: 'My beloved Wife and children were all lost at sea in the steamer *Pulaski,* on the night of Thursday the 14th of June, 1838, going north to visit my wife's aunt in Maryland. They parted from me, here in Savannah, on the morning of the 13th, leaving me happy for them and certain of meeting—them again—in the fall.' "

When William stopped reading, Jack said, "It's—just right, brother. Seems to me what you've done is—just right."

"That's not all. This—is the part—I struggled over such a long time: 'Father, receive them with Mercy and—call me soon—to follow them. Let—this heavy affliction—turn my heart to Thee.' "

When a choking sob stopped the reading, Jack got up quickly and embraced his brother. "You're—a beautiful human being, William. A—real man. A—Christian man."

"That's not all," William whispered. "This was—the hardest part. I guess I must have sat here for nearly a week, trying—to get myself to be willing to put this next part down and mean it: " *'Thy—will—be done.'* "

Without a word, Jack sat down again. Finally, he said, "I—wish this—had happened to me, William. You're too good. It shouldn't have happened to you. Not ever. I don't think I could endure any of it—without being bitter."

For a time, the brothers sat in silence. Then Jack said, "Except when we lost Father, I never paid much attention in church to saying 'Thy will be done.' I said it then because Mama wanted me to, but to this day, I wonder if I meant it. I haven't stopped missing Papa. Robert Lee still writes to me of how much he goes on grieving for his mother. It—it must be even worse when it's—your wife, your own children."

William was staring at the wall, now almost as though Jack weren't there—as though he sat alone, or with someone unseen. Finally, he whispered, "Thy—will—be done. *Thy will be done!*"

There was nothing to say. Jack waited.

His brother got up at last, held out his thin hand and smiled weakly. Taking William's hand, Jack kept watching the grief-lined face and, as he watched it, he believed the weak smile. Believed it to be the outward sign that—at that moment—some inner struggle had ceased. Oh, plainly the grief remained. William, he thought, will go to his grave with the grief. But even though the painful words had been written several days ago, Jack was somehow sure that—right now—and not one moment earlier, William had managed to *mean,* "Thy will be done."

Once more, Jack embraced him. "I'm downright proud of you."

As though drained of every ounce of strength, William fell across his bed and lay staring up at the ceiling. "Jack?"

"What is it, old brother?"

"Tell Mama—I'm going to—make it now. And—tell her to be sure, when Mark comes to visit her tomorrow morning, to send him right up to see me."

"Man, she may swoon with joy when I tell her that!"

"I know she'll be glad," William said, still staring at the ceiling. "But Mama won't swoon. She doesn't do that."

"How would you like me to run over to Mark's house and tell him right now? I know he'll be here as fast as he can ride over on one of those blooded horses of his. You've always been Mark's favorite."

"I expect he's suffered some. I'll apologize. But—until a minute ago, I—couldn't face seeing him. I can now, but I think I'd rather wait till tomorrow morning. I've shut him out for so long, I guess one more night won't matter."

"Whatever you say. Well, I'll go back downstairs now." At the bed, Jack leaned down and patted his brother's cheek. "No one ever needs to know your reason, William, but—might it help if you told me why you—refused to see Mark all this time?"

"It might. I—blamed him. Blamed him—and every other stockholder in—the *Pulaski,* including W.H., for—what happened."

"And you no longer do?"

"Yes. I still blame all of the stockholders for carelessness. They hired the best chief engineer, and until his off-duty time came and his second engineer took over, things were fine. No one bothered to test the second-shift crew, though." William's face grew taut. "Jack, the boiler blew up—because that second engineer let it go dry—and then added—cold water to hot copper!"

"They know that for certain now?"

William nodded. "There's blame all right. My family—didn't need to die." He took a deep, uneven breath and turned his face to the wall. "But all of a sudden—a while ago here—when I heard myself say 'Thy will be done' the second time, a knot came loose inside somewhere. The first thing I knew, I wanted to see Mark. I—don't despise him anymore."

"He'd never commit such a wrong—if he knew it."

His face still turned to the wall, William murmured, "No, he wouldn't, if he knew it. I'll be mighty glad to see him now."

TWENTY-THREE

TO EVERYONE'S SURPRISE, the Stileses reached Savannah just before noon the next day and finding W.H.'s father, Joseph Stiles, ill, went to his house in the Yamacraw section of town to stay as long as needed. Jack knew of his sister Eliza Anne's fondness for the old gentleman, but since his own time at home was so short, prevailed upon her to go riding with him after dinner in Joseph Stiles's trim one horse buggy.

"I guarantee to lift your spirits, Sister dear," he said, as they drove away from the Stiles mansion. "No guilt for leaving W.H. and his brother alone with their father now. They need to be with him. Come on, give your old brother a smile?"

"And is it all right," she asked, "if I'm as proud as a peacock to be riding beside such a dashing army officer, Captain Jack?"

"I expect you to be proud—and to concentrate only on our being together. After all, I bought this new uniform in New York to impress all of you."

"You're as handsome as Papa and Mark used to be when they strutted out to parade with the Chatham Artillery in the old days. Remember?"

"You bet I do."

"You winced. Why? Because you still miss Papa too?"

"Partly. And because undoubtedly poor old William is facing Mark right now."

Eliza Anne sat bolt upright. "Oh, Jack! Really? Is he seeing Mark this morning?"

Carefully, Jack tried to tell her exactly what happened in William's room the night before, but words seemed to fail him. Before his eyes, he had watched William—not only accept his tragedy, but let his bitterness against Mark drain away too. "I'm not the—spiritual kind," Jack said. "I don't need to tell you that. Still, I know what I saw happen, Sister. Normally, I exaggerate. I'm not exaggerating this. Not any of it."

"I'm so happy for Mark, I could cry. He's suffered over William—and on top of his estrangement from Natalie, it's been almost more than poor Mama could bear. She loves Mark Browning as though he were really our brother."

"Well, at least William and Mark are going to be all right from now on. William needs Mark. But what's this about the redhead, Natalie? With so many people lost on the *Pulaski*, I'd think Mark would be so happy she's—"

"Oh, he is, he is! If he'd lost her, I don't know what might have happened to him, but—well, she'll be pestering you, too, so I might just as well tell you."

Jack listened as Eliza Anne recounted the story of Natalie's romance with a perfect stranger: "On a makeshift raft in the middle of the ocean—alone together for five whole days and nights! Now, her Mr. Burke Latimer has vanished into thin air and she refuses even to address her father as Papa—only 'sir'—because he won't send at least the entire Chatham Artillery to search for him."

"I take it the child fancies herself in love."

"You're way behind, Jack. She means to marry this man the minute she finds him. Natalie's barely turned seventeen, and her parents haven't even laid eyes on the fellow. When she left our house an hour or so ago, W.H. and I felt as though we'd been in court under vicious cross-examination. Natalie vows that her lover—"

Jack laughed. "Her lover?"

"Well, she calls him that. She's an overindulged child still, but—seventeen isn't too young to know. Natalie vows he's going to settle up in Cass County near where W.H. and I will build our house someday. She had us looking for him everywhere! It seems that before the wreck, he'd been scouting land—in Florida, too, I think she said—but he'd decided on the Georgia upcountry."

"How can she be sure of all this when the young man vanished right after they were rescued? How sure, I wonder, is *he?* Maybe she was good company on a raft in the middle of the Atlantic, but—"

"Jack Mackay, none of this is a joking matter! You'll find out firsthand when Natalie corners you with her barrage of questions. She knows you've been stationed in Cherokee country, don't forget. W.H. and I had to tell her in detail about the manner and appearance and age of every person we met while we were up there. It's not likely, because all Burke Latimer's money went overboard in the wreck, but he could have been in the vicinity, according to Natalie, even before W.H. and I went. While you were still there."

"Uh-oh, look!"

"All right. You'll find out right now what I mean. Here she comes!"

Jack slowed the horse and pulled to one side of Congress Street, peering at a gig heading toward them, a young man driving, Natalie standing—waving wildly.

After introducing Jack to Olin Wheeler, Natalie ordered that Miss Lib permit Olin to take her to Joseph Stiles's house since she, Natalie, absolutely had to confer with Jack. As always, when Natalie ordered, the three obeyed, Olin helping Natalie into the seat beside Jack.

"Sure you don't mind if I steal your lovely companion, Mr. Wheeler?" Jack asked with mock gallantry.

"Of course I mind," Olin Wheeler said pleasantly. "But I also want her to be happy—at whatever cost to me." He bowed to Natalie. "Good day, beautiful lady. I'll see you at dinner." To Jack, he said, "Your charming sister will be in good hands, Captain."

Before Jack could say a word and as though the two of them had been seeing each other regularly over the past two years, Natalie began: "All right, Jack, I want you to start thinking."

"Don't you want to take a buggy ride with me?" he teased.

She tossed her hand. "I don't mind. Drive or stay right here. What matters is that you start thinking back. Listen carefully and then think back to when you were still stationed in the Cherokee Nation."

Starting the horse, Jack asked, "How far back am I being ordered to remember?"

"Don't be condescending. Think back to early July." And then, he began to listen, to be less and less amused, as she recounted the thrill and the anguish of her experience on the raft with Burke

Latimer. From her reticule, she drew the now worn and tattered letter that Burke had written and read it aloud—every word. When she had finished, she leaned toward him. "What do you think, Jack? You do agree that he loves me, don't you? My aging father just does not understand. I read the letter to him, too, but he goes right on being a stubborn old fogy about it. You're younger than my father. You're a man of the world. I know you can tell that Burke loves me!"

"I thought you were asking my opinion."

"I am."

"Yes, I'd say he does. But I'd also say he's a man with a mind of his own, and that until he's ready to see you again, even your powerful, persuasive father couldn't budge him."

She fell back against the seat, disgusted, Jack was sure. "I've annoyed you," he said.

"You certainly have. You sound just like my father."

"I'm proud if I do."

Sitting upright again, she repeated. "Think back, please! Think back and picture a tall, wide-shouldered, marvelously built man of twenty-four—maybe twenty-five by now. Curly golden hair, no frills, no blathery gentlemanly speeches—just sure and strong-minded. No. *Bull-headed.* But dear, brave, gently rough . . . manly, intelligent, tender, unafraid . . ."

"Does he spring, perhaps, from Mount Olympus?"

Jack fully expected her to hit him, as she'd done dozens of times in the old days. She didn't. Instead, she looked straight into his eyes, her own abruptly filled with tears. "Jack, I love Burke Latimer. I—grew up with him—when we both almost died. If you don't take me seriously and try to help, I'm going to run away with Olin Wheeler! He cares about me. Olin cares about me enough to help me find the —only man I'll ever love."

Slipping the reins into his left hand, Jack took one of hers. "Forgive me, darling. What does your Burke Latimer do for a living?"

"He's an expert carpenter and cabinet maker."

"You're in love with a man who works with his hands?" Beyond a still somewhat tearful, but defiant look, she didn't honor that with an answer, so Jack went on a bit more seriously. "Truthfully, there were a few rather decent white men settled there when I left, but precious few. It was the Cherokee's land for hundreds of years. A white man had to be married to a Cherokee woman in order to settle there before the removal."

He watched the defiance change abruptly to a look of sorrow—or at least sympathy. "Oh, Jack—you had to be one of the military who drove the Cherokees out, didn't you? How could you bear that?"

"A soldier obeys orders. I confess, at night I can still see some of those tragic faces. Especially the children. Natalie, we herded them into stockades like cattle. And how they loved their land! I wonder often where some of them are now—right now, today. A few are still hiding in the hills, I suppose. The elderly begged to be left behind to die in peace beside the little waterfalls and mountain caves. General Winfield Scott did allow some to stay. Georgia was so determined, though, to get them all out, the federal government had no choice, beyond going to war with our home state. I'm not proud, I can tell you, of the brutality of some of the Georgia Guard."

Up on the edge of the buggy seat now, she exclaimed, "Burke feels about the Cherokees exactly the way you do, Jack! I never gave Indians much thought, but he talked a lot about how, since the Georgians were forcing them off their land, he meant to move there —to love and protect and care for the land the way they did." She was quiet a moment. "Burke isn't like most Savannah men. I honestly don't think he'd like it here. He's—not purse-proud like Savannahians." Then: "Jack, if the Cherokees aren't all gone yet, might you have to go back up there?"

"No, I'm afraid not. They are all—officially gone. White men now have free access to their land, which is what they wanted. Any stray Cherokees who might have stayed back are in hiding or—passing as Georgians." He laughed a little. "I wish I might be ordered back up there. I'd choose that mountain air anytime over muggy, buggy Florida where I'm headed. But orders are orders."

He could tell she was not really listening. "I'm sorry for the Cherokees now," she said, "but since they're mostly gone, don't you think a man good with his hands could make a lot of money in their country? Uncle W.H. and Mr. Barnsley will need new houses. They can't be the only white men going. Burke doesn't want a lot of money—just enough to buy a piece of land and build a house. You do think he must be up there somewhere, don't you?"

"He could be. How much work he'd be getting I don't know. My dear girl, that's wild country. Most of the buildings are now empty

Indian log cabins—huts, some of them. Oh, I saw a few fairly good cottages belonging to white men. I stopped once in one built six or seven years ago by a white fellow married to a Cherokee, but I was as comfortable as a man can be up there at Cherokee Chief John Ross's two-storied log house. Logs are the style," he chuckled, "except for one mansion owned by Chief Joseph Vann, the wealthy, hard-drinking quarter-breed son of old James Vann, a Scot who was shot to death in a tavern brawl. The old man did finance the Moravian school for young Cherokees, though, and his son carried it on. That is, until he made the mistake of hiring a white man to run his vast plantation."

"What's wrong with that?"

"Nothing, except that secretly, in order to rid themselves of all Cherokees, the Georgia legislature had passed a law forbidding a white man to work for an Indian. Vann—Rich Joe Vann, as they called him—innocently broke that law and was forced to leave one of the most stately and magnificent federal-style mansions I've ever seen. The brutish Georgia Guardsmen fought one day with a white boarder at the Vann house, who also claimed the property. While they battled it out, the Vann family huddled together in the house. Finally, the Guard built a fire on Vann's handsome stairway in the front hall and smoked the boarder out. I've seen the burned scars on the stair landing."

"Well, whatever happened to the Vann family?"

"Turned out of their home on a cold March day, they somehow made their way to a farm Rich Joe owned in Tennessee. They will undoubtedly end up out west with the other Cherokees now."

"It—is a terrible part of Georgia, isn't it?"

"Yes. It's frontier country, honey. Does it scare you?"

"Of course it does! But I could love it with Burke. By now, he and I aren't afraid of anything if we're together."

Jack studied her intent face. "I believe you mean that."

"Oh, Jack, how am I going to find him?"

"You can't run away with Wheeler. That much I know."

"Why not? No one else will help me."

"It wouldn't look right for two unmarried people like you and Wheeler to—"

She turned in the buggy to glare at him. "Have you ever been near death, Jack Mackay?"

"I've had some—risky times up there, but no, I guess not. Not as near death as you were."

"As Burke and I were. If you had been, you wouldn't worry much about how anything *looks*. You'd just be grabbing at—all life can give you."

"Do you talk this way to your father?"

"I don't talk to him because he refuses to help me."

"You don't think he may be right to give Latimer time to work this out his own way?"

"No."

"I see. Could I say one more thing about conditions in north Georgia?"

"Yes, yes! I'm dying to know all about it."

"In even a year or two, your young man might do exceedingly well in that area. Once it's known the Indians are really gone, all sorts of white men will pour into the old Cherokee Nation. You know W.H. and Mr. Barnsley are not going to want mere cottages. They'll want mansions. Men will bring their families from coastal Georgia, from the Carolinas, from Virginia. Burke won't be able to keep up with the offers. This could well happen within two years, Natalie."

"That's a lifetime!"

"It seems that way only because you're barely seventeen."

"I hate being reminded of that."

"Honey, I've known your father since I was a little boy. He wants only what is best for you." She made a scoffing sound. "He does, just the same. Even though I'm sure neither of your parents dreamed you'd not marry well here in town—live here, raise your children here—I am absolutely certain that if Latimer is a gentleman from a good family and can take the kind of care of you that—"

"Let me out!"

"What?"

"Let me out. Stop the buggy and let me out this minute!"

Jack laid a restraining hand on her, but when he saw she meant it, pulled to one side of Bull Street.

Glaring up at him from the deep sand into which she'd jumped without his help, Natalie shouted: "Love has nothing whatever to do with 'good family.' Burke is Burke and that's all I care. I expected more of you, Jack Mackay. I'm sorry to have bothered you. Good day."

"The Stileses are going back up there in the spring," Jack called after her as she cut along the street. "Can't you at least wait till spring? They could easily meet up with him by then. . . ."

As best she could in her dress slippers, Natalie hurried along Bull toward Commerce Row on Bay. This time, she was not going to see her father. Only one choice remained—Olin Wheeler's offer to take her or to go himself to find Burke in north Georgia.

Hearing voices inside Olin's office, she waited to knock, listening instead, staring at the oak panel of the closed door. The voices were unmistakably Olin's and that of Kottie's friend, Little Domer. There was no mistaking Little Domer's voice—unfinished, like his dwarfed, lopsided body. Domer must be pretty old, she thought. Lots older than her father. She'd seen him around the city all her life. Kottie had told her once that he'd known Domer since they both came out of Bethesda Orphanage, where he and poor Kottie had grown up. Like Kottie, Domer had no family that Natalie had ever heard of. He just did odd jobs and limped and twisted along the streets and lived in a shack on the river, but she liked him because he almost worshiped Kottie. And Kottie trusted him. He'd told her so many times.

Both men on the other side of the closed door were talking in such low voices, she had trouble catching what they were saying. Funny, she thought, to be standing here like this. Why don't I just go on in? They're both my friends.

Then she heard Olin raise his voice in amazement: "And you've had Miss Natalie's money in your possession all this time, Domer?"

She wondered *what money* Olin was calling hers. And how did he know Domer well enough to call him Domer? Most people did, of course, and Natalie hadn't even wondered whether Domer was Little Domer's first or last name.

"Where did you keep such a huge amount of money?" Olin asked.

"I kep' it for her safe, sir, in my shack on the river."

"And why have you brought it to town only today? Miss Natalie's been home more than five months."

"Just had t'be certain Osmund Kott was really dead. Kept hopin' he'd turn up one day."

Natalie gasped. Kottie had left her his money! Suddenly she felt as though her heart might break with love for him. Then a sickening wave of loneliness swept over her. She had never felt so lonely.

"How much did you say you have there in that wooden box?" Olin asked.

"Pert near thirty-seven thousand dollars. Thirty-six thousand six hunnert dollars an' forty-nine cents. I counted las' night."

"Why are you telling me about this? Why not her father?"

"He ain't chere, that's why."

"Oh, I suppose he's paying his slavish daily visit to the Mackay house."

What did Olin mean—*slavish?* Didn't Papa have a right to visit Miss Eliza and William anytime he wanted to? Natalie pressed her ear to the door because Olin had begun to speak in a peculiarly quiet voice—almost a whisper. All she could make out were the words "Leave the box here with me." And, "Don't worry, Domer, you've done exactly the right thing to bring it to me. I'll see that both Mr. Browning and Natalie understand the whole thing."

Quickly Natalie moved back a few steps down the hall to make it appear, should Olin open the door, that she was just arriving. The door opened, but it was not Olin. Crooked, crippled Little Domer ducked out into the hallway and, in his usual manner, beamed upon her with an almost toothless smile and backed toward the outside door, his face glowing, pleased and proud to be on such an important mission.

"Little Domer, what are you doing here?" she asked. His only response, as he moved toward the building's entrance, was his happy, wheezing laugh.

Natalie knocked sharply at Olin's door, opened it without waiting and went in. She was both angry and confused. For a moment, she and Olin stood there looking at each other.

Then he rushed to greet her. "What a surprise to see you! I thought I'd have to wait for dinner. Sit down, sit down."

"What was Little Domer doing here?"

"Please sit down," he said warmly, as he whisked the wooden crate off and under his desk and, as an afterthought, began to rearrange some papers neatly on the desk. "Excuse my office," he said. "I've been hard at work."

"What was Domer doing here?"

Holding a chair which she ignored, Olin said casually, "Oh, I don't know exactly what he wanted." He tapped his own head. "Isn't the man a bit touched?"

"He's a cripple, that's all. I'm waiting, Olin. I want to know why he was here!" For some reason she suspected Olin, but hadn't yet figured out why. Kottie had left her over thirty thousand dollars. Olin should have told her right off.

"I gather he meant to see your father, actually. Mr. Browning, of course, is paying his daily homage to the Mackays."

"Papa is like a member of the Mackay family! They were his only family long before he married my mother."

Olin, still standing, laughed pleasantly. "I swear you sound almost protective of your father. That's the first time I've heard you say anything in his defense in weeks."

For an instant her head spun so, she steadied herself on the corner of Olin's desk. He was acting just the opposite of the way he should be after what she had just overheard! He was saying nothing that he should be saying! She had run to him as a last resort, as the only person who loved her unselfishly enough to help her find Burke—even if they had to run away to do it. All she could think to say was, "Why did Domer want to see my father?"

"Oh, something about a job. Nothing important. Certainly nothing to bother your beautiful young head about."

"I'm sick of being called beautiful and I'm sick of being called young and I demand that you tell me what's in that box you hid under your desk!"

As though he'd just remembered it, Olin glanced at the floor beneath his desk. "I'm not sure what's in the box. One of the clerks brought it up from the dock. Something about not having a bill of lading and—"

"You're lying! Your mouth curls on the left side when you lie."

He moved toward her. "Natalie, I'm the one person who loves you enough to—"

"To lie! Domer brought that box and what's in it is for *me*. You are lying to me, Olin and—I don't think I can bear that."

In one graceful motion, he took her in his arms. When she jerked away, he backed up, both hands raised as though she held a gun on him. Then he smiled the wholesome smile she'd counted on ever since he'd brought her home. "I can see you're not going to let me —carry out the surprise I had planned for you."

"What surprise?"

"I beg you to give me that small pleasure at least," he said earnestly. "I know you don't love me in the way I love you, Natalie, but can't you—because I still mean to help you find Latimer—give me just this one small pleasure? I've planned a—special way of presenting a gift for you. And, yes, it is in that box. But can't you grant me that small—"

Without waiting for him to finish, Natalie rushed from the room, ran out of the building and up onto Bay Street. For a terrible moment, she stopped, feeling more trapped than when she and Burke had been trapped in the middle of those ugly waves on that flimsy settee. Home was the last place she could go. No one there would understand. Jack Mackay had called her young and now Olin was—no longer Olin. There was only one person left. Running again, she headed toward Vale Royal, the Joseph Stiles house at Yamacraw, where she knew Miss Lib was visiting. She would tell her exactly what happened while she eavesdropped and then faced Olin with his lie.

"Oh, Papa!" she gasped aloud, pushing herself to keep running. "Papa, where are you?" Her lungs felt as though they would burst, but she made herself run all the way.

TWENTY-FOUR

IN THE wide front hall of Vale Royal, Joseph Stiles's big house at the edge of town, Natalie pushed past the ancient butler, who tried vainly to tell her that something was wrong in the family.

"Something's wrong for me, too, Samson," she said, heading for the parlor. "Miss Lib won't mind if I go on in. She cares about me—at least, I think she does. And I need to talk to her."

At the parlor double doors, Natalie stopped. Eliza Anne, Uncle W.H. and his brother, Benjamin Stiles, sat silently staring at the carpet. When they saw her, the two men got up, but for a long, awkward moment, no one spoke or even smiled a greeting.

"What is it, Natalie?" Miss Lib asked, almost irritably. "Is something the matter?"

Looking from one to the other, Natalie murmured, "Yes, Miss Lib. Oh, I can see I've done a terrible thing rushing in here like this—but yes. Something is very wrong."

"Here too, Miss Natalie," Benjamin Stiles said sadly. "Our father is dying upstairs."

"Mister Joseph—is dying?"

"That's right, my dear." Uncle W.H. went to her. "Won't you sit down? It's just a matter of time, the doctor says. We've—told him good-bye. Our stepmother is sitting with him, but he's aware of nothing here now. We're all just waiting."

Feeling out of place, ashamed of her rudeness, Natalie took a step back toward the door. "I'm sorry. Truly I am. What an awful thing

I've done! I—I just felt I'd—die, too, if I couldn't talk to you for a few minutes, Miss Lib. All of you please forgive me."

She saw the loving look Miss Lib gave her husband when she asked, "You won't mind, will you, dear, if I step into the hall with Natalie? I won't be long."

In his familiar, warm voice, now tinged with sadness, Uncle W.H. said, "By all means, Lib. Take your time." Bowing to Natalie, he added, "Regards to your parents, my dear."

In the high-ceilinged entrance hall, Miss Lib didn't wait for Natalie to explain. "What on earth is wrong, child? You're so out of breath and you look like a frightened rabbit!"

"I am frightened. You know I wouldn't come barging in like this if I'd known Mr. Stiles was so sick."

"Get to the point, Natalie. You had no way of knowing how ill he is."

Feeling more alone now than ever—and even more embarrassed at what she'd done, Natalie blurted, "Miss Lib—it's getting harder every day!"

"Being away from Burke? Not knowing where he is?"

"Yes, and except for you—I'm so alone."

Miss Lib took her hand. "I ache for you, I really do, but you've put us all in a dreadful predicament. All of us who love you so dearly. Especially your father. No one wants to help you more than your wonderful father."

Lips trembling, Natalie said, "I'll go now."

"No, wait. I really can't think what your dear father might do for you if you'd begin to treat him in a civil manner again. If you'd treat him with just a hint of the old warmth, he'd move heaven and earth to find a way to help. He's frightened of *you* now! Don't give me that look—he is. Grown-ups get scared, too." When Natalie turned toward the door, Miss Lib grabbed her arm. "I know how I sound to your young ears, but I intend to go right on loving you no matter how rash you are. I will love you no matter how unreasonable you are with your father. With any of us. I honestly don't know how you bear not knowing where Burke is. I *don't* think that what you feel for him is merely young love to be scoffed at. W.H. and I will be going back to Cass County in the spring if he can settle up his father's estate by then. Can't you help me through this sad day, Natalie, by trying just a grain of common sense about this whole thing?"

Fighting tears, Natalie asked, "You—need me? You want me to—*help* you?"

"Yes, yes. We all need you to be our friend. Just because it is the adult's unhappy lot to discipline and suggest doesn't mean adults don't need friends. Your father is even needier than W.H. today. Elderly people do die. But because of you, your father lives daily with a sorrow in his heart far worse than death!"

Natalie stood looking for a long time at the worn, elegant oriental carpet. Finally she said, "Miss Lib, will you tell me once more that you *do* believe my love for Burke is—real and forever?"

"I do believe it. Since you let me read the letter he wrote you, I also think he deserves a *woman*, not an unreasonable child lacking the patience to understand what it is he's trying to do before he comes here to see you again."

The red-gold eyebrows pulled together sharply. "I'll think about what you've said. I promise. If I can figure out a way *to* think about it. Nothing makes much sense to me." Her hand on the big brass doorknob, she added in her most well-bred manner, "I'm sure my parents would send their condolences in your time of sorrow. I'm—sorry too."

"Thank you. But one question before you go. If you don't know how to love your father after all these years, how can you be sure you will really know how to love Burke day in and day out, when things might not be especially romantic or to your liking?"

Miss Lib had said one thing too much. On the steps outside the big front door, Natalie said—far more sharply than she intended, "Miss Lib, things weren't especially romantic or to my liking on that makeshift raft!"

The sound of the heavy door closing behind her made her feel lonelier than ever. Head down, she hurried along the dusty street, barely damp from a light rain that had fallen while she was in the Stiles house. Then, feeling too lost and weak to keep walking, she crumpled—good dress and all—on a fallen tree in the vacant lot near the corner. She had run to Miss Lib meaning to pour out the story of Olin's troubling behavior over the money Kottie had left her. Somehow she had not done it and it wasn't only because Uncle W.H.'s father was dying. Miss Lib had insisted upon lecturing her about the way she had been treating her father, and for some reason, Papa was all she could think about now. With all her heart, she longed for a way to go back to him. Miss Lib might really understand how she loved Burke, and that had helped. There would, if she put her mind to it, be a way to handle Olin so that he would keep his promise to go with her to hunt for Burke. But even if Olin hadn't been so peculiar about Kottie's money, even if he was really trying to plan a romantic way to surprise her with it, she now admitted that only Papa could truly help. She was suddenly appalled that she and Olin had been stupid enough to believe they could manage to sneak away together. Nothing made sense at this moment but finding a way to get Papa to begin to act like himself again.

Walking now toward home, she remembered that it was Saturday, that her family and Olin were taking Sunday dinner at the Mackay house tomorrow. Jerkily, her thoughts began to assemble themselves. She had run out of Olin's office in a state of panic and fury, but she'd always been able to handle Olin. The two of them were attending a piano concert tonight. She'd be on her best behavior, act as though the scene in his office hadn't even taken place. Bide her time. Wait for Olin to make the next move. He either had an innocent, if silly plan to surprise her, or he was a rat under all those wholesome smiles and declarations of undying love. Did he really mean to give her Kottie's money? There would be time to think that through. None of it mattered in the long run anyway, if she could find a face-saving way to make up with Papa. Papa could help find Burke if he only would. And maybe she *had* frightened him.

Even though the sky was darkening again and it looked like more rain might fall, she walked slowly, giving herself plenty of time to try out her own feelings about changing her attitude toward Papa. There would be no need to do anything yet today. She would go right on calling him "sir" at supper. She would be vague and indefinite with Olin at the concert tonight. A way to discover what Olin was really up to would come to her.

Except to start her thinking still more about Papa, Miss Lib hadn't really helped much, but she *did* understand about the way she loved Burke. "Miss Lib doesn't really understand *me*," she said aloud as she quickened her steps toward home, "but she seems to grasp how I love Burke—at least a little."

• • •

Caroline was waiting in the small drawing room when Mark let himself into their Reynolds Square house that night. As always, she ran to meet him.

"Darling, you look exhausted. Is everyone holding up well at the Stileses'? I understand the old man died easily, but I'm sure you were a great comfort, especially to Eliza Anne. She's depended on you for such a long time. It must have meant a lot that you went by after your meeting."

Sighing heavily, he hung up his hat and sprawled on the parlor sofa. "Sit here beside me, please, ma'am?"

"I have no intention of doing otherwise. Now, put your head in my lap."

He sighed again. "Better. Much better. To answer your question, yes. Everyone is all right at Vale Royal. Lively old Joseph Stiles seemed to fool everyone, though, by actually dying. Such a strong-bodied, strong-willed old man. Do you know that W.H. told us tonight when we were reminiscing about his father that he, William Henry, had once asked the present Mrs. Joseph Stiles to marry him? Of course she refused because she was already promised to his father." Mark laughed a little. "The old fellow was a magnificent man. He had to be to have won a beautiful young lady such as Margaret Vernon Adams—ahead of his own handsome son."

"I never knew any of that! Tell me—did Eliza Anne hear W.H. tell that story?"

Mark laughed more easily now. "No, there were only gentlemen present. W.H., his brother Benjamin, Jack Mackay, Mr. Smets, Mr. Tefft, William Thorne Williams. Eliza Anne knows it, though. W.H. vows he uses the story when she needs to be kept in line."

"Do you have any idea how wonderful it is to hear you laugh?" Immediately she saw his eyes cloud over. "Don't, Mark—don't get that look again, please."

"Is—Natalie in her room?"

"No, she's out with Olin. At the piano concert."

"That's right. Smets and Tefft and Williams were going. We held only an abbreviated meeting on the Historical Society charter because of that concert. Your husband's memory is short these days."

Working as he'd been doing with Savannah's "literary men," as they jokingly called themselves, had undoubtedly helped Mark endure the misery Natalie was causing him. The idea of forming the

Georgia Historical Society had seemed to spark a kind of interest Caroline hadn't seen in her husband since their daughter's wretched pout over Burke Latimer began. His longtime friendship with William Thorne Williams deepened as they worked night after night with the other founders, drawing up the charter and the by-laws of the new society. Mark, she knew, had always admired A. A. Smets, the energetic Frenchman who spoke English with such a delightful accent and who was not only an astute businessman, but collector of one of the country's most important libraries. Alexander Smets adored Natalie, and she treated him with the affection and charm Mark longed for from her, no matter how removed it was from their old closeness. She seemed to go out of her way to beguile Mr. I. K. Tefft, too. When Caroline invited members of the new society to their home, Natalie plied Tefft with flattering questions about his superb collection of autographs and documents on Colonial and Revolutionary Georgia. From Smets, Williams, Tefft, William Stevens, Robert M. Charlton, the lawyer-poet son of the late T. U. P. Charlton, Mark seemed to draw a measure of strength as well as stimulation. Caroline was thankful for that, but she'd never seen him so weary, the dear, sensitive face so drawn and lined, the deep eyes so haunted.

"I'm proud of your work with the new Society," she said after a time, "and I know how important it is to preserve that valuable store of books and documents, but—are you giving more time than you need to, darling? I can't bear your tiredness."

He looked up at her. "Those gentlemen have kept me going through the past weeks. Those gentlemen and—William. William does help so much."

"What does he do—or say that helps you?"

Mark closed his eyes. "He listens. Or we just sit there in his room understanding each other. His little Delia can't grow up to—despise him. But somehow he understands. I can say anything to William. I can tell him anything without feeling unmanly or—weak. I can even—shed tears."

"Mark, do the men in the Society know that you and Natalie are not on good terms?"

When his eyes flew open, she could see in them only anger. He pushed her away and jumped to his feet. "What a stupid question!

Do you think for a minute I'd admit to any of those men that I'm—helpless with my own daughter?''

When he grabbed a sofa pillow and slammed it across the room, Caroline waited, trying to think what to say. His self-control had always been so reliable that after such an uncharacteristic outburst she dared do nothing but wait, hoping he would speak first. He simply stood, his back to her, both slender hands making and unmaking fists, fighting himself—as she fought once more against actually *disliking* their daughter for what she was doing to him.

Finally, she said, "If Natalie didn't love you more than anyone on earth, she wouldn't be so angry with you for not launching a foolish search for Burke Latimer. You're being wisely firm with her—maybe for the first time, Mark. You're proving your love for her. Not only do we know nothing whatever about this young man, we dare not allow Natalie to risk her own happiness by chasing after him when he so plainly means to decide his own future himself." Her voice wavered. "Oh, Mark, it's almost as though we're suffering because of a—ghost. Or a figment of Natalie's imagination."

A dog barked outside in the Square. A lone rider galloped by—the hoofbeats faded. Mark had said nothing. Then, still not facing her, he spoke passionately. "I can't stand any more of it, Caroline. I —*can't*. W.H.'s father's estate is so large, the assets and properties so diverse, as executor, I don't see W.H. being free to go back to Cass County for a long time. Surely not by spring. I've begged Natalie to be patient until then. Now I'm sure they won't be going. I've—got to do something else." He turned so that Caroline could see tears streaming down his face. "I still don't see forcing Latimer into something he's not ready for—and God knows I don't want her to marry him or anybody yet. But I can't stand any more of this! I've —got to do something. I can't live with this conviction that—I've failed Natalie."

"You could never fail her."

"Oh yes, I could. I have. Maybe we both have—you far less than I. In letting her have everything her heart desires, I've ruined her for facing life's—disappointments, heartbreaks. You've tried and I've opposed you—you, whom I love so much—I've resisted almost at every turn. I've opposed you in favor of our child."

"Mark, dearest . . ."

"Let me finish. There's another way we both may have—failed

her. You and I were not on that ship—when it exploded. I'm sure I've failed to grasp how much the whole horrifying tragedy might have changed her." He stretched both hands in a helpless gesture. "Caroline, I've *never* been a good father to our daughter. Not only have I given in to her, I see now that I really *haven't* understood until the past day or so what—that ghastly experience might have done to her." He sat down again, face buried in his hands. "You're right, I have given too much time to the Society. More than was needed, I know. But my self-loathing drove me to the flattering escape of those learned gentlemen. Is still driving me to spend too much time on it all, to be picky and labored in my contributions to the charter— what little those contributions might be worth. In fact, Tefft and Williams are beginning to tease me about what an old woman I've become. I don't want the charter work to end. I'd be lost without that constant escape into their company. My self-loathing over Natalie has driven me to those fine, erudite gentlemen for selfish reasons."

"Foot, Mark. Just plain—foot."

"Don't—you belittle me, too!"

Trusting no more careless words, Caroline took him in her arms and held him until he pulled away. Finally, she said, "I love you, Mark Browning. I've never loved you more than—right now."

His attempt at a smile tore at her heart. "You love me—even when I'm being—so dreary?"

"You've loved me through endless dreary times. And yes, I love you when you're dreary. I don't need to tell you I wasn't belittling. You know that."

He nodded yes.

"And I'm as glad as you are that you've had the charter work to— occupy you. The men may tease, but they value you. Few have given as much time, and no one as much financial help."

"I needed the work—the men, more than they needed me. They preserved what little self-respect I have left."

"I won't hear you talk like that!"

"Then stop your ears."

"You sound like Natalie."

"I do? Good. Because I'm trying, Caroline, with all my mind and heart—to understand her. You've been patient with me—God knows William has listened by the hour to my self-pitying tirades about how that girl abuses her poor adoring father. I'm sick of pitying myself. The time has come for me to—*do* something about Natalie and Burke Latimer."

"But, Mark—what?"

"I think William could be my solution. Tomorrow, when we take Sunday dinner with the Mackays, I'm going to beg William to make the trip to the upcountry for me. To go for one reason only—to find Burke if he's there. William no longer blames me for what happened. We're closer than ever. The trip might be good for him. *If* I can get him to leave his mother's house."

She looked at him for a long time. "Mark, why haven't we thought of William before? I've been *so worried* that Natalie might really talk Olin Wheeler into going to find Burke." She paused. "Am I wrong to—like Olin less and less?"

"Olin Wheeler is not in question." Mark was firm now, in charge, without self-pity or the bitterness that so frightened her. "Wheeler's doing a fine job for me at the office, but we need to concentrate on William. He's the right one to go, and I'm going to give it a try—tomorrow."

TWENTY-FIVE

IT WAS AFTER ELEVEN that night when Olin Wheeler let himself into the Browning Company on Commerce Row and walked boldly along the center hall to his own office at the rear of the building. A window was open, and in the dark, he gave sharp attention to the now familiar smells of the waterfront—river stench, the pleasant aroma from a leaking keg of rum, the dry, sweet pungency of molasses spilled onto the hot planks of the wharf that day during a measuring process. In every scent, Olin smelled money. Living as a guest at the Browning home had left him with almost his whole generous salary. He'd performed well for Mark Browning, but two hundred dollars a month was a ridiculously high figure.

He lit one candle, enough light to count by, and smiled. His goal was being reached far faster than he'd hoped when, back in Wilmington, before he and Natalie left, his plan had begun to form. Squiring Natalie, proclaiming undying love for her had been only enjoyable. Even listening to her almost incessant talk of Burke Latimer amused him. Her blind infatuation with Latimer in itself was part of Olin's guarantee that once he'd reached his money goal, he'd be free to go on his own way with no obligation to Natalie.

Hauling the small wooden crate from under his desk, he could not stifle a short laugh. Good old Kottie had managed remarkably to speed up his plans. His aim was to accumulate a stake of thirty-five thousand dollars. He had already won nearly seven thousand at the race track and at Savannah's gentlemanly gaming tables. With no room and board to pay, by the start of the new year, 1839, he would have nearly another thousand in salary. The crate contained, Little Domer had declared, almost forty thousand. Olin could afford to be generous with Natalie when he executed his new scheme tomorrow in the presence of the Brownings and Mackays at Sunday dinner on Broughton Street.

Earlier this evening, before he left the office, he'd hidden a claw hammer and a chisel in his bottom desk drawer, along with a handful of nails for refastening the wooden box.

Now, in the silent building, the crooked lid gave a loud *sk-r-e-e-k* as he pried it open to expose a white oilcoth bundle tied around and around with strong cord. With his pocket knife, Olin cut the cord and lifted the bundle onto his desk. When the oilcloth was removed, he stood looking at more money than he'd ever seen at once in his entire life—packets and packets of perfectly stacked bank notes— each tied neatly with what appeared to be fishing line. For a time, he stared at the pleasurable sight, his thin fingers shaking with excitement, passing up and down the stacks, caressing the packets of fives, tens, twenties . . . for him a sensuous gratification.

He intended, first of all, to buy shares in the Central Railroad and Banking Company. Once the rail lines were completed to Macon— with Savannah's cotton and rice shipments moving to the interior of the state—dividends would soar. He thought also of the future possibility of a position with the railroad company itself. As Natalie's escort, he had listened attentively to conversations in the homes of Savannah's business leaders and had absorbed what he'd overheard. W. W. Gordon, president of the company, the Habershams, Mark Browning, Godfrey Barnsley, W. H. Stiles, William Thorne Williams—nearly every prominent man in town held some interest in the Central Railroad and Banking Company. Undoubtedly, the future of the city lay there.

"You've reached Savannah at the end of her long slumber," Godfrey Barnsley had told Olin. "Our future is brighter than at any time in history." Barnsley had then laughed his cultivated, cordial laugh and added, "I have no intentions, when I move my family to the upcountry, of severing my Savannah connections. Stiles and I will need all the Savannah money we can make to build our dream estates up there."

Olin meant to stay at the heart of where the profits would generate—in Savannah. If Natalie should outgrow her passion for her laboring man, Latimer, well and good. Olin wouldn't mind marrying her in order to stay close to her father's power in the city. If she did marry Latimer, also well and good. With financial success, Olin could marry any Savannah belle whose family coffers might further fill his.

Somewhat more calmly now, he untied the first packet of cash and counted it. Five hundred dollars. Perhaps the money was tied in five-hundred-dollar bundles. He'd soon know.

Moving the candle closer, he had just begun to lift off the top layer of packets when the heavy footsteps of the waterfront watchman stopped him—and his heart. Surely, the watchman would notice a light in the Browning offices at such a late hour. With feverish deftness, he retied the one packet, replaced it on the stack, wrapped the whole in the square of oilcloth, stuffed it back into the wooden box and blew out the candle. For two or three minutes, he waited without moving, picturing the watchman on his rounds; moving west, one door at a time, along the section called Commerce Row. When the steps had finally died away, Olin, the crate under one arm, crept down the hall and let himself out the front entrance.

The door safely relocked, he picked his way in the dim light of the oil-burning street lamp to a wooden walkway that connected the steep bluff where the office building stood to another wooden walk on the Strand. His careful footfalls echoed like gunshots in the still night. When he reached the sandy street, he would breathe more easily. Far safer to count the money in the privacy of his own room at the Browning home.

He was smiling to himself confidently when the thud of running boots and the watchman's shout stopped him.

"Who goes there?" The harsh voice roared.

"Oh, good evening, my man," Olin called back pleasantly. "I'm Olin Wheeler, sir. Mr. Browning's assistant. You're going to chuckle when I tell you my romantic reason for having been in our counting-house at this unseemly hour."

The watchman huffed up to him, aiming his lantern up close to be sure it was Olin Wheeler. "Oh, evenin', Mr. Wheeler. Sorry, sir, I was just doin' my duty, you know. Romance? I welcome it. Gits mighty lonesome walkin' these old streets alone at night."

The wooden crate under his left arm, Olin shook hands with the man. "Can I trust you with a secret?"

"Indeed you kin, Mr. Wheeler!"

"Well, as I'm sure you know, Captain Jack Mackay is in town visiting his family."

"Known Captain Jack since he was a shaver."

"A charming gentleman. Well, he did some shopping for me while he was in Washington City receiving his new orders." Olin tapped the wooden crate. "A present for Miss Natalie Browning. I plan to wrap it properly in my room tonight and give it to her at the Mackay house tomorrow at Sunday dinner."

"Oho," the watchman chuckled. "Now I can see why you're slippin' round here after hours! That little girl must be hard to take by surprise. Her papa's spoiled her rotten all her life. I guess he's spoilin' her worse than ever these days, he's so happy she got off the *Pulaski* alive."

"Oh, sir, we're all happy about that."

"And you're the young gentleman who brought her home, eh?" He shook Olin's hand again. "She's a perky little thing for sure, and the prettiest young lady on the coast—north to south. An' that father of hers don't have an enemy in Chatham County. We're all happy for Mr. Browning that she wasn't lost." He saluted Olin, chuckling again. "Good luck to you, sir. I hope Miss Natalie likes your present. She wouldn't be easy to please, I'd think."

In his room, an hour later, Olin had counted all the money. Little Domer was right. Thirty-six thousand, six hundred dollars and forty-nine cents—to the penny. The coins were tied in a small chamois bag. And at the very bottom of the crate, under the last row of packets, lay a letter, evidently in Osmund Kott's handwriting:

For my beloved Natalie Browning, the entire contents of this package. At my death, it is for you, blessed child, as a small token of my appreciation for the joy and gladness you have given me by your love and devotion for all the years of your life. Think of me always as Kottie, not as anyone else might ever describe me to you. Except for my own mother, who died when I was a child, I have never loved another person. Only you. At my death, which has occurred by the time you read this, I want you to know that I am your great-uncle. Your father's mother, Melissa Cotting, was my little sister. She and I are the illegitimate offspring of your mother's (and father's) late grandfather, Jonathan Cameron, and his indentured servant, Mary Cotting. I pray that this blood relationship, even out of wedlock, may help you understand what you have meant to me and will go on meaning to me throughout eternity.

Devotedly,
KOTTIE

Olin read and reread the note. Old Kott had handed him still another plum—in case he needed to use it. Was this scandal known in town? he wondered. Well, it needn't be, if Mark Browning went on being so kind to him. As he refolded the note, a smaller slip of paper fell to the floor, obviously stuck by dampness to Natalie's letter from Kott. It read: "The amount of money in this package is, as of 12 June, 1838, before my departure on the *Pulaski*, $36,600.49." Slowly, carefully, Olin tore the second slip of paper into tiny shreds, dropped them in his candlestand and burned them to ashes.

He then counted out exactly five thousand dollars, divided into packets of one hundred dollars each. Painstakingly, he tied each packet with the cord, of which where was plenty now, rewrapped the money in the square of oilcloth, put the entire package, with the chamois bag of coins, back into the crate and slid it under his bed. Tomorrow, he'd renail the lid when the house began to stir. The remaining $31,600 he tied in a clean nightshirt and shoved the bundle to the back of the bottom drawer of the tall armoir. At some point, he would transfer it to his trunk stored in the cellar where Browning kept his wine.

In his comfortable bed, Olin felt the fine linen sheets. Quality, quality all the way, these Brownings. And tomorrow at the Mackay house, he'd make a touching presentation of old Kottie's five thousand dollars and forty-nine cents to Natalie. He could even count on her being deeply affected, not only because she adored Kott, but because five thousand would strike her as little different from nearly forty thousand. He dropped off to sleep satisfied. To Natalie, money grew on trees anyway.

Olin rode in the family carriage with the Brownings from Sunday services to the Mackay house the next day, the wooden crate stowed safely—just after dawn—in the luggage carrier. Affably as always, he agreed that the Reverend Edward Neufville had preached a searching sermon and showed as much enthusiasm as the Brownings in the prospect of the new Christ Church building, the cornerstone of which had been laid back in February. Everyone seemed pleased, Olin too, that the Mackays' longtime friend, Mr. James Hamilton Couper—also rescued from the *Pulaski*—was designing the church.

Throughout Mrs. Mackay's superb meal, prepared around two fat stuffed hens, the talk moved rather easily from how they missed Jack, visiting his own Savannah River plantation that day and Jonathan, who was dining with the family of his friend, Ralph Meldrim, to the recent death of Joseph Stiles. Eliza Anne and W. H. Stiles were there, not feeling it in bad taste to accept the invitation, because the Mackays and Brownings were family. There was an underlying sense of sorrow, of course, and everyone repeated what Olin had already heard a dozen times, that "it still seems strange, because Joseph Stiles was such a vital man, the epitome of vigor." Obviously, to the end, the old man had held them all in a kind of virile thrall. In fact, Olin guessed that old Stiles had dominated the lives of all of his nine children, by both wives. Bored with their talk as usual, he studied W. H. Stiles, son of Joseph's first wife, Catherine Clay. As striking-looking as a romanticized Greek god, slight of build, with almost delicate hands, discriminating, keenly sensitive. No hint of the aggressive manliness of old Joseph Stiles in Eliza Anne's husband, but she plainly adored him, independent though she appeared to be. Olin had long ago made a point of finding out about William Henry Stiles because he was an important young professional in town—in Georgia, for that matter. At twenty-four, Stiles had been appointed solicitor general in his district and, as a distinguished lawyer and U.S. district attorney, elected also to the city council. Stiles, Olin knew, had driving political ambitions that could well be one of the reasons he was moving to the still unsettled upcountry.

Olin's own musings were only slightly disturbed by Mrs. Mackay's tiring talk of her cavalier son Jack's latest earth-shaking assignment for the Army Department of Engineers. Who could possibly care that Captain Jack Mackay was about to build an obscure road from St. Augustine, Florida, to an unknown spot on the St. Johns River called Picolata? Still, to hear them all rave, one would think such a feat had never before been accomplished. Jack Mackay was not one of Olin's favorites. Everyone appeared to adore this Mackay son, to hang on his every word, and it had sickened him. Oh well, no one had guessed Olin's real thoughts or how he actually felt about anything, and he intended to keep it that way.

Now and then, during the meal, he caught Natalie's eye and smiled. She was seated between Kate and Sarah Mackay across the table. However she interpreted his smiles, as always, he made them inviting. As she had last night at the concert, Natalie appeared distracted, more so than usual, and did not really return even one. Only when the talk veered to the Stileses' plans to move to Cass County did she appear to listen. And when Mr. Stiles announced that, due to his duties as executor of his father's will, they would not be returning to north Georgia in the spring, Natalie dropped her fork so that it clattered against Eliza Mackay's best Meissen china.

"Do be careful, darling," Natalie's mother scolded.

"Oh, no harm done, Caroline," Mrs. Mackay offered quickly.

"Oh yes, there is harm done—to me," Natalie cried. "I knew you wouldn't be going to the upcountry. It was too good to be true, Uncle W.H.—Miss Lib—why do people love doing things like that to me?"

Her sudden cry of protest brought a dead silence all around the table, during which the Mackays' two aging servants, Emphie and Hannah, were removing plates. This, Olin decided, could well be his moment to act, while everyone's attention was focused on Natalie. Almost unnoticed by the others, he excused himself and hurried outside for the wooden box, hidden under a heavy lap robe in the rear of the carriage.

During the awkward moments after her outburst and Olin's departure, Natalie sat miserably in the heavy silence. Of course everyone stared at her with disapproval, and she was so heartbroken and confused and scared because the Stileses had changed their plans, she was having trouble looking defiant as she intended. Around the familiar table sat a whole group of people who seemed bent on thwarting her—determined that she would never see Burke's face again. That was enough, she thought, hating the wretched way she must appear to them all, to *scare* anybody!

Without any warning, she felt her father's hand on hers. He had dared to reach across Kate Mackay and pat her in front of a whole table full of people! Suddenly longing to grab his hand, instead she jerked hers away.

"Natalie, my dear," Miss Eliza said, "you scarcely touched your meal."

Ignoring the inane comment, Natalie said weakly, "Miss Lib, somehow I thought you—and maybe even Uncle W.H.—did really understand."

"We do, Natalie. We both understand how you feel. We just couldn't help it that—W.H.'s father died."

She was ignoring her father, but out of the corner of her eye, Natalie saw him get slowly to his feet and move to stand behind her chair. "I'm going to help you, honey," he said. "Your old papa thinks he may know a way to help."

It had been months since she'd heard that firm, comforting tone in his voice. She could almost feel her defenses crumble. She hated *and* liked the feeling and began to twist her big linen napkin until it was a hard cord in her hands. Why did Papa have to wait until they were in front of everybody who knew them so well to—to stop being bull-headed and offer to help her? In the old days, she would have turned and fallen into his arms. She couldn't now. Even if she did want to do it, too much had happened between them. One dumb public announcement like this wasn't going to change anything!

"I don't have things all worked out yet, Natalie," Papa was saying, "but I will help—I promise you, I will."

"I can't believe you anymore," she said. "I want to, but I can't believe you or anyone else. I don't think I'll ever—believe any of you again."

When her father didn't answer, abruptly—irrelevantly—she wondered where Olin had gone. What difference did it make? She no longer trusted or believed him either. Not after what she'd overheard when Little Domer had brought the box of money Kottie left her. She'd decided last night that Olin was up to something. What good was money anyway? Even dear Kottie's money. Money didn't help a thing. There had always been money everywhere, and look at the trouble all around. She fully intended to confront Olin, but there was certainly no hurry.

Her father still stood silently behind her chair. Instead of helping, his standing there only made her feel more defenseless against them all. If Papa touches me, I'll hit him, she thought. He didn't.

The helplessness—a feeling she hated more than any other—seemed about to engulf her when she heard Olin let himself in the Mackay front door. She jumped to her feet, her back to her father, steeling herself. For what? She had always been able to snap her fingers and watch Olin jump. Suddenly—this minute—she was almost afraid of him and hoped wildly that no one sensed her inner cry for Papa. For Papa at least to lay his hand on her shoulder. To—protect her.

To protect her from what?

"You're back, Olin," Eliza Mackay said—the polite hostess.

"Indeed I am," Olin answered, entering the dining room, the wooden crate held out as though he carried a silver serving tray.

Natalie stared at him—glared at him. "Olin Wheeler, you—wouldn't dare!"

"Natalie," her mother scolded again softly. "None of this is Olin's fault."

"Olin, not here! *Not now.* You're not usually—so stupid."

He was smiling at her—the wholesome, trustworthy smile on which she'd depended to get her through the ghastly months without Burke. "Papa?" she heard herself say—almost pleadingly.

"What, Natalie dear? What can I do for you?"

"Nothing," she said, closing her heart to him again. "Nothing at all."

Her father stepped away, back toward his own chair, but remained standing, as Olin bore the wooden crate toward her.

"I feel I've proved to you, Natalie," Olin began, "that I—care. I hope, at least, that I have been able, because of my own deep love for you, to help smooth your difficult way since I've been in town. I have something for you here in this wooden box. If I was wrong in choosing this time to present it, I'm truly sorry. But"—he paused, took in the entire table with a tender glance—"these are the people who love you most in all the world. I—I've tried not to pry, but I've been unable not to sense that—some of them, at least, did not feel warmly toward your beloved late friend, Mr. Osmund Kott."

Natalie could feel the blood pound in her ears. "Olin!" She was almost crying now. "Take that box right out of here! Do you hear me? I said take it—"

"Natalie, wait," her mother interrupted. "Don't be rude to Olin. Whatever he has in that box, I think he has good intentions in giving it to you now, and—"

"Since when are you defending Olin, Mama?" Natalie demanded. "Every single person at this table knows you don't care a fig for him. That you despised Kottie. Why don't people say what they mean? Olin—why don't you say what you mean instead of all this—pa-laver?"

"I am saying what I mean," he went on evenly. "I didn't have the pleasure of knowing Mr. Kott, but I have seen your grief over his death—your reverence for his memory. Remember, my dear, I'm the one who's gone with you each time you've visited Knightsford. I've seen how you miss him. In this box, Natalie, is a gift to you from Mr. Kott. A bequest of money. A token of his undying devotion to you." Olin opened the loosened lid and handed her Kott's note.

Natalie read it through tears that streamed down her face no matter how she fought them. The startling revelation that Kottie was her great-uncle brought still more tears. Then, her face grim and closed, she looked deliberately from one person to another, pausing long enough to let the true, loving import of what Kottie had done soak in, to indict each one there. Not trusting herself even to bring up the blood relationship to Kottie now, she asked, "Olin, have you read this letter?"

"Yes. I had to be sure the rather odd little man who brought it to my office was telling the truth about its contents of money. About the—donor."

Still reeling from having read in Kottie's own handwriting that, through Papa, he had been her own great-uncle, Natalie felt wholly lost, isolated—a stranger, in no way related either to her own parents or to their closest family friends. All this time, Kottie had been her great-uncle, and no one—not even Papa—had told her! Soon, a kind of pride began to course through her whole being. She was proud, *proud* of being a blood relation of Kottie's. Prouder than she'd ever been of being related to anyone. Still standing there in the silence, she went on studying Miss Eliza, Mama, Papa, Miss Lib, Uncle W.H., the other Mackay sisters, unable to say a word to any of them. Easier to keep her kinship with Kottie to herself—right now, at least. She decided to say nothing until she'd had time to—think, to be rid of Olin for humiliating her like this. Not one person around the table said anything that might help her through this awful minute. True, only Olin knew what she'd just read in Kottie's note, but she was sure they'd all known about his being her great-uncle. From deeper down than ever before, she longed for Burke. . . .

I don't belong here with these people, she thought. I belong with Burke. Tears were coming down again and nothing she could think to do or say would stop them.

"Osmund Kott had a—good side to him," Miss Eliza said finally.

"And he did love you, Natalie," Miss Lib echoed.

Ignoring both useless remarks, Natalie demanded, "Where did you get this, Olin?" She knew, of course, but meant to make him tell them too. "Where did you get this box?"

"Oh, as I said, a strange little deformed man brought it to my office. He came, I'm sure, to see you, Mr. Browning, but you were paying your daily visit here at the Mackays'."

"And you took it upon yourself not to tell me about it?" her father asked in a stern voice.

"Yes, sir. And perhaps I was wrong. But all a man can do is lay out the truth. From my heart, I only meant to be giving your daughter a chance to show everyone that the old gentleman she adored was— also a man with a generous, loving nature."

Natalie gave Olin a look that should have shattered anyone's composure. It did not faze Olin. He responded with a smile. She knew perfectly well that Little Domer had brought the box, but she pressed her question. "Olin, who brought—Kottie's gift to your office?"

"I believe he said his name was Domer."

"You *know* his name was Domer!"

"That's what I said, Natalie."

Her father was still standing beside his own chair, listening, saying nothing. Papa, her heart called to him. Papa, please—help me! Olin's lying! Domer did bring him the box, but—oh, Papa, I don't know what it is—except something's *terribly wrong.* Help me, Papa. . . .

As though he had heard her silent cry, her father asked, "Olin, have you examined the money in that box?"

"Domer opened it and showed it to me, sir. He told me how much is there and that he's been keeping it, hoping that Mr. Kott might not have really been—lost. That the old gentleman just might turn up someday, alive and well. He told me that the money is for Natalie, all of it."

"Go get Little Domer, Papa!"

"Today, darling? Now?"

"Yes—*now.*"

"But why, Natalie?" Her mother was standing too. "This is your father's only day to rest. Domer might not even be in his cabin up the river."

"Go get him, Papa, please! If you never do another thing for me— go get Little Domer."

Turning to Miss Eliza at the head of the table, her father asked, "Do you think William would go with me?"

"He might," Miss Eliza said eagerly. "Oh, I'd be so glad if he would. He couldn't face dinner with us today, and he hasn't been out of the house except to help me in the yard. Go ask him, Mark. For you, he just might agree to go. And—tell Domer we'd like to give him his dinner when he gets here."

"How much money is in that box, Olin?" Natalie demanded.

"Exactly five thousand dollars and a small chamois bag containing forty-nine cents," he answered easily.

Now she knew what was so wrong! The childhood urge to pound Olin—to pound his quiet, composed face—tempted her. Instead, she sank weakly into her chair. "Get William and go, Papa. *Please.*"

Her father hurried back to where she sat, but said nothing. Then, after a few seconds, she felt his hands resting lightly on her shoulders. Still, he did not say a word. She grabbed one strong, familiar hand and held it in both of hers. "Go, Papa. Bring Domer back here —and hurry!"

TWENTY-SIX

WILLIAM STEERED as they skimmed Mark's light sailboat over the mile or so of river to Domer's rickety one-roomed cabin. As usual, William asked no questions, but before they came in sight of the shack on the south bank of the river, Mark had told him the whole story of what had happened at the dinner table.

William shook his head. "Osmund stole from you and left it to Natalie, eh?"

"That's right. I doubt that it all came out of my pocket, though. At least, the weighted bales I know about didn't amount to as much as five thousand dollars. My friend, I was furious at Kott the day he left on the *Pulaski*. I had a hard time even being civil with him. You can believe I'm glad now I managed to be."

"I expect a lot of his chicanery can be blamed on his loneliness."

"Loneliness?"

"A man's likely to do anything if he's lonely. Kott was by himself all his life, the way I've heard it. At least, after the orphanage."

"I honestly hadn't thought about that."

"Glad you told me the whole story," William said, easing the boat toward the south bank. "I—missed a lot all those weeks I wouldn't let you in my room." Mark had seen William smile so seldom since the tragedy, the half-smile helped more than anything William might say. It reached Mark's heart and comforted him. He was still more comforted when his friend added, "I think your little girl's coming back to you. Just the fact that Natalie asked you to fetch Little Domer looks promising to me."

"I hope you're right."

"Why do you think she's demanding to see Domer in person?"

"I have no idea, William. Sounds peculiar, I know, but I'm still almost afraid to ask her much. I'd give *anything* to have her back again the way she and I have always been."

When William didn't answer, Mark was sorry for what he'd said. He had reason to hope that Natalie might come back. She was alive. She *could* come back.

"I see Domer now, fishing off his dilapidated old dock, Mark. We're in luck."

On their way back to town, Mark and William got Little Domer's story. At least, he told them all he knew of the money bequest from his friend, Osmund Kott. "A man living in a shack like yours," Kott had said to Domer, "won't be robbed. In my good overseer's house at Knightsford, I'm not so safe. I trust you, Domer. I trust you and no one else to look after this money. Never mind how I got it. All that matters is that I'm giving it to you to keep because when I die, it goes—every cent—to my beloved Natalie Browning."

Since Kott had been Domer's best friend, Domer had never needed to know where the money came from. He had just been glad to look after it, count it often to be sure it was all there, and wait happily for Kott's twice-a-year visit to his cabin to add to the treasure.

"It took me a while," Domer confessed, "to be sure he wasn't ever gonna' come back alive. I woke up last week knowin' Kott's gone forever. He won't be comin' to my shack no more. That's when I brung the box into town. You wasn't there, Mr. Browning. I give it to the young feller in charge."

Back on the porch of the Mackay house where all the guests except Natalie were gathered waiting, W.H. told Mark that Natalie had insisted upon being alone in the parlor the whole time he and William were gone. "She's even given us orders that you and Domer —and Olin Wheeler—are to come to her at once. No one else."

"Where is Olin?" Mark asked.

"Walking around by himself in the backyard the last time I saw him," Miss Eliza said.

Caroline stood up. "I'm going to the parlor with you, Mark."

"No. We do exactly what Natalie wants now." He turned to William. "Thanks, thanks more than I can say—for going along to Domer's place."

William nodded, then stretched out his hand to the earnest little cripple, "Good to see you again, Domer. I'll go on back upstairs."

"Oh, William, dear," Miss Eliza said, "we're going to feed Domer. Please have your dinner now, too."

"Thanks, Mama. Not now. I'll go fetch Wheeler, though, before I go back to my room." To Mark, William said, "Let me know what happens in the parlor."

"I will. I certainly will."

In the Mackay parlor, roseate light from the setting sun gave the faded wallpaper and the now shabby furniture a beauty and gentility that sent Mark's mind racing back to the good years in which he'd lived in the house. Especially to the nights spent in this room with his late friend, Robert Mackay, who had always, it seemed to Mark, shown Little Domer unusual kindness.

Domer, who had followed Mark into the parlor, stood now, frayed cap in hand, ill at ease in the direct path of the sunset glow. W.H. had said that Natalie was waiting in the parlor. She was nowhere in sight. "I'll be right back, Domer," Mark said. "I have to find my daughter."

"Here I am, Papa." She spoke in the small-girl voice that always dissolved any intention of his to be strict with her. "Here, on the stair."

Mark hurried to sit down on the steps beside her, but kept himself from embracing her. "Domer's in the parlor, honey, waiting for us. William's gone to get Olin. Are you—crying?"

"No. And I don't want you to do anything terrible to Olin when you find out."

"Find out—what, Natalie?"

In the dusky light, he could barely see that she shrugged. She said nothing.

"I just want him out of my sight for good, Papa. I don't care about —*anything* else. Absolutely nothing else that has to do with Olin—or his wooden crate. You see, I've been sitting here making decisions."

His heart pounded. Natalie was coming back to him! She was. He could tell by her voice, and twice she had called him—Papa. He longed to hug her, to welcome her back, to tell her how much her shutting him out had hurt. He said only, "You've been—making decisions?"

"Yes. I want Olin Wheeler out of our house by tomorrow. Tonight, if you'll send him to a hotel. You and Mama have been terribly stubborn with me about Burke, but Olin's a snake. I'm too tired, though, for you to yell at him or have him arrested or anything like that. I just—want him to be *gone.*"

"But what has he done?"

"You'll see. Then you'll discharge him."

"You want me to—fire him from his position at the firm?"

"Immediately. Oh, you'll want to anyway. But, Papa, I am tired. I stay tired—without Burke. I miss him so much, I wouldn't be at all surprised if I got quite sick. I just want you to get rid of Olin right away. Without any fuss."

"If he's done anything to be discharged, darling, I will most certainly let him go, but—"

"You've made me very angry lately, but Olin's a snake. He's been so beautiful and graceful—the way snakes are. They are beautiful, you know."

He didn't agree, but kept quiet. In her way—a way he might never truly understand—she *was* coming back to him. He meant to listen to her, praying that somehow the coldness might never return.

"Remember when we saw that coral snake move his graceful head back and forth so that he mesmerized the silly phoebe bird at Knightsford when I was little?"

"Of course I remember."

"I've been that silly phoebe bird. I'm not now. Papa? Will you do something for me?"

He longed to say, "Yes, yes—anything." Instead, he said, "I'll always try, Natalie."

"Will you let me be a silly phoebe bird when I feel that way and a soaring wide-winged hawk when I don't?"

Mark took a deep breath, struggled to mask it when he exhaled so that she wouldn't think him annoyed—wouldn't pull away again. She was his own daughter, but *he did not know this young woman.* With all his being he loved her, but after seventeen years as her father, he knew very little about her. "Natalie, I'll always try to—be—the way you need me to be."

They heard the back door bang shut. William, so quiet in other ways, had always banged doors. He was coming with Olin Wheeler.

"Domer's waiting for us in the parlor," Mark said. "Probably still standing there in the middle of the floor holding his cap."

Natalie got up. "Oh, Domer won't mind. He loved Kottie. Domer and I were the only two people on earth who really loved him."

"Mr. Wheeler was taking a walk," William explained, when he and Olin came toward them down the center hall. "I had to go hunt for him. See you later, Mark."

As William mounted the stair to his room, Mark openly studied Olin Wheeler's calm, pleasant, aristocratic face. He had no idea—none whatever—why Natalie was now calling Olin a snake, but he felt sure that his daughter wouldn't wait long to inform him.

"In the parlor, Olin," Natalie said in the same chillingly polite voice she had used with Mark for so long.

Indeed, Little Domer was still standing in the center of the parlor floor, cap in hand. The minute he saw them, a snaggle-toothed smile lit his homely face and he thrust a friendly hand toward Olin, who returned the greeting warmly.

"Pleased to see you again, Mr. Wheeler," Domer said. "I guess you done give Miss Natalie her—surprise."

"Yes, I certainly have. At dinner today—right here at the Mackays'." Then, holding a chair for Natalie, Olin asked, "Shall we all be seated?"

"No." She bit off the word. "There won't be time to be seated, Olin. I want you to tell me again how much money Kottie left me in that box. Tell me *in front of Little Domer.*"

Mark did not once take his eyes from Olin's face. For the merest instant, the almost perpetual smile vanished. Then, as to an intimate friend, looking straight at Natalie, Olin said, "So that's why you left me alone in the backyard for so long while your father and Mr. Mackay were away?" He moved toward her. "I was worried. I thought it might be something—serious between us."

Her pale eyes narrowed, Natalie repeated her question: "How much money was in that box when Domer gave it to you?"

"Five thousand dollars—oh, and the chamois bag of change. Forty-nine cents, I believe."

Natalie turned to Little Domer. "Domer, *you* tell us how much money my dear Kottie left me!"

Mark watched Domer now. His bushy eyebrows shot up and down a few times in total surprise, he opened his mouth, then closed it, then opened it again, but no words came. Finally, Domer turned to Olin. "Mr. Wheeler, you—you was so—kind to me that day—in your office!"

"Never mind that, Domer," Mark said, taking a step toward Olin. "Don't let his kindness cause you to lie to us. I've always been your friend, don't forget."

Domer was nodding rapidly now, nodding and nodding. "Oh yes, sir, Mr. Browning. Yes, sir. You always been kind to Domer."

"How much money?" Natalie shouted at the nervous little man. "If you were really Kottie's friend, tell us exactly how much money you brought to Mr. Wheeler's office that day."

Beginning now to stutter, Domer said, "Wh-wh-why, just like I— t-t-told Mr. Wheeler—that d-day, nearly f-forty thousand—"

Mark saw Olin Wheeler begin to inch closer to the double door-way that led to the hall, his eyes still on Natalie's white, stricken face.

"I was eavesdropping outside your office, Olin," she said, her words falling like ice into the warm, dim room. "I heard Domer tell you exactly how much money Kottie left to me. Thirty-six thousand, six hundred dollars and forty-nine cents! He's a thief, Papa—*fire him.* I want him out of my sight forever. . . ."

Before she finished speaking, Olin had darted into the hallway and out the front door, Mark after him. But Mark had waited a few seconds too long. By the time he raced across the porch, down the steps and into Broughton Street, Olin Wheeler was nowhere in sight. Rounding the corner into Abercorn, he could hear Natalie call: "Papa! Papa!" He did not stop. Surely, he thought, Olin would head for their house on Reynolds Square. Even if he meant to leave town, all his new clothes were there and a large trunk. The remainder of Natalie's money, too, he was now sure.

Natalie's calls remained close as Mark kept running. She was still calling frantically, and when he turned to look, he saw her hurrying and stumbling toward him along the sandy street.

"Wait, Papa—please wait!"

Mark rushed back to her.

Natalie threw herself into his arms. "Let him go! I told you I wanted him out of my sight. Papa, please, please—just *let him go!*"

"But your money, darling—he'll take that money with him."

"I don't care! Kottie—thought about me—that's all I care. You've got plenty of money. I don't care about money anyway, because Burke doesn't." She dissolved into tears and clung to him.

"Natalie, oh, Natalie," he breathed. "You are back, aren't you?" He was hugging her now, kissing her red curls, hugging her.

"Let—him go, Papa. . . ."

"All right. All right, we'll let him go—if that's what you want. Everybody in town will call your father six kinds of fool for throwing away more than—thirty thousand dollars, but—"

"Who cares?"

"I ought to have Olin arrested."

"No! They'd just—keep him here." She reached to take his face in both her hands. "Papa, we're together again—the way we used to be. What matters most—being together? Or a pile of money?"

In answer, he held her bright head hard against his chest. "My dear, let's go back and tell the others. I know they saw us both racing down the street after Olin."

After she blew her nose hard, she said, "I wasn't racing after *him*. I was racing after my—beautiful father!"

For a long moment, he stood looking down at her upturned face. It was still wet with tears, but she was smiling—giving him a real Natalie smile. "I missed you so desperately," he said.

"I missed you, too, but you deserved to be punished."

A firm, responsible father wouldn't have laughed, but he did. "I—suppose so."

Arm in arm, they began to walk back toward the Mackay house, now and then giving each other an affectionate squeeze.

Just before they reached the gate, Natalie asked, "Now, when will we leave for the upcountry to find Burke?"

Mark managed not to show too much surprise, he hoped, and felt a touch proud of himself when he said firmly, "We—you and I—won't be going, honey. But I've decided to ask William if he'll go for the sole purpose of finding Burke."

She stopped walking, let go of his arm and stood looking off down Broughton Street. Mark's heart was pounding again. Her pale eyes told him nothing. Then, as though she were twenty-seven or thirty-seven and not seventeen, she said slowly, thoughtfully, "*Yes* . . . why didn't I think of William a long time ago? It will do him a lot of good to make the journey. He really needs to get away from—

Savannah. He'll go, too, for my sake. I'm just sure William will go."
Seventeen again, she flashed her irresistible smile. "Why are we just
standing here in the street? Come on, Papa. We have to tell William!"

"Darling, we have to be—careful with him."

"Don't explain William Mackay to me. If anyone knows about his
—broken heart, I do."

TWENTY-SEVEN

NATALIE'S eager, hopeful look when she and her father had rushed into his room with her big plan, still haunted William hours later. Sitting by his window open to the chilly night air, he wondered why her hopefulness troubled him more now than had her crestfallen little face when they left. He had not refused; he'd just said he needed time to think about making that long ride to the upcountry alone. He felt bad about Natalie, he decided, because she'd been so sure he'd agree right off to go.

William took a deep breath and let it out on a sigh. Sighing had become almost an expression for him—sighing and deep breaths, although he never seemed to get enough air into his chest. There wasn't room, he guessed. The heavy weight in his heart took up most of the space. Still, since Natalie had insisted that she needed him, he felt somehow helped. And instead of slumping in his chair now, he was sitting straight, almost alert.

No one enjoyed bucking Natalie Browning. No one ever had. He certainly hadn't enjoyed being firm with her earlier tonight. He'd tried, oh, how he'd tried to "hear" Virginia's voice again, to remember the sweet caress of it when she spoke his name. He couldn't, but he could still hear Natalie pleading with him, telling him over and over how much she needed him. That he was the only hope she had of ever seeing Burke Latimer again. Poor Mark. What a load the man carried these days. It was plain that he and Natalie were reconciled and for that William gave thanks, but humiliation was a load too, and that scoundrel Olin Wheeler had certainly humiliated Mark.

If I could get my hands on Wheeler right now, I'd make him sorry for what he tried to do to Mark and Natalie, he thought. I wonder if they found him still at the house. Mark said Wheeler had hightailed it up the street like a bat out of the hot place. Most likely he'd gone to collect his belongings—and the remainder of the money poor old Kott left Natalie. He'd likely stolen one of Mark's horses and headed for Augusta.

William's mind went to Little Domer and Kott's box of money. At least, Osmund had proved he loved Natalie. Even if he did steal the money from Mark, and heaven only knew from whom else through the years, he didn't keep it for himself. Maybe everybody but Natalie and Little Domer had been wrong about Kott. Maybe.

Chilly now, William slipped into his old wool jacket, but left the window open. As usual, he felt tired. He'd been tired, bone-tired since his last sight of Virginia and the babies. His mother would say he needed food. "Oh, Mama," he said aloud. "I'm in need of—everything!"

William reached for his pipe, filled it, lit it from a candle burning on the table beside his chair and thought about Natalie's pitiful pleas. All he'd promised was to give the trip some thought. There wasn't, he knew, any use whatever to expect a young girl in love—certainly not a Natalie Browning in love—to understand that just talking to people was still too hard. He *was* hungry, but he'd refused dinner because talking, even to loved ones, was too hard. Maybe it would always be. At least, a mere five months and two weeks hadn't been long enough to catch on again to how folks just sat around and said things to one another. He'd lived in his room because a walk anywhere in town was still too painful. It didn't help at all that so many other people were grieving too. It certainly didn't help when someone sympathized. He could shield himself from that, anyway, by sticking to his own room—alone.

There was only one person on earth other than his mother and Mark and Jonathan with whom he longed to talk, and that was Cousin Margaret McQueen, who had deeded her plantation at Causton's Bluff to him "for love and affection," but also because, as she'd confessed in her straightforward way, she couldn't live there again after Uncle John McQueen had died. It seemed to William that Margaret McQueen couldn't even bear living in America anymore. Months ago, she'd gone to visit their Jamaica relatives. Now she was in England, still postponing her return. Mama didn't believe him, but William knew deep inside that Cousin Margaret would never be back. She'd written to him only once since his loss. He'd answer someday when he could, but Cousin Margaret'd never made him feel guilty. He'd always liked her, but the real bond between them had formed in those days and weeks right after Uncle John died, way back, more than twenty years ago. Barely sixteen then, William had walked with her every day the weather permitted, from the Mackay house, where Cousin Margaret was staying, to Colonial Cemetery and Uncle John's grave. William hadn't really done or said anything on those walks, but she swore it helped her just having him there.

He needed Cousin Margaret.

Natalie needed—*him.*

From the small drawer in his night table, he took out Cousin Margaret's short letter. He knew every word by heart, but it helped to look at the spidery, elegant handwriting—words directed only to him. Not merely as a grieving family member, but as a friend:

It doesn't end, William. The pain, in some form, will always be with you, but will you take my word that the sooner you begin to be William, with even one other person, the sooner the pain will ease? In you, if one has the spiritual sight to see, is a vast store of strength. No one, and I do mean *no one,* could have done for me what you did when John left me. As you know, dear William, I have never been recognized in the family as a religious person. My continuing loneliness for John has, I confess, somewhat changed that. I have come to see that God meant what He said when He told us to bear one another's burdens. He did not, I feel, intend to be heaping more burdens upon any already burdened heart. He instructed us to reach out to help others because He knows us better than we can ever know ourselves. God knows that bearing someone else's burden lightens our own. I doubt that He gave such a command in order to display His authority. He gave it for love's sake. His love for each one of us, I am beginning to see, is beyond our frail abilities to understand. Savannah must be filled with need these days. Do share yourself with someone. If you trust me at all, take my word that only in sharing yourself does relief come.

When you begin to share, you will understand what I mean. I can feel your need of even a small *relief.*

William sat staring out into the early winter darkness long after his pipe had gone cold. Relief was a feeling he had almost forgotten. Until now, he had supposed that the heavy strain of grieving would never end. That there would be no relief. He must have read Cousin Margaret's letter fifty times, but sitting there at this minute, staring into the cold black night, he felt as though he'd just broken the seal —just seen the glowing words for the first time. He'd certainly known he needed Cousin Margaret, but all he'd thought of was seeing her, walking beside her again. Would she have been able to tell him face-to-face what she'd just told him on the one page of this letter—worn when he received it from its long sea journey?

Natalie needs me; the thought was as though a strong hand had jerked him out of the old chair. On his feet, still holding the letter, he spoke aloud: "All right, Cousin Margaret. I've finally got it through my skull what you wrote about!"

He'd go to the upcountry and do his level best to find Burke Latimer.

Not till spring, though. Even Mark, this very evening, in the middle of Natalie's pleading, had said several times that he should wait for the roads to get better with spring. But William had his answer ready tonight and he saw no reason to keep Natalie or Mark waiting. They both needed to know now. Knowing would help Mark because it would help Natalie.

He held the letter under the circle of candlelight and hunted until he found one line Cousin Margaret had written: "Savannah must be filled with need now. Do share yourself with someone."

That "someone" was Natalie. And he recognized a hint of the promised relief. Relief that seemed almost to make him a little less tired.

He closed the window, pulled on his overcoat, slipped quietly downstairs and out the front door. Mark and Natalie—Caroline, too —deserved to know his decision tonight. Then, he thought, walking almost briskly along Abercorn, I can come home and tell Mama the latest news about Olin Wheeler. Burke Latimer could turn out to be a scoundrel, he supposed, like Wheeler. Natalie was capable of all kinds of wild allegiances, but William had made a decision. Right or wrong, good results or bad, Natalie needed him—*him, William.* Besides, Natalie had tried as hard as she could to—help Virginia and the babies.

The girl would raise a ruckus, no doubt, because he wasn't going till spring. No matter. He'd simply tell her the facts, make it short and sweet and walk right home again.

Striding along outside the Mackay property wasn't so hard after all. In the silent, dimly lit street, over his footsteps, he heard his stomach grumble. I expect Mama will be mighty glad when I tell her I'm hungry, too.

Mark answered William's knock and greeted him with such warmth and eagerness, William had to fight himself not to turn and leave when his sister, Eliza Anne, W.H. and Caroline rushed out of the family parlor to join in the welcome.

"I'm not here for a visit," William said. "Mama doesn't even know I left the house. I'm here only to give you and Natalie my decision, Mark." Silence fell over the little group standing in the spacious entrance hall. William broke it by saying bluntly: "I'm going to try to find Burke Latimer, but not till spring. If I make the long trip, I want to be able to use the roads after I get there. I mean to find him. Mama will want me here for Christmas. I need to be here. They tell me the first Christmas—after death in a family—is the hardest."

"Oh, of course," Mark said. "Just the fact that you'll go is—the best news I could have!"

"But do you suppose Natalie will understand the delay? Will she sit still for all that time?" Eliza Anne wondered.

"Where is Natalie?" William asked.

"In her room upstairs," Caroline said, a little anxiously. "She—insisted upon being alone this evening. William, we're trying to show her understanding. What Olin Wheeler did—was a terrible blow to her, I'm sure, although she hasn't said one word about him since we left your mother's house."

"Where is Wheeler?" William asked.

"Probably well along his way north," Mark said. "At least, he took one of my best horses."

William studied the pattern in the hall carpet for a moment, then said, almost as to himself, "Wheeler's pitiful."

"Pitiful?" W.H. sounded incredulous.

"I think so," William said quietly. "I always feel sorry for anybody who steps on other folks' faces to get what he wants. Did he take the money, Mark?"

"No. He left that in his room. I don't feel quite so foolish for giving in to Natalie again, because he did leave the money."

"Good," William said. Then he glanced up the stair. "I'd—hoped to be able to tell Natalie that I'm going."

"We—we could go get her," Caroline offered, "but she—she was so adamant about being alone. She won't even allow Jonathan in, and Mark and I think he could help her so much."

"Does Jonathan know what Olin Wheeler tried to do?"

"He knows. He was back from the Meldrims' when Wheeler threw his things together and flew the coop. I wish Natalie would let her brother in to see her, too," Mark said. "The boy seems always to know just what to say and what not to say."

"You don't have to tell me about Jonathan," William agreed. "But, in my book, that girl's all right, too."

"Can't we all sit down awhile?" Eliza Anne urged. "You probably haven't eaten a bite, have you, William?"

"Mama will fix me something when I get home. And I'll go now. I just came to tell Natalie I'll do my best, come spring, to find her young man."

"Sh! Listen—I think I heard her door open upstairs."

"You did, Mother," Natalie said from above them on the stair landing. "And—I heard what William just said, too."

She spoke in such a subdued voice, they all stood staring up at her. Finally, Mark rushed partway up the steps. "William—is going, darling," he said eagerly.

"But you must understand, Natalie," Eliza Anne put in, "William wants to go when the roads aren't quite so bad and—"

"Those roads won't be passable now," W.H. said. "It's plainly sensible to wait for spring."

William hadn't taken his eyes off Natalie's surprisingly calm face. She was coming slowly, steadily down the stair now, in full control.

"You all look as though you're seeing a ghost," she remarked almost casually. "Spring will be fine, William. All I've ever wanted was a promise—from someone—to look for him. I won't like waiting, but spring is all right. And, William, I'm so relieved that you're the one who's going."

"You are, Natalie? Why is that?" William asked almost anxiously.

"Because you'll tell me everything—just the way it is. You won't try to gloss anything over or sound alarms. You'll just tell me."

His mind raced back to the hot July day when Natalie had told him everything about how his little family died. William bowed slightly and said, "That's what you did for me, Natalie. I'll do the same." Then he added, "I admit I thought you might raise sand when I told you I can't go till spring, though. I won't underestimate you again. You're—a real little lady now."

"I'm glad someone realizes that," she said.

After a pause, W.H. cleared his throat and declared, "Well, I can see all sorts of possibilities in your spring trip, William. Since I can't get away as planned, you can inspect some property up there for me. I want to add to my Etowah River land and can give you names of people in Cassville—"

"Wait, Uncle W.H.," Natalie interrupted. "The deal I made with my father when he thought of asking William to go was that he would make the trip for one reason only. To find Burke."

"That's right," Mark said.

"If he's up there, I'll find him, Natalie."

"He's there, William. That's just something I know. If there's time later on, then I give you permission to make deals for Uncle W.H. But what I need you to do first and foremost is find out if he—still loves me—the way I love him."

"I'm honored that—you trust me, Natalie."

Caroline saw William to the door, shaking her head, smiling helplessly. "Thank you, William," she said just above a whisper. "This whole thing may be a wild-goose chase, but Mark and I are so relieved *you're* the one who's going."

Part II

TWENTY-EIGHT

BENDING WILLOW MCDONALD, legs wrapped against the early April cold in worn strips of buckskin, wearing a skimpy rabbit jacket and a coonskin cap that almost hid his broad, open face, sat hunched on the low flat rock that roofed the entrance to a wide cave. In his hands, he held the treasured flintlock with which he'd managed to feed and clothe himself and his young sister, Mary Willow, for more than eight months. The gun was loaded and cocked. Ben Willow hated guns, but Mary was not back yet from her necessary, though dangerous, cooking time. At least every two days, with her big cook pot and whatever meat Ben had found for them, Mary walked the half mile to a spring deep in the woods. Ben's reason for living these days, and for every day since July of last summer, was his fifteen-year-old sister, and he was proud of her. Mary had learned to cook from their mother, Green Willow, and after her death four years ago, learned more from an aging neighbor, dead too, by now, Ben was sure.

On her way from their cave home near New Echota, which had been the capital of the Cherokee Nation, to the safer cooking place beside the spring, he knew Mary had picked every edible green thing—cresses, in the coldest part of the winter past, then ramp and So-cha-ni, the green-headed coneflower, lamb's-quarters, wild onions, and now the tiny green shoots of poke. He smiled a little. Mary's delight was to surprise him with her discoveries, "good gifts for us from God," she called them. In the hot summer and warm, gentle autumn months, they had eaten well of wild fruits and berries

—flowering raspberries, the fruit of the passion flower, sometimes called old-field apricots, and the fleshy linings of the seed pods from honey locusts. They still had a hoard of chestnuts, and Mary cooked them in venison broth, as she "imagined a new soup" to surprise Ben. Venturing into the woods for surprises, with the one strong basket he'd found in the deserted cabin he'd raided right after their escape from the stockade, was Mary's favorite game to play. She worked hard and showed the bravery of a grown woman, but a child would always live in little Mary. At least, Ben hoped so.

He had, with his flintlock and the three horns of gunpowder also found in the empty cabin, been able to keep them fairly well supplied with rabbit for stews, with squirrel meat and venison. Through the days when there had been no meat, they had eaten from their store of chestnuts, walnuts, hickory and butternuts and chinquapins. Today, Mary was cooking the last of the deer meat with wild onions. Although he seldom mentioned it, Ben still missed the civilized taste of salt in their food. He'd forgotten to look for salt in the empty cabin that day after their escape from the stockades. He had remembered a cooking pot, though, pewter spoons, a pillow for Mary, the flintlock and powder and plenty of flint and steel. How the soldiers had overlooked the gun he still had no idea. Thank God they had.

From habit, he scanned the woods now, north, south, east and west, looking behind him often in the direction of the overgrown path to the spring where Mary Willow was cooking. The cave was not safe for cooking—for living—located as it was, less than a mile from New Echota. They would have stopped, he supposed, in whatever cave they found that was large enough, no matter its location. For the first weeks after their July escape from the federal stockade near their old home at Spring Place, they had slept side by side on the warm ground. Perhaps, though, Ben had chosen this cave wisely. The very fact that it was so near New Echota, now temporary headquarters for some of the U.S. Army, caused him to feel relatively safe. They had not known real safety since the Georgia guardsmen had routed them from their family cabin last summer, but it seemed likely that troops would not be hunting for Cherokees so close to their own headquarters. Actually this was the only cave he'd found, and it was large, with a low, nearly hidden entrance beside a rather deep, protective ditch. At least, they had not been discovered. During the long, bitter, snowy winter, he had been forced to build a small fire at the cave's entrance at night, but they both felt it far safer for Mary to do her cooking a little ways into the woods. Smoke from her cook fire, glimpsed or smelled by any remaining members of the cruel Georgia Guard, could mean his and little Mary Willow's death —or torture.

Crouching on his silent watch, Bending Willow let his mind run back over the nightmare through which he and his sister had lived since last summer. Federal soldiers under General Winfield Scott had begun to round up their people back in June while Ben's idol, Chief John Ross, was still in Washington City trying to reason with the men of the federal government who called themselves civilized. Hope that the chiefs of the Cherokee Nation might be dealt with as equals had faded long ago when Major Ridge and Elias Boudinot had signed the bad treaty, expecting, Ben supposed, to feather their own nests, and had left the Cherokees' beloved Georgia hills— traveling west in luxury and ease, their journey well paid for by the United States.

Ben made a scoffing sound, broke off a sweet-gum switch and began to twist it angrily between his fingers. "The powerful, *flinching* federal government!" He spit the words. So "powerful" it was that the last two Georgia governors had made officials in Washington cringe and act against the Cherokees on the flimsy excuse of "protecting states' rights." A government had to be cowardly to send two thousand U.S. soldiers to rout one Cherokee! Ben and Mary had no way of knowing what moon it was when the last of their people had been herded across the Tennessee River toward Ridge and Boudinot's "promised land" in the west. Winter, he was sure. He smiled a little. Well, the Cherokees were not all gone. He and Mary Willow were still here, and sturdy old Dancing Waters had overnight become the "aunt" of Mr. Robert Baines near Spring Place. A few other white settlers had opened their homes to favorite Cherokees because they had been unable to face seeing them driven like cattle from their land and homes. Some white men and women were kind. But the kind ones were few in number, and it took a long time to learn about their hearts.

Ben shuddered, remembering, as Mary said he did too often, the brutality they had seen with their own eyes. He felt again the bayonet jabs and heard the curses and laughter of the guardsmen as they dragged family after family—theirs among them—out of their cabins and drove them toward the nearest federal stockade. "Cherokee removal forts," the U.S. Government called the crude pens built by soldiers in the Department of Engineers. So far as Ben knew, he was not bitter, but he seemed to remember more painfully than Mary Willow did. Perhaps because his own body had felt the jab and tear of those bayonets. Ben had worried through every day since their miraculous escape from the stockade near their old home in Spring Place, but he felt he was not bitter. Afraid of being caught, worried about where he would find a place for them to live before another winter came, but at least, he did not feel bitter.

Ben had become a Christian at the Moravian school at Spring Place, and one of the benefits of that act of faith had been to give him a truer look at people and life in general. One of the hard things about being a Christian was that he felt the suffering of others more than before, but at times, he had even been able to laugh at the overwrought, greedy behavior of white men, who didn't rest until they had robbed the Cherokees of their rightful land and home. Now and then, he was still tempted to hate the well-fed, well-clothed Army Engineer officers who stalked about or rode their good horses as they supervised the building of the despised removal forts. He had seen a few smile now and then at their captives, and not unkindly, he thought. After all, the officers were only obeying orders, as the men under them obeyed their orders to cut and shape Cherokee trees into logs that formed the ugly stockade walls.

Where he and Mary would go from their present cave home, he had no idea. Both were sure God knew. For nearly nine months they had lived in this low cave which stretched deep inside a hill. The cave home was only twenty miles or so south of their old home at Spring Place where the Moravian school had stood until four years ago, when Rich Joe Vann, the drunken but good-hearted Cherokee-Scot, had been driven by the Georgia Guard from his mansion on a hilltop half a mile from their school. The Moravians, Ben remembered, had had mixed feelings about Chief Vann. His drinking dismayed them and he showed little interest in their Gospel, but he was generous with money and supplies for the education of young Cherokees. Rich Joe Vann's father, James, had been killed in a tavern brawl. Like father, like son, the Moravians had said, but both men had cared about young people such as Ben and his sister. Thanks to their schooling, Ben and Mary Willow McDonald could read, write and cipher. They could converse intelligently even with such wise, respected men as Ben's hero, Chief John Ross.

Every thought of John Ross stirred Ben. Until the last possible moment, the strong, educated, loyal Scottish gentleman—only one-eighth Cherokee, but dedicated to their cause—had fought the federal government during the terms of several U.S. Presidents in the only way Ross believed in, through the courts. He had lost in the end, and Ben shuddered trying not to imagine what horrible fate might by now have befallen the man he admired above all men. John Ross, married to quiet, gentle, full-blood Quatie, had thrown in his lot with her people, and considering the distance, from the Cherokee land in Georgia, across the Mississippi River all the way to Oklahoma, could now be dead. John Ross was no longer young. The ugly journey, Ben was sure, had dragged on through the cold winter months. Could still be dragging on now, into early April. Ben tried to accept the fact that he might never know what happened to Chief John Ross or to Quatie.

He checked the sun. Mary Willow had been away at their cooking place for nearly two hours. Soon, he would hear her signal, their special whistle—the high, clear, eager notes of a winter sparrow repeated three times—and would run to meet her to be sure she reached the cave safely and to carry the heavy pot filled with venison and wild onions and whatever surprises Mary might have picked for him on her way.

Through one more cooking time, Ben had seen no sign of a white man or a guardsman from New Echota. He thanked God and relaxed his watchfulness a little to look around him on the ground across the deep ditch that gave their cave home some protection, at the violets, trilliums and lady's slippers spread over the uneven earth like bright bows of ribbon and lace. He stretched a hand to touch a swelling wild azalea bud beside him. Ben had touched a new bud at least once every spring for as long as he could remember. Touched and marveled. In his childhood the feel of a swelling bud had meant the Great Spirit never failed to send signs of life. Now, knowing the Christ of God, the bud's Creator, the sticky, flame-green promise stirred a fresh rush of faith and assurance.

He stood up, stretched, and before his lean, responsive muscles could relax into waiting, he heard Mary's whistle. Three times.

Before the third note ended, Ben had bounded down from the cave roof and was running toward the spring behind a steep rise in the protective hill that sheltered them.

Mary Willow, her body no longer thin and child-flat, but shapely in spite of the long, icy winter days of hunger, moved quietly along the path beside her brother as he carried the heavy pot with care so as not to spill a drop of broth. Now and then Mary looked up at him —he down at her—and they smiled. She was four years younger than Ben and spoke English only fairly well. But she knew Ben was doing his best to teach her to speak so as not to let it be known that she was Cherokee. Ben had gone to school longer and, being a girl, she'd stayed at home much, in the company of their mother, Green Willow, a full-blood. Even their light-haired Scottish father, Tom McDonald, so loved their mother that he roared with fury when Mary or Ben spoke English at home. He wanted them to be like Green Willow, hating the English as he did. Only when Mary and Ben started at the Moravian school did they begin to use the name McDonald, so deeply did their father prefer their mother's Cherokee name, Willow. At home, they were Merry Willow and Bending Willow. Merry had changed the spelling to Mary as soon as she found out that the mother of Jesus was called Mary. Their father couldn't object by then. He had died from too much firewater drunk with white neighbors in the McDonald log cabin. Within half a year, Green Willow had sickened and joined their father. For four years, Ben and Mary had been orphans. Ben had turned fifteen a few days before their mother's death, and every minute of his life since had been given to caring for his young sister. Mary's heart was always mingled with Ben's heart, and to make him happy was the best thing she did with her days.

"It is not so cold today," she said, smiling up at him again. "I not shiver much while our food cooked."

"You *did* not shiver much," he corrected her. "Next month will be May and still warmer." He swept his free hand about. "And there will be still more flowers."

"And then we will find a real house, Ben?"

He frowned. "Maybe. Will you be afraid to stay alone in the cave while I look around?"

She shook her head. "I not afraid. I never afraid!"

"You should have said, 'I *am* not afraid. I *am* never afraid.' "

"Sure," she laughed. "Sure" was a word she loved to use. "Maybe by June we live in a real house again." Then she asked, "Could we be family with white family, you think?"

Ben's answer was serious. "Only friends become family with white people, Mary. No one knows us here, so far away from Spring Place. I think we're even in another county now."

"But you find friends, Ben! Everybody love you."

He laughed and touched his head. "With this straight, black Cherokee hair of mine? My telltale skin? You are blessed by Father's fair skin and soft, curly brown hair. It would be easy for us if I'd been blessed with our father's hair, too. We could pass as whites."

"Better for you, a man, to be brown and curly and not me. A man can do more. A man can work with his hands and build us a cabin."

Inside their cave, the hot venison and tender wild greens in his stomach, Ben settled himself against his favorite hollow place in the cave wall as Mary watched. After a moment, he mused, "You must understand that there is no need to build a cabin, Mary. The countryside stands full of good, empty Cherokee cabins. But I'll have to be seen in order to buy lumber and other materials to repair one. We must buy supplies in order to live." They sat in silence for a time, then Mary was glad when she saw Ben lean his head back and smile to himself. That meant he would be talking to her of things he knew, but she did not. "I was once in Cass County as a boy with our father," he began slowly, remembering. " 'In these parts, there is almost always,' he told me, 'an Indian village built in a most beautiful spot.' One I recall so plainly, Mary, built on high cliffs above a little river called Etowah. Father traded skins we'd trapped with the village chief in his good house above the Etowah River. A man of means, this chief was called Chief Two Bears." Ben sighed. "Gone now. Chief Two Bears is gone now with the others on the long march, his good cabin standing empty on the cliffs, I'm sure."

They sat quietly together for a time, and then Mary asked, "How can you—ever go among the white men, Ben Willow? You with the hair and eyes and skin of our mother? I afraid."

"I *am* afraid," he corrected gently. "I will just have to go out first, as our mother said, 'with the sun behind the night sky' or early in the morning. I may not have to go far to find a cabin. Mary, don't press me for answers. I don't know what we will do, but I will pray. Every step I take while I look for a home, I'll pray to God that somewhere a —kind white man will—need me to work."

"One who will take us to be family in his house?"

"Or hire me and not make trouble if we live in a cabin of our own. We're willing to renounce our Cherokee blood and live as a white man and woman. Chief John Ross told us at school one day that if he failed in Washington City, we would have to be willing to—renounce our ancestors. He did fail. Hard as it is, we'll obey him. But we'll wait here for one more moon. One more moon and then I'll find a home. Maybe in the strawberry moon."

To show Ben that she was not afraid now, Mary took one of his hands in hers. "You got us from stockade—that night, my brother." Her fingers tightened over his. "I still tremble for that night. My legs were stiff like poles. You carried me away from the—soldiers with ugly eyes and dirty faces!"

"That night was a miracle, Mary. A miracle that some careless soldier failed to nail down that bottom log at the corner of the stockade where you and I—happened to be." He hugged her. "That's all past. Don't think of it again. Spring is coming—to help us."

Her heart was too full for words. In answer, she squeezed his hand harder.

"Will you mind so much being called only Mary McDonald? And never Merry Willow again? Will you mind that I'll be only—Ben McDonald? And never Bending Willow?"

"Yes," she whispered. "I will mind, but I will do as you say I do."

"Good girl."

"And—after one more spring," she said in a little burst of cheerfulness, "I will have salt to spill in your supper!"

Ben laughed. "The word is 'sprinkle.' You sprinkle salt."

"But the rain sprinkles."

"What will I do when the day comes that you love a man and leave me to marry him? I'll miss your laughter, Mary, and your funny words for things."

She sat up straight. "I will never leave you!"

"So you say." Ben laughed again, springing to his feet. "But I'm leaving you now. There's work to do. You need your new skirt. That deerskin must be dry enough for me to work today. I want you to save and take care of the white girl's skirt you're wearing. We'll need you to look—British or Scottish like our father any day now."

"But what will you wear? White men see you in leggings and skin jacket and—Mama's black hair and—" She stopped, heartsick that she had been so careless as to bring up the fate of Ben's one pair of trousers, which he wore the day of their capture—the terror-filled day when a guardsman, just for sport, had poked at Ben's buttocks with a bayonet, then, laughing—had torn off Ben's trousers and forced him to march half-naked and bleeding. Ben had a shirt, but no white men's trousers of the kind Cherokee boys always wore to school. She was still pained to remember the sight of poor Ben, the sleeves of that shirt tied around his waist to hide himself as he tried to obey by marching briskly with the blood streaming from those vicious bayonet wounds.

"We'll think about my trousers later," he said firmly. "Oh, when I remember the stacks of britches and shirts I had to leave back in our cabin, I could—"

"Don't remember," she scolded. "Don't remember, Ben! Please —don't remember back to that—day."

He pulled her to her feet and hugged her again. "You're right. No more remembering. We're here, not trudging to the west with our poor friends and relatives. We're still here. Right here in our fine cave, our stomachs full of venison and broth. We'll think only of the future. And that the Great Father is in charge. He is, you know. God is in—full charge."

TWENTY-NINE

AT THE TOP of the rise behind their cave in the warmth of the afternoon sun, Ben knelt over the deer hide he'd tanned and stretched across two forked branches of a sweet gum to dry and began to work it. There had been no trick at all to working leather to a supple softness while they still lived in their good cabin with an attic for drying. In fact, they'd worn white man's clothes most of the time. But now and then, wanting his family to keep their Cherokee heritage alive, Ben's father had insisted that the children wear hand-dyed, beaded jackets to school, and he had taught Ben the plants and barks to use in preparing hides. Ben was glad now. His prayers for sunshine to dry the deer skin had been answered. Except for one shower, the weather had been dry and clear.

Grasping a smooth round rock in his right hand, he settled to the long job of rubbing soft the stiff, dried skin. And as he worked, his mind could not keep away from that bright hot summer day when the guardsmen had broken into their house while he and Mary and their old uncle, Running Deer, were eating their meal at the strong plank table Ben had built. The day they'd managed to save only their lives and the clothes on their backs by going willingly to join their captured neighbors on the sorrowful march to Fort Haskins at Spring Place. For nearly four miles they had trudged along, some women weeping, although not Mary. Uncle Running Deer kept stumbling, and each time, a guardsman struck him across the back or face. Just after the old man crumpled for the last time, Ben had felt the first rip of the bayonet across his own backside. "Break line to help a useless old man, will you?" a pimply-faced guardsman had yelled and then jabbed Ben again, forcing him back into the line of march.

Rubbing the skin with his rock now as though he were attacking the weasel face of that guardsman, Ben fought, as he'd done so many times since, his own terror-filled imaginings of what might have happened, finally, to dear, wise old Uncle Running Deer. Night after night, in the past months, he and Mary had prayed that their uncle had been able to die quickly—right there on the ground where he'd stumbled and fallen. If he'd died, they didn't need to worry about him anymore. Uncle Running Deer would be with God.

Still rubbing the softening skin, he did his best to end such memories by thanking God that he and Mary had been driven into the same stockade, and that one bottom log had *not* been nailed down. By what had to be a miracle of God, Ben had been able to roll and shove Mary under that loose log and follow her into the black night.

They had not been shot dead in their tracks, and after an hour's stealthy run through the dense woods behind the stockade, they had slept in each other's arms until first light. For three days and nights, God had protected them as they traveled through wild country, avoiding settlements—even deserted Cherokee villages—eating only plants and berries. It was summer, and at night the warm ground welcomed them to sleep. Sassafras leaves and berries and wild onions held far more nourishment than Ben had ever thought, and they ate them freely. God had helped them survive, and then one day He caused Ben to think a bit more clearly. To think about how they would need a cook pot and spoons, a gun and powder and flint and steel and a pillow for Mary's head. God might have tried to remind him of salt, too, but Ben evidently wasn't listening. The thought of his own raid on an empty Cherokee cabin made him sad now as he rubbed the deerskin with the round rock and remembered his fine leather tools back in the attic of their cabin at Spring Place.

The hide was softening. It would make Mary a good skirt to wrap around for everyday use. With all his heart, Ben meant to remain hopeful for Mary's sake, but without another miracle, he had no idea—no idea at all—what their next move might be. He longed to find work, and soon, if not now, there would be work in the area.

In the days and weeks before they'd found their cave near New

Echota, he and Mary had, from various hiding places, seen gangs of Negroes and white men opening up new paths and roads across the valley or around a hill. This was enough to tell Ben that the white men were not waiting long to swarm over the just-emptied Cherokee land. There would be work. He could build, his back was strong and he was smart enough to learn any trade, but would he ever be safe? He could cut his hair short, but it would always be black and coarse and his skin was copper even in winter. He could wrap his head in a cloth, but it was widely known that some Cherokee men had at times worn turbans. Were soldiers arresting suspected Cherokees on sight? He expected abuse. Georgians hated Cherokees. But wasn't it only the Cherokee *land* the Georgians coveted? Did they really care about the blood of a good carpenter if they needed a store built or a house or a church? His main hope now was that they would not care. He could tolerate abuse.

Ben rubbed the leather against his cheek. It was almost soft enough, even for sweet Mary to wear. His hand and arm ached from the rubbing, his legs cramped from having sat cross-legged for so long. Slowly, holding the softened leather in one hand, he got to his feet and, as was his habit, listened to the sounds around him. On the rising wind, he could hear pounding all the way from the old Cherokee capital of New Echota. He listened more closely. It was either a man hammering or what Rich Joe Vann's Negro slaves used to call the Lord God Bird, the huge woodpecker with a flaming crest that could hammer at a dead tree so that it imitated almost exactly the sound of a man pounding a nail. When the unmistakable sound of sawing reached him, he knew men were at work. Building had already begun taking place in New Echota, where stood the Cherokees' proud Supreme Court Building, the old print shop where Elias Boudinot had published the *Phoenix,* Tarvin's Tavern, the good houses of Boudinot and of the missionary Samuel Worcester. Did he dare venture into New Echota? How would he find out what lay in store for him and Mary if he kept putting it off? Went on hiding in their safe cave? Maybe he should go—tomorrow morning, first thing. His heart quickened at the thought.

And then, body tense with alarm, all his senses keenly alert, Ben held his breath. Much nearer than the hammering and sawing, he plainly heard the beat of a galloping horse—nearer and coming nearer! On impulse, he half turned to flee in the direction of the

cave, then stopped. His feet crashing through the forest undergrowth would only attract more attention. In one swift movement,
he leapt over a fallen log and flattened himself on the ground beside
it. He piled as many old twigs and cones and mulch over himself as
he could before falling as silent as a hidden deer.

The galloping slowed to a trot, so near now, he could smell the
horse's sweat, slowed to a walk and then, not ten feet from where he
lay, a man's voice said, "Whoa, Judge, whoa, boy." The horse
snorted, pawed the soft earth once or twice, gave a little sideways
dance and stopped. "I smell smoke," Ben heard the man say. "It
smells like old smoke. Like a fire's been doused somewhere close by.
Do you smell it, Judge?"

Mary's cook fire, Ben thought. The rising breeze is wafting the
acrid stench of those damp coals! To protect their hiding place, she
always doused her fire with water from the spring. They'd been able
to keep secret the small fires he'd built at the mouth of their cave
through the long winter months. There was no road to their cave,
though, and so he hadn't worried. No road! Why was this lone rider
out here in these unmarked woods? The horse snorted again and at
a click of the man's tongue the animal began trotting in the direction
of the cave.

Ben turned his head just enough to see that astride the broad
chestnut back of the horse sat a young white man, curly yellow hair
long on his neck, almost to his brawny shoulders. He wore a wide-
brimmed felt hat at such a rakish angle that Ben could glimpse only
one side of his face, but the young man was smiling to himself,
unmistakably pleased about something.

At the top of the rise in the land above their cave, the rider halted
the horse again and whistled admiringly. Still talking to the horse,
he said, "I'm a son of a gun, Judge. Here we are at another spot so
beautiful I could put roots down here too! How many does this
make? All the way from Sparta, where I got off that stage and bought
you, we've been finding real beauty spots. You bring me luck. And
do you hear that hammering and sawing down there in the valley?
There's building going on. Work to do. Could you be happy here,
Judge?"

Then, as though a spell of boyish abandon overcame him, the
young man gave a lusty whoop and urged the horse to a gallop down
the slope, heading straight for the cave.

The abrupt charge away by the horse and rider brought Ben to his feet, one thought pounding in his mind: Mary Willow alone in that cave—unprotected.

Just as the man rode up to the deep ditch that ran along in front of the mouth of the cave, Ben raced to the wide, dark opening in the rocky cliff and spread his arms and buckskin-covered legs to bar the entrance—black eyes fixed on the startled, ruggedly pleasant face of the stranger. Ben stood there, catching his breath in long, noisy gasps.

"Hello," the stranger said, still astride his horse.

Ben said nothing.

"Where did you come from?" the man asked. "I just rode down from that ridge. I didn't see you up there."

His eyes riveted on the intruder, Ben still did not speak.

"You live around here?"

When Ben remained silent, the stranger let his gaze roam leisurely about the thick stands of gums, buds greening—clumps of mountain laurel, also big of bud, some showing color against the dark pines and oaks.

"You must live in that cave, then. Do you?"

While Ben was still trying to decide how to answer, Mary, in one, quick, graceful motion, ducked under Ben's outstretched arms and stepped into the sunlit space before the cave entrance. Smiling at the yellow-haired man, she curtsied as the Moravians had taught her to do in the presence of older, respected people.

Ben slipped a protective arm about her shoulders. She was still smiling, her dark eyes dancing. The rider returned her smile, then leaned down to shake Ben's hand. Ben held back, tightening his grip on Mary.

Hand still extended, the man said, "I'm not your enemy. If you both really live in this cave, I fully understand the fix you're in. You're Cherokees, aren't you?"

Ben took an involuntary step back.

"Are you married to this pretty little lady, sir?" the man asked.

"Oh no," Mary said. "He my brother. I his sister. You need us work for you, white man?"

The rider threw back his head and laughed. "Maybe, but not unless your brother agrees to shake my hand."

The young stranger's firm, friendly grip was like a comforting balm to Ben. Not since last June had he felt a friendly human touch except from Mary. "I'll shake your hand, sir," Ben said. "But after so many months, I—find trust hard."

"Of course you do," the rider said, sliding easily down off the horse. "And—I am white. But I'm not a Georgian. I was born in Baltimore in the state of Maryland. I'm moving here, though, to spend the remainder of my life." When Ben made no comment, he went on, "I've heard how your people were treated. It's disgraceful. I—want you both to know that—I'm sorry." Kicking at a pine cone with the toe of his boot, he added earnestly, "It must not seem to you as though I—care, barging in here this way so soon after your people were driven out." He looked straight at Ben now. "I'm not like the others, though. You'll have to take my word for that. It's just that I need to begin a new life on some frontier. I traveled Florida first. Didn't like it." His gaze now swept the rolling land and took in a mountain rising in the distance against what was now a reddening afternoon sky. "I love this land. I can—almost feel the agony of your people having to—leave it. You two took a terrible chance hiding out."

Ben's fear was waning. "Yes, sir," Ben said. "We took a chance. But we will find a way to work in order to stay. God will help us."

A slow, easy smile lit the man's agreeable features. "You could suddenly become my—cousins from Florida, I guess."

"Florida?" Mary asked.

"Lots of sun there, little lady. Your brother's dark complexion could be from the sun." The smile widened. "I'll tell you what—you could be my—Minorcan cousins from St. Augustine!"

The knot of fear that had become like a part of Ben's body loosened a bit more. He couldn't help grinning at this hopeful, energetic young man. "Some white people in Spring Place, our old home, cared enough for three Cherokees—an old woman, a mother and child, to let them become family," he offered. A distressed look clouded his face. "But—only if they renounce their—Indian blood forever. Our white name is McDonald. My sister is Mary, I am Ben. Our father was a Scot. She even has his hair—and pale skin."

"So I see," the man said, giving Mary an admiring glance. "Now that you've told me your names, I'll tell you mine. I'm Burke Latimer."

"Burke?" Mary asked in an awestruck whisper. "No. Not—Burke."

"You don't like my name, Mary?"

"You not be called—only Burke. You be called Mister Good Angel Burke!"

Ben found himself responding to Latimer's infectious laughter. Who could help it?

Abruptly, Mary clapped her hands with joy. "I go. You wait, Mister Burke."

When she had vanished inside the cave, Burke Latimer asked easily, "What's your little sister up to, Ben?"

"To serve you what little we have, I'm sure."

"All right. Fine. Haven't eaten yet today. I'll hitch my horse to one of your pine trees and relish whatever she brings. We have a lot to talk about. It's pretty obvious that you need me. And I wouldn't be a bit surprised to find out that I need you." He looped the reins around a branch, patted the horse's long, white-blazed face and said, "Judge, we're in luck today for sure."

When Mary returned from the cave bearing one of the two shallow wooden bowls Ben had found in the deserted cabin, the two men were admiring Mister Burke's horse, smiling and talking together as though they had been friends for a long time before this day dawned. Mister Good Angel Burke Latimer is good, Mary thought, eagerly handing him the bowl of broth. "You eat," she said sweetly. "You good to my brother. You eat my venison broth."

"You've both been in school somewhere," the man said, taking a big swallow of broth.

"Moravian school at Spring Place," Mary said. "I no speak good like Ben, but he older."

"He *is* older," Ben corrected her. "I'm almost twenty, sir, and I can work long hours. I don't tire soon."

"Good," Burke Latimer said, wiping his mouth on a jacket sleeve. "What kind of work do you do, Ben?"

Mary saw Ben look away, but only briefly. Then he said, "Carpenter."

Mister Burke's smile delighted Mary. "A carpenter, eh? This is without doubt my luckiest day since I was rescued from a shipwreck last June!" he said. "I'm a carpenter too. Actually, I have big hopes for contracting—houses, stores, churches. That's why I rode on here to New Echota. Settlers are coming all the time. You haven't ventured as far as the old Cherokee capital at New Echota, Ben?"

"No, sir."

"I afraid Ben go there. Better with my hair and skin that I go first," she said. "Ben refuse me."

"But you can't just stay on here." He was addressing Ben, giving him his direct, clear-eyed look. "Are you afraid to be seen in public? Are you, Ben?"

Ben nodded. "I'm ashamed to say yes. I'm full of fear—to go there—among them."

"No need to be ashamed of that kind of fear. It's probably sensible."

The three sat cross-legged on the ground for a long time, one idea leading to another, most of which were discarded because of Ben's Cherokee appearance. Then Mary said with sudden urgency, "Do not stop speaking! Do not stop thinking, Mister Burke. You are —good. God will give you idea what we do. Talk more. Ben, talk more."

Mister Burke chuckled softly. "Stop worrying, little Mary. The three of us are going on—*together*."

She beamed at him. "You say. We do!"

"Good," he replied absently, his mind, she could see, fixed on the problem of their next move. "Your brother and I are going to work together—build together. We just have to decide where we'll be safest—and do best—from our hard work. What comes to me now is that as soon as I can find another horse cheap enough to afford, we'd better get away from New Echota. I heard that a few Georgia guardsmen are still hanging around here—and anyway, this isn't the only beautiful spot I've seen. By the way, Ben, do you know anything about Cassville?"

"Not much, sir," Ben said.

"It's about twenty or so miles south of here. The county seat. I've heard talk about it. Cassville is going to be a real town, I think. They've already built a brick courthouse and a jail."

"They'll put me in the jail," Ben said, trying to joke.

"Over my dead body," Mister Burke snapped. "Don't forget, you're my *Minorcan cousin* from Florida."

"What is Minorcan?" Mary asked.

"Any person who came himself or whose family came in a group from Greece, Italy or the island of Minorca way back before the American Revolution to colonize a place they called New Smyrna. Things didn't work out too well. Some say the people were horribly mistreated. At any rate, they ganged up on the overseers and left. Walked up along the coast for miles to St. Augustine."

"Did Minorcans look like Indians?" Ben asked and Mary was glad, because she wanted to know the same thing.

"Well, let's say Minorcans don't look too Anglo-Saxon. Some have dark skin. I suppose, to the average American, they look somewhat foreign."

"You know much," Mary breathed, then asked, "Mister Burke, did God send you here?"

He laughed, not at her. His laughter, she thought, merely joined them all three together. "Whether God sent me or not, I'm here," he said. "And I hear there will be plenty of work soon in Cassville. I guess I didn't go there first, because I just plain wanted to see more of this beautiful Cherokee country. Before I found the two of you, I was considering settling near here. Cassville will do fine, though. And I feel it might be safer for Ben, since there's a chance those guardsmen are still around New Echota." She watched his smile widen. "I'm really not particular. I love every inch of this land."

"You Cherokee!" Mary joked.

Quite solemnly, he answered, "I'd be proud to be."

"Proud and scared," Ben said with a sly grin.

"You're probably right." There was an easy pause before Burke asked, "How long do you think you might be safe here in your cave, Ben? Long enough for me to go back to New Echota and earn enough extra money to buy a horse for Mary to ride on the trip to Cassville? I don't want to spend any of what little I've saved."

"I walk. Ben ride," she said.

"All right. You can take turns. Will you feel reasonably safe for another week or ten days, Ben?"

Ben only shook his head the way he did when he was uncertain.

"We be safe, Mister Burke," Mary answered firmly.

"I lost every cent I had in that shipwreck last summer," he said. "Afraid I can only afford one more horse, but we'll get along." Burke Latimer got to his feet, strode briskly to the horse and swung up into the saddle.

"You—have purpose," Mary said.

"That's right, little one, I do have a purpose now. You two wait right here—and be careful. I'll be back as soon as I can and you can both count on it." He leaned down to shake hands with each of them, doffed his wide brimmed hat and galloped out of their sight into the spring-green forest toward New Echota.

For a long moment, Mary and Ben stood looking after him. Finally, Mary said, "He will return to us. I love Mister Burke, Ben. My —love will bring him back."

Ben threw his arms around her. "Oh, Mary Willow, you love too easily! But—I also think Burke Latimer is good."

"He come back."

"I hope so. I pray so. But—your Good Angel Burke almost seems —too good to be true."

Hugging her brother with all her might, she said, "He too good— *not* to be true, Ben. You see."

THIRTY

FROM THE WINDOW of his upstairs room, William watched Mark lift his daughter down from the gig. He noticed that Natalie was smiling up at her father, so she must still be in her pleasant, obedient frame of mind. Good, William thought, because I've certainly put her through some real suspense this winter by not making up my mind when to start to the upcountry to find her young man.

The whole town was talking about Natalie's reform, which had begun, Mark had told him, almost at the moment William agreed to look for Latimer in the spring. William had been taking meals with his family a little more often these days—although he still refused to go out socially—and sometimes his mother and sisters had actually made him laugh with their Natalie tales.

"It's been like a conversion of sorts," Kate declared. "She began on New Year's Day by making, without a word of complaint, all those social calls with her parents."

" 'Dull social call after dull social call,' Natalie used to call them," his mother said. "If she felt bored and dull this year, she certainly fooled me."

"And she's still doing everything possible to please Caroline." Sarah laughed. "I honestly think she's too much for both parents sometimes. Caroline says she needs a course in how to be a mother to a perfectly well-behaved young lady!"

All I can say, William thought, watching Mark and Natalie stroll arm in arm up the front walk, is that she really loves Burke Latimer to be able to hold her little self under such tight control all this time, just on my promise to go.

He had honestly hoped to get away late this month, but there were now only seven more days left in March, and although he was going, William still had nervous spells alone in his room, so that his hands shook at the thought of leaving the safety of the house. If one of his spells came on downstairs with the family, he would quickly excuse himself and hurry upstairs. They all loved him—even nosy Kate—because no one asked any questions.

Today, though, he meant to give Mark and Natalie the news: If Mark would lend him one of his good geldings to ride, he'd made up his mind to leave at the end of the first week in April.

Father and daughter had disappeared from sight down below. They would both be inside the house now, talking to his mother. William took a deep breath and drew on all the courage he could muster. Mama will be calling me any minute, he thought. I won't mind telling Mark and Natalie that I made my decision based on riding alone instead of taking the stage. Talking to people some when I stop at night will be hard enough. Not as hard, though, as being trapped inside a stage where there would surely be another passenger who—knew about the *Pulaski* and might talk about it.

He heard his mother's call from downstairs. It was time to tell them all that his plans were set. For an instant, he felt an almost dizzying sense of anticipation. It had been so long since he'd looked forward to anything, and even now he wouldn't be honest if he said he did. But he was interested—interested to see the empty Cherokee land W.H. was so fired up about and interested to see for himself—if he could locate him—what Burke Latimer was really like.

Making his way slowly down the stairs, he was still more aware of the expectant stirring inside. There would be no backing down once he'd given Mark and Natalie his word. The near anticipation helped, even though it was probably no more than the relief anyone feels once a decision has been made.

From the landing, he saw Mark and Natalie standing side by side in the lower hall, peering anxiously up at him. "Good morning," he called down and felt as though he were about to present them with a gift.

· · ·

For more than a week, Burke had searched for a horse through every free hour away from the temporary work he'd taken at the construction site of Byrom and Kirkham's store at New Echota. Within two days, he'd been offered twice the money if he would agree to supervise the ragtag crew working with him. He refused. More money would help, but from listening to the ignorant whites on the job, he was more certain than ever that Ben McDonald had to stay away from New Echota. If Ben and his little sister were not safe, Burke had no intention of remaining there. With all his heart, he hoped Mary would find a good husband to care for her, but it was Ben who haunted him at night as he lay on his side of the hard bed shared at Tarvin's Tavern with a repulsive, fast-talking land speculator bent on making "a killin'" on Cherokee land.

"Ain't no way Georgia could ever have her just due as long as them savages was here smellin' up the place," the man had said. "Georgia's a white man's state—with rights. States' rights. They's so little to do around these parts so far, though, wouldn't bother me much if I was to run into an Injun or two. Be good sport to show him with my fists what we think of savages on what had oughta' be white man's property."

When Burke had asked him if Georgians might now more or less ignore a stray Cherokee who'd managed to stay behind, the man drawled, "Aw, I dunno. Why don't cha bring one around an' find out? Like I said, spillin' a pint or so of native blood would help pass some time."

Still, Burke kept hearing tales of the Cherokees who had safely escaped into North Carolina, living on the way in caves, as Ben and Mary now lived. There could be a few nearby, but none in New Echota so far as he knew.

"Jist lookin' at their uppity Supreme Court Buildin' here makes a white man's bile rise," his roommate assured him. "Seein' that an' their fancy printin' press—whew! Makes a white man wanta' rough up their ugly red faces!"

Beyond his careful questions, Burke had said nothing of his own feelings of grief for the Cherokees. Since meeting Ben and Mary, the grief had intensified. The grief and his own growing attachment for their gentle, wild, rich land. This was only his second trip to the Georgia upcountry. His feelings toward it were even stronger now than they had been after his first visit. On their makeshift raft, he had meant every word he'd said to Natalie about the Cherokees and what they had called their "enchanted land."

The time had come. He had to find a horse *tomorrow*, quit his job and hurry back to the cave. Wide awake, as far on the other side of the bed as possible from the snoring speculator, he couldn't dispel the haunting fear that Ben, so responsible for Mary, might risk a trip into New Echota without him if he waited any longer. Horses were as scarce as hen's teeth, it seemed, although one of the workmen that day had mentioned a Mr. Jones, who lived in an Indian cabin out in the country, who might just have one for sale.

The land speculator was snoring so loudly that Burke felt safe in turning over. He cringed at the thought of rousing the oaf, for fear he'd start talking again and not stop till morning.

Lying on his other side now, eyes still wide open, he glimpsed the sharp, bright tip of a sickle moon out the open window. "Natalie," he groaned. "Oh, Natalie . . ." Had he dreamed his love for her? Had he only dreamed it—confused by the unrelenting sun, the sickening swells of the sea, the incessant danger? Had he merely imagined that the spoiled rich girl named Natalie had actually begun to change out there before his eyes? Had he really written all the things he now seemed to remember writing to her in that letter he'd sent? Did he actually order her to go back to Savannah and pick up her gay social life in order to find out if she knew what she was saying when she vowed love for him? Did he actually tell her *not* to wait for him—that he would come for her someday when he had earned back his fortune and risk finding her still free? He had written the letter so soon after their rescue that now, almost a year later, the facts were blurred in his mind.

Only Natalie herself was not blurred, not dim, not confusing. Riding Judge on any day across the countryside, he could remember her lovely face as clearly as though she were standing before him. On his bed at night—now, this minute—he could see that face, not blistered and burned and swollen as it had been under the merciless sun, but young and perfect, feature upon feature, the whole of her form so beautiful as to stop a man's heart. He could see her as she had been at dinner at the Captain's table on the *Pulaski* the night Burke purposely tried to shut her out of his mind by ignoring her. He'd succeeded too, until the explosion had brought her back to possess him so that his own safety had meant nothing. Nothing that frightening night had mattered but finding her again in the black water. Finding her alive. Finding her and keeping her with him forever, so that at any time for the remainder of his life, he would only have to open his eyes in order to see her face.

He saw it now, just above the curve of the spring moon outside in the night sky, and he tried to turn his thoughts back to New Echota and the horse he had to find tomorrow, before poor Ben McDonald did something risky.

Astride Judge so early the next morning that the sun was just spreading its blush behind the distant mountains, Burke felt still more urgency to get back to Ben and Mary. The strong-smelling man in the bed beside him was still snoring when Burke opened his eyes and ended a dream of Natalie that he now couldn't remember. As he bathed quickly and dressed himself, he scolded her, ordered her to go away, to leave him alone today because he had important business. Beating the speculator to the washbowl in the morning had been no problem. The man, so far as he knew, didn't wash or shave.

"I'll never have to lay eyes on him again," he said to Judge as they galloped along an eight-mile trek to the area where he had been told Jones lived—Jones, the man who might have a horse to sell. "We're going to find a horse, Judge. Today, we're going to find something with four legs that can help you get us all three to Cassville."

His dream and last night's restless thoughts of Natalie seemed safely remote now, almost harmless, as he set his mind on one thing and one only—finding a horse.

In sight of the ample log cabin where he had heard Albert Jones lived, he slowed Judge a little and wondered at his own sanity. He'd been with Ben and his sister only a few hours. Desperate people did desperate things. What made him so certain that, once riding together through the wilderness on the way to Cassville, Ben wouldn't kill him in order to steal the horses?

Am I an outright sucker? he wondered, frowning as he neared the cabin. Have I been reading too much of the eastern press's railing against Georgia and the federal government in defense of the Cherokees so that I've gone soft in the head over their tragedy? Were Cherokees really as intelligent, as fair-minded as Jeremiah Evarts, the Boston missionary, had claimed?

Burke could trace his first interest and pity for the Cherokees to his reading of the Evarts' essays written under the pseudonym William Penn. Evarts had certainly been right that the Cherokees had patterned their own government somewhat after that of the United States. Leaving New Echota, he'd ridden past their empty Supreme Court Building only this morning. He'd also passed the printing press where they'd once published a bilingual newspaper. Newspapers prospered only if people read them. Savages couldn't read! He shook his head to clear it. He cared about the Cherokees, whatever the reason. And if he failed to find a horse now, he was going back to the cave tonight to get Ben and Mary anyway. They could take turns on Judge, if worse came to worse. After all, Cassville was only twenty or so miles away.

Burke walked his horse cautiously up to the porch of the log cabin, feeling a wave of shame for his country, whose national government had knuckled under to the land-hungry Georgians. Maybe, he thought, I'm also a little ashamed of myself for wanting so much to own some of the Cherokees' land. Am I, after all, so different from these other white settlers, many of whom turn my stomach?

He halted Judge and called, "Hello! Anybody home?"

A thin spiral of smoke from the single mud-and-stick chimney drifted on the quiet air, but for a full minute or so, as Burke sat his horse, he heard only the crow of a single rooster and a handful of hens clucking about the yard. Somewhere off in the woods that surrounded the cleared land, a dog barked. Burke called again, and from behind a faded blue curtain at the single front window, he saw movement. The curtain parted just enough for him to glimpse a woman peeking at him from inside.

"Is Mr. Jones—Albert Jones—at home, ma'am?"

"I'm acomin'. I'm acomin'."

Around from the rear of the cabin, a fat-bellied, middle-aged man, wearing a greasy deerskin jacket, ambled slowly into view. Plainly, he was in no hurry to welcome his visitor.

"Good morning," Burke said. "My name's Latimer. Are you Mr. Albert Jones?"

"The same. State yer business."

"I hear you might have a horse for sale. Tarvin, the tavern owner at New Echota, said he'd heard you have one you don't need."

"Got two. Horse and a pony."

"Could I see them, Mr. Jones?"

"You got eyes, ain't cha?"

Burke decided to go on trying to be pleasant. "You have the finest weather around these parts I've seen anywhere."

Jones spit a squirt of tobacco juice. "Once we git shed of the smell of Indians, I guess it'll be tolerable. My wife was sayin' this morning, it could take a year to git shed of their stench."

"This was—until recently—a Cherokee home, eh?"

"If you can call a place where animals rut a home. I been waitin' more'n five years to get my hands on this land. You'd think them heathens figgered they owned the whole United States of America the way they fought to stay here."

Half a dozen sharp retorts were on the tip of Burke's tongue, but he needed another horse. Best to keep his opinions to himself. "I don't have a lot of time, sir. Are the horses nearby?" Burke dismounted.

"Course they are. If you was to move five feet that way, you'd see 'em grazin' back there behind the shed. Come on."

Burke followed the man, hoping to keep conversation to a minimum by lagging a step or two behind.

"Over there." Jones pointed across a meadow to where a large dappled gray horse and a brown-and-white pony grazed on a patch of new spring grass. "One horse, one pony. That pony's worth more'n the horse, I'll warn ya. Horse has been good stud in years gone by. Still strong and easy to ride, but teeth shows his age. Pony's worth a lot of money. Both worth a lot of money. Horses ain't easy to come by. Took so many to haul them savages west. You want the pony or the horse—or both?"

"I'd like to have both," Burke said, "if they seem sound after I've tried them out. I probably can't afford but one. Do you have a saddle in the shed?"

"Got one, but a man gets a better feel of a horse between his legs without all that leather. If you really want to test a horse, ride him bareback. I'll fetch ya a rope."

No point in making an issue of the saddle, Burke thought, wanting only to buy one or both of the animals and get away—*if* he felt either was worth the asking price. While Jones was in the shed, Burke went up to the big dappled gray. The horse whinnied gently at the touch of Burke's hand on his forelock. "Let me see your teeth, old fellow?"

he asked, unable not to notice the fear in the big, dilated eyes. "Come on, now, I'm a friend." He lifted the horse's head, pried open the mouth and saw what Jones meant. This was no young animal. Still, a tug at Burke's heart reminded him that nothing mattered as much as getting Ben and Mary safely away. That had become paramount. Not too sensible, he supposed, but he meant to do it. Examining the horse, he shook his head at his own impetuous action. He knew nothing about either of his new Cherokee friends. Still, here he was risking being cheated out of hard-earned cash, heart pounding to get back before Ben gave him up and did something foolish.

He liked the big horse, liked him a lot, was still smoothing the strong, unkempt neck when he heard the pony canter up behind him and felt a nudge in the seat of his trousers. He whirled around and there was the chunky, sturdy little fellow up on his hind legs, happily pawing the air and all but talking.

"Hey, young sir," Burke laughed, reaching for the pony's mane. "You're doing quite a selling job on yourself. Do you know that?" Now the playful animal was nuzzling Burke's neck, pushing at his shoulder—a show of instant affection. "And look at that white star between your big eyes! You know you're a beauty, though, don't you, boy?"

"Which one you wanta ride first?" Jones asked, handing him the rope. "You'll have to put this on. I hate both animals and they know it."

Burke gave him a puzzled look. "You—hate these fellows?"

"They still stink of Cherokees!"

Mounted first on the dappled gray, Burke gave Jones a hard look. "These—belonged to a Cherokee?"

"Course they did. Every horse in these parts was bought or stole from an Indian, 'ceptin' the ones we rode in on, or the teams that pulled in our wagons. Most whites ain't been here long enough to raise horses. Lot of us just got here early last fall—or later."

While Jones was still mouthing, Burke galloped off. Better to get out of earshot. The horse galloped evenly, then slowed, at one tug of the rope, to a smooth trot. This is the horse Mary should ride, he thought, but wondered if the gray's back was too broad for her. For half a mile or so, he trotted, galloped again, then walked the aging animal. He could hear Jones yelling something, but took his time about rejoining him.

When at last he loped back and dismounted, the pony was up on his hind legs again, showing off, and Jones was muttering: "I might have knowed I made a mistake buyin' this durned, rearin', hard-headed pony. Hard-headed and mean as an Indian!"

Burke removed the rope and strode toward the frisky little animal. "If this pony's mean, I'm a jackrabbit."

"He'd as soon throw ya as look at cha."

On the equally mangy, tick-infested, but strong back of the pony, Burke called, "What's the matter, Jones? You that eager to sell the old one?"

Before Jones could answer, the pony and Burke were off at a gallop and out of hearing.

Burke smiled to himself. He liked the old horse, but he shouldn't spend his cash for both animals. Without a doubt, he would buy the pony.

Astride Judge and leading the pony by a piece of frazzled rope Jones had deigned to give him, Burke rode back toward New Echota. He had undoubtedly paid more than the going price, but at least he had avoided punching Jones on his fat face.

Remembering the man enraged Burke all over again, and without realizing, he caught himself galloping Judge too fast for the eager pony on the rope. He slowed to a trot and half wished he'd bought the old horse too, to save it from Jones. It had been wiser not to, of course. He was headed back to New Echota to quit his job. He and his Cherokee friends would need every dollar he had. By quitting the work on Byrom and Kirkham's store earlier than planned, he didn't expect Byrom, kind as he was, to pay him the agreed-upon amount.

He wiped his brow on his sleeve. Ben and Mary had certainly changed his plans, but his determination to save them was now stronger than ever. He laughed at himself a little, wondering if indeed he felt heroic for his trouble. He was rescuing Ben and Mary, though, as surely as the men on the *Henry Cameron* had rescued him and Natalie and the others last summer.

Nearing New Echota, the urgency to get back to the cave was so strong, he felt he'd give almost anything not to stop at the old

Cherokee capital. He had to, though. Byrom had been a friend. Riding as briskly as the pony could follow, Burke had reached the town and passed Tarvin's Tavern on his way to see Byrom, when he heard ugly voices and saw a gang of whites walloping the daylights out of what appeared to be a young Indian. Shouting, laughing and cursing, the angry men were beating their helpless victim over the back and head with fists and boards, so that the boy could no longer stand, but crawled frantically about on the ground.

Burke slowed, then on impulse urged Judge to a fast trot, hoping to slip past the brutal scene without being noticed—without seeing too much of it himself. If he was to make it back to the cave in time to get Ben and Mary out of the New Echota vicinity before dark, he dared not stop to go to the Indian's defense. Still, there was no way to avoid a glimpse of the desperate, bloody face as he passed, and before he'd ridden ten yards, he knew the face belonged to Ben!

By the time Burke dismounted and pushed his way through the crowd of onlookers, the attackers had begun to lose interest. "I've had enough," one of them said. "He ain't worth the trouble to haul him to the Army Post." Another brushed off his own clothes, took one more swing at Ben and knocked him down again. It took little effort. Ben was badly hurt.

"I oughta have you all arrested," Burke shouted as he helped Ben to his feet and began to drag him toward the pony.

"What're you doin', Latimer? You a Indian lover?"

When respected Charles Byrom came out of his half-finished store building to help him hoist Ben onto the pony, Burke was sorrier than ever to be quitting. "I hate to tell you this, Mr. Byrom," he said as they lifted, "but these roughnecks have just lost you a good carpenter. Me. This young fellow they've been beating is no—Cherokee. He's my Minorcan cousin from Florida. Came up with me. I can't hang around a place like this one more day!"

Byrom looked skeptical when he asked, "This boy's your—cousin, Latimer?"

"Yeah," one of the gang yelled, "that red-skinned, black-headed Indian's your *cousin?*"

Burke was on Judge now. "He's closer than a cousin," he called down to the ruffian. "And he happens to be—a Florida Minorcan, not a Cherokee! I planned to bring him to work with me tomorrow at Mr. Byrom's store. Not now." It was a lie, but in a good cause.

Hoping with all his heart that Ben could hang on to the pony once the little animal began to follow, Burke rode slowly toward Byrom and Kirkham's to pick up his tools. Charles Byrom, he noticed, had run on ahead and into the finished part of the store. Dismounting, Burke spoke some encouraging words to Ben, who sat there, bleeding and staring, unable to speak. Where had Byrom gone? Afraid to leave Ben until the sympathetic storekeeper returned, he waited, supporting Ben as best he could, hoping to save a little of the injured boy's energy for the ride to the cave.

In a few minutes, Byrom was back with a gunnysack of supplies which he himself tied on to Judge's saddlebags. "You'll need these," he said. "Go get your tools, Latimer. I'll wait with your—cousin."

As quickly as possible, Burke went for the tools, came back to stow them in his saddlebags and shook hands with Byrom. "You're a kind man, sir. I am sorry to have to quit on such short notice. I don't expect any pay."

Without a word, Byrom began counting out bank notes. "Just the same, I'm paying our full agreed amount," he said, handing Burke the money. "You'll need it. Hate to lose a good man like you, Latimer—and my deep apology for the brutality of the residents of New Echota. I hope your cousin isn't too injured to travel."

"So do I," Burke said, pocketing fifteen dollars—exactly the cost of the pony.

Byrom grinned at him. "Are you sure this poor fellow's your cousin? You don't take after each other."

"Cousins seldom do," Burke answered. "Thank you for my pay. Thank you still more for being—human."

"I keep still about it mostly, but I feel the way you do about how we've treated the Cherokees. Not that I think there could have been any other solution with Georgians so hot after their land. You know, Latimer, there are a few Cherokees still around here. I pray to God the time will come when whites more or less forget about them. Take them for granted. After all, it was their *land* they were after." He sighed deeply. "I had friends among the Indians before they left. I think about them now, wonder how many have died on the way west. You sure this—cousin of yours is able to ride?"

"No, but I've got to try."

"How far you aiming to go today?"

"That depends on—my cousin's condition, I guess. Ben? Ben, do you think you can ride?"

In response, Ben tried to lift his head, then, in a dead faint, slid abruptly sideways off the pony's back onto the ground.

Byrom helped Burke lift the limp body back onto the pony and hurried to the store for rope. Together, they lashed Ben, face-down, across the pony's back.

"If this pony's as steady as he seems, those ropes should hold for a time," Byrom said. "I wish you success, Latimer. Not asking you to tell me your destination, but my guess is Cassville. There's bound to be plenty of work there for a skilled craftsman like you. Cassville's burgeoning, I hear."

Back on his horse, Burke touched the wide brim of his hat. "I'm counting on a lot—from Cassville," he said. Before riding off, he took one more look at Ben on the sturdy little animal's back. "Good pony," Burke told Byrom.

"He does seem to be doing his best to help you. I never saw such a patient fellow in the midst of all that yelling and fighting." As though he hated to see them go, Byrom reached up once more to shake Burke's hand. "Good luck. I'm sure you know that what you're trying to do for your—cousin—could be risky for you, too."

"I know."

They shook hands again and then Judge and the pony began the slow, painstaking mile-and-a-half journey back to the cave where Burke hoped—even prayed—that Mary was still all right.

THIRTY-ONE

THREE DAYS before William planned to leave for Cassville, Eliza Mackay greeted young Julia Scarbrough Barnsley's husband, Godfrey, at her front door.

"What a pleasant surprise, Godfrey," she said, allowing the flawlessly dressed, cultivated gentleman to kiss her hand. "Please come in and sit down. This chilly spring day calls for hot tea. I'll order some."

"No, thank you, Mrs. Mackay," Barnsley said in his clipped British accent. "Forgive my being blunt, but I'm here on what to me is an urgent mission. I'm just relieved to find you at home."

Preceding him into the parlor, Eliza said, "Oh, I'm at home most of the time these days. You see, my son, William, is traveling to the upcountry soon, and mothers never outgrow their hope of being useful when a child has a project underway. Do sit down."

"Thank you. Tell me, how is William? He suffered such a dreadful loss, I find myself wondering how he really deals with it."

"William—is better, I think, although it's always hard to tell with him. But he's agreed to make this journey for Mark Browning—a personal matter—and I cling to the hope that his going is a good sign."

"I wonder if a man or a woman ever truly recovers from the loss of a mate. I say, do forgive me. I know you suffered that same loss, but your husband died so long before I left England for Savannah, I—"

"Don't apologize, Godfrey. The answer is no. One never fully recovers. One does eventually learn how to live a half-life. In spite of the heartbreaks she's had, which so few seem to realize, your dear mother-in-law, Julia, Sr., will learn how to live without her beloved William one day."

Eliza noticed Barnsley's somewhat skeptical smile. "I hope so. And that's part of my mission here today. You're an old friend of the Scarbrough family, Mrs. Mackay. You've known her daughter, Charlotte Taylor, longer than I, although I've known her quite long enough. My sister-in-law, Charlotte, is a brilliant woman, perhaps even an important writer and scientist, but she continues to make it plain every day, by some means, that her sister, my wife, and I are— only by her largesse being allowed to live in The Castle on West Broad. Her poor, grieving mother too. I mean to do something to put an end to her—haranguing us all."

"Oh dear," Eliza said. "I suppose Charlotte's still more domineering since the courts gave her full possession of the Scarbrough house."

"She is indeed, and I intend to put a stop to it—for my Julia and our family, and for her mother—just as soon as possible. I'm going to leave Savannah, establish our residence elsewhere. Perhaps near the Stiles property in the upcountry, in fact. I was as captivated with Cass County as was your son-in-law, W.H. That's the thrust of my visit today, Mrs. Mackay. I knew William was going up there. I wonder if it would be possible for me to see him?"

"Oh, I'm afraid William isn't at home this morning. He and the Browning girl are on a shopping expedition—William's first since the—tragedy."

"Good. I'm glad he got out of the house. And I must say, he's in entertaining company with Miss Natalie."

Eliza laughed. "Highly entertaining." Glancing at the clock on the mantel, she added, "They should be back by now, though. Wouldn't you care to wait for him?" At that moment, she heard the front door bang—unmistakably William. "Oh, here they are now, Godfrey. Natalie's so happy over William's trip, I don't know how she'll survive until he leaves on Friday. William? You have a caller. In the parlor, dear."

In the big double doorway, William and Natalie appeared, both laden with packages and boxes of all shapes and sizes. After a pleasant exchange of greetings with Barnsley, Natalie exclaimed, "Miss Eliza, I think I may die any minute now! I've never been so happy in all my seventeen years. Not about anything! Wait till you see all we've bought.''

"About two tons more than I can carry on horseback," William said, grinning. "I did finally convince her she'd have to ship this stuff up later when—*if* my trip's successful.''

"What on earth did you buy?" Eliza asked.

"And are you planning to stay for some time in the upcountry, Mackay?''

"Not that I know of, Godfrey.''

"Natalie, what's in all those boxes and bundles?''

"Why, blankets, Miss Eliza, bed linens, table linens, shirting, work clothes, a few fancy foods and supplies one can't possibly buy on the frontier. Just some necessary luxuries.''

"Where do you plan to stay up there, William?''

"I'm not sure. My mission is just not the kind you can plan that far ahead.'' William barely glanced at Natalie. "Only time will tell.''

"I'm sure this all sounds terribly mysterious," Natalie said, looking directly at Barnsley, "and even though my parents don't seem to want to tell anyone why William is going, I don't mind at all. On the *Pulaski* my life was saved by a young man named Burke Latimer. I'm sure he is now in the upcountry. Uncle W.H. says a place called Cassville has the most new settlers and is the most likely place for Burke to find work. You see, Burke Latimer's the man I'm going to marry, and temporarily I've lost him. William is going to find him for me. That's why I want William to go well supplied.''

The adults exchanged amused, somewhat uneasy looks.

"So you'll be heading for Cassville, then, William.''

"I figured I might go there first, yes.''

"Godfrey came by today to talk to you, son," Eliza Mackay said. "Something concerning your trip, I believe.''

"Frankly," Barnsley began, "W.H. told me you were going, William, although not why. I was hoping you might have time to look over some land for me. You see, I plan to move my family up there, too. Somewhere near the Stiles property—allowing room between for our spreads of land. My Julia and Eliza Anne are, as you know, such close friends, we'd like to be neighbors.''

"I suppose you've seen W.H.'s Etowah River purchase," William said.

Godfrey laughed. "Indeed I did see it on our last trip upcountry!

It was nearly dark before I could persuade him to leave his chosen spot high on those cliffs overlooking the picturesque little river. I've never known a man so taken with a piece of land. But look here, I'm sure you'll have no trouble learning what else might be available, especially if you're going to Cassville, the county seat. I—hadn't quite decided to make the move when W.H. and I were there." He looked at Eliza Mackay briefly. "Your mother can tell you why I've definitely made up my mind since. I want to leave Savannah. I like the country up there as much as W.H. likes it."

"When I marry Burke, we might all be neighbors!" Natalie exclaimed.

Eliza forced a laugh. "You can see how—lonely Savannah is going to be someday, Godfrey."

"But we can all visit one another, Miss Eliza," Natalie said. "I'm almost certain Burke's already bought at least one of those lots drawn in the lottery. Papa told me about all that. Each lot was a hundred and sixty acres. Burke isn't rich. He wouldn't be able to afford but one. You see, Mr. Barnsley, his savings were lost on the *Pulaski.* But he's a splendid carpenter and I'm sure he's earned back enough for at least one lot."

Eliza Mackay could see that Godfrey was taken aback at the idea of Mark Browning's daughter married to a man who worked with his hands. "Natalie's young man," she explained, "doesn't sound like a run-of-the-mill person, Godfrey."

"No. No, he certainly doesn't. Well, unless Stiles and I are sadly mistaken, he should find ample work in that area." Barnsley turned to William. "What do you say? Will you find out what you can for me about land near the Stiles tract?"

Eliza Mackay watched her son's face closely. Such a short time ago, William couldn't converse at all with anyone but Mark, Jonathan and the family. Did he still feel that the world was rushing at him?

"All right," William said finally. "After I take care of my business for Natalie, I'll see what I can do."

While William, to his mother's delight, was seeing Godfrey to the door, Natalie, all but dancing with joy, surveyed the stack of merchandise she and William had bought. "I can't wait to show it all to you, Miss Eliza. And you must promise to tell me what I've forgotten. Burke's going to need just about everything for his house up there."

Eliza took her hand. "My dear, aren't you allowing yourself to soar a little too high until William's had time to see if your young man is really there? Oh, I know he's determined to settle on the Indians' old land, but the Cherokee Nation covers a lot of territory. There's always a chance William won't be able to find him."

Natalie jerked her hand away. "Not you, too, Miss Eliza! Mama and Papa keep trying to discourage me by saying things like that. I really don't like people who disagree with me. I never have. Your very own daughter, Miss Lib, thinks I should have faith that William will not only find Burke, but that he'll find him *soon.* That's what I'm doing—having faith. You're always telling people to do that, aren't you?"

Deciding to ignore the question, Eliza sank into her favorite chair. "I know you don't like people who disagree with you and I'm not disagreeing. I'm just trying to protect you from what could be a big disappointment. You and Burke were in such danger on that raft, you were both so—ill, he may have said many things he—he—"

Natalie stamped her foot, then turned her back to face William, who was reentering the parlor. "Come in here, William," she demanded, "and help me with your mother. She's really being awfully difficult—and old."

"I reckon Mama is old enough to have quite a lot of wisdom," William said evenly. "You don't have to agree with her, but I've always thought it was smart to listen to what she has to say."

"William Mackay! Now you're turning against me—just when you and I were having such a good time together!"

"Natalie," Eliza said, "please listen to me."

"A sermon, I suppose."

"No, not a sermon. With all my heart, I want William to find Burke. I want Burke to turn out to be the kind of young man your parents will approve—and I want him to be truly in love with you."

Slowly, the girl's scowl faded. "You do know that I'm in love with him, don't you? Miss Eliza, that's the most important thing for everybody to know."

"Yes. I believe you are."

"I do want to be taken seriously. Whether my parents like him or not doesn't matter one whit. I love him. And he loves me." She paused and the tiny frown, so like her father's, came and went. "At least, he did love me last summer. . . ."

"You simply have to find out, don't you?"

Embracing her, Natalie said, "Thank you! No one *needs* to understand, but I—I like it when someone does."

The slow ride to the cave from the Byrom and Kirkham building site at New Echota seemed endless. Judge moved carefully, the pony walking steadily alongside on the short rope, so that Burke could keep an eye on Ben's still unconscious body lashed to its back. As they had crossed the cleared area, inside New Echota, men, women and children stared at them, punching each other, nodding and whispering. There was a way to go yet, when finally they entered the woods on the other side of the town, but Burke felt some relief. At least, they were alone, away from the people.

At last they reached the flat, thick, uneven slab of rock that roofed the cave entrance. Beside the gully that fronted the cave, he brought Judge to a stop. The pony stopped too. Burke would need Mary to help him lift Ben to the ground, somehow get him across the ditch and into the shelter of the cave itself.

He slid from the horse, sniffed the pure, sunny air. No scent of smoke. Good. Mary had not tried to cook. Undoubtedly Ben had warned her not to leave the cave while he was away at New Echota. What a reckless thing Ben had done. Why couldn't he have waited one more day for Burke to return?

He tried the thin sparrow's whistle that brother and sister had demonstrated to him the one time they'd been together. His version sounded all wrong. Burke tried again. No sound, no movement from inside the cave.

"Mary?" His voice was barely above a whisper. "Mary! Are you in there?"

He waited. The sudden movement of a ground bird in the nearby bushes sounded as loud as a pistol shot. He leaped the gully and peered into the low, dark entrance. In the cave's darkness, he could see nothing, but distinctly, though ever so softly, he heard the clear, sure sparrow's whistle.

"Mary," he called a bit more loudly. "Mary, it's Burke Latimer. Come out and help me with Ben! He's been hurt."

Her dark eyes wide with fear, the girl climbed out of the cave, jumped the ditch and flew to her brother, still draped over the pony.

"Bending Willow, oh, Bending Willow, my brother . . ." She seemed at once to moan and to sing his name, as she cradled Ben's head in her arms, touching his battered face, blood still seeping from one of the deeper gashes. Then, looking up at Burke, she asked, "Who hurt him? *Who?*"

"I'll explain it all later," he said, hurriedly cutting the ropes with his hunting knife, loosing Ben so that Burke had to support the sagging body in his arms.

"Bending Willow, my brother," she sang and moaned again and again, as she lifted and pulled along with Burke until they'd managed to carry and drag Ben down the gully slope, up the other side and into the safety of the cave. At least, Burke hoped it would be safe. With two horses tied outside, the almost hidden cave seemed no longer a refuge.

While Mary bathed and cleaned her still unconscious brother's wounds, Burke examined the bag of provisions Byrom had quickly gathered. There were two loaves of bread, several slabs of cooked ham, butter, a small jug of molasses and some apples. Enough, if they were careful, to last through the remainder of today and maybe for a day or two after they reached Cassville, should they still have to hide.

After a time, he heard Ben begin to groan. Then, lying on his own pallet on the cave floor, the boy opened his eyes. With Burke and Mary reassuring him, Ben tried to smile. Soon, he could even say a few words through smashed lips and seemed mainly intent upon promising Mary that he would be fine again.

"I—remember a pony." He looked up at Burke. "You bought a—pony?"

"Yes, Ben. A fine little fellow, too," Burke told him. "He carried you almost as though he had a longtime, injured friend on his back."

"Pony?" Mary asked. Burke saw her eyes fill with tears. "We—once had—pony. Little Star . . ."

"Well, the original owner of this little fellow must have loved him," he said. "I never saw such a playful animal when he and I first met."

She said no more as she set to work making root poultices for

Ben's cuts and bruises. Burke sat to one side of the cave, watching, thinking. The devotion between brother and sister touched him deeply. Mary had been terrified at first sight of Ben's face, but she had not wept. Rather, she had seemed to take control, as though aware that any sign of panic on her part would only harm Ben. Young as she was, Burke saw at once that he had no reason to worry that Mary might be a helpless burden.

When, at last, Ben dozed a little, she turned to Burke. "The man who sell you the pony love him?" she asked.

"*That* man had no love for anything but the dollars I put in his fat hand." Burke thought a minute, then decided to tell her that the pony had belonged to a Cherokee who lived at Spring Place, their old home. As he talked, Ben opened his eyes and listened too.

Mary stared at Burke, glanced at Ben, then got up and hurried outside.

"She shouldn't be out there, Ben!" Getting to his feet, Burke asked, "What got into your sister?"

And then they both heard her peal of merry laughter from outside and her voice, excited, tender with endearment: "Little Star! Little Star, my love! You come back to us—Mister Good Angel Burke bring you back to us!"

Ben tried to raise himself on one elbow. "Did she say—Star?"

"I think so," Burke said, crouched at the low entrance. "Mary! Come back in here!"

The girl seemed almost to float back into the cave, pouring out a joyful stream of Cherokee to her brother, embracing him, hugging herself. Then, in her child English: "It is Star, Ben Willow! Mister Burke buy Little Star for us! God hear my prayer—I pray every night for Little Star!"

Ben was staring at her, unbelieving. "Maybe—the pony—just looks like Star, Mary."

"No, no, no! He *be* Star. He kiss me, like always."

Burke then listened transfixed as Ben helped Mary recount their capture by the Georgia Guard that ghastly late summer day at Spring Place. With both parents dead by then, brother and sister and crippled Uncle Running Deer, their mother's brother, had been sitting at the dinner table in the cabin their Scottish father had built for his Cherokee wife before they were born. Sitting together talking, laughing and eating—Mary even remembered what they ate—

roast pig and potatoes, carrots and cornbread. Uncle Running Deer, once a tall, strong full-blood, had been shot in the thigh on a hunting trip and crippled for life, but he helped Mary around the house and he was gentle and loved to laugh. Three times Running Deer had been knocked down by guardsmen that day and never seen again in the stockade.

"He dead," Mary said just above a whisper. "With God now. Uncle could never make long walk—west."

After Ben helped her tell of their miraculous escape through the loose lower log of the stockade fence, the young man sank back onto his pallet, tears streaming down his swollen cheeks.

"They take our horses and—they take Little Star," Mary whispered. Then, suddenly, the smile came. "But you buy back Little Star!"

Burke could only give her a dumbfounded grin. "Piece of good luck, little Mary. Just plain good luck."

"No. God."

He laughed. "All right, God." He got to his feet. "We need some luck right now. Ben, how about trying to get up? I—hate to say this, but you know we need to get as far away from New Echota as we can —yet today."

"I'll—ride—as far as I—can," Ben said faintly.

With Ben riding the pony and Mary and Burke the horse, and their precious provisions, the thick bearskin blanket and Mary's white-woman's shirt and skirt secured to Judge's back, the little trio moved cautiously, steadily away from the sheltering cave in the direction of Cassville.

Ben surprised Burke and Mary by holding out, upright on Little Star's bare back, until only an hour or so remained before dusk. All along the way, Burke had watched for a cave where they might spend the night. There was none, because they rode over a kind of plateau surrounded by low, rolling hills.

Well, Burke thought, as Ben slumped wearily across the pony's neck, we'll sleep on the ground. We have Ben's old mud-caked bearskin, Mary's deerskin skirt and my greatcoat. His coat now hung around Ben's shoulders, and although she made no complaint, Burke knew Mary had to be chilled through. He was. Fearful of building a fire, he portioned out their food, urging Ben to eat as much as he could. And then, with Ben between them for what they hoped would be healing warmth to his injured body, Mary and Burke stretched out too, on the hard, cold earth.

For a time, only night sounds stirred the black silence that seemed to lie over them like a moist blanket.

Then, his voice weak, but almost vibrating with what to Burke seemed a sudden and surprising confidence, Ben murmured: " 'For he shall give his angels charge over thee, to keep thee in all thy ways.' " A moment passed in which there was only the silence again and the night sounds. Soon Ben whispered, "Mary? It's your— turn."

As though she'd waited for Ben to tell her to begin, Mary spoke softly and clearly: " 'The angel of the Lord encampeth round about them that fear him, and delivereth them.' " Then she explained: "We say that before sleep each night, Mister Burke."

Such a long time passed without anyone speaking, he was sure his new friends had fallen asleep, when Mary said, "It is good to trust God, the Great Spirit." Then she sighed contentedly, curling her body closer to Ben's. "It is—good to trust Mister Burke."

THIRTY-TWO

COMFORTABLY MOUNTED on Mark Browning's fine chestnut gelding, William smiled a little at the still fresh memory of his final glimpse of Natalie beside her father in the middle of the road when he left early this morning on the long-awaited trip. Riding two other Browning horses, father and daughter had gone with William as far as the Louisville and Savannah Road, which would take him that first day to Statesboro, Georgia, where Sheftall Sheftall had told him he'd find the only decent hotel. After a ride of six or seven hours, he'd be ready for a night's sleep. Oh, he'd stop some to rest and eat. His mother and Hannah had packed enough food for a regiment—fried chicken, boiled eggs, fruit, biscuits, cornbread and, at Hannah's insistence, half a coconut cake.

Rob, Mark's blooded horse, was surely a strong, steady animal, his red-brown body aglow from the special grooming for what to all the Brownings was a special journey. The day was clear and sunny, with just enough breeze to make riding pleasant. William felt far better than he'd expected to feel heading away from the shelter of his familiar room.

"That girl Natalie," he said aloud to himself, "bouncing up and down in the saddle, waving both hands over her head as I rode off. Hard to tell about her. A lot must go on deep down inside that people would never suspect." Speaking aloud gave him a kind of pleasure. No one could hear, or think him peculiar. No one there but the horse, Rob, who seemed exhilarated, glad to stretch his legs on the open road. For the fun of it, and to match Natalie's excitement, William had galloped Rob until he could no longer see his friends when he looked back over his shoulder. The trip was a long one. He'd hold Rob to a steady pace most of the three hundred-plus miles to Cassville.

Of course, he meant to begin asking around after Burke Latimer tonight in Statesboro. Still a long way south of the old Cherokee boundary, but William had promised Natalie not to leave a single stone unturned. His sister Kate had teased Natalie about looking for Burke under a stone. William loved Natalie too much to tease her at a time like this, but then Kate had never minded too much when she hurt somebody, if she got off what she thought was a good joke. He was fond of Katie, but Sarah had always been William's favorite.

Earnestly, during the days of preparation for his trip, William had prayed that the smothering, thick hood of his grief would not—out of the blue—fall over him during the lonely ride. But suddenly there it was! As always, with no warning. Everyone had kept saying the trip would help lighten the sorrow. Not for one minute did he really expect that. He was making the long journey only to find Burke for Natalie's sake. Nothing could ever lessen his sorrow because nothing could ever bring Virginia back, or the children. Lately, though, he thought maybe he could find a sort of peace in seeing Natalie happy with her young man. He supposed few people who knew her would believe him, but William had seen a change in Natalie since the day she'd come to Causton's Bluff to tell him about his family's last moments. He would never forget that she had held his baby son all night long in that mean, black water, even after the little fellow was dead.

He stopped when the sun was directly overhead and ate part of his picnic lunch. Hard to understand how spring had just quietly slipped back to the woods again with Virginia and the children gone, but it had.

The picnic lunch tasted mighty good.

It would have taken a healthy rider only half a day to cover the twenty miles from New Echota to Cassville, but by daybreak on their second day, when it began to storm, Burke realized that Ben was not going to be able to go much farther. And, as though Mary's prayers had really been answered, they had found a cave—a low-ceilinged, tiny cave, but for most of two rain-drenched days and two nights, it had been home. A dry place, at least, where Ben could lie quietly on the bearskin and rest.

On Friday morning, they ate the remainder of the food Charles Byrom had given them, but the sun was out at last. Burke went hunting and shot a big buck rabbit, and with a handful of wild onions Mary picked, the last meal in their temporary cave home wasn't bad at all. Ben seemed so happy to have Burke's salt in his rabbit stew again, they all took heart. Ben was definitely improving.

"I'm riding on into Cassville in a few minutes," he told his two friends when they had almost finished eating. "We can't be more than a couple of miles from there and we've got to establish ourselves today—out in the open, so there'll be no more hiding. They told me back at New Echota that settlers are coming to Cassville from other parts of Georgia, even North and South Carolina, without homes to live in. What they do is hunt till they find an empty Cherokee cabin and move into it. They learn later who claims to own it now and then they buy. I don't much like just taking over a place, but we're going to do it."

"Whatever you say, Mary and I will do," Ben said, finishing the last bite of stew.

Burke got to his feet. "You two stay right here in the cave, Mary. Let Ben rest as long as he can. No more fires. Just stay inside until I come back." He grinned at them. "Can you trust me—once more?"

Big, hard scabs had formed on Ben's mouth, but some of the puffiness around his eyes had gone down. His smile, as he reached for Burke's hand, looked a little more like Ben. "We trust you, Burke."

Clinging to his other hand, Mary said, "I trust you like God."

"I wouldn't go that far," he said, smiling down at her, "but you can be sure I'll get back sometime today, so we can sleep in our new cabin tonight—if I'm lucky enough to find one."

"You feel lucky today, Mister Burke?"

He laid his hand on the soft, curly brown hair. "Yes, little one. I've decided you're my good-luck charm."

"You love me, Mister Burke?"

After a surprised laugh, Burke asked, "*What?* Why, yes, Mary, I guess I do."

• • •

"Nothing fancy," Sheftall Sheftall had warned William, "but the hotel at Statesboro is—a shelter of sorts. A place to lay your head. Watch for the good wooden bridge over the Ogeechee. Cross the Ogeechee River and go north. You'll be traveling parallel to the river, over higher ground. The swampy land will be on your right as you ride. Then just head for Statesboro and hope for the best. There's only one hotel. Just pray to find only a few bugs in the room they give you."

William liked old Cocked Hat Sheftall a lot. He always had. The aging Jewish gentleman had such authority when he explained something, you caught yourself not wondering how he knew so much until later. William wondered now how Sheftall happened to know that much about roads leading west when he had seldom left the streets of Savannah except in the early days when he used to make an occasional trip by water to Charleston.

By the time he'd crossed the Ogeechee, William was more certain of Sheftall's advice. The bridge was a good one and the road paralleled the river on the other side, with swampy land to his right. Mark thought a lot of old Sheftall too, in fact, had told William that one reason he'd been able to hold out and not look for Burke Latimer sooner was Sheftall's support in the decision to honor Latimer's own wishes. At Natalie's insistence, William had read Latimer's letter only last week and believed Sheftall to have been right in convincing Mark that Burke needed time to set his own affairs in order, no matter what Natalie said or did.

William remembered the girl saying when she'd handed him her letter that his trip would be a lot easier if he could know for sure that she had been right about Burke all along. William smiled to himself as he rode along, thinking about the letter. It seemed to him that only a strong, honest man could have written it. A man with a mind of his own, though. A proud man with no intention of living on the Browning fortune. Mark had been right to make her wait. Heaven knew, it had cost him dearly. Undoubtedly, Natalie would never admit he'd been right, but he had been. The girl just didn't have the patience to give anybody enough space, even her beloved Latimer. William shook his head. She just might have to learn how, if I read his letter right, he thought.

At the fork in the road, William turned off and covered the few remaining miles to Statesboro right at sundown. In the town itself,

he saw that there were only two buildings of any size—the courthouse and another two-storied block-shaped frame house a little
beyond it. The frame building had to be what was going to pass for
his home for the night. It was.

He was in some luck—to William, a lot of luck. There were so few
visitors in town, he actually got a room to himself. It cost a little
more that way, but he'd be better off by far if he didn't have to talk.
One sniff of the greasy cabbage odor inside the hotel settled his
mind, though, about food. He'd take the rest of his picnic lunch
from home to his room for supper.

Burke had galloped Judge about a mile or so toward Cassville
when he saw the first small log cabin. Slowing his horse, he circled it
carefully, listening, watching, making sure it was deserted. At one of
the two paneless window openings, he shaded his eyes against the
bright afternoon sun and peered inside. Rats and mice, coons, too,
he supposed, had done their destructive work among the still rumpled beds along one wall. Scraps of dry, moldy bread and what he
took to be meat—at least, parts of a dead animal of some kind—had
been chewed and dropped over the dirt floor. A table still held
upended bowls and cups and a piece or two of flatware. Burke
frowned. He'd lay a healthy bet that this Cherokee family, like Ben,
Mary and the uncle they never saw again, had been captured while
eating. Weathered, stringy, once striped curtains still hung at the
two small windows, and plain but sturdy furniture stood about the
room—a rocking chair, four straight chairs, a low cupboard—and
showed that the Cherokee family had been among the typical hard-
working farmers who had loved and tended the good Cass County
earth.

More troubled than he wanted to be, Burke rode slowly away from
the little cabin and headed Judge toward town. If possible, he hoped
to find a larger house, even though he meant it to be only temporary. He had no intention of staying for long in an Indian cabin. Oh,
he meant to buy one, if he could find one for sale, but with any luck
and plenty of hard work, he'd be able to save enough in a year or so
to build a good place of his own. Long before he'd fallen in love with
Natalie, he'd drawn detailed plans for the house he wanted. He
would teach Ben how to build a solid house—furniture and cabinets
too.

He heaved a disgusted sigh. How did Natalie get into his mind today—of all days? How would she ever, ever fit in with life here? With Mary and Ben? For that matter, with him?

Natalie . . . Natalie Browning. Sometimes at night, before sleep came, she was *not* Natalie Browning the rich Savannah beauty, whom he was trying desperately *not* to love. At those times, she was—just his Natalie, brave, hurt, burned, tired, clinging, helping him, loving him—possessing him again as she did on their blessed raft. He slept well on those nights; deep, certain, restful nights when she was just —his. His to touch, to kiss, to hold, to work for, to look after, to live for. To belong to. Next month, it would be a year since the two of them had lived so concentratedly—every minute of every hour—for and because of each other. A year since those brief, eternal five days in which they simply stayed alive together, in which they let love grow, shared thoughts, dreams. *Dreams.* He urged Judge to a gallop. They had shared *only*—dreams. Vague, shapeless ones, at best. No plans. No firm plans at all. Unlike now, though, on the raft, there had been no need to struggle against loving each other . . . not as he was struggling now, this minute, sitting Judge's broad, hard, rounded back—bent on his crazy mission of finding a cabin where he and Mary and Ben could sleep tonight. He was *not* hunting a house for Natalie—but for himself and two lost, helpless Cherokees.

He'd just decided that Natalie had probably never even seen an Indian, when up ahead—around a slight bend in the narrow road, he saw a fairly large cabin in an almost weedless clearing. Behind the well-built log house stretched old cornfields, unplanted. He must clear his mind of Natalie, as someone needed to clear that cornfield of weeds . . . there were more urgent things to think about today than that beautiful face he so longed to see again, that sun-bright, curly hair . . . those pale, translucent eyes that had looked at him with laughter and anger and longing and annoyance and willfulness and—on the raft, even ill and hurt—with love.

Galloping straight down the lane that led to the good cabin, he tried not to remember what she'd said about the Cherokees: "Don't Indians just cause trouble, Burke?"

"Shut up, Natalie!" he shouted, riding up to the front porch. "The more I try to put you out of mind, the plainer I see you—hear you! Not now . . . not *now.*"

He looped Judge's reins around a porch post and tested its

strength. Only a little wobbly. Stepping back a few feet, he looked at the single stick-and-mud chimney. Chimney seemed all right, but the porch roof probably leaked or those floorboards wouldn't be rotting. On the whole, though, the house was sturdily built. Old, but cared for. And cared for fairly recently, if the condition of the hewn logs stopped with hard upcountry mud was any indication. Few cracks, no empty spaces. Sun glinted off real glass windowpanes, too. Glass was surely a rarity up here. He stepped up onto the porch —two wooden steps above the ground—and examined the wide, solid, sturdy front door; its leather hinges were in good shape. This had been the home of a prosperous Cherokee, he decided, and would take only a modest amount of repair.

No smoke curled from the chimney, but suddenly he felt as though he were trespassing. The ample front door was closed, and because of the clean, neat yard and garden, he made no move to try it. Instead, he knocked. There was no answer. Still, he did not go inside. His breathing was short and quick. Why? Was he only excited because he had probably found a suitable cabin? Or was he intruding?

He jumped off the porch and walked rapidly around to the back. Almost at once, he felt somewhat easier. A huge iron kettle was turned over on its side. Against the wall of the house leaned two hoes and a shovel. A corn-husk broom lay on the ground as though it had just been dropped. Soaked from the heavy rains for the past three days, but still unopened, he found three bags of grain piled one atop the other by the back door. A good bucket still hung above what appeared to be a deep, tended well. He'd been told that whatever could be damaged or stolen, the Georgia Guard damaged or stole. There was not one broken window anywhere. No guardsman could have resisted smashing an Indian's windowpane, if he was well off enough to have glass panes. Then Burke saw the neat row of plants in buckets and kegs lining the path to the well. The plants were all blooming.

Back at the front of the house, he noticed the clean, well-made flowered curtains at the wide window off the porch, but they covered the window so that he could see nothing inside. Up on the porch, he knocked harder this time. Listening, he could hear no sound but a nearby mockingbird, singing so loudly that the gray-and-white bird, wherever it was perched, seemed about to burst itself wide open.

The horse whinnied restlessly. "Hush, Judge."

His ear against the door, Burke listened for another few seconds, then—in spite of believing now that the house was empty—he knocked once more. There was still no answer, and because the sunset light on the windows was beginning to turn crimson, slowly, quietly, he lifted the iron latch and pushed open the door. It didn't creak. The leather hinges were soaked in oil. Recently oiled.

"Hello!" His own voice sounded as though it belonged to someone else. "Anyone home?"

There was still no answer, and yet he felt such a sense of intruding that he waited again. And then he heard a clock ticking somewhere in the shadows of the large, neatly furnished room. A clock had to be wound at least once a week. If no one lived here now, the homey place had surely not been deserted for long. He stepped inside and looked around. There were two rockers and, around a square table, four straight chairs. A chest and a bureau with doilies stood against two walls and he counted four bedsteads with mattresses—one bed unmade, a woven coverlet merely thrown up over the pillows, the others carefully made up with Indian blankets smoothed and tucked in around other pillows. Still on the table, all washed and stacked, were six pottery cups, six pewter plates, forks, spoons and two knives. Pots and kettles and two iron spiders hung or stood on the hearth of a good, wide fireplace.

He touched nothing, but stood in the middle of the well-laid split-log floor and marveled at how right the cabin was for their needs. He and Mary and Ben would each have a bed and one to spare! After their primitive winter in the wilderness, Mary and Ben would consider the cabin a mansion, and he could see Mary's smile at her first sight of that fireplace and all those kettles.

He knew for a fact that white settlers who rode into Cherokee country these days were simply occupying empty Indian cabins and seeing later to their purchase. This place had been too recently lived in to risk that, but with all his heart, he did want it. In his own way, Burke believed in God, but prayer was such an infrequent and inward thing with him, he felt a little guilty asking God now to fix it so that he and his new friends could move in. He had no idea how much land lay around the house, no idea at all that he would be able to afford the property even if it turned out to be for sale. But he had no doubt at all that Mary and Ben were praying this minute that he'd find a place for them. He decided to leave prayer to them and hurry into Cassville for some firsthand, factual information.

Back on Judge, he got his bearings and headed for town. From New Echota, they had traveled south and slightly east to the Cassville vicinity, which lay near the head of a level valley about three quarters of a mile wide, he supposed, flanked by almost parallel ranges of hills and closed by a cluster of lower hills to the north. Everything about the outlying area through which he now rode told him that Cassville was not only situated in a picturesque spot, but that its terrain was more than suitable for growth. Within a few minutes, he could see buildings up ahead and knew that, just south of the town, there had to be the important junction of the Alabama with the New Echota Road over which Judge galloped now.

Entering the town, Burke could see that Cassville was well planned. The dirt streets were at least forty feet wide, bordered on each side by ample space for sidewalks. Even the cross streets were wide and provided room for walking. He was not surprised—delighted, spirits soaring, but he was not surprised. He'd heard talk of the concentration of lawyers in Cassville, many still busily occupied handling transfers and sales of the recently emptied Cherokee lands. Lawyers lived well and collectively had enough power to keep a place growing.

In town, Burke headed straight for the new two-storied brick courthouse, which spread over much of the town square, passing thirty or forty new or fairly new houses on the way and some stores. Work for him would be plentiful in Cassville, he thought, dismounting and looping the reins over a peg on the courthouse hitching post. He glanced around, then went briskly through large double doors and stood admiring the interior of the courthouse, taking in the flurry of activity. Another good sign. Prosperous-appearing men moved up and down the stair to the second floor or stood in deep conversation in the small vestibules inside what he now could see were four sets of elegantly made double doors giving the building entrance from all sides of the town square. Most of the lower floor was given over to the courtroom, and a sign indicated that offices could be found upstairs.

Taking the steep stair two steps at a time, Burke found the room marked "Clerk" and went inside.

"Afternoon," a middle-aged, balding man said, peering over his spectacles. "Another new face in Cassville, eh? What can I do for you, sir?"

"It so happens I'm from Baltimore, but as of today I'd like to be from Cassville. I'm looking for information about the fair-sized cabin less than a mile north of town. I couldn't find anyone around, the fireplace and chimney are cold, but it doesn't quite look like an Indian cabin deserted last year."

"It is an Indian cabin, though," the clerk said. "Ol' Miz McNally died day before yesterday. Don't believe she was a Cherokee, but her husband was an eighth-blood. General Winfield Scott showed mercy on her last year when they removed the Cherokees. Mr. McNally just up and died of heart failure when the guardsmen first broke into their place. That left Miz McNally alone, old, partly crippled, but neat as a pin about her cabin. The General left her back by herself in the house. No heirs. The state owns the property if that's what you want to know."

"Is it for sale? If so, how much, and how much land around the cabin?"

"It was the regular size of one Cherokee lottery tract—one hundred and sixty acres. The old man had sold a hundred acres of it. You can buy the house and what's left of the lot right here from me if you've a mind to." The clerk busied himself in the pages of a large deed book. "Hold your horses a minute and I'll tell you how much."

Burke waited impatiently. The man seemed in no hurry as he slowly ran his finger up and down rows of careful script and figures. Finally, without looking up, he said, "Lot 356 with house sells for a total of four hundred and fifty dollars."

Property so close to a growing town, Burke knew, would be higher than wild land, but he had no intention of paying out nearly a third of what he'd managed to save. "Tell me the name of a prominent man in town," he said. "Someone involved in working to see Cassville grow. Could you do that?"

The man peered up at him for a moment, then said, "Mr. Fred Bentley's our brainiest lawyer. Got his office in a little building next to the jail. Fine gentleman. Got a lot of git-up-and-go, but he's busy. Don't see the reason to bother him. I got the figures right here."

"Is the jail nearby?"

"Four blocks east of the courthouse. Another fine brick building."

"Thanks," Burke said. "I may be back later."

"Better be soon. I close at five o'clock sharp."

Knocking on the new, still unpainted pine door of Fred Bentley's law office, Burke hoped he was doing the right thing. He meant to be completely forthcoming about his Minorcan cousins from Florida—if saying they were his cousins *was* forthcoming—but he also intended to make friends, if possible, with Bentley, who undoubtedly could steer him toward work, and a better price on the cabin. Cassville looked promising. He liked the town fine, but it wasn't the only settlement in Cherokee. Ben was stronger. They could move on, if Bentley couldn't or wouldn't help him get the property for less money in order to get Burke to settle here. Waiting for an answer to his knock, he fidgeted. It was getting late. He'd have to ride hard in order to get them moved into the empty cabin tonight. Even if Bentley couldn't help, he fully meant to borrow the McNally place temporarily. No more risk in that than he'd been taking from the moment he'd begun to feel responsible for Ben and Mary McDonald.

Rather abruptly, the door swung open and a tall, pleasant-faced, dark-haired gentleman, slightly out of breath, held out his hand. "Sorry to keep you waiting," he said. "I do manage to have myself trapped under a pile of law books every time someone knocks on my door, it seems. Fact is, I was on a stool trying to replace a stack on the top shelf. Come in, come right in."

Burke liked his handclasp, liked the man himself, but vowed to try, at least, to be cautious. He had hunted so long for the right place to settle, it wasn't easy now to conceal his growing enthusiasm for Cassville.

"My name is Burke Latimer, Mr. Bentley," he said, taking a chair beside a newly varnished, rather poorly made desk. "I need some help—not exactly legal help yet—but if it entails legal work, then I'm a prospective client." That didn't sound very cautious.

"Legal or not, I relish giving advice," Bentley said warmly. "I take it you're new in town?"

Burke explained his background and his purpose as briefly as he could, then asked, "Is the word of your county clerk final on real estate transactions, Mr. Bentley? I find I'm interested in Cassville as a place to live and work. I can contribute some good buildings to this town, but I'm not rich. I was shipwrecked last summer and every dollar I'd saved—ten thousand in all—went down with the ship. I've worked hard at my trade of carpentry since then, saved every penny possible, but the asking price of the McNally place is too high for me." He looked directly at Bentley. "I think I want to settle here. My cousin, Mary McDonald, can handle my housekeeping. Her brother Ben is also a carpenter. They're of Minorcan blood. Joined up with me in St. Augustine, Florida, last year." He felt no uneasiness in the lie. The times made deceit a necessity. "I plan to teach Ben cabinet-making, to make a first-class craftsman of him. I'm a master carpenter. I'd like to be a part of Cassville's future."

Bentley studied Burke for a while, half-smiling. Then he began to run his hand over the corners and top of his desk. "I think you can see by the botched-up job I got on this desk that we need at least one good craftsman in town. You can bet your bottom dollar that there's going to be a lot more building done here. Building of all kinds. I don't hesitate a minute to tell you you'll be needed. How much are they asking for the McNally place?"

"Four hundred and fifty. I assume that includes the furnishings in the cabin. It may be worth that much, but I can't pay it."

Burke could almost see the wheels spinning in Bentley's head, as he sat tapping the desktop with his fingers. Then he pursed his mouth in a way Burke imagined must mean he'd made up his mind. "Would you pay three hundred twenty-five, Latimer?"

"Yes, sir!"

"You'd be getting a bargain. That's a good cabin. The McNallys were fine folk. Took care of their place. Except for his one-eighth Cherokee blood, they might both still be there, enjoying it, as they always did." Bentley shook his head a bit sadly. "She died alone day before yesterday, probably of a broken heart. They always had Indian help on the place. The help was removed last summer. McNally must have been nearly eighty. Those bayonets only had to threaten him. He keeled right over dead the morning they came to remove him and the old lady."

"I was told that the kindness of General Winfield Scott allowed Mrs. McNally to stay," Burke said.

"I guess you could call it kindness. She might have had no Cherokee blood, but the truth is, she would simply have been too much trouble on the long trek west. We think she could have been dead a full day when her body was found. But the floor of that cabin was swept so clean you could eat from it."

"Her clock is still ticking," Burke said.

"You've been inside the cabin?"

"Yes, sir. You see, Mr. Bentley, I need—my cousins and I need a place to stay tonight."

Without a change of expression, Bentley asked, "You're sure those cousins aren't Cherokees?"

"Yes, sir."

"I just thought I'd ask. Although I doubt if anything would be done if a Cherokee did turn up in Cassville now. Especially under a white man's supervision. We've got their land. Nobody wanted them. But any—Cherokee should be careful living around here. Be on good behavior."

Bentley did not sound antagonistic. Burke felt the gentleman was merely warning him. He had no intention of admitting the truth, though. "You may already know the St. Augustine residents they call Minorcans are Italian, Greek and Minorcan. My cousins are—Greek."

"I see. Well, I just thought you should be informed."

"I understand."

Bentley gave him a long look. "Somehow I think you do." He got to his feet, a sly smile on his good face. "All right, Latimer, I'll go with you to the courthouse. Our clerk, Jackson, wouldn't have his job except for me."

THIRTY-THREE

MARK AND HIS FAMILY sat at dinner on the afternoon of what should be William's second day on the road, if everything had gone well. Neither Mark nor Caroline mentioned William's trip—just in case Natalie didn't feel like hearing it discussed. Since late last year, in fact, they had both tried valiantly to show her only love and understanding. The hardest of all, especially for Caroline, Mark knew, was not to have asked even once about the contents of Kott's note found in the box of money. Either Kott had told her of the blood relationship, or he hadn't. She had given no hint. When and if Natalie wanted to tell them, she would. Together, he and Caroline spoke often of the precarious, thin line between spoiling their daughter and allowing her room to grow up. Most of the time during the long, chilly winter months, they had felt fairly comfortable with her. The girl was trying to be agreeable and both parents meant to respect her effort. In one sense, they supposed, Natalie would always live in her own world—alone.

At table today, instead of speaking of William's journey, Mark had been bringing Caroline up to date on the recent boom in the cotton market, enjoying, as he always had, her keen interest in his business.

"I really think we should build another row of good, modest houses," he said, helping himself to more of Maureen's creamed chicken. "Savannah still has poor families who would live far happier, healthier lives in well-built, clean houses."

"That's a wonderful idea," Caroline agreed. "I wish I could tell you how proud you make the children and me."

"I know I'm proud of you, Papa," Jonathan said. "But we both keep our family secret about who owns your low-rent places. Don't we, Sister?"

When Natalie didn't answer, but went absently on pushing food around on her plate, Caroline said, her voice quite lowered, "Our Maureen was telling me, Mark, just last week that her cousin and his family—he's not at all well—moved into one of your other buildings and they are ever so much better off."

"Is that a fact? Good."

"But the truth is, the family had to wait for more than a year. We do need more."

"It's sure not easy to keep our secret, Papa," Jonathan said just above a whisper. "I know it's hard for me 'cause I'm so proud of my father. But I haven't breathed a word to anyone. Have you, Natalie?"

"Hm? What, Jonathan?"

Mark reached to pat his daughter's hand. "Your sister's mind is definitely not in Savannah right now, son."

As though they'd been talking about it all along, Natalie mused, "William stayed in Statesboro last night." Mark could tell that throughout the meal she'd been going over William's planned route. She knew every road by heart. "Not a very good hotel," she went on. "But that's behind him. Today, he backtracked to the Savannah Road, going parallel to the Ogeechee River again. William said he was sure he'd be able to see the remains of last year's tornado up there. You know, twisted trees, houses not rebuilt yet. I wonder if he did." She looked at Aunt Nassie's gold pendant watch, which Mark had given her on her seventeenth birthday. "William's through Queensboro by now. In fact, he could be in Louisville in a couple of hours."

"He'll find three good hotels there," Caroline said. "One in particular is quite nice, I think. Ladies like to stop in Louisville because of it. Mrs. Habersham says there's a big yard and lots of live oak trees for shade. A fine place to rest for a day or so on such a long journey."

"Oh, William promised me he'd travel every day," Natalie said.

"I'm sure he will if he can," Caroline agreed, "but we want him to rest if he needs to, and even though Louisville's no longer the capital, a lot of people still go there because of the slave market."

Mark had learned to keep quiet when Caroline made one of her casual remarks about buying and selling slaves. They had never quarreled over the subject, but he had been forced to accept that she actually thought of owning slaves as an ordinary part of life. It was, he supposed, and turned the conversation back to William.

"Good old William is so careful with money, I wouldn't be surprised if he stops tonight at the cheapest of Louisville's three hotels, even though I urged him to stay in the best."

"Papa, he will find Burke, won't he?" Natalie's lovely, anxious face tore at his heart. "William won't begin looking for land for Uncle W.H. or Mr. Barnsley and fail me, will he?"

"I can't promise he'll find him, darling, but I can promise he won't let anything he can help stop him."

"Papa?"

"Yes, son?"

"What if you and Mama don't like Burke Latimer? What if, when William finds him, he turns out to be a—not very nice man?"

Glaring down at her brother, Natalie jumped up. "Mama and Papa *will* like him!"

"But if he turns out to be the kind of man they wouldn't want you to marry, Sister—"

"I'm no dunce! And I'm the one who's going to marry him. Not Mama—not Papa. Certainly not my nosy little brother."

"I thought you were so grown up these days," Jonathan teased. "You surely don't sound like it. You sound just the way you've always sounded."

"Only a mature woman knows when she really loves a man, dummy."

"Natalie, sit down and finish your meal," Caroline scolded. "William isn't anywhere near Cass County yet, where you're so sure your Mr. Latimer will be. There's no way anyone can know exactly what he'll find—or how it will all turn out. We simply have to wait."

Mark watched his beloved daughter sit back down, unwillingly, of course, her face so furious it would have been ugly on anyone but Natalie. "Your mother and I are, in our ways, as anxious as you are, dear," he said, trying to keep his voice calm.

"You are?"

"We're anxious in many more ways than you. You seem to have no reservation about anything. We all still have questions."

"I guess that just shows you don't trust me."

"We sent William to try to find him, didn't we?"

"Yes, *finally,*" she said. Her anger was gone now, the partial smile almost an apology. "It took long enough, but you're sweet, Papa. You're sweet too, Mama. I just love Burke so much it—hurts. Not just some of the time. It hurts all the time!"

On his way to Greensboro, after a good night's rest in Louisville, William, traveling northwest, crossed the Ogeechee for the last time over a sturdy old bridge pronounced "Fann's Bridge," but spelled Fenn's, after the Fenn family. He was told that Zechariah Fenn had built the bridge himself in the 1780s, and William paid a toll to his descendants, who still kept it in excellent repair. He was able to buy a good meal at Sparta toward the middle of the day, since it was the crossing point for the east-to-west Milledgeville–Augusta Road. He'd be glad to reach Greensboro—another sixty miles—where Sheftall Sheftall vowed he'd find the best choice of hotels anywhere on the entire journey.

Creek Indians had once burned Greensboro—sacked and burned it almost to the ground—William knew. Undoubtedly, he'd see the evidence when he got there in spite of the new activity he'd heard was going on in Greensboro these days. He thought for a while, as he rode along, about Indians in general. It seemed a pity for them to be driven out of their homes, off their land because white men wanted it. Still, the United States did belong to the white man now. It had taken the federal government a mighty long time, actually, to clear them all out of the Southeast. He wondered how much truth there was in the rumors that the Cherokees, especially, were a highly intelligent, pretty well-educated people. Mostly farmers—peace-loving, willing, they claimed, to share the country with the whites, so long as they could stay on their forefathers' property. That, of course, was impossible. Until they'd been driven out, the Cherokees had allowed no white person to settle in their Nation unless he or she was married to a Cherokee or had mixed blood.

After galloping Mark's gelding, Rob, for a stretch, William slowed the horse to a steady trot and went back to his thoughts. How fair was it, he wondered, for one race to prosper at the expense of another? Until now, he'd never really questioned that the Creeks had been long ago run out of his own region of coastal Georgia.

Actually, he didn't question removing the Indians from anywhere in the booming, growing United States these days. It was just part of living in the year 1839. Bad to break treaties, but, he supposed, unavoidable.

What actually happened in human history and what was right didn't always match. Life wasn't fair. So far as he'd heard, though, the Creeks had burned and sacked no other town in the whole state of Georgia but Greensboro. He didn't feel that one sacking showed them to be especially warlike. Well, he held his opinions to himself. Too much questioning got a man nowhere and made enemies. He had worked so hard at curbing his own questions after he lost his family, he was certainly not going to begin torturing himself with unanswerable ones about a bunch of Indians he didn't even know. Natalie swore that her Burke Latimer was on the side of the Indians, the Cherokees, at least. He has a funny way of showing it, William thought, if he's headed straight for his own piece of their empty land up there.

He was getting closer to "up there" all the time now. Tomorrow's long ride of seventy-five miles—all the way to Decatur—would put him almost into the old Cherokee Nation. The country through which he and Rob traveled now was rolling. There was no more gray, loamy coastal soil. Even the earth itself had changed to red clay. Pretty color, he decided. There were no more palmettos, no more Spanish moss hanging from the trees, and they looked kind of naked. The word "naked" shot his mind unwillingly to—Virginia and the children—their dear bodies, almost naked when they died, he was sure—since the *Pulaski* had blown up at night with them in bed, surely only in their nightclothes. Asleep, for all he knew. He'd never done harder work than to force himself to turn away from useless speculation about those blessed, nearly naked bodies tumbling helplessly, in the dark, impersonal sea. . . .

He must be getting tired of the journey. Always good on a horse, William had never made such a long ride before. Dark-sided thoughts would help nothing, though. Would only make him more tired.

For several miles, he made himself concentrate on Natalie and what was beginning, by now, to seem her wildest idea yet. At his insistence, any specific plans, even the first stopping place once he reached the old Cherokee territory, had been left indefinite. "I'll have a chance on the way to discuss what's going on up there since the removal," he'd told Mark. "I know Natalie wants to know my every move ahead of time, but how can I know till I get there?" He had agreed to write to her, though, on his first night in Cherokee country.

He would be taking Montgomery's Ferry above Decatur, in order to cross the Chattahoochee into what had been the Cherokee Nation. The talks he'd had with men at his various stops so far indicated that Cassville, the county seat, might be as good a place as any to ask questions about newcomers to the area, but he'd have to see how tired he was after tomorrow's long ride. He could honestly tell Natalie that he'd begun to hunt for Latimer just outside Savannah. He'd seen no wide-shouldered, yellow-haired young men anywhere. No one had heard the name Burke Latimer. Well, there was still a long way to go, a lot of places to look, a lot of people to ask.

Crazy as Natalie's dream appeared, at least it gave him something to try for again.

Through their first night in the clean, roomy cabin—now Mister Burke's very own property—Mary slept so soundly and so long, the next sun was up and shining before she awoke.

Slowly, her dark eyes opened, and at first, fear engulfed her. Through the long, icy months of waking up in the New Echota cave, she had been afraid on every new morning, until Ben spoke to her. She felt afraid now and stiff from such a long, deep sleep. Involuntarily, her eyes squeezed shut again from the fear, she stretched her legs under Mrs. McNally's warm comforter, then touched the bed with her hand—once, twice. Real sheets! Her fingers moved over real sheets, smooth, of the kind her mother had spread over their beds when she and Ben were growing up. Then she listened, eyes open now. By the way they sounded, the birds outside had been singing for a long time. It was late. Still she lay there, trying to believe she was safe. Except for the birds and the spit and crackle of a nearly burned-out fire in the fireplace, she could hear only deep, regular breathing. Sleeping breath. The breathing of the two she loved most on the earth—her human saviors, Ben and Mister Good Angel Burke, who did not like her to say "angel" of him. She closed her eyes again and folded her hands together. "Thank You, God, for both, for gift of both men to me. For safe night. For safe morning and no need for fear. For new day to make happiness for them. For —no more cave!"

Soundlessly, she slipped out of the warm, cozy hollow in the bed and wrapped around her new deerskin skirt, then slipped a large white cotton blouse over her head. In Mrs. McNalley's cupboards and drawers she had found white-woman's clothes, too large, but not Cherokee. She had found also tea and coffee and sugar and flour and lard. Now, in the morning sunlight, she saw, for the first time, a salt dish. No meat, but she could make hoecakes for her men. Hot hoecakes and hot coffee, and hot tea, too, if Mister Burke liked. Anything, she thought, clasping her hands together in joy, oh, anything I long to do for him!

Over a year ago, Merry Willow had, at not quite fourteen, looked upon Swift Bear, a neighbor's son, who sat across the room from her in the Moravian school, with shy longing. She had longed only for him to smile at her. But . . . now, overnight, over the very first night . . . perhaps even at the first minute her eyes had seen Mister Burke—she was no longer a tender girl. She was a woman.

She must mix dough for hoecakes, but first, she must go to the far end of the cabin where Mister Burke slept. He lay on his back, the thick golden curls spread on his pillow, mouth a little parted. One husky forearm covered with curly golden hair hung over the side of the bed. She drew in her breath sharply, sick with a strange, heavy longing. Golden. He was golden. Her good God could have given Mister Burke only *golden* hair. Not black, not brown.

The new, unfamiliar longing frightened her, made her ashamed and yet not ashamed. She lifted her head. Love is not to be ashamed. Love is to cherish. To give more—to give more than there is to give, she thought, her head seeming almost giddy. God is love. God gives. God gave. She was taught that God gave His Son for her sins.

Her dark eyes still fixed on Burke's strong forearm, she said inside her heart, I do not sin to love him! I am in God's love. To give. Not to take from him—to give. Oh, Mister Burke, her heart cried, let me give to you . . . let me give to you what—I cannot. She frowned in dizzy confusion. Let me give to you what I—do not even know to give. . . .

THIRTY-FOUR

OVER THE NEXT FEW WEEKS, Burke and Ben worked at repairing the front porch, the old shingle roof and recaulking some chinks in the logs of their new home. Then they built a small back porch and a new room adjoining it where Burke could live in a semblance of privacy. Except for an occasional trip into town for supplies in trade for a divided bin he'd built for food staples and a new door at Hawke's Store, Burke stayed close to the cabin, not minding at all. Even on rainy, dark days, the mood in their home was sunny. Ben was learning the fine points of cabinetmaking as naturally as a squirrel buries nuts and enjoying it as much, too. For Burke, the work of teaching him was pure pleasure. Both laughed a lot at Mary, who seemed not to sit down all day except to eat or sew, happily using the needles, spools of thread and calico Burke had bought in town. Her delight in the new scissors brought smiles every time she picked them up, which she did at the slightest excuse.

"You know, you're quite a pretty young lady, Mary," Burke told her when she twirled out onto the back porch in a bright flowered dress she'd just finished making. "Did you realize your sister was such a beauty, Ben?"

"Always. She was curly and pretty as a tiny baby."

"Do not speak of me then," she scolded. "I grown woman now."

"I *am* a grown woman," Ben corrected.

"You no look like a grown woman, Ben!" Breaking into peals of laughter, Mary twirled again, so that the long, full skirt billowed about her delicate ankles. "All my life, I think my brother, Bending Willow McDonald, to be a man!"

Burke laughed too. But Ben frowned. "You made a good joke, Mary, but what do I have to do to teach you to stop talking like a Cherokee who cannot speak English? Do you want to get Burke into trouble by your broken talk?"

When Mary wilted, Burke went to her, lifted her chin and said gently, "You're doing fine, Little One. We're all doing fine."

"She should be careful, though," Ben said. "Especially should she stop all Cherokee talk. Do not call me Bending Willow, even here at home. I no longer call you Merry Willow—not ever." Burke saw tears spring to Ben's eyes. "It is—sad, little sister, but for all Burke has given us, we must protect him. Not sometimes. All the time."

She scowled at Ben, then lifted her face to Burke's. "I am—doing fine, Mister Burke?"

"Indeed you are, Little One."

"To you I am a—grown woman?"

He laughed. "Well now, I'd have to give that some thought. What I said was that we're all doing fine, and we are. Ben and I are undoubtedly the best-fed and best-mended men in Cassville, and we live in the cleanest, neatest house. How's that?"

She shrugged and went slowly back inside the cabin.

"What do you think that meant?" Burke asked.

"Who knows about Mary? She's changing every day."

"Oh?"

"At times I feel I do not know my own sister. You haven't noticed?"

"No, I can't say that I have. She's probably just at the age when being a little girl is no longer comfortable—and being a woman is new territory. Unknown territory. A little scary."

"You had a sister once?"

Burke laughed. "No. I have known a few girls, though. And—women."

Burke picked up his hammer to finish nailing a strip of molding around the ceiling of the new porch and Ben began to saw. Suddenly, the sawing stopped.

"Something wrong, Ben?"

"You will get married soon?"

Stunned by the question, Burke laughed again somewhat awkwardly. "What ever made you ask a question like that?"

Ben merely shrugged.

"I swear, I didn't know Cherokees shrugged so much," Burke said.

Smiling up at him, Ben quipped, "Not Cherokees. It is Minorcan cousins who shrug."

With no word at all from William for almost a month, Mark had begun to dread the end of a workday because neither he nor Caroline could any longer find ways—valid or imaginary—to calm Natalie's growing fears. That there were good reasons for those fears he had no doubt. William, who always kept his word, had promised to write as soon as he'd reached Cherokee territory. If he had written, the letter was at least two weeks late. There was reason to worry.

Mark went over and over his own concerns for William's safety. Was he ill? Rob was the best of riding horses, but had he thrown William on a lonely road somewhere with no one to help? Or had William found out something about Burke Latimer too terrible to report by letter? Natalie, poor child, not only worried about William, her dream of finding Latimer hung suspended in the torment of such a long wait for word of any kind. There had even been time for Eliza Anne to write to the Brown family with whom she and W.H. had stayed last year during their trip to Cass County. Time to write and to have received a reply—yesterday. The Browns had heard nothing about William. No word at all of anyone from the coast visiting in those parts. Kate Mackay tried to toss off her anxiety by saying that William was probably just dawdling around in one of his moods, but the Mackays were all uneasy about him.

When Caroline met Mark at the front door one soft, early May evening, he could tell there was trouble.

"It's Natalie," she whispered. "Natalie's taken to her bed. And, Mark, I think she's really ill over all this. I wish we'd never heard the name Burke Latimer!"

He led her into the parlor. "You know you don't mean that. Latimer saved our little girl's life."

"And now he's ruining it. Hers and ours too. Miss Eliza had a mild spell with her heart last night—worrying about William. Kate was here for a few minutes. Even Kate, who loves to badger William, is

terribly upset over what might have happened to him. Mark, she is
sure he's been killed by the Pony Boys!"

Mark stared at her. "The Pony Boys?"

"There's another piece in today's paper about them. You remember we read not long ago of that gang of cutthroats—highway rob-
bers, actually—who attack travelers on the roads around the Chattahoochee River or somewhere up there in the wilds. They struck
again."

"They killed somebody else?"

"Shot two men from South Carolina right off their horses. It
happened near a place called Pumpkinvine Creek. Took all their
money. Oh, Mark, should you have allowed poor William to make
that dangerous trip? Couldn't Natalie have found it in her teeming
little head to fall in love with a civilized gentleman with ambitions to
succeed in a civilized society? What if something did happen to
William? How would we ever face Miss Eliza?"

"Here, sit down, darling. Posing all those unanswerable questions
won't help anything. We need now, of all times, to be calm and—
and—"

"And what?" She did sit down, but on the edge of the love seat.
"Calm and what, Mark?"

"You were as willing to let William go as I. It won't help a bit to
push the blame off onto me."

"I know it won't." She sighed heavily. "What can we do?"

Sitting beside her, he took her in his arms for a moment, then
pulled away. "I can't think until I've been upstairs to see Natalie. I'm
sure she needs me."

"I need you too," she said, clinging to him. "Can't you just sit
here and hold me a minute?"

"Yes, yes. Of course."

Their embrace was cut short by rapid banging of the front
knocker. They both rushed to open the door. It was William Henry
Stiles, who strode quickly inside.

"I have news," he blurted. "Miss Eliza has had this letter from
William."

Seated anxiously in the family drawing room, Caroline demanded, "Where is he? Where's the letter from, W.H.?"

"In the name of heaven, read it, W.H.!"

Unfolding the letter, Stiles began at once: " 'Cass County, Sallie's

Ferry, Etowah River. Dear Mother and All, I know you have been worried and I expect Natalie is fit to be tied.'" W.H. stopped. "Natalie should hear this too," he said.

"She's ill in bed," Mark explained. "The child has worried herself sick."

Caroline jumped up, calling back as she hurried into the hall: "Maybe she isn't really ill. Maybe this will perk her up."

"You're right, Mama," Natalie said from the top of the stair, then ran down the steps, pushed past her mother and into the parlor. "I heard your voice, Uncle W.H. Give me that letter!"

"Natalie, don't be rude."

"I can read aloud too, Mama," she snapped. "Where on earth is Sallie's Ferry?"

"Not far from the land I've bought," W.H. said. "Sallie Hughes was a wealthy Cherokee, who for years ran the ferry across the Etowah. She's been removed west now, of course, but I'm sure it will go on being called Sallie's Ferry."

Natalie reread William's opening sentence and hurried on:

" 'For most of my final long day on the road, it poured rain. I caught a bad cold. So bad that by the time I took the ferry across the Etowah River, still some fifteen miles or so from my planned destination, Cassville, the county seat, I was too sick to continue. A kind, Christian gentleman, whose fertile land lies near the ferry, took me in. A good thing, since I was sick enough not to be able to remember much about the first week or ten days in his comfortable house. His name is Arnold Milner, of English parents. He came to Georgia from South Carolina some five years ago in search of health, bought this land, built a good log house—now, he owns the States' Rights Hotel in Cassville and—' "

Natalie stopped and said, "*Who cares?*"

Smiling a little, W.H. said comfortingly, "Read on, Natalie. William does get to the part that concerns you."

Natalie's sigh was so loud, all three adults smiled a little. She continued:

" 'Milner's house slaves, two kind and faithful Negro women, have taken the best care of me. I owe them much. It is likely that I may be able to ride the remaining distance to Cassville by next week.' "

"When did he write this?" Natalie demanded. She flipped the pages to find a date. "April the twentieth, Papa. William wrote this more than a month ago! Why did it take so long to get here?"

"Undoubtedly no one was riding to Cassville just when he wrote it, darling. That's where letters are posted up there, isn't it, W.H.?"

Before W.H. could answer, Natalie said, "Never mind. Listen to this.

" 'All along my journey, from the outskirts of Savannah, I have inquired at every opportunity about Burke Latimer. Of course, once I regained my senses from the illness, I asked Milner if he'd heard of a young man from Baltimore answering Latimer's description. I fear he has not, although there is one new resident rumored to be in Cassville, who has bought a deserted Indian cabin for himself and his two cousins from Florida. I am not hopeful about this, except that, according to the rumor, the young man seems somewhat to resemble Latimer in appearance.' "

"Oh, Papa—Mama—did you hear that?" She rushed on. "There's more.

" 'As I understand it from Natalie, Latimer is from Baltimore, not Florida, but be sure that I will follow every rumor to its source once I reach Cassville. My strength is ebbing now, so tell Natalie to trust me to do my best as soon as I am able. Do not worry, Mama, since I am improving every day and would improve faster if I could sleep without coughing at night. Your affectionate son, William Mackay.' "

"Now, doesn't that make you feel a little better?" W.H. asked.

Natalie sighed again. "A little. And I do trust William." She looked beseechingly at her parents. "I'm trying. I really am trying to be patient. It's—it's just been so long. So horribly long. Next month, it will be a whole year since I've seen Burke's face!"

William didn't feel strong enough to make the fifteen-mile ride to Cassville until the much warmer third week in May. Even then, he dismounted often, ate frequent small portions of the food Milner's cook had packed for him, then rested for long periods stretched out on a blanket. He would lie there, giving himself a few more and then a few more minutes, until the spring-cold ground began to chill him, before he could make the enormous effort to remount and ride on.

Had he felt well, he would have covered the distance with some ease in a little over half a day. When the setting sun began to paint copper-bright patterns among the dark foliage of laurel and pine, he pushed himself to ride for longer periods without resting. He had come through wild country most of the way, with no landmarks along the narrow clay trail, but felt he must be within a few miles of Cassville, and though dizzy at times in the saddle, he pressed on.

His nose was still swollen from his deep cold, but on the light, gentle wind, with darkness perhaps still an hour away, he thought he could smell whiffs of wood smoke. Cassville must be nearby. Just ahead, he could hear the rhythmic splash of a small waterfall. Perhaps if he dismounted and took a good drink, bathed his face a little, he would feel refreshed enough to make it all the way. At the waterfall, he could see that the icy mountain water tumbled down from twenty or thirty feet above the trail off a jutting of mossy limestone into a straight, almost gentle stream. He drank, then splashed two or three handfuls over his face. It helped some and eased the burning in his eyes.

Back on Rob, he felt more hopeful that he would sleep tonight in a bed, under warm covers. The sound of the waterfall faded behind him as he trotted Rob rapidly now, determined to reach Milner's States' Rights Hotel in Cassville by dark. Rob's steady clop-clop on the hard red clay was soothing. Cardinals and brown thrashers in the woods about him were giving their sleepy evening ticking sounds and a whippoorwill began to call in the distance. In his weakened condition, William tried to concentrate on the peace, the soft, wild calls, the fact that he did have a chance to reach his journey's end tonight. But after half an hour or so, he was again so exhausted that he could feel hope fade along with the dying light.

Although the land was too hilly to see the sun, it must be sinking fast. At home, in the low country, one could watch the huge, fiery ball until it vanished into the flatness of sea or marsh. Not up here. A man had to find an opening between hills in order to see the sun actually set.

He felt dangerously drowsy, his eyes no longer refreshed by the icy water. Then a distant thudding noise, flatter than thunder, broke into his consciousness. Or was he—having another nightmare? A quick glance at the sky brought on a dizzy spell so severe, he grabbed for the saddlehorn. The thundery noise, not loud, but steady now and somehow ominous, was coming closer and closer. A horse! A galloping horse. More than one—a band of horses galloping up behind him—and a rough man's voice shouted: "Halt, or we'll shoot!"

The gravelly command still grated in William's ears after the heavy blow struck the back of his head. As he lay sprawled on the hard ground, he could hear cursing, mumbled talk. Could hear men dismount . . . one of them growling, "Whoa! Whoa!" at Rob. Then a blessed fog, thick, painless, somehow easy—shrouded William's mind.

Soon after she washed the dinner dishes that afternoon, Mary announced to Ben that she was going into the woods to pick poke greens.

"Not today. Tomorrow, when I'm finished with this," Ben said, sanding the skillfully made lid of the coffin Burke had been asked to build for the body of an old man who had died in Cassville that morning. "You know I don't like you to go into the woods alone, Mary."

"You are coward for me."

"That makes no sense. Say it in better English. For Burke. We have to try harder for him, Mary."

Picking up her basket, she said wistfully, "We alone now. Mister Burke in town. Can I not be Merry Willow to you, my brother? Our mother's clan still strong in our blood—your blood and mine. Can blood run out and change?"

"You must form the habit," he said sternly, laying aside his work. "If you aren't careful with me alone, you will not be able to be careful when someone else can hear. Georgians—white people— use verbs when they speak. They do not say, 'We alone now.' They say, 'We *are* alone now.' You know that."

She took a deep, disgusted breath and blew it out noisily. "You not love Mister Burke above my love for him!" Smiling now, teasing, she added, "White people not always solemn like you, either.

Mister Burke laugh much. You *are* solemn. Do not frown so, Bending Willow."

"*Ben!*"

"I do better. But I go now to pick poke greens to cook for him tomorrow. And sassafras roots for tea. He like it."

Ben was smiling at her now. "I know how hard it is for you. You were with our mother so much and I with our white father when we were growing up. It's easier for me to speak English. And what I say to you in plain English this minute is that you cannot go into the woods alone. Let me finish sanding this end of the coffin lid and we'll both go. But you must have picked all the poke. Don't you know that?"

"I know wild onions be there beside creek."

"You know wild onions *will* be there beside *the* creek."

She hit Ben playfully with her empty basket and sat down on the new back porch steps to wait for him.

By the time they'd walked a half mile or so into the woods, she'd found only a handful of poke shoots and Mary headed them toward a sassafras grove that bordered Burke's property. Her basket was almost full, though, because, as usual, she couldn't resist picking branches of dogwood, which Mister Burke liked.

"I put flowers on our table and he not notice we find so little poke," she called back from the sharp rocky rise in the land above the road where Ben was stooping now to examine the packed red clay. "You hear me, Ben? I fool Mister Burke with dogwood and—"

"Come back down here, Mary," he shouted. "Hurry! Look what I've found!"

The bright-patterned skirt flying about her, Mary sprinted lightly down to the road and bent to look where Ben's brown finger was pointing. "Horses," she said, not very interested. "You bring me here for horse tracks, Ben? I see more flowers for Burke up there— golden groundsel. Like his hair. I pick!"

"No, wait. You stay right here with me. This road is little-traveled. I don't like the looks of so many tracks—all riders, too. These are not the tracks of a wagon and team. They are from galloping riders!"

She knelt beside him. "They are bad, these tracks?"

"I don't know." He sat back on his heels in deep thought.

"They're fresh. No later than yesterday. See? The clay is still standing up in broken pieces around each track. There was no rain last night. They're fresh tracks."

"Men go to Cassville. Mr. Burke say more and more they go."

"*Listen.* I hear something!"

They stood, both as straight as pines, alert to every crackle in the tranquil afternoon woods, instinctively turning their heads slowly this way and that, in order not to miss a scent or sound from any direction.

"There it is again," Ben whispered. "A moan! A man moans."

She nodded rapidly and pointed ahead along the trail to the south of where they stood. The moan came again, more a grunt now, as though someone struggled to move a heavy object. Then a broken, short cry and a hoarse voice called weakly, "God help me! God send me—help—from somewhere!"

Ben bounded away in the direction of the voice. When Mary caught up with him, he was kneeling, holding the head of a thin, pale, wounded man, maybe some older than Mr. Burke. Mary knelt too and laid her hand on the man's forehead.

"This man no die, God! This man no die," she murmured.

Blood soaked his collar from a gash in the back of his head and his face was cut and bruised, as Ben's had been the one day he dared to venture into New Echota among white men.

In an instant, Mary had ripped away a piece of her new muslin petticoat and was running to the creek over the low hill from the trail.

"I hate to leave you alone," Ben said, when she came back and began to bathe away the blood on the white man's face. "We can't leave him here. He'll die. I'll run to our cabin and ride back on Star. Little Star will take him carefully to our home."

Mary stayed willingly, her heart aching for the pain the poor man must be feeling. He lay there, his eyes closed, making no sound. Only after Ben's crashing, running footfalls had faded away did she feel afraid. This was a *white* man! A strange white man . . .

But when he finally opened his eyes, she saw only misery and gratitude. "Who—are you?" he whispered. "Where did—you come from?"

"I *am* Mary," she said, secretly proud that she'd remembered her verb. With all her heart, she meant to save Mister Burke from trouble with any white man. "Sure. I *am* Mary," she repeated.

The man nodded weakly, then fainted.

In the time that she knelt beside him, waiting for Ben, she was afraid for this white man. No longer for herself.

THIRTY-FIVE

A WEEK LATER, leaving their injured visitor in the capable hands of Mary and Ben, Burke rode through a light spring shower to the law office of Fred Bentley. The sky, when he'd stepped outside the cabin, had seemed ready to deluge the countryside, but so far the rain was merely steady and his appointment in town was important. His friend Bentley had arranged a meeting with a Mr. John Cummings and his wife, who were looking for "the best carpenter" to build "the best house in town." "Not a large house," Bentley had said, "but what Mrs. Cummings considers the best. You're just the man, Latimer, with the skill and charm to win her over. Cummings has money and he comes well recommended from North Carolina and with the reputation of being almost sickeningly honest. In my opinion, you're about to land your first good job."

Handling an opinionated woman didn't faze Burke. If Cummings had the money to pay, he'd please the lady. Once he had the job, he meant to bring Ben into town for the first time. Sooner or later, the people of Cassville had to have a chance to accept or reject Ben's Indian appearance. Bentley had urged Burke to break the ice right away—to march right into town with Ben in tow as though he had nothing to hide.

"I've never said I had anything to hide, sir," Burke had protested.

"You didn't need to say it. Not to me. Don't forget, Latimer, I'm on your side. So far as I'm concerned, I'd swear your cousins are Florida Minorcans."

Mary and Ben's recuperating stranger at the cabin, who called himself William McQueen from Savannah, had appeared not to suspect the truth about them either. At least, he had given no sign that he suspected them of being Indians. Of course, for the first several days, McQueen had been only partly conscious, aware of his own bodily pain and little else. There was no doubt in Burke's mind that William McQueen had been attacked and robbed by the Pony Boys. He'd heard they were working the Cassville vicinity but felt certain no one would ever know, since it would certainly be front-page news in Cassville's *Georgia Pioneer* if a Pony Boy were caught and arrested. The kind of justice their guest had known in Savannah simply did not exist up here. What seemed to worry the injured man more than the money of which he'd been robbed was the horse. "That horse belonged to one of the finest men in Savannah, Latimer," he'd said. "Belonged to my best friend, in fact."

The name McQueen had not aroused Burke's curiosity until he'd overheard the man tell Mary that he had no family of his own, that his wife and two children were all dead, lost at sea. At that moment, Burke was sure that William McQueen from Savannah was really William Mackay, who, for a reason of his own, did not want his name to be known—or his mission. No one pressed him about anything after he'd told Ben that he was in the upcountry "just to look around." They all three liked the mild-mannered, uncomplaining gentleman. He'd shown real courage and didn't seem at all bitter over his bad luck with the Pony Boys. "It's far from the worst thing that's ever happened to me," he'd said.

Trotting Judge into town past Courthouse Square toward Bentley's law office, Burke smiled a little at the game he and the man who called himself McQueen were most likely playing with each other. For some reason, William Mackay did not want Burke to know who he was. Burke would have sworn that it was his pale, exhausted visitor's son whose little dead body had vanished into the water the day he'd found Natalie in her wooden box. He marveled that the injured Mackay could manage to hide such grief from Ben and Mary, who knew nothing of Natalie or the wreck.

Hitching Judge outside Bentley's office, the thought struck: Had Natalie sent William Mackay to Cassville to find *him*? Stomping his wet boots on the tiny front porch, he scoffed at such a thought. Pure arrogance. Even Natalie wouldn't do such a wild thing. Still, she'd told him that her powerful father and William Mackay were like brothers. He vowed to be more than careful until he'd had time to observe Mackay awhile longer.

The Cummingses were waiting in Bentley's office when Burke entered, brushing rain from his new redingote. Rain or no rain, he'd worn his new clothes today. The Cummings job was going to be the beginning of success in Cassville, where he fully intended to make a name for himself as the best contractor this side of Augusta.

"We got here just before the rain," Cummings said in his amiable way, after introductions. "My lovely wife insisted we be early. She was right, of course."

"No sense in spoiling our good clothes," Mrs. Cummings said in a voice that to Burke was as puzzling as her face.

She was not pretty, not homely, not young, not old. Her slightly pointed features did not give her a sharp, repelling look, but neither did they put a man at ease as did the broad, pleasant face of her husband.

Mrs. Cummings turned in her chair to face Burke directly. "I trust you are in the contracting business, Mr. Latimer, for more than mere money."

Burke gave her his most winning smile and answered, "Yes, Mrs. Cummings. I trust I am, too."

The smile appeared to have worked. At least, she almost returned it. Still excluding her husband and Bentley, she added—only to Burke, "I sincerely hope you are of a mind to please your clients before you please yourself, Mr. Latimer."

"That's an interesting thought," he said. "Yes, I am, within limits."

"And what are those limits?"

"Quality. I would certainly hope to make you entirely happy with your new home, but not at the expense of building it right—from the ground up."

Cummings slapped his knee. "Well said, Latimer! Wouldn't you agree, my dear?"

Now she did smile at Burke and he took it to be genuine. "Yes, I would agree—within limits."

Was this a flip answer or did she have humor?

"The Cummings tell me they have two basic requirements," Fred Bentley said. "But I feel they should explain to you."

"The first is that you give me a guarantee that the house will fall within my means."

"Not your means," his wife interrupted. "The set limits of what you are willing to spend."

"Very well, my dear. Can you make an accurate estimate, Mr. Latimer? My wife can give you details of what we want. A cottage, but a good cottage."

"After I've had time to check my costs, sir, yes, I can make a reasonably accurate estimate. Will you be taking bids from other contractors?"

"Good heavens, Mr. Latimer, we've done that! But we've also seen samples of their work." Mrs. Cummings was directing her words to Burke again. "Our second requirement is quality. Mr. Bentley here admits you haven't built a house in the area, but we trust Mr. Bentley's judgment."

Bentley bowed. "My gratitude to you, Miss Elma. Since Mr. Latimer has only been here a short time, he's had no chance to build yet. But a man in my position in a growing town like Cassville must often act on his instincts. If I were building a house, I would give the contract to Mr. Latimer without consideration of any other builder."

Surprised, Burke said, "You flatter me, sir."

"I do use flattery at times," Bentley replied. "This time, no. You have the best head, the most ambition to succeed, the strongest will to work of anyone in your trade who's come this way. The cottage you build for the Cummings will be inspected by everyone in town— from the first nail driven. I simply feel you're smart enough not to tackle it if you think there's a chance you'll fail."

"Oh, I don't intend to fail. Could I let you know my price in about two weeks, sir?"

Turning to his wife, Cummings asked, "Will two weeks be satisfactory, my dear?"

"We've waited for more than four years for those stubborn Cherokees to be removed. I think we can wait another fortnight."

"Will you be farming hereabouts, Mr. Cummings?" Burke asked. "Or are you in another business?"

"Mr. Cummings is in hotel management," she answered for him. "In Cassville, he will not only manage, but build his own establishment." Her half-smile appeared again and again, only for Burke.

"Yes, Mr. Latimer. Mr. Cummings will be needing a contractor for his own hotel one day. *After* we're completely satisfied with our new cottage, of course."

The sun came out about noon and William felt well enough to urge Latimer's cousins to leave him alone while they went to search for wild mint. Little Mary's poultices of crushed mint, steeped first in hot water, seemed to help the steady head pain, which was still so severe he had trouble focusing his eyes to read or even to look for long at anything at close range.

"I'll be all right," he said, when Ben brought him a cup of sassafras tea before they left. "Take your time. I'm stronger today. Over that sickness I had at Milner's place, I'm sure. Once this head quits hurting, I'll be able to move on."

"We'll be sorry to see you go, Mr. McQueen." Ben's soft, low voice was calming, William thought. He found the young man pleasant to have around, good to his sister, and he seemed almost to worship Burke Latimer.

"I expect you'll be glad to have a little more room in this cabin," William said, as Ben spread a light cover over him where he lay across the spare bed. "I aim to see that you're rewarded for the care you've given me."

Ben stared at him. "Rewarded? No, no, no, sir. We did not care for you with a reward in our minds. Not one of the three of us."

"You're Minorcans, eh?"

Ben's smile vanished. He merely nodded.

"If Burke Latimer's from Baltimore and you're both from Florida, how did you happen to move up here together?"

"Burke went first to the Florida Territory to see if he would want to settle there."

William noticed in passing that, except to nod when he'd asked about their Minorcan descent, Ben had not really lied. Hadn't even said that Burke actually found them in Florida. Just that he'd gone there to inspect the territory. William liked the dark-skinned, reserved young man. Not being one to judge any man by where he came from, he chose to leave well enough alone. William was dead certain that Ben and Mary were Cherokees, but that was none of his business. They'd saved his life, just as Burke Latimer had saved Natalie's.

He lay thinking for a long time after brother and sister had left for the woods that joined the ten or fifteen cleared acres of Latimer's land. There was a lot to think through. He had picked out the last name of McQueen, his mother's maiden name, without much thought except that he'd never asked Natalie how familiar Burke might be with the name Mackay. He meant to get to know Latimer a lot better before he revealed his own identity and his mission in the upcountry. McQueen had seemed safer, since William was all but certain that in the dark ocean at the moment he'd rescued Natalie, Burke Latimer had at least glimpsed the tiny dead body in her arms. Natalie hadn't thought to tell William whether Latimer would or would not relate that tiny body to the name Mackay, but he did think she had told him that Burke and Virginia had met at dinner that one night at sea.

It was going to be June now in no time. Almost a full year since he'd held Virginia in his arms. . . . Not in the habit of questioning God much these days, he turned his face to the log wall and tried to smother the fire of physical longing that still swept over him so often, so unexpectedly. While he had lain ill at Milner's place by Sallie's Ferry, he had been dismayed to find his body—ill and weak as it was—aching for Virginia's tenderness, her warm, quick response to his every touch. Wasn't grief enough? Did a man have to go on fighting desire, too, in the midst of grief? During those first weeks without her, he'd rebelled at God until he was blue in the face, but somehow what he'd written in Virginia's Bible had put an end to the questioning. He had accepted the fact that there were no agony-free answers, and that maybe God did let his little family die in order to bring William closer to Himself. When he was absolutely honest now, almost a year later, he had to admit that such an explanation did not exactly make him love God more. Still, his need went on being too great not to keep trying to depend on Him more and more. What other way did a man have to get through his days—and nights—alone?

Deliberately, he turned his thoughts to Natalie. He had been fairly sure that she did indeed love Burke Latimer, even before he'd met the man. Now, in spite of all that had happened to stop him, William had found Burke, and could understand for himself why Natalie might well love him. And need him. He felt pretty sure there weren't many young men like Latimer around these days. If the truth were known, William was having some trouble restraining himself—what stopped him from writing Natalie and Mark to tell them he'd not only found Burke, but understood why Natalie wanted to marry him, and could give his own heartfelt approval? Of course, haste was not one of William's traits. But maybe he wasn't just being cautious for Natalie's sake now. Maybe it was because he was already genuinely fond of Burke, was allowing his affection and admiration for the strong, pleasant fellow to develop into a kind of loyalty. There was a surprising gentleness about Latimer which somehow didn't match his remarkable physique, but which was certainly there. Natalie had always been able to cut her gentle father to the quick with a look, or to twist him around her finger without half trying. William felt almost sure that she could not manipulate Burke. Was he right? He honestly didn't know, and in a way, none of that's my business, he thought, turning back to finish off Mary's tea, now tepid. He drank it, though, because he couldn't bring himself to hurt the feelings of little Mary McDonald. Funny name for anyone of Minorcan descent, and he'd heard that a lot of Scottish men had married Cherokee women. Well, maybe only their mother had been Indian— or Minorcan. For the first time since he'd been robbed and beaten, William felt a little like smiling. If he didn't already like so much about Burke Latimer, he'd have to respect him for daring to be kind to two Cherokees.

From the table beside his bed, he picked up the worn Bible Mary had brought him, but only riffled through the pages, testing his eyes. They were somewhat clearer today, but still not clear enough to write to Savannah. His mother would know by his large handwriting that he couldn't see too well. Burke and the Cherokee brother and sister would have done anything he asked of them. Mary and Ben had some education. They could both write. He dared not ask anyone to write for him. No matter how deeply he was beginning to feel about Burke and his "cousins," he was far from ready to let it be known why he was there. He was going to be cautious, careful. Not only for the sake of Mark and Natalie, but also for Burke. After all, he had read the letter Burke had written to Natalie in North Carolina. The boy was not ready to send for her—to go to her. Not yet. He had told William that the cabin and its surrounding acres had cost him almost a quarter of his savings.

At first, after William had begun to recover from the Pony Boys' attack, he'd marveled that Burke hadn't come right out and asked if he, being from Savannah, knew the Browning family. Now that he knew Burke better, saw how hard he was working to build a reputation for himself, understood something of the real excellence of the man, he realized that simply would not have been a thing Burke Latimer would do.

He would remain William McQueen for a while, because every day, he was learning more about the young man he had come to find.

THIRTY-SIX

ONCE JUNE CAME, William grew restless to be moving on. Every day the cabin seemed to shrink. He had enjoyed his three angels of mercy and owed them much, but now that it was June again, he longed for time alone. By June 14, marking the end to the day of the first year of life without his family, he would *have* to be in a room by himself at Milner's States' Rights Hotel in Cassville. Kind Mr. Milner at Sallie's Ferry on the Etowah had guaranteed him a private room. He would have but to tell the clerk when he got there.

Alone in the cabin on June 7, he took quill and paper and sat down at the table to write the letter he'd been prevented from doing. Today, he felt he had no choice. Sitting there, he could picture his mother standing on their big side porch staring into the yard, wondering about him, trying not to worry, trying to trust him to God.

He took a deep breath, dipped the quill and began to write:

States' Rights Hotel
Cassville, Georgia
7 June, 1839

Dear Mama and All,

Once more I owe an apology for my long silence, but during the ride from Milner's place here, I was robbed by the renegade Pony Boys. Please send more money to the above address. They took every cent I had, mine and Mark's and, sorry to report, Mark's fine horse, Rob, too. They also roughed me up quite a bit, but two young Minorcans from St. Augustine and their cousin took me in and gave me wonderful care. I am leaving their cabin in a few days, for the hotel in Cassville, where I will be able to be alone on 13 and 14 June, days I dread most grievously. Please tell Natalie and Mark that although deterred in my efforts, due to the robbery, I have not forgotten about Burke Latimer. At a Cassville hotel, I will meet more people and can make many more inquiries. I can also go to the courthouse and investigate property for sale so that I can finally report to W.H. and Barnsley. Remember me to all the Brownings, to my sisters and to Jack when you write. I vow to let you hear again soon. Hard trip, but I am all right and will be better once June is behind me.

> Yr loving son,
> WILLIAM MACKAY

William was sitting on the back porch steps when Mary wandered into sight from the direction of the woods, her river cane basket filled with wildflowers. He had to smile when he saw her begin to skip as soon as she saw him sitting there. She's a mighty warm, loving little thing, he thought, giving her a brief, friendly wave.

"You are waiting for me, Mister William?" she called, breaking into a run.

"Why, yes, I guess you could say that."

"I bring flowers—see?"

"They're pretty. I'll miss your flowers after I leave, Mary."

Her smile vanished. "You—go away from us?"

"That's right. Come and rest awhile."

Rushing to sit beside him on the step, she said eagerly, "You friend of Mister Burke. I happy over you. Sure!"

"Could I ask you something about you and your brother? He's been in school a lot longer than you, I think. What kind of school did you attend in St. Augustine?"

Her face fell. She thought for a long time, then, not really answering—asking, she said in a tentative voice, "Moravian?"

William knew he had been right. There was now no doubt about it. There were no Moravian schools in St. Augustine. In the Cherokee Nation, yes. And Arnold Milner had told him that some white

families in the area were passing off Cherokees as relatives these
days. One thing was certain—Burke Latimer had a kind heart.

"I go to Moravian school in—Florida, Mister William," she said
firmly now. "Sure."

Too bad, he thought, for a pure-hearted little thing like Mary to
be forced to lie outright in order to save herself and her brother,
and probably Burke, too, from a few mean-spirited folks. Milner,
otherwise a Christian man William knew, had no use for Cherokees
either. Well, every man to his own way of thinking.

"You're a lot younger than Ben?" he asked, wanting to ease her
obvious anxiety.

She nodded. "Ben talk better too. You like Mister Burke?"

"Why, yes. Yes, I like him more every day."

"I love him. I die for him."

Her dark eyes shone so when she said that, William waited awhile
before saying anything more. Then he tried to pass it off lightly.
"Well, you just spoke quite a mouthful, young lady."

"My mouth is full of Mister Burke. My head is full of him. My heart
is full of him. The Moravian teachers convert me to loving Jesus
Christ." Quickly, she added, "In—Florida. But next to Jesus, I love
Mister Burke."

A warning flag went up so fast in William's mind now that he fell
silent, remembering Natalie's earnest, solemn eyes when she'd told
William that if she could have saved Burke's life on that raft by dying
herself, she'd have done it gladly. If Burke intended to go on living
with these young Cherokees—after he married Natalie, more than
sparks could fly. William felt even more certain now that he'd been
right not to have told them back in Savannah that he had already
found Latimer. Right also, to have called himself McQueen up here.
He'd have to register at the hotel by his right name, because Milner
had guaranteed his private room in the name of William Mackay, but
Burke didn't need to know yet. Not yet.

"Why you leave us here, Mister William?"

"I need to be in Cassville. I've got a lot of things to do there at the
courthouse. Two of my close friends back in Savannah want to buy
property up here."

Mary looked off into the woods. "White men buy all of Cherokee
land now," she said.

"In a year or so, I look for them to come in droves."

"Ben say many Cherokees—die on the long trail west."

"I expect that's right."

"To die means not to live again."

He waited for a time, then said, "Unless you believe people who die go to heaven, Mary. Didn't you learn that in school—that there's a heaven where people go on living right with God?"

She nodded. "I learn that. But, in heaven—how can they be—touched? To—touch Mister Burke—would be—heaven!" Her eyes lit up. "One day I touch his lips—I kiss him."

This so startled William that he was relieved when Mary went right on. "You need my help when you go to Cassville? I help you. But I wish you not go." She reached for his hand. "Nice man. Good, gentle man, Mister William." When he didn't answer, she asked, "You go to town with Ben at your side, too? You will have Ben and Mister Burke to take you by daylight in the new wagon?"

"Why, certainly Ben can go too. If he wants to."

"Oh, he wants to. Last night, at our well, I hear Ben and Mister Burke say it be good if Ben be seen in Cassville at your side."

His heart turned over at this. He'd never actually objected to either the federal or the state governments removing the Indians from Georgia so white men could resettle the area, but then he'd never before thought about Cherokees as real people. Now this guileless girl was almost pleading for him to allow her capable, warm-hearted brother to be seen in his company! It was a shame. He got to his feet and crossed the porch to go back inside, thinking of what his mother had so often reminded him—that life just isn't fair.

"We have a good talk together?" she called wistfully.

"Yes, Mary. A good talk. I—learn quite a bit talking to you."

THIRTY-SEVEN

ON THE MORNING of June 13, for the first time, Mark dreaded his daily visit to Miss Eliza. What, he wondered, as he walked slowly toward the dear old house on Broughton Street, could he possibly say to her on a day that would surely heighten her anxiety over William? The *Pulaski* tragedy was no worse because June 13 happened to mark a year since the ship had steamed away from Savannah's waterfront, but this morning, it was certainly on everyone's mind. The mournful ceremony planned for later in the day would help, he supposed, but it would also renew anguish.

At the corner of Broughton and Abercorn, he stopped trying to think of words to comfort Miss Eliza. He'd simply have to allow her mood to govern him. If she wanted to weep, his shoulder was hers as it had always been. If she wanted to relive it all, he would listen. Still, he stopped on the corner to delay the moment when he faced her need, whatever it was. He was going to see her, but first, he needed to find strength for himself.

Almost since his first day in the city, he had, in his own times of distress, somehow been able to isolate his troubled mind and draw sustenance from Savannah herself. Savannah—more than ever, since he was older—his one place to be. There was now a magnificent Catholic Church in town, St. John the Baptist. With the country's financial problems coming to an end, Savannah was beginning to boom more than at any other time since he'd come there to live. Handsome buildings were going up all around. One in progress on the other side of town was Mark's own three-storied tenement, where a few more of the city's poor would be able to live within their means. He took a deep, grateful breath. In one way, all the new buildings were his, because they belonged to his city.

Natural, he was sure, that he'd awakened this morning with Savannah more pronouncedly in his thoughts. Until late last night, he'd worked at writing a paper he would be reading tomorrow evening at the first open meeting of the new Georgia Historical Society, a paper called "Savannah, 1837–1839." In it, he had covered the exhilarating change in the temper of the town from the Van Buren Panic of 1837 right up to today. A change that resembled the mood of a man who had just drunk deeply of a rare wine. The limits of the city extended beyond Liberty to Jones Street. Savannah's security made some sense at last. A nightwatch communicated from one man to another by a recognizable means now when trouble arose. If a watchman heard the wooden-rattle signal of another in the night, he understood and responded without confusion. The city was not only more alertly guarded, it was, at last, rather evenly lighted. There were lamps at the City Exchange, the market, at each public pump in the squares, at the courthouse and the public docks. Even the guardhouse and the engine house were well illuminated. Strict laws were on the books to handle still more expansion.

Earlier this year, before William left for the upcountry, the ramshackle old colonial Filature Building had burned down, along with a ship in dock and several houses, but the advances made since then in fire-fighting equipment were astounding. There was also talk of deepening the channel in the river so that more and larger ships could enter. But in everyone's opinion, the big reason for Savannah's rush of prosperity was the new Central of Georgia Railroad. Sixty-seven miles were already graded and the superstructure laid for at least twenty-six miles from the city, so that trains were running, bringing passengers and carrying away cotton to the interior of Georgia, which had never been important to Savannah before.

As always, prosperity or trouble in town made Mark think of his late friend, Miss Eliza's husband, Robert Mackay. How Mackay would have reveled in all that was happening in the old city today! Slowly, head down, Mark walked toward the Mackay house. He'd delayed his visit as long as he dared. Mounting the front steps, his heart lifted. He could tell Eliza Mackay exactly what he'd been doing —dreaming about Savannah—and she'd understand not only why he'd taken the time to do it—but the depth of meaning the dream still held for him.

Over tea in her parlor, Eliza Mackay listened as Mark told her of his moment spent on the corner, alone with the city, her smile letting him know that indeed she did know what he meant by all of it. That such communion with his city had calmed him. That it had also caused him to miss Robert Mackay—even after more than twenty years.

"Time itself, Mark, is becoming more and more perplexing to me as I grow older," she said, turning her cup in its saucer. "We should all stop more often and let our minds do exactly what you've just done. We might be better able to put events into some sort of perspective. It often seems that William's grief has been going on forever and that Robert went away only yesterday." She sighed. "Sometimes I try to imagine how long it will take us—who have listened for so many years to the Exchange clock in order to learn just where we are in our days—to adjust to eternity, where there is no time. Without time, will we ever feel as though we're accomplishing anything? Or—would I be so worried about William now if I couldn't tell from a calendar how long he's been gone, how long we've waited for that second letter?"

He thought a moment, then asked, "Are you more or less impatient now than you were twenty-seven years ago when I first met you?"

"I don't know. I honestly don't know. Except for my stiff joints when I get up in the morning, I don't feel much different. Do I seem more impatient to you, Mark? Oh, I'm sure knowing my years are numbered makes me want to hurry things up a bit, so as not to miss too much. That's *time* again. Would you and I be trying quite so hard to be careful in what we talk about today if we didn't know that this is June 13, 1839—exactly one year after the *Pulaski* left Savannah?"

"I wish I could make today easier for you," he said simply.

"I know you do, with all your heart." She finished her tea. "Tell me, how did Natalie seem this morning? Did you talk to her? Is—today bothering her in any more noticeable way?"

"She was at breakfast with us. Quiet, as she's been now for the past week or so. She did ask if I thought Burke might also be thinking about last June 13."

"Oh, that child! That poor, pining-away child. But, Mark, Natalie and Burke may have lived a whole lifetime together on that piece of wreckage. Have you thought of that? A whole lifetime compressed into five days! We must never again take her feelings for him lightly."

"I don't. I think I did at first, mainly because I had always adored Natalie as a charming, self-absorbed child. My little girl isn't a child anymore." He tried a short laugh. "That may be part of what bothers me about all this Latimer business. She evidently was ready to burst out of childhood. Her father was far from ready to have her do it."

Hurrying footfalls up the wooden front steps brought Mark up from his comfortable chair to look out the high front window.

"Who's coming, Mark?"

"W.H. and Eliza Anne. They seem to be in a hurry, too."

The Stileses rushed into the parlor, both out of breath and anxious. In his hand, W.H. held William's letter—unopened. "It's for you, Miss Eliza," he said, giving it to her. "I was in the midst of writing a brief at my office, when my clerk came in waving it. It seems he'd had a visit from a friend just in on the Augusta coach, bringing mail from the upcountry. My clerk's friend thought—"

"For heaven's sake, W.H., that's ample explanation," Eliza Anne interrupted sharply. "Mother's waited long enough for William's letter, what difference does it make how you got it? I'm sorry, darling, for sounding cross, but—open it, Mother, and read it aloud to us—every word!"

"All right, all right," she said, breaking the seal. Then, after a deep breath, she unfolded the single page and began to read the letter William had written at the cabin table.

"Well," Eliza Anne said when her mother had finished, "at least we know where he is. We can all write to him at the States' Rights Hotel in Cassville. The hotel's new. They were building it when we were up there. And—we know William's all right." Moving abruptly to take her mother's hand, she added, "Oh, Mama, today is the day he 'grievously dreads.' June 13. William needs us with him this minute!"

"Yes," W.H. said. "You're right, Lib. He does."

"It's—my fault he's up there by himself," Mark said.

"Hush," Eliza scolded. "It's no one's *fault.*"

"Barnsley and I were keen to have him inspect some land for us," W.H. offered. "It's not all your doing, Mark."

Eliza Mackay wiped her eyes. "We're all talking like children. What we should be deciding is *who* is going up to see about William firsthand?"

"I could send my senior clerk," W.H. said.

"No! It has to be one of us—someone close to William, doesn't it, Mama?"

"Yes, Eliza Anne, but there couldn't be a busier time here in town for both W.H. and Mark. I know you're reading your paper on Savannah tomorrow at the Historical Society, Mark—and W.H., you have all that estate business of your father's on top of the biggest law practice in town. Could Eliza Anne and I go up on the stage?"

"Never," her son-in-law said. "I'd never permit either of you to go without a man to escort you. That's frontier country! The Pony Boys rob more stagecoaches than lone riders like William."

"Jack isn't due for a furlough again anytime soon, is he, Miss Eliza?" Mark wanted to know.

"Not for six months or more."

For a moment no one spoke, then Mark said, "Because of business, I shouldn't, but I'll go. Caroline and I will go—once I give my paper tomorrow night."

"Oh, could you, Mark? Would you really?" Eliza Anne asked eagerly.

"Dear boy, your business is so demanding these days, are you sure?"

"Yes, Miss Eliza. I'm sure. Someone close to William has to go. I'm the one." He smiled a little. "I volunteer Caroline because I know she won't let me go alone."

"She surely won't," Eliza Anne said firmly. "After all, William may have turned up Burke Latimer by now—that letter took days getting here. For all reasons, Caroline will go, too. And—"

"And—Natalie," Eliza finished.

Mark sighed heavily. "Yes, and Natalie."

"Oh, Mark, Natalie will soar like an eagle when you tell her!" Eliza Anne's voice grew abruptly tender. "This is the perfect day to tell her, too. I was on my way to see her when W.H. found me, to give her an understanding ear if she needed to talk about a year ago today. She'll want to go for William's sake too. Natalie and William have a—kind of bond only Natalie and William could have."

Eliza Mackay went to Mark, laid her hand on his arm. "Dear Mark, thank you. I'll feel the same about your seeing to William as if Jack were free to go. And I'll pray all the while you're gone. You know—if William's found the young man, this could bring everything to a head far sooner than any of us expected."

"I know," Mark said. "And yes, you'd better pray, Miss Eliza."

"Will you write to let William know you're coming?" W.H. asked.

"If you want my opinion, no," Miss Eliza said. "William will write back to dissuade us. I say we don't give him a chance. He doesn't lie, but I have a strong feeling that he hasn't told us everything. That someone needs to get there as soon as possible."

"We'll leave the day after tomorrow, if Caroline and Natalie can be ready that quickly. We'll take our own carriage and money for William."

Eliza Anne laughed. "I expect Natalie will want to leave this afternoon."

"If William has found Latimer by the time we get there—well, it has to be faced sooner or later," Mark said. "Caroline and I are the people who have to face it."

"Not necessarily alone, Mark. If W.H. will agree, I'd like to go with you." Eliza Anne looked at her husband. "I have one of my hunches, darling. I feel I should go. Will you make a big fuss if Mother and my sisters keep Mary Cowper, Henry and Baby Robert?"

Eliza Mackay watched her son-in-law carefully, knowing the problem he had always had in accepting her daughter's sudden "inspirations." He was frowning. "Kate and Sarah and I will gladly look after the children, W.H."

"And I certainly don't object to that," W.H. answered, "but why, Lib, do *you* have to go too? The country's beautiful once you get there, but the journey is certainly not pleasant."

"I've made the journey, my love, remember? With you. Anyway, this isn't a pleasure excursion. I'm going to—to—" She broke off.

"To what?" W.H. asked.

"To—find out about William, but I think I'm going so I can—be close to Natalie if she needs me. She and I are friends now. If Caroline needs me—I'll be on hand for her. And Mark." She grew annoyed. "For goodness' sake, I can't explain why I'm going in legal terms, but please, dear—will you agree?"

Pouting, he said, "It's a ten-day trip up and back. At least ten days. You could be gone a whole month."

She kissed his cheek. "And I could also come back with a deed to that adjoining property we want on the cliffs overlooking your Etowah River." Eliza Anne turned to Mark. "Do you want me? Will I be in the way? Why do I feel such a need to go, Mark?"

"I don't know, but I'm using enormous restraint to keep from begging you. Natalie may well need you, but probably not as much as her parents will. Especially if her young man is really up there by the time we arrive. W.H.? I'd be ever so grateful if you'd agree to let your Lib go. I'm nervous about what we might find. More nervous every moment we all stand here. Having Eliza Anne would help."

"But—can you prepare the children to come over here and still be ready yourself—so soon?" W.H. asked.

"My sisters can pack the children's things this afternoon. And—dearest husband, a lady has no need for an extensive wardrobe where we're going. Even the new States' Rights Hotel can't be very plush. The children will be lovingly cared for. There is absolutely no problem but your consent. Do say yes, darling!"

Eliza Mackay thought she'd never known her son-in-law to be so attractive, so winsome as when he smiled his slow, adoring smile and said, "If I live as long as my father lived, I'll never learn how to refuse you, beloved Lib. By all means—go."

THIRTY-EIGHT

BY TEN O'CLOCK on the morning of June 13, William rode toward Cassville in the driver's seat of the new wagon beside Burke. Ben stood behind them in the wagon bed, not talking much, but there, in case one of them spoke to him. Burke had the contract to build the Cummings house and Ben was making his first, all-important trip into town to help stake out the foundation.

"I hope the Cummings will drop by the house site," Burke was saying. "Ben's going to be my good right hand and I want him to meet them right off. Especially Mrs. Cummings."

William looked back at Ben. He was smiling, but the dark eyes were not. He's half afraid to meet them, William thought.

"I'm all Burke's got," Ben said, as though he felt William's glance required him to say something. "They've hired him. They'll have to put up with me, I guess."

"None of that talk," Burke said firmly. "No hanging back when I introduce you. I want you to step right up and shake hands with Cummings."

"And if Mrs. Cummings is as much a lady as Burke says she tries to be," William said, hoping to lighten the talk a little, "you'd better bow to her, Ben. Ladies like to be bowed to."

Burke changed the subject. "Mary did a pretty good job of patching up your travel clothes, Mr. McQueen. The way those Pony Boys mussed you up, I thought we'd have to get you a new wardrobe before you could come to town."

Burke was right. For two days, Mary had sponged and mended the torn trousers and jacket. She'd washed and ironed his one remaining shirt. He did feel fairly presentable. Presentable enough to register at the States' Rights Hotel until he could use the fifteen dollars Burke insisted upon lending him to buy a valise and some new clothes. But first, he'd have to make it through today and tomorrow—alone again in a room of his own.

There was space right in front of the new hotel for Burke to pull the wagon to a stop. The place looked all right to William. Milner's States' Rights Hotel was pretty much as he'd described it. A block-shaped frame building of three stories—three rooms across—with a front porch and a tavern on the ground floor where the registry book was kept.

He had nothing to take in with him but the clothes on his back, so he shook hands with Burke and Ben outside, preferring to go in alone. He would not be fit company until tomorrow was past. The clerk did not ask him to pay in advance. The mere mention of Milner, William Henry Stiles and Godfrey Barnsley brought all the credit he could possibly need.

At a long table in the tavern, he ate what he could, went to his room, locked the door at a little past noon, with no intention of talking to anyone until the day after next, when June 14, would be behind him.

It was somehow comforting to be alone within four walls again. The return to four walls and silence brought a smothering rush of the old sadness, but even that somehow calmed him. He could deal with silence—even the sadness—so long as he didn't have to talk to anyone. Burke and Ben and Mary had treated him like a king, but it was a relief now no longer to have to keep saying thank you, thank you.

He took off his jacket and hung it up on a wall peg beside the one chest of drawers, then sat down in a wooden rocker and stared out the open window overlooking the red clay street. He didn't much notice the occasional ox-drawn wagon that rumbled by, the men on horseback, the sunbonneted women, the mostly young men hurrying for their own reasons in and out of the handful of Cassville business establishments.

He was not seeing a Cassville street at all. In his mind's eye, he was seeing his own front yard at Causton's Bluff again—the pines standing straight and black against an indigo night sky flung with

stars. . . . The Causton's Bluff sky right after the nightmare that
had sent him racing down the stairs and outside. The sun was
shining on frontier Cassville, but to William it was dark and the stars
were out and just the act of breathing was hard and rough because
the explosion in his dream—louder than thunder—was filling him
again with terror. Today was only June 13. Desperately, he tried to
focus his mind's eye on the snapping flags and the glistening water
and the happy throngs of well-wishers and passengers on the day
one year ago when last he saw Virginia and the children. But he
could see only that indigo night sky and the stars. He could feel only
the terror.

The Pony Boys had taken his gold watch. He didn't know how
long he'd sat by the window, but when a soft knock came at his door
about sunset, he had cried so much his eyes ached—and his head.

In the passageway outside William Mackay's door, Burke waited.
Mackay had called out, "Be there in a minute," so he didn't knock
again. From inside, he could hear Mackay blow his nose several
times and clear his throat. There was a splash or two of water,
another moment's silence and footsteps across the floor. Then the
door opened just a crack.

"I hope I'm not disturbing you," Burke said, "but what I came for
is important—to me and I feel sure to you also."

"All right. Come in," Mackay said, his thin face drawn, eyes red
and swollen. "Sorry to keep you waiting." Motioning to the one
rocker, he added, "I haven't told you—I'm surprised I'm telling you
now, but today's a—hard day for me, Latimer. I guess June 13
always will be." Tears spilled down his face, but he kept his voice
fairly steady. "One year ago today, my family left me on a voyage
north. Steamship exploded off the North Carolina coast. I lost my
wife and two babies."

Still standing, wide-brimmed hat in hand, Burke said, "I know.
The *Pulaski*."

Mackay sank onto the side of his bed. "I guess—a lot of people
know about it. I wish you'd take that rocker."

Sitting down, Burke said, "I was on the *Pulaski*."

For a full half minute or so, Burke waited as Mackay sat looking at
him. Finally, in a quiet voice, Mackay said, "I was wondering if you'd

ever tell me. You saved the life of a young lady very dear to me, Burke. You see, my name's not McQueen. It's Mackay." Without pausing for Burke to respond to that, he went right on. "There's no way Natalie's parents—any of us—can ever show you our gratitude, and now, I owe you still more thanks. You and Mary and Ben. Natalie's father sent me up here to find you. Mark Browning is like my own brother. He'll want to show you his appreciation."

Not trusting himself to respond, Burke said nothing. This reserved, gentle, tragic gentleman had lived right in his cabin without once hinting that he knew Natalie—or her parents. With his own grief held deep inside. Burke got up abruptly and went to the window. A man cursed loudly from the street below and a woman shrieked her displeasure, but neither man in the second-floor room spoke a word.

Finally, William blew his nose again, wiped his eyes and said, "I gave you several chances to ask questions about Natalie—about her family. I kept bringing up my home town, Savannah."

Turning to face him, Burke said, "Yes, sir. I know you did."

"Did you come here to find out about Natalie?"

"I'm—not sure," Burke said, frowning. "I did come to see if I could do anything for you today. You see, I've suspected from the time you told us your name was McQueen, that it wasn't. Natalie and I talked a lot on the raft, if you could call it that. I knew your mother was Don Juan McQueen's daughter. They still talk about him in St. Augustine. I also knew you were William Mackay. Natalie described you to a *T*. I knew also that you would have to be dreading today, June 13—and tomorrow. I didn't think you were well enough to leave our place, but I knew why you had to. You see, when I found Natalie in the water—she was still holding your—little son." When Mackay only nodded, Burke asked, "Is there—anything I can do for you? I—know how useless that must sound, but I just couldn't bring myself to ride back to the cabin without—telling you that I know about the *Pulaski*. Sometimes it helps a little if someone else—knows."

He watched Mackay—still sitting helplessly on the side of his bed, hands hanging between his knees. After a time, he lifted his face to look at Burke. Tears were flowing again as the grieving man nodded his head. "It helps some," he said.

"Would you like for me to stay awhile—or leave?"

The thin shoulders slumped, then, with effort, straightened. "Where's Ben now?"

The thin shoulders slumped, then, with effort, straightened. "Where's Ben now?"

"Waiting in the wagon. Ben's all right."

"He looks Cherokee, Latimer. There are those in Cassville who will know he is. Some may not be kind about it."

"I'm aware of that. But Ben and Mary and I are here to stay and we just have to bull it through. So far, no trouble at all."

Mackay pulled himself to his feet. "Then, since Natalie and Mark Browning sent me up here to find you," he said, "maybe today's as good a day as any for us to talk. Could we go down to the tavern? A little brandy might steady me. At least, in public it might be easier to act like a man. Stop these tears."

"You're one of the strongest—and best men I've ever known," Burke said, handing him the door key from the small bedside table. "Better lock your door when we go. Every kind of person you can imagine hangs around Cassville these days."

William found a small, narrow table to the rear of the crowded States' Rights tavern and the two sat across from each other. William ordered a brandy, Burke a mug of ale. Until their drinks came, neither spoke.

Then, raising his glass, William said, "I'm not very quick with a toast, Burke, but here's to your—kind heart. I'll do my best to find a way to repay you and your—cousins."

Only sipping his brandy, he noticed that Burke drained over half the strong ale.

"You—guessed about—Mary and Ben, didn't you?" he asked.

"Yes, but your secret's as safe with me as it is with the Lord Himself. Georgians who haven't had any contact with Cherokees don't even think of them as human beings. Even respectable, well-intentioned Georgians don't. I didn't. I do now. Natalie told us all that you cared about the Indians. I was never sure she understood just what you meant, but she told us over and over that you intended to see that the Cherokee land you finally bought would be looked after."

"She—told you *that?*"

"You must have let her know your feelings about them."

"Yes, I guess I did. It just—dumbfounds me that she remembered. There were a few times on that piece of wreckage when I thought she did understand what I was saying to her, but that was a year ago. Since then, I've pictured her back in her father's mansion, safely returned to the elegant society of Savannah's wealthy class— oblivious of everything and everybody but—Natalie. Living a life of ease. I've never known a life of ease, Mr. Mackay. I don't want to know it."

William thought a minute, then said, "I declare, Burke, I believe Natalie got to know you better than you got to know her." He noticed Burke's arched brows, the full, well-shaped mouth drawn to a firm line.

"Mr. Mackay, how—is she? Did her feet get well? Is—Natalie—all right? Is she happy being home—safe?" He tried a short, sarcastic laugh. "I suppose her parents are so glad to have her home again, she's even more spoiled than ever! The toast of every ball in town and—"

"Yes," William said. "Natalie's had her seventeenth birthday, for one thing, and she is always the belle, but I'd say she hasn't gone to very many parties this year past. There haven't been many. A lot of folks lost loved ones on the *Pulaski*. Oh, Natalie tried for a time to go out with Olin Wheeler, the young North Carolinian who brought her back after the wreck. They saw a lot of each other. He lived at the Browning home. Her father hired him. But I'd say Natalie despises Wheeler now. At any rate, after he showed his true colors, he left town for good. So far as I know she saw so much of him because, liar that he was, he claimed he loved her enough to run away with her to help find you. Or, come himself to look for you."

Burke stared at him. "To—look for *me?*"

"To be as smart as you are, you can be awfully dumb in some ways, Latimer. Her poor father and mother—and all the rest of us who love Natalie—have lived in continuous turmoil over that girl because of you! Stop looking out the front door, Burke, and look at me. *Natalie loves you.* At least, my sister, Eliza Anne Stiles, my mother and I are convinced that she does. I think she even convinced my brother, Captain Jack Mackay, and he's yet to take any young woman more seriously than the next dance."

Burke drained the mug of ale and stood up. "If you're really grateful for what Mary and Ben and I did for you, Mackay," he said in a hard voice, "you'll forget all about Natalie and me. You'll go back to Savannah and tell them you couldn't find me!"

"I'd rather take a beating than to lie to Mark Browning—or Natalie. I've had to come close to it in a letter, but I won't lie to them outright."

"But I'm not ready for Natalie! Can't you get that through your head?"

"You mean you don't yet own a mansion up here?"

"Mansions don't interest me except to build them for other men. I'm just—not ready for Natalie."

"Sit back down, Burke. I don't intend to shout, and today, my temper is apt to be short."

Sinking down again uneasily, Burke said, almost as to himself, "It's only been a year. . . ."

"Take my word for it, we've all done well, mighty well, to keep Natalie even reasonably restrained this long. Her poor father's been through a living hell with her over this thing."

Burke's short laugh was not amused. "Please take my deepest sympathy to poor, powerful Mr. Browning, Esquire. I'm sure he's had time from his busy mercantile life to lose lots of sleep over me."

"Not over you. Over Natalie. The man all but worships her. He's suffered."

"Tsk, tsk, tsk."

"I'll thank you not to make light of him, Latimer. Except for my mother, he's the best friend I've got." William fought back fresh tears. "Natalie and I were both cruel to him for a time. At first I blamed him for the *Pulaski* explosion—blamed Mark and all the other owners of the company that built it. These days Mark and I are closer than ever, but I wouldn't even speak with him for weeks. Latimer, I don't know you too well yet. If it had been any other day but today, we wouldn't even be talking together like this. You caught me when I—was all to pieces anyway. I let my—grief get the best of me. It's just not easy to be strong and—lonely at the same time. It seems to me you should know that I intended to watch you a while longer before I told them I'd found you. I will say that what I know of you, though, I like. Mostly you've been fair-minded, but you can't poke fun at Natalie's father with me. I won't stand for it."

William thought Burke's grin was a little less derisive. "Browning's the perfect gentleman, eh?"

"No. He's far from perfect. He has one glaring weakness—Natalie. Money's not his weakness, nor power. The girl is."

"Tell me, Mackay, why *didn't* he send out a search party?"

"She let him read the letter you sent her up in North Carolina."

"I suppose she's passed it among all of you!"

"Nope. But what you don't seem to see is that the little thing was desperate, trying to convince *somebody* that you love her as much as she loves you. Trying to get her way about finding you. Mark could tell from your letter that you're a man with a mind of your own. That you had no idea of coming to Savannah to ask for Natalie's hand until you could earn back your lost fortune. Mark Browning honored that. Stood firm to the extent that he endured the torture of her icy treatment for all those months. Like me, she wouldn't even talk to him." William finished his brandy. "That girl can freeze a man's heart solid."

"I'm sure she can."

"Why are you so against her father, Latimer, when you don't even know the man?"

Burke held out his strong, wide hands. "I don't have anything in common with men who don't earn a living with their hands. Browning and I could never see eye to eye."

"Do you love Natalie?"

William waited so long for him to answer that even he, who could annoy others with his own long silences, grew irritated.

Finally, looking into his empty mug, Burke said, "I—love her so much, I have to—risk losing her forever—rather than go to her before I'm—ready."

"By 'ready,' I take it you mean something more to offer than your cabin—with a Cherokee brother and sister."

Burke buried his head in both hands. Then he looked straight at William. "Can you see little Miss Savannah Belle—darning my socks by the fire at night in that drafty place? Can you see her digging sassafras roots? I *like* sassafras tea! I'll always like it. Can you picture Natalie milking a cow—even when I can afford to buy one? Or scrubbing the cabin floor on her hands and knees?"

"No," William answered quietly, "but you won't live in that cabin long. You'll be well off up here in three or four years. Good carpenters and furniture makers are so scarce, you can all but set your own price right now."

"Three or four years is not now, Mackay. Go back to Savannah and tell them you couldn't find me, *please.*"

"Can't do that."

"Mr. Mackay, I had no idea I'd be responsible for—Mary and Ben —when I wrote that letter to Natalie."

"I know that. What I don't know is why you saddled yourself with them. I'm sure you felt sorry for them and they're fine young people, but—"

"I *don't* feel sorry for them!"

"Then what do you feel?"

Burke sighed heavily. "I don't know."

"Little Mary's in love with you."

"Like a child, she thinks she is. I take her Scottish father's place. I more or less saved their necks. Time may ease things off for the Cherokees who stayed behind, but when I found them near New Echota, their lives weren't worth a cent. They were living in a big cave—like animals."

"And you rescued them." When Burke didn't answer, William leaned back in his chair. "If you think Natalie loves you only because you saved her life, you're dead wrong." When again Burke didn't answer, William asked, "Don't you think you at least owe her an explanation of why she hasn't heard a word from you in a whole year?"

"I—don't trust myself to explain—anything to her. Even when I let myself think about her at night—in my bed, or riding my horse, or—even when I'm working, I—lose my bearings." He was giving William his direct look again. "My—memories and my heart and my mind and—my body are so full of her to this day, Mr. Mackay, I dare not make one move until—the right time. My chances of ever making her happy are mostly in my imagination anyway—and hers. Even if I lose her forever, I don't have the courage now to make a single move."

William weighed what came to his mind to say, then said it: "Natalie has surprised all of us back in Savannah in more ways than one. She could surprise you too. She's almost a grown lady now."

"And ladies fall in love and marry within their own social class! I'm no fool. Her parents will never give me their approval. I love her enough not to want to come between her and her family."

"That sounds pretty noble."

Burke jumped up again. "If I didn't like you, Mackay, I'd break your jaw for that!" William did what he felt like doing. He smiled at

Burke with all the understanding he really felt for the man. In a moment, Burke laughed a little. "I did sound—noble, didn't I? Well, I'm not. I'm sensible. My chances with her are so thin to begin with, I'm scared to stretch them any thinner. It was one thing having her alone on that raft in the Atlantic. It would be another thing entirely to watch her struggle at being my wife—up here." Towering above William, who was still seated at the narrow table, Burke asked, "Mackay, what are you going to tell them about me?"

"I'm not sure, and that's the truth. They've all waited so long now, I guess a few more days won't matter. I have to give it a lot of thought." On his feet too now, William held out his hand. "For today, Latimer, I owe you still more thanks. The day's not over yet, but you've given me quite a bit to think about—besides myself."

THIRTY-NINE

JUPITER was driving as steadily as possible, Eliza Anne knew, but even Mark's luxurious carriage was no match for the rough dirt road. Pressing her aching back hard against the tufted seat about midmorning on the third day of the long trip to the upcountry, she tried to think of something cheerful to say. After all, she and W.H. had, along with Godfrey and Julia Barnsley, made the more than three-hundred-mile journey last year.

"The trip does end," she said to no one in particular. "I admit tomorrow's the longest day of all—that seventy-five-mile stretch between Greensboro and Decatur—but, cheer up, Mark, Caroline. It does end."

"And isn't the hotel at Greensboro supposed to be the best of all?" Natalie asked, her weary little face suddenly eager. "Miss Lib says we'll have a fine night's rest in Greensboro tonight, Mama."

"I know, dear," Caroline answered absently. "If I can just learn to sleep while the bedbugs march up and down."

"I'll rub your back for you," Natalie offered.

Poor child, Eliza Anne thought, giving Natalie a smile. She's trying so. I hope she isn't feeling guilty about this hard trip. After all, we're going to see William as well as to find Burke Latimer. Always fond of her, Eliza Anne had grown still closer to Natalie. She liked it that the girl called her Miss Lib, W.H.'s own name for her. Somehow it strengthened the bond between them and Eliza Anne wanted the bond strong, especially now.

That night, Natalie did indeed insist upon massaging her mother's back. The Greensboro hotel, at least, by comparison, was quite comfortable. As they'd been forced to do all along the way, the three women shared a room, while poor Mark tried to sleep in an even smaller cubicle down the hall with four unkempt men.

Just before they blew out the candles, Eliza Anne was touched when Natalie murmured, "I wish I could rub Papa's back too."

"Well, you can't, my dear," Caroline said sharply. "And, thank you for my massage, but having you so attentive is making me quite uncomfortable. If you really do love this Latimer person, Natalie, you can't help it. Don't feel guilty. Do be yourself. You *never* rub my back at home!"

Bumping along the Madison Road the next day, some seven miles or so after the smooth, peaceful moments while the carriage floated across the Oconee River at Carson's Ferry, Eliza Anne thought about the look on Natalie's face after her mother had spoken so sharply last night. On impulse, Natalie had jumped to her feet, pale eyes blazing. Then, in an instant, the blaze had turned to a weary half-smile. "I'm not going to remember any of what you've just said, Mama," the girl had whispered. "Or how cross you sounded. I know how tired you must be. After all, Miss Lib and I are still young."

Nasty, Eliza Anne thought, but true, of course. Her mother *is* forty-four and I'm thirty-one. She studied Caroline's lovely, even features, pronounced now in profile. Showing almost no expression, Caroline was gazing off into the woods that bordered an old field past which the carriage moved. Mark was deep in his own thoughts too.

They are both obviously dreading the whole idea that William might have found Burke Latimer by now. No one had anything against the young man because no one but Natalie knew him, still the Brownings' anxiety must be devouring them. Eliza Anne could feel it in the cab of the rattling, jerking carriage, which had seemed so comfortable when the journey began.

How, she wondered, would I deal with it if my little daughter, Mary Cowper, were old enough to fall in love with a young man—a stranger—who worked with his hands? I'd like to believe I'd be understanding. I doubt I could be. That sort of thing just isn't what one spends all the childhood years expecting for a daughter who has grown up with every advantage. I doubt I'll ever have to face that dilemma with Mary Cowper, though, she decided. No two children

were ever more unlike than Mary and Natalie when she was Mary
Cowper's age. My child is so docile and well balanced, she resembles neither W.H. nor me.

Eliza Anne caught Natalie smiling at her—almost conspiratorially.
She smiled back, remembering that even when Natalie was a tiny
girl, they all knew she wasn't going to be like anyone else's child.
Eliza Anne had been partial to the vixen in Natalie then. She was
almost always partial to it now. Of course she could be, since she was
not the one who had to rear Natalie. Everyone well remembered
that, while other children ran from Osmund Kott, and hung their
heads when in the formidable presence of Caroline's grandmother,
Ethel Cameron, Natalie had adored them both. At times, Eliza Anne
was almost consumed with curiosity about what Osmund Kott had
written in the note left with his money. She had promised Caroline
and Mark not to ask. So far, she had kept the promise.

"Turn around and look, Papa," Natalie broke the silence brightly.
"We're coming to another ferry. Look, Mama—another smooth
ferry ride ahead."

"That must be the Apalachee River and Reid's Ferry," Mark said,
almost as hopefully as Natalie. "I think it's large enough for us all to
get out while we're crossing and stretch a little. Does that make you
happy, Mrs. Browning?"

Eliza Anne, who had thought Caroline's smiles to be rather forced
all day yesterday, suddenly thought otherwise. The smile she gave
Mark now quite obviously came from the heart.

Well, Eliza Anne hoped, maybe Caroline isn't as distraught as I
imagined. At any rate, she loves Mark and I'm going to believe will
rally in the end. Whatever "the end" may be.

Mark knew that Madison, Georgia, was a quite prosperous town,
with some fine houses and cultured residents. Seated in the dining
room of one of the two good hotels, he fully expected their Madison
stop to refresh them all. Smiling at his wrinkled, weary traveling
companions, he said, "No doubt that today is our longest ride, but
isn't it lucky we've reached Madison in time for a good midday
meal?"

"Oh yes, Papa." Natalie joined in a show of extreme amiability.
"We haven't been able to do this but once before. And I'm starved! I
might eat some of everything they have to serve." On the edge of

her high-backed chair, she beamed around the table. "Are you hungry, Miss Lib?"

"Perishing of it!"

"Mama? Doesn't this nice place make you feel cheerful? It makes me so cheerful, I could get right up and dance with Papa if they had music."

Caroline didn't answer at once, but she did pat Natalie's hand and smile at her in a way that Mark felt took most of the sting out when she said, "Darling Natalie, do stop trying so hard. We all appreciate how much you mean to help, but we're fine. I'm fine, dear, really. And not feeling one bit *old* today." She paused. "I'm—anxious. I admit that, but I haven't *felt*—cross about anything. Why is it that I always feel you'll think I'm cross?"

"I'm not sure," Natalie said thoughtfully. "But I suppose it has something to do with mothers—in general."

Mark laughed. "Not fathers?"

"No," Natalie answered easily, thinking aloud in what Mark knew she considered her most mature manner. "No, Papa, fathers are different. Oh, they can be difficult, but you expect fathers to love you. Of course, you know mothers love you, too, but you're not always sure they approve." Giving no one a chance to interject a word, she added, "I wish I could confide in you more, Mama. I guess I just can't risk displeasing you."

Mark reached for Caroline's hand. After a long, heavy silence broken only by the clatter of dishes from the kitchen to the rear of where they sat, he looked helplessly at Eliza Anne.

"Does a mother's approval mean all that much, Natalie?" Eliza Anne asked.

"Didn't it mean a lot to you when you were seventeen that Miss Eliza approved of you?"

"Yes. I confess it did. And, Caroline, I don't think we mothers need to feel insulted. When I was a child I don't think I wanted my father's approval any more or less than Mother's. I just—always felt I might think of a way to *persuade* him."

Mark was looking at his wife now, still holding her hand. Her fingers tightened on his.

"You have to remember, Natalie," Caroline said finally, "that I—never knew my mother. Can you be a little patient with me while I learn?"

"You had darling old Grandmother Cameron," Natalie needled. "I don't think you liked her very much, Mama, but I loved her. She could have been your mother if you'd—"

"That's enough, Natalie," Mark interrupted. "You're growing up so fast, both your parents are having to run to keep even with you. But one thing I know—and you'd better realize too—you can always count on *your* mother's intelligence. I don't remember my mother either, but I do know yours. Mothers and fathers need to be patient, but so do—daughters. We're all here, aren't we? Trying to find your Burke Latimer?"

"That's right," Eliza Anne joined Mark eagerly. "You're—a blessed girl, whether you know it or not."

"Oh, I know it, Miss Lib. I'm just trying to help Mama understand about being young. About being in love."

Mark saw his wife tense a little. "You well may love your Mr. Latimer deeply, Natalie, but young or not, you can't love him any more than I love your father!"

"*Really,* Mama?"

"Surely you knew that."

"Oh yes, I know you love each other the way parents are supposed to. You've both inspired me to believe in love, but—"

"But you haven't stopped long enough yet to realize—that these two handsome people are also *in love?*" Eliza Anne asked. "In love the way you are with Burke?"

Mark saw his daughter sink back against her chair, taking in what obviously was a brand-new thought. Then she began to smile the smile that always turned him weak and sometimes Caroline, too.

"Why, this is marvelous!" the girl gasped. "I don't have to worry at all about your disapproval of Burke, do I, Mama, now that I know you—you" For once, without words, Natalie jumped up to hug her mother. "Oh, Mama, I've been terribly stupid, haven't I? Was I so stupid because you and Papa are—older?"

Caroline laughed weakly. "Older than *what,* Natalie?"

"I don't know," Natalie said, sitting back down after she'd hugged Mark, too. "I know Miss Lib is madly in love with Uncle W.H., but I —I guess I just thought—"

Mark laughed. "You didn't think, honey."

"That's right," Caroline said. "I knew I was in love with your father *long* before he knew he loved me. You didn't know that, did you?"

"How could I know it? I wasn't born yet!" She sighed. "I've told Miss Lib, but now I can tell you—Mama, Papa—how wonderful it was kissing Burke—on that rickety wreckage out in the sea even with both our mouths burned by the sun. I can tell you things now, Mama, and you'll understand, won't you? You'll be glad for me! You won't be dubious any longer—that little frown on your face—giving me no clue as to what you're thinking. Making me fidgety inside for fear you won't approve of him."

"Understanding the wonder of being in love doesn't necessarily guarantee—approval," Eliza Anne said carefully. "Mark, Caroline— should I not have said that?"

"I'm glad you did," Caroline answered for them both. "Your father and I want your happiness above everything else, Natalie. There's just one thing I hope you'll remember, and that is that neither of us knows Burke Latimer. We are neither disapproving nor approving. We're just here."

Their meal was being served and no one said anything for a time. Mark saw Natalie's slightly deflated look, but was relieved when she said sweetly, "Well, Mama, your last splash of cold water didn't cause quite the damage your splashes usually cause. I think maybe I've made a little progress with you."

Caroline's resigned sigh, because she smiled as she sighed, didn't concern Mark too much either.

"I don't think your mother splashed a drop of cold water," Eliza Anne said, passing the enormous platter of baked hen and dressing.

"Well, maybe not," Natalie agreed. "I'm glad you're here, Miss Lib. It's just not easy for young people to understand older people."

Smiling, Mark said, "I do think you're trying, though."

"Yes, Papa, but I seem to have the hardest time of all. Of course, older people have been young once, so that maybe they can— remember. I can't possibly know what it's like to be old, though." She began to eat as though famished. Then, giving them all a melt- ing smile, she carefully swallowed a bite and said, "What matters now is eating our dinner. We can't get any closer to Burke just sitting here, can we? My chicken is delicious!"

• • • •

From Madison, they traveled the Hightower Trail to the point where the road forked at Rock Bridge—a natural spot on the Yellow River so full of rocks no ferry was needed. Mark directed Jupiter to take the left fork called the Rock Bridge Road into Decatur, where Eliza Anne assured them they'd get their first whiff of real upcountry air.

"I warn you," she said, as they came in sight of a small, primitive village, "that we will undoubtedly find bugs, hard beds and no carpets of any kind on the floors of our Decatur hotel. I well remember it's far more a frontier town than any we've been through so far. So do be warned."

"Oh, how exciting," Natalie cried, sitting bolt upright in the carriage. "Burke would love Decatur!"

"I—did feel, when we stopped here before," Eliza Anne said, "that there was a—different spirit. W.H. vowed he could smell the exciting Cherokee land just ahead. I can still see him and Mr. Barnsley, dressed like Savannahians, but striding as they thought frontiersmen would, up and down Decatur's muddy main street—both teeming to become part of the new land."

"Could you and I stride a little before we leave tomorrow, Papa?" Natalie demanded. "Decatur sounds exactly like a place Burke might be!"

"I doubt we'll have much time there, darling," Mark answered. "But we'll see."

"Papa, if we find him in Decatur, we won't have to make the trip all the way to Cassville!"

"We're on this journey to find William, too," Caroline reminded her.

"I knew you'd say that, Mama."

"William's endured a lot for you, Natalie, all these weeks," Eliza Anne ventured, because she knew neither Caroline nor Mark dared. "And don't scold me for saying that. It's true."

"Of course it is, Miss Lib. It isn't that I don't want to know about him, but—"

"But—you tend to forget poor William now that we're getting so close to Burke's Cherokee country."

Natalie laughed a little sheepishly. "Does Uncle W.H. know— does he really know what a—clairvoyant wife he has?"

"I think he does. I can see through him the same as I see through you, Natalie dear."

After a last futile search for Burke in Decatur, they climbed into the carriage and Jupiter headed the team northwest to Montgomery's Ferry on the Chattahoochee. Natalie wasted no time in quizzing the ferry operator, James Montgomery, about Burke.

"Sorry, ma'am," he said, poling them toward the far side of the river, "don't recollect ever hearin' the name Burke Latimer. But if he can build, he could be a rich man someday in these parts. Over there on that riverbank, you're lookin' right at the old Cherokee Nation now."

"You mean that's *it?* That's really—Cherokee land?" Natalie was breathless. "Papa! Those trees are growing right on—the—Indians' poor land!"

"It's far from poor, though, darling," her father said, trying, Natalie supposed, to keep the talk away from what he knew to be still controversial up here. "This is some of the richest land around, as I understand it."

"Of course it's rich," she said. "Burke wouldn't decide to settle on poor land, for goodness' sake! I meant the poor Indians and you know it. I wasn't even talking about the land. We've treated the Cherokees like—dogs!"

Catching the sudden scowl on ferryman Montgomery's face, Natalie recognized an instant enemy when he said, "You been listenin' to them easterners, young lady. Gawd Almighty knows it took us long enough to run the savages out of here. This is Georgia now, for *whites.* The Cherokee land's part of our state. White man's got a right to every square inch of it!"

"That's your opinion," Natalie replied. "My opinion is that there is at least one white man up here who—cares about both the Indians and their land. They loved their land. One man, at least, is going to love it and care for it the way they did."

Montgomery let the ferry bump the bank so hard, Jupiter had to grab the horses to keep them from bolting.

"You're going to get paid for ferrying us across the river, Mr. Montgomery," Natalie said, pulling herself up to her full height. "I consider you quite rude for causing such a bad landing simply because you—despise Cherokees and we don't."

"Natalie!"

Ignoring her mother, she plunged on. "You must know a wealthy Indian woman named Sallie Hughes, Mr. Montgomery. I've been told she's not only wealthy, she owns lots of land, and also operates a *good*, safe ferry across the Etowah River. Do you consider Sallie Hughes a savage?"

"Ol' Sallie?" he growled. "Had a voice like a mountain lion! Long gone. They drove her out—*removed* her, you polite folks would say— just last year, along with the rest. A *white Georgian* operates Sallie's Ferry now."

"Then why do you still call it 'Sallie's Ferry'?"

"I don't know!" Montgomery was livid now. "How do I know that? Just been called Sallie's Ferry fer so long, I reckon."

As her father was paying Montgomery for the trip across the Chattahoochee, she heard the ferryman say, "Best to watch the lip of that daughter of yours. Ain't nobody around these parts wants to hear even a pretty girl take up for the Cherokees. Oughta' drove 'em all out three years ago when that fancy Boudinot and ol' Major Ridge signed the treaty with Washington City. Been too danged good to 'em as it is. Paid 'em a fortune, too, for their precious land."

The road on the Cherokee side of the Chattahoochee, called New Echota or New Town Road, ran on northwest toward the Etowah River and what had been Sallie Hughes's Ferry. The last ferry poor sick William crossed, Mark thought. William had grown too ill at Sallie's Ferry to continue his journey to Cassville and had been well cared for by a gentleman named Arnold Milner.

Mark had written briefly to Milner before they'd made their hasty departure from Savannah, in case a night's lodging might be needed before they could reach Cassville. He smiled at Natalie now, hoping to keep her in a good humor so that she wouldn't be too impatient to spend one more night on the road should Eliza Anne and Caroline prefer to rest until morning. He'd written to the States' Rights Hotel, too. Reaching for Caroline's hand now, he thought how good it would be to sleep beside her in the same bed again once they reached Cassville. Milner owned the hotel, and whether they spent tonight at his house or not, Mark meant to pay a brief visit, to thank him for all he had done for William.

Watching Natalie struggle to stay cheerful had not been easy for

Mark. Once more he pushed aside the thought that things might not work out to her liking with Latimer. God knew Mark didn't want her married to a man who would take her away from Savannah to this dangerous, primitive part of the state, but even more, he dreaded further heartbreak and disappointment for her.

"Are your thoughts as interesting as they appear to be, Papa?" she asked pertly, her eyes light, light blue today, as always penetrating his heart.

"Of course they are. I was thinking about you."

"Do you realize, all of you, that this very night it's possible I could actually *see*—Burke again? Think about it! After a whole, endless, tragic year!"

Eliza Anne looked at Mark, then at Caroline. "*Tonight*, Natalie? Mark, aren't we still more than fifteen miles from Cassville when we reach Milner's place? We are. I remember clearly. And over quite a dreadful stretch of road."

Without giving Mark a chance to answer, Natalie demanded, "Don't tell me *you're* going to be the one who makes us stop tonight for just fifteen miles, Miss Lib!"

"I'd think you'd want to arrive at the States' Rights Hotel fresh and rested," Eliza Anne answered firmly. "Burke might even be living there."

"William *is* living there," Caroline said sharply. "It's William we're looking for first, Natalie. It's William who needs us."

When Natalie gave Caroline her icy look and turned her face to the woods they were passing, Mark reached for his wife's hand. There would be far less likelihood of friction ahead if Natalie had argued a little.

After a long, unpleasant silence, he was relieved when Eliza Anne said, "Natalie, if you'll accept a friend's opinion, it seems to me we'd all four better continue communicating with each other. Your chilly silence at the tired end of such a long trip won't help a thing. Do you agree?"

Mark saw the flicker of a smile on Natalie's face. She said nothing, but he had seen the smile. His girl was going to keep on *trying* to contain herself.

"Well, if my opinion is of any consequence," Caroline said, "I, for one, want a night's sleep at Mr. Milner's house before we reach Cassville. That is, if he'll have us."

Mark and Eliza Anne exchanged looks. He was sure she was also waiting for an eruption.

Instead, Natalie swept the three with a smile and said calmly, "Stop fretting, Mother—all of you. I've rearranged things in my mind now. I won't like it, but I guess I've known all along we'd have to stay tonight with Mr. Arnold Milner. And I promise I'll do my level best *not* to quarrel with him when he says ugly unfair things about Burke's Indians, as I suppose he will." She took a deep breath. "I'll just—sit there like a bump on a log—and dream. Dream and be charming—a perfect little Savannah lady."

The twisting New Echota Road sloped gently down a tree-bordered incline until the carriage reached the south bank of the Etowah River. Dark, cozy shadows fell from the trees across the narrow stretch of the curving stream where Sallie Hughes's Ferry lay tied on the other side. No one was in sight as Jupiter reined the horses and jumped down from his high seat.

"You want me to call for the ferry, Mister Mark?"

"Fine," Mark said. Using Jupiter's hand to brace himself, he jumped to the ground, glad to stretch his cramped legs. "You go on down to the water's edge and call. I'll help the ladies."

"Oh yes, please do, Mark," Caroline moaned. "I don't think I ever want to sit down again."

By the time they were all out of the carriage, Jupiter had hailed the ferry operator, and while a short, stocky young man, plainly visible across the narrow stretch of dark green-brown water, slowly untied the ferry, Jupiter vanished into the woods to relieve himself, Mark knew, as he looked about for a suitable spot for the ladies to do the same.

When they had all returned to the carriage, Mark pointed out to them that from his own vantage point in the woods a moment ago, he had been able to see Milner's good house across the river. "And it looks quite prosperous. I feel sure he'll have room for us tonight."

Natalie stood gazing up and then down the winding, gentle river, her mind plainly far, far away from them all—and yet, present as Mark had seldom seen her on the entire trip. It was as though she had suddenly, but not surprisingly, come at last to a long-familiar place.

"Caroline—Mark," Eliza Anne cried, "we *have* to be very near W.H.'s beloved spot on the Etowah! I'm so nearsighted, can either of you see cliffs anywhere up or down the river?"

"No," Natalie said quietly. "No, Miss Lib, your beautiful cliffs aren't in sight from here, but you're—already a part of all this too, aren't you? I can tell. You're a part of all this beauty and—now, oh, now—so am I!" No one spoke, and after a time, Natalie sighed. "We —both belong up here, Miss Lib. You and I both—truly *belong* to the Cherokee land."

Mark moved to Caroline's side. "What do you think of it, my dear?" he asked, only half smiling. "Am I losing you as well as Natalie and Eliza Anne and W.H. to the upcountry?"

"You are not," Caroline answered, taking his hand and looking up at him. "So, don't worry. My heart is still exactly where yours is—on Reynolds Square. There is a kind of—untamed awesome beauty here, though." She turned back to the river. "I think the ferry operator has finally headed this way. He certainly seems in no hurry."

"Natalie?"

"What, Miss Lib?"

"Suppose Burke isn't anywhere around here. Would you still belong to the Cherokee land?"

Without a moment's hesitation, Natalie said, "No. But he's very nearby."

"We all hope so," Mark said.

"Thank you, Papa. You're being sweet." Her eyes moved up and then down the river again, and as though remembering that her mother was there too, added, "You, too, Mama. I'm going to marry Burke, no matter what. But it will be even more wonderful having you and Papa here with me when I do."

"Here?" Caroline asked, struggling, Mark knew, to keep her voice calm.

"Oh yes. Almost as soon as I find him. If he's really in Cassville, as I'm somehow sure he is. There'll even be a courthouse for a license. After all, it's the county seat."

Mark slipped his arm around Caroline. "I hope Milner heard Jupiter call for the ferryman. We need some rest. You suddenly look exhausted, my dear."

"I am. I'm tired all the way inside my bones."

He could tell Natalie hadn't heard a word either of them had said. She was leaning dreamily against a sweet-gum tree, its vivid, spring-green leaves and her crown of lustrous red curls lit by a waning ray of sunlight. He was losing his adored girl. Even if they never found Burke Latimer—even if he didn't love her as she remembered and believed—Natalie was never going to be willing again to be only the shining center of her father's universe. He would have to learn to love and respect her as a woman, who perhaps—no matter how deeply she loved—would always belong only to herself.

"You're frowning, Mark," Eliza Anne said.

"Just wondering how a sturdy young man like that ferry operator out there in the middle of the river can pole so slowly!"

"What's your hurry, Papa?"

"Aren't you in a hurry, darling?" He hoped the words came out in their old teasing way.

"Not to get to Milner's. The longer we can stand here on Uncle W.H.'s pretty little river, the less we'll have to listen to Mr. Milner berate Burke's Indians."

"He may not do that at all," Caroline said. "William said he was a respected gentleman in the community. Certainly, he was terribly good to William."

"How do you know you'd like Indians?" Eliza Anne asked.

"Burke convinced me."

"And do you always agree with Burke? If you say you do, I simply don't believe it."

"Of course I don't! He can be terribly bull-headed. We quarreled a lot—especially at first. But he made me understand how cruel and greedy white men can be where Indians are concerned. Until he began to tell me about them, I never even thought about Cherokees before."

"But isn't Burke buying Indian land the same as any other white Georgian or Carolinian or Virginian?" Caroline wanted to know. Mark wished she hadn't asked, because Natalie withered her with one flick of her suddenly angry eyes. "If he reveres the Indian culture so much, how can he be so determined to get his hands on their land?"

"Forgive me, Mother," Natalie replied evenly, "But I refuse to honor that with an answer."

Looking up at him, Caroline whispered quite audibly, "I won't say another word, Mark. I promise. When our daughter calls me *Mother*, I know I've already said too much."

FORTY

AT AN EARLY afternoon dinner in Arnold Milner's two-storied clapboard house, their host explained that he had built around an old Cherokee cabin on the property back in 1834, when he'd purchased the land from a Georgia lottery winner. Milner was a gracious man, but Eliza Anne—remembering Natalie's near argument with Ferryman Montgomery as they crossed the Chattahoochee yesterday—decided to stay alert through dinner in case the subject of Indians came up directly.

"My brother William wrote us that you're the owner of the States' Rights Hotel in Cassville, Mr. Milner," Eliza Anne said when he seemed finished telling them about his move to north Georgia for his health back in 1834. "We do hope there'll be vacancies to accommodate our party."

"Oh yes, Mrs. Stiles," Milner said expansively, "I've already seen to that. Mail comes into Cassville before it reaches me here. I was in town all last week. As soon as I read Mr. Browning's letter, I took care of everything. Two corner rooms have been reserved for you. You'll be properly cared for."

"Oh, you didn't tell my brother we were coming, I hope!"

Milner laughed. "Surprising him, eh? Well, I might have told him. Be the natural thing to do—*if* he'd been in town."

"You mean William Mackay isn't in Cassville?" Caroline asked.

"That's right. He's away on business."

"We're sorry to hear that," Mark said. "You see, one of the main reasons we made the long trip was to see Mrs. Stiles's brother. After the good care you gave him, he was waylaid and robbed by a band of renegades and—"

"Have you seen him since then, Mr. Milner?" Eliza Anne asked.

Milner raised his hand to stop their questions, in full charge, she thought, relishing every moment. "Indeed, I have seen him. Pony Boys got him on a deserted road behind a cabin just outside Cassville. That new builder in town found him, or I should say, two illegal Cherokees found Mackay and brought him back to the builder's cabin to get well."

"But is my brother all right now, really?" Eliza Anne pressed.

"Seemed fine to me. Downcast, lonesome, I'd say, but he's sound as a dollar otherwise."

"Where is he, Mr. Milner?" Eliza Anne wanted to know. "Did he happen to tell you where he was going?"

"He did. Off to inspect some land for a prosperous Savannah merchant named Godfrey Barnsley. Friend of yours, Mr. Browning, I'm sure. Wealthy as all get out, they say."

"Yes," Mark said. "He is both wealthy and a close friend. Do you know when Mr. Mackay is due back in Cassville?"

Eliza Anne heard Natalie clear her throat, demanding attention. Her eyes were narrowed so that they looked only light—almost without color. Mark and Caroline were watching her, too.

The girl cleared her throat again. "Mr. Milner, sir, might I ask you the name of this—*new builder* in Cassville? The one who helped take care of Mr. Mackay after he was robbed?"

"Anybody can tell you that young buck's name, Miss Browning. He's building a cottage for the Cummingses now, and they say he's the most skilled carpenter and furniture maker to hit these parts. Mr. and Mrs. Cummings swear by the man. Got almost everybody in town thinking he's the best thing ever to ride into Cassville. Turning jobs down already. He's got Fred Bentley, our best lawyer, on his side, and when you get old Fred on your side, you're—you're set. Fred got him the Cummings job."

"I asked you his name," Natalie reminded firmly.

"So you did, pretty little miss. It's—Latimer. Burke Latimer. Claims to be from Baltimore—but he also claims to be from Florida and—"

Natalie had jumped up. "Papa," she gasped. "Papa, did you hear that? *It's—Burke!* Oh, Papa, he's—he's in Cassville. Burke's really in Cassville!"

Mark got up to hug her. "I heard, darling. I heard! But can't we sit back down now and find out a little more about—"

"I don't need to find out one other thing except that he's in Cassville! I knew we should have gone on tonight. I knew we shouldn't stop here. I knew—"

"Natalie," Eliza Anne broke in. "Would you have wanted Burke to see you tired and in that wrinkled travel suit? Won't it be far better tomorrow—after a good rest and—"

Natalie literally charged Eliza Anne, throwing both arms around her, laughing now. "Do you really think Burke cares what I have on? For heaven's sake, Miss Lib, we lived together on that raft out in the ocean with almost nothing on—either of us—for five whole days! The last time—he saw me, my face was burned and blistered and—peeling and—" She stopped abruptly and stepped back from hugging Eliza Anne to look straight at their host. "Mr. Milner, I hope you can forgive me," she said in an almost contained voice. "I assure you that my parents did not rear me to behave in this—uncontrolled manner. But you see, Mr. Milner, sir, I'm in love with Burke Latimer. I'm going to marry him and—well, I haven't seen him for over a year!" She smiled sweetly at the gaping Milner. "How can I ever thank you for telling me where he is? Just state what my father can do for you and I promise he'll do it at the earliest possible moment!"

For some reason, Eliza Anne did not hurry after Natalie when, after giving Milner a surprise kiss on the cheek, she whirled and ran from the room. They heard an upstairs door slam and in a silence so thick it could be stirred, Mark and Milner sat back down. No one spoke until Caroline said to no one in particular, "Well, it's really happened. She's—found him."

Eliza Anne looked at Mark, who sounded almost apologetic as he addressed Milner. "You see, we—we have found far more than excellent hospitality here with you, sir. We're—grateful."

Milner, evidently completely perplexed, spoke bluntly. "Well, I just hope once you've caught up with Latimer, you still feel inclined to thank me."

"Could I ask you to tell us exactly what you mean by that?" Eliza

Anne asked. "From what you've said, Mr. Latimer sounds quite successful."

"I have nothing whatever against the young man, Mrs. Stiles, except that—he's a lawbreaker. Took in two escaped Cherokees. A brother and sister, he claims. Calls them his cousins. Swears they're Minorcans he brought from St. Augustine."

"Well," Eliza Anne said, "Natalie did tell us that her young man had been looking over the Florida Territory before he decided to settle up here."

"Did your daughter tell you Latimer had two Minorcan cousins with him, Mr. Browning?" Milner wanted to know. "Of course she didn't. They're no more Minorcan than I am! These two 'cousins' of Latimer's are out-and-out Cherokee."

"Does everyone in the area think of Burke Latimer as a law-breaker?" Mark asked. "You also said he was well liked, much in demand as a builder. I still don't quite understand."

"Oh, the Cummingses—especially Mrs. Cummings—will flare right up when anyone even mentions that Latimer's harboring Cherokees. They think he brings up the sun."

"Well, suppose you're right in thinking Mr. Latimer's cousins are not Minorcan," Eliza Anne said, "is it really illegal to have Cherokees in your house if you're a white man? Wasn't it actually the Indians' *land* that was wanted?"

"In a manner of speaking, yes."

"My husband, W. H. Stiles, has handled many legal cases over the Indian land. He doesn't seem to think anyone minds much that a few Cherokees managed to stay. Is Mr. Latimer the only white man with suspected Indian houseguests?"

"Well, uh—no, he isn't," Milner admitted grudgingly. "There are a few others."

"You've been so kind to us, sir," Mark said, "I assure you, none of us wants to argue with you over the Indian problem. Could you be specific and tell us outright if Mr. Latimer is really breaking the law?"

Eliza Anne watched Milner closely, as he rubbed his chin, mulling over his answer to Mark's question.

"I suppose you couldn't call Latimer an outright lawbreaker, Mr. Browning. As long as the renegade Cherokees behave, work, don't cause trouble, act, at least, like citizens of Georgia, likely they'll be

left alone." Milner grinned. "Well now, wouldn't you people care
for some pie?"

"Oh, I'd love some," Eliza Anne said quickly, eager to change the
subject.

"All right, thank you," Mark agreed.

"I couldn't eat another bite," Caroline said, getting up from her
place at the table. "You and Eliza Anne enjoy your dessert, Mark.
I'm going upstairs to Natalie. I think she—needs her mother."

Eliza Anne saw at once that she'd done the wrong thing by accepting the pie. Caroline and Natalie—in Natalie's cloud-high state
of mind—might get into a real quarrel up there alone. Too late,
though. She took a deep breath, smiled at Milner, and folded her
hands in her lap to wait for dessert.

When Caroline went upstairs, she found that in the flurry of
excitement, Natalie had run by mistake into her parents' room instead of the room she was to share with Eliza Anne. When Caroline
found her there, her daughter was standing at the window. "Natalie?" There was no answer. Neither did Natalie turn around. "I
thought you might—need me," Caroline said.

"No, Mama. I don't need you." Her voice was quiet, dreamy,
distant, but not annoyed. "I don't need anyone now. I just need this
—interminable night to pass."

"Could we talk?" Caroline asked, sitting down in the room's one
chair. "I won't be—prying. There's something I've—wanted to tell
you for a long, long time. I—haven't had the nerve, I guess. And I
confess I had no intention of telling you when I left the table just
now."

Slowly, Natalie turned around. "Is it something about Burke?"

"No. But I do hope you believe I'm very, very glad we know where
he is."

After a wait, Natalie said, "I do believe you." Then, abruptly on
her knees beside Caroline's chair, she repeated, "Oh, Mama, I do
believe you! And I'm—I'm sorry for all the—cutting things I've said
about your being too old to understand about love."

Lifting the bright head so that she could look straight into her
daughter's face, Caroline said, "I do understand, my dear. I don't
always understand you, but I do know about—being in love." Then

she took the plunge. "I—also understand, finally, about—*forgiveness,* Natalie."

"Forgiveness?"

"Telling you this is so long overdue; I beg you to—bear with me while I try to put it into words. Your dear father has wanted me to tell you—all this time, but—"

"Mama, listen to me. I'm so happy that we know exactly where Burke is, I can't imagine that I'll ever be unkind to anyone again— about anything! Not ever. All that matters is—"

"Natalie, wait. And please listen carefully. This isn't about Burke at all. It's about—Osmund Kott." The girl's face flushed. Her eyes turned cold. Her smile vanished. "I know you and I have never been able to talk about him," Caroline went on. "I—couldn't help that. I tried. I was—powerless. *I feared that man more than anyone on earth.* Darling, please don't give me that—contemptuous look. I'm being truthful with you. Long before you were born—for all my young life at Knightsford, he—mistreated Grandfather Jonathan Cameron. I tried, for your father's sake, to—to let go of my resentment toward your—Kottie. I did try. I couldn't do it—until one night, with your father present, I—forgave him."

Natalie hadn't taken her eyes from her mother's face. She was still looking at her now, but the coldness was gone. It was as though the girl were weighing and reweighing what Caroline had just said. For what seemed an endless moment, they studied each other.

Finally, Natalie asked, "When? When—did you forgive him? After he—died trying to save my life?"

"Yes. I'm ashamed that it took so long, but—yes. I forgave him— deep in my heart—after he was gone."

"Do you—think he knows it—wherever he is now, Mama?"

The poignant question so moved Caroline, she could only take Natalie's face between her hands and whisper, "I—hope so. With all my heart, I hope so!"

"I know now, he was—my great-uncle, but I couldn't have loved him more than I did—even if someone had told me while he was still alive."

Caroline's hands dropped to her lap. She sat staring at Natalie, unable to say anything.

As though actually trying to help *her* now, Natalie said quietly, "For a reason that—had to do with my love for Kottie—I'd decided never to tell you and Papa. But in that letter Kottie put in the box of money he left me, he told me about being my great-uncle. Papa's own mother was—his sister. Their father was—your grandfather Cameron. Their mother was a servant, not my blessed old grandmother Cameron. Kottie was *always* loving to me. It was like him to let me know about—all that. I don't suppose you and Papa ever would have told me. I don't hold it against you, because knowing it before Kottie—went away—couldn't have made me love him any more than I already did. I thought that all through, Mama, long ago, and decided just to—let it go."

Tears filled Caroline's eyes as she reached for her daughter's hand. "Thank you," she said. "You—are growing up."

"Only because of Burke, Mama. Only because of—Burke."

"Will it be all right if I tell your father about our talk, Natalie? You've been so fair and forbearing with me, but I won't tell *anyone* if you'd rather I didn't."

"Oh, I don't mind. Tell anyone you like. Just don't expect me to—talk about Kottie at all. Maybe I can talk about him again—someday. Maybe never. Only one thing truly matters now. Seeing Burke. If it makes you feel better, tell Papa. Tell Miss Lib, too. But I don't want them to bring it up with me. Everything about Kottie—is deep inside me, where I keep—all my treasures. Keep them to myself—away from everyone but Burke."

Stretched on her side of the bed she would share tonight with Natalie, curtains drawn against the bright spring sunlight, Eliza Anne waited for Natalie to come for what she'd always disgustedly called "a lady's nap." Far from sleepy, even after the heavy meal, Eliza Anne waited alertly, listening for any sound of raised voices in the adjoining room. There were none. Then she heard the latch lift. The door squeaked open and Natalie slipped in quietly.

"I'm not asleep. No need to tiptoe. I've been waiting impatiently to know about your—talk with your mother. Did it go well?"

With a weary sigh, Natalie fell onto her side of the bed. "Mama's a dear," she said. "We're—very close now." When Eliza Anne made no comment, Natalie sighed again. "Oh, Miss Lib, Miss Lib, my wait—my eternal wait is almost over! Can you believe that tomorrow—*tomorrow*—I'll be able to look at Burke again? To touch him, to—feel those big, hard arms around me?" Abruptly, she was up on her elbow. "Do you know that only part of me really believes it? That—another part of me is—*scared?*"

"Scared? Because of your parents?"

"Oh, heavens no! They're harmless. Mama's trying awfully hard to be glad for me. I don't think she really is, but I'm tolerant with anyone who tries. I know Papa will love Burke. I love him. That means he will, too. I can almost always count on Papa. And Miss Lib, you are truly going to adore Burke! I predict you won't be able to take your eyes off him."

"That's quite a prediction for a woman married to a gentleman with the looks of William Henry Stiles. Still, I've never been more eager to meet anyone."

Natalie lay back and sighed contentedly.

"You and your mother didn't have any problems in her room just now?" Eliza Anne asked.

"Not really. I didn't snap at her and she didn't snap at me. I was just very *reasonable,* and Mama loves that."

"But is it all right if I ask what she did say when she first came upstairs?"

"About Burke—or what?"

"About Burke, of course."

"Just that she thought I might need her."

"And did you?"

"No. But Mama was—trying, Miss Lib. Didn't you expect her to be relieved that we've almost found Burke?"

"Yes. Oh yes. But I'm proud of her."

"So am I. I don't think she's going to tip over a single apple cart. Of course, I went out of my way to reassure her of my maturity, my newly acquired common sense and all that."

"And are you sure you have 'all that'?"

Natalie's quick laughter tinkled. "What do you think?"

"Frankly, I'm trying not to think. I'm simply wondering how I can wait to find out." After a pause, she asked, "Natalie, did you know Burke had two Minorcan cousins from St. Augustine?"

"No, because he hasn't. He has no family at all." After a deep breath, which she exhaled in what was rather a happy little hum, she said, "But he'll have me, and I'm going to be better for him and more exciting than a huge, huge family. . . ."

"I have no doubt whatever."

"My plans are all made. Before Mama came upstairs, I made a complete plan for when we get to Cassville tomorrow."

"Would you care to tell me about it?"

"Sorry, no."

"Just—no. Is that the end of it?"

"That's the end of it, Miss Lib."

Feigning injured feelings, Eliza Anne said, "And I thought you trusted me."

"I do trust you, but if Burke himself were right here this minute, I wouldn't even tell him!"

FORTY-ONE

JUST AFTER DAWN, Jupiter Taylor left the pallet he'd been given in the Milner slave quarters. On the narrow porch of the cabin, he washed and shaved, and because only some fifteen or sixteen miles remained until they would reach Cassville at last, he changed into the extra dark blue frock coat he'd brought along and brushed his black felt top hat. *Mister Mark not gonna be ashamed of his driver when we roll into the county seat,* he thought, hunting around in an old box on the porch for some rags. *Gotta get some of that mud off the carriage too.*

At full sunrise, a little before six by his cherished Christmas watch from the Brownings, Jupiter had done all he could do for the carriage and was currying Mark's matched pair of dappled grays when behind him, from the open stable doors, he heard "ps-st!"—then his name. Before he turned around, he knew it was Miss Natalie. In the dark interior of the stable, he couldn't see her for a few seconds, but she whispered, "Over here, Jupiter! Sh-h! Don't talk to me. Whisper!"

"What you doin' out here this time of morning, Miss Natalie?" he whispered, obeying her as almost everyone always did. "You gonna get caught by somebody."

"No, I won't," she said. "Milner's people haven't gathered yet to go to his fields. I made sure of that. Now, listen carefully. When we get to Cassville, I'll see to it that my father decides he'd like to drive around the town for a while. We just have to hope and pray and cross our fingers that my mother will want to go with him. I'll go to our room at the States' Rights Hotel and pretend to take a nap with Miss Lib Stiles. Do you understand so far?"

"Why, yes, ma'am, I do, but why you tell me all this? Course, I'll drive your folks anywhere they want to go. Still and all, do you think they'll want to feel one more turn of them carriage wheels?"

"I told you I'd think of something to persuade my father."

Jupiter chuckled. "I 'spect you will."

"Sh! Now, what I want you to do after they've driven around awhile is—well, get stuck in the mud or something to keep them out longer. Can you do that? You can, can't you?"

"I can, but I wouldn't want to."

"I didn't ask if you wanted to."

"That's right, you didn't." She was stroking the handsome mare, from which Jupiter had already combed all ticks and brambles. He grinned at her. "What you gonna be doin' all the time I'm gettin' your poor folks stuck in the mud, Miss Natalie?"

"Never mind. What I'll be doing is the most important thing I've ever done in my whole life!"

Jupiter grinned at her, exposing an empty space in the front of his mouth where two teeth had been. "Wouldn't have nothing to do with that fine yellow-headed young man that save' your life, would it?"

She gave him her most dissolving smile. "Jupiter Taylor, how could you even think of such a thing? Just do as I've instructed now and no more curiosity. Later"—she hugged herself with excitement —"later, all your questions will be answered, but not until after we're in Cassville."

"Well," Caroline said, taking off her shoes and travel hat when she and Mark reached their plain, square, uncarpeted room at the States' Rights Hotel, "the ride here from Milner's wasn't half bad, was it? And, with some adjustments, I think we'll be fine in what Mr. Milner called this 'spacious' corner room, don't you, dear?"

She went willingly into his arms. "Of course we'll be fine," he said. "I imagine Natalie and Eliza Anne's room is identical to ours, don't you?"

"Mark, does Natalie seem to you to be behaving with a bit too much restraint and poise? She worries me, being so calm when we know she's too excited to get her breath. And why do you suppose she's so interested in our touring the town this first afternoon?"

He laughed. "Her facts are right, of course. The county seat is an extremely important place to inspect in a newly opened territory. She was even right about the large number of lawyers already settled here."

Caroline, at the other side of the room, was unpacking toilet articles—comb, brushes, hand mirror, hair-container, talc, toilet water. "But how does any of that concern you and me? We are certainly *not* considering a move to the upcountry."

"No, we're not. I miss Savannah already."

"I've missed it since we left the city limits. She's up to something. You know that, don't you?" Turning to look at him, she asked, "Is that sigh the only answer I'm going to get?"

He grinned.

She let him help her arrange the toilet articles on the common sturdy oak dresser. Finally, Mark said, "I do think she's trying awfully hard, though, to let us see that she's—mature and in control of her emotions. Shouldn't we return the favor by not being suspicious of everything she brings up?"

"I'm not being!"

"I didn't say *you*, darling, I said *we*. I'm watchful too. I also know she wants to find Burke Latimer alone—without us."

"But she's still only seventeen, and we *are* her parents."

"Wouldn't you want to find me alone—under the same circumstances?"

She threw her arms around him. "Oh yes! Do you remember, my darling, how we used to sneak off on that little bypath at Knightsford when you and the Mackays would come to their place at The Grange to visit? You always docked at Grandfather's wharf and we did everything but push the others in the river so we could get away—alone— to kiss and kiss and kiss. . . ."

They kissed now, long and tenderly. Caroline, pulling back finally to look at him, whispered, "You're deliberately distracting me from worrying about Natalie."

"Yes, ma'am, I am. Natalie's with her friend, Miss Lib. She'll be fine while we all rest awhile before dinner."

"That little vixen is scheming this minute, even if she's pretending to take a nap with Eliza Anne. Mark, I don't want her slipping out in this frontier town alone. It's not Savannah, you know."

"Listen to me," he said gently. "We have to trust her some. Within reason." He turned Caroline toward him. "She certainly is no more in love than her mother was at her age. Don't forget, Mrs. Browning, I was there. I remember how much in love you were."

Caroline touched his cheek. "Oh, darling, yes! At seventeen, her mother was hopelessly in love with her father. But our daughter isn't much like either of us. You know that better than I."

Opening his own small valise now, Mark took out his brushes and smoothed his thick, dark, wavy hair. "What you're really saying is that I know her because I'm the one who gives in to her most often. And you're right. I am."

As soon as she and Miss Lib were somewhat settled in their corner room at the other end of the States' Rights Hotel, Natalie feigned extreme sleepiness and fell across the bed, still dressed in a carefully selected blue-and-tan-striped cotton dress. During the carriage ride from the Etowah River to Cassville, they had all admitted to sleeping very little at Milner's place. Natalie had felt cheered when her mother said, "I'm sure you didn't sleep, darling. You were just too excited." It always helped enormously when Mama seemed to understand how she felt.

Natalie's eyes did feel sandy, but sleep was the farthest thing from her mind now as she lay checking and rechecking Miss Lib's closed eyes. When people were just resting, not asleep, their breathing was quicker and shallower than when real sleep came. Her pendant watch, which she was barely able to see in the shuttered room, told her it was exactly seven minutes past one o'clock. Miss Lib's breathing grew a little heavier and deeper. She was already safely asleep.

Mr. Milner might have built his States' Rights Hotel so the floors don't creak so much, Natalie thought, picking up her straw bonnet as she crept in long, careful steps toward the door that led to the hall. She'd have to pass her parents' room in order to reach the stair to the street, then she could put on her blue slippers. For some reason Mr. Milner's hallway didn't make quite so much noise under her feet. She didn't pause to listen at their door, but she heard her father laugh and he sounded easy and unsuspecting.

Outside in the clear late June sunshine, she smoothed her dress and petticoats, hurriedly tied her tan straw bonnet by its ribbon under her chin and began to look around for someone who might know the location of the Cummings house site. Her heart had nearly burst with excitement during Mr. Milner's dinner-table talk about Burke and what he was doing in Cassville, but she hadn't missed a word. He was right now building a new cottage for people named Cummings and she meant to find it!

Walking carefully to avoid mudholes left from yesterday's rain, she headed toward the part of town where the brick courthouse stood, peering into the face of every person she passed. She peered also at the drivers and passengers in the occasional wagon or gig that rattled by. Up ahead, leaning against a hitching rail, stood a rather presentable-looking gentleman who was staring at her in a curious way. She was accustomed to that. Even in Savannah, gentlemen, in particular, turned to admire her because she was, as she well knew, always the prettiest girl around. She expected it here, too, and they did look—gawk was a better word.

Walking a little faster now so as to reach the man before he walked on, she suddenly thought of removing her hat. Ladies did not go out in the summer sun—anytime, for that matter—without a hat, but Burke, except for the few times he'd seen her aboard the *Pulaski* before the explosion, might not recognize her in a hat. She wanted her bright, red-gold hair plainly visible in case—dear Lord!—in case Burke himself might drive by.

The loud clatter and rattle of an empty wagon going far too fast, sent a shudder of fury through her as she ran toward the nearest building to avoid being splashed. When the wagon and its three passengers drew abreast of where she stood she saw a dark, Indian-looking young man with straight, cropped black hair riding in the empty wagon bed, his legs swinging free. In the driver's seat a heavy-shouldered man under a wide-brimmed hat urged the horse to a still more disgusting speed and beside him a pretty girl laughed her delight, clinging for dear life to the boorish driver's arm.

They were gone too soon for her to see the driver's shaded face, but she saw the yellow longish curls below the hateful hat and her heart stopped. Natalie stopped too and fell back against the building she'd been hugging to avoid the mud. When the contraption passed, she forgot the mudholes and ran after it. Just at the moment she saw the wagon slow suddenly and pull toward the side of the clay road, she splashed into a mudhole any fool should have seen by only half-watching. The ruffles at the hem of her petticoats and beautiful blue-striped skirt felt suddenly heavy—they were. With mud. "Foot!" she said aloud. "Now, look what that wagon made me do!"

Her shoes were heavy, too, and she could feel the oozy clay seep around her stockinged feet, but she was hurrying faster than ever now because the wagon had come to a halt some yards ahead. Her legs ached as she kept running toward it, but it stopped only long enough for the pretty girl to jump out, return the men's waves and stand watching while wagon and both men disappeared over a small rise in the rutted street.

"Hello!" Natalie called, still running toward the girl who'd been clutching the driver's arm. *Burke's arm,* she thought over and over as she ran, then said it aloud to herself: "It's Burke! That was Burke driving that dumb, rattly wagon like an idiot. I know it was Burke!"

Again, she shouted, "Hello!"

The girl, carrying a bucket, turned now and smiled. "You call to me?"

"Who else is nearby?" Natalie said, out of breath.

"No other one," the girl said, still smiling. She shifted the empty pail to her other hand and held out her right one to Natalie.

Natalie smiled, but asked in her most cultivated manner, "Do woman shake hands with each other up here on the frontier?"

"I do not know," the girl answered, only a little embarrassed. She then withdrew her hand and used it to brush back her light brown curls, damp with perspiration after the wild ride. "Mister Burke shake hands a lot. I watch him."

Faced now with *proof,* Natalie swayed a little in the hot sun and felt not only foolish but scared again. "Did—you—say—Mister *Burke?*" she gasped, her cultivated manner forgotten.

The friendly, earnest girl nodded vigorously. "Mister Burke Latimer. My brother and me, we live in his cabin."

"You—*live* with him?"

Again the vigorous, happy nod. "Safe—with Mister Burke. My brother, Ben, build house with him."

"Where is—he now? Where did they go when they drove off in that ramshackle wagon?"

The curly-haired girl laughed. "Mister Burke and Ben build the wagon. It strong."

"And dangerous. Where is Burke Latimer now? I have to find him —*at once.*"

The happy smile faded from the girl's face. "You—know my Mister Burke?"

"*Your* Mister Burke?" Natalie had found her cultivation again. "Tell me where he went!"

"To sawmill for lumber. I come to town to get milk for Mister Burke to drink. He buy us another horse and a cow, but in two weeks, the cow die. No milk. Mister Burke love to drink milk when he eat the good food I fix for him."

Fear enveloped her now. Except for that one dinner on the *Pulaski*, when Burke had been so rude, she had never even eaten a meal with him! He'd so annoyed her then, she'd paid no attention to what he did or didn't eat. This simple, smiling, eager girl knew far more about what Burke liked. During their five-day lifetime together on the raft, there had been nothing to eat. Only those few drops of precious rainwater one stormy Sunday afternoon.

"I say wrong?"

"No. No, of course not. Where is the sawmill? Is it here in town?"

The girl shook her head no and pointed toward the little rise in the road over which Burke had vanished like a dream that ended too quickly because you woke up. "Two mile that way. Come with me. I take you to house he builds with my brother. Mister Burke and Ben, they come there with lumber in only one hour." The girl's smile returned. "Come with me. We buy Mister Burke's milk together." She pointed across the street. "Over there lives Mister Mullins with cows that give milk."

On the Mullins front porch, Natalie watched and listened to every word that passed between snippy Mrs. Mullins and the smiling girl. I wonder, Natalie thought, as they waited for the woman to fill the pail, if everyone is as rude in this town as that woman is. The thought of anyone living right in the same cabin with Burke infuriated her, but this girl certainly was polite with the woman who treated her as though she were scum. Mrs. Mullins took her money, though, and handed her the filled pail of milk. When the girl gave a fancy curtsy and thanked her, the woman looked at Natalie for the first time. Looked her up and down, in fact, but since Mrs. Mullins hadn't introduced herself, Natalie didn't bother either. Mama would definitely not approve, but right now, ordinary, crude Mrs. Mullins mattered not at all.

FORTY-TWO

THE DISTANCE to the Cummings house site wasn't nearly as far as Natalie expected, and although the girl smiled at her often, they said nothing until the new clapboard structure appeared around the bend in the road—Burke's house nestled in a grove of tall, straight pine trees. The wagon was nowhere in sight. Natalie sighed. More waiting.

"My name is Mary McDonald," the girl said simply, when they found a clean stack of lumber on which to sit. Natalie ignored her because she felt scared again, scared and so nervous, she thought she might be ill.

This was not the way she meant it to be when she'd sneaked away from Miss Lib earlier—to find him. To embrace him, to be *with him* after all the dragging months—the only way she knew to be with Burke Latimer. He had admitted on the raft that he hadn't liked her at dinner at the Captain's table that one evening. "I loved you, I guess, even then," he'd confided. "But I didn't really like you much. You were arrogant." Oh, Burke, she thought now, uncomfortable on the pile of boards, I don't feel arrogant anymore. I'm just yours, and I need to be with you—oh, I need you so much this minute. Need you to be—*my* Burke. I need you to help me learn again how to be with you. I'm really furious that you're living in the same house with this—this girl. I'm furious about that! How would you like to endure all those back-breaking days jouncing over the roughest roads in Georgia to find me under the same roof with—a strange man? She hadn't even shown the girl the courtesy of acknowledging her irritatingly simple announcement that her name was Mary—whatever it was. Even Papa would think me rude, she thought. She forced herself to say, "Excuse me, Mary. My name is Natalie. Natalie Browning."

"You beautiful," Mary breathed.

"Thank you. I'm here with my parents—from Savannah." She certainly didn't care, but asked in what she meant to be a polite tone, "Have you always lived in the upcountry?"

Mary waited a long time before she answered. "My brother, Ben, he—uh, we—Minorcan—from Florida—in St. Augustine."

"Florida isn't in St. Augustine," Natalie said. "St. Augustine is in Florida!"

Mary nodded, agreeing and smiled again, this time a bit tentatively. "I from there also. Sure!"

Like a flash, Natalie remembered Milner's somehow double-edged statement last night at the table to the effect that Burke claimed to be from both Baltimore *and* Florida. She decided to try an experiment with Mary. "Tell me, is Mister Burke Latimer—from Florida too?"

For an instant, panic flared in Mary's eyes, but she only frowned and thought for another awkward time before she said, "You will be kind and—ask—him—yourself, Miss Natalie Browning?"

The peculiar question was barely out when Natalie heard the steady rumble and creak of a loaded wagon bearing down on the Cummings house site.

"They come!" Mary almost shouted, relief and joy in her voice and on her face. "Mister Burke and Ben—they come!" Then she laughed. "Big load of lumber, see?"

On her feet, Natalie stared at the wagon, heading straight toward them. She fluffed her bright red curls and stepped out from the shade of the pine grove into the sun so that Burke could not possibly miss her. At the same moment, her heart turned over. *What if only she, Natalie, still loved Burke?* She loathed tears, but felt them stream down her cheeks. The young man on the driver's seat beside Burke waved, and with both arms, Mary waved back.

Natalie wanted to wave too, but she couldn't move. Under the wide-brimmed hat was Burke's face! *There was his face* and all she could do was look and look at him, hating the tears she kept trying to wipe away.

Running toward Burke's side of the wagon the minute it ground to a stop, Mary called, "Milk, Mister Burke. You drink milk now!"

Once he'd reined the team, Burke just sat—not moving a muscle. As though she did it all the time, Natalie saw Mary reach her hand to touch Burke's muscular forearm; its downy golden hair—just as Natalie remembered it—brought more tears.

She was not going to give way to one single sob and she couldn't smile. She could only stand there looking at him, while he looked at her, saying nothing, making no move to jump down from the wagon.

"Her name," Mary said a bit hesitantly, "is Natalie—Browning."

Finally, Burke shoved the wide-brimmed hat to the back of his head, still looking down at her. He looked only at Natalie, and if her life depended upon it, she could not have guessed even one of his thoughts.

The earth seemed to be sliding sideways and she could only swipe at her eyes with the back of her hand. He must be angry. He almost seemed to be scowling. But why, when her heart was pounding with joy?

"You hear me, Mister Burke?" Mary said again. "Her name is—Natalie Browning. From Savannah."

Without taking his eyes from Natalie's face, Burke said, "I know her name, Mary. I—also know where she's from." He jerked his hat back firmly on his head and said, "Savannah's exactly where she should be this minute! You couldn't wait for me—or trust me either, could you?"

Before she could think of even one word to say, he bounded down out of the wagon, grabbed her and held her to him so hard she made no more effort to control her tears—tears from the security of his steely arms and her own overflowing heart.

To Natalie, Mary and Ben were no longer there. They—she and Burke—were once more in the world alone. Not under pine trees, not even on that sinister ocean. For this minute, they were alone in a world where no one else had ever been. And then she found herself waiting for his kiss—Burke's perfect mouth, no longer swollen and burned from the sun. Burke could kiss her at last—freely and forever. Her hands stroked his broad, hard back, touched the dear, moist curls on his neck, but he did not kiss her—hadn't loosed his

arms except to knock his hat onto the ground when its wide brim
kept getting in the way of holding her.

"Burke," she whispered. "Oh, Burke—it's *you!*" She clung to him
but he didn't kiss her.

Instead, he dropped his arms suddenly, then seized her shoulders, pushed her away so he could look at her, and asked solemnly,
"Natalie—how are your poor little feet? Your—face is all healed
from the burns, but how are—your little feet?"

"Mister Burke," Mary interrupted. "Mister Burke!"

Ignoring Mary, he demanded again to know if "those hurt little
feet can walk all right."

"Mister Burke." Mary was insistent now. "*People* here!"

Burke whirled around, one hand still on Natalie's shoulder. She
turned with him and saw her mother and father and Miss Lib.

"Papa! I thought Jupiter was taking you for a ride!"

"We'd ridden quite enough," her mother said sharply, then
dropped the sharpness to add, almost too brightly, "And since you
did disappear from the hotel like a wraith, Natalie, even you should
have expected us to come looking for you."

"We—thought a good walk would get out the kinks," her father
said, not really covering her mother's gibe. Just showing his own
anxiety.

Burke glanced at Mama, then Papa, then Miss Lib before he said,
"You felt you had to sneak away to find me, Natalie?"

Blessedly, Papa stepped forward, his hand out to Burke, so there
was no need for her to answer. They shook hands and Burke said in
what seemed an unnatural voice, "I'm Burke Latimer, sir. I take it
you're Mark Browning, Esquire."

"That's right," Natalie broke in. "This is my father." Then, talking faster and faster, she introduced him to her mother and to Miss
Lib and thought he bowed as elegantly as any Savannah gentleman
—better in fact, since Burke never bothered with exaggerated flour-
ishes over anything.

"This is a moment we've all waited for," Miss Lib said in her
forthright way. "I admit to a bad scare when I awakened from my
nap to find you'd vanished, Natalie. But"—she turned back to Burke
—"we're all so very glad to meet you at last, Mr. Latimer. To have
this chance to try, at least, to express our gratitude to you."

"Believe me," Papa said, "I do mean to try, but there can be no adequate means to thank you—ever, for saving our daughter's life. It hasn't been easy not knowing where you were. Natalie's mother and I have longed to—"

"It certainly has *not* been easy," Natalie blurted.

"However, Natalie managed to find you today," her mother was saying, "I'm glad she did. Gratitude, Mr. Latimer, doesn't begin to describe our feelings for what you did."

Natalie wanted to hug her, grasping at the smallest hint that Mama might like him.

Quietly, Burke said, "I'm just sorry we couldn't save Mr. Mackay's son. Natalie did her best, but—" When he fell silent, looking at the ground, Natalie felt she might die of love for him. "You see," he went on, "I'm partial to Mr. William Mackay. He's a fine, steady man —in spite of his tragedy. And all the trouble he's had up here."

"Now, let me thank you," Miss Lib said, taking a step toward Burke. "Not only for saving our beloved Natalie, but for all you've done for my brother. You're right about William. He's a deserving man. Our mother, the whole family thanks you."

"I hope you and I will be able to have a good talk, Mr. Latimer," Papa said. "My time while we're up here is freer than yours. Will you let me know when a meeting might be convenient for you?"

Natalie was watching Burke. He'd never, never let Papa thank him in any material way, but she prayed he wouldn't get that obstinate, closed look on his face or make Papa wait too long, the way he sometimes made her wait for an answer. He was just looking at her father, not smiling, not frowning, just looking at him with those direct brown eyes, but he didn't say a single word.

Finally, when the silence grew awkward, Miss Lib said, "So this is the new house you're building. My eye *is* unpracticed, Mr. Latimer, but from what I can tell at this stage, you must have quite satisfied clients. The finished house should be most attractive. Don't you agree, Mark? Caroline?"

They both did agree, but it seemed to Natalie it was not without effort. Almost everything was turning out to be an effort. What a cruel, clumsy thing for them to break in on Burke and me like this! How can I just stand here and do all this dumb socializing so soon after—finding him again?

"We'd like to meet these two young people too," Miss Lib was saying, smiling at Mary and the dark young man.

"I apologize," Burke said. "I would like all of you to meet my—cousins, Mary and Ben McDonald. They're from St. Augustine, Florida. Ben's working with me."

"St. Augustine," her mother addressed Burke's friends pleasantly. "We're practically neighbors. By water, St. Augustine isn't far from Savannah. How interesting that you're both here in the up-country."

"I'd say it's fortunate for Burke that he has such a skilled cousin to help him," Miss Lib said. Then she laughed. "You'll have to forgive me, Mr. Latimer, for using your first name. You see, Natalie and I are quite close. I'm sure you can imagine how often she's spoken to me of you as—Burke. I'm afraid I think of you that way."

"That's all right, Mrs. Stiles. Quite all right." He sounded, Natalie thought, more like himself now, more at ease. "Your husband's name is already familiar up here. William Henry Stiles is a highly respected gentleman in these parts. I hear he's already begun building your new home over on the Etowah River cliffs. The only cliffs of that size between here and Mobile, I'm told."

Natalie was staring at Miss Lib, who was staring at Burke—for once, practically speechless.

"My—husband is—already—*building* our house? I think you must be mistaken, Mr. Latimer!"

"I'm sure I'm not. The man who's begun it tried to get me to work for him. I was already busy here," Burke said, glancing back at the Cummings house. "But everyone's expecting Mr. Stiles to influence other well-to-do Savannahians to follow suit. I hope to get my share of the future building."

"W.H. must have been planning to surprise you, Eliza Anne," Natalie's mother exclaimed. "You know how he loves to surprise you."

"I'm sure Caroline's right," Mark agreed. "In a small settlement like this, he must have worried that you'd find out. Do you remember how long he hesitated before letting you come up here with us? He didn't want to risk your learning about his surprise!"

"I'm controlling myself with enormous effort," Miss Lib said, her mouth pursed tightly. "You're right, Mark, I'm sure. And I know W.H.'s heart—but I'd also like to shake him!"

Natalie's mother reached a hand toward Miss Lib. "A house *is* such a personal thing to a woman."

"Of course it is!" Miss Lib didn't sound angry, just startled. "I could shake him cheerfully," she went on, "but if he were here this minute, I suppose I'd give him a big hug, too." She looked, in her open, unaffected way, at Burke. "You must excuse me—you and your friends—for airing my domestic dilemma. Your news so stunned me, I—I—"

Burke smiled the broad, irresistible smile Natalie had remembered through all the long months away from him. His smile hadn't changed. For her, it brought out the sun.

"It's you who should excuse me, Mrs. Stiles," he said. "Perhaps someday I can apologize to your husband for spoiling his surprise." All business suddenly, he glanced at the dark young man. "We'd better get back to work, Ben. The Cummingses haven't missed a daily inspection yet."

"I'm sure they're pleased with all they see," Mama said. "They're going to have a handsome place here."

Burke merely nodded.

"Do you have any problem getting well-seasoned wood?" Papa asked.

"Not so far, sir. I've managed to make friends with two mill owners."

Papa laughed. "Keeps them both on their toes, eh?"

"Spoken like a true businessman, Mr. Browning."

Natalie wondered if Burke meant that as a compliment, or if he was poking fun at Papa for being rich. He must have meant it. Burke meant everything he said.

"We'd better go now," Mama said. "Nothing would do Natalie," she went on, as though needing to explain their presence to Burke, "but we tour Cassville, but if I don't get some rest soon, I'll—spoil our trip."

"I'm ready to go too," Miss Lib said to no one in particular, still flabbergasted, Natalie was sure, that Uncle W.H. was actually building them a house up here on the frontier without telling her. But, being Miss Lib, she managed a charming laugh and held out her hand to Burke. "Don't worry about spoiling the surprise. A surprise is a surprise no matter when it's discovered. Good luck to you."

Burke didn't bow over her hand. He shook it warmly. He likes Miss Lib, Natalie thought. Good. We'll need her. He nodded to both her parents, then turned to her.

"How long do you expect to be here, Natalie?"

"Oh, we don't have any definite plans," she said. "We have to wait for William Mackay to come back." Then, lightning-quick, the thought flashed: If the brother and sister who lived with Burke were really his cousins, why had they said nothing all this time? Why had he waited so long to introduce them? They'd both just moved silently to one side and stood there. Suddenly, she heard herself demand: "If Mary and Ben McDonald are your cousins you brought from Florida, why weren't they with you on the *Pulaski?* Have you been back to Florida since—"

"—since the wreck? No, Natalie, I haven't." Abruptly, he turned to the others and asked, "Would you excuse us for a few minutes? I'd like to speak with Natalie alone."

"Certainly," her father said quickly. "We haven't been very considerate, I'm afraid. Natalie, we'll begin to walk slowly back toward the hotel."

"Better yet, we'll wait over there on that corner," Mama said.

"I am seventeen!" Natalie said, grabbing Burke's hand, as she pulled him around the wagon and behind the Cummings house.

Safely out of hearing, she said, "I don't need to know about—where you got your cousins now. Tell me later. But I *do* want to know: Why you didn't kiss me when you—first saw me again?"

"I was afraid," he said simply.

"Afraid? Of—kissing *me?*"

In answer, he kissed her so hard, she gasped for breath. Then he stopped and held her at arm's length. "I'm—not ready to—be with you yet," he said. "I told you in the letter that when I was ready—when the time was right—I'd come to Savannah. Don't you remember what I wrote in that letter?"

"I can recite every word of it this minute."

"I know what I said. I wish you hadn't come up here."

"Give me one good reason!"

"I'm not ready yet."

"What about me? *I am.* What about me?"

"You couldn't live the way I'm living now."

"Try me!"

"And take a chance on—losing you forever?"

She threw both arms around his sturdy waist and buried her head on his chest. "Oh, Burke, I love you so much, I've been so—miserable being away from you, I almost forgot how bull-headed you can be!"

"I'm just older than you."

Her arms still around him, she pounded him in the small of his back. "I forbid you ever to mention that again! Do you hear me? I forbid it!"

When he laughed, she turned her back and began to cry. "What's —so funny?"

"Nothing, except that no one forbids me to do anything." And before she could turn and face him, his arms went around her, crushing her to him so desperately that fresh anger flared through her because she could not reach any part of him except his forearms.

The anger turned to stormy longing when, his mouth close to her ear, still holding her to him, he said softly, "Natalie Browning, I love you, too."

"Enough to marry me?"

"Yes, but not for a long time."

She jerked free. "You make me just as furious as ever!"

"I make the pampered child in you angry," he said evenly. "It was that pampered child who forced your parents to bring you to look for me."

"Just who is that—Mary McDonald? You said on our settee that you'd never lie to me. She can't be your cousin. Burke, who is she?"

"Why can't she be my cousin?"

"Because you said you had no family."

He led her to a giant fallen white oak tree on which they sat down side by side, and Natalie listened all the way through his story of finding Mary and Ben in the cave, of Ben's beating by white men at New Echota, of how Mary and Ben had found William—had saved his life after the Pony Boys' attack. He also told her how lonely he himself would have been without the Cherokee brother and sister. Natalie listened without a word, and by the time he'd finished, she felt as though she'd lived through every minute of his strange, difficult year with him.

"Ben has all the makings of a fine carpenter," Burke went on. "I need him. I need Mary to cook for me and keep my cabin and my clothes clean." He hadn't touched her all the while he'd been talking. Now, he lifted her face and looked down at her. "Without them, it will take me a lot longer—to be ready."

"Ready—to marry me?"

"To marry you."

"But what am I supposed to do all the time it's taking you to get ready? Why can't you build an extra room on your cabin *now*—for us? I'd need someone to cook for me, too!"

He laughed. "I'm sure you would."

"Well, what's wrong with that? People have Negro servants to cook. You happen to have Indian servants."

"Mary and Ben are *not* servants."

"Then what are they? Not cousins, not servants—what?"

"They're like my brother and sister."

"Is—Mary always—sweeter than cane syrup?"

"I don't find her so."

She hugged one of his arms in both of hers. "Oh, Burke, you've gotten yourself into such a—a peculiar situation, how will my parents ever—understand it?"

"I'm not hoping to marry your parents. They're pleasant people, but—"

"Is that all they seem to you? Just 'pleasant'?"

"That's all I know of them. Mackay's sister's a nice lady, too, but I don't live in the same world with your parents or Mrs. Stiles. Her brother and I hit it off fine, but—"

"William grew up in the same house on Broughton Street back home as Miss Lib—my own father lived there for years too."

"The fine, expensive Mackay mansion didn't seem to hurt William Mackay any."

"It is *not* a fine, expensive mansion!" She was flaring at him again and she didn't mean to. "It's—just a big, rambling frame house under the trees, and it's full of love and good food. Oh, Burke, after all this horrid time away from each other, why can't we—be close now that I've found you? Why are we talking about the Mackays or anyone else but us?"

"You rushed things. You—you showed up before—I was ready."

Natalie jumped to her feet. "I'm tired being told that everything's my fault!"

"I expect it does get tiresome."

"You're supposed to stand too, when a lady gets up!"

"You only jumped up because you were annoyed."

"Living here with these—tacky, illiterate people is making you mean."

Still seated on the tree trunk, he grinned up at her. "I don't have that much to do with anyone. I stay pretty much to myself. Besides, not everyone up here is tacky or—ignorant."

"Burke? Have you—do you—go to those places where a man can —pay a woman to be close to him? I've heard—men do that."

"I tried it once or twice when I was younger."

"Is there—one up here?"

"Sure. More than one." He got up now. "Natalie, I have to go back to work. The Cummingses will be here in less than an hour. Mrs. Cummings all but counts the nails Ben and I drive. She'll know right off we haven't been driving any since we got back from the mill."

"Will you come to the States' Rights Hotel to see me tonight? We can go for a ride in Papa's carriage. I'm sure our driver has it all shined up by now."

He stood looking down into her eyes for such a long time without saying a word, Natalie thought she might die. Finally, after the longest kiss she'd ever had in her seventeen years, he said, "Not tonight, Natalie."

"What's *wrong* with tonight?"

"Nothing. I just need to think."

"Will you see Papa? He's asked you to tell him when you have time for a talk."

"I'm not one of your fancy Savannah gentlemen," he said, "but neither am I rude. I'll think about when I should do that, too." He loosed her arms from around his neck. "You'd better go. They'll be worried. Natalie—I haven't even kissed another woman since the last time I kissed your poor blistered mouth. I've been truer to you than you have to me."

The now repulsive thought of Olin Wheeler kept her silent. Not one thing came to mind to say.

"William Mackay told me you'd at least been paying attention to part of my letter," he went on. "I wanted you to go back to Savannah and live the way you'd always lived until—and if I saw you again. I'm glad you went to all those balls and concerts and parties with the North Carolina fellow."

"He was a snake!"

"So Mackay told me. But at least, you did part of what I asked. Natalie, listen to me. The final choice about us—won't be up to me. It will be up to you."

"I want to marry you *now!*"

"I know you do, but you'd be jumping into as—foreign a way of life as that sea we were tossed into. Natalie, please go. *Go!*"

"Kiss me once more!"

"I—can't. I don't dare. . . ."

After finally convincing Mark and Caroline that Natalie would find it easier to talk to someone other than parents right now, Eliza Anne stood waiting alone on the corner.

Burke does love her, she thought, her parasol open against the blazing sun, her body growing hot and sticky as the wait grew longer. He's having a hard time letting her go, I'm sure.

Eliza Anne certainly had no problem understanding Natalie's blind love for him, now that she'd finally met the man. He was nothing like W.H., but if a woman found herself drawn to a golden-haired giant, as Natalie helplessly was, she'd drown in the physical and inner magnetism of a Burke Latimer. Over and over, Natalie had told her that Burke was no "Savannah gentleman" and seemed proud of it. "Oh dear," Eliza Anne spoke aloud, walking up and down under the shade of a sycamore tree. "Oh dear . . ."

How, she wondered, would Natalie—so sheltered, obviously so uninformed about love between a man and woman—deal with her own passionate emotions in such a relationship? Burke Latimer overwhelmed the child—just by being present! Natalie had never known a man this way. She had never known a man like Burke. Was the contrast from the other young swains of the Browning's own social class—what attracted her to him?

Pointless question, she decided. Who knows why a man over-whelms a woman? Especially who knows about Natalie, who, from her own first day on earth, has done the overwhelming?

Somehow, suddenly, she thought of her own early suitor—Jack's closest army friend, Captain Robert Lee. She sighed. Lee had certainly overwhelmed Savannah's young ladies, Eliza Anne included, when he'd first come to stay at the Mackay house while he was surveying the land for Fort Pulaski. That was before she had been swept away with love for W.H. Robert Lee, taller, stronger in body, strikingly handsome and roguish, had seemed drawn to her, too. "And I to him," she spoke aloud again. "But not as I was finally drawn to W.H.!" Her slender, graceful, poetic-looking husband had, once she'd faced the fact that she and Lee were not meant for each other, truly overwhelmed her. To this day, even a brief time away from W.H.'s fiery gentleness could make her heart and her body ache. The love they shared was forever, and it ran deep, deep now, especially since the children had come. But, waiting in the wretched heat, Eliza Anne felt she understood, as though it had all been written out for her—word for word, motion for motion, longing for longing—Natalie's wild restlessness away from Burke.

Oh, she hadn't mentioned any of this to Mark and Caroline, but her own sure conviction that she did understand how much their daughter loved this man had moved her to insist that she wait alone. In a way, Mark and Caroline seemed almost helpless with Natalie. Both had admitted freely that, at times, they felt as though she were a stranger in their house. Beloved and cherished, but a stranger.

When Eliza Anne saw Natalie coming slowly toward her, head down, she called, "I'm over here in the shade." Lowering her parasol because Natalie, even with her fair skin, hated them, her thoughts were no longer on Mark and Caroline. More keenly than before, she was sure that Natalie needed a friend, and she hoped she was up to it.

Natalie had seen her, but unmindful of how warm and miserable Eliza Anne might be waiting in the hottest part of the day, she didn't bother to quicken her step. Neither did she smile.

"We're alone," Eliza Anne said. "I sent your parents on to the hotel. It seemed as though this might be a time for two—friends to be together."

Still without a word, Natalie threw her arms around her and began to weep. In spite of the suffocating heat, Eliza Anne held her and asked no questions. Finally, she said, "He's wonderful, Natalie. I think your Burke Latimer is not only gorgeous as you said; I like him. I'm sure things aren't the way you imagined they'd be. They seldom are, but—we've found him." When Natalie still said nothing, Eliza Anne asked, "Do you want to tell me about your time alone with him?"

In response, Natalie stepped back, flipped a handkerchief from the matching sash of the blue-striped dress, blew her nose, wiped tears from her face and declared, "Miss Lib, I don't approve of things not being the way they should be!"

"How were they wrong? He kissed you, didn't he?"

"The—longest, most divine, most—upsetting kiss I've—ever had," she said, her voice barely audible.

"You don't look particularly happy about it. Or was it too—perfect for—mere happiness? Now and then a kiss can be almost too—unexpected, too awesome—even from a dearly loved. . . ."

"That's it! You're exactly right. It was awesome! But, Miss Lib, everything seemed so strange. After all Burke and I went through together, after all those long, empty months of trying to imagine his face and mouth and arms—how could it seem strange finally to be with him?"

Eliza Anne thought awhile, then said, "Well, except for that single meal you had together on shipboard, you and Burke have never been together under anything resembling ordinary circumstances."

"These weren't ordinary circumstances today! Why *did* Mama and Papa have to follow me? You, too, for that matter."

"I swear to you we didn't follow you. We were concerned about you, but we were also obeying your orders to see the town."

"But I meant for you to *ride.* Jupiter was supposed to get stuck in the mud. Miss Lib, it was a horrible shock seeing you. I'd just been with him for a few minutes when there you all were! And those two Indians. Oh, Burke taught me to care about Cherokees, but I don't like them underfoot. Ben and simpering little Mary follow him around as though he were a royal prince and they his hounds! Especially Mary."

They were sauntering toward the hotel during Natalie's tirade against Burke's so-called cousins. "Natalie, did you call them Cherokees? I thought they were his Minorcan cousins from St. Augustine."

"Well, they're not. I pinned him down on that. He just has to say they're Minorcans or some of these white brutes up here will beat Ben again. They did once. And Burke says it's hard to tell what they might do to his precious Mary."

"His 'precious' Mary?"

"She lives under the same roof with him, doesn't she?" Natalie jammed the wet handkerchief back under her sash. "And surely you didn't miss seeing the way she looks at Burke."

"I didn't notice."

"Smart as you are about everything else?"

"You're jealous of little Cherokee Mary, aren't you?"

"Ha!"

"Did Burke tell you how he happened to be with Mary and her brother?"

"Evidently, he makes a habit of going about saving lives."

"I see. But I don't see how you could dislike those young people. Neither of them said more than two words after we arrived."

"Who said I dislike them? I just want to marry Burke and not have anyone else around!"

"And who will clean and cook for you?"

"I can tell you I don't intend to! Miss Lib, if Burke weren't so pigheaded, he'd go right back to Savannah with us, get rich building houses and then, if he has to live up here, we could bring a whole wagonload of servants."

"Have you approached him with that idea?" Surprisingly, Natalie gave her only a fleeting smile. Actually a somewhat shy smile. Coming from Natalie, it was startling. "I take it you haven't mentioned it to him."

Natalie's reply was an almost pathetic plea. "Could we please— just not talk about any of it? I'm so—mixed up. And I was so sure that if only I found him—"

"Natalie, you need to talk about it. Give Burke time. He did hold you and kiss you—passionately. He wouldn't have done that if he weren't as desperate as you, would he?"

"I don't know. Don't ask questions! Those—kisses almost scared me!"

"I thought so. I'm not trying to pry, Natalie, but I do think, because you're young and—"

"I'm not young! I'm seventeen."

"Well, because you—you've never been in love with anyone as you are with Burke, you—need someone to talk to who has been in love, don't you think?"

"No. I don't want to talk about it. I don't want things to be the way they are—all scary and strange."

"Didn't you like being close to him?"

"I told you I don't know! I'm—mixed up."

"You're avoiding the question and I think—I need to know. Just tell me. Did you like the way Burke kissed you?"

"No. Yes!"

"Which?"

"No, I didn't like it because he wouldn't—go on kissing me. He wouldn't even kiss me when I left. . . ."

FORTY-THREE

ON THEIR THIRD AFTERNOON in Cassville, Mark sat alone in the hotel dining room, sipping a glass of cider and waiting for Caroline and Eliza Anne to join him later for the main meal of the day. Since their arrival, they had done almost nothing but wait. They were still waiting for William to return and for some word—any word—from Burke Latimer. Mark had heard nothing concerning the private talk he'd requested, but his real heartache was that the young man had also ignored Natalie.

"The child just sits by our window looking out at nothing," Eliza Anne told him yesterday, when Natalie had again refused to come downstairs for meals. "I try to talk to her. She answers me politely, but, Mark, she's crushed!"

He had never seen his daughter behave as helplessly as during these past three days. Had Natalie met her match in Burke Latimer? Was she really helpless? Oh, she'd frequently pulled her wide-eyed, helpless manner on Mark when she failed to get her way with her mother, but this was no trick. The girl seemed not to know which way to turn. For the entire year since she'd come home, he and Caroline had watched her move her small mountains this way and that with only one goal in mind—to find Burke Latimer. As long as Natalie was bent on shifting obstacles out of her path, they felt on familiar territory. Often difficult, but at least familiar. This was different. Even Caroline could not plead for her to be reasonable. Reason seemed to have nothing to do with Natalie's present mood. She simply wasn't being Natalie.

Last night had made all this clear to him. Against the two ladies' better judgment, Mark had insisted upon seeing her alone. Natalie had given him several small, halfhearted smiles, but had scarcely spoken. When he hugged her good-night, her arms had tightened a little, but her mind was not on him.

"I can't talk about Burke yet, Papa," she'd said. "I have to trust you not to hurry me. I can't say anything because there isn't anything to say. Everything's up to him."

How did a father just stand aside and watch his own daughter struggle from childish dependence upon him into what was likely to be real heartbreak from an almost total stranger, who held her happiness in his strong, work-hardened hands? Still waiting for the ladies to appear, one of his own smooth hands kneaded the other. Without realizing it, he had literally been sitting there wringing his hands.

Why, he thought, don't I just go to the Cummings house site and talk to him? The boy's going to remain unknown, a stranger to all of us but Natalie, until someone talks to him.

At that moment, he heard the street door open, and in a few strides, Burke, in his work clothes, stood beside the table, holding his hat.

Mark got up to shake hands, and without being asked, Burke sat down across the table. "I've come to talk," he said. "I hope I haven't picked a bad time. Natalie isn't anywhere around, is she?"

"She's upstairs in her room. She doesn't even come down to meals with us. Mrs. Stiles has been taking a tray up to her—three times a day."

"She isn't—sick, is she?"

"Like the rest of us, she's confused as to why there's been no word from you."

"It's only been three days."

"We did make the long journey up here hoping to find you."

"And Mr. Mackay," Burke said.

"True. But I sent Mackay expressly to find you," Mark said. "Inspecting land for Barnsley and Stiles was incidental."

For the first time, Burke smiled. "Has your daughter always been so hard to manage, Mr. Browning?"

Dumbfounded at such directness from a younger man, Mark answered carefully, "Natalie has always needed a lot of—of—"

"Of what?" Burke pressed.

Unexpectedly, Mark felt his own first genuine, warm response to this surprising fellow—a kind of relief. "I'll give you a direct answer. Yes, Latimer, she has always required some—handling."

"You mean giving in to her, don't you?"

"I know I've given in to her much of the time. I, more than her mother. I suppose I should be ashamed to admit it."

"Why? What can we accomplish by this talk if we're not honest with each other?"

"You're right. Would you like some cider, ale—anything?"

"No, thank you. I came to talk. Ben will be needing me on the job in a little while. We're raising the roof beam today."

"I see."

"What do you see, Mr. Browning?"

Mark studied the broad, even-featured, clean-shaven face. "I—I see my adored daughter at the first real impasse in her entire life."

"I don't agree." When Mark looked surprised, Burke went on, "I don't think there's an impasse in anyone's life to compare with—facing death. I saw her face death for five long days and nights. She didn't break once. Natalie isn't only too beautiful, she's got guts." An amused smile flicked across Burke's face. "I'm sure my use of that word 'guts' in speaking of your daughter, the Savannah belle, surprises you. Offends you?"

"Neither. It relieves me. Look here, Latimer, from Natalie I gather that you have some rather distorted ideas of what our family is like. Of what Savannahians are like. We happen to live in a now booming city, in a good house, but we're people too." When Burke said nothing, he asked, "Do you love my daughter? I know you're undoubtedly infatuated by her beauty, but—do you love her?"

"She wasn't exactly a beauty on that raft. I was with her there more than I've been with her anywhere, you know." He paused. "Yes. I love her. And in case you're too much the gentleman to ask outright, I also want to marry her. If I can't marry Natalie, I doubt I'll ever marry anyone. I—want Natalie to be my wife—more than I've ever wanted anything. As much as I want to—make my own success up here as a builder. If you knew me better, you'd know I couldn't want her more than that."

"Are you—asking my permission to marry her?"

"No. I've come to ask you to help me convince her that we *can't* get married now. Maybe not for several years." Burke's eyes filled with quick tears, but his voice sounded almost hard as he added, "If you won't help me, I can buck her alone."

"You sound awfully sure."

"I am."

Mark looked down at his hands. "I've never been much good at—bucking her, as you say."

"I know that."

"Who told you?"

"No one needed to tell me. Any fool could see in five minutes how spoiled she is. As rotten spoiled as she is—beautiful. A girl can't be more spoiled than that."

"Just what is it you want me to do? What is it, for that matter, that you want Natalie to do? Since she saw you three days ago, she's done nothing but sit alone by a window and hurt. I can't watch that much longer. What is it you really want?"

"I want to marry her, Mr. Browning. I've told you that. At best, our marriage would be a long shot. So I want to wait until it will at least have—half a chance to work."

"Well," Mark said, "we agree on that much. But you'll have to be more explicit. By that, I mean you'll have to give me more details of what would be needed in order to make your marriage succeed."

Burke grinned. "You don't need to explain that word 'explicit,' sir. Just in passing, you might like to know that my father, who didn't die until I was nearly ten, was a respected schoolmaster back in Baltimore."

"I'm sorry. I meant no offense. My wife and I have noticed how well you speak."

Now Burke laughed. "Do you mean—well? Or simply fairly well for a man who works with his hands?" At that, Burke held up his hand. "I shouldn't have said that. Excuse it. My parents are dead, but they would have been as much against my working with my hands as you and Mrs. Browning are."

"But we're not!" Mark stopped. He was beginning to like this man, to like him sincerely, but he meant to be aware of Burke's sudden, seemingly pleasant traps. "It was merely an accident of birth that I inherited money," he went on. "I'm a merchant, as you're a builder, because being a merchant is what I wanted more than any other line of work. Mrs. Browning and I do not consider ourselves superior in any sense whatever. If you and Natalie do really love each other, I have to believe you'll learn to accept us, too."

For a time, Burke studied him. "You're a—surprising gentleman, Mr. Browning. Is there even one more wealthy merchant or professional man in Savannah as—human as you seem to be?"

"Of course," Mark answered easily. "But only this one happens to be Natalie's father. Do you disapprove of men who *don't* earn their living with their hands?"

A slow smile spread over Burke's face. *"Touché,"* he said.

"Do you fence?" Mark asked, on a soft laugh. "Don't answer that question. Obviously, you could."

"Parrying has always made me uneasy," Burke confessed. "Even with words. My father did fence, expertly. With words and foils."

"Latimer, there can never be an adequate way to thank you for—giving Natalie back to us. Still, what I'm about to say is not only out of gratitude. I'm merely making a suggestion, and before you refuse outright, I hope you'll do me the honor of giving it some hard thought. I am a man of some means and influence in Savannah. Our city is indeed expanding and prospering these days."

"Natalie told me. Sitting beside me on our settee in the water, she did her best to convince me that I should forget about this area and move to Savannah. That I could make a fortune practically overnight building all those new houses and churches and the Lord knows what else. Is that what you're about to suggest?"

Deflated, Mark said, "But you came here instead, is that it?"

"That's it. I can't explain it, but this is my part of the world now. Now and always. Natalie said you would understand that."

"She told you that too, eh? That I felt about Savannah when I was young exactly as you feel about Cass County?"

He nodded. "At the risk of sounding ungrateful, my answer is *no*, Mr. Browning. If you were about to make me a generous offer to give all this up and come to Savannah, no. I have to refuse." When Mark only frowned, Burke went on, "I'm far more certain than Natalie that I've found the one person with whom I want to spend the remainder of my life. I'm older than she is. Eight years older. I know myself better than she does. I love her more than I—want to love her at this time in my life, but *I can't marry her*. Not now. Not for three or four years. God knows I want to, but can your daughter sew and cook and milk a cow and mend torn britches and mop floors? Can Natalie even make her own bed?"

"I don't suppose she's ever tried. She could learn, but I'd—I'd—"

"You'd hate to see her have to do it."

"Yes. I would hate to see her have to do it." Mark stopped, then decided to be as blunt with Latimer as Latimer had been with him. "The truth is, I wonder if I do know my daughter very well. I've all but worshiped the ground under her feet since the moment I laid eyes on that bright, curly red head, but I—I have always given her everything she's wanted, and because I have, she behaves around me most of the time in a way she knows will only—charm me. Her mother and I have spoken of this, but until now—talking to you, I doubt that I ever fully realized how little I understand her. It could well be that in just five days on that makeshift raft, you came to know her far better than I."

"You really don't like to parry either, do you, sir?"

"No. As for helping you buck her, as you say—convincing her to wait until you can afford the kind of life she knows how to manage with the proper grace, I—"

"I don't give a hoot whether or not she manages with proper or improper grace—I just don't want her to come to despise me and the frontier life I stand for!" He brought both fists down on the table. "I don't want to risk turning her against me. If my work goes well here, I can build her a good house—not a mansion—I don't want a mansion. But a good house. I can hire a couple of servants and—"

"No slaves?"

"No. We're together there, Mr. Browning. I don't believe in owning other human beings either."

"How did you know I don't?"

"Natalie talked a lot about you. In fact, she scorched me good for underestimating you as just another soft-handed, paternalistic, slave-owning gentleman."

"Well, that pleases me," Mark said.

"Will you talk to her? Will you help me convince her to wait? I won't even ask her to be true to me while she's waiting. I'd rather risk her finding someone else than to jump into a fire neither of us could survive." Burke stood up. "I do have to get back to work. What do you say?"

Mark stood too. "I'd say we've had a most unusual conversation between a suitor and a girl's father."

"Please answer my question. Will you talk to her?"

Mark clasped Burke's outstretched hand. "I'll try. But I think you should know that Natalie won't listen to anything I have to say unless I can tell her that you've refused my offer to finance you in your own contracting business in Savannah. I am making that offer again. Whatever you need to get started would be yours. After what you did for Natalie, your acceptance would give me a great deal of happiness."

"Tell her I refused. Point-blank. But can I count on you to try to convince her that we *cannot* get married anytime soon?"

"On one condition. That you'll tell her first. That you'll tell her what you've told me."

"I intend to. Tomorrow afternoon. I'll have to work late today because of our talk here. May I call for her tomorrow about four o'clock?"

"I'll tell her you're coming," Mark said. "I can't imagine that I'll ever like her living up here in the wilds, but I want you to know that I do feel better, now that we've talked. Your head is very squarely on your shoulders, Latimer."

"I think it is, sir."

"I also feel you're basically unselfish and probably quite a strong man."

Picking up his hat, Burke smiled wryly. "I just hope I'm strong enough."

During dinner, Eliza Anne mainly listened, as Mark tried to tell her and Caroline some of what Burke had said and of his own reaction to the young man who, though absent, had kept their Savannah household in turmoil for a year.

"He does work with his hands," Mark explained, "but he was born into a proud and cultivated family. He told me that both his parents, dead now, would disapprove of his being a carpenter—especially his schoolmaster father."

"Mark, that is not what bothers me," Caroline said. "Isaiah Davenport was a builder, a superb carpenter. Eliza Anne and I have been discussing Burke Latimer's lack of *courtesy*. That *does* bother me."

"Speak for yourself, Caroline, on that subject," Eliza Anne said.

"All right, I will. None of us made this long trip up here to enjoy the dubious comforts of the States' Rights Hotel. Why has he gone on pounding nails and sawing his planks as though he's hiding from Natalie? I'll try to like him, Mark. I want her to be happy as much as you do, but he's turning her into someone her own mother doesn't recognize!"

"He asked permission to see her tomorrow," Mark said. "He'll leave work early and come here to the hotel."

"You mean he's finally behaving like a gentleman?"

"That isn't fair, Caroline," Eliza Anne said. "We did take him by surprise."

"Mark, did you even ask him why he's been so cruel to her? Why he—"

"Excuse me, Caroline," Eliza Anne interrupted quietly but firmly. "I have to say this. You two are on the verge of quarreling over something that has no bearing on the real problem."

"The real problem," Caroline flared, "is that Natalie is scared half to death that she might lose this golden-haired, boorish young man. I'm quite bewildered at her being submissive this long! Obviously, he doesn't know Natalie at all."

"My dear," Mark said, "he knows her far better than we do."

"What?"

"I mean that, Caroline. He knows—a different Natalie from the girl we know and love."

"Burke watched her face—death," Eliza Anne said slowly.

"That's it exactly." Mark sounded relieved. "And—he loves her, probably more than she understands how to love yet."

"He has an odd way of showing it!"

"Dear Caroline, it does seem that way," Eliza Anne said, "but could we just listen while Mark tells us what else Burke had to say? Mark, something tells me you like him."

"I do," he said. "I honestly didn't know what I felt about him when he first sat down, but I know now. Actually, it was an astounding experience. The young man who is in love with our daughter calling on her father, not to ask permission to marry her—to ask me to help him convince her that they can *not* marry anytime soon."

"He—doesn't want to marry her, Mark? What arrogance! Did he give you a reason?"

"Several reasons," Mark went on. "Burke sees things as they are, not as our dear Natalie mistakenly believes they can be."

Mark went through all of Burke's reasons, Eliza Anne nodding encouragement and approval as he talked. When he reached Burke's list of questions: Can Natalie mop a floor? mend torn trousers? darn socks? cook? make beds?

Caroline's eyes widened in surprise. "Is it carved in stone that they *have* to live up here?"

"This is the life Burke's chosen. As I chose Savannah, he's chosen Cass County. Natalie's told us that all along."

"Oh, she's been so starry-eyed over him, I paid no attention to that."

"Well, I did," Eliza Anne said. "As much as I love Savannah and want my children to grow up near Mama, I am willing to live up here because W.H. wants it more than anything else. Men have dreams, Caroline. W.H.'s dream is to live here. He's my life. I listened to Natalie because I'll have to learn how to live up here too. Burke evidently knows what he wants. Give Natalie credit for realizing that."

"Darling," Mark said, more boldly now, Eliza Anne thought, "Latimer knows his own mind, but he also has good sense. He's bluntly honest. In fact, he reminds me of you before we were married. Back in the days when it was still hard for you to go to Knightsford because your grandmother was living there. You said exactly what you were thinking. Your honesty was one of the many reasons I loved you. It still is."

Eliza Anne saw Caroline's brief smile and knew Mark had said the right thing to help her regain perspective.

"You still know how to handle your wife when she's fighting windmills, don't you, Mr. Browning?"

"Your fairness allows me to be—straight with you, darling," he said.

"Will he try to convince her tomorrow that they should wait?" Caroline asked.

"I expect him to do just that," Mark answered.

Eliza Anne looked from one to the other. "It sounds to me as though you're both reconciled to the marriage."

In the silence that followed, she watched Caroline take a sip of tepid tea, make a face and push the cup away. Mark was watching her, too.

Finally, Caroline said, "Miss Eliza keeps reminding me that Natalie isn't much like either Mark or me. She is our child, even though I've wanted to reject that at times. But, Mark"—her eyes looked so troubled, he laid his hand over hers—"she is awfully like my grandmother!"

"Caroline, no!" Eliza Anne exclaimed. "I've never thought of Natalie as an unhappy child."

"Well, she certainly fights everyone who displeases her."

"But Ethel Cameron was a bitter old woman, closed away in her own private world. I know Natalie is keeping to herself now, but—"

Mark interrupted. "She *isn't* closed away, darling."

"In a way, she's always been. Why do you deny it? When does she hatch all her schemes and plans?" Eliza Anne couldn't be sure because Caroline was looking at Mark, but she thought her voice sounded on the verge of tears. "It's—as though she's just waiting out the years until she'll be free of both of us. It—it seemed to run off her, like water off a duck's back, when I told her I'd forgiven Osmund Kott!"

Eliza Anne caught her breath, but said nothing.

Mark stared. "Caroline—you told her that?"

"Yes. At Milner's. She also knows he was her—great-uncle. Osmund wrote it all in that letter he left. Don't gape so, Mark. She took it very calmly, really. Natalie had evidently made up her mind never to mention the contents of that letter to anyone—but Burke. It didn't particularly upset her and I think she believed me when I vowed I'd forgiven him. She spoke of it quite calmly. Told me I could tell the two of you, if I liked, but that she never wanted to discuss it with anyone."

"And did it make you feel better—having told her?" Mark asked.

"Of course it did. She was quite mature about the whole thing. I—thanked her for it. But she means to keep Osmund to herself. In a secret place. Where she keeps—all her 'treasures,' as she put it. It's that strange, secret place that makes me think of how much she might be like—my grandmother."

"I simply can't follow you there," Mark said.

"Well, I've thought of the comparison a dozen times since we've been up here. Mark, what would we do if Natalie *is* like—Ethel

Cameron—in any way? Look at her now, withdrawn from all of us, shut up in her room!"

"Stop it," Eliza Anne ordered. "What you're saying isn't fair to Mark or to you. Forgive me, but you're not thinking clearly. I—I wouldn't be either, I suppose, if my daughter were as—upset as Natalie seems to be now, but your nerves are getting the best of you, Caroline."

"They're my nerves; don't you think I know it?"

"Listen, both of you," Eliza Anne said, taking charge because someone had to. "I have an idea. I may be quite crazy to offer it right now, but I do offer myself along with it. Natalie and I are friends. I think she trusts me. She talks to me some, at least."

"But not her parents," Mark said helplessly.

"For goodness' sake, her silence with the two of you isn't an insult, nor is it a compliment to me when she talks in our room. I'm simply not her parent. You remember, Mark, how I used to tell you things when I was young and you were living with us—personal things and just plain gossip I wouldn't have thought of telling either Mama or Papa?"

"I remember," he said impatiently, "but what are you driving at?"

"Lookout Mountain isn't far from here. You have Jupiter and your own carriage. W.H. and I didn't mind the hotel there. Why not leave Natalie with me for a few days and have a second honeymoon?"

"You're suggesting that her parents should just go off and leave her—now, of all times?" Caroline was incredulous.

"That's exactly what I'm saying. Natalie isn't all child anymore. Give her a chance to think like the woman she's trying to become. Not a sheltered little girl."

"But she is still part child!"

Eliza Anne nodded. "Yes, in that terrifying limbo between the two. The woman in her loves Burke Latimer. She's torn apart inside by what we all know is her first experience of loving—of longing for someone. A child can't deal with that kind of—torment. A woman at least has a chance. With all your good intentions toward her, the two of you being near keeps the child Natalie alive. I beg you to give her a chance to—move into womanhood. She is old enough now."

"Eliza Anne's right," Mark finally agreed. "A good friend may well be able to help her far more than anxious, troubled parents."

He tried to give Caroline a reassuring smile. "Even loving parents like us."

"But, Mark, we brought her all the way up here to find him. Surely she knows we only want the very best for her. We *did* make that long, ghastly trip when you were so busy and—"

"She knows all that," Eliza Anne broke in. "Even in her present misery, she knows how much you love her, but because she also loves you, your anxious faces only add to her burden. Oh, I scare myself witless promising to look after Natalie while you're gone, but I do promise. I'll try not only to keep an eye on her, but I'll also try to give her room to find her own way. Frankly, I think Burke stands a far better chance of convincing her to wait if neither one of you is here when he sees her tomorrow." Eliza Anne paused, then dared to ask, "You know, don't you, that you're both almost as—lost as Natalie right now?"

"I know that," Mark said. "I'm not proud of it, but I know it."

"Time alone together will help you, though. I feel so sure of it."

After looking long at Mark, Caroline tossed her napkin onto the table. "All right. All right, we'll go, if you're sure, Eliza Anne, that you really want to tackle what might lie ahead. I know she came here with the idea of marrying him—not back in Savannah at some future date—but right here, in Cassville, *now*. Shouldn't we wait at least until she's seen him?" Then Caroline laughed at herself. "No, don't listen to me. Find Jupiter, Mark. If he can be ready to start tomorrow, we'll go."

FORTY-FOUR

BURKE was not yet back at the Cummings house site when two hired white men arrived to help raise the roof beam, so Ben was forced to face the men alone. For weeks now, with a minimum of trouble, Ben had come openly into town to work alongside Burke. He would, he supposed, never grow accustomed to being treated as though he were the scrapings of the earth, but his position as Burke's helper—because Burke was so respected in Cassville—had made life bearable. For the most part, people either glared at him or ignored him. He had not learned how to converse with white men and had formed the habit of standing off to one side or disappearing when they came around.

The uneasiness he felt today, though, was far worse than at any other public encounter because his own heavy heart seemed to have robbed him of his innate courage. Where courage had been, today there was anxiety and swelling anger. He was angry with himself for being anxious, and his heart was heavy because he suspected the real reason Burke had left him alone to talk to Mr. Browning of Savannah—*her* father.

For the half hour or so as Ben and the white workmen waited, there was no talk whatever. Ben sat alone on a pile of lumber at the back of the house, the men on the cottage steps out front. When Burke did return at last, their combined efforts made possible the raising of the roof beam in a relatively short time, and Ben was relieved when the two men left. He was even more relieved when Burke asked him to taper cedar shingles on the far side of the cottage from where Burke would be working. Ben had tried to act as usual with Burke, but he could never again know the old peace and trust in the company of the man he had so admired and trusted since the day Burke rescued him and Mary from the cave. The thought that Burke Latimer, his best friend, had just been with her father—speaking personally of her—lay like a stone in the heart.

The heavy shaving block on which Ben fastened the shingles for tapering could not be moved. He would have to work there alone. At least, he would not be near enough to talk to Burke. Hands shaking, Ben braced the first cedar shingle with a block hook, pressed his own body against the other end of the shingle and began to taper its edges with a drawknife. He groaned at the botch he was making of such a simple task, but the groan came less from his clumsy work than from the heaviness in his heart.

From the moment he had glimpsed her standing there three days ago, pretty bonnet in hand, red-gold hair gleaming in the sunlight, the heaviness had entered his heart. "Love does not bring despair," his Cherokee mother had always told him. For the first time, he had found his mother to be wrong. Love did bring despair, when a man loved a woman he could never, never know.

Rooted to the ground at this very house site, those few days ago, he had stood to one side with his sister and watched the beautiful one fly into the arms of the man Ben loved more than he might have loved a blood brother. Burke's own arms had held her! Burke, who had saved him and Mary from the cave—who would, this minute, fight, if need be, to his own death for Ben—or for Mary. Burke had become his beloved enemy. . . .

Ben's hands, when he worked, had always been sure, expert. Burke's teaching had improved their skill. Today, they felt stiff and clumsy. The shingle slipped and he let the drawknife fall to the ground. Ben covered both eyes. Her beauty remained! If he never saw her again in this life, the perfect face and crown of shining hair would surely fly beside him through eternity. Would fly beside him through the Cherokee's Spirit world *and* the white man's heaven. He could never touch her, never have her, but he could never again be free of her beauty.

That her name was Natalie Browning seemed of no importance. To Ben, her name was Beauty. Beauty that sprang from the pure heart of both worlds—from this world, where, in sun and shadow, grew pine trees and sycamores and wild lilies and children and rabbits and birds . . . Beauty that sprang from the next world where God and the Spirit made light shine even when it was night.

Four days ago, he had nodded politely to her mother and father, to the other white lady named Stiles. But not to her. A mere mortal Cherokee half-blood does not address Beauty. He had felt his fists harden when Burke took her in his arms, but he'd kept silent and must remain silent forever.

"Ben!" Burke's usually welcome voice calling his name was now a burning arrow. "Ben! Is anything wrong around there? I don't hear your drawknife."

"You need me?" he called back, his voice tight and unfamiliar.

By the time Burke rounded the corner of the cottage, Ben was busy again, fitting another red-brown wedge of cedar against the block hook.

"Just wanted to be sure you're all right. You almost never stop working. I got worried."

Ben tried to return the smile. "Everything is all right. I promise."

Giving him a friendly wave, Burke returned to his own work. Ben sighed. Burke was not the stone in his heart. The stone was his heart itself. He grasped the drawknife handles again and his thoughts flew to Mary. Now, there were *two* hopeless loves. Since before they'd left the cave at New Echota, Ben had known that Mary loved Burke. With his own heavy heart, he would find it far harder to watch over his sister in her futile love. The burden would be doubled, because he, too, would have to make his own way without hope.

In spite of Burke's strange, unsmiling silence since the strangers from Savannah had come, Mary sang a little song that evening as she washed the dishes in a pan of steaming soapy water. When Burke called her to "leave the dishes alone" and sit back down at the table with him and Ben, her heart sang too. Obeying him would mean heating more water, but when Mister Burke wanted her with him, nothing was trouble.

Drying her hands on her apron, she beamed at him and sat down in the chair Ben had painted willow-green because of their mother's name, Willow. "From now on, Mary," Burke once teased, "neither Ben nor I will dare sit in that chair. It's yours—all yours."

Mister Burke, by saying that, had turned it into her throne. "I am here, Mister Burke," she said brightly.

Tonight, he did not tease, but frowned when he spoke. "I've put off telling you both a story I probably should have told you long ago," he began. "But sometimes, certain things are so—deep in a man's soul, he—well, he keeps them secret."

Mary glanced at Ben, wondering if he felt nervous and scared too. The thought crossed her mind that she had never, until now, seen her brother seem so much like their mother. Even she could not tell what Ben was thinking. That look is why they know Ben is Indian and not I, she thought. Like our father, I tell my thoughts on my face. Her mind and her attention rushed back to Mister Burke, who seemed to be thinking how to tell them his story.

"A little over a year ago," he said, "I took a boat called the *Pulaski* at Savannah..I'd docked there the day before from St. Augustine"—his quick smile sent a thrill through Mary, and she smiled too. "You both remember St. Augustine, I know." He is teasing now since we are said to be his cousins from that city, she thought, happy that he was teasing because that most always meant Mister Burke was happy.

But his face was solemn again when he returned to his story, and for over an hour she and Ben sat motionless, listening—more than listening—they clung to every word of the tragic tale of the explosion in the black of night that ripped apart the fine ship and killed so many frightened, helpless men and women and little children. He spoke of kind, sad Mr. William Mackay's dead family, and Mary's heart ached to realize how much sorrow the good man had kept inside himself while being so courteous and appreciative of their care after the Pony Boys beat him.

When Mary could no longer stifle a sob, Mister Burke said, "I understand how you feel, Little One." He only called her Little One when he understood her in a good way. "I guess a man or a woman just—goes on because there isn't anything else to do after a loss like that, but Mr. Mackay may be the strongest, bravest man I know."

"We would have been kinder to him, if we'd known," Ben said, and just having him say that much relieved Mary. It always troubled her when Ben fell silent, as he most surely had been so far this week.

"Now," Mister Burke went on, "I'm coming to the part that may concern the three of us later on. Miss Natalie Browning and I ended up together after the shipwreck—on a makeshift raft—a wooden settee and a barrel—out in the Atlantic Ocean. When I found her, she was still holding on to the tiny dead body of Mr. Mackay's son. The wooden settee I'd found couldn't have floated us both with one more pound on it. Anyway, the baby had been dead all night."

When she saw tears fill Mister Burke's eyes, Mary's hands squeezed together so hard, her fingers hurt.

"I persuaded—Natalie—to let the little fellow slide into the sea. For the first several hours people were shouting and praying and crying for help in the water all around us. Natalie and I—sat there, unable to help and—watched most of them—drown, right before our eyes."

"But—you no die," Mary said just above a whisper.

"No, I didn't die, and neither did Natalie Browning. We nearly burned to death under the sun by day, we nearly starved, we nearly died of thirst, we nearly froze at night—but we didn't die."

When Ben got up and walked to the open door while Mister Burke was still talking, Mary felt vexed with him, but she couldn't take her eyes off Burke's face. Ben was still standing there now, his back turned to them, but she stared only at Mister Burke's troubled face —so troubled by remembering that he looked almost old.

Then, for a long, long time, there was no more telling of the story. No more sound but the ticking of the clock, until the sudden scatter of a squirrel's feet as it dropped to the roof from the big white oak that shaded the cabin. The shout of a wren nearby, into another choking silence, seemed so harsh, so out of place, it startled her.

Finally, when she heard Ben clear his throat, Mary glanced at her brother. He was staring out the door, his shoulders drooping in such dejection that she grew afraid because at that minute, Ben looked like an old man too.

He cleared his throat again and said, in the most hopeless tone Mary had ever heard from him, even during the hardest time in the cave, "You told us this, Burke, so you could also—tell us that you have—loved her ever since."

"That's right," Mister Burke said, sounding relieved. "I have loved Natalie every minute since. I will always love her."

Mary stifled a cry. Not once had she suspected! Even though Mister Burke had embraced the beautiful girl with hair like the sun on a red oak leaf, she did not suspect that he loved her as a man loves a woman, because in the stockade many people embraced each other. At the house site that day, she'd tried not to listen to what the visitors and Mister Burke said because her mother had taught her not to eavesdrop.

"Yes," he was saying now, almost as though she and Ben were not there, "I love her. More than I ever intended to love anyone. She loves me too. Her father told me just today that she plagued her parents until they brought her up here to find me."

"You—you were lost, Mister Burke?"

"I guess you could say, Little One, that I saw to it that I was lost to her for a year."

Her mind grabbed at the endearing name. He loves her, but he called me Little One!

He was talking now about his own money problems. All his money had gone down when the ship wrecked. Natalie Browning was a rich girl who could never deal with the kind of life they all lived. He said Natalie Browning lived every day of her life expecting mountains to move at her slightest whim.

"Mountains do not move," Mary said.

He was looking at her now. "You're right, Little One. Miss Natalie's educated, but not wise like you."

Mary tried to smile, but it was too late. He had seen her tears.

"Are you crying over poor Mr. Mackay?" he asked.

She nodded yes as hard and as fast as she could.

"I want you both to know that Natalie's heart is tender, too. She grieved deeply for the Mackays, and how she tried to save that little boy! She's also brave. For five days and nights, she and I were only one swamping wave away from death. I told her father today—she didn't break once." He took a deep breath. "She's—too many things. A man can't think straight."

"You think, Mister Burke," she said. "You think—good."

"Not when I'm near her. I do all right as long as she's out of sight. One look and—a man's mind goes haywire."

Mister Burke slapped, then rubbed his knees, seeming to jerk himself back to the present, to the cabin, to Mary and Ben. "I've told you both this story because one day—I mean to marry Natalie Browning."

The silence that followed stretched and stretched and stretched.

Finally, from the doorway, Ben asked, "You'll move to Savannah then?"

"No sirree, Ben! If I marry her, she will live here—with me."

"In—our cabin?"

"No, Little One. Never in our cabin." He groaned. "God knows I want her here, but she couldn't live the way we live. She's been waited on hand and foot all her life. She'd hate it in no time here with us."

"Her father—agrees with you?" Ben asked.

"He most certainly does. In fact, he isn't at all the way I thought he'd be."

"You—ask him, Mister Burke, to marry—his daughter?"

"I did not! I asked him to convince her to wait until I say I'm ready to marry her. And that won't be for a long time. I want you two to understand that we won't be together like this for always, but if I married her now, I'd lose her. I can't face that. I hope to build a good house for her someday, but it will be at least a few years yet."

Mary sat straight in her green willow chair, hands in her lap, her heart clinging to the one comforting thing Mister Burke had said: *It will be at least a few years yet.* She, Mary, would be the one to care for him, to cook for him, to mend his shirts, to gather sassafras for his tea—for a few more years.

Longing, suddenly, to say something that would make him smile again, she whispered, "Miss Natalie Browning be—beautiful in the rooms of—the house you build someday—for her—Mister Burke."

But before he could respond, she ran across the room and threw herself into Ben's arms, sobbing.

Hour after hour that night, Burke lay awake—keeping himself awake actually by trying so hard not to toss and turn. At the slightest sound of restlessness from him, Mary was likely to appear in his doorway, wanting to know what she could bring him, do for him.

He felt better having told Mary and Ben that he hoped someday to marry Natalie, but Mary's weeping and their quick, frantic embrace when he'd finished, still troubled him. Almost from the first day he'd found the two in their New Echota cave, he'd known something of the extent of their gratitude; gratitude he'd watched turn to devoted dependence. The expression in their eyes, when they looked at him now that he'd found a real home for them, made plain their devotion. Burke counted on that devotion. Brother and sister were as necessary to his life as he to theirs. He could not have pleased the Cummingses without Ben's growing skills as a carpenter. Certainly Mary took care of his house, his clothes, his meals and even on dark, rainy days filled the cabin with light and happiness. Not a day passed that he and Ben didn't have a good laugh because of something Mary said or did. She had been perfectly named by her Cherokee mother—the girl was truly merry. Too bad, he thought often, that she can never again be called *Merry* Willow.

Maybe learning of his future dream of marrying Natalie—crazy as it still seemed—had merely stunned them. Possibly it had even frightened them a little. Burke knew better than anyone else some of the horror and misery of the winter spent in that cave, the hunger when ice and snow had kept Ben from hunting, the panic at the risk of being discovered by white men. Undoubtedly, neither had yet thought about life in the future, when the three of them might not be together. They had made no plans at all, no commitments, but, he reasoned, his story had simply taken them off guard. At first, he thought Mary had seemed somewhat satisfied when he assured them that he could not marry Natalie for a few years—but then she had broken into sobs in Ben's arms.

Turning in the bed, he punched up the pillows and tried to settle his restless body between Mary's newly hemmed muslin sheets. To be truthful, far more than perplexity over Mary and Ben was keeping him awake. *He would be with Natalie—tomorrow.* After a whole year, he was going to be with her—off that raft! In strange surroundings for them. Living from moment to moment, as they'd done on the rolling, threatening water, seemed, in retrospect, to have been almost simple. It was simple compared to learning how to be with her again now. By appearing in Cassville, she had forced them both into a sea of problems. The real sea was, at least, the sea. It was there, all around them, merciless in its motion, relentless in its danger, but also holding them together, centered on each other, clinging to each other for life itself. Nearly naked in body and mind and soul, he had—for those days and nights—thought of nothing, of no one— but Natalie. He dwelled tonight on those terrifying, cherished hours . . . days, spiced by mutual independence of spirit, yet bonded by a love that seemed created only for them. He'd been sure of that, then, and so had she, through all those strange, uncluttered hours of knowing each other as a man and woman seldom had a chance with the pressures of ordinary life bearing in upon them. He could admit tonight, lying in his rumpled bed, that out there on the water, even he had refused all thought of—later. All thought of what might lie ahead if they were, indeed, rescued. Somehow there hadn't seemed to be time then for the future. Only toward the end, just before the *Henry Cameron* picked them up, had he faced even the almost certain loss of all his money. Money that might have made it possible for them to stay together.

Again, he punched the pillows. Would any amount of money have made that possible? With another kind of woman, maybe. But with Natalie? Glorious, beautiful, self-willed, childlike Natalie? Being together, for Burke, meant living on *his* frontier. The irresistible girl-woman, Natalie Browning, in the north Georgia wilderness? On a water-logged settee in the Atlantic it had almost made sense. In her were all the qualities for survival, even for buoyancy in the face of death. But she didn't have to cook on that raft—or clean house or wash dishes or sew or make a garden. He was far more afraid of life with her in the real world. He was afraid now . . . far more afraid, perhaps, than Ben and Mary. True, he had surprised himself by rather liking her father, but the thought of trying to keep their love alive in the company of her parents and their socialite friends frightened him far more than had the water, where there had been only one danger to face. Death, he now knew, would be preferable to watching Natalie's love die. . . .

Out there, *in his arms*, even Mark Browning could do nothing to help her, to shield her, to rein the free, brave spirit about which only Burke knew.

He sighed heavily. Natalie in his arms . . . it was she who was robbing him of sleep tonight. Not Ben or Mary—*Natalie*.

With the realization, the year-old, cherished memory of her came clear again, clearer and sharper now that he'd seen her once more—dressed in the latest fashion, almost a stranger, her face no longer blistered or swollen, and surrounded by three people from the privileged world Burke despised. The memory of Natalie in his arms on the sea had tortured him wherever he had lain alone this year past—in a bed or on a blanket spread on the ground. She had not come to him then in fashionable gowns, but as she had been on the raft . . . his burned and swollen mouth kissing her, kissing her until, arms encircling him, she had begun to kiss him, to cry, to cling to him, to—ask for him. Had Natalie really asked for him? Had they both really known *longing* out there? Had she recognized her asking as longing? Had physical longing been possible, so weak from hunger and thirst, so burned by the sun? As he remembered, there had been no more than those few moments—or were they hours?—of clinging and kissing. Had she actually wanted him as he wanted her? As he wanted her now?

How did she want him now? Why had she forced both him and her father into such a predicament? He had cared enough to stay away from her—to disappear from sight—until the time was right to claim her. Could Natalie be as innocent as he—suspected? Did she have no apprehension at all about being with him now? Was he the only one who feared it?

He sat up in bed, admitting to himself again what he'd known for a year, that the only way he could resist taking her for himself forever, was by staying away from her! Were she in this room now, he would not—could not—resist her. A man can endure just so much beauty, so much spirit—so much human magnetism. Natalie, even if she turned out to be as innocent as he suspected, possessed all those charms, possessed them in fuller measure than any woman he'd ever seen—anywhere.

If he had tried to ascribe loftier motives to leaving her as he had in North Carolina, he was facing now that he had done it because he had been afraid to be with her—sound of body and healthy again.

"Dear God, help me," he moaned. "Help me when we're together tomorrow afternoon. . . ."

From beyond the doorway in the old part of the cabin, he heard the floor creak and Mary's voice whispered, "You are—troubled, Mister Burke? I—help you—*any way you need!*"

He knew full well that Mary was too much a child to mean that, but just in case, he sat up and began to rub his foot. "No, Mary, I'm fine," he lied. "I—don't need a thing. Just had a—cramp in my foot. Go back to sleep."

When he was sure she'd returned to her own bed, he turned his face to the wall and lay clutching a pillow until the agonizing need of his body and at least some of the turmoil in his mind quieted.

I am going to talk to Natalie alone—without her parents and their family friend, Mrs. Stiles. But, he vowed, we are *only* going to talk.

He would demand—not merely suggest or insist—*demand* that they see each other in the safety of the hotel dining room. He would demand it because mere insistence got a man nowhere with Natalie.

When the first light of dawn fell across the new split-log floor of his room, Burke was still vowing to himself that Natalie was not going to make a fool of him—or of herself, if he could help it. "I've got to believe," he formed the words again as he'd done often in the night, "that here, through the long, dark hours, alone, I have conquered myself. If she and I can ever find a semblance of—peace or contentment together—I have to walk into that hotel believing in my own victory before she has a chance to say a word."

Slapping lather on his face with his shaving brush, he informed himself of one more thing: If I can't make her happy, I'd far rather lose her now, before I've known her as my wife, than—later.

FORTY-FIVE

NATALIE had agreed so readily, so sweetly to their abrupt departure for Lookout Mountain, that Caroline, though nagged by suspicion, worked at being cheerful with Mark, as Jupiter drove them out of Cassville early the next morning.

"You actually seem relieved that we're leaving," she said, as they sat side by side, jolting and swaying along the bumpy road that led north into Murray County.

He laughed. "I'm always relieved, dearest, when any problem with our daughter gets resolved. And what a happy solution Eliza Anne had—a surprise holiday with you!"

"She does seem sure that Burke has a far better chance of convincing Natalie to simmer down with us out of the way," she said. "I'm sure we pull the child in two directions."

"Don't fret, my darling." He took her hand and his gray eyes were so tender, so earnest, Caroline moved closer on the carriage seat. "We can't be expected just to forget about her," Mark went on, "but we can trust Eliza Anne. I find I rather trust Latimer, too."

"Oh, Mark, I hope we're right to be going."

"We are right. Now listen. I promise to put my countinghouse out of my mind. Couldn't you concentrate on your husband now, please? A second honeymoon just might cause you to fall in love with him."

He was teasing, but she pressed her head hard against his shoulder and whispered, "Don't tease about that! I've been in love with you forever. And somehow all this romantic turmoil with Natalie just makes me realize that without you—I'd have only half a life. I think I get cross and overly strict with her because at times, I actually resent her taking up so much of our time and energies—by being Natalie. Mrs. Meldrim wrote that Jonathan is looking after her frail fifteen-year-old Ralph like a father. Why wasn't Natalie born more like Jonathan? Don't you miss him terribly? Just terribly?"

"You know I do. But it may be good for us both to have to do without him for a while. I've said this often, I know, but we both lean on Jonathan too much."

"We wouldn't if Natalie were more like him."

For a time, they rode along deep in their own thoughts, Caroline only half hearing Jupiter hum his soft, rumbling tunes from the high front seat. He was deep in his own thoughts, too, she supposed. At least, being Jupiter, he did his usual wily job of pretending that the carriage wheels scattering stones, the harness jangle, the regular squeak of the leather straps that held their luggage in place kept him from overhearing one word they said.

Go on, sing, Jupiter, she urged silently. You are calming me down a little. She smiled up at Mark. Returning her smile, he tightened his fingers on hers.

"Could I ask one more question about Natalie?"

"Of course."

"Did she seem a little too glad we were leaving?"

"To me, she just seemed pleased for us. Didn't you notice her sweet smile when we told her?"

"But what did the smile say? Or demand? Or—appear to hide?"

"To me, it just said, 'All right, Papa, Mama—have a beautiful time. I'll be fine.'"

"And that doesn't worry you one bit?"

"Caroline, we have to believe that Natalie can—grow up."

After a while, she asked, "Mark, do you want her to grow up?"

He seemed to take his time in answering. Finally, he said, "Yes. Yes, I do. You see, I'm convinced that she loves this man. I believe he loves her. And if Natalie doesn't mature, I predict Burke Latimer won't put up with it."

Caroline sat up. "What do you mean by that?"

"I don't know exactly, but—hard as it would be, you and I just might have to stand aside and watch. You see, I'm dead sure now that our little girl has met her match."

• • •

Once her parents were gone, Eliza Anne could not believe Natalie's behavior, in view of her moody suffering the past few days. She was so amenable, so willing to fall in with whatever plans Miss Lib thought best, that Eliza Anne found herself quickly rearranging her own thought. She had prepared herself to listen, to comfort, to dry tears, to try to understand—even to give the girl time alone if that's what she seemed to need. She had made no preparation, though, for the lighthearted suggestion that the two of them dress and go downstairs for an early midday dinner.

Dressing in Mark and Caroline's empty room, Eliza Anne decided that so far, all was well. Even the first uneasy moment, when Natalie insisted that they make use of both rooms, had passed. "I've heard you say, Miss Lib, that except for W.H., you'd always rather sleep alone. Please let me honor that. Papa's paying for both rooms. Why shouldn't we use them?"

The question had made Eliza Anne curious, of course: What does Natalie have planned for herself when I might be napping, or even sleeping at night in another room? And then she'd felt ashamed, because there'd been no hint—not one—that Natalie had anything up her sleeve.

"I know what people always think of me," Natalie confided at one o'clock dinner. "They always expect me to do the selfish thing. Anyone else on earth but you, Miss Lib, might even suspect me of wanting to be rid of my darling parents." And then she leaned toward Eliza Anne, the pale eyes sincere. "My parents do act as though I'm still a little girl, but I'm adult enough to know they are a lot more than just the handsome Brownings who live on Reynolds Square. They're really in love! I realize that now. I don't always let them know it, but they're the ones who made me believe that two people can go on loving for always and always. Burke owes them far more than he thinks. I'm able to love him as unselfishly as I now do, Miss Lib—because of what *they* taught me about loving."

Eliza Anne's mind was reeling too fast to think of a plausible response to such sane, mature insight, and so she just listened, moved the snap beans about on her plate and beamed.

"You know Burke's coming to see me later today." Natalie went on. "I expect we'll talk right here in this stuffy dining room, but he's going to encounter—a new woman in me. Oh, he'll have to do some explaining about why he's stayed away for all this time, but I guarantee you he's going to find me totally irresistible . . . mature, poised." She laughed. "Even 'reasonable.' "

When Eliza Anne allowed that she was sure Burke had long ago found her irresistible, Natalie waved aside the remark with "What you and Mama and Papa might not realize, Miss Lib, is that Burke and I have never been together socially. But I know him like a book. I learned a lifetime about him in those five days on our raft. For one thing, he's so pigheaded he really thinks his life and mine don't go together." She sighed. "During the hours I've spent in my room in this hotel—suffering alone—I did a lot of thinking. My duty to Burke, because I love him, is to prove to him now—fully dressed in good clothes, wearing perfume and sitting with him in public—that because we do love each other, he and I can be together *anywhere.*"

Still Eliza Anne could think of nothing to say except "Natalie, you amaze me!"

"I know I do. Three long days of thinking that maybe Burke didn't love me—changed me, Miss Lib. For almost all of that horrible time alone, I was afraid he didn't want me anymore. I couldn't see how he could just go on hauling boards—ignoring me right here in the same town!"

"What do you think makes you feel so confident about him now?"

Natalie glanced heavenward. "A flash of pure wisdom—yesterday afternoon while you were taking a nap. There it was—truth. *Everything* that has ever come to me has always come in a sudden flash—like gunpowder. Right then, that minute, I stopped suffering."

Carefully, Eliza Anne asked, "And do you know why?"

"Yes. That instant, I knew that Burke was suffering too! And all my suffering stopped."

Keeping in mind Natalie's extremes, Eliza Anne asked, "Do you know why it stopped?"

"No. But does that matter? When dear Papa and Mama came to have their little talk with me and told me about your wonderful plan for their second honeymoon, I knew that with both of those clucking old darlings safely away at Lookout Mountain, it would be only a matter of time."

"What will be only a matter of time?"

"I left my watch upstairs. What time is it now?"

"Almost two. I had no idea we'd been in this dining room so long.

Uh, Natalie—what are your plans for this afternoon—until time for
Burke to get here at four?''

Relishing the last bite of soggy peach cobbler, Natalie leaned back
in her chair and glanced casually out the small window by their
table. "I think it could rain. Look at that sky—the sun's all gone.
Why don't we just enjoy a restful afternoon? I have a new Jane
Austen book. Shall we read in your room or mine?"

"Doesn't matter to me. Which do you prefer?"

Natalie only shrugged, giving Eliza Anne a smile that dissolved
the last fragment of suspicion that anything resembling a secret plan
was afoot. Arm in arm, they wended their ladylike way up the flight
of stairs to Natalie's room, where they decided to spend their "quiet
afternoon."

"Not slipping on a negligee?" Eliza Anne asked, when she saw
Natalie changing instead into a cool, pale green walking skirt and
blouse.

"I'm sick of my negligee! If you'd spent the last three days flop-
ping around in the same old lavender silk thing, you'd be sick of it,
too. I'm comfortable in this new blouse and skirt. Do you like the
color, Miss Lib?"

Eliza Anne looked up from her book. "No one has to tell you how
stunning that shade of green is with your hair. Admit it."

"Oh, I do admit it," she laughed. "And I mean to treat your eyes
to it all afternoon."

"Thank you."

"You're welcome."

For nearly half an hour, they read in silence—Eliza Anne
stretched on the bed, Natalie in the rocker by the window.

"I hope you like your Jane Austen novel better than I like this
one," Eliza Anne said, yawning. "Everyone in it is so good and
Christian, I simply don't believe them."

"Are you sleepy?" Natalie asked.

"I hate to admit it. No rain yet, but the air is close and oppressive.
And it's getting almost too dark in here to read."

"Miss Lib, do you have any idea how much I—love you? How—
grateful I am that you seem to—like being my friend?"

Eliza Anne laid down her book. She could not be exactly sure in
the half-light, but Natalie's eyes appeared to have filled abruptly
with tears. She jumped from the bed to hug her. "Darling girl," she

449

whispered, "thank you for—loving me, for liking to be *my* friend. I need you to be. Do you ever think how much your friendship means to me?"

"I hope it will mean—a lot more someday." Natalie was smiling again now and a quick brush with the back of her hand banished one tear that had slipped down her cheek. "You were as drowsy as a kitten a minute ago—now look at you! But isn't it a sleepy day?"

Stretched again on the bed, Eliza Anne stifled another yawn. "Oh, excuse me. It's the day. Not the company. I thought surely the rain would have come by now. Look out there—suddenly not a leaf stirring, but it's so dark."

"I absolutely adore this day," Natalie said, hugging herself. "Sunshine is fine, but a cloudy, shut-away day like this is—cozy. Makes me want to take a nap too, and I even think you believe me. Mama never does."

"I don't wonder," Eliza Anne said softly, eyes closed. "You hated naps even when you were a baby."

"Funny you should remember me as a—baby."

"Why?"

"I don't know. You don't seem that old to me."

"I'm being grateful for the compliment, even if I sound so—fuzzy with—sleep." Eliza Anne felt herself dropping off, but she peeped at Natalie—just to be sure she really was as quiet inside as she seemed. Her bright head was leaning against the high back of the hotel rocker, eyes shut.

Eliza Anne drifted into sleep thinking how amazing that the girl was so calm and contained with Burke Latimer due to visit her in something less than two hours. . . .

FORTY-SIX

AFTER THE OBSEQUIOUS CLERK at the hotel helped her mount the borrowed horse, Natalie walked the animal sedately through Cassville, then—out of sight of the last house, gave the mare her head.

Hatless, loosened flame hair whipping in the wind, she galloped now, away from town. The mare seemed as exhilarated as she to be free and flying. Dark, leaden clouds hung close to the earth, but astride the horse, feet securely in both stirrups of the old army saddle, she laughed and let go a thoroughly unladylike whoop.

When she had slipped the note onto Miss Lib's pillow just before tiptoeing from the room, Natalie felt satisfied that her timing was going to be almost perfect. She had planned it all carefully. Burke would go home about three to clean up and dress for their meeting at four. On that first day in town, Mary McDonald had even told her the exact location of his cabin. No more than half a mile remained, if she kept to the road. That meant there was plenty of time to indulge herself in a short, hard run through the woods and still reach the cabin before or just after he got there. This minute, she was more than ready for such a gallop—the kind she and Kottie used to take in the Knightsford woods, when both had reveled in the thrill of jumping their horses over fallen logs and tangled vines—free of a road or even a path.

Such a ride through Burke's woods alone would be even more exciting.

Natalie felt only momentary annoyance that undoubtedly Mary

and Ben would be somewhere around his cabin when she found him. Oh well, she thought, Burke would think of something. He'd be as desperate by now to hold and kiss her as she was to feel his arms again, his mouth. Of course, there would be the pain, because loving Burke hurt in the deepest place in her heart and the freest, wildest place in her brain.

"Burke is in the most secret part of my brain forever!" she shouted against the rising wind that swept over her now from the hills and woods beyond the cleared fields. "I'm myself again," she called. "I'm not sitting in that old rocker by the window anymore! I'm not afraid. He loves me, wind! Trees—Burke loves me!"

Joy exploded from the wildness loosed in her. A wildness against which everyone had always railed, which everyone but Kottie had tried to tame . . . the wildness that drove her now toward Burke as surely as she drove the broad-backed mare.

A thick woods lay just ahead to her left. She swung the horse away from the road, across a field and plunged into it, shouting, "Kottie, here we go!"

Galloping over a soft carpet of fallen needles through a long stand of tall pines, she remembered word for word what she'd written in Miss Lib's note—Natalie's own new declaration of independence:

I have gone to Burke. I think you knew I would because you are my friend and because you understand that no two people in love could possibly be together in that ugly dining room. I demand that you do not send for me. Prove your friendship by trusting me. The minute I return, even if I have to wake you, I will tell you everything.

The note was just right. If she could trust anyone on earth, it was Miss Lib. Should she not understand and try to spoil things by hunting for her, well—so be it. By then, she would be with Burke. . . .

Basket in hand, Mary skipped along under the sullen sky toward the deep woods behind Mister Burke's fields—fields standing now with green corn almost to Mary's waist. Even after she'd crossed his cornfield, she could hear the wind rattle through its stiff, perfect stalks and green spear leaves. Good, she thought. Robust, noble

corn—like Mister Burke. Mary was practicing hard today, the day
after he'd told her and Ben of his love for the beautiful Miss Natalie.
Mary was practicing with all her might to think only good, helpful,
happy thoughts. It was happy to admire his corn from which she
would roast plump hot kernels—tender and milky—for his mouth so
that when his white teeth burst them, juice would overflow and spill
down his perfect chin. To be happy is still good, she reminded
herself, and two or maybe three more fields of his corn will grow
before he tells us good-bye.

She was disobeying Ben and Mister Burke, though, by taking the
lonely path made by the feet of her people through the long years
when all the deep woods above the small valley had been Cherokee.
Mister Burke's corn and trees and bushes and wildflowers and berry
vines sent their roots down today into Cherokee land. "As long as
you skip over it, Little One," Mister Burke had said, "it is still
Cherokee land." But then he had at the same time warned her to
stay away from the deep woods path because of the undergrowth
where rattlesnakes hide. "Not just rattlesnakes," he had said.
"There's an old catamount in that swampy section not a hundred
yards from where the path begins. I heard about him the second day
after we hit Cassville. As a rule, catamounts leave people alone if
people have enough sense to leave them alone, but this old boy's
been known to attack a horse and rider." Mister Burke lectured to
her like a teacher but he also laughed when he said, "Just think how
he'd lick his chops over a savory little morsel like Mary Willow!"

Not often, but about as often as he called her Little One, when
they were alone or only with Ben, Mister Burke would say Mary
Willow. That pleased her, and she had not forgotten his warning
about danger in the woods, but today, even though rattlesnakes
come out on a cloudy afternoon and even though the old catamount
might mistake the low-hanging sky for coming darkness, she was
skipping along the forbidden path because of her love for Mister
Burke. Cheerful red and yellow rock-bells would be blooming just
this side of the swampy place where the catamount's run crossed
over and up the side of a cliff. Her heart was set on picking a bunch
of pretty rock-bells. Mister Burke's eyes would shine to be handed
the flowers when he had bathed and shaved and dressed to ride back
to town to be with *her*. Because Mary loved him more than her own

breath, in his hand, instead of nothing, he could take Miss Natalie Browning the dear flowers.

At the Moravian school she had been taught that God protects His children. She would have faith that the catamount would still be sleeping. Sure. Darkness would not begin to fall for a long time. She would be safe, and in minutes, she would skip back along this same path to the cabin. And in her basket, the flowers for helping his heart with Miss Natalie. Skipping was easier when practicing good, happy thoughts.

She had just glimpsed the mass of red and yellow rock-bells up ahead, when a piercing scream filled her with such terror, her feet tangled in a berry hoop and she fell—face-down in a watery mud-hole.

Again, the chilling scream! Mary sucked in a mouthful of choking mud. . . . The scream came again and this time she froze. Because she dared not make a coughing noise, the mud and fright almost shut off her breath as she listened.

Then, from some distance up ahead, she heard a large animal crash toward her—the undergrowth breaking and cracking as it came closer and closer so that instinct forced her to struggle to her feet. Another scream! This one thinner—surely a woman crying for help! Choking, running, Mary headed in the direction of the last scream.

The large beast kept coming, and with the sound of it, short, thin, desperate cries. She stopped to listen and from somewhere nearby, Mary could hear low, thick breathing that was almost a growl. She looked up. Not twenty feet above her, peering over a cliff, crouched a tawny, full-grown panther—the size of a wolf, shoulders heaving with each grating breath. It was Mister Burke's *catamount*. Thick, ropy saliva hung from the snarling mouth—lips drawn back so that long, sharp fangs gleamed even in the dim woods light. Again she heard the thinner cry nearby and saw a green-clad body strike the ground and roll under a clump of sumac. What was plainly a run-away horse thundered straight at Mary, who was so paralyzed by the sudden rush of danger, she was unable to move. As it galloped past, the riderless horse veered in time to miss running her down, but one swinging stirrup struck her in the face.

The pain was sharp, then only hot—and she forced herself to

stumble ahead in the direction of the woman's voice and follow it to the thicket of sumac bushes.

Mary was now sure that someone had been thrown from the terrified horse. Wiping what she thought was mud from her blinded right eye, she saw blood—fresh blood on her hand, but she dived to the ground near the pale green heap in the bushes. A slender woman lay there, face-down, crying and pounding the earth with both fists. Crawling, Mary reached her, and in God's strength, turned her over on her back.

"It is you! You—are Mister Burke's—shining woman!"

Pale, almost colorless eyes looked up at Mary, who began to tremble. Nothing scared her so much as not knowing, and peering as hard as she could into those light, compelling eyes told her nothing. Miss Natalie just lay there on her back in the old pine cones and dead sticks and last year's fallen leaves—the not-green, not-blue, not-gray eyes—glaring.

"You—are angry?" Mary ventured.

There was no answer, but the eyes looked down at one ankle and foot, twisted under her. Pity flooded Mary's heart. Mister Burke would hurt because she was hurt.

Reaching to touch the injured ankle, Mary said, "I bind it." She ripped at her own blue-flowered skirt. Still trembling so that her hands felt helpless and unsure, she began to wind a folded strip of calico around and around Miss Natalie's foot and leg. When she had wrapped a second strip carefully over the first, she tied the bandage with two torn ends of the material.

Daring to look into Miss Natalie's eyes again, she found them still a riddle. A riddle with no answer.

"That—ghastly heavy scream," Natalie gasped. "What was it?"

"Panther—catamount." Mary's heart pounded, remembering that only a few yards away, the big cat must still be watching. She looked back in the direction of the cliff. The catamount was there—silhouetted against the forbidding sky—bushy tail flailing.

"No. No, Mary, it sounded like a woman screaming."

Mary shook her head. "Catamount. Mister Burke warn me." Suddenly she was weeping, unable to help herself.

"Stop that—do you hear me, Mary? Stop crying!"

Mary could not. She rocked herself, the sobs hurting her torn face and head. The more she wept, the more the blood dripped down onto her ripped skirt, staining its blue flowers.

"What happened to your face, Mary?"

"Running horse. Too scared to—see me."

"Oh dear, oh dear! Well, can't you do something at least to stanch that blood? Can't you use another piece of your skirt?"

So angry did the shining woman sound when she spoke, Mary's sobs grew harder. Somehow she had done wrong to anger her and began to let out her fear and regret so that she wailed out of control.

Miss Natalie sat up and tried to quiet her. Mary could feel the hands, gentle at first, on her shoulders. Then the hands shook her hard . . . slapped her. Desperately, Mary tried to choke back the sobs, but to choke hurt her face and her head began to swim, swim. . . .

"You're going to faint, Mary, if you don't do something to stop that blood! I don't suppose there's any water in this godforsaken place." Miss Natalie scrambled to her feet, thrown off balance with every step by the injured ankle, but she began to limp about, going this way and that in a circle around where Mary sat.

"Even the horses are stupid up here," Natalie grumbled, for no reason that Mary could imagine.

"Horse—scared," she said, struggling to hold back more tears.

"Mary—do you think Burke's home yet? Do we have to pass that —big cat to get to his cabin? I've got to get there. Please try to—help me, Mary! What are you doing out here anyway? I thought you knew so much about—frontier life. Why didn't you bring water? Do something to help me!"

Mary stared back at her. Unexpected anger flared inside her own whirling head now and grew until it seemed about to burst her skull. She reached for a young scrub pine, pulled herself to her feet and cried: "You no shout rudeness to me! Not one time more!"

Still angry, but unable to look away, Mary watched Natalie as though under a spell. Miss Natalie's annoyance melted like an icicle in the sun. The pale eyes, so lately a riddle, grew tender and sorry. She smiled. A smile more heart-lifting, more cheering than first light. A smile to give hope and—balm. Neither spoke. In spite of the hot pain in her torn face and eye, Mary did her best to smile back.

"I come here—to find flowers for Mister Burke—to bring to you," she whispered. When Miss Natalie held out her arms, Mary stumbled into them.

The panther screamed again, but from a long way off—and fading. They both laughed weakly.

"I go to—cabin," Mary whispered, still in Natalie's arms. "I get Mister Burke and Ben. They bring my pony, Little Star, to carry you. You cannot walk."

Abruptly Natalie released her—almost pushed her away. "I *can* walk! Come on—we have to hurry!"

A stiff wind, blowing rain pushed against them as they hobbled toward the path. Natalie slipped now and then on the wet, pine-straw-covered ground, stumbled over fallen branches, tripped often on her own long, wet skirt, but fiercely determined to keep going, she dragged the Indian girl along. Over and over she repeated every encouraging word she could think of. Mary's moans and soft cries, each time she felt herself about to faint, were stimulants to Natalie. She could never take care of that bleeding face and eye out here in the woods. Mary had to keep walking. They both had to keep walking—because one more minute lost could mean that Burke might be on his way to the States' Rights Hotel.

At the very moment Natalie glimpsed the steep roof and chimney of a cabin through a break in the rainy mist and trees, Mary sagged against her and crumpled to the ground.

"No," Natalie cried. "Mary—no! Get up—get up now! I can see the cabin. Please, get up—*please!*"

Thwarted, staring down at Mary's still body, Natalie vowed to give that simpering hotel clerk a piece of her mind for putting her on such a skittish horse. Trying to decide whether to stay with Mary or leave her and limp ahead to find Burke, she listened—and blown on the wind, muffled by thunder and rain—she heard his voice.

"Mary! *Ma-ry Willow* . . . Mary, where are you?"

Burke, calling not for her, but for Mary. A second voice called—desperate, penetrating: "Mary Willow—little sister! Answer us, Mary Willow—in God's name, call to us!"

There followed the keen, thin notes of three long whistles—high-pitched, shrill, like a bird calling for help. A signal of some kind, Natalie was sure. Did she dare leave Mary alone on the wet ground in the rain? Could she limp on far enough to reach Burke? On instinct, she hobbled ahead, slipping often, half falling, but driven toward his arms.

She could hear heavy footfalls now, hurrying toward her. "Burke," she screamed. *"Burke!"*

Pushing herself harder, she vowed not to cry. Rain and tears and mist so blinded her that she was startled when around a bend in the old path, Burke heaved into sight, Ben right behind him.

In an ecstasy of relief, she lunged toward him. The ankle gave way and, before she reached him, she fell in a soggy heap at his feet. "Burke, oh, Burke," she sobbed. "I found you—I found you!"

He knelt in the mud beside her, held her in his arms, pressing her body hard against him as though he'd waited through the last bearable moment to do what he was at last free to do. "Natalie," he breathed. "Natalie, what in God's name are *you* doing out here in this storm?"

Ben gasped her name too, but she ignored him, her hands reaching for Burke's wet face as he bent above her. "Burke, I—love you! Burke, kiss me, please kiss me—before I die!"

She felt him stiffen, pull away. "Where's Mary?" he demanded roughly. "Natalie—did you see Mary?"

He isn't even glad to see me, she thought. Her temper flared, even as she clung to him. "Yes, I—know where she is. She's right back—there—on the path. She—fainted, I think."

"You *think?*"

"I was—trying—to help her, to get her to your cabin. I was, Burke! Hold me again—Ben can find Mary. She's his sister. She—just fainted because she's lost so much blood and—"

Burke was on his feet now, glaring down at her. "Why is she bleeding? What happened?"

She stretched both arms toward him. "Help me up! Send Ben for Mary. She needs help. We both do!"

"Can you walk?"

"No!"

Burke whirled on Ben. "What's holding you, Ben? Don't just stand there! Go find Mary. . . ."

Natalie was struggling to get up on her own now. "What about me?"

"Ben—did you hear me? Mary's bleeding. Go find her! I'll get Miss Natalie back to the house."

Without a word, Ben swooped down on Natalie, lifted her in his strong arms and started out, half walking, half running, in the direction of the cabin.

"Put me down," she screamed and pummeled Ben's back and shoulders, kicking as hard as she could in spite of the now searing pain in her ankle. "Burke! Help me—I'm scared. *Burke!* . . ."

"All right, Ben," she heard Burke call. "Be careful with her. I'll get Mary."

Ben plowed steadily ahead, talking softly to Natalie in his low voice, scarcely out of breath from the exertion. "My sister will feel better—happier," he said, "to have Burke bring her home. *This one thing*—I can do for you. Please do not fight me—do not fight—me. I will only be good to you."

In a moment, she stopped struggling, but she was stiff with terror. A savage Indian was running with her through the dark, stormy woods—without Burke! Burke had deserted her . . . had made not one move to stop Ben. *Everything was all wrong.* Burke was looking after Mary—not her. He'd deserted her for Mary—without a thought of what Ben might be planning in his Indian mind!

A sheet of white lightning lit the sky. For an instant she could see bright green leaves above her head, as though it were noon on a sunny day. And in that instant, a clarifying thought—like the flash of light—changed her fear to hope. More than hope—she had the beginning of what could be a plan.

"Trust me," Ben said, after they'd moved into a cornfield. "I mean you—only good. I mean you only—good."

How had she been so slow to see that Ben was plainly in love with her? He was still a savage Indian, but young men always fell in love with her, and young men under her spell had always been easy to handle—all except Burke. Ben just might fit quite handily into her plan, which so far was not very clear except that she saw in it a chance to teach Burke a lesson.

By the time they were trudging through the cornfield, she lay limp in Ben's arms—limp and silent, convinced, not only that Indian Ben was smitten with her, but that he meant her no harm. She wouldn't give Burke the satisfaction of knowing, but the fact that he had trusted Ben to take her had calmed her a little. It would be good for Burke to have seen with his own eyes that Ben did choose to rescue *her* while his own sister still lay unconscious on the trail. She felt fairly safe now. After all, Ben was little more than a servant. She certainly knew how to deal with servants.

"You feel sick?" Ben asked.

"Because I'm—quiet? No. I've just—suddenly begun to trust you."

"You're not afraid?"

She laughed a little. "Afraid of you? I admit I was. But not now. You're being very kind to me, Ben. And you'll see—you'll see very soon, how—kind I'm going to be to—all of you." They were through the rain-drenched cornfield now and in full view of the back of Burke's cabin. "Will you promise to believe, Ben, that everything I do from now on, will be because I—mean to prove how helpful I can be?"

She felt no tightening of his arms, but she could read his meaning as though it were printed on the page of a book: "I promise you—*anything!*"

FORTY-SEVEN

THE RAIN had stopped by the time Ben kicked back the half-open door and carried her into the scantily furnished, plain cabin that was Burke's home. For a moment, Natalie felt afraid again as Ben stood in the middle of the main room still holding her in his arms. I must stay calm, she thought. Calm and pleasant.

"Welcome to our home," he said softly. "I put you on—my bed."

"No!" she protested, but quickly changed her tone. "I mean—just put me in that rocker, please. I—I'm not hurt as severely as Mary. We must definitely put her right to bed, though, when Burke gets here with her."

"My—sister is—hurt bad?"

"I'm not sure, but—put me down, Ben! I'll explain how it all happened—when Burke gets here." He didn't move a muscle. "I demand that you put me down. Do you hear me?"

"Yes, ma'am."

His voice sounded both ashamed and sad, as he lowered her carefully—as though she might break—into the rocker. "Now, Ben, if you'll fetch me a footstool so I can prop my injured ankle on it, I'll be ever so grateful. Oh, and also a bowl of warm, soapy water and a cloth. A towel, too, of course. I want to wash my face before they get here. I must be a mess!"

"No," he murmured, still standing beside her chair, his black eyes seeming to burn into her. "You look—too beautiful to be on this earth."

"That's sweet of you, but I am very much on this earth and I'd like the footstool first, please. Then, the soapy water."

"I can build a footstool for you—even tonight, but there is not one here."

She hoped her "Oh, I see" did not sound too annoyed. "Well, you do have soap and water and a towel, haven't you?"

Just then, Burke's heavy footsteps crossed the porch and he stood in the doorway holding Mary's sagging body in his arms. There was blood on the front of his checked shirt, on the collar where her wounds had bled as he struggled with her dead weight along the forest path. Mary's face was as white as death.

"Here she is, Ben, in case you're interested," Burke said, his voice thick with anger and exhaustion.

"Is—she dead, Burke?" Ben asked.

"No," he said, grunting as he lay Mary gently on the bed that stood across the narrow room. "She's still breathing, but she's—lost a lot of blood. Bring me a bowl of cold water, Ben. No soap—just cold water and a soft cloth. First, I have to clean her face before we can see how deep this cut is."

"Burke?" Natalie whispered. "Burke!"

He merely glanced at her, with no expression on his face, then turned to Ben. "Hop to it, Ben! What's the matter with you?"

Holding her injured foot up off the floor with both hands to ease the throbbing, Natalie bided her time. She remembered, from their days on the raft, that Burke talked little or not at all while he was working. At least, then, he had been working for them. Poor, blood-soaked Mary had his full attention now. Carrying out her new plan was not going to be easy, but it was the only way: She meant to show every courtesy, and right now, the best method to handle Burke was to sit still and say nothing until he'd finished tending Mary's wounds.

I wish I were bleeding, too, she thought, watching as Burke, seated on the side of Mary's bed, sponged her face with the cool water Ben had brought.

"Rain falling all that time she lay on the ground kept the blood from caking too much," he mumbled to himself as he worked, his wonderful hands gentle and tender. "I dread cleaning her eye," he went on, to no one in particular.

"Is her eye bad?" Ben asked.

"Can't tell yet. What stanches bleeding, Ben? Does Mary have any roots or herbs around for that?"

"Our mother's remedy, button snakeroot," Ben said numbly. "Mary keeps some in a little skin bag. I'll find it."

On his way to the kitchen end of the cabin, Ben stopped briefly to give Natalie a look that said: I'd be helping you if I could. She smiled at him and whispered, "I'm—fine, Ben. You help Burke with Mary. I'm sure I'll be able to help too, very soon now."

Burke glanced at her again. "You'll help more by just—staying put," he said and went right back to pressing the gash on Mary's face with the cool compress. In a moment, he called, "Ben? Can't you find it? She's bleeding more. I need that stuff now!"

Ben smiled a little at Natalie as he took the dried leaves and stems in the hollow of his hand to Burke. "It's got to be chewed," Ben said. "Can't put it on her until somebody chews it good."

"Well, do it!"

"I can't," Ben answered, embarrassed. "It always made me sick— I throw up when I chew it."

Burke sighed in disgust. "We don't need you sick right now. Give it to me. I'll chew it."

"No, Ben!" Natalie cried. "No—bring it to me, please!"

"Natalie, don't be crazy," Burke scolded. "I can't let go here, Ben. Will you drop that stuff in my mouth?"

Pulling herself quickly out of the rocker, Natalie hopped to where Ben stood, grabbed his hand, dumped the dried leaves and roots into her own mouth and began to chew as hard as she could, while hobbling back to her chair.

Still holding the cold compress in place with both hands, Burke turned to stare at her. Chewing with all her might, she smiled at him, though the sickening, bitter taste made her eyes water. Finally, as her mouth filled with root-steeped saliva, she could smile only with her eyes, but she kept trying and never once allowed her gaze to leave his face.

He hadn't smiled back at her, but in a voice that was no longer cross, he said to Ben, "How long does she have to keep chewing? Can't you get her something to spit in? A cup—a saucer? Do something, Ben, besides gawk at Natalie. Help her a little!"

Darting to the cupboard beside the open fireplace, Ben hurried back with a small crockery bowl into which Natalie gladly spit the nauseous contents of her mouth.

"All right, Ben, don't just stand there—bring it here. Now, when I clean the last of the blood and lift this cloth, I want you to pack the snakeroot into the gash before it fills up with blood again."

Ben obeyed without a word. Burke folded a dry cloth and laid it over the poultice, his hands carefully placing it just right. That finished, he turned all the way around and gave Natalie his full, though grave, attention.

"Thank you," he said. "You're—still the same plucky girl, aren't you?"

She nodded, tried to give him a loving look, but her ankle hurt so, only pain distorted her face as she grabbed and lifted her leg with both hands.

"Do you feel—sick, Natalie?" Burke asked. "I know Mary's got some wild mint tea around."

Her stomach was churning, but she shook her head no. Burke had spoken his first kind word to her since he'd reached the cabin, and she fully intended to be the "same plucky girl" he'd loved and cared for on their raft. "I'm—fine. Just fine. What else do you need to— help Mary? I look awful, I limp—but I can do lots of things to help."

Burke set Ben to holding the herb compress on Mary's eye and face, then, without a word, he crossed the room to where Natalie sat, picked her up and carried her out the door and onto the porch into the rain-washed, early evening air. Natalie kept still. She knew him. The best way was to let him say something first. She would wait, if it killed her.

With his foot, he pushed a high-backed, obviously newly built rocker to the far end of the porch, sat down with her on his lap, her head held against his shoulder, but said nothing at all for a long, long time.

When he did speak, his voice was just above a whisper. "It seems I've done nothing for a whole year but worry about your—poor little feet. Now, you've hurt one of them again. . . ."

There was no time to answer. Burke was crushing her in his arms, kissing her—kissing her mouth, nose, eyes, cheeks, forehead, hair, mouth again . . . then, just when she felt she would surely die of ecstasy, he stopped himself, held her hard against his big, firm chest and began to sob.

She lay against him, clinging as though she might fall into a bottomless gulf of emotion . . . unable to form one clear thought. Her plan lay in shambles in her mind. A few minutes ago, she had been determined to prove to him how lucky he was to have her there —to prove that, city-bred and rich, she could help around a house as well as anyone. She had vowed to herself that Mary would have the most efficient nurse any sick person ever had—in her. She had formed no idea of how to go about this, but she *had* chewed that foul mixture and reasoned that keeping house and cooking and sewing and nursing must be easy, or one wouldn't find uneducated, simple people doing it. There had been no place in her plan, though, for Burke to kiss her as he had—or to *weep*. Was he weeping with exhaustion from carrying Mary's unconscious body for such a long way? From worry over Mary? From irritation because Ben had grabbed her, Natalie, instead of finding his sister? Because Ben hadn't stopped gawking at her with those love-sick eyes? Or was he —weeping from wanting her? She had cried at home into her pillow at night when the ache swept through her. For every day of every month through the whole year, loving Burke had hurt. She hurt now, in spite of being near him again. More than once, Natalie had almost dared to ask Miss Lib *why* there was so much—hurt in loving. Surely, Miss Lib knew.

Burke was no longer sobbing, but his arms had not relaxed. *He knows.* He knows why it hurts, she thought. He knows so much that I don't know, but he thinks I'm too young to understand. Instead of asking him, she whispered, "Don't worry, Burke. Only strong men —cry." The very thought made her feel a strange reverence. Did he feel it too?

He released her enough so that in the dim, cloudy, late afternoon light, she could look up at him—could see his golden hair, even curlier because it was damp. His face was tear-streaked.

"Burke? Does everyone in love—hurt so much?"

He made a harsh, laughing sound, but she could tell he wasn't laughing. "I can't keep up with everyone else," he said hoarsely. "I can't—even keep up with us."

"Do—you know why you—cried?"

He groaned. "Dear God, yes, Natalie!"

Young or not, she heard herself ask, "Why? Tell me why we hurt like this! I've *found* you. Why, Burke? Why doesn't—it stop?"

Lessening the pressure of his arms suddenly, he held her with a new tenderness, cradling, reassuring her. "Hurting is part of loving, I guess," he said, much as one would speak to a child. "You'll understand—someday."

"I want to know now!"

"I know you do."

"Then tell me. I feel so—empty inside. Burke, this is worse than—just being hungry or thirsty!"

She had never heard such a deep, tearing sigh. "You hate hearing it, but—you *are* young."

Her body tensed in response. That one word—that dreadful word "young" shattered the spell of her wonder. She had no intention of proving him right and so did the most grown-up thing she could think of. She jumped to her feet, nearly fell—but when he tried to catch her she jerked free and forced her wretched, numb ankle to stand. "I'm going inside to see to Mary," she announced. The ache in her was still so strong, her voice shook, but she limped across the porch and into the cabin, fully expecting him to follow. When he did not, she stopped in the middle of the room where Mary lay, Ben kneeling beside her, and tried to think what to do next.

"Miss Natalie? . . ."

The sight of Ben's agonized face made her feel weak, almost too weak to stand. "How is she, Ben?"

"Still not fully conscious, but stirring a little."

Meaning to hurry to see for herself, the numb foot—on the first step—sent her sprawling. Like a cat, Ben was beside her.

"I'm all right, Ben." She spoke sharply and from somewhere found the strength to pull herself up, using his shoulder as a prop. "Get away. I'm going to take care of Mary!"

Before Ben could stop her, she had hopped to the bed, quickly removed Mary's poultice and, at the sight of the fresh gush of bleeding she had caused, she fainted.

FORTY-EIGHT

BEN'S SHOUT for help brought Burke rushing into the cabin to find Natalie on the floor, her face as white as Mary's and, spreading across Mary's pillow, a bright stain of fresh blood.

"Did Natalie take off that poultice?" When Ben only nodded, Burke groaned, "What next? What new trouble will she cause us next?"

Kneeling beside Natalie, Ben whispered, "She means to do good."

"I know, I know." Burke's voice softened. "I—hate it, but she just goes on proving me right."

"Right?"

"How could I marry a helpless city girl and expect her to learn— ever—to live up here?"

Burke saw his friend's puzzled frown before Ben ran outside to the well, and by the time Burke had carried Natalie to his own bed in the new addition, Ben was back with cool water to bring her around.

"We should be ashamed, Ben," Burke said, bathing Natalie's face. "Mary's the one who needs attention and we both leave her alone in the next room because this beautiful, helpless girl did the wrong thing again." He smacked Natalie's cheek lightly. She began to stir. "All right, Ben. She's coming around. Get more of that dried snake-root. I'll chew it this time. We've got to replace Mary's poultice—we had the bleeding slowed until—" He broke off, listening intently. "Do you hear a wagon heading down our road? Way off yet, but—"

"Yes. Coming hard! I'll go."

"Get the snakeroot first, so I can begin chewing. Whoever it is can wait. Mary can't."

Ben was no sooner out of the room than Natalie opened her eyes. "Somebody's coming, Burke! *Don't tell them I'm here.* Just get—help for Mary. I—shouldn't have ripped off that poultice."

"That's right, you shouldn't. You don't know how to help—you mean well—but why do you try?" Before he said more to hurt her, Burke hurried with the water to where Mary lay and began to clean away the fresh blood from the ugly gash that appeared so close to her right eye, he dared not think of the consequences.

Hopping on one foot, Natalie followed him into the main cabin. "I know who it is coming," she said meekly.

"Who?"

"It's Miss Lib. She's missed me at the hotel."

"I don't suppose it occurred to you before you made that wild ride out here that she might follow, did it?"

Her meekness vanished. "How did I know that panther was going to give that bloodcurdling scream and scare my horse?"

When Ben brought the snakeroot, Burke tossed it into his mouth and began to chew.

"You did that on purpose," Natalie accused. "You fixed it so you wouldn't have to answer me. I understand you far better than you think I do, Burke Latimer. Just because you happen to be eight years older doesn't mean my woman's intuition isn't working. Men seem to think women don't see right through them. Women do! You're not really angry with me. You're as much in love with me as I am with you, and I'm going to show you once and for all that I can learn how to be—a frontier woman! I'm not going to let you ruin our lives."

As he worked ever so gently at cleaning blood out of Mary's hair and eyebrows, Burke chewed faster. The snakeroot must be a hundred years old! His hands were steady, but his thoughts were shooting off in all directions. As usual, Natalie was both right and wrong. Dead right that he loved her with all his heart and dead wrong that she could ever learn to make it up here without servants.

"Burke—whoever's coming in that wagon is already out in front of the cabin!"

He only nodded and went on chewing.

"Ben," Natalie ordered, "go out and tell them I'm not here—that you haven't even seen me! Just say your sister had an accident and that they have to take her into town to a doctor. Then, you go with her, Ben. Burke and I will be just fine here. If it's Miss Lib Stiles, she'll be sure to want to help poor Mary."

The snakeroot was finally soft enough, and Burke spit it out in his hand, spread it on a clean cloth and, as carefully as his surging emotions would allow, laid the soggy poultice over half of Mary's face.

"I'll hide in Burke's room at the back," Natalie was saying, looking almost ridiculous in her damp, mud-streaked green skirt, the bright hair tousled so that one clutch of curls stood straight up on the top of her head. "Go on, Ben—I'll hide in Burke's room."

"You'll do no such thing," Burke said, crossing the room to spit the rest of some of the raw, sickening root juice into the fireplace.

"That's a vulgar thing to do—spitting in a fireplace," she said.

"It's where we spit up here," he answered evenly, taking her arm and guiding her, limp and all, out onto the front porch to face with him whoever it was just climbing out of a wagon in the early dark.

"Burke, let me go!"

He tightened his grip on her arm. "Good evening," he called to the man and woman making their way along the path that led to the cabin.

"I see you, Natalie," Mrs. Stiles called. "I've never been so worried in my whole life!"

"Evening, Mr. Bentley," Burke said to the man helping Miss Lib up the two porch steps. "This is an unexpected pleasure. And Mrs. Stiles, welcome to my cabin. I'm—just sorry you had to come under such—annoying circumstances." He and Fred Bentley shook hands, but Mrs. Stiles just stood looking at Burke, then Natalie.

He waited for some sort of explosion—at least a cooked-up story from Natalie. She said nothing at all.

"You're very courteous, Mr. Latimer," Mrs. Stiles said finally. "But what I must have is an explanation of why you chose to sneak off like this with a young girl left in my care. I do think you owe me an explanation."

"Burke did nothing wrong, Miss Lib," Natalie said in her most poised manner. "There's been a dreadful accident. You're wasting time with idle talk."

Mrs. Stiles stared at her. "*Idle* talk, Natalie?!"

"We have to make a bed in the back of your wagon, Mr. Bentley,"

Natalie went on, "so you and Miss Lib and Ben can rush little Mary McDonald to a doctor."

"Is this true? Mr. Latimer—was there an accident?"

"Yes, ma'am. But, so far, we're managing. Mary McDonald is— hurt—but there is no doctor in Cassville now."

"What happened to Mary?" Mrs. Stiles directed her question to Burke. "Can someone please help me understand what's happened?"

"I'll explain it all tomorrow, Miss Lib," Natalie put in quickly. "I do count on your understanding. But what matters now is—Mary. I want you and Mr. Bentley—and Ben to take her back to Cassville. There must be a doctor somewhere!"

"We are—uh—between physicians right now," Fred Bentley said, "but it so happens I have a young physician as my houseguest this week."

"Then get Mary in your wagon," Natalie ordered, "and take her to him!"

Burke saw Mrs. Stiles give Natalie a long, penetrating look. Finally, she said, "I'm sure you're furious with me for asking Mr. Bentley to bring me out here, Natalie. But I don't think you're really surprised to see me. As for my understanding, we'll discuss that when we're both back in our rooms *tonight.*"

"Mary's the one who needs to go back with you—not me!"

"You're smart enough to know when I have the upper hand," Mrs. Stiles said quietly. "And, Natalie—I do have it right now." She turned to Burke. "May we step inside? Even at this inappropriate time, I have one important word of business to discuss with you. I'd also like to have a look at the injured girl." Before Burke could apologize for leaving them on the porch in the damp night air, she turned again to Natalie. "You can't object to my coming in, can you, Natalie? You know I'm quite good with the sick—and I do need a word with Burke. I'd expected a few minutes with him at the hotel. I need to ask him about building our new house up here."

Burke saw Natalie's eyes narrow and could tell she was trying to think of a way to take charge again. When she only stood there, though, he invited the two guests inside. "My manners suffer when —so much goes wrong," he said, gesturing toward the open cabin door. Seeing Natalie struggle to hide her limp from Mrs. Stiles, he took her arm and helped her.

All eyes went to Mary, tossing and moaning on her bed now, obviously completely conscious. Burke's heart ached for her having to open her good eye with strangers standing over her bed. "Little One," he whispered. "It's Burke. Ben's here too. You're in your own bed—at home."

Abruptly, Natalie hobbled forward, knelt beside Mary and took her hand. "And *I'm* here, Mary. Your friend, Natalie, is here too. These other two people are my friends. They're going to take you to town so a doctor can care for you. Please, don't worry about a thing!"

What *will* she do or say next? Burke thought.

He walked away so abruptly, Natalie apologized for him. "I hope you'll excuse Burke, Miss Lib and Mr. Bentley," she said, in full charge again now. "You see, he's worked so hard to—save Mary's life—he's exhausted. Far too tired, Miss Lib, to discuss any sort of house business now, I'm sure."

"I can see that, Natalie. But can anyone tell us—what did happen?"

From across the cabin, Burke said, "There was an accident, Mrs. Stiles. In the woods. Natalie's horse ran away. Mary was struck in the face by a stirrup."

Instead of the string of questions almost any other woman would have asked, Burke was relieved to see Mrs. Stiles simply lay her hand on Mary's forehead and say quietly, "I don't think she has much fever—if any." Then she asked Mary, "Can you—see out of the eye not covered with the poultice, my dear?"

"Yes, ma'am," Mary whispered weakly. "I—see you. Thank you."

"Good. Does the injured eye hurt so much?"

In response, Mary forced a little smile. Her pain, Burke knew, had to be bad. He'd seen the ugly ragged gash down her cheek and up into the corner of her eye. "The poultice," he explained to Mrs. Stiles, "is an old remedy for stanching blood."

"And it seems to be working," she said.

"Oh, Miss Lib, I—almost spoiled everything," Natalie blurted.

Burke stared at her. She meant it! Natalie was truly sorry she'd jerked off that poultice, and he longed, suddenly, to tell her that he knew how she felt. That his own feelings were driving him in all directions too. Instead, he heard himself say awkwardly, "Mrs. Stiles

—could I drop by your hotel tomorrow to discuss the business you spoke of?"

"By all means," she said. "I've written my husband that I want you to finish building our new home on the Etowah River, but for now, we'll say no more about it."

"Look here, folks," Fred Bentley said, "it seems to me we'd better get the girl to young Dr. Brown right away. If he can treat her soon, she may avoid a bad scar on her pretty face."

The look of alarm as Mary's hand flew quickly to her cheek tore at Burke's heart. Desperate to change the subject, he heard himself say, "Mary's brother, Ben, and I *will* be needing another house to build, Mrs. Stiles." He stopped short. "I—I don't know what made me bring that up again, ma'am. I'm sorry." Then he made it worse by repeating, "I don't know what made me—bring up business again at a time like this."

"I do," Natalie said, giving him an earnest, adoring look missed by no one in the room.

Burke knew too. The prospect of more work would bring him closer to the day when he would be free to ask her to marry him. I'm as crazy as she is, he thought. We're crazy to be together. Natalie's as innocent as a child but—clever as a courtesan. I've got to keep *my* head.

Nervously, Burke glanced around the room. Ben was standing off by himself in the shadows beside the fireplace. Lawyer Bentley leaned against one wall, arms folded, wise, knowing eyes taking in everything. And Natalie—Natalie was still standing on her swollen ankle, still looking at him so appealingly, so earnestly, his desire to hold her again made him feel weak.

Mrs. Stiles turned from Mary to Burke. "Business can wait," she said, "we must get Mary to town. Nothing is important right now but Mary."

"Miss Lib, I'm hurt too!" Natalie exclaimed.

What next? Burke thought, knowing full well that until that minute, she had tried to hide her swollen ankle from her friend.

"I can't possibly make it back to town tonight, Miss Lib." Natalie lifted her skirt to show the puffy ankle and foot.

"And why have you waited so long to tell me?"

"I'm trying—I'm really trying not to be—selfish. To cause more worry."

"I see," Mrs. Stiles said, and knelt to examine the injury. In a moment, she stood and looked Natalie in the eye. "You certainly are injured," she said in a controlled voice that said far more than if she'd shrieked at her.

On Natalie's face—so earnest a moment ago—Burke saw impudence. Pure impudence.

"We'll take care of your ankle later, back at the hotel," Mrs. Stiles said, still calm. "And we will also discuss what we both thought was our mutual trust. Heaven knows what else you're trying to hide from me."

"Miss Lib—it's just that I care so much about you, I—didn't want to worry you—over any of this."

Instead of impudence, there was now such instant sincerity, Burke could have kissed her right there before everyone.

Bentley cleared his throat again. "If I'm not intruding, Latimer— Mrs. Stiles," he said, moving closer to the bed where Mary lay, "I'd like to urge that we make up a pallet in my wagon and get this young lady right into town to Doc Brown."

"No!"

The strength in Mary's voice surprised them all. It also brought Ben hurrying from the shadows of the far end of the room to kneel beside his sister.

"Why?" he asked bluntly. "Why don't you want us to get the best care for you, Mary?"

"Mister Burke—give me best care!"

Burke waited, wanting Ben and Mary to settle it between them.

Ben stood up and glared down at his sister, his black eyes angrier than Burke had ever seen them.

"Mister Burke give me—best care." Mary said again.

"*Damn* Mister Burke!"

Mary's hands flew to her mangled face. "No, Ben! No!"

Burke grabbed Ben's shoulder. "What did you say?"

"Damn you, Burke Latimer! You are—God Himself in your own eyes!"

Burke felt as though his friend had struck him. He said nothing because he could think of nothing to say.

"I tell you, you are *not* God," Ben went on. "You are only a man— like me. Because you are boss, because you have money, because"— he gave Natalie a long, piercing look before his dark eyes shifted to his sister—"because you are—so *loved,* you are still not God!" In two long strides, Ben reached the open door, then whirled on Burke again. "My sister *worships* you and that is a sin. We are to worship only God. You cause my good little sister—to commit sin! To be hurt, to be punished by God with a—torn face. Miss Natalie worships you! You cause—Miss Natalie to—commit sin, too! So I leave it to you, *Mister God Latimer,* to take care of them both!"

No one spoke until the sound of Ben's running footsteps outside had faded. Burke could picture him pounding through the cornfield and into the woods. Apologetically, he glanced at Mrs. Stiles, then at Fred Bentley.

"It's—being a difficult evening, Burke," Mrs. Stiles said.

"Do you have that kind of temper to contend with in Ben often, Latimer?" Bentley asked.

"No. No, Mr. Bentley, he does not," Natalie offered quickly with the air of one who had spent years with Burke and Ben. "Ben McDonald is—just very worried about his sister. He's a quiet, kind person when he's himself. The truth is, Ben is the one who worships Burke." Hopping to the bed, Natalie laid her hand on Mary's head. "Don't cry, Mary. Crying will only make the pain worse. You know Ben isn't—bad-tempered, don't you?"

Each sob from Mary stabbed at Burke's heart, but he made no move toward her.

"Ben say—you—sin! Ben say—I sin," Mary gasped, her good, uncovered eye seeming to plead with Natalie. "We do wrong to—go into woods—where catamount hunts, but—we not *sin!*"

"Of course we didn't," Natalie said quickly, as though twenty years separated them instead of only two. "Did you ever see Ben act that way before in your whole life, Mary?"

Mary shook her head no.

"I honestly don't know what got into Ben," Burke said softly. "I wonder if I should follow him." And then he surprised himself by asking, "Natalie? Should I follow Ben and try to help?"

From the tone of her response, she might have been quite accustomed to Burke's asking her advice. "No," she said. "No. Leave him alone, Burke. He's just—jealous."

"Jealous?" Mrs. Stiles asked.

"Yes," Natalie answered firmly. "Ben is, I now see, insanely jealous of Burke."

"That's enough silly talk," Burke said, determined now to take charge himself. "You people don't know Ben the way I do. You don't know him either, Natalie. I'll talk to him in the morning. Bentley's right. What matters now is Mary." Almost effortlessly, he picked Mary up and headed for the door, calling back to Natalie to bring pillows and a blanket.

"I'm not your servant, Burke Latimer!"

"I don't need a servant," he called over his shoulder. "I just need those pillows and a blanket."

FORTY-NINE

AT FRED BENTLEY'S HOUSE in Cassville, dour, young Dr. Lester Brown cleaned and dressed Mary's face and eye and told them all—in Mary's presence—the discouraging news that she would surely be left with a severe scar. As they left Bentley's home, Burke carrying Mary, the tactless doctor said, "I'll be in town for another week. Bring her back in two days. Before, if she worsens. Change that bandage no earlier than tomorrow evening." He addressed everyone but Mary, speaking as though she weren't even present. "I've done all I can do, but she may have lost the sight in that eye."

Because Natalie insisted, Eliza Anne finally agreed that she and Natalie would ride back to the cabin in Bentley's wagon with Mary and Burke. Her heart ached for little Mary—so pretty, so young to be scarred and maybe partially blinded. Eliza Anne rode beside the girl in the wagon bed and held her hand. "Does your head ache, Mary?"

"It ache some, thank you."

"We should all be thanking you for being so brave! And that pickle-faced young doctor wasn't at all sure you've lost the sight in your eye. He's so gloomy, I honestly don't see how he expects to cure anyone. I think you're going to fool him. I predict, if we all pray and take the best care of you, that you'll be able to see again once the bandage is removed. Do you pray, Mary?"

"I pray. And I believe I see again. Do not worry. If not with two eyes, with one."

* * *

At the cabin once more, while the Browning girl and Mrs. Stiles put Mary to bed, Fred Bentley made a point of looking around for Ben. Carrying a lantern, he walked the entire cleared area around the log house, and as he started along the path to the barn, he was glad when Latimer joined him.

"You looked tired," Bentley said, lifting the lantern to light Burke's face.

"And disgusted. I've just had to mop the cabin floor. Miss Natalie spilled a basin of water."

Bentley chuckled. "Still trying to help, eh?"

"Still being headstrong. She can scarcely walk on that twisted ankle. But I suppose it's possible she never tried to carry a basin of water before—even on two good feet. No sign of Ben?"

"Not yet. He could be in the barn. That beautiful Browning girl makes a man want to—spank and then hug her, doesn't she?"

In the flickering lantern light, he saw Latimer nod his head.

"How long have you been in love with Natalie Browning?"

"Probably from the moment I first laid eyes on her."

"One reason I like you so well," Bentley said, "is your confounded, admirable honesty. I'm glad you're going with me to look in the barn for your helper."

"I wonder, though, if you might not get farther with Ben alone."

"I may get nowhere in either case. But we'll try."

They had reached the far end of Burke's cleared land where the barn stood in total darkness. At the door, Bentley held his lantern high. "McDonald? McDonald!" When there was no answer, he whispered, "You call him, Latimer."

"Ben? You out here?"

Burke's horse, Judge, and the new mare he'd bought stamped in their stalls, and almost at once, Little Star was eagerly on his hind legs.

"All right," Burke addressed the animals. "Quiet—quiet. No trips tonight." He called again, "Ben?"

When there was still no answer, Bentley pushed ahead, lantern high to spread the light. The two men walked past the stalls to the back of the barn. In a far corner, on a bed of straw, Ben lay curled and silent, his face to the log wall.

A finger at his lips to keep Burke from speaking, Bentley said in a businesslike tone, "It's Fred Bentley, Ben. Latimer and I want to talk to you." Ignoring Ben's failure to respond, he went on, "Your sister's all fixed up. The two women are putting her to bed inside. We're hopeful she's going to make a good recovery. Say, you'll be shirking your job tomorrow if you catch cold sleeping out here tonight. In just a few minutes, I'll be driving the two Savannah ladies back to town. I want you to tell me before I go that you'll get up off that pile of straw and head for the cabin. I went out on a limb with the Cummingses to get them to hire Latimer to build their house. You're a big part of pleasing them. Burke needs you in good shape tomorrow. Can we count on you?"

Without moving, Ben answered, "I plan to go to work tomorrow. Same as always."

"Then, on your feet," Bentley said. "I want to see you in that cabin before I go."

"You won't see me there, sir."

"Why not?"

"I'm sleeping here."

"And let your little sister spend the night alone in the cabin with Latimer? How will that look?"

Slowly, Ben turned toward them. In the yellow lantern light, his face was a mask, his black eyes dark sockets beneath swollen eyelids. "Who will see?"

"Probably no one," Bentley said, still all business. "It's the principle of the thing."

"I'll be close by—to watch over her," Ben said.

"You can save your worry over Mary's safety, Bentley," Burke said. "She's—like my little sister. Ben's—upset now, but he trusts me. Ben? Tell him you trust me."

"For one reason, I trust him." Ben's voice was hard. "His head is too filled with—Natalie Browning to—think of any other woman."

The Browning girl had been right, Bentley thought. Ben is jealous of Latimer. All Fred Bentley said was, "I'll bring a blanket out to you, then. Gets too chilly at night to sleep without a cover. And you can count on the fact that I'll stop by the Cummings house site tomorrow—just to be sure you're there, Ben, doing your usual fine work."

Inside the cabin, Natalie, hobbling over the split-log floors—the injured foot bare now—picked up a splinter. With one of Mary's precious needles, Eliza Anne dug it out. "You're going to stay in bed at the hotel all day tomorrow, young lady," she said, wiping a drop of blood from the sole of Natalie's foot.

"I'll do no such thing! Isn't it enough I've agreed even to leave here tonight, Miss Lib?" She hopped to Mary's bed. "You sleep now, Mary, do you hear me? Miss Lib and I will be back early in the morning to fix breakfast for Burke—for you and Ben, too, of course."

"No! I cook," Mary protested.

"Nonsense. Miss Lib and I will be here right after first light, and that settles it."

"And how will we get out here?" Eliza Anne wanted to know.

Natalie flipped a hand at her. "We'll ride, of course. I'll get two horses. That hotel clerk will move heaven and earth for me. My powers of persuasion are considerable. Even you and Burke would have to admit that."

After a futile attempt to discuss everything with Natalie once Bentley had seen them back to their hotel, Eliza Anne sent her to bed, then lay awake in her own room, feeling helpless. What on earth, she thought, made me think I could cope with her? The girl's been beyond her own parents' control for nearly eighteen years. When she's eighteen in a few months—legal age—what on earth might she do then?

Eliza Anne sighed and tried to find a comfortable place in the lumpy bed. What makes me think reaching legal age would have any effect on her one way or the other? *I* obviously have none. She pulled the light cover over her face, hoping to induce sleep. Undoubtedly Natalie would be knocking at her door before dawn.

As always, though, when she tried to drop off, her thoughts rushed to W.H. How she missed him! But, with the missing—now that she'd learned from Bentley of the poor workmen he'd hired— was lingering irritation. Still, her letter to him recommending Burke had been all loving. Burke did seem most interested, and Mrs. Cummings had praised him to the skies. If her beloved husband agreed to retain him, they might cut most of their losses of time and money from the present builder's botched-up work. It was not a woman's place to do it, or she'd ride to Etowah Cliffs herself and fire that jackleg carpenter.

Eliza Anne threw off the cover. Burke would not only build the kind of house they both wanted, keeping contact with him could well work to the advantage of everyone—Natalie, Mark, Caroline—the young man himself. She sighed.

After tonight in his cabin, no one could ever convince her that Burke Latimer did not love Natalie, was not as driven by that love as Natalie certainly seemed to be. For all reasons, it seemed right that Burke should build their new house.

Feeling chilly without a cover, she pulled it back up. Poor Mary McDonald. Poor distraught Ben—lost, because the inevitable banditry of history had robbed him of everything but his own responsible manhood. In the face of what she'd seen and heard tonight, even that seemed precarious. The capable young Cherokee would lose everything if he lost Burke. Natalie had innocently thrust herself between the two friends, just by being Natalie. Insane, of course, for Ben to allow himself a second look at Mark Browning's daughter.

She turned in the bed again. Poor Burke, to be faced with outrageous jealousy from the helper he so needed to succeed as a builder. Even Mrs. Cummings permitted herself to praise Ben's skills.

Was Mark right? Had Natalie met her match in Burke? Deep down, Eliza Anne felt a surprising confidence that Burke was strong enough to accomplish what no one else, including her parents, had ever managed with Natalie. Eliza Anne liked Burke Latimer, truly wanted him to build their home. Heaven knew living on the frontier was going to be hard enough for her, even in a good, well-built house.

FIFTY

SMOKE ALREADY CURLED from the wide stick-and-mud chimney when, at sunrise the next morning, Natalie and Eliza Anne rode up the lane that led to Burke's cabin.

"Foot, Miss Lib," Natalie shouted over her shoulder, "I thought we'd be early enough for me to slip in and kiss Burke awake!"

"Well, we're not," Eliza Anne called back.

Whipping her horse to a gallop, Natalie yelled, "Hurry! Burke might even be cooking breakfast—and I wanted to prove I can do anything a frontier woman can do!"

Still groggy from an almost sleepless night, Eliza Anne allowed her to forge ahead. Allowed? How could she have been stopped? Kiss Burke awake indeed, she thought, walking her own horse toward the front porch, where Natalie had already dismounted—her injured ankle hampering her only a little—and disappeared into the cabin.

At the porch herself now, Eliza Anne frowned. Not one of us really *knows,* she thought, how that man fills Natalie's horizons. In her mind, they're already married. The shocking idea of slipping into his bedroom to kiss him awake seemed perfectly natural to Natalie. I've known she loves him, but until this minute, I don't think I've realized how like one person they must have become on that raft! To fight closeness like that now that they're together again must be dreadful—almost unnatural.

Dismounting, Eliza Anne wished for her brother. William is so sensible about things, she thought. Why doesn't he get back to

Cassville? And why didn't I take Mama's advice and learn to cook? I can't think what a mess Natalie might make if she tries to fix breakfast—and she will try.

Eliza Anne walked to the end of the porch and glanced toward the barn, wondering if Ben was still out there, then, gathering her courage, went inside.

In the main, older part of the cabin, Natalie was nowhere to be seen. But there was Mary, a flowered cotton dress pulled over her nightgown, struggling, in her weakness, to lift a heavy coffee pot onto an iron grill over a half-burning fire.

"Mary, my dear," Eliza Anne called, hurrying to her. "You shouldn't be out of bed!"

The girl turned to greet her, the big coffee pot tipping dangerously in her hands. "I—cook for—Mister Burke," she said in a quavering voice and then slumped to the floor—spilling the contents of the pot.

"Mary," she cried. "Oh, Mary—!"

Burke, still in his nightshirt and barefoot, rushed from his room at the rear of the house, Natalie right behind him.

"I don't think she fainted," Eliza Anne said as Burke knelt beside Mary. "She's just so weak." To Natalie, she added sharply, "So, you passed right by poor Mary to kiss him awake, did you? I suppose you feel proud of yourself."

"Hush, Miss Lib! This is no time for a sermon. Do you know how to make coffee?"

"Yes, I do know how to do that."

Burke carried Mary back to her bed, his face grim and worried.

"Then make it," Natalie ordered. "Burke will need a good hot cup of coffee—after an ordeal like this. Can you have it ready by the time he bathes and dresses?"

Hands on hips, furious because she couldn't think of anything forceful enough to say, Eliza Anne muttered, "Natalie—you're not helping *anything.* You know that, don't you? Mary needs the attention now—not Burke."

"They both need attention," Natalie countered. "Oh, Burke, why in heaven's name don't you have at least one servant?"

After a brief glance at Natalie, which Eliza Anne could not quite decipher, Burke appeared to ignore her. It was clear, however, that indeed Natalie had kissed him awake. The man was, after all, still in his nightshirt.

While Burke dressed, Eliza Anne busied herself with a fresh pot of coffee and, after first protesting, decided to let Natalie plunge ahead —to let her prove to herself once and for all that she was as out of place in a primitive kitchen as a fish out of water. Within a few minutes, the flower-sprigged dress Natalie wore was spattered with grease, because—all in the same skillet—she tried to fry enough bacon for a regiment and a whole dozen eggs. The floor in front of the open fireplace was already white with spilled flour because she was also determined to "whip up" biscuits. She tried to turn the mound of bacon and the skillet's contents flared up. When Natalie screamed, Burke appeared—buttoning his work shirt.

"Natalie, no!" he shouted, springing to haul the blazing skillet off the fire and out onto the hearth.

Natalie rushed to him, grabbed his hand and began to kiss his singed fingers. "Don't you know men should stay out of a woman's kitchen when she's cooking breakfast?"

Burke jerked back his burned hand, and for a long moment he just stood there, glaring at Natalie, who glared back.

"Leave a woman alone," he barked, "and let her burn a man's house down? This mess you've made just proves you could never live up here without a houseful of servants!"

Eliza Anne saw Natalie's eyes draw to mere slits—her fury-look that intimidated everyone except Burke Latimer.

"Get a broom," he ordered, "and sweep up that flour! I don't mean spread it around, Natalie, I mean sweep it up. If you can't get it all out of the split-log cracks, then get a brush and scrub it out."

Seeming to ignore what he said, Natalie breathed, "You've really burned yourself, Burke. How can you pound nails and things today with those fingers?"

"Sweet bass ointment on shelf you build by hearth, Mister Burke," Mary said from her bed. "In green bottle."

At least, Mary's conscious, Eliza Anne thought, sipping fast at a cup of strong coffee.

"My hand's all right, Mary," Burke said, his voice suddenly gentle. "But I'll use some ointment before I leave for work, thank you." Glaring at Natalie again, he repeated—not so gently, "I'll get the ointment. I certainly don't intend to add to the trouble around here by refusing to use *my* head!"

"You warned me you weren't a—Savannah gentleman," Natalie snapped, "but you don't need to be—crude."

Eliza Anne felt she should say something, but what? Then Natalie's eyes filled with tears and she threw herself into Burke's arms. Threw herself so hard, he caught her involuntarily, but quickly pushed her away.

"That won't work with me this time," he said.

In response, Natalie slipped both arms around his neck and laid her head on his shoulder, much as a chastened child might. "I—only meant to help you. To help—Mary. Ben needs breakfast too, before you take him off to town to saw boards."

Eliza Anne saw Burke's quick, sheepish glance just before he caught Natalie in his arms and held her to him. Then, slowly, he pulled her arms from around his neck, led her to a chair beside the table and sat her down. "Stay right there. Just—please—sit there, while I clean up this floor. I can cook breakfast. I've done it for years."

With Eliza Anne helping, in no time at all, Burke had the floor swept and scrubbed, the charred contents scoured from the iron skillet, biscuits baked, newly sliced bacon fried and six eggs instead of twelve. Eliza Anne found it hard to believe, but Natalie kept her place by the table in sweet silence, her eyes—widened now—in awe of Burke's easy, graceful movements. When breakfast was on the table, he headed for the porch to call Ben.

"Let me go get Ben," Natalie offered, jumping up.

"On that poor little swollen foot? I'm no Savannah gentleman," Burke said, half smiling, "but I'm no brute, either. Please sit back down." She remained standing. "Natalie, I said—*sit down!*"

To Eliza Anne's amazement, she sat.

Almost an hour later than usual, Ben rode in silence beside Burke on the high wagon seat, as they hurried to town. In sight of the courthouse, Burke broke the silence.

"Whatever it is that's happened between us," he said, "we'll straighten out somehow, Ben. I'm going to trust you to tell me what I've done to turn you against me. Not now, necessarily. Just when you can."

"Mrs. Stiles will stay with Mary today?" Ben asked.

"That's right. She and Natalie will be there to look after her." Burke tried a short laugh. "I guess I should say—Mrs. Stiles will be there all day to look after them both."

Ben said nothing.

"How was your breakfast?"

"Not so good as when Mary cooks it, but Mrs. Stiles did fine."

"Mrs. Stiles can't cook. I don't think her family was as rich as the Brownings, but she said servants did the cooking in the Mackay family when she was growing up. Some southern white ladies don't learn how to cook."

Burke felt Ben looking at him for the first time. "Miss Natalie—cooked my breakfast?"

"Sorry to tell you, but I fixed it. Miss Natalie managed to ruin nearly a half side of bacon and a whole dozen eggs." When Ben remained silent, Burke asked, "I don't suppose you're going to tell me why you're—treating me like this."

"No."

"Haven't I earned your friendship, Ben?"

"Yes."

"But you won't tell me what's wrong?"

"I can't. Not ever."

At the Cummings house site, Burke pulled the wagon up in its usual place under the sycamore tree. "I—dread not being able to enjoy working together as usual today, Ben. I—thought we were family, you and Mary and I. I really dread a whole day of—silence."

Jumping to the ground, Ben said, without looking at him, "I dread it too."

Mary did her best to give Eliza Anne instructions about how to fill and hang a pot of stew ingredients—dried beef, potatoes, onions, turnips, carrots—on the heavy hook above the wood fire. She had never known of a woman who could not make a pot of stew. Mrs. Stiles was so kind, though, so willing and so pretty, even when she frowned. With her good eye, Mary saw that both Mrs. Stiles and Miss Natalie frowned a lot all the while she tried to explain about how much salt and onion and water. Finally, Miss Natalie got out Mister Burke's quill and paper and wrote it all down to read from as they cooked.

"We're going to need water from the well, Mary," Mrs. Stiles said. "There's plenty on the porch, but all three buckets have flies in them!"

"How dumb of Burke and Ben not to get fresh for us," Miss Natalie complained, but quickly gave Mary her beautiful smile, and added, "Men can be awfully dumb, can't they?"

"Ben is smart. Mister Burke is—even smarter than Ben."

The sound of Miss Natalie's laughter was as bright as her hair. "It doesn't matter," she said. "I can draw water from a well. There's really nothing to it. I've watched the servants draw water lots of times at Knightsford."

"For heaven's sake, Natalie, you talk as though your foot and ankle weren't swollen to twice normal size. I've drawn water a hundred times myself at The Grange when I was a girl. Don't forget my family once owned a plantation on the Savannah River too."

"What is—Knightsford?" Mary asked.

"My family's plantation," Natalie tossed over her shoulder, still wiping and wiping at the breakfast plates Miss Lib had just washed.

"You really don't need to rub holes in those plates, Natalie." Mrs. Stiles laughed. "I think she's trying to convince Burke Latimer that she can turn into a high-grade frontier woman, Mary. What do you think?"

"I can think only how beautiful is Miss Natalie."

Ignoring what she'd heard so often in her life, Natalie said, "Miss Lib, if you won't allow me to draw that water, will you kindly get it yourself? Stew, I would imagine, has to cook a long, long time."

FIFTY-ONE

THE CUMMINGSES arrived shortly after noon for their daily inspection of the cottage and Burke noticed that, as usual, Ben managed to disappear.

"I wish that young man felt more comfortable with us," Mrs. Cummings said, running her hand over the railing Burke had ready to install on the wide front porch.

"Smooth enough to suit you, Elma?" her husband teased.

"I think I'll ignore that," she said, giving Burke a rare smile. "Of course it's smooth. Mr. Latimer allows no inferior work. Tell me, why *does* your helper make himself so scarce when we come around? I'd think he'd want to hear how pleased we are."

"Stuff and nonsense, my dear," Mr. Cummings said. "The boy's an Indian. Why wouldn't he keep out of sight? Correct, Latimer?"

"I know that's the rumor in town," Burke said calmly, looking first at Cummings and then at his wife. "Ben McDonald and his sister are my cousins from Florida. They're Minorcans."

"Still sticking with your story, eh?"

"Yes, Mr. Cummings. I am."

"I don't see what difference it makes," Elma Cummings said, more interested in the stack of spindles piled against the house at the back of the porch. "I simply can't wait until you get these in place, Mr. Latimer."

"With Ben helping, you should find the porch finished when you come by tomorrow."

"I don't see any reason for McDonald to hide who he is by now,"

Cummings persisted. "Georgians only wanted the Cherokee land—not the Cherokees. I've seen a dozen or more red-skinned people since we've been here. The Cassville folks mostly take 'em in stride. Why don't you just drop this Minorcan business?"

"We retained Mr. Latimer to build a good house for us," Elma Cummings said firmly. "*Not* to run his personal life. And, by the way, I gave you a splendid recommendation a day or two ago, young man. You've met Mrs. W. H. Stiles, I'm sure. She's in Cassville with those wealthy Brownings from Savannah. The red-haired daughter is still here, I believe, in Mrs. Stiles's care while Mr. and Mrs. Browning are at Lookout Mountain."

"Mrs. Stiles inquired about me?" Burke asked carefully.

"The rumor is that some dreadful builder has made a perfectly terrible start on the Stiles house over on the Etowah River. She came right out and asked what we thought of you as a builder. It seems she's already written to Savannah for her husband's permission to retain you to build a place for them just as soon as you're finished here. Mrs. Stiles hasn't even mentioned it to you?"

"Uh—not in any detail."

Cummings laughed. "I know it's hard for you to believe, my dear, but most ladies consult their husbands before taking such an important step."

When the Cummingses had gone, Ben walked out from the parlor onto the porch. "Burke?"

"You were hiding close by this time, weren't you? Did you hear everything we said?"

Frowning, Ben only nodded. After a moment, he asked, "You going to take the Stiles job over on the Etowah?"

"I haven't been offered any job. But would moving over there for several months interest you?"

Ignoring the question, Ben said, "I'll help you with the spindles and railing today. Thank you for lying again about Mary and me. I want to help with the railing, but—don't expect me to talk to you. I can't."

For the life of him, Burke could not think what might be wrong. He reached through the window opening to lay his hand on Ben's shoulder. "Whatever you say, Ben. What matters most to me right now is for you to know how much you—and Mary—mean to me."

In response, Ben backed away, so that Burke's hand slipped free.

"As soon as I finish sanding the front door," Ben said, "I'll be out to help with the porch."

Back in Savannah, Eliza Mackay had read and reread her daughter's letter to W.H., who would be coming by any moment, to ask if she thought he should agree with Eliza Anne about retaining Burke Latimer to build the new Stiles home in the upcountry.

Dear me, she thought, when W.H. has never once asked my opinion about anything of consequence, why does he do it now? I suppose because there could be ramifications in so many directions. Eliza Anne seems absolutely certain that Burke Latimer would build them a fine house, but I do wish she'd waited for William to get back to Cassville. He would know in a minute if the present builder is botching the job. Well, my daughter, Eliza Anne, is not blessed with an ounce of extra patience. Never has been. If Burke Latimer were to build their house up there, it would give Natalie still more contact with him, still more reason to push for an early marriage. Poor Mark. Poor Caroline. I'm glad they went away alone for a time, but I wonder what on earth is happening while they're gone.

Eliza Anne's reasoning in the letter did seem practical. "Good builders are as scarce as hen's teeth up here," she had written. "Except for Burke Latimer and his helper, one can hire capable carpenters only by bringing them from Augusta. How much saner, it seems to me, to hire the one responsible contractor who already lives in the vicinity. He could repair one of the several Cherokee cabins standing on our Etowah River land for himself. He lives in one here, with a Cherokee brother and sister. The brother is Burke's helper."

Burke Latimer must have a most generous heart, Eliza thought, to have taken in those homeless young people. Evidently, he's also an excellent craftsman. Mark had written just before he and Caroline left for Lookout Mountain that, indeed, they both thought highly of Natalie's beau—if five days spent on a raft with a girl made an eligible man a bona fide *beau*. On the other hand, how many young men had actually saved the life of the young woman they courted? Nothing in Natalie's intense, extraordinary relationship with Burke Latimer fit into any pattern at all, but why should they expect it to?

Eliza had prayed that God would give Mark and Caroline His wisdom while they were away. They needed it.

She looked at her watch. W.H. was already late. I do hope he gets here, she thought, before Kate and Sarah come home from the market. Kate, especially, is good at asking the wrong questions at the wrong time. Slowly, Eliza Mackay refolded the letter. Come on, W.H., I'm ready with my answer—for whatever it's worth. Why *not* retain Burke Latimer to build your new home? There would be nothing fair in depriving him of such a big job simply because Natalie will undoubtedly go right on—being Natalie.

She had no way of knowing, but at the exact moment in which her mother, sitting on her porch back in Savannah, was thinking of "Natalie being Natalie," Eliza Anne was having the same thought. And being Natalie, of course, was—never to be predictable. There the girl sat now, across the room, her chair pulled near Mary's bed, sewing away on the torn lining of Burke's good jacket. Natalie had always done beautiful fanciwork, but so far as Eliza Anne knew, she'd never *mended* anything. Studying Natalie's composed, soft expression at this minute, she found herself hoping with all her heart that somehow things would work out with Burke. She loves him, she thought. He loves her. I see no reason why they wouldn't be supremely happy once he's financially able to support her in the customary ways. Can she wait till then? Who knows?

"What are you smiling at, Miss Lib?" Natalie asked, glancing up from her sewing. "I don't think I look a bit awkward mending a coat."

"You don't, my dear. As usual, you simply look—beautiful."

"More beautiful than usual?"

"Maybe."

"I should be. Can you honestly believe that this is Burke's very own jacket lining I'm mending? I've never been so happy in my entire life!"

Eliza Anne glanced at Mary, who lay with her face to the wall. "I'm sure Mary's relieved to have your help with the mending, aren't you, Mary?"

"No, ma'am."

"Oh, but I'm doing a skillful job, Mary," Natalie exclaimed. "Just wait till I'm finished. You'll see."

Abruptly, Mary sat up in the bed and looked with her one good eye at Natalie. "You very kind to me," she said, "but you take my joy away."

"Don't be ridiculous."

Natalie's voice was so impersonal, so intent upon her mending, Eliza Anne felt sure Mary was going to cry—and crying could bring on a dreadful headache.

"You take away my joy," Mary repeated, "but I make one thing plain to you. You leave my brother—alone! You stay away from Ben!"

Eliza Anne stared at Mary, who was definitely *not* going to cry. She had merely stated a fact, and in spite of her clumsy English, for the first time Eliza Anne caught her meaning—caught the full impact of it. "I think I'd better go tend the stew," she said quickly, hoping to divert Mary. "Does it smell right, Mary?"

She hurried over to the fireplace and began to stir so fast, some of the broth sizzled onto the open fire. Until this moment, she had given no thought whatever to the fact that Ben—Indian Ben—might also be in love with Natalie. Did Natalie know? True, the girl had declared Ben to be jealous of Burke last night, but Eliza Anne had supposed that to be mere prattle and had promptly forgotten it until this minute. Her thoughts whirled. This was too farfetched to believe—every bit of it! Anyone could see that Mary adored Burke Latimer, but Ben—*in love with Natalie?* Had she read it in a romantic novel, she would have rejected it out of hand.

"I'm sure we'll need more water from the well," Eliza Anne remarked. "This beef's tougher than leather." As she picked up a bucket, she saw that Mary had again turned her face to the wall. Natalie was still happily mending and humming.

"Will you be all right while I'm gone, Mary?" Her question was superfluous, of course—she'd be gone only a few minutes—but felt compelled to keep including Mary.

"Take your time, Miss Lib," Natalie said, not looking up. "Mary and I will be fine. In fact, you've been cooped up in this cabin all morning. Why not take a little walk before the sun gets too hot?"

"I'll do no such thing," Eliza Anne called back from the front door. "As soon as I can haul that heavy bucket up the forty or fifty feet from the bottom of Burke's well, I'll be right back. And Natalie —don't even get up from your chair! You've been sitting there so long, your ankle might give way."

• • •

Once Miss Lib's footsteps had crossed the porch, Natalie whispered, "You can stop worrying about your brother's obvious infatuation with me, Mary. I've known it all along, but there is and will always be only one man in my life. Burke. I also know you fancy yourself in love with him, but you must put such thoughts completely out of your mind. He belongs to me. Burke thinks of you as his little sister—no more. You have to be satisfied with that." She held up the jacket, smoothing it. Then she hugged it to her and kissed the collar where it touched his neck. "I hate to say it, but I'm finished with the mending. So now, with Miss Lib's cold well water going into that pot, I think I'd better put on more wood, don't you?"

Without turning in the bed, Mary said, "No, Miss Natalie. The coals are right. No more wood."

"Nonsense. There's a nice little stack right there on the hearth. Short, knotty pieces I can handle easily." She hobbled to the fireplace and began tossing on chunk after chunk of fat pine.

"No!" Mary shrieked, as she crawled out of bed and, after two or three lunging steps, collapsed on the floor.

"Now, look what you've done, Mary!" Scared and angry, Natalie grabbed two more knots of pitch-laden pine and hurled them into the great black cloud of smoke already billowing out into the room.

When the fat pine caught and began to blaze, the explosion in the chimney was so loud, Natalie—terrified—lost her balance and fell too, so near the raging fire, she had to crawl quickly away or be burned by it. The roar was deafening, and down over the front porch, through the open door, she could see thick, blown gusts of black smoke, and red embers sweeping about on the hot blast of wind from the blazing chimney.

With all her might, she screamed for Miss Lib, then crawled as fast as she could to where Mary lay.

When Burke and Ben drove in sight of the still smoking ruins just before dark that evening, Ben jumped from the wagon and began to run like a crazy man toward where the cabin had stood. Burke whipped the team frantically and hung on for dear life while the empty wagon rattled and banged over the rutty road behind Ben. If anyone was still alive, they'd need the wagon. When he reached the sweet-gum tree near the well, Ben was already kneeling on the ground beside the bodies of the three women.

Reining the team so abruptly the horses stumbled, Burke jumped from the moving wagon, yelling "Whoa!" His own terror seemed to go on sounding in that panic-stricken "Whoa!" as he ran toward the tree under which Ben was on his hands and knees, going from one prone figure to the other.

Ben gave him no signal at all, but he could hear Mrs. Stiles's strained, weary voice say, "We're—all here, Burke. We're—all here. No one—is dead. . . ."

"Natalie," Burke breathed, as he dropped to the ground beside the tiny crumpled figure in the smudged flower-sprigged dress. "Natalie, oh, Natalie—thank God!" For that first agonizing moment of relief, he could only hold her in his arms and smooth her sooty, singed hair. "Your—your hair's burned," he gasped. "Your—hair, Natalie! It's—all stiff when I—touch it."

Both her arms were around his neck, pulling him close. "Hair grows," she whispered.

"You're alive," he groaned. "Oh, Natalie, I—was so scared!"

"I wouldn't die, Burke. I—belong to you!"

"Yes, yes! You do belong to *me*. . . ."

"*I—did it,*" she said, her voice remarkably firm. "I set the fire."

He turned to Mrs. Stiles and Mary. Ben was holding Mary's hand. "Mrs. Stiles," Burke managed, "what *is* Natalie saying?"

"I caused the fire," she repeated. "I was trying to—prove to you, Burke, that I could be a housekeeper—and I—I—"

"She did! She threw a whole stack of fat pine on the burning coals, Burke, dear," Mrs. Stiles explained.

"Dear Lord in heaven," he moaned. Weak himself from the scare and shock, he lowered Natalie to the ground and sat back on his heels.

"Oh, forgive me," Mrs. Stiles said, embarrassed. "I'm so sorry for you, Burke—I believe I called you 'Burke, dear.' "

"You might as well call me anything you like, Mrs. Stiles. If the Stileses and Brownings are—like one family, as you say—just get used to me, lady. I—I've tried, but *I—can't live* without Natalie."

"I know," Mrs. Stiles said.

"She's telling you the truth, Burke," Natalie spoke quietly. "Miss Lib—understands about us."

"Natalie, don't say any more!" He looked at Mary's blackened face. The bandage was gone. The injured eye was swollen shut.

"Mister Burke," Mary whispered so that he had to lean closer. "Miss—Natalie, she—save me—from—death."

"She did that, too," Mrs. Stiles confirmed quickly. "I was at the well for water when the chimney exploded in flames. On that— injured ankle, Burke, Natalie dragged Mary out of the cabin—just in time. The—roof had begun to burn by then. Great chunks of it were falling in—around them. Natalie dragged Mary—both blinded and choking from the pitch smoke—out onto the porch, where I could get to them—just in time."

Burke's eyes went from one to the other. He saw Ben get slowly to his feet and, without a word, go straight to where Natalie lay on the bare ground. He knelt beside her, and after gazing down at her for a long time, kissed his fingers and placed them tenderly on her fore-head. Plainly it was more than a gesture of gratitude. Ben held his fingers to her face for so long, Natalie began to cough, then pushed him away.

"Anyone would have done what I did, Ben, to save your sister," she said. "Don't you dare do that again!"

Ben touched Natalie's hair just once—then leaped to his feet and raced away, out of their sight, into the darkening woods.

"Mary," Burke asked, his voice wooden. "Will he come back? Will Ben—come back to help me get—all of you into town? Or—do you think he just—left us for good?"

"The stars are out," Eliza Anne Stiles said. "Couldn't we—sleep right here, Burke? I'm so—tired."

Burke repeated his question. "Is Ben gone for good, Mary?"

She was crying. "I do not know, Mister Burke—and I am— afraid."

"Afraid Ben ran away forever?" Natalie demanded.

"Just—afraid—of all things."

For a long moment, Burke stared at the smoldering ruins of his cabin. Even the stick-and-mud chimney had collapsed. He'd tried his best to be sure the old mud lining of that chimney had no breaks left in it, but Natalie's raging fire must have licked at bare logs somewhere to set them ablaze. Then he looked at her. She lay exhausted, but smiling at him from the stubbly ground.

Pointing to something dark rolled up under her head, supporting it, she asked, "See what I managed to save from the fire, Burke? Your good jacket! I mended the torn lining in the sleeve just before —just before—" Her hands flew to her face and she broke into sobs.

He gathered her into his arms and held her, rocked her as though she were a small child. Her willful determination to try to do what she was incapable of doing infuriated him, but she had saved Mary's life—she had rescued his good jacket—and she could have died trying to do either one.

"Thank you for—mending my sleeve. For—saving Mary—and the jacket." He frowned. "But don't cry anymore, *please*. I need you to help me think what to do, Natalie. Can you understand that I—need you—now?"

"He does," Mrs. Stiles said firmly. "Burke needs you to be grown up and helpful, Natalie. I want you to stop crying this minute, do you hear me?"

"I—hear—you, Miss Lib," she choked, "but I don't think—I can ever—be helpful to—anyone!"

"Nonsense."

"If you're going to be my wife and live up here in this rough country," Burke said, his voice more reproachful than he felt, "you're going to have to *learn how*—to help me. God knows I want you here with me—God knows I want you to grow up!"

"I—don't—think even God cares—about us anymore. . . ." Uncontrollable weeping shook her whole body.

"Natalie, that's enough!" Eliza Anne Stiles stood up. "Burke has more to face right now than he deserves—his home is gone, Ben's gone—it's getting dark and he and Mary have no place to sleep tonight. *Stop crying.* Do you hear me? Prove to us, Natalie, once and for all, that you're made of the stuff to be Burke Latimer's wife! Are you going to do that or are you going to lie there—sobbing for attention?"

Still holding her, Burke could feel the sobs begin to subside. Natalie wasn't merely holding them back, they were subsiding. Slowly, she disengaged his arms and struggled to her feet—refusing his help. Mary, who had also been weeping, stopped too.

A screech owl called from the woods where Ben had vanished.

Still squatting on the ground, Burke looked up at Natalie. She was disheveled, soot-streaked, almost pathetic in her wobbling, yet determined effort to stand. He could not have explained any of what he saw in her face, but he sensed that, deep inside Natalie—something was *happening*. With all his heart, he longed to reach toward her, to help her. He could not. He was rooted by the look on her face —a look he had never even glimpsed before.

"I—I think I've just—*seen me*—for the first time," she said, her voice faint, but far from tentative. "*I* caused all this—trouble for you, Burke. Mary and Ben didn't cause it—I did! Miss Lib only tried to help us. To—help me." Dark was falling so quickly now, her face was shadowed, but Burke had seen the mysterious change in her expression. He was nearly frightened by it. "Everyone has always tried to help me," she went on. "Except for Kottie, I—hated it when they did." She took one limping step back—away from all of them. "Miss Lib, your mother told me once that pampering is not helping. I didn't know what she meant. I didn't! I swear I didn't." She took another step back. "I—I'm not sure I want to know now, either."

"But you do know what Mama meant?" Mrs. Stiles repeated her question: "Do you know now what my mother meant, Natalie?"

"Yes," she said simply, just as the screech owl—this time directly overhead—shrieked again. Without warning, Natalie laughed. It was her familiar bell laughter. "I've—been as *obnoxious* as that— screech owl!"

Burke leapt to his feet.

"Don't you dare take me in your arms, Burke Latimer," she ordered. "And don't think whatever—ugly thing—this is I've discovered in myself is going to stop me from being *me*. It isn't! I'll—just be less trouble from now on in the way I go about things." She flung one arm toward the wagon. "Now, we're going to ride back to town —all of us. Mary, you're going to help us get you up into the wagon bed, aren't you?"

For the first time, Burke noticed that Mary was sitting bolt upright on the ground. "We—leave Ben, Mister Burke? And Little Star?"

"We'll have to for tonight," he answered. "He'll see to Little Star. Thank God, the barn's all right."

In full command now, but somehow gentled, Natalie went on with her instructions. "I'll sleep with you in your room, Miss Lib—Mary can have my bed at the hotel. Burke can take William's room. Tonight is what we have to get through now. And we've wasted enough time. Is there a lantern in the wagon? We have to see where the horses are going!"

Dumbfounded, Burke managed to say, "Yes, Natalie. Ben and I always carry a lantern. But I don't need a hotel room. I'll sleep in the wagon bed."

"You'll do no such thing!" She turned to look at the burned-out cabin. For a long moment, she looked at it. In the gathering darkness, live embers glowed more brightly around the foundation. "Wait. Before we start helping Mary into the wagon, I want one more thing understood."

Burke thought he heard just a hint of amusement in Mrs. Stiles's voice when she asked, "And what is that, Natalie?"

"When Mama and Papa come back to Cassville, I'm—ready to go home with them. I—I hate it, but, Burke, I know I'm *not* ready—to be your wife—up here. I will be someday, and I won't like doing the sensible thing in the meantime, but—" She took a deep breath. "I'm telling all of you that whatever Burke thinks is best, *I'll do.*"

He could only stare at her.

"Natalie," Mrs. Stiles said—in some awe, "I must say I think—you're wonderful!"

"I know you do. So do I, Miss Lib." A small smile played at her mouth. "Although I am—kind of weak in the knees from—whatever just happened to me a minute ago. And that was a pretty dangerous thing I just said because Burke is so mulish. But . . ." She limped toward him. "I meant it, dear Burke. You're a—peculiar man, you know. *Peculiar.* But, I—love you. There just isn't any way I could ever stop loving you."

His arms were around her again. "Natalie, oh, Natalie—I'll work harder than ever, so we don't have to wait too long. I promise!"

Hugging him back, right in his ear, she said, "I'll be good from now on. I have the whole thing planned. You'll see. I'll be really—good."

He tried to laugh. "I'm not sure I can—deal with you that way, either."

A sigh went through her. He felt it. "I will be good and I certainly hope I won't be too dull." Abruptly, she let him go. "Now, the three of us should be able to find a way to get Mary into the wagon bed." Limping to where Mary lay, she bent over her. "And, Mary, I might as well be honest with you, too. I told you before the fire that I know you love Burke. I'm just terribly sorry, but you'll have to try to overcome it. You're going to find someone else to love—someday. I know you will." She took Mary's hand. "I don't think this should keep us from being friends, do you?"

If there had been a deep hole nearby, Burke would gladly have crawled into it. Poor Mary! Even if Natalie was right that Mary loved him, did she have to say it right out in the open? This new, changed, honest girl could well be more difficult for him than ever. And still harder to resist.

FIFTY-TWO

EARLY THE NEXT MORNING, Burke sat hunched at a corner table in the States' Rights Hotel dining room, forcing himself to eat at least some of the hard, dry ham and overdone biscuits. Throughout the night spent in William Mackay's room upstairs, he had come awake—quickly and often—each time fighting a sense of unreality. Only day before yesterday, he had awakened in his own familiar room at the rear of his own cabin, the energizing aroma of Mary's good coffee and bacon telling him at once that he was home—in his own place—ready to begin another day's work with Ben.

Ben . . . Would he find time today to look for Ben in the woods in back of the cabin's ruins? It was not yet 6 A.M. No chance of seeing Natalie so early, but he might allow himself an hour, at least, to look around his burned-out place. There was a chance that Ben's deep attachment to the home they'd shared might draw him back. There had not been time to examine the ruins last night, but Ben might come back today to look around, to feed and water Mary's pony, Little Star. Ben had to eat, after all, wherever he was hiding. And Mary's pots and pans would still be there in the blackened remains of the cabin.

Burke downed the coffee left in the cup and was reaching for his hat when Eliza Anne Stiles, looking tired, but fashionable in a striped gray dress, walked directly to his table.

"I see I've just caught you, Burke. Do you have to leave this minute?"

He stood to greet her. "Morning, Mrs. Stiles. Uh—no. I guess I don't have to go quite yet." After he seated her across the narrow table, he asked, "Is—she still asleep?"

"Natalie? Or Mary?"

He grinned. "Natalie."

"Still sound asleep, I'm sure. Not only because she's exhausted. Something real did happen to her yesterday, Burke. She can be a fine actress, but—I know the child. She wasn't acting. In all her life I've never seen her really—peaceful before."

"I'm glad to hear you say that. She—certainly caught me off guard. I—I don't think I handled any of it too well."

Eliza Anne Stiles ordered only coffee, and a sleepy waiter filled both their cups. "You did all a man could do under such surprising circumstances," she said when the waiter had gone. "I must say, though, you seem awfully downcast this morning." She smiled weakly. "And why not? Burke, I'm so sorry about your cabin. Do you suppose it took a catastrophe like that to bring Natalie to her senses?"

"Whatever that means," he said. "I don't want her to—leave for Savannah anymore than she wants to go, Mrs. Stiles."

"I know. I do think she'll go, though."

He nodded. "If you'd asked me yesterday, I'd have said she *has* to. I've been stubborn with her at times on that." He looked straight at her. "Mrs. Stiles, I—don't want all the—spirit to go out of Natalie. I —love the fire in her."

"I can practically promise you that she'll never lose the fire." After a pause, she asked, "You were planning to hunt for Ben before work, weren't you? And then I arrived. Surely, he'll be at the job."

"I don't think so this time. And I'd give anything to know why."

She leaned toward him. "Don't you honestly know what's wrong with poor Ben?"

He only frowned.

"You do know. On top of all that's happened—you just can't face it, can you? To me it's as plain as the nose on your face that Ben's in love with Natalie."

He pushed back his coffee. "I *can't* face that kind of—heartbreak for Ben! His life's been too tragic. He and Mary were barely existing when I found them. The whole removal was a desperate thing for him. It still is. I've seen Ben's scars. All of them. What can I do to—"

He broke off. "Mrs. Stiles, do you think Natalie knows he's—in love with her?"

"Of course she knows. She's accustomed to young men falling hopelessly in love with her. I doubt she's paid much attention, though. But she's not to blame. This time Natalie did nothing to cause him to be infatuated with her."

Burke shook his head. "Ben isn't the kind of man to be—infatuated. He wouldn't know how to do anything but love her with all his heart."

"Nor would Mary. It's really an excruciating coincidence, isn't it? You and Natalie—stumbling onto the same problem with your Cherokee brother and sister. Natalie's right. Mary is in love with you."

"Mary's young—younger than her sixteen years. I've got to believe she'll find someone else, grow out of it. There's—no one for me but Natalie."

"And I think I believe that by some means—eventually, you and Natalie will be together. My mother would say that it was God who gave Natalie a good, honest look at herself out there beside the smoking ruins of your cabin. Maybe it was. However it happened, I know—the change in her was real. It's going to help somehow. In fact, she's been so amenable since, I almost don't know how to act with her."

He gave a short laugh. "Neither do I." He waited a moment, then said, "Mrs. Stiles—"

"Can't you at least call me Miss Lib?"

"I'd like that. Miss Lib, I want you—and Natalie's parents—to know that I do *not* intend ever to live and work in Savannah. Mr. Browning's offer was most generous, but I'd hate city life, even after such a short time up here. For some reason, I also want—all of you to know that if it turns out I can't marry Natalie—I doubt I'll ever marry anyone else. It's important to me that you, at least, know that."

"I do," she said. "And, almost from the beginning, I've been on your side, Burke. Yours and Natalie's. More than that, it pleases me no end that you're determined to live up here."

"It does?"

"Yes. You see, I had an ulterior motive for meeting you this morning. I know you're eager to get to work, but on my way down-

stairs just now I met Mr. Milner, the owner of this luxurious establishment. He saw my brother, William, last week in Macon. William
is due back here in less than three weeks."

"That means I'll have to find another room."

"I'm sorry. William does like solitude."

"Bentley has a bed at his house."

"Good. When William returns, I'll have irrefutable proof that the
man my dear husband hired to build our house on the Etowah River
is as shoddy as I've heard. I'm still expecting a letter from Mr. Stiles
agreeing that you should take over. If there's any hesitation on his
part, my brother will settle it. William's been to our Etowah River
property. W.H. has utmost respect for William's opinion. You are
interested, aren't you?"

"I certainly am, but—I need Ben."

"How long will it take you to finish the Cummings cottage?"

"Without Ben, more than a month. Maybe two. I'm going to scour
the countryside. If I can't find him, it will take time to locate another
skilled helper. If you plan a large house, I'll need two or three."

"I do want W.H. to be the one to explain all that to you, but
knowing him, yes, he'll want a mansion eventually. My husband
meant to surprise me with the frame portion of the house that's all
botched up. He's devastated, I'm sure, that I found out, but thank
heaven, I did. I do want him to make all future contacts with you,
though." She laughed. "I'm far from a submissive woman, Burke,
but my strongest desire is that W.H. and I go on forever being
happily married. We're close. He's my life."

"I'm glad to hear that."

"Oh yes, if my plan works out—if things work out for you to build
it—you'll be working on a truly happy house over there on those
gorgeous cliffs. We want it to be a place where our children will *want*
to put down roots."

"I hope your dream comes true," he said and reached again for
his hat. "I really must go, Miss Lib. I hope you have some idea what
it means to me that—you're my friend. And, lady, I'm so glad—
Natalie has you." He escorted her to the door. "I'm more than
grateful, too, that you're here to—take Mary to the doctor. If she—if
she gets worse during the day—send for me at the Cummings
place."

"You'll stay on in William's room until he gets back, won't you?"

"I suppose so, yes. Natalie would raise Cain if I didn't." He grinned. "When she wakes up, tell her—tell her I'll see her late this evening. I'm going to hunt for Ben, though, after work."

For over two weeks, Burke spent every free daylight hour searching the woods from Cassville to his burned-out property north and as far as five miles south of the town. He caught Natalie using a few tricks to keep him with her now and then, but not once did she demand to go along, and although the steady search kept their meetings to a minimum, for the most part, she was understanding. Miss Lib ate with them much of the time, but at other times she insisted upon taking her supper with Mary.

Although Burke still could not be absolutely sure she meant it, Natalie gave almost full attention to Mary. True, Natalie had agreed only twice for Burke to visit Mary, but he sensed during those two visits that—as much as she could be, shut up in a stuffy hotel room—Mary was somewhat peaceful, and praying she would see again with her injured eye.

"I wonder if Mary agitates to see you more often?" Miss Lib dared to ask Burke.

"Natalie says not," he said. "As long as she knows I'm hunting for Ben, Mary seems satisfied. She's also happy that the fire didn't reach the barn. Her pony's safe."

On the day William Mackay was due to come back, Burke decided not to look for Ben before work. Nearly three weeks had passed with no sign of him. An extra hour or so at the Cummings cottage would move him that much closer to being free to consider the Stiles offer once Mackay returned. Miss Lib seemed sure that her husband and Mackay had been corresponding, and Natalie, of course, had the entire deal all arranged in her mind. She thought it utterly ridiculous that Burke had to leave the hotel and move in with the Bentleys' once William got back, but she'd agreed with far less resistance than he expected. He'd found no direct way to ask her if she had any idea how difficult it was for him these days—not knowing ahead of time whether she'd resist or cooperate. Now and then, he felt that he and Natalie were almost strangers . . . except during the few times they'd been alone. Miss Lib was right—the fire in her was still there.

No one knew exactly when William Mackay would ride in today, but Burke would be glad to see him again. Needed to see him, in fact. Mackay had been the only other white man with whom Ben had felt comfortable besides Burke. It would help to be able to talk to him about Ben, to tell Mackay how he missed the help and friendship.

By noon, Burke was struggling to set the Cummings parlor mantel in place, when a familiar man's voice called his name. He propped up the unattached, plain wooden mantel with a two-by-four and went outside to greet William Mackay, tanned and looking, for him, quite hale and hearty.

"Sorry to hear about your cabin, Latimer," William said as the two shook hands. "My sister tells me our little princess managed to burn it down by throwing on fat pine instead of oak."

Burke gave a short laugh. "It wasn't my idea of a permanent home, but I hadn't planned to move any time soon."

"Mighty fine piece of work you've done for the Cummingses here," William said, examining the evenly spaced clapboard exterior, running his hand over Burke's porch railing. "Owners happy, I suppose."

"They seem to be. Was your trip a success?"

"I'd say so. Bought up some property for my brother-in-law, Stiles, adjoining what he already owns on the Etowah River. Barnsley's gone to England. All I was authorized to do for him was look around. I found some fine land roughly twenty miles from the Stiles place. Barnsley's wife, Julia, and Eliza Anne have been friends for years. He wanted to be fairly nearby. Found it in Cherokee District 3, Section 16. He wants several thousand acres eventually. Plans to build a real mansion, he told me. I found the perfect site for it, owned by a fellow named McBride." William glanced at Burke, a half-grin on his face. "My sister tells me you spoiled her husband's surprise he had planned."

"You knew about his surprise, eh?"

William nodded. "Are you going to take over the botched-up job?"

"You haven't lost any time catching up on Cassville gossip, have you?" It was fine to see Mackay laugh. The trip had done him a lot of good after the bad, bad time he'd had on the first anniversary of the *Pulaski* tragedy.

"Eliza Anne's taken quite a shine to you, Latimer," Mackay said. "She knows how to handle W.H. He wrote me that he was pretty riled up when he first found out she knew he had started the house, but whatever she wrote to him smoothed it all over. In fact, Eliza Anne heard from him today. She let me read his letter just as I was starting over here to see you."

"His response to the idea of hiring me?"

William grinned. "To read his letter, you'd think the idea was his all along. He kept her waiting for his reply, though, until he heard from me on the road. I recommended you highly. And I'm authorized by W.H. Stiles, as of right now, to retain you. The fellow he hired hasn't done much, but what he has done, you'll have to tear down, and start over. Worst foundation I ever saw. But I paid him off. He's gone."

"Mr. Stiles works fast, doesn't he?"

"Wants everything done yesterday. You'll like him, though. Fine lawyer, honorable, just always in a hurry. My sister and W.H. are closer than most couples. She understands him a lot better than he understands her, but that's better than the other way around. Eliza Anne's smart. She'll know exactly how to hold him down to what they can afford."

Burke grinned. "I've always heard the man had to hold down the wife's extravagance."

"Reverse is true here. W.H. was born to money. Lots more than our father ever had, although Papa was a highly respected merchant."

For a time, they said nothing, Burke seated on the porch railing, William leaning against a post.

"You need a place to live, Latimer. You're almost finished here. What do you say to building the Stiles house over on the Etowah?"

"You think I should, don't you?"

"Might solve some knotty problems for you. I looked at three or four vacated Cherokee cabins over at their house site—what my sister is now calling Etowah Cliffs. There are two good cabins. One about the size of yours Natalie burned down. Plenty of room for you and your two friends, Mary and Ben." William looked around. "Ben still gone, I see."

"Yes. Miss Lib told you, I guess."

"She told me all about it. Sorry. I didn't think that of Ben. I liked the boy. You were turning him into a fine craftsman, too." He shook his head. "Natalie stirs things up, doesn't she? Even when she doesn't know she's doing it."

"I—I keep thinking he'll come back before I finish here. I find myself watching for him—every day. He loves his sister. He seemed to like me. He and Mary both pray a lot. The Moravians taught them about God and they take Him seriously. I go on hoping he's just— well, praying about everything, thinking his deep thoughts. I need him, but he also needs me. Mary needs him."

"Eliza Anne says Mary cries when Ben's mentioned, and that's bad for her injured eye. I guess Natalie caused her accident too." When Burke looked away, William asked, "You planning to marry Natalie, Latimer?"

"Yes, sir." He sighed heavily. "I don't seem to see any other way now that we've been together again. I was doing pretty well until she showed up here in Cassville."

"You're right about waiting, though, until you can afford a house and servants. Is it your opinion that burning your cabin down really brought about a change in Natalie?"

Burke shrugged. "Miss Lib thinks so. Have you seen Natalie since you got back?"

"I have."

"Do you believe she's—growing up?"

"I haven't seen that much of her, but I know she's prettier than ever and so sweet and submissive and gracious. Her poor parents are going to be mighty mixed up when they get back."

"Soon now, I guess," Burke said. "I—suppose they'll want to be leaving then in a day or two for Savannah."

"Most likely. Mark should get back to his factorage. Business is brisk at home. What beats me, though, is that Natalie vows she's going back with them. Insists she's taking Mary along."

Burke stared at him. "What? Take Mary back to Savannah?"

"It's Natalie's idea. We do have good doctors there. Who's going to look after her up here when Natalie and my sister leave?"

"I—I planned to take care of her. Mrs. Bentley thinks Mary should move right into their place."

"Whatever change she's had, Latimer, Natalie is no fool. The Cherokee girl loves you."

"Miss Lib's caught you up on everything, hasn't she?"

"Natalie told me that herself."

"I see."

"What do you see, Latimer?"

Burke shook his head. "I can't answer that. I'm not that sure. I wish Mary could have a good doctor. At best, she'll be left with a bad scar. She might even lose the sight of that eye. I care a lot about the girl, but—Mackay, if Natalie had never been born, I'd care about Mary only as the young sister I never had. I feel about her, minus the blood ties, much the same way Ben does."

"You plan to stand in the way of the Brownings taking Mary back to Savannah with them when they go?"

"I have no right to do that."

"And Ben may be a hundred miles from here by now."

Burke was silent a moment. "He could be. I hope not. Oh, how I hope he's—still around here. I've hunted for him every day. Mackay —I never saw more misery in a man's eyes than when he gave me one last look that night before he ran crashing off into the woods."

"A man has to learn to battle misery alone. You may be right. Ben could be off—learning, as you say. Talking it over with God. I know that's the way I managed finally. Do you pray, Latimer?"

"As much as most men, I guess. Not like Mary or Ben, though. What will the Brownings think of taking Mary back with them?"

"If Natalie's got her mind made up about it, you know that's a foolish question." After a pause, Mackay said, "You need to think awhile on the matter of my hiring you to build the Etowah house, I suppose. As my brother-in-law's agent, I've got a one-thousand-dollar retainer back at the hotel."

Burke said nothing for a time. "Would the fact that I'd be building the Stiles house help keep Natalie patient about waiting until I can afford to marry her? Mackay, she doesn't know *how* to be a poor man's wife up here in the wilds!"

"I know that. Everybody who's watched her from babyhood knows that. She vows she knows it too now. As for her patience— that could be asking a lot of the Almighty. The fact that you'd be in constant touch with W.H. and Eliza Anne, though, might help some. How long do you need to decide? I look for Mark and Caroline Browning to come rolling in here any day now. I'd like to send word by them to W.H. back in Savannah."

Burke looked around the secluded house site. "I'll be by myself working here today, with plenty of time to think it through. I'll meet you in your room a little before sundown with my answer."

Again they shook hands. "I know how worried you must be about Ben," Mackay said. "You don't think he'll do anything—crazy, do you?"

"Until this happened, I haven't seen anything in him but a kind of steadiness and loyalty almost unheard of these days—especially around here. Now, I don't know any more than you know."

"Just how devoted *is* Ben to his sister?"

"Mackay, you're not worried that Ben might do away with himself, are you?"

"I don't know. Just an uneasy feeling in my gut. He's been through more than most young men could bear. See you this evening, Latimer."

FIFTY-THREE

BEFORE MACKAY'S VISIT, Burke had felt lonely enough in the empty Cummings cottage. With Mackay gone, the swish of his plane, as he evened up the mantelpiece, made an even lonelier sound. Ben's hammer, Ben's saw answered from nowhere nearby or out back. A good sharp saw slicing through a fresh-smelling plank had always struck Burke as a merry noise. To him, hammering rang like an insistent bell. The sounds of his work were good. Between them, he and Ben had made fine music.

Sultry waves of afternoon heat swept against his face and neck and bare arms as he strained to lift the mantel into place—testing the fit. It was a sturdy, plain mantel with no frills about it, but fitting it was a job for two men. And Ben was not there. The upper edge hung a little and, with one brawny arm trembling under its weight, he held the fixture out from the wall, reached for his plane and slid off an eighth of an inch. Good. The mantel slipped into place so exactly, it would have held without being fastened. Burke stood back to inspect the work, to catch his breath. More than a month ago, Ben had crafted the paneled, wide front door. That still had to be hung.

He strolled to the entrance and stood in what warm, muggy breeze blew off a stagnant pond on the far side of the town road. Ben's door stood solid and ready against a wall just inside the small foyer. He was proud of the door. Ben had been too.

Burke sighed heavily. He was so hot, perspiration dripped from his elbows. Wiping his face and neck and arms did no good because the blue-and-white faded cotton square was already soaked with his sweat. The sun was down, he noticed, behind one tall pine at the west end of the house. That meant he had enough water left until quitting time. At the water bucket on the shady end of the porch, he poured a little onto the bandanna and refreshed his face and his bare, heavily muscled chest.

He surely needed Ben to help hang that heavy door, but before he left today, somehow, the door would be hung. There might even be time, he thought, to put on the ornate brass lock, Mrs. Cummings's "touch of excess," as she said. The handsome lock was going to look pretty silly on the modest cottage. It was more the kind of hardware he might use on the Stiles house over on the Etowah. *If* he decided to build the house at all. There were still so many unanswered questions. Did he really want to take on such a big job without Ben? Would it be wise to sign a contract that would keep him in almost constant touch with Savannah? Had Natalie really made up her mind to go back peacefully once her parents returned?

Resting on the front steps before tackling the heavy door, he groaned, "Natalie—oh, Natalie!" The sound of his voice speaking her name brought back an earlier afternoon soon after he and Ben had laid the foundation for the Cummings cottage when Ben had caught Burke saying, "Natalie—oh, Natalie!" Ben had teased him that afternoon, but that was before his friend had seen her.

Lost in thought, he picked up a handful of curled shavings and inhaled their pungent rawness.

"Ben, Ben, *Ben* . . ."

Steady, always sensible Ben had let himself fall in love with someone so far out of his reach as to drive him to—to what? Certainly, to make him lose every shred of common sense. Still, Burke thought, what in blazes does common sense have to do with love? Nothing. Nothing at all, or he, Burke Latimer, would never have kept the vision of the graceful body, the blistered, beautiful face, the sun-bleached, glowing hair in his own heart through the long year in which he'd forced himself to stay away from her. If anyone understood the fever in Ben's soul, he did. His heart ached for Ben—ached at the thought that Mackay's gut feeling might be right. . . .

He got to his feet and went into the small foyer where his tool chest stood in one corner. From it, he took a hammer, two chisels—one a half-inch, the other an inch—then began to size up Elma Cummings's thick, wide front door. Too wide and too heavy for the general proportions of the cottage, but on such minor points as the size of the door and the brass lock, in order to get his way on larger structural details, he'd given in to the lady. The Cummingses would be dropping by later on. He meant to have that outsized door hung, even without Ben. It took all his strength to lift it, but lift it he did, carried it to the entrance and set it down briefly before attempting to hold it up over the sill to check the fit.

With every passing hour, although not exactly concentrating on it, he found his interest in the Stiles house mounting. It might be a relief, he thought, not to have the owners coming by daily to pass judgment on every nail driven and every plank sawed. He'd never actually seen the picturesque Etowah River cliffs, but he knew the Stiles land had once been the site of a thriving Cherokee village. His deep attachment to Ben and Mary, the firsthand knowledge from them of the peaceful, civilized way of the Cherokees, had strengthened his already pronounced sympathy with them in their tragedy. Most people now knew that some four thousand had died on the long march west. The thought of their deserted cabins over on the river haunted him. If he did make up his mind to take the job, he'd surely be living in one of the old cabins, among the ghosts of people who had once been happy and productive when the good, rich farmland around the cliffs was theirs.

He had lived in an Indian cabin with Mary and Ben, but somehow, because the old lady had died of natural causes, he hadn't thought in terms of Cherokee ghosts. The still sharp memory of his cabin crumbled into a black, smoking heap—of Miss Lib and Natalie and Mary lying on the ground—of the pony whinnying in fear from the barn out back—of Ben's dark face—still drained even Burke's physical energy. The heavy door loomed larger, the task of hanging it alone almost insurmountable.

Leaning against the door frame, he felt painfully alone. He had no home now—no home anywhere on the face of the earth. A stark loneliness he'd never experienced even in his solo wanderings, gripped him. Maybe he should just pack up and hit the road again. Ben might never come back. Natalie, maybe even Mary, would be gone soon. Where—dear God, *where* would he find the strength to watch Natalie drive away, out of his sight—now that he'd held her in his arms again?

He'd seen her every day since the fire, but they seldom mentioned it. Was he angry over what she'd done? Had he ever been? No. Exasperated, yes, because anyone with a nose knew fat pine from oak. Natalie simply had never learned that too much resin-filled pine exploded in a fire. And the reason she hadn't learned was simple—a servant had always built and tended fires for her.

Taking a deep breath, he hoisted the door into place. As nearly as he could tell in the few seconds he was able to hold it, not much trimming would be needed. Ben, as always, had his measurements accurate. Time now to set the hinges.

As he worked, Burke's mind went again to Natalie. In one of their few talks alone, she'd left no doubt whatever that *she* wanted him to build the Stiles house. "I know Miss Lib and Uncle W.H.," she'd said, full of anticipation. "They'll make lots of trips up here to see how you're doing. And you know I'll come with them—every time, don't you?"

They had been standing together on the hotel porch one evening, when she'd urged him to take the job, and as she spoke, her hands held his face. The memory of that touch, instead of helping, deepened his loneliness. She had promised him that she'd go back to Savannah with her parents and wait until he was ready to marry her. He knew she might still scheme, was cunning and ingenious, but Burke took the promise seriously. He had to. He believed her. He knew she was going.

Both hinges firmly in place on the door, he oiled them, worked them back and forth, his mind still on the incredible fact that soon Natalie would be gone. The thought of more weeks, months without even a glimpse of her, without her nearness was becoming unbearable. Holding his face between her dear hands, her eyes holding his, she had promised so sensibly, so sincerely to go away, that he had longed to embrace her right there on the hotel porch and beg her to take back the promise!

He measured the door and its frame and tried the fit again, only now facing the impossible problem of attaching it without Ben to hold it in place. There was, after all, no law that said he *had* to have the door hung by the time the Cummingses arrived. Tomorrow, he could pick up a man in town to work for a few hours. It wouldn't seem right for a stranger to help hang Ben's beautifully built door, but he'd never allowed his feelings to interfere with a job to be done.

Face beaded with sweat, Burke leaned the door against the foyer wall and went to refresh himself again from the water bucket on the porch. The shadow of the big sycamore reached all the way to the roof of the cottage. The Cummingses would be here within the hour, for sure. As though disciplining himself—for what, he didn't know—he lifted the door again into its frame. Muscles trembling, he was struggling once more to center the thick door when two strong, brown hands lightened its weight.

He had not heard a sound, but there was Ben, helping him settle the door in place. . . .

Accepting the help in silence, Burke quickly began to drop in the hinge pins, swung the door a couple of times, then stepped back into the foyer and stared at his disheveled, dirty, almost wild-eyed friend. *Were* Ben's eyes—wild? Or were they simply blacker than ever with anger or jealousy or rejection? The word *rejection* stuck. And, abruptly, Burke remembered the ugly, crooked scar across Ben's buttocks where the Georgia guardsman's bayonet had ripped him. Except for his friendship, Mary's devotion and what had seemed a staunch faith that God still loved him, Ben's life, he knew, had, for the past year, been one of rejection.

Neither had yet spoken. Each stood, staring at the other. Burke dared not take his eyes off Ben because, unreal as it seemed, he was afraid of what his friend might do.

Hoping to break the heavy silence, he held out his hand to Ben, who made no move to take it.

Finally, Burke said, "I've—really missed you. That door's heavy as lead."

"You need me!" Ben's voice was a taunt.

"Yes. I need you bad. Right this minute, in fact." Still without taking his eyes from Ben's, he reached down for the big plane and handed it to him. "Want to try your hand at shaving off a little on that far side? When it swells it still has to clear."

He was taking a chance. Aware that Ben knew the door could be ruined by two or three plane strokes too many—having no idea whether Ben meant him harm or good—he still held out the plane, waiting. "Well?"

The merest frown drew at Ben's brow. "You—trust me to do it? The Cummingses will never pay for another door if I spoil this one."

"I know that. Go ahead."

The brown fingers closed over the handle of the tool as Burke swung the door a few more times to verify the dragging edge. Then, with no help from Ben, he removed the pins, heaved the door up and off the hinges and laid it with a thud across the sawhorse. "All right," he said. "See what you can do with that far edge."

"You're—not going to ask me where I've been?"

"I can see you haven't been near a basin of water." There was another long silence and Burke added, "I'm just glad you're here. Go on. Fix the door for me."

As deft as ever, with his usual intense concentration, Ben planed the far edge of the door—just so. This time, he helped Burke rehang it, then reached himself to swing it back and forth over the wide-board floor. The fit was perfect.

A little less apprehensive now, Burke managed a smile. "I see you haven't lost your skill. Welcome back."

Ben whirled and landed one heavy blow on Burke's chin that sent him sprawling against the rear wall of the foyer.

For a moment, he lay there, rubbing his chin—glancing at the blood on his hand where he'd touched it—then, fearing the worst again, scrambled quickly to his feet.

Ben was standing in the open doorway, the anger, the wildness, the rejection—or all three—gone from his dark eyes.

"I had to—do that," he said softly.

Burke asked, "Do you know why?"

Ben nodded. "Yes, but I'm sorry I had to. No one has been such a friend to me. No one will ever be."

"What did you do all the time you were gone?"

"Prayed to God to cleanse my heart of hatred for my only friend, Burke Latimer."

"I see." Burke thought a minute, then decided the question had to be put to Ben: "You—love Miss Natalie, don't you?"

Seeming to ignore the question, Ben said, "I did not pray all the time I was gone. I listened, too. God told me to come back to help *you.* In a dream, I learned that I will never have another friend as true as you, Burke. And that is all that matters now. I will accept what I have."

"Did you eat anything while you were gone?"

"Mostly berries. And I know I—stink."

"You do. But we can take care of that. We can feed you, too."

Ben's eyes brimmed with tears. "We have no home, Burke. No place to—wash or sleep."

"The Cummingses, I'm sure, will let you sleep here. I've got a bed at the Bentleys' house. We'll find another home. Don't worry. There's a little water left in the bucket on the porch. No soap, but the way you look, even plain water will help."

"My sister—where is Mary Willow? How is her poor eye and cheek?"

"She's in a room at the States' Rights Hotel. Natalie and Miss Lib and now, her brother, are looking after her. Mr. Mackay came back today."

"Mary will see from her eye again?"

"We don't know about that yet. But they took her to a doctor three times to have it treated and dressed. She's—all right, Ben. Up and around a lot of the time now, Natalie tells me."

"You have not seen—Mary?"

"I visited her twice."

"Good." The look Ben gave him was a heart-searing mixture of resignation and plainly visible pain. "Mary Willow is better than I am," he said. "She would never do what I did. Thank you for visiting her. I know what it meant to her to see you."

Burke gave him an affectionate poke on the shoulder. "Come on, I need a little of that water to clean the blood off my face and then see what you can do for the dirt on yours before the Cummingses get here."

"I am back to stay by your side."

"I know that. I know that, Ben. And we just may have big things to do up ahead. I'll tell you about it later. For now, we both need to wash up."

FIFTY-FOUR

WHEN JUPITER drew the carriage up in front of the States' Rights Hotel that afternoon, Caroline saw their daughter first. Even before Natalie leaped from a porch rocker and hurried, still limping a little, down the wooden steps, she noticed how short her hair had been cut. Eliza Anne and William were still on the hotel porch, but Natalie headed for the carriage, both arms open in welcome.

"Mama, Papa," she cried, her face glowing.

"She seems to be limping," Mark said, "but I guess nothing went too wrong. Look at that happy face, Caroline."

"And that cropped hair! What on earth made her do that?"

Beside the carriage, they hugged all around—Eliza Anne and William there too, now.

"The return of our honeymooners!" Eliza Anne said, kissing Caroline. "Tell us, did you two have a beautiful holiday?"

"We did indeed," Mark said, embracing her. "But oh, my poor business back in Savannah! I dread to pick up the mail that must be waiting. We shouldn't have stayed so long." He shook William's hand. "I'm glad you're here, William. Was your trip successful?"

"Hush, Papa," Natalie ordered, hobbling ahead as they climbed the steps. "We have far too much to tell you to talk about William's business trip."

"You're limping, Natalie," Caroline said. "How did you hurt yourself? And what have you done to your hair?"

Natalie plopped down in a porch rocker. "Oh, a dumb accident in the woods, Mama. I wasn't hurt at all compared to poor little Mary

McDonald. She's still upstairs in my room—in bed. She can get up some now, but she lost a lot of blood and has to rest most of the time yet."

"What kind of accident?" Mark asked. "What were you doing in the woods with Mary?"

"Well, Papa, there was this wild cat or panther or something that screamed and screamed—the mare I was riding got scared and started to run. She threw me off and then when she raced past Mary —Mary was hunting flowers for Burke to bring me that night—one of the stirrups hit her in the face. She'll probably have an ugly scar for life and may even lose the sight of one eye. But we're taking care of her and Burke is almost finished with the Cummings house and Miss Lib and Uncle W.H. are going to hire him to build their big house over on the Etowah River!"

"Natalie, please slow down," Caroline pleaded.

"By all means, darling," Mark urged. "Give William and Eliza Anne a chance to fill us in a little. Latimer is really going to build your house, Eliza Anne?"

"I certainly hope he'll agree," Eliza Anne said. "He's done a remarkable job on the Cummings cottage. Wait till you see it."

"Burke's thinking it over," William explained. "Meeting me here today after work with his answer."

"You see, William is acting as W.H.'s agent," Eliza Anne said, "with full authority to close the deal. I'm really awfully pleased."

"But, Natalie, how does it happen that Mary is here at the hotel and not at Burke's cabin?" Caroline asked, trying her best to sort things out. "And will the child actually be blind in one eye?"

In a torrent of earnest explanation, Natalie told them that she had burned down Burke's cabin, and that Ben had just run away into the woods, so that they had to bring Mary to town in order to look after her. "Burke thinks Ben is gone for good," she went on, "so I've decided we'll take poor Mary back to Savannah to live with us until she's well again. You see, there's no doctor here. Oh, there was a grumpy young one who was visiting the Bentleys, but he's gone now, so there's no sense leaving Mary here alone in her condition. I'm sure she's in love with Burke—or thinks she is—but that's all right. I expect that, and I don't necessarily like my big decision, but it's final. As I told Miss Lib—"

"Natalie!" Caroline interrupted. "What decision? What on earth are you talking about? *Slow down!*"

"My decision to go back to Savannah with you. It's really Burke's doing. Oh, Mama—Papa, to me, he's the world's wisest, most splendidly superior man!"

"We gathered that," Caroline said, "but—"

"I do need a chance to explain, you know—without so many interruptions, Mama. So, please, will you both listen carefully?"

A smile was playing at the corners of her daughter's mouth now—an easy kind of almost modest smile Caroline did not find at all familiar.

"Burke is convinced that I'm just not ready to manage a household up here in his beloved wilds," Natalie went on. "He's right. It kills me to admit it, but he is. After all, I did burn down his cabin—all the way to the ground—the one time I was trying to help. He's just as determined to marry me as I am to marry him, but as he says, someone has to show common sense, and I've decided to be the one. *I'm going back to Savannah,* take cooking lessons and sewing lessons from Maureen and Gerta and—"

"Darling," Mark broke in, to Caroline's relief. "Your mother and I are doing our best, but could you slow down just a little?"

"Why? I've waited all this time to tell you about the enormous change in me—to show you that I'm a woman now, with a sane, practical viewpoint, who means to be the most efficient, capable wife a man ever had!"

Dumbfounded, Caroline said weakly, "I—I'm trying to understand, Natalie."

"Oh, Mama, I hope you can. It's all as plain as the nose on your face." Turning to her father, she added, "Papa, I'm sure *you* understand every bit of what I've said. You always do."

Caroline decided to wait for Mark to respond to the too-familiar trap Natalie had laid for him.

With a half-laugh, he said, "I'm—trying, too, little girl. I'm really trying."

Natalie let a few seconds tick by before she said doubtfully, "Well, I don't think you're trying very hard, or you wouldn't call me 'little girl.' Miss Lib, please tell them—you try convincing them that they simply have *not* come back to the same daughter they left."

"I—I have to admit," Eliza Anne said carefully, "that this is the first I've heard of your plan to take Mary back to Savannah with us, Natalie, but—"

"William knows," Natalie interrupted. "I told William. He came out here on the porch earlier today and I was sitting right here—in my new way—thinking things through. So I told William all about it."

Caroline was watching Eliza Anne's face closely, hoping for a clue. Either Natalie was being extraordinarily clever with all this mature, reasonable talk—or something *had* happened to her. Eliza Anne did seem to be taking the child seriously.

"I guess I'm not quite accustomed to your—'new way' yet, either, Natalie," Eliza Anne said, "but"—she turned to Caroline—"you and Mark have a lot to be thankful for. In the face of quite upsetting events, Natalie has been remarkable. I hope you will both take my word for it that I actually *saw* her begin to change right while Mary and I were still lying flat on our backs on the ground beside the smoldering cabin."

Mark looked from William to Natalie, to Eliza Anne, then asked, "Why in the world were you lying on the ground?"

"Papa, I told you—I'd just burned down Burke's cabin!"

"Natalie saved Mary's life," Eliza Anne said. "I was outside struggling to draw a bucket of water from the deepest well in the world when the cabin burst into flames. I couldn't believe my eyes! There she was—through all the fire and thick smoke, dragging Mary outside to safety. It's a wonder they weren't both—cremated! The fire, of course, is why we had to cut Natalie's hair."

"Where were Burke and Ben when the place burned?" Mark asked.

"At work, Papa! Miss Lib and I were at Burke's cabin caring for Mary."

"As I understand it," William said, "Burke and Ben came home in the wagon and found the house in smoking ruins and the three women on the ground."

"And that's when Ben just ran crashing into the woods and disappeared," Natalie explained.

"Does anyone know why?"

"No, Caroline," William said. "Pulling a trick like that isn't like the Ben McDonald I know, but he's gone just the same."

"Leaving his sister alone and injured?"

"It's all right about that, Mama. We're taking Mary home with us."

"That's a charitable impulse, Natalie," Caroline said, controlling her voice, "but we'll have to talk more about that later."

"I certainly don't intend to leave her alone with Burke! So, there's nothing to discuss. It's all settled. And since I'm going back with you to learn all about how to do everything, I'll see to it that Mary's no trouble to you or Papa. Honest, I will."

"You know your father and I will want to do the charitable thing, Natalie, but—"

"Mama, it is not charitable! It's my new common sense—plain and simple. The poor girl may go blind in that eye, she fancies herself in love with Burke and I'm not leaving her here alone with him. Charity has nothing whatever to do with it. Charity would insult both Mary and Ben anyway. Indians are human beings—just like us. Burke says the Cherokees are proud people."

On a sigh, Caroline muttered, "I'm sure they are."

"You say, William, that Latimer is coming here this evening?" Mark asked.

"Yes," Eliza Anne answered for her brother. "I've written to W.H. He's responded quite positively to Burke's building our house, *if* Burke agrees. That's just one of the many tragedies of Ben's disappearing the way he did. Burke needs him. You know neither W.H. nor I will settle for inferior work, and Burke says Ben's turned into a real craftsman."

"You're calling him—Burke too, now, Eliza Anne?"

"Oh, Caroline, yes. I like him so much! Really, such a lot has happened while you were gone, we've all gotten very well acquainted. I'm sure it's being hard for you both to catch up."

Trying to sound somewhat pleasant, Caroline said, "Yes, it's quite the most monumental effort I've made in a long time."

"What about Mary, Natalie?" Mark asked. "Does Mary want to go back to Savannah?"

"Oh, I haven't told her yet, Papa, but she'll have to agree. I'll just inform her that since her brother vanished and since the cabin's gone, we're taking her home with us. I'll tell her tonight after she and I have gone to bed. There aren't any extra rooms in the hotel. Miss Lib and I will move in with Mary. Poor Burke has to stay at the Bentleys'. Mary may not want to go to Savannah, but I'll handle that. We're friends."

While the carriage was being unloaded, Eliza Anne and Caroline mounted the stair inside the hotel to wait for the trunks in the Brownings room. Still flabbergasted, Caroline said, "Evidently, the minute we drove out of sight, things began to happen here."

"The minute I fell asleep for my first afternoon nap, to be exact," Eliza Anne said, unlocking the door. "I don't suppose I need to tell you that I'm not at all sure sending you both away was the best idea I've ever had."

In the room, Caroline gave Eliza Anne her direct look. "On the contrary, it may have been one of your very best. *If* you really see a change in her for the better. Do you?"

"I certainly see the beginning of a change. She now seems perfectly peaceful about marrying Burke much later on. Oh, she will marry him. I'd wager my spotless reputation on that. But, Caroline, she burned down the cabin because she's totally unequipped to manage a house. Like you and me, Natalie hasn't needed domestic skills ever before. Our servants have spoiled us—we tell them what to do, but they're the ones who know *how*."

Caroline sighed. "I'm aware of all that. Tell me, how did—Burke take it? What on earth did he say when she burned down his house?"

"He was astonishingly gentle with her. That log cabin was all he had, but he—he wasn't angry with her. You see, she disarmed us all by taking full blame. Oh, being Natalie, I expect her idea of what she now calls 'common sense' to be somewhat different from ours. But also, being Natalie, she will learn fast. That ghastly day, she seemed to see herself as totally inadequate to life up here. She admitted it, too. I think she really saw her selfishness. And isn't seeing oneself usually the first step toward changing?"

Caroline fell across the bed. For a time, neither spoke. Finally, she said, "You were right to send us on the trip. We might have kept her away from Burke's cabin had we been here, but undoubtedly we'd also have shielded her from seeing how headstrong she's always been." She paused. "Remember what your wise mother says when something dreadful happens? 'God makes redemptive use of—everything.' I've made up my mind to rely on that."

"What about this grand gesture of taking Mary back to Savannah? Or are you too weary and stunned to think about that yet?"

"Yes, I am. What's more, I intend to let Mark make that decision. If our daughter is finally growing up, both her parents had better grow up too. Mark tends to leave the hard decisions to me and I tend to accept them too readily." She took a deep breath. "I will not be the one to decide about Mary. Natalie and her father are welcome to the full responsibility for Burke's little Cherokee maiden. I'll just keep still about it—now and forever."

"Good luck," Eliza Anne said. "Good luck to us all—especially to Natalie."

Caroline sat up. "Especially—to Natalie?"

"You and Mark have had to absorb so much—in such a short time, but I've been here, right with her—through almost everything. And I confess my heart is somehow—breaking over her. I can't explain it, so don't ask. But maybe for the first time in her life, she's—truly vulnerable."

Just before sundown, William jumped to his feet when Burke knocked at the door of his room.

"Ben came back," Burke announced, as soon as they both sat down. "This afternoon, just when I was struggling with that heavy front door, there he was—helping me lift it into place."

"Did he say why he ran off—and stayed so long?"

"He told me in part."

"But you're not saying, is that it?"

"That's it."

"Looks like somebody hit you on the chin pretty hard. You two didn't come to blows, did you?"

"No. He knocked me down, but we didn't fight. And he's facing facts. He needs me. I need him. I haven't told him any details about the Stiles job, but he'll go with me. He and I can fix up one of those empty Cherokee cabins over there to live in. Oh, and by the way, I've just told Mary Ben is back. Eliza Anne went with me to see her. Mary hadn't heard a word about Natalie's plan to take her to Savannah. I guarantee she won't go. She's too happy to be moving to Etowah Cliffs to live."

William gave him a sly smile. "I take it that means you're going to accept the job."

"Yes, sir, I am," Burke said. "With Ben."

"Where is he now?"

"Back at the Cummings house. They agreed to let him sleep there until we're finished with the work."

"And when will that be?"

Burke stretched both arms over his head and thought a minute. "Even if we get some rain, most of our work is inside from now on. With luck, Ben and I could be finished in a month. It'll take another month, at least, to round up more carpenters. I may have to go to Augusta myself. I want to see a sample of their work before I hire them on."

"So, a couple of months yet, anyway."

"Correct. I mean to build a good house for Miss Lib's family. I want high-grade supplies and dependable men who know what they're doing."

"I expect W.H. will settle for two months. I'd do my best, though, if I were you, not to wait any longer than that to get started. You should know, Burke, that one of the big reasons he's moving his family up here is political ambition. He's only one of several outstanding lawyers in Savannah. There won't be much opposition in these parts and he intends to get himself elected to the U.S. Congress. Wants to be living in Cass County by the end of next year—1840. That will give him time to move around the countryside and make himself known. Can you finish one wing of his house in a year?"

"I can certainly try."

"Good." William told him then that the Brownings were back from Lookout Mountain.

"I saw a fine carriage in the street outside the hotel. I figured it had to be theirs."

"They got in early this afternoon, but Natalie had such a story for them, I figure they're both still reeling from it. You might be interested to know she told them she's willing to go home to Savannah until you're ready for her—until she's learned how to keep house."

"She really told them that?"

"That's right. I heard it myself."

Burke was silent for a time. Then, frowning, he said, "I—I guess she means it, doesn't she?"

"You don't look too happy or relieved. I thought that's what you wanted."

Burke shook his head. "Aw, Mackay, it isn't what I *want!* It's the way it has to be for now. Where is she?"

"We all came upstairs and left her rocking away on the front porch. You didn't see her when you came in?"

"No."

"Most likely Eliza Anne will know where she is. Maybe in her room getting all spruced up for you. Natalie knows you were coming to talk about the Stiles house. Which reminds me, we'd better settle our business. Let me get the contract W.H. drew up, get you to sign it and give you the tidy sum of one thousand dollars to start you out." From a drawer, William took a long legal paper, unfolded it, handed it to Burke and sat down to wait while he read.

"Well, I certainly never read such an elaborate contract! I didn't even have one with the Cummings." Burke grinned. "But this looks all right to me. I'm ready to sign it."

William opened the inkwell and gave Burke a quill. "You or I could have put it all into about six lines, but W.H. is a lawyer. He can't resist those splendid archaic phrases. You're going to like him, even though he seems at first somewhat aristocratic in his tastes. He's literary, revels in elegant furniture, china, crystal, and, I should add—excellent architecture."

"I'll take my chances on pleasing him," Burke said, as he signed the agreement with a flourish. "And I'll probably like him." He blew on the signature, handed the papers to William and stood up, a big smile on his face. "Miss Lib likes him. That's enough for me."

From his jacket pocket, William produced a bank draft, which Burke looked at proudly for a moment, then slipped in his shirt pocket. "I should have apologized, Mackay, for keeping our appointment in my shirt sleeves. You see, just before she set my cabin afire, Natalie was evidently mending the torn lining in my one good jacket. That jacket, along with Mary, was all she managed to save. I fully intended to wear it this afternoon. Thought she'd be pleased." Burke grinned. "I couldn't."

"Why not?"

"She'd sewed the lining together. Couldn't get my arm in the sleeve."

William laughed, gave Burke an encouraging pat on the shoulder and sent him off to find Natalie.

FIFTY-FIVE

BURKE had only to step outside William's room in the narrow hall. She was waiting for him—in something filmy and cream-colored, face glowing, cropped hair a mass of curls so lustrous she seemed to light up the dingy passageway. For an instant they stood, not five feet apart, beaming at each other. Then, still limping a little, she rushed into his arms.

On impulse, he picked her up and carried her down the hotel stair, out onto the porch and up the street. In plain view of hotel guests and townspeople, he strode past the shoemaker's, the newspaper office, two churches, a row of low shops and houses, Natalie clinging to him, both unmindful that pedestrians and storekeepers, men on horseback and in wagons, all gaped at the sight.

She didn't fuss or kick or rebel. She cared no more than he that people would talk and stare because a grown man was carrying a grown woman in his arms along the main street of Cassville at sundown. His impulse seemed as right, as natural to Natalie, as to him. Neither had said a word, but he could tell. Who cared what people thought? They were alone again. Alone—even on a public street, almost as they had been on the raft. And suddenly, for no reason he could explain, they were in less turmoil than they had ever been. He was holding her. She was holding him. Nothing had been said to tangle things, to cloud the moment. For this instant there were no threats. Beyond this, Burke refused to think. He was not thinking now. He was aware only of loving her. Of her loving him.

He was headed for one certain white oak tree at the edge of town and the wide rock shaped like a seat that had pushed its way out of the earth beneath the enormous tree. He was taking her to a spot where he had often found refuge during the months in which he and Ben had worked on the Cummings house. Troubled times that had sent him striding alone toward this spot under this tree.

He had tried to make a good home for his two friends. Had tried to teach Ben all he knew about the work. But, when longing for Natalie had seemed almost to choke him, Burke had fled even from the pleasant company of Ben to the tree and its hollowed-out rock. There was a spring in his step now and she felt as light as a leaf in his arms. Somehow it was right—at last—to be taking Natalie there.

Striding past the last weed-choked open field, he reached the tree and stopped. He held her, gazed down at her, as she looked, unsmiling, up at him, her arms still around his neck. Gently then, he lowered her onto his rock under the thick, summer-green branches of the big oak and eased himself down beside her. For a long moment, they sat there, drinking in the joy of being alone.

"This is my favorite spot," he said, "how do you like it?" Before she could answer, he was kissing her. Kissing her too long, too deeply, but unable to think beyond the bright conviction that no woman ever responded to a man's kisses as Natalie responded to his. The bright conviction stretched into an almost blinding light that revealed to him, without his needing to ask, that she had never kissed another man as she had freely, eagerly kissed him from the first.

"Burke," she breathed. "Burke, I don't want to—leave you again! And I'm—going to. I'm going—back—to Savannah with my parents. . . ."

"Don't talk about that now. Not yet, please!"

"But I think it's going to be soon. From what my father said after he read his mail. Burke, I'm so afraid it's going to be the day after tomorrow."

He kissed her eyes, so round, so dear with shining, so full of sky. Then he stopped to hold her, desperate to ease a little of the pain for himself—for her. Pain that could not really be satisfied for a long, long time.

"Papa hasn't said yet, but—"

"Don't talk, Natalie. Just let me hold you." The silence, her dear closeness were torment and enchantment. She belonged to him—to him alone. He held the perfect head against his chest, his hand tingling at the touch of curling copper hair.

"Burke . . ."

"Sh-h. Wait. Don't say anything. Just be here, Natalie. Just be here —with me."

She grabbed one of his hands and began to caress each finger, then, quite violently, she bent back one finger, then another. "I know I'm hurting you," she breathed, her arms around him again, head pushed bone-hard into his breast. "But I—have to! I didn't know growing up would be so—awful! It's—awful, just awful. Don't make us wait, Burke," she pleaded. "Don't, don't, *don't!* Nothing could be harder than this, could it? Could anything be worse than this?"

With a wild little cry, she shoved him away and jumped to her feet. For a moment, she stood above him, while he sat there, caught by those beautiful eyes—pale, almost catlike—but so innocent, he was held motionless on the rock, unable to do more than look up at her. Only once before, on the cabin porch, had her young, urgent passion reached for him as it was reaching now, all of it there—in those eyes, never so maddening. Never so *innocent.* It was the innocence that kept him rooted to the rock. Dear God, his heart cried, what can I do with *innocence* in a woman who looks the way she looks, feels the way she feels?

"Burke," she whispered, her eyes darkening with something akin to fear. "What makes—loving hurt so much? *Why won't you tell me?*"

A gentleman would stand because a lady was standing. He still sat, his eyes fixed on the child-woman who, by her bewildered question, was telling him that when, at long last, he did take her, he would be the first . . . the first. His voice faltered. "You—really don't know, do you? You—really don't know!"

When, without a word, she crumpled onto the rock beside him again, he struggled to quiet himself, to remember that he longed for far more than the unaffected response of her body; that he loved all of Natalie—the quicksilver mind, the abandoned heart, the wild, free spirit.

"Do you think we could—talk now?" she asked, her breath still uneven, her voice misty.

"Yes, dearest girl. We can talk now. We'd better."

The reddening sun was beginning to sink so low in the cloud-streaked summer sky that, here and there in the woods beyond his rock, shafts of light picked out one tree to touch, then another— then a short, thick bush—as though a heavenly finger pointed here and there and there.

"Look, darling," he said. "Right beyond that dead sycamore. Do you see?"

"Flowers," she gasped. "Burke, it's a whole tree full of—pale pink flowers!"

He smiled down at her. "That's exactly what I hoped you'd see."

"How could I not see? In all the time I've been up here, I've never seen a tree full of pale pink flowers. . . ."

His own pain eased, and as though she had spoken the words, had told him, he knew that her pain, which she did not understand, was easing too. Motionless, full of wonder, she sat watching the tree. Burke watched her. Then he saw the slow, delicate change of expression on her face—and, in pure delight, she turned to him.

"They're gone! The flowers are—just *gone!*"

"That's because they were never really there—except in our eyes," he said.

"But I want them back! Burke, they were the most beautiful flowers I've ever seen. . . ."

He took her hand. "We won't ever forget them. But they couldn't last. Maybe because God knows we can't stand such beauty—for long at a time."

Her fingers tightened on his. "The pain you won't explain to me —was beautiful, too, wasn't it?" Giving him no time to answer, almost as though she sensed that he couldn't, she whispered, "What caused the flowers?"

"The sunset. Just for that short time, a shaft of light made plain old leaves look like flowers."

After a moment, she said, "Leaves will never be plain old leaves to me again. Not ever." Then, in her straightforward way: "Burke, I'm going back to Savannah to learn how to live in a log cabin with you."

He laughed softly. "Without burning it down?"

She hit him, but not very hard. "Our nurse, Gerta, can mend better than anybody in town, and Maureen, our Irish cook, can teach me how to make—everything to eat. Old Prince at Knightsford can teach me how to find things in the woods, can explain all about digging sassafras roots to make tea for you. Mary says you love

sassafras tea. So do I, but I never thought about digging it or—
anything. I will—I'm going to learn it all."

Right now, far more than in the storm of their passion, he loved
her. "You won't ever stop being Natalie, though, will you?"

The tiny frown—Burke had noticed that her father frowned in the
same fleeting way—came and went. "Was I, Natalie, on the raft?"

"Oh yes! You were the—very best Natalie. The one I love."

"Good, because now that I'm older, I'm sure that's the way I
really am. You see, when we were out there alone—on the ocean—
there wasn't anyone trying to make me—what I'm not. I had only
you out there, not parents, dear as they both are. Not even Miss Lib
being wise and careful with me." She kissed his hand. "I'll be back
up here all ready to marry you and take care of you and your house
in no time, I'm sure. You'll see. I learn fast."

"But, dearest girl, don't you understand? *I* won't be ready anytime soon."

"I will be, so you don't need to be. 'Being ready' to you means
getting rich enough to build us a big house and hire a whole army of
servants. I don't want either. A huge house would be silly—I loved
you on our raft." She patted the still-warm rock. "I love you right
here under this tree. A big house has too many rooms, all too far
apart. I need to be close to you. Servants swarming all over the place
would mean we weren't absolutely—alone. I want to be absolutely
alone again, Burke, the way we were in the middle of the ocean.
Every minute out there—danger and blisters and all—was better
than ducking around hotel rooms and hallways and hunting rocks to
sit on! Out there on those big waves, we were—us. It would even
have been all right if we died, because we'd have died alone—
together."

"Natalie . . . do you know what you're saying?"

"If I don't, who does?" He had no answer for that. There wasn't
time anyway, because she was already leaping ahead in her plans.
"And I want you to help me with Mary, too. I informed her that we
were taking her back to Savannah to a real doctor and that she could
live in our house as long as she needed, so as to save her sight in that
eye, but Indians can be so stubborn. She vows she's staying right
here until Ben comes back. I came right out and told her that I had
no intention of leaving her up here alone with you and—"

"Wait a minute, hold your horses. Ben is back. He just appeared—dirty and smelling to high heaven—at the job today."

She heaved a sigh of relief. "Well, that takes care of everything."

"It does?"

"I won't worry as much about Mary's being here, if Ben is too. And you need him, don't you?"

"I certainly do. Even more now that I've signed a contract to build Miss Lib's mansion on the Etowah River."

Both arms circled his neck with joy. "Burke! That's the best news of all, because I do know Miss Lib and Uncle W.H. They'll be rolling up and down those roads from Savannah to the upcountry all the time! And you know who'll be with them—*every time,* don't you?"

"Maybe that's part of the reason I agreed to build their house. Do you suppose it could be?"

Not bothering to answer, she grew quite stern. "Miss Lib said that if you did decide to build their house, you'd fix up a cabin over there to live in, so I want you to have one thing straight."

"What's that?"

"I don't want either Ben or Mary living in the same cabin with you —or with us when I come back to marry you—even if you find an empty Indian cabin over there with twenty rooms!"

Joking seemed the best way to respond. "I doubt I'll find a Chero-kee—mansion."

"I'm serious. I don't want anyone around but us."

"Natalie, listen to me. They'll *have* to live with me at first, anyway. Mr. Mackay says Stiles is in a hurry for his house. I won't have time to remodel a whole Indian village before I get started. We won't have to decide anything else till later."

"That's right, because I've already decided."

He turned her face to him. "Natalie, you said you'd wait until I was ready for us to get married. You're sounding now as though you're the one to know when that is. It isn't going to be that way. I'll be the only person to know when. Agreed?"

"But I do learn fast," she argued, turning away. "How long do you expect me to endure all that Savannah social whirl and dullness once I know how to sew and dig sassafras?"

"Natalie, look at me. Do you trust me?"

"Yes."

"Then you have to trust me to know the right time for us. Just the same as you trusted me with your—life on that raft."

Looking straight up at him now, she thought for a while, then said, "Oh."

"What does 'oh' mean?"

"I thought you were waiting for lots of money and servants only because I don't know how to keep house."

"Darling, in my way I am, but—"

"I mended your jacket lining, didn't I?" When he smiled broadly, she asked, "What's funny? I not only mended your lining, I saved the jacket from the fire!"

"You also sewed the lining together front and back so I can't get my arm in the sleeve."

"I—did?"

He hugged her. "I shouldn't have told you. And it doesn't matter a bit. Mackay paid me the first money on the Stiles house. I intend to buy a new jacket and keep that one forever to remind me that you loved me enough to try to fix it anyway."

With a little smile, she said absently, "That's a sweet thought." Then, her mind going like the wind, he could tell, she sat for a long time looking off into the now darkly shadowed woods. Finally, she said, "All right. I'll wait—awhile—for you to say you're ready. But, when it gets to be too long, I'll simply tell Papa to bring me back up here. Burke, what you don't seem to understand is that I can bear it only so long without being near you."

She reached to touch his face and the awesome longing for her overpowered him again.

After several minutes in his arms, while he kissed her and held her and caressed her, she gasped, "Burke, I *can't* do it. I—thought I could, but—I can't leave you now!"

Ashamed, helpless, he held her closer, but said nothing.

"Can you—let me go, Burke? Can you really let me—go?"

He groaned, "I don't know—*I don't know*. . . ."

Darkness was filling the woods around them, still they clung together. Never had he known such desperation. "I—*have* to let you go. I have to, my—terrible, wonderful girl, but I—don't know *how* I can do it. . . ."

"You can't! And I can't—go!" Clinging to him, but turning her face away from his kisses, she said, "I—know I've told everyone I would go back and—learn about things. But I just can't do it now. I —meant it, too, when I said I would. You know I meant it, don't you?"

"Yes." His voice was low and tortured. "I know you did." He was trying to disengage her arms. She clung more closely. "Natalie, we've got to stop this!"

"Listen to me, Burke. There's a justice of the peace at the courthouse. Mr. Bentley introduced Miss Lib and me to him. Why can't we—get married up here—let me sleep beside you—just for one night, the way I slept beside you on the raft. Burke, please let me wake up and see your face just once and then, I *promise* I'll go home and—learn about sweeping floors and fat pine and sassafras and linings—everything! Wouldn't it help if we did that? Wouldn't waking up just once together help us both wait for whatever it is you have to accomplish? Wouldn't it—make this awful—hurt go away?"

Roughly, he pulled her arms from around his neck, pinned them to her sides and looked straight at her. "Would your parents give their permission? You're not eighteen yet."

"Yes! Oh yes, they would."

"How do you know?"

"I've known them for nearly eighteen years!"

He took a deep, deep breath and leaned back against the trunk of the tree. Feeling more helpless than at any time in his life, he said hoarsely, "Maybe that's—what we should do. But not unless you promise me you'll still—go back to Savannah when they leave—day after tomorrow."

She was on her feet again now. "I will! I will go back—as *Mrs. Burke Latimer.* Then, I'll be—safe."

He sat up. "Safe? From what?"

"From all those stupid balls and parties. From those—silly Savannah boys. Burke, if I'm *not* Mrs. Burke Latimer when I go home, I'll still be expected to go to—dances and parties and—"

He stood now, too. Scarcely realizing what he was doing, he gripped her shoulders and shook her. "That's exactly what I wanted you to do when I—left you in North Carolina. I can't bear the thought of any of it now! If you think they'll agree, we'll find a way to get married—tomorrow." Suddenly, he pulled her to him. "Then, oh, Natalie—then, I can—forbid you ever to look at another man."

FIFTY-SIX

ELIZA ANNE was proud of her peacemaking brother William when, the next afternoon, head held high, he stood with their small party in the tiny sanctuary of the frame church facing Courthouse Square. He'd agreed at once to act as Burke's groomsman in the hastily arranged ceremony that was about to begin. She knew taking part in a wedding was hard for him, but he had done a masterful job of bringing about the somewhat haphazard event. She was proud of Caroline and Mark too. They had agreed far more willingly than she'd dared hope. But it had been William's steady persuasion that had brought about the compromise—almost at the last moment—that had shifted the setting from the office of the justice of the peace to the plain, quaint altar of the Methodist Church where they all stood now, waiting for the minister to find his place in a book he held in his hands. The tall, balding man had been notified, after all, less than an hour ago that he had a wedding to perform.

Standing just behind Natalie, as her only attendant, Eliza Anne marveled that the one person in the party who did not appear nervous was Natalie. Wearing the only good gown she'd brought—a saffron-yellow silk with ribbon bandings and bows—she radiated quiet happiness as she held Burke's hand. The groom, obviously uncomfortable in a new dress coat, looked happy too. The sleeves of his coat were too short, but William had been unable to find another in town large enough to span the massive shoulders. For sentimental reasons, Burke had refused to allow anyone to rip out Natalie's unwearable mending in his other jacket. He does love her, Eliza

Anne thought. And so do her parents. Both had seemed more upset that—after only one night with Burke—Natalie would have to leave him, than at the sudden wedding itself. They love her unselfishly, but she pitied Mark, especially, because it was the press of his business that would force the cruel separation.

If the bumbling preacher ever found his place, the newlyweds would have tonight—one night—and then an absence whose end no one could foresee. To look at them now, though, no one would have guessed. Had those five uncertain days and nights at sea given Natalie and Burke a perspective on time itself—unknowable to the rest of them?

Eliza Anne caught Caroline's eye. The two exchanged weak smiles. Caroline, she noticed, clung even more tightly to Mark's hand than Natalie clung to Burke's.

Feet shuffled on the bare board floor of the church, as they all waited and waited. The minister evidently had been hunting for the wedding ceremony in the wrong book. After an embarrassed word of apology, he now mounted the pulpit and bent down to search for another book on a shelf beneath it. No one said a word. They all just shifted their feet again softly and waited.

I did all I could, Eliza Anne thought, to help, but it's been William who has kept us calm through the wild day of preparation that had the whole town talking. William and kind Mr. Fred Bentley, who secured the marriage license on such short notice. Mark had succumbed first, of course, but it had been William who hit upon the one way of persuading Caroline to agree to what was rapidly beginning to resemble a tragi-comedy. William had taken Caroline to the simple church, pointed out the intimacy of the sanctuary, the green blinds that would mellow the midafternoon light. But William had shown a stroke of genius when he told the Brownings that Natalie, even Burke, had agreed to still another ceremony back in Savannah at some future time—a proper, formal wedding in Christ Church.

As the nervous minister went on leafing through a second book— still up behind his pulpit—Eliza Anne's thoughts flew to Ben and Mary. It had also been William who went to see Ben at the Cummings cottage to break the news of the wedding. At the thought of Ben's agony, Eliza Anne sighed more loudly than she intended and the minister glanced down at her over his spectacles. Both Cherokee young people must be, right now, enduring the same heartbreak.

Ben, alone at the cottage, so loved Natalie. Mary, alone at the hotel, so loved Burke. Both had been invited. Both had refused. Everyone knew the truth now and everyone pitied them. Even Natalie had said at least three times during the hectic day that life just isn't fair. "Life is wonderful, Miss Lib, but it isn't a bit fair!" She *was* beginning to feel for someone else besides herself. She had even given in, finally, to Burke's living, temporarily at least, in the same cabin at Etowah Cliffs with his two Cherokees, so the big house there could be started as soon as possible.

Feeling wrinkled in her much-worn green silk—after all, they'd been in Cassville a long time—Eliza Anne gave her full attention to the minister, who had finally found his place in the right book and was back standing before the wedding party—ready to begin. He cleared his throat repeatedly and finally embarked on the familiar words of the ceremony that—for better or for worse—would make everyone's beloved Natalie Burke Latimer's wife.

The newlyweds left the wedding dinner given in their honor by the Bentleys and returned early to the hotel to spend their first and only night together in William's room. Eliza Anne would spend the night alone in the room with Mary. Knowing she had kept Caroline and Mark talking at the Bentleys' table far longer than either wanted to stay, she felt a bit guilty as she told them good night. She had lingered over dinner because she so dreaded facing heartbroken, injured Mary, the badly torn eye unbandaged now, but still sightless.

After leaving the Brownings, she knocked softly at the door of the room where they had left Mary, and when there was no answer, opened it to find her gone. The sagging bed had been neatly turned back for Eliza Anne, but Mary's one cotton dress, scorched from the fire, was not there. Needing desperately to tell someone, she hurried to the room William had been forced to share for that one night with two other men.

Agitated, she knocked on the door. When her brother, pulling on a dressing gown, joined her in the hallway, she whispered the bad news that Mary was missing. In no time, fully dressed, he rejoined her, and together, they walked hurriedly, lantern in hand, to the Cummings cottage.

Eliza Anne tiptoed inside after William, who had quietly pushed open the wide front door. There, on the floor in one corner of the small entrance hall, Mary lay on a pile of tree branches spread with the blanket Natalie had given Burke for Ben to sleep on. Beside her sat Ben, keeping watch.

Slowly, the young man lifted his head to look at them. In the light from William's lantern, Ben's eyes were black wells of anguish.

"Sorry if we woke you, Ben," William said gently. "My sister was worried when she didn't find Mary in their room at the hotel. We just came to be sure—you were both all right."

"You woke my sister, I guess," Ben said. "I wasn't asleep."

Eliza Anne hurried to kneel beside Mary, who looked up at her for a long moment, a long, difficult moment, during which Eliza Anne was unable to think of anything to say. Finally, she laid her hand on Mary's head. Surprisingly, but with total sincerity, Mary smiled at her.

"Thank you," the girl whispered. "We be—all right here—together. Sure. Ben always take care of me."

"I—suppose you've got something to eat for breakfast," William said, sounding as helpless as Eliza Anne felt.

Ben nodded. "Both of you—leave us alone, Mr. Mackay. Tonight, only my sister and I—can help—each other."

"We—help each other," Mary agreed, seeming truly eager to reassure them. "Do not worry. Ben will not leave me again."

After another awkward silence, William said, "I expect Burke will be here fairly early in the morning, Ben. He told me he plans to get in a good day's work."

"You see, we're all leaving for Savannah tomorrow right after breakfast," Eliza Anne offered.

"Except me," William said. "I'm staying to do what I can to help Burke round up supplies for the new Etowah River job."

"That's right," Eliza Anne said, longing to give them something to cling to. "Burke will be staying too, of course. And soon, the two of you—and Burke—will move to the Etowah River." She brightened her voice. "I'm sure Burke told you, Ben, that you'll be his right hand again when he builds the new house for my family and me. I'm awfully pleased about it."

"Yes, ma'am," Ben said flatly. "He told me."

Eliza Anne pushed William's arm up a little so the lantern light would fall on Mary's face. The girl said nothing, but Eliza Anne's last glimpse of her, before she and William left, helped a little. Mary was smiling and wiggling her fingers the way a small child waves good-bye.

Just after seven the next morning, Eliza Anne sat with Caroline on the hotel porch, while Mark and William supervised Jupiter's packing of the Browning carriage. She thought she'd never seen Caroline so tense, and although Eliza Anne tried, she found it hard to make conversation. It was a relief when Mark and William came for them. William, she noticed, didn't try to say anything. They all dreaded the departure. It was going to be terrible for everyone, so why try? Still, Eliza Anne couldn't help admiring Mark—and pitying him—because he was trying.

"It won't be long, Jupiter," he promised. "I know you're eager to be on the road. The newlyweds should be coming down any minute now."

As Mark settled the two women so that they faced each other in opposite carriage seats, Eliza Anne's throat tightened at the way Mark looked. Through most of the night, she'd heard him pace the floor. Now and then, in the quiet hours, she'd caught a snatch of low, restless talk between him and Caroline. Neither, she was sure, had slept any more than she had.

William gave some comfort, as they waited, just by being there.

"I wish you were going home with us, William," Eliza Anne called from her seat in the carriage. "Mama will be so disappointed."

"She'll understand," her brother answered. "W.H. said in his letter that he'd kept her informed about all the doings up here. She already knows I'm staying to see to Burke's supplies. Don't worry about Mama."

"I can just see her face when we tell her Natalie got married," Caroline said in a dazed voice. "She'll act happy about it, but I can't imagine what she might think of us for allowing it."

"If Natalie's happy, Miss Eliza will be satisfied," Mark said.

They were all working at being pleasant. They had to, because Natalie and Burke were still nowhere to be seen. Eliza Anne had ordered breakfast sent up to them in their room, giving them every possible final moment alone. Again and again, inwardly, she had shuddered to think of the agony they must be feeling—certain that

she could never, never have made herself leave W.H. the morning
after their wedding night.

I'd better gird myself, she thought. There's no telling what condition poor Natalie will be in when they do appear. No telling what
might happen when the time actually comes for her to say good-bye
to Burke.

"Have you seen anything of my daughter's luggage, Jupiter?"
Mark asked.

"Oh yes, sir, Mister Mark. Miss Natalie send it down more'n a
hour ago. I pack' it already."

After a nervous sigh, Caroline said, "Then she isn't up to anything like refusing to go with us. Mark, why don't you climb on into
the carriage too, so we can settle these small valises around our feet?
Jupiter can take Natalie's—when she gets here. It can ride up there
under the driver's seat."

"Caroline," Mark said. "I am not getting in until they come down.
I feel bad enough to be dragging her off today. Try to be patient. Try
to think how—you and I would have felt if we'd had to—"

"I don't *have* to try," Caroline said sharply. "I'm already—suffering with both of them!"

"Mama? Papa? We're coming," Natalie called from the hotel
porch.

Her voice sounded heavy with misery, Eliza Anne thought, but
firm. Natalie was not weeping and she was coming toward them now
across the porch, Burke beside her. He held her as close as he could,
as they moved slowly down the steep wooden steps.

"Sorry, Mr. Browning," Burke said, when they reached the carriage. "We—we tried not to keep you waiting too long."

Burke was in a far worse state than Natalie. Her lovely face was
drawn and tense, but determined to prove to them all that she was
not only grown up, but strong. A grown-up, married woman ready
to face—oh my Lord, Eliza Anne thought—she's facing one of the
cruelest moments a woman could ever be asked to face right now!
Much harder than most far older women could endure. . . .

Holding his hat, Mark stood to one side, as did William, when
Burke took her in his arms for the last time and kissed her long and
deeply.

Caroline reached across to grab Eliza Anne's hand. "I don't think
I can—stand this," she gasped. "It's—too terrible. Help me, Eliza

Anne—help me! *This is—cruel.* I know she brought it on herself, but would it have been this hard to tell him good-bye if they—weren't married?"

"I don't know," Eliza Anne whispered. "It's—just something we all have to—get behind us. This is what Natalie wanted." She squeezed Caroline's hand. "We'll simply have to—support her in every way we can—help her stay strong."

"Mark! Come here, Mark!" Caroline too was whispering now, as though fearful of disturbing the lovers, who were still clinging to each other. "I think I'll sit beside Eliza Anne. Move these valises. I'm sure Natalie's going to need your shoulder to cry on once we're on the way."

"Good idea, darling," Mark whispered nervously as he reached in through the open carriage door. "I'll move these so you'll have more foot room on the other seat."

They were all whispering a lot, Eliza Anne thought, explaining actions that needed no explanations. Caroline settled herself beside Eliza Anne, as much as anyone could settle under such dreadful circumstances, and for what seemed one of the longest silences ever, they waited again—all trying not to look at Natalie and Burke —yet all stealing anxious glances.

Out of the corner of her eye, Eliza Anne saw Burke hold her away from him for a moment, saw his lips move, saw tears begin to flow down his cheeks. Then—unabashedly staring—Eliza Anne glimpsed Natalie's glorious smile. Sensed, more than saw them, embrace once more, and as Natalie walked, head up, out of his arms and toward the carriage, all three of them were dumbfounded to hear her say quietly, "I'm ready, Papa. I'm ready to go home—for a while."

When Mark reached to help her into the passenger section of the carriage, she shook her head no.

"But, Natalie, you said you were—"

"I am ready to go home with you, Papa, but help me up onto the driver's seat, please."

"But, it's—so rough up there, Natalie."

"Help me up beside Jupiter, please!"

It was a command. On the edge of her seat, Eliza Anne watched. If Mark just keeps standing there gaping at the girl, she thought, I'm going to get out and help her up myself.

Still clinging to her remarkable control, Natalie said, "Papa, if you refuse to help me up onto the driver's seat, Burke will!"

"I'll do it, darling." Mark leaped to her side, his face wet too, with tears. "I'm sorry. Of course, I'll help you up beside Jupiter."

Eliza Anne was still holding Caroline's hand when Mark lifted their daughter onto the high seat.

"Are you sure you'll be all right up there?" Mark called.

Eliza Anne had to lean out the carriage window now in order to see Natalie. The girl ignored her father's question—ignored her father. Turned sideways in the seat, but erect, she was looking and looking and looking at the tall, golden-haired young man who stood apart—alone—unashamed of his still flowing tears. In one hand, he held his wide-brimmed straw hat. The other was raised to her in the torment of good-bye, but also—in salute.

"I love you, Burke," Natalie called down to him from her perch. "I—love you with all my heart . . . *I love you!*"

His hand still raised, Burke called back, "I love you, too. We belong to each other now—don't forget it for a minute. Not for one minute, Natalie!"

Caroline was leaning across Eliza Anne, watching as Mark and Burke shook hands, Burke giving his father-in-law only a part of his attention. As Mark climbed quickly into the carriage and gave Jupiter instructions to start the team, Burke's eyes were on Natalie—and if the look on his face was any sign, Eliza Anne knew that Natalie was smiling and waving and being strong.

No one said a word when the carriage clattered away from the States' Rights Hotel, along the main street of Cassville and headed in the direction of Milner's house at Sallie's Ferry, some fifteen miles away. No one knew what to say. Once, Eliza Anne saw Caroline try to give Mark a reassuring smile.

They had traveled almost two miles, when Natalie called down in a voice that told them everything—at least, everything they needed so desperately to know: "Please understand—all of you—that I have to sit up here for a while, because I need to be—only myself. Don't remind me that Jupiter is here. I know he is. But Jupiter knows exactly how to leave people—alone."

AFTERWORD

ABOUT MIDWAY through the first draft of what you have just read, I realized the impossibility of finishing the Browning-Mackay-Stiles story into the Civil War in only two novels, as indicated when I wrote *Savannah. To See Your Face Again,* therefore, is now the second in a planned quartet of novels laid in the old city.

As must be obvious, Natalie Browning, only three years old at the end of *Savannah,* simply took over this book. My own keen interest in her even then was shared by hundreds of readers who wrote urging me to hurry with novel number 2 so it could be known just "how the little red-haired vixen turned out." In case her survival for five days on a makeshift raft with Burke Latimer struck you as unlikely, let me assure you that the entire *Pulaski* tragedy was recreated from actual newspaper accounts and the writings of survivors themselves, including Rebecca Lamar and James Hamilton Couper. In one news story, a young man Burke's age saved a girl Natalie's age from the ocean, and after five days on a piece of wreckage, they were rescued and eventually married. I am indebted for all the *Pulaski* material to the archives of the Georgia Historical Society in Savannah.

Of course, the enormous loss to William Mackay is authentic in every way. I have used William's own words from the Society's Walter C. Hartridge Collection in the telling of what he wrote in the front of Virginia's Bible. Graves of the Mackay and Stiles families can be found in Savannah in Colonial and Laurel Grove cemeteries. Eliza Anne Mackay Stiles's grave I have also seen in the tiny, tree-shadowed family plot near the ruins of her beloved home, Etowah

Cliffs, near present-day Cartersville, Georgia. The stories of all the Mackays, the Brownings, Natalie and Burke Latimer and the Cherokee brother and sister will, of course, continue through the remaining two novels of the Savannah quartet.

I confess that I have become profoundly involved with the history of the remarkable Cherokee Indians who once called the upcountry setting of this novel their "enchanted land." Their treatment both by the federal government and by the government of Georgia was shameful, and a study of it leaves the Cherokees looking somewhat superior both in intellect and spirituality to the whites who drove them away from their ancestral home. I was already much attached to my niece Cindy's husband, Mike Birdsong, who can boast of Cherokee blood. Now that I know something of the fiber of these people, I am prouder than ever to have an eighth-blood in my family, even by marriage.

If you are as hazy about the Cherokees in Georgia as was I, let me urge you to visit the remarkable New Echota Historic Site near Calhoun, where you will find, along with other buildings of interest and an excellent museum, the Cherokee Supreme Court Building and the print shop where the bilingual *Cherokee Phoenix* was printed. Then, after you've seen New Echota, the old Cherokee capital, it is but a few miles on Georgia Route 225 to present-day Chatsworth and the handsome federal-style mansion of Rich Joe Vann, who so generously supported the Moravian schools for the education of young Cherokees at nearby Spring Place, where Mary and Ben McDonald were born. Both sites are marvelously maintained by the state of Georgia.

In the museum at New Echota, I hope you will be able to meet the director, Ed Reed, to whom I give deep thanks for his important help in my own research of the area. I must also thank New Echota ranger Vernon Timms, for his part in "locating" the cave where Burke found Mary and Ben.

At the Vann House, you will be fortunate if you can talk with the director, Patricia Hall, who helped and encouraged me more than she realized. I predict that you will never forget your first sight of the handsome Vann House on its little hill overlooking the land where Ben and Mary grew up.

Through Mrs. Elizabeth Clark of Cartersville, I was privileged to know and be marvelously helped by the kind heart, agile mind and local-history expertise of the late Mr. Clyde Jolley who, with his charming wife Marjorie, gave us more than an entire day of touring and explanation of old Cassville and the Etowah River Valley area. It was because of his enthusiasm and love of the land there that I chose to set my story in and near Cassville. Mr. Jolley also gave me the rare experience of a personal meeting and informative visit with Mrs. Frederick W. Knight III (Julia) at her historic later Stiles home, Malbone, near Cartersville. From there, Julia took us to see the ruins of the first Stiles home, Eliza Anne's Etowah Cliffs, overlooking the unforgettable Etowah River. Sometime later, I was able to speak with Julia's pleasant father-in-law, Mr. Frederick W. Knight, Jr., a Stiles descendant, who had answers to my every additional question. Here, I must also mention my gratitude to my friend, the late Audry Knight Blackburn (Joyce Blackburn's mother), and her traveling companion, Ruth Lundy. They "discovered" Elizabeth Clark who, because of Clyde Jolley, brought me and my story to that part of Georgia. For the loan of their valuable book on Cass County (now Bartow) for study while I was there, I am also indebted to Susan Turner and Gwen Richards of Cartersville. For further help I thank Jolley's friends, Robert White of Cartersville and Professor J. B. Tate of Kennesaw College. Through the courtesy of the late Lee J. Hark of Rome, Georgia, husband of Mary Ann Drasnin Hark, my high school Spanish teacher, I am grateful for the contact and assistance of Dr. Robert Norton of Rome and Valley View, his beautifully preserved mansion located near Etowah Cliffs.

During the writing of *To See Your Face Again*, I was invited to speak at the Cobb Symposium at Kennesaw College in Kennesaw, Georgia, and there I met a charming gentleman named Fred Bentley, who instantly became, not only a happy acquaintance, but an enthusiastic helper in certain areas of research. En route to the Atlanta airport after my lecture, Fred surprised me with his detailed knowledge of the architecture of Etowah Cliffs. I not only named a Cassville attorney for Fred in this book, I expect to annoy him and his wife Sara for further help on the Etowah Cliffs house during the writing of book 3 of the Savannah quartet.

My longtime friend, archivist David Estes, and his staff at Robert W. Woodruff Library of Emory University, greatly assisted me in obtaining excellent material on W. H. Stiles; Dr. Richard Shrader, reference archivist, Southern Historical Collection, University of

North Carolina at Chapel Hill, did me the favor of a long-distance meeting with an astute research specialist, Dr. Linda McCurdy. For days, Linda read and summarized dozens of Stiles-Mackay letters housed at Chapel Hill. Linda will, I'm sure, be even more invaluable to me in the research for the next two novels. I tremble at the thought of not having her work for me again because I simply could not, no matter how hard I tried, decipher Eliza Anne Stiles's handwriting! Linda "translated" admirably.

Once more, I am indebted to Brenda Williams, now of Augusta, Georgia, to Scott and Frances Smith of Old Fort Jackson, to Gordon Smith of Savannah and to Lila Blitch, great-great granddaughter of A. A. Smets. Everyone is always indebted to Lilla M. Hawes, Savannah historian, and again, so am I. For their consistent help to me through many books and on many subjects, I thank Jim Darby, director, Dorothy Howseal and Marcia Hodges of the Brunswick-Glynn County Regional Library.

I am permanently devoted to the person most plagued by me for research help during the writing of the Savannah sequence—Barbara Bennett of the Georgia Historical Society. As always, Bobby helped quickly, accurately and professionally. She and Mary Harty, of Historic Savannah's Davenport House staff, are two cherished friends without whom I can't imagine tackling even one more Savannah novel. Thank you, Mary and Bobby, for your separate, singular help throughout every phase of the long task.

Two other marvelously cooperative and stimulating descendants of W. H. Stiles—Elizabeth Stiles Layton of Deland, Florida, and Hugh Golson of Savannah—gave me far more than creative and factual help. Both have remained interested, involved and most encouraging. I'm also grateful to Malcolm Bell, Savannah historian, author and kind gentleman, as well as Karen Osvald, Susan Floyd Murphy and Anne Smith of the Georgia Historical Society, and Gene Wadell, director of the South Carolina Historical Society. And my warm thanks also to a few personal friends who stand by from a distance and give to me in ways only I understand and appreciate— Frances Pitts, Reba Spann, Easter Straker, Ellen Urquhart, Jimmie Harnsberger, Mildred Price, Dr. Anna B. Mow and Lorrie Carlson. Nancy and Mary Jane Goshorn, who live in my hometown, through still another book have not only been there urging me on, but go on being truly my remaining "family." On the island where I live, along with Joyce Blackburn, my closest friend, was Sarah Plemmons, with favors, reference books and nature knowledge, as well as Sarah Bell Edmond, Ruby Wilson, Monroe Wilson, Gwen Davis, Beth Edwards, Joe Whittle, Jr., and the late, so beloved Elsie Goodwillie, who died as I was finishing the final chapter of *To See Your Face Again.*

For a quarter of a century, Joyce Blackburn has done all and more for me than even a "Joyce" could do with her intelligent expertise in editing, plot counsel, constructive criticism—*and* her flare for holding together the author herself through the writing of manuscript after manuscript. To say thank you is to say nothing of any consequence. To say I wouldn't want to try even one more book of any kind without her is to understate the truth.

Once more, with the help of her husband, Dr. James Humphlett, and her children, Mark, Beth and Jay, Eileen Humphlett has worked sacrificially, professionally and always cheerfully to transform my huge stack of scratched-up yellow pages into a splendid typescript. But she has done even more on this one. Due to certain pressures in my own life, she caught me in—not one but five plot contradictions! From now on, for me, she is *absolutely essential Eileen.*

At my publishers, Doubleday & Company, Inc., I thank my longtime friend and editor, Carolyn Blakemore, one of New York's best and busiest senior editors. I do wish she would believe me when I say that even during the long silences when I am simply here writing another book *for* her, I am continually receiving *from* her. An editor who never dims for an author at work is rare. From my heart, I thank Carolyn for bringing me to Doubleday and for keeping me there. At the publishing house also, deep thanks to her assistant, Karen Suben, to my special friends, Peter Schneider and Ed Waters, and to Patrick Filley. Gratitude also to my expert copy editor, Erika Schmid, to Libby St. John, to art director Alex Gotfryd and book designer Barbara Rasmussen.

After more than thirty years as a working author, I finally have an agent-manager. Her name is Lila Karpf, and she is a gift to me in all ways. For getting Lila and me together, I deeply thank our valued mutual friend, Faith Brunson, Rich's book buyer supreme, who keeps me believing in what matters most in books and in the people who make them and sell them.

To See Your Face Again is dedicated to a warm-hearted, knowledgeable gentleman, Marion Hemperley, deputy surveyor general of the state of Georgia. Back during the writing of my novel *Lighthouse*, in 1970, I met Marion at the State Archives in Atlanta. From the first, he and I were blessed with friendship and I with his amazing expertise on Georgia history. During the writing of this book, no one pestered this busy, important gentleman more than I, but not once did I find him too busy to give me his full and constructive attention. Out of the blue, I could call him long-distance and ask: "How tall would corn be in a field near Cassville, Georgia, in July?" Marion could tell me. I could ask how to taper a cedar shingle. He knew that too. Marion is responsible for the routes taken by my characters from Savannah to the upcountry—for the location of old inns—for the depth of coastal wells as against deep upcountry wells—for the names of old roads and what might be seen as one jostled over them. I simply do not see how I could have handled the upcountry sequences without his wide, deep knowledge of the state as it used to be. If these lame words in any way rouse Georgians to their enormous debt to Marion Hemperley, I will have accomplished one goal at least. In customary modesty, he claims to be honored that I have dedicated this book to him. In this one area, he is wrong. I am the honored person because Marion is my friend.

The people in the pages of this book are my friends now too, and for this, I give thanks. I wouldn't have missed them for anything. As always, at this point, I again feel lost without them, and in spite of general urging to take a long, long time away from the typewriter, I know myself too well to believe that I will. Right now, I simply can't wait to begin novel number 3 of the Savannah quartet. For this continuing involvement of mine, I thank my loyal readers. Perhaps, above all, I thank them.

EUGENIA PRICE
St. Simons Island, Georgia
January 1985